little
brother &
homeland

also by cory doctorow

little
brother & homeland

cory doctorow

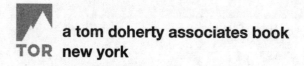
TOR a tom doherty associates book
new york

LITTLE BROTHER & HOMELAND

Little Brother copyright © 2008 by Cory Doctorow; Afterword by Bruce Schneier © 2008 by Bruce Schneier

Homeland copyright © 2013 by Cory Doctorow

Introduction copyright © 2020 by Edward Snowden

A Tor Book
Published by Tom Doherty Associates
120 Broadway
New York, NY 10271

www.tor-forge.com

Tor® is a registered trademark of Macmillan Publishing Group, LLC.

The Library of Congress Cataloging-in-Publication Data is available upon request.

ISBN 978-1-250-77458-3 (trade paperback)
ISBN 978-1-250-78040-9 (ebook)

Our books may be purchased in bulk for promotional, educational, or business use. Please contact your local bookseller or the Macmillan Corporate and Premium Sales Department at 1-800-221-7945, extension 5442, or by email at MacmillanSpecialMarkets@macmillan.com.

First Edition: 2020

Printed in the United States of America

0 9 8 7 6 5 4 3

contents

introduction

by Edward Snowden

When I was working at the CIA, if you had told me that there would soon come a youth rebellion that relied on lasers and traffic cones as sword and shield, and that it would come to paralyze one of the world's richest and most powerful governments, I would have—at the very least—raised an eyebrow. And yet as I write these words nearly a decade later, this is exactly what's happening in Hong Kong, the city where I met with journalists to reveal the secret that would transform me from an agent of government into one of the world's most wanted men. As it happened, the very book that you now hold in your hands lay on the desk, the desk of the last hotel room I would ever pay for with a credit card.

What I showed those journalists was proof, in the form of the government's own classified documents, that the self-described "Five Eyes"—the state security organs of the United States, United Kingdom, Australia, New Zealand, and Canada—had together conspired to weaken their laws. They had forced clandestine access to the networks of their largest telecommunications and Internet titans (some of whom hadn't needed much in the way of arm-twisting) in pursuit of a single goal: the transformation of the free and fragmented Internet into history's first centralized means of global mass surveillance. This violation of our fundamental privacy occurred without our knowledge or consent, or even the knowledge and consent of our courts and most lawmakers.

Here's the thing: although the global response to this violation was furious, producing the largest intelligence scandal of the modern age, mass surveillance itself continues to work today, virtually unimpeded. Nearly everything you do, and nearly everyone you love, is being monitored and recorded by a system whose reach is unlimited, but whose safeguards are not.

But while the system itself was not substantially changed—as a rule, governments are less interested in reforming their own behavior than in restricting the behavior and rights of their citizens—what *did* change was the public consciousness.

The idea that the government was collecting the communications of those who had done nothing wrong had once been treated as a paranoid conspiracy theory (or as the subject of instructive fiction, such as the work you're about to read). Suddenly, this prospect had become all too real—the sort of universally acknowledged truth that can be so quickly waved away as obvious and unremarkable by the crooked timber of our political operators.

Meanwhile, the corporations of the world digested the realization that their darkest shame—their willful complicity in crimes against the public—had not been punished. Rather, these collaborators had been actively rewarded, with either explicitly retroactive immunity or informal guarantees of perpetual impunity. They became our latest Big Brother, striving to compile perfect records of private lives for profit and power. From this emerged the contemporary corruption of our once-free Internet, called surveillance capitalism.

We are coming to see all too clearly that the construction of these systems was less about connection than it was about control: the proliferation of mass surveillance has tracked precisely with the destruction of public power.

And yet despite this grim reading from my seven years in exile, I find more cause for hope than despair, thanks in no small part to those lasers and traffic cones in Hong Kong. My confidence springs not from how they are applied—to dazzle cameras and, with a little water, to contain and extinguish the gas grenades of a state gone wrong—but in what they express: the irrepressible human desire to be free.

The problems that we face today, of dispossession by oligarchs and their monopolies, and of disenfranchisement by authoritarians and their comfortably captive political class, are far from new. The novelty is in the technological means by which these problems have been entrenched—to put it simply, the bad guys have better tools.

You have heard that when all you have is a hammer, every problem looks like a nail. Herein lies the folly of every system of rule whose future relies more heavily on the omnipotence of its methods than the popularity of its mandate. There were times when empires were won by bronze and boats and powder. None survive. What outlasts each forgotten flag is our greatest technology, language: the empire of the mind.

It is true that we have been thrust, like Marcus Yallow and his friends, into an unequal battle. But no amount of even the most perfect surveillance, no amount of repression or rent-seeking can or will change who we are. From brave students in Hong Kong to brilliant cypherpunks in San Francisco, there is not a day that passes without individuals searching for the means to restore and improve the systems that govern our lives. We have seen ingenuity and invention give rise to systems that keep our secrets—and perhaps our souls—systems created in a world where possessing the means to live a private life feels like a crime. We have seen lone individuals create new tools—better tools—than even the greatest states can produce. But no technology, and no individual, will ever be enough on their own to curtail for long the abuses of our weary giants, with their politics of exclusion and protocols of violence. This is the part of the story that matters: that what begins with the individual persists in the communal.

The changing of an age takes more than lasers and traffic cones: it takes the hands that hold them.

It takes you.

little brother

For Alice, who makes me whole

I'm a senior at Cesar Chavez High in San Francisco's sunny Mission district, and that makes me one of the most surveilled people in the world. My name is Marcus Yallow, but back when this story starts, I was going by w1n5t0n. Pronounced "Winston."

Not pronounced "Double-you-one-enn-five-tee-zero-enn"—unless you're a clueless disciplinary officer who's far enough behind the curve that you still call the Internet "the information superhighway."

I know just such a clueless person, and his name is Fred Benson, one of three vice-principals at Cesar Chavez. He's a sucking chest wound of a human being. But if you're going to have a jailer, better a clueless one than one who's really on the ball.

"Marcus Yallow," he said over the PA one Friday morning. The PA isn't very good to begin with, and when you combine that with Benson's habitual mumble, you get something that sounds more like someone struggling to digest a bad burrito than a school announcement. But human beings are good at picking their names out of audio confusion—it's a survival trait.

I grabbed my bag and folded my laptop three-quarters shut—I didn't want to blow my downloads—and got ready for the inevitable.

"Report to the administration office immediately."

My social studies teacher, Ms. Galvez, rolled her eyes at me and I rolled my eyes back at her. The Man was always coming down on me, just because I go through school firewalls like wet kleenex, spoof the gait-recognition software, and nuke the snitch chips they track us with. Galvez is a good type, anyway, never holds that against me (especially when I'm helping get with her webmail so she can talk to her brother who's stationed in Iraq).

My boy Darryl gave me a smack on the ass as I walked past. I've known Darryl since we were still in diapers and escaping from play-school, and I've been getting him into and out of trouble the whole time. I raised my arms over my head like a prizefighter and made my exit from Social Studies and began the perp-walk to the office.

I was halfway there when my phone went. That was another no-no—phones are muy prohibido at Chavez High—but why should that stop me? I ducked into the toilet and shut myself in the middle stall (the farthest stall is always grossest because so many people head straight for it, hoping to escape the smell and the squick—the smart money and good hygiene is down the middle). I checked the phone—my home PC had sent it an email to tell it that there was something new up on Harajuku Fun Madness, which happens to be the best game ever invented.

I grinned. Spending Fridays at school was teh suck anyway, and I was glad of the excuse to make my escape.

I ambled the rest of the way to Benson's office and tossed him a wave as I sailed through the door.

"If it isn't Double-you-one-enn-five-tee-zero-enn," he said. Fredrick Benson—Social Security number 545–03–2343, date of birth August 15, 1962, mother's maiden name Di Bona, hometown Petaluma—is a lot taller than me. I'm a runty 5'8", while he stands 6'7", and his college basketball days are far enough behind him that his chest muscles have turned into saggy man-boobs that were painfully obvious through his freebie dot-com polo shirts. He always looks like he's about to slam-dunk your ass, and he's really into raising his voice for dramatic effect. Both these start to lose their efficacy with repeated application.

"Sorry, nope," I said. "I never heard of this R2D2 character of yours."

"W1n5t0n," he said, spelling it out again. He gave me a hairy eyeball and waited for me to wilt. Of course it was my handle, and had been for years. It was the identity I used when I was posting on message boards where I was making my contributions to the field of applied security research. You know, like sneaking out of school and disabling the minder-tracer on my phone. But he didn't know that this was my handle. Only a small number of people did, and I trusted them all to the end of the earth.

"Um, not ringing any bells," I said. I'd done some pretty cool stuff around school using that handle—I was very proud of my work on snitch-tag killers—and if he could link the two identities, I'd be in trouble. No one at school ever called me w1n5t0n or even Winston. Not even my pals. It was Marcus or nothing.

Benson settled down behind his desk and tapped his class ring nervously on his blotter. He did this whenever things started to go bad for him. Poker players call stuff like this a "tell"—something that lets you know what's going on in the other guy's head. I knew Benson's tells backwards and forwards.

"Marcus, I hope you realize how serious this is."

"I will just as soon as you explain what this is, sir." I always say "sir" to authority figures when I'm messing with them. It's my own tell.

He shook his head at me and looked down, another tell. Any second now, he was going to start shouting at me. "Listen, kiddo! It's time you came to grips with the fact that we know about what you've been doing, and that we're not going to be lenient about it. You're going to be lucky if you're not expelled before this meeting is through. Do you want to graduate?"

"Mr. Benson, you still haven't explained what the problem is—"

He slammed his hand down on the desk and then pointed his finger at me. "The *problem,* Mr. Yallow, is that you've been engaged in criminal conspiracy to subvert this school's security system, and you have supplied security countermeasures to your fellow students. You know that we expelled Graciella Uriarte last week for using one of your devices." Uriarte had gotten a bad rap. She'd bought a radio-jammer from a head shop near the 16th Street BART station and it had set off the countermeasures in the school hallway. Not my doing, but I felt for her.

"And you think I'm involved in that?"

"We have reliable intelligence indicating that you are w1n5t0n"—again, he spelled it out, and I began to wonder if he hadn't figured out that the 1 was an I and the 5 was an S. "We know that this w1n5t0n character is reponsible for the theft of last year's standardized tests."

That actually hadn't been me, but it was a sweet hack, and it was kind of flattering to hear it attributed to me. "And therefore liable for several years in prison unless you cooperate with me."

"You have 'reliable intelligence'? I'd like to see it."

He glowered at me. "Your attitude isn't going to help you."

"If there's evidence, sir, I think you should call the police and turn it over to them. It sounds like this is a very serious matter, and I wouldn't want to stand in the way of a proper investigation by the duly constituted authorities."

"You want me to call the police."

"And my parents, I think. That would be for the best."

We stared at each other across the desk. He'd clearly expected me to fold the second he dropped the bomb on me. I don't fold. I have a trick for staring down people like Benson. I look slightly to the left of their heads, and think about the lyrics to old Irish folk songs, the kind with three hundred verses. It makes me look perfectly composed and unworried.

And the wing was on the bird and the bird was on the egg and the egg was in the nest and the nest was on the leaf and the leaf was on the twig and the twig was on the branch and the branch was on the limb and the limb was in the tree and the tree was in the bog—the bog down in the valley-oh! High-ho the rattlin' bog, the bog down in the valley-oh—

"You can return to class now," he said. "I'll call on you once the police are ready to speak to you."

"Are you going to call them now?"

"The procedure for calling in the police is complicated. I'd hoped that we could settle this fairly and quickly, but since you insist—"

"I can wait while you call them is all," I said. "I don't mind."

He tapped his ring again and I braced for the blast.

"Go!" he yelled. "Get the hell out of my office, you miserable little—"

I got out, keeping my expression neutral. He wasn't going to call the cops. If he'd had enough evidence to go to the police with, he would have called them in the first place. He hated my guts. I figured he'd heard some unverified gossip and hoped to spook me into confirming it.

I moved down the corridor lightly and sprightly, keeping my gait even and measured for the gait-recognition cameras. These had been installed only a year before, and I loved them for their sheer idiocy. Beforehand, we'd had face-recognition cameras covering nearly every public space in school, but a court ruled that was unconstitutional. So Benson and a lot of other paranoid school administrators had spent our textbook dollars on these idiot cameras that were supposed to be able to tell one person's walk from another. Yeah, right.

I got back to class and sat down again, Ms. Galvez warmly welcoming me back. I unpacked the school's standard-issue machine and got back into classroom mode. The SchoolBooks were the snitchiest technology of them all, logging every keystroke, watching all the network traffic for suspicious keywords, counting every click, keeping track of every fleeting thought you put out over the net. We'd gotten them in my junior year, and it only took a couple months for the shininess to wear off. Once people figured out that these "free" laptops worked for the man—and showed a never-ending parade of obnoxious ads to boot—they suddenly started to feel very heavy and burdensome.

Cracking my SchoolBook had been easy. The crack was online within a month of the machine showing up, and there was nothing to it—just download a DVD image, burn it, stick it in the SchoolBook, and boot it while holding down a bunch of different keys at the same time. The DVD did the rest, installing a whole bunch of hidden programs on the machine, programs that would stay hidden even when the Board of Ed did its daily remote integrity checks of the machines. Every now and again I had to get an update for the software to get around the Board's latest tests, but it was a small price to pay to get a little control over the box.

I fired up IMParanoid, the secret instant messenger that I used when I wanted to have an off-the-record discussion right in the middle of class. Darryl was already logged in.

> The game's afoot! Something big is going down with Harajuku Fun Madness, dude. You in?

> No. Freaking. Way. If I get caught ditching a third time, I'm expelled. Man, you know that. We'll go after school.

> You've got lunch and then study hall, right? That's two hours. Plenty of time to run down this clue and get back before anyone misses us. I'll get the whole team out.

Harajuku Fun Madness is the best game ever made. I know I already said that, but it bears repeating. It's an ARG, an Alternate Reality Game, and the story goes that a gang of Japanese fashion-teens discovered a miraculous healing gem at the temple in Harajuku, which is basically where cool Japanese teenagers invented every major subculture for the past ten years. They're being hunted by evil monks, the Yakuza (aka the Japanese mafia), aliens, tax inspectors, parents, and a rogue artificial intelligence. They slip the players coded messages that we have to decode and use to track down clues that lead to more coded messages and more clues.

Imagine the best afternoon you've ever spent prowling the streets of a city, checking out all the weird people, funny handbills, street maniacs, and funky shops. Now add a scavenger hunt to that, one that requires you to research crazy old films and songs and teen culture from around the world and across time and space. And it's a competition, with the winning team of four taking a grand prize of ten days in Tokyo, chilling on Harajuku bridge, geeking out in Akihabara, and taking home all the Astro Boy merchandise you can eat. Except that he's called "Atom Boy" in Japan.

That's Harajuku Fun Madness, and once you've solved a puzzle or two, you'll never look back.

> No man, just no. NO. Don't even ask.

> I need you D. You're the best I've got. I swear I'll get us in and out without anyone knowing it. You know I can do that, right?

> I know you can do it

> So you're in?

> Hell no

> Come on, Darryl. You're not going to your deathbed wishing you'd spent more study periods sitting in school

> I'm not going to go to my deathbed wishing I'd spent more time playing ARGs either

> Yeah but don't you think you might go to your deathbed wishing you'd spent more time with Vanessa Pak?

Van was part of my team. She went to a private girl's school in the East Bay, but I knew she'd ditch to come out and run the mission with me. Darryl has had a crush on her literally for years—even before puberty endowed her with many lavish gifts. Darryl had fallen in love with her mind. Sad, really.

> You suck

> You're coming?

He looked at me and shook his head. Then he nodded. I winked at him and set to work getting in touch with the rest of my team.

I wasn't always into ARGing. I have a dark secret: I used to be a LARPer. LARPing is Live Action Role Playing, and it's just about what it sounds like: running around in costume, talking in a funny accent, pretending to be a superspy or a vampire or a medieval knight. It's like Capture the Flag in monster-drag, with a bit of Drama Club thrown in, and the best games were the ones we played in Scout Camps out of town in Sonoma or down on the Peninsula. Those three-day epics could get pretty hairy, with all-day hikes, epic battles with foam-and-bamboo swords, casting spells by throwing beanbags and shouting "Fireball!" and so on. Good fun, if a little goofy. Not nearly as geeky as talking about what your elf planned on doing as you sat around a table loaded with Diet Coke cans and painted miniatures, and more physically active than going into a mouse-coma in front of a massively multiplayer game at home.

The thing that got me into trouble were the minigames in the hotels. Whenever a science fiction convention came to town, some LARPer would convince them to let us run a couple of six-hour minigames at the con, piggybacking on their rental of the space. Having a bunch of enthusiastic kids running around in costume lent color to the event, and we got to have a ball among people even more socially deviant than us.

The problem with hotels is that they have a lot of nongamers in them, too—and not just sci-fi people. Normal people. From states that begin and end with vowels. On holidays.

And sometimes those people misunderstand the nature of a game.

Let's just leave it at that, okay?

Class ended in ten minutes, and that didn't leave me with much time to prepare. The first order of business was those pesky gait-recognition cameras. Like I said, they'd started out as face-recognition cameras, but those had been ruled unconstitutional. As far as I know, no court has yet determined whether these gait-cams are any more legal, but until they do, we're stuck with them.

"Gait" is a fancy word for the way you walk. People are pretty good at spotting gaits—next time you're on a camping trip, check out the bobbing of the flashlight as a distant friend approaches you. Chances are you can identify him just from the movement of the light, the characteristic way it bobs up and down that tells our monkey brains that this is a person approaching us.

Gait-recognition software takes pictures of your motion, tries to isolate you in the pics as a silhouette, and then tries to match the silhouette to a database to see if it knows who you are. It's a biometric identifier, like fingerprints or retina-scans, but it's got a lot more "collisions" than either of those. A biometric "collision" is when a measurement matches more than one person. Only you have your fingerprint, but you share your gait with plenty other people.

Not exactly, of course. Your personal, inch-by-inch walk is yours and yours alone. The problem is your inch-by-inch walk changes based on how tired you are, what the floor is made of, whether you pulled your ankle playing basketball, and whether you've changed your shoes lately. So the system kind of fuzzes out your profile, looking for people who walk kind of like you.

There are a lot of people who walk kind of like you. What's more, it's easy not to walk kind of like you—just take one shoe off. Of course, you'll always walk like you-with-one-shoe-off in that case, so the cameras will eventually figure out that it's still you. Which is why I prefer to inject a little randomness into my attacks on gait-recognition: I put a handful of gravel into each shoe. Cheap and effective, and no two steps are the same. Plus you get a great reflexology foot massage in the process. (I kid. Reflexology is about as scientifically useful as gait-recognition.)

The cameras used to set off an alert every time someone they didn't recognize stepped onto campus.

This did *not* work.

The alarm went off every ten minutes. When the mailman came by. When a parent dropped in. When the groundspeople went to work fixing up the basketball court. When a student showed up wearing new shoes.

So now it just tries to keep track of who's where, when. If someone leaves by the school gates during classes, their gait is checked to see if it kinda-sorta matches any student gait and if it does, whoop-whoop-whoop, ring the alarm!

Chavez High is ringed with gravel walkways. I like to keep a couple handsful of rocks in my shoulder bag, just in case. I silently passed Darryl ten or fifteen pointy little bastards and we both loaded our shoes.

Class was about to finish up—and I realized that I still hadn't checked the Harajuku Fun Madness site to see where the next clue was! I'd been a little hyperfocused on the escape, and hadn't bothered to figure out where we were escaping *to*.

I turned to my SchoolBook and hit the keyboard. The web browser we used was supplied with the machine. It was a locked-down spyware version of Internet Explorer, Microsoft's crashware turd that no one under the age of forty used voluntarily.

I had a copy of Firefox on the USB drive built into my watch, but that wasn't enough—the SchoolBook ran Windows Vista4-Schools, an antique operating system designed to give school administrators the illusion that they controlled the programs their students could run.

But Vista4Schools is its own worst enemy. There are a lot of programs that Vista4Schools doesn't want you to be able to shut down—keyloggers, censorware—and these programs run in a special mode that makes them invisible to the system. You can't quit them because you can't even see they're there.

Any program whose name starts with SYS is invisible to the operating system. It doesn't show up on listings of the hard drive, nor in the process monitor. So my copy of Firefox was called

SYSFirefox—and as I launched it, it became invisible to Windows, and thus invisible to the network's snoopware.

Now that I had an indie browser running, I needed an indie network connection. The school's network logged every click in and out of the system, which was bad news if you were planning on surfing over to the Harajuku Fun Madness site for some extra-curricular fun.

The answer is something ingenious called TOR—The Onion Router. An onion router is an Internet site that takes requests for web pages and passes them onto other onion routers, and on to other onion routers, until one of them finally decides to fetch the page and pass it back through the layers of the onion until it reaches you. The traffic to the onion routers is encrypted, which means that the school can't see what you're asking for, and the layers of the onion don't know who they're working for. There are millions of nodes—the program was set up by the U.S. Office of Naval Research to help their people get around the censorware in countries like Syria and China, which means that it's perfectly designed for operating in the confines of an average American high school.

TOR works because the school has a finite blacklist of naughty addresses we aren't allowed to visit, and the addresses of the nodes change all the time—no way could the school keep track of them all. Firefox and TOR together made me into the invisible man, impervious to Board of Ed snooping, free to check out the Harajuku FM site and see what was up.

There it was, a new clue. Like all Harajuku Fun Madness clues, it had a physical, online and mental component. The online component was a puzzle you had to solve, one that required you to research the answers to a bunch of obscure questions. This batch included a bunch of questions on the plots in dōjinshi—those are comic books drawn by fans of manga, Japanese comics. They can be as big as the official comics that inspire them, but they're a lot weirder, with crossover storylines and sometimes really silly songs and action. Lots of love stories, of course. Everyone loves to see their favorite toons hook up.

I'd have to solve those riddles later, when I got home. They were easiest to solve with the whole team, downloading tons of dōjinshi files and scouring them for answers to the puzzles.

I'd just finished scrap-booking all the clues when the bell rang and we began our escape. I surreptitiously slid the gravel down the side of my short boots—ankle-high Blundstones from Australia, great for running and climbing, and the easy slip-on/slip-off laceless design makes them convenient at the never-ending metal detectors that are everywhere now.

We also had to evade physical surveillance, of course, but that gets easier every time they add a new layer of physical snoopery—all the bells and whistles lull our beloved faculty into a totally false sense of security. We surfed the crowd down the hallways, heading for my favorite side-exit. We were halfway along when Darryl hissed, "Crap! I forgot, I've got a library book in my bag."

"You're kidding me," I said, and hauled him into the next bathroom we passed. Library books are bad news. Every one of them has an arphid—Radio Frequency ID tag—glued into its binding, which makes it possible for the librarians to check out the books by waving them over a reader, and lets a library shelf tell you if any of the books on it are out of place.

But it also lets the school track where you are at all times. It was another of those legal loopholes: the courts wouldn't let the schools track *us* with arphids, but they could track *library books*, and use the school records to tell them who was likely to be carrying which library book.

I had a little Faraday pouch in my bag—these are little wallets lined with a mesh of copper wires that effectively block radio energy, silencing arphids. But the pouches were made for neutralizing ID cards and toll-book transponders, not books like—

"*Introduction to Physics?*" I groaned. The book was the size of a dictionary.

"I'm thinking of majoring in physics when I go to Berkeley," Darryl said. His dad taught at the University of California at Berkeley, which meant he'd get free tuition when he went. And there'd never been any question in Darryl's household about whether he'd go.

"Fine, but couldn't you research it online?"

"My dad said I should read it. Besides, I didn't plan on committing any crimes today."

"Skipping school isn't a crime. It's an infraction. They're totally different."

"What are we going to do, Marcus?"

"Well, I can't hide it, so I'm going to have to nuke it." Killing arphids is a dark art. No merchant wants malicious customers going for a walk around the shop floor and leaving behind a bunch of lobotomized merchandise that is missing its invisible bar code, so the manufacturers have refused to implement a "kill signal" that you can radio to an arphid to get it to switch off. You can reprogram arphids with the right box, but I hate doing that to library books. It's not exactly tearing pages out of a book, but it's still bad, since a book with a reprogrammed arphid can't be shelved and can't be found. It just becomes a needle in a haystack.

That left me with only one option: nuking the thing. Literally. Thirty seconds in a microwave will do in pretty much every arphid on the market. And because the arphid wouldn't answer at all when D checked it back in at the library, they'd just print a fresh one for it and recode it with the book's catalog info, and it would end up clean and neat back on its shelf.

All we needed was a microwave.

"Give it another two minutes and the teachers' lounge will be empty," I said.

Darryl grabbed his book and headed for the door. "Forget it, no way. I'm going to class."

I snagged his elbow and dragged him back. "Come on, D, easy now. It'll be fine."

"The *teachers' lounge?* Maybe you weren't listening, Marcus. If I get busted *just once more,* I am *expelled.* You hear that? *Expelled.*"

"You won't get caught," I said. The one place a teacher wouldn't be after this period was the lounge. "We'll go in the back way." The lounge had a little kitchenette off to one side, with its own entrance for teachers who just wanted to pop in and get a cup of joe. The microwave—which always reeked of popcorn and spilled soup—was right in there, on top of the miniature fridge.

Darryl groaned. I thought fast. "Look, the bell's *already rung.* If you go to study hall now, you'll get a late slip. Better not to show at all at this point. I can infiltrate and exfiltrate any room on this campus, D. You've seen me do it. I'll keep you safe, bro."

He groaned again. That was one of Darryl's tells: once he starts groaning, he's ready to give in.

"Let's roll," I said, and we took off.

It was flawless. We skirted the classrooms, took the back stairs into the basement, and came up the front stairs right in front of the teachers' lounge. Not a sound came from the door, and I quietly turned the knob and dragged Darryl in before silently closing the door.

The book just barely fit in the microwave, which was looking even less sanitary than it had the last time I'd popped in here to use it. I conscientiously wrapped it in paper towels before I set it down. "Man, teachers are *pigs*," I hissed. Darryl, white-faced and tense, said nothing.

The arphid died in a shower of sparks, which was really quite lovely (though not nearly as pretty as the effect you get when you nuke a frozen grape, which has to be seen to be believed).

Now, to exfiltrate the campus in perfect anonymity and make our escape.

Darryl opened the door and began to move out, me on his heels. A second later, he was standing on my toes, elbows jammed into my chest, as he tried to backpedal into the closet-sized kitchen we'd just left.

"Get back," he whispered urgently. "Quick—it's Charles!"

Charles Walker and I don't get along. We're in the same grade, and we've known each other as long as I've known Darryl, but that's where the resemblance ends. Charles has always been big for his age, and now that he's playing football and on the juice, he's even bigger. He's got anger management problems—I lost a milk tooth to him in the third grade—and he's managed to keep from getting in trouble over them by becoming the most active snitch in school.

It's a bad combination, a bully who also snitches, taking great pleasure in going to the teachers with whatever infractions he's found. Benson *loved* Charles. Charles liked to let on that he had some kind of unspecified bladder problem, which gave him a ready-made excuse to prowl the hallways at Chavez, looking for people to fink on.

The last time Charles had caught some dirt on me, it had ended with me giving up LARPing. I had no intention of being caught by him again.

"What's he doing?"

"He's coming this way is what he's doing," Darryl said. He was shaking.

"Okay," I said. "Okay, time for emergency countermeasures." I got my phone out. I'd planned this well in advance. Charles would never get me again. I emailed my server at home, and it got into motion.

A few seconds later, Charles's phone spazzed out spectacularly. I'd had tens of thousands of simultaneous random calls and text messages sent to it, causing every chirp and ring it had to go off and keep going off. The attack was accomplished by means of a botnet, and for that I felt bad, but it was in the service of a good cause.

Botnets are where infected computers spend their afterlives. When you get a worm or a virus, your computer sends a message to a chat channel on IRC—the Internet Relay Chat. That message tells the botmaster—the guy who deployed the worm—that the computers in there are ready to do his bidding. Botnets are supremely powerful, since they can comprise thousands, even hundreds of thousands of computers, scattered all over the Internet, connected to juicy high-speed connections and running on fast home PCs. Those PCs normally function on behalf of their owners, but when the botmaster calls them, they rise like zombies to do his bidding.

There are so many infected PCs on the Internet that the price of hiring an hour or two on a botnet has crashed. Mostly these things work for spammers as cheap, distributed spambots, filling your mailbox with come-ons for boner-pills or with new viruses that can infect you and recruit your machine to join the botnet.

I'd just rented ten seconds' time on three thousand PCs and had each of them send a text message or voice-over-IP call to Charles's phone, whose number I'd extracted from a sticky note on Benson's desk during one fateful office visit.

Needless to say, Charles's phone was not equipped to handle this. First the SMSes filled the memory on his phone, causing it to start choking on the routine operations it needed to do things like manage the ringer and log all those incoming calls' bogus return numbers (did you know that it's *really easy* to fake the return number on a caller ID? There are about fifty ways of doing it—just google "spoof caller id").

Charles stared at it dumbfounded, and jabbed at it furiously, his thick eyebrows knotting and wiggling as he struggled with the demons that had possessed his most personal of devices. The plan was working so far, but he wasn't doing what he was supposed to be doing next—he was supposed to go find some place to sit down and try to figure out how to get his phone back.

Darryl shook me by the shoulder, and I pulled my eye away from the crack in the door.

"What's he doing?" Darryl whispered.

"I totaled his phone, but he's just staring at it now instead of moving on." It wasn't going to be easy to reboot that thing. Once the memory was totally filled, it would have a hard time loading the code it needed to delete the bogus messages—and there was no bulk-erase for texts on his phone, so he'd have to manually delete all of the thousands of messages.

Darryl shoved me back and stuck his eye up to the door. A moment later, his shoulders started to shake. I got scared, thinking he was panicking, but when he pulled back, I saw that he was laughing so hard that tears were streaming down his cheeks.

"Galvez just totally busted him for being in the halls during class *and* for having his phone out—you should have seen her tear into him. She was really enjoying it."

We shook hands solemnly and snuck back out of the corridor, down the stairs, around the back, out the door, past the fence and out into the glorious sunlight of afternoon in the Mission. Valencia Street had never looked so good. I checked my watch and yelped.

"Let's move! The rest of the gang is meeting us at the cable cars in twenty minutes!"

Van spotted us first. She was blending in with a group of Korean tourists, which is one of her favorite ways of camouflaging herself when she's ditching school. Ever since the truancy moblog went live, our world is full of nosy shopkeepers and pecksniffs who take it upon themselves to snap our piccies and put them on the net where they can be perused by school administrators.

She came out of the crowd and bounded toward us. Darryl has had a thing for Van since forever, and she's sweet enough to pretend she doesn't know it. She gave me a hug and then moved onto Darryl, giving him a quick sisterly kiss on the cheek that made him go red to the tops of his ears.

The two of them made a funny pair: Darryl is a little on the heavy side, though he wears it well, and he's got a kind of pink complexion that goes red in the cheeks whenever he runs or gets excited. He's been able to grow a beard since we were fourteen, but thankfully he started shaving after a brief period known to our gang as "the Lincoln years." And he's tall. Very, very tall. Like basketball player tall.

Meanwhile, Van is half a head shorter than me, and skinny, with straight black hair that she wears in crazy, elaborate braids that she researches on the net. She's got pretty coppery skin and dark eyes, and she loves big glass rings the size of radishes, which click and clack together when she dances.

"Where's Jolu?" she said.

"How are you, Van?" Darryl asked in a choked voice. He always ran a step behind the conversation when it came to Van.

"I'm great, D. How's your every little thing?" Oh, she was a bad, bad person. Darryl nearly fainted.

Jolu saved him from social disgrace by showing up just then, in an oversize leather baseball jacket, sharp sneakers, and a mesh-back cap advertising our favorite Mexican masked wrestler, El Santo Junior. Jolu is Jose-Luis Torrez, the completing member of our foursome. He went to a super-strict Catholic school in the Outer Richmond, so it wasn't easy for him to get out. But he always did: no one exfiltrated like our Jolu. He liked his jacket because it hung down low—which was pretty stylish in parts of the city—and covered up all his Catholic school crap, which was like a bull's-eye for nosy jerks with the truancy moblog bookmarked on their phones.

"Who's ready to go?" I asked, once we'd all said hello. I pulled out my phone and showed them the map I'd downloaded to it on the BART. "Near as I can work out, we wanna go up to the Nikko again, then one block past it to O'Farrell, then left up toward Van Ness. Somewhere in there we should find the wireless signal."

Van made a face. "That's a nasty part of the Tenderloin." I couldn't argue with her. That part of San Francisco is one of the weird bits—you go in through the Hilton's front entrance and it's all touristy stuff like the cable car turnaround and family restaurants. Go through to the other side and you're in the 'Loin, where every tracked out transvestite hooker, hard-case pimp, hissing drug dealer and cracked up homeless person in town was concentrated. What they bought and sold, none of us were old enough to be a part of (though there were plenty of hookers our age plying their trade in the 'Loin).

"Look on the bright side," I said. "The only time you want to go up around there is broad daylight. None of the other players are going to go near it until tomorrow at the earliest. This is what we in the ARG business call a *monster head start.*"

Jolu grinned at me. "You make it sound like a good thing," he said.

"Beats eating uni," I said.

"We going to talk or we going to win?" Van said. After me, she was hands down the most hardcore player in our group. She took winning very, very seriously.

We struck out, four good friends, on our way to decode a clue, win the game—and lose everything we cared about, forever.

The physical component of today's clue was a set of GPS coordinates—there were coordinates for all the major cities where Harajuku Fun Madness was played—where we'd find a WiFi access point's signal. That signal was being deliberately jammed by another, nearby WiFi point that was hidden so that it couldn't be spotted by conventional wifinders, little key-fobs that told you when you were within range of someone's open access point, which you could use for free.

We'd have to track down the location of the "hidden" access point by measuring the strength of the "visible" one, finding the spot where it was most mysteriously weakest. There we'd find another clue—last time it had been in the special of the day at Anzu, the swanky sushi restaurant in the Nikko hotel in the Tenderloin. The Nikko was owned by Japan Airlines, one of Harajuku Fun Madness's sponsors, and the staff had all made a big fuss over us when we finally tracked down the clue. They'd given us bowls of miso soup and made us try uni, which is sushi made from sea urchin, with the texture of very runny cheese and a smell like very runny dog droppings. But it tasted *really* good. Or so Darryl told me. I wasn't going to eat that stuff.

I picked up the WiFi signal with my phone's wifinder about three blocks up O'Farrell, just before Hyde Street, in front of a dodgy "Asian Massage Parlor" with a red blinking CLOSED sign in the window. The network's name was HarajukuFM, so we knew we had the right spot.

"If it's in there, I'm not going," Darryl said.

"You all got your wifinders?" I said.

Darryl and Van had phones with built-in wifinders, while Jolu, being too cool to carry a phone bigger than his pinky finger, had a separate little directional fob.

"Okay, fan out and see what we see. You're looking for a sharp drop-off in the signal that gets worse the more you move along it."

I took a step backwards and ended up standing on someone's toes. A female voice said "oof" and I spun around, worried I was about to get stabbed for breaking someone's heels.

Instead, I found myself face to face with another kid my age. She had a shock of bright pink hair and a sharp, rodentlike face, with big sunglasses that were practically Air Force goggles. She was dressed in striped tights beneath a black granny dress, with lots of little Japanese decorer toys safety pinned to it—anime characters, old world leaders, emblems from foreign soda pop.

She held up a camera and snapped a picture of me and my crew.

"Cheese," she said. "You're on candid snitch-cam."

"No way," I said. "You wouldn't—"

"I will," she said. "I will send this photo to truant watch in thirty seconds unless you four back off from this clue and let me and my friends here run it down. You can come back in one hour and it'll be all yours. I think that's more than fair."

I looked behind her and noticed three other girls in similar garb—one with blue hair, one with green, and one with purple. "Who are you supposed to be, the Popsicle Squad?"

"We're the team that's going to kick your team's ass at Harajuku Fun Madness," she said. "And I'm the one who's *right this second* about to upload your photo and get you in *so much trouble*—"

Behind me I felt Van start forward. Her all-girls school was notorious for its brawls, and I was pretty sure she was ready to knock this chick's block off.

Then the world changed forever.

We felt it first, that sickening lurch of the cement under your feet that every Californian knows instinctively—*earthquake*. My first inclination, as always, was to get away: "When in trouble or in doubt, run in circles, scream and shout." But the fact was, we were already in the safest place we could be, not in a building that could fall in on us, not out toward the middle of the road where bits of falling mortice could brain us.

Earthquakes are eerily quiet—at first, anyway—but this wasn't quiet. This was loud, an incredible roaring sound that was louder than anything I'd ever heard before. The sound was so punishing it drove me to my knees, and I wasn't the only one. Darryl shook my arm and pointed over the buildings and we saw it then: a huge black cloud rising from the northeast, from the direction of the Bay.

There was another rumble, and the cloud of smoke spread out, that spreading black shape we'd all grown up seeing in movies. Someone had just blown up something, in a big way.

There were more rumbles and more tremors. Heads appeared at windows up and down the street. We all looked at the mushroom cloud in silence.

Then the sirens started.

I'd heard sirens like these before—they test the civil defense sirens at noon on Tuesdays. But I'd only heard them go off unscheduled in old war movies and video games, the kind where someone is bombing someone else from above. Air raid sirens. The wooooooo sound made it all less real.

"Report to shelters immediately." It was like the voice of God, coming from all places at once. There were speakers on some of the electric poles, something I'd never noticed before, and they'd all switched on at once.

"Report to shelters immediately." Shelters? We looked at each other in confusion. What shelters? The cloud was rising steadily, spreading out. Was it nuclear? Were we breathing our last breaths?

The girl with the pink hair grabbed her friends and they tore ass downhill, back toward the BART station and the foot of the hills.

"REPORT TO SHELTERS IMMEDIATELY." There was screaming now, and a lot of running around. Tourists—you can always spot the tourists, they're the ones who think CALIFORNIA = WARM and spend their San Francisco holidays freezing in shorts and T-shirts—scattered in every direction.

"We should go!" Darryl hollered in my ear, just barely audible over the shrieking of the sirens, which had been joined by traditional police sirens. A dozen SFPD cruisers screamed past us.

"REPORT TO SHELTERS IMMEDIATELY."

"Down to the BART station," I hollered. My friends nodded. We closed ranks and began to move quickly downhill.

We passed a lot of people in the road on the way to the Powell Street BART. They were running or walking, white-faced and silent or shouting and panicked. Homeless people cowered in doorways and watched it all, while a tall trans sex-worker shouted at two mustached young men about something.

The closer we got to the BART, the worse the press of bodies became. By the time we reached the stairway down into the station, it was a mob scene, a huge brawl of people trying to crowd their way down a narrow staircase. I had my face crushed up against someone's back, and someone else was pressed into my back.

Darryl was still beside me—he was big enough that he was hard to shove, and Jolu was right behind him, kind of hanging on to his waist. I spied Vanessa a few yards away, trapped by more people.

"Screw you!" I heard Van yell behind me. "Pervert! Get your hands off of me!"

I strained around against the crowd and saw Van looking with disgust at an older guy in a nice suit who was kind of smirking at her. She was digging in her purse and I knew what she was digging for.

"Don't mace him!" I shouted over the din. "You'll get us all, too."

At the mention of the word mace, the guy looked scared and kind of melted back, though the crowd kept him moving forward. Up ahead, I saw someone, a middle-aged lady in a hippie dress, falter and fall. She screamed as she went down, and I saw her thrashing to get up, but she couldn't, the crowd's pressure was too strong. As I neared her, I bent to help her up, and was nearly knocked over her. I ended up stepping on her stomach as the crowd pushed me past her, but by then I don't think she was feeling anything.

I was as scared as I'd ever been. There was screaming everywhere now, and more bodies on the floor, and the press from behind was as relentless as a bulldozer. It was all I could do to keep on my feet.

We were in the open concourse where the turnstiles were. It was hardly any better here—the enclosed space sent the voices around us echoing back in a roar that made my head ring, and the smell and feeling of all those bodies made me feel a claustrophobia I'd never known I was prone to.

People were still cramming down the stairs, and more were squeezing past the turnstiles and down the escalators onto the platforms, but it was clear to me that this wasn't going to have a happy ending.

"Want to take our chances up top?" I said to Darryl.

"Yes, hell yes," he said. "This is vicious."

I looked to Vanessa—there was no way she'd hear me. I managed to get my phone out and I texted her.

> We're getting out of here

I saw her feel the vibe from her phone, then look down at it and then back at me and nod vigorously. Darryl, meanwhile, had clued Jolu in.

"What's the plan?" Darryl shouted in my ear.

"We're going to have to go back!" I shouted back, pointing at the remorseless crush of bodies.

"It's impossible!" he said.

"It's just going to get more impossible the longer we wait!"

He shrugged. Van worked her way over to me and grabbed hold of my wrist. I took Darryl's and Darryl took Jolu by the other hand and we pushed out.

It wasn't easy. We moved about three inches a minute at first, then slowed down even more when we reached the stairway. The people we passed were none too happy about us shoving them out of the way, either. A couple people swore at us and there was a guy who looked like he'd have punched me if he'd been able to get his arms loose. We passed three more crushed people beneath us, but there was no way I could have helped them. By that point, I wasn't even thinking of helping anyone. All I could think of was finding the spaces in front of us to move into, of Darryl's mighty straining on my wrist, of my death grip on Van behind me.

We popped free like champagne corks an eternity later, blinking in the gray smoky light. The air raid sirens were still blaring, and the sound of emergency vehicles' sirens as they tore down Market Street was even louder. There was almost no one on the streets anymore—just the people trying hopelessly to get underground. A lot of them were crying. I spotted a bunch of empty benches—usually staked out by skanky winos—and pointed toward them.

We moved for them, the sirens and the smoke making us duck and hunch our shoulders. We got as far as the benches before Darryl fell forward.

We all yelled and Vanessa grabbed him and turned him over. The side of his shirt was stained red, and the stain was spreading. She tugged his shirt up and revealed a long, deep cut in his pudgy side.

"Someone freaking *stabbed* him in the crowd," Jolu said, his hands clenching into fists. "Christ, that's vicious."

Darryl groaned and looked at us, then down at his side, then he groaned and his head went back again.

Vanessa took off her jean jacket and then pulled off the cotton hoodie she was wearing underneath it. She wadded it up and pressed it to Darryl's side. "Take his head," she said to me. "Keep it elevated." To Jolu she said, "Get his feet up—roll up your coat or something." Jolu moved quickly. Vanessa's mother is a nurse and she'd had first aid training every summer at camp. She loved to watch people in movies get their first aid wrong and make fun of them. I was so glad to have her with us.

We sat there for a long time, holding the hoodie to Darryl's side. He kept insisting that he was fine and that we should let him up, and Van kept telling him to shut up and lie still before she kicked his ass.

"What about calling 911?" Jolu said.

I felt like an idiot. I whipped my phone out and punched 911. The sound I got wasn't even a busy signal—it was like a whimper of pain from the phone system. You don't get sounds like that unless there's three million people all dialing the same number at once. Who needs botnets when you've got terrorists?

"What about Wikipedia?" Jolu said.

"No phone, no data," I said.

"What about them?" Darryl said, and pointed at the street. I looked where he was pointing, thinking I'd see a cop or a paramedic, but there was no one there.

"It's okay buddy, you just rest," I said.

"No, you idiot, what about *them,* the cops in the cars? There!"

He was right. Every five seconds, a cop car, an ambulance or a firetruck zoomed past. They could get us some help. I was such an idiot.

"Come on, then," I said, "let's get you where they can see you and flag one down."

Vanessa didn't like it, but I figured a cop wasn't going to stop for a kid waving his hat in the street, not that day. They just might stop if they saw Darryl bleeding there, though. I argued briefly with her and Darryl settled it by lurching to his feet and dragging himself down toward Market Street.

The first vehicle that screamed past—an ambulance—didn't even slow down. Neither did the cop car that went past, nor the fire truck, nor the next three cop cars. Darryl wasn't in good shape—he was white-faced and panting. Van's sweater was soaked in blood.

I was sick of cars driving right past me. The next time a car appeared down Market Street, I stepped right out into the road, waving my arms over my head, shouting *"STOP."* The car slowed to a stop and only then did I notice that it wasn't a cop car, ambulance or fire engine.

It was a military-looking Jeep, like an armored Hummer, only it didn't have any military insignia on it. The car skidded to a stop just in front of me, and I jumped back and lost my balance and ended up on the road. I felt the doors open near me, and then saw a confusion of booted feet moving close by. I looked up and saw a bunch of military-looking guys in coveralls, holding big, bulky rifles and wearing hooded gas masks with tinted faceplates.

I barely had time to register them before those rifles were pointed at me. I'd never looked down the barrel of a gun before, but everything you've heard about the experience is true. You freeze where you are, time stops, and your heart thunders in your ears. I opened my mouth, then shut it, then, very slowly, I held my hands up in front of me.

The faceless, eyeless armed man above me kept his gun very level. I didn't even breathe. Van was screaming something and Jolu was shouting and I looked at them for a second and that was when someone put a coarse sack over my head and cinched it tight around my windpipe, so quick and so fiercely I barely had time to gasp before it was locked on me. I was pushed roughly but dispassionately onto my stomach and something went twice around my wrists and then tightened up as well, feeling like baling wire and biting cruelly. I cried out and my own voice was muffled by the hood.

I was in total darkness now and I strained my ears to hear what was going on with my friends. I heard them shouting through the muffling canvas of the bag, and then I was being impersonally hauled to my feet by my wrists, my arms wrenched up behind my back, my shoulders screaming.

I stumbled some, then a hand pushed my head down and I was inside the Hummer. More bodies were roughly shoved in beside me.

"Guys?" I shouted, and earned a hard thump on my head for my trouble. I heard Jolu respond, then felt the thump he was dealt, too. My head rang like a gong.

"Hey," I said to the soldiers. "Hey, listen! We're just high school students. I wanted to flag you down because my friend was bleeding. Someone stabbed him." I had no idea how much of this was making it through the muffling bag. I kept talking. "Listen—this is some kind of misunderstanding. We've got to get my friend to a hospital—"

Someone went upside my head again. It felt like they used a baton or something—it was harder than anyone had ever hit me in the head before. My eyes swam and watered and I literally couldn't breathe through the pain. A moment later, I caught my breath, but I didn't say anything. I'd learned my lesson.

Who were these clowns? They weren't wearing insignia. Maybe they were terrorists! I'd never really believed in terrorists before—I mean, I knew that in the abstract there were terrorists somewhere in the world, but they didn't really represent any risk to me. There were millions of ways that the world could kill me—starting with getting run down by a drunk burning his way down Valencia—that were infinitely more likely and immediate than terrorists. Terrorists kill a lot fewer people than bathroom falls and accidental electrocutions. Worrying about them always struck me as about as useful as worrying about getting hit by lightning.

Sitting in the back of that Hummer, my head in a hood, my hands lashed behind my back, lurching back and forth while the bruises swelled up on my head, terrorism suddenly felt a lot riskier.

The car rocked back and forth and tipped uphill. I gathered we were headed over Nob Hill, and from the angle, it seemed we were taking one of the steeper routes—I guessed Powell Street.

Now we were descending just as steeply. If my mental map was right, we were heading down to Fisherman's Wharf. You could get on a boat there, get away. That fit with the terrorism hypothesis. Why the hell would terrorists kidnap a bunch of high school students?

We rocked to a stop still on a downslope. The engine died and then the doors swung open. Someone dragged me by my arms out onto the road, then shoved me, stumbling, down a paved road. A few seconds later, I tripped over a steel staircase, bashing my shins. The hands behind me gave me another shove. I went up the stairs cautiously, not able to use my hands. I got up the third step and reached for the fourth, but it wasn't there. I nearly fell again, but new hands grabbed me from in front and dragged me down a steel floor and then forced me to my knees and locked my hands to something behind me.

More movement, and the sense of bodies being shackled in alongside of me. Groans and muffled sounds. Laughter. Then a long, timeless eternity in the muffled gloom, breathing my own breath, hearing my own breath in my ears.

I actually managed a kind of sleep there, kneeling with the circulation cut off to my legs, my head in canvas twilight. My body had squirted a year's supply of adrenaline into my bloodstream in the space of thirty minutes, and while that stuff can give you the strength to lift cars off your loved ones and leap over tall buildings, the payback's always a bitch.

I woke up to someone pulling the hood off my head. They were neither rough nor careful—just . . . impersonal. Like someone at McDonald's putting together burgers.

The light in the room was so bright I had to squeeze my eyes shut, but slowly I was able to open them to slits, then cracks, then all the way and look around.

We were all in the back of a truck, a big 18-wheeler. I could see the wheel wells at regular intervals down the length. But the back of this truck had been turned into some kind of mobile command-post/jail. Steel desks lined the walls with banks of slick flat-panel displays climbing above them on articulated arms that let them be repositioned in a halo around the operators. Each desk had a gorgeous office chair in front of it, festooned with user-interface knobs for adjusting every millimeter of the sitting surface, as well as height, pitch and yaw.

Then there was the jail part—at the front of the truck, farthest away from the doors, there were steel rails bolted into the sides of the vehicle, and attached to these steel rails were the prisoners.

I spotted Van and Jolu right away. Darryl might have been in the remaining dozen shackled up back here, but it was impossible to say—many of them were slumped over and blocking my view. It stank of sweat and fear back there.

Vanessa looked at me and bit her lip. She was scared. So was I. So was Jolu, his eyes rolling crazily in their sockets, the whites showing. I was scared. What's more, I had to piss like a *racehorse*.

I looked around for our captors. I'd avoided looking at them up until now, the same way you don't look into the dark of a closet where your mind has conjured up a boogeyman. You don't want to know if you're right.

But I had to get a better look at these jerks who'd kidnapped us. If they were terrorists, I wanted to know. I didn't know what a terrorist looked like, though TV shows had done their best to convince me that they were brown Arabs with big beards and knit caps and loose cotton dresses that hung down to their ankles.

Not so our captors. They could have been halftime-show cheerleaders on the Super Bowl. They looked *American* in a way I couldn't exactly define. Good jawlines, short, neat haircuts that weren't quite military. They came in white and brown, male and female, and smiled freely at one another as they sat down at the other end of the truck, joking and drinking coffee out of go-cups. These weren't Ay-rabs from Afghanistan: they looked like tourists from Nebraska.

I stared at one, a young white woman with brown hair who barely looked older than me, kind of cute in a scary office-power-suit way. If you stare at someone long enough, they'll eventually look back at you. She did, and her face slammed into a totally different configuration, dispassionate, even robotic. The smile vanished in an instant.

"Hey," I said. "Look, I don't understand what's going on here, but I really need to take a leak, you know?"

She looked right through me as if she hadn't heard.

"I'm serious, if I don't get to a can soon, I'm going to have an ugly accident. It's going to get pretty smelly back here, you know?"

She turned to her colleagues, a little huddle of three of them, and they held a low conversation I couldn't hear over the fans from the computers.

She turned back to me. "Hold it for another ten minutes, then you'll each get a piss-call."

"I don't think I've got another ten minutes in me," I said, letting a little more urgency than I was really feeling creep into my voice. "Seriously, lady, it's now or never."

She shook her head and looked at me like I was some kind of pathetic loser. She and her friends conferred some more, then another one came forward. He was older, in his early thirties, and pretty big across the shoulders, like he worked out. He looked like he was Chinese or Korean—even Van can't tell the difference sometimes—but with that bearing that said *American* in a way I couldn't put my finger on.

He pulled his sports coat aside to let me see the hardware strapped there: I recognized a pistol, a Taser and a can of either mace or pepper spray before he let it fall again.

"No trouble," he said.

"None," I agreed.

He touched something at his belt and the shackles behind me let go, my arms dropping suddenly behind me. It was like he was wearing Batman's utility belt—wireless remotes for shackles! I guessed it made sense, though: you wouldn't want to lean over your prisoners with all that deadly hardware at their eye level— they might grab your gun with their teeth and pull the trigger with their tongues or something.

My hands were still lashed together behind me by the plastic strapping, and now that I wasn't supported by the shackles, I found that my legs had turned into lumps of cork while I was stuck in one position. Long story short, I basically fell onto my face and kicked my legs weakly as they went pins-and-needles, trying to get them under me so I could rock up to my feet.

The guy jerked me to my feet and I clown-walked to the very back of the truck, to a little boxed-in porta-john there. I tried to spot Darryl on the way back, but he could have been any of the five or six slumped people. Or none of them.

"In you go," the guy said.

I jerked my wrists. "Take these off, please?" My fingers felt like purple sausages from the hours of bondage in the plastic cuffs.

The guy didn't move.

"Look," I said, trying not to sound sarcastic or angry (it wasn't easy). "Look. You either cut my wrists free or you're going to have to aim for me. A toilet visit is not a hands-free experience." Someone in the truck sniggered. The guy didn't like me, I could tell from the way his jaw muscles ground around. Man, these people were wired tight.

He reached down to his belt and came up with a very nice set of multipliers. He flicked out a wicked-looking knife and sliced through the plastic cuffs and my hands were my own again.

"Thanks," I said.

He shoved me into the bathroom. My hands were useless, like

lumps of clay on the ends of my wrists. As I wiggled my fingers limply, they tingled, then the tingling turned to a burning feeling that almost made me cry out. I put the seat down, dropped my pants and sat down. I didn't trust myself to stay on my feet.

As my bladder cut loose, so did my eyes. I wept, crying silently and rocking back and forth while the tears and snot ran down my face. It was all I could do to keep from sobbing—I covered my mouth and held the sounds in. I didn't want to give them the satisfaction.

Finally, I was peed out and cried out and the guy was pounding on the door. I cleaned my face as best as I could with wads of toilet paper, stuck it all down the john and flushed, then looked around for a sink but only found a pump-bottle of heavy-duty hand-sanitizer covered in small-print lists of the bio-agents it worked on. I rubbed some into my hands and stepped out of the john.

"What were you doing in there?" the guy said.

"Using the facilities," I said. He turned me around and grabbed my hands and I felt a new pair of plastic cuffs go around them. My wrists had swollen since the last pair had come off and the new ones bit cruelly into my tender skin, but I refused to give him the satisfaction of crying out.

He shackled me back to my spot and grabbed the next person down, who, I saw now, was Jolu, his face puffy and an ugly bruise on his cheek.

"Are you okay?" I asked him, and my friend with the utility belt abruptly put his hand on my forehead and shoved hard, bouncing the back of my head off the truck's metal wall with a sound like a clock striking one. "No talking," he said as I struggled to refocus my eyes.

I didn't like these people. I decided right then that they would pay a price for all this.

One by one, all the prisoners went to the can and came back, and when they were done, my guard went back to his friends and had another cup of coffee—they were drinking out of a big cardboard urn of Starbucks, I saw—and they had an indistinct conversation that involved a fair bit of laughter.

Then the door at the back of the truck opened and there was

fresh air—not smoky the way it had been before, but tinged with ozone. In the slice of outdoors I saw before the door closed, I caught that it was dark out, and raining, with one of those San Francisco drizzles that's part mist.

The man who came in was wearing a military uniform. A U.S. military uniform. He saluted the people in the truck and they saluted him back and that's when I knew that I wasn't a prisoner of some terrorists—I was a prisoner of the United States of America.

They set up a little screen at the end of the truck and then came for us one at a time, unshackling us and leading us to the back of the truck. As close as I could work it—counting seconds off in my head, one hippopotami, two hippopotami—the interviews lasted about seven minutes each. My head throbbed with dehydration and caffeine withdrawal.

I was third, brought back by the woman with the severe haircut. Up close, she looked tired, with bags under her eyes and grim lines at the corners of her mouth.

"Thanks," I said, automatically, as she unlocked me with a remote and then dragged me to my feet. I hated myself for the automatic politeness, but it had been drilled into me.

She didn't twitch a muscle. I went ahead of her to the back of the truck and behind the screen. There was a single folding chair and I sat in it. Two of them—severe haircut lady and utility belt man—looked at me from their ergonomic superchairs.

They had a little table between them with the contents of my wallet and backpack spread out on it.

"Hello, Marcus," severe haircut lady said. "We have some questions for you."

"Am I under arrest?" I asked. This wasn't an idle question. If you're not under arrest, there are limits on what the cops can and can't do to you. For starters, they can't hold you forever without arresting you, giving you a phone call, and letting you talk to a lawyer. And hoo-boy, was I ever going to talk to a lawyer.

"What's this for?" she said, holding up my phone. The screen was showing the error message you got if you kept trying to get into its data without giving the right password. It was a bit of a rude message—an animated hand giving a certain universally recognized gesture—because I liked to customize my gear.

"Am I under arrest?" I repeated. They can't make you answer any questions if you're not under arrest, and when you ask if you're under arrest, they have to answer you. It's the rules.

"You're being detained by the Department of Homeland Security," the woman snapped.

"Am I under arrest?"

"You're going to be more cooperative, Marcus, starting right now." She didn't say, "or else," but it was implied.

"I would like to contact an attorney," I said. "I would like to know what I've been charged with. I would like to see some form of identification from both of you."

The two agents exchanged looks.

"I think you should really reconsider your approach to this situation," severe haircut lady said. "I think you should do that right now. We found a number of suspicious devices on your person. We found you and your confederates near the site of the worst terrorist attack this country has ever seen. Put those two facts together and things don't look very good for you, Marcus. You can cooperate, or you can be very, very sorry. Now, what is this for?"

"You think I'm a terrorist? I'm seventeen years old!"

"Just the right age—Al Qaeda loves recruiting impressionable, idealistic kids. We googled you, you know. You've posted a lot of very ugly stuff on the public Internet."

"I would like to speak to an attorney," I said.

Severe haircut lady looked at me like I was a bug. "You're under the mistaken impression that you've been picked up by the police for a crime. You need to get past that. You are being detained as a potential enemy combatant by the government of the United States. If I were you, I'd be thinking very hard about how to convince us that you are not an enemy combatant. Very hard. Because there are dark holes that enemy combatants can disappear into, very dark deep holes, holes where you can just vanish. Forever. Are you listening to me young man? I want you to unlock this phone and then decrypt the files in its memory. I want you to account for yourself: Why were you out on the street? What do you know about the attack on this city?"

"I'm not going to unlock my phone for you," I said, indignant. My phone's memory had all kinds of private stuff on it: photos, emails, little hacks and mods I'd installed. "That's private stuff."

"What have you got to hide?"

"I've got the right to my privacy," I said. "And I want to speak to an attorney."

"This is your last chance, kid. Honest people don't have anything to hide."

"I want to speak to an attorney." My parents would pay for it. All the FAQs on getting arrested were clear on this point. Just keep asking to see an attorney, no matter what they say or do. There's no good that comes of talking to the cops without your lawyer present. These two said they weren't cops, but if this wasn't an arrest, what was it?

In hindsight, maybe I should have unlocked my phone for them.

chapter 4

They reshackled and rehooded me and left me there. A long time later, the truck started to move, rolling downhill, and then I was hauled back to my feet. I immediately fell over. My legs were so asleep they felt like blocks of ice, all except my knees, which were swollen and tender from all the hours of kneeling.

Hands grabbed my shoulders and feet and I was picked up like a sack of potatoes. There were indistinct voices around me. Someone crying. Someone cursing.

I was carried a short distance, then set down and reshackled to another railing. My knees wouldn't support me anymore and I pitched forward, ending up twisted on the ground like a pretzel, straining against the chains holding my wrists.

Then we were moving again, and this time, it wasn't like driving in a truck. The floor beneath me rocked gently and vibrated with heavy diesel engines and I realized I was on a ship! My stomach turned to ice. I was being taken off America's shores to somewhere *else,* and who the hell knew where that was? I'd been scared before, but this thought *terrified* me, left me paralyzed and wordless with fear. I realized that I might never see my parents again and I actually tasted a little vomit burn up my throat. The bag over my head closed in on me and I could barely breathe, something that was compounded by the weird position I was twisted into.

But mercifully we weren't on the water for very long. It felt like an hour, but I know now that it was a mere fifteen minutes, and then I felt us docking, felt footsteps on the decking around me and felt other prisoners being unshackled and carried or led away. When they came for me, I tried to stand again, but couldn't, and they carried me again, impersonally, roughly.

When they took the hood off again, I was in a cell.

The cell was old and crumbled, and smelled of sea air. There was one window high up, and rusted bars guarded it. It was still dark outside. There was a blanket on the floor and a little metal toilet without a seat, set into the wall. The guard who took off my hood grinned at me and closed the solid steel door behind him.

I gently massaged my legs, hissing as the blood came back into them and into my hands. Eventually I was able to stand, and then to pace. I heard other people talking, crying, shouting. I did some shouting too: "Jolu! Darryl! Vanessa!" Other voices on the cell-block took up the cry, shouting out names, too, shouting out obscenities. The nearest voices sounded like drunks losing their minds on a street corner. Maybe I sounded like that, too.

Guards shouted at us to be quiet and that just made everyone yell louder. Eventually we were all howling, screaming our heads off, screaming our throats raw. Why not? What did we have to lose?

The next time they came to question me, I was filthy and tired, thirsty and hungry. Severe haircut lady was in the new questioning party, as were three big guys who moved me around like a cut of meat. One was black, the other two were white, though one might have been hispanic. They all carried guns. It was like a Benetton's ad crossed with a game of Counter-Strike.

They'd taken me from my cell and chained my wrists and ankles together. I paid attention to my surroundings as we went. I heard water outside and thought that maybe we were on Alcatraz—it was a prison, after all, even if it had been a tourist attraction for generations, the place where you went to see where Al Capone and his gangster contemporaries did their time. But I'd been to Alcatraz on a school trip. It was old and rusted, medieval. This place felt like it dated back to World War Two, not colonial times.

There were bar codes laser-printed on stickers and placed on each of the cell doors, and numbers, but other than that, there was no way to tell who or what might be behind them.

The interrogation room was modern, with fluorescent lights, ergonomic chairs—not for me, though, I got a folding plastic garden chair—and a big wooden boardroom table. A mirror lined one wall, just like in the cop shows, and I figured someone or other must be watching from behind it. Severe haircut lady and her friends helped themselves to coffee from an urn on a side table (I could have torn her throat out with my teeth and taken her coffee just then), and then set a styrofoam cup of water down next to me—without unlocking my wrists from behind my back, so I couldn't reach it. Hardy har har.

"Hello, Marcus," severe haircut lady said. "How's your 'tude doing today?"

I didn't say anything.

"This isn't as bad as it gets you know," she said. "This is as *good* as it gets from now on. Even once you tell us what we want to know, even if that convinces us that you were just in the wrong place at the wrong time, you're a marked man now. We'll be watching you everywhere you go and everything you do. You've acted like you've got something to hide, and we don't like that."

It's pathetic, but all my brain could think about was that phrase, "convince us that you were in the wrong place at the wrong time." This was the worst thing that had ever happened to me. I had never, ever felt this bad or this scared before. Those words, "wrong place at the wrong time," those six words, they were like a lifeline dangling before me as I thrashed to stay on the surface.

"Hello, Marcus?" She snapped her fingers in front of my face. "Over here, Marcus." There was a little smile on her face and I hated myself for letting her see my fear. "Marcus, it can be a lot worse than this. This isn't the worst place we can put you, not by a damned sight." She reached down below the table and came out with a briefcase, which she snapped open. From it, she withdrew my phone, my arphid sniper/cloner, my wifinder and my memory keys. She set them down on the table one after the other.

"Here's what we want from you. You unlock the phone for us today. If you do that, you'll get outdoor and bathing privileges. You'll get a shower and you'll be allowed to walk around in the exercise yard. Tomorrow, we'll bring you back and ask you to decrypt the data on these memory sticks. Do that, and you'll get to eat in the mess hall. The day after, we're going to want your email passwords, and that will get you library privileges."

The word "no" was on my lips, like a burp trying to come up, but it wouldn't come. "Why?" is what came out instead.

"We want to be sure that you're what you seem to be. This is about your security, Marcus. Say you're innocent. You might be, though why an innocent man would act like he's got so much to hide is beyond me. But say you are: you could have been on that bridge when it blew. Your parents could have been. Your friends. Don't you want us to catch the people who attacked your home?"

It's funny, but when she was talking about my getting "privileges" it scared me into submission. I felt like I'd done *something* to end up where I was, like maybe it was partially my fault, like I could do something to change it.

But as soon as she switched to this BS about "safety" and "security," my spine came back. "Lady," I said, "you're talking about attacking my home, but as far as I can tell, you're the only one who's attacked me lately. I thought I lived in a country with a constitution. I thought I lived in a country where I had *rights*. You're talking about defending my freedom by tearing up the Bill of Rights."

A flicker of annoyance passed over her face, then went away. "So melodramatic, Marcus. No one's attacked you. You've been detained by your country's government while we seek details on the worst terrorist attack ever perpetrated on our nation's soil. You have it within your power to help us fight this war on our nation's enemies. You want to preserve the Bill of Rights? Help us stop bad people from blowing up your city. Now, you have exactly thirty seconds to unlock that phone before I send you back to your cell. We have lots of other people to interview today."

She looked at her watch. I rattled my wrists, rattled the chains that kept me from reaching around and unlocking the phone. Yes, I was going to do it. She'd told me what my path was to freedom—to the world, to my parents—and that had given me hope. Now she'd threatened to send me away, to take me off that path, and my hope had crashed and all I could think of was how to get back on it.

So I rattled my wrists, wanting to get to my phone and unlock it for her, and she just looked at me coldly, checking her watch.

"The password," I said, finally understanding what she wanted of me. She wanted me to say it out loud, here, where she could record it, where her pals could hear it. She didn't want me to just unlock the phone. She wanted me to submit to her. To put her in charge of me. To give up every secret, all my privacy. "The password," I said again, and then I told her the password. God help me, I submitted to her will.

She smiled a little prim smile, which had to be her ice-queen equivalent of a touchdown dance, and the guards led me away. As the door closed, I saw her bend down over the phone and key the password in.

I wish I could say that I'd anticipated this possibility in advance and created a fake password that unlocked a completely innocuous partition on my phone, but I wasn't nearly that paranoid/clever.

You might be wondering at this point what dark secrets I had locked away on my phone and memory sticks and email. I'm just a kid, after all.

The truth is that I had everything to hide, and nothing. Between my phone and my memory sticks, you could get a pretty good idea of who my friends were, what I thought of them, all the goofy things we'd done. You could read the transcripts of the electronic arguments we'd carried out and the electronic reconciliations we'd arrived at.

You see, I don't delete stuff. Why would I? Storage is cheap, and you never know when you're going to want to go back to that stuff. Especially the stupid stuff. You know that feeling you get sometimes where you're sitting on the subway and there's no one to talk to and you suddenly remember some bitter fight you had, some terrible thing you said? Well, it's usually never as bad as you remember. Being able to go back and see it again is a great way to remind yourself that you're not as horrible a person as you think you are. Darryl and I have gotten over more fights that way than I can count.

And even that's not it. I know my phone is private. I know my memory sticks are private. That's because of cryptography— message scrambling. The math behind crypto is good and solid, and you and me get access to the same crypto that banks and the National Security Agency use. There's only one kind of crypto that anyone uses: crypto that's public, open and can be deployed by anyone. That's how you know it works.

There's something really liberating about having some corner of your life that's *yours*, that no one gets to see except you. It's a little like nudity or taking a dump. Everyone gets naked every once in a while. Everyone has to squat on the toilet. There's nothing shameful, deviant or weird about either of them. But what if I decreed that from now on, every time you went to evacuate some solid waste, you'd have to do it in a glass room perched in the middle of Times Square, and you'd be buck naked?

Even if you've got nothing wrong or weird with your body—and how many of us can say that?—you'd have to be pretty strange to like that idea. Most of us would run screaming. Most of us would hold it in until we exploded.

It's not about doing something shameful. It's about doing something *private*. It's about your life belonging to you.

They were taking that from me, piece by piece. As I walked back to my cell, that feeling of deserving it came back to me. I'd broken a lot of rules all my life and I'd gotten away with it, by and large. Maybe this was justice. Maybe this was my past coming back to me. After all, I had been where I was because I'd snuck out of school.

I got my shower. I got to walk around the yard. There was a patch of sky overhead, and it smelled like the Bay Area, but beyond that, I had no clue where I was being held. No other prisoners were visible during my exercise period, and I got pretty bored with walking in circles. I strained my ears for any sound that might help me understand what this place was, but all I heard was the occasional vehicle, some distant conversations, a plane landing somewhere nearby.

They brought me back to my cell and fed me, a half a pepperoni pie from Goat Hill Pizza, which I knew well, up on Potrero Hill. The carton with its familiar graphic and 415 phone number was a reminder that only a day before, I'd been a free man in a free country and that now I was a prisoner. I worried constantly about Darryl and fretted about my other friends. Maybe they'd been more cooperative and had been released. Maybe they'd told my parents and they were frantically calling around.

Maybe not.

The cell was fantastically spare, empty as my soul. I fantasized that the wall opposite my bunk was a screen that I could be hacking right now, opening the cell door. I fantasized about my workbench and the projects there—the old cans I was turning into a ghetto surround-sound rig, the aerial photography kite-cam I was building, my home-brew laptop.

I wanted to get out of there. I wanted to go home and have my friends and my school and my parents and my life back. I wanted to be able to go where I wanted to go, not be stuck pacing and pacing and pacing.

They took my passwords for my USB keys next. Those held some interesting messages I'd downloaded from one online discussion group or another, some chat transcripts, things where people had helped me out with some of the knowledge I needed to do the things I did. There was nothing on there you couldn't find with Google, of course, but I didn't think that would count in my favor.

I got exercise again that afternoon, and this time there were others in the yard when I got there, four other guys and two women, of all ages and racial backgrounds. I guess lots of people were doing things to earn their "privileges."

They gave me half an hour, and I tried to make conversation with the most normal-seeming of the other prisoners, a black guy about my age with a short afro. But when I introduced myself and stuck my hand out, he cut his eyes toward the cameras mounted ominously in the corners of the yard and kept walking without ever changing his facial expression.

But then, just before they called my name and brought me back into the building, the door opened and out came—Vanessa! I'd never been more glad to see a friendly face. She looked tired and grumpy, but not hurt, and when she saw me, she shouted my name and ran to me. We hugged each other hard and I realized I was shaking. Then I realized she was shaking, too.

"Are you okay?" she said, holding me at arms' length.

"I'm okay," I said. "They told me they'd let me go if I gave them my passwords."

"They keep asking me questions about you and Darryl."

There was a voice blaring over the loudspeaker, shouting at us to stop talking, to walk, but we ignored it.

"Answer them," I said, instantly. "Anything they ask, answer them. If it'll get you out."

"How are Darryl and Jolu?"

"I haven't seen them."

The door banged open and four big guards boiled out. Two took me and two took Vanessa. They forced me to the ground and turned my head away from Vanessa, though I heard her getting the same treatment. Plastic cuffs went around my wrists and then I was yanked to my feet and brought back to my cell.

No dinner came that night. No breakfast came the next morning. No one came and brought me to the interrogation room to extract more of my secrets. The plastic cuffs didn't come off, and my shoulders burned, then ached, then went numb, then burned again. I lost all feeling in my hands.

I had to pee. I couldn't undo my pants. I really, really had to pee.

I pissed myself.

They came for me after that, once the hot piss had cooled and gone clammy, making my already filthy jeans stick to my legs. They came for me and walked me down the long hall lined with doors, each door with its own bar code, each bar code a prisoner like me. They walked me down the corridor and brought me to the interrogation room and it was like a different planet when I entered there, a world where things were normal, where everything didn't reek of urine. I felt so dirty and ashamed, and all those feelings of deserving what I got came back to me.

Severe haircut lady was already sitting. She was perfect: coifed and with just a little makeup. I smelled her hair stuff. She wrinkled her nose at me. I felt the shame rise in me.

"Well, you've been a very naughty boy, haven't you? Aren't you a filthy thing?"

Shame. I looked down at the table. I couldn't bear to look up. I wanted to tell her my email password and get gone.

"What did you and your friend talk about in the yard?"

I barked a laugh at the table. "I told her to answer your questions. I told her to cooperate."

"So do you give the orders?"

I felt the blood sing in my ears. "Oh come on," I said. "We play a *game* together, it's called Harajuku Fun Madness. I'm the *team captain*. We're not terrorists, we're high school students. I don't give her orders. I told her that we needed to be *honest* with you so that we could clear up any suspicion and get out of here."

She didn't say anything for a moment.

"How is Darryl?" I said.

"Who?"

"Darryl. You picked us up together. My friend. Someone had stabbed him in the Powell Street BART. That's why we were up on the surface. To get him help."

"I'm sure he's fine, then," she said.

My stomach knotted and I almost threw up. "You don't *know*? You haven't got him here?"

"Who we have here and who we don't have here is not something we're going to discuss with you, ever. That's not something you're going to know. Marcus, you've seen what happens when you don't cooperate with us. You've seen what happens when you disobey our orders. You've been a little cooperative, and it's gotten you almost to the point where you might go free again. If you want to make that possibility into a reality, you'll stick to answering my questions."

I didn't say anything.

"You're learning, that's good. Now, your email passwords, please."

I was ready for this. I gave them everything: server address, login, password. This didn't matter. I didn't keep any email on my server. I downloaded it all and kept it on my laptop at home, which downloaded and deleted my mail from the server every sixty seconds. They wouldn't get anything out of my mail—it got cleared off the server and stored on my laptop at home.

Back to the cell, but they cut loose my hands and they gave me a shower and a pair of orange prison pants to wear. They were too big for me and hung down low on my hips, like a Mexican gang kid in the Mission. That's where the baggy-pants-down-your-ass look comes from you know that? From prison. I tell you what, it's less fun when it's not a fashion statement.

They took away my jeans, and I spent another day in the cell. The walls were scratched cement over a steel grid. You could tell, because the steel was rusting in the salt air, and the grid shone through the green paint in red-orange. My parents were out that window, somewhere.

They came for me again the next day.

"We've been reading your mail for a day now. We changed the password so that your home computer couldn't fetch it."

Well, of course they had. I would have done the same, now that I thought of it.

"We have enough on you now to put you away for a very long time, Marcus. Your possession of these articles"—she gestured at all my little gizmos—"and the data we recovered from your phone and memory sticks, as well as the subversive material we'd no doubt find if we raided your house and took your computer. It's enough to put you away until you're an old man. Do you understand that?"

I didn't believe it for a second. There's no way a judge would say that all this stuff constituted any kind of real crime. It was free speech, it was technological tinkering. It wasn't a crime.

But who said that these people would ever put me in front of a judge.

"We know where you live, we know who your friends are. We know how you operate and how you think."

It dawned on me then. They were about to let me go. The room seemed to brighten. I heard myself breathing, short little breaths.

"We just want to know one thing: what was the delivery mechanism for the bombs on the bridge?"

I stopped breathing. The room darkened again.

"What?"

"There were ten charges on the bridge, all along its length. They weren't in car trunks. They'd been placed there. Who placed them there, and how did they get there?"

"What?" I said it again.

"This is your last chance, Marcus," she said. She looked sad.

"You were doing so well until now. Tell us this and you can go home. You can get a lawyer and defend yourself in a court of law. There are doubtless extenuating circumstances that you can use to explain your actions. Just tell us this thing, and you're gone."

"I don't know what you're talking about!" I was crying and I didn't even care. Sobbing, blubbering. "I have *no idea what you're talking about!*"

She shook her head. "Marcus, please. Let us help you. By now you know that we always get what we're after."

There was a gibbering sound in the back of my mind. They were *insane*. I pulled myself together, working hard to stop the tears. "Listen, lady, this is nuts. You've been into my stuff, you've seen it all. I'm a seventeen-year-old high school student, not a terrorist! You can't seriously think—"

"Marcus, haven't you figured out that we're serious yet?" She shook her head. "You get pretty good grades. I thought you'd be smarter than that." She made a flicking gesture and the guards picked me up by the armpits.

Back in my cell, a hundred little speeches occurred to me. The French call this *esprit d'escalier*—the spirit of the staircase, the snappy rebuttals that come to you after you leave the room and slink down the stairs. In my mind, I stood and delivered, telling her that I was a citizen who loved my freedom, which made me the patriot and made her the traitor. In my mind, I shamed her for turning my country into an armed camp. In my mind, I was eloquent and brilliant and reduced her to tears.

But you know what? None of those fine words came back to me when they pulled me out the next day. All I could think of was freedom. My parents.

"Hello, Marcus," she said. "How are you feeling?"

I looked down at the table. She had a neat pile of documents in front of her, and her ubiquitous go-cup of Starbucks beside her. I found it comforting somehow, a reminder that there was a real world out there somewhere, beyond the walls.

"We're through investigating you, for now." She let that hang there. Maybe it meant that she was letting me go. Maybe it meant that she was going to throw me in a pit and forget that I existed.

"And?" I said finally.

"And I want to impress on you again that we are very serious about this. Our country has experienced the worst attack ever committed on its soil. How many 9/11s do you want us to suffer before you're willing to cooperate? The details of our investigation are secret. We won't stop at anything in our efforts to bring the perpetrators of these heinous crimes to justice. Do you understand that?"

"Yes," I mumbled.

"We are going to send you home today, but you are a marked man. You have not been found to be above suspicion—we're only releasing you because we're done questioning you for now. But from now on, you *belong* to us. We will be watching you. We'll be waiting for you to make a misstep. Do you understand that we can watch you closely, all the time?"

"Yes," I mumbled.

"Good. You will never speak of what happened here to anyone, ever. This is a matter of national security. Do you know that the death penalty still holds for treason in time of war?"

"Yes," I mumbled.

"Good boy," she purred. "We have some papers here for you to sign." She pushed the stack of papers across the table to me. Little Post-its with SIGN HERE printed on them had been stuck throughout them. A guard undid my cuffs.

I paged through the papers and my eyes watered and my head swam. I couldn't make sense of them. I tried to decipher the legalese. It seemed that I was signing a declaration that I had been voluntarily held and submitted to voluntary questioning, of my own free will.

"What happens if I don't sign this?" I said.

She snatched the papers back and made that flicking gesture again. The guards jerked me to my feet.

"Wait!" I cried. "Please! I'll sign them!" They dragged me to the door. All I could see was that door, all I could think of was it closing behind me.

I lost it. I wept. I begged to be allowed to sign the papers. To be so close to freedom and have it snatched away, it made me ready to do anything. I can't count the number of times I've heard someone say, "Oh, I'd rather die than do something-or-other"—I've said it myself now and again. But that was the first time I understood what it really meant. I would have rather died than go back to my cell.

I begged as they took me out into the corridor. I told them I'd sign anything.

She called out to the guards and they stopped. They brought me back. They sat me down. One of them put the pen in my hand.

Of course, I signed, and signed and signed.

My jeans and T-shirt were back in my cell, laundered and folded. They smelled of detergent. I put them on and washed my face and sat on my cot and stared at the wall. They'd taken everything from me. First my privacy, then my dignity. I'd been ready to sign anything. I would have signed a confession that said I'd assassinated Abraham Lincoln.

I tried to cry, but it was like my eyes were dry, out of tears.

They got me again. A guard approached me with a hood, like the hood I'd been put in when they picked us up, whenever that was, days ago, weeks ago.

The hood went over my head and cinched tight at my neck. I was in total darkness and the air was stifling and stale. I was raised to my feet and walked down corridors, up stairs, on gravel. Up a gangplank. On a ship's steel deck. My hands were chained behind me, to a railing. I knelt on the deck and listened to the thrum of the diesel engines.

The ship moved. A hint of salt air made its way into the hood. It was drizzling and my clothes were heavy with water. I was outside, even if my head was in a bag. I was outside, in the world, moments from my freedom.

They came for me and led me off the boat and over uneven ground. Up three metal stairs. My wrists were unshackled. My hood was removed.

I was back in the truck. Severe haircut woman was there, at the little desk she'd sat at before. She had a Ziploc bag with her, and inside it were my phone and other little devices, my wallet and the change from my pockets. She handed them to me wordlessly.

I filled my pockets. It felt so weird to have everything back in its familiar place, to be wearing my familiar clothes. Outside the truck's back door, I heard the familiar sounds of my familiar city.

A guard passed me my backpack. The woman extended her hand to me. I just looked at it. She put it down and gave me a wry smile. Then she mimed zipping up her lips and pointed to me, and opened the door.

It was daylight outside, gray and drizzling. I was looking down an alley toward cars and trucks and bikes zipping down the road. I stood transfixed on the truck's top step, staring at freedom.

My knees shook. I knew now that they were playing with me again. In a moment, the guards would grab me and drag me back inside, the bag would go over my head again, and I would be back on the boat and sent off to the prison again, to the endless, unanswerable questions. I barely held myself back from stuffing my fist in my mouth.

Then I forced myself to go down one stair. Another stair. The last stair. My sneakers crunched down on the crap on the alley's floor, broken glass, a needle, gravel. I took a step. Another. I reached the mouth of the alley and stepped onto the sidewalk.

No one grabbed me.

I was free.

Then strong arms threw themselves around me. I nearly cried.

chapter 5

But it was Van, and she *was* crying, and hugging me so hard I couldn't breathe. I didn't care. I hugged her back, my face buried in her hair.

"You're okay!" she said.

"I'm okay," I managed.

She finally let go of me and another set of arms wrapped themselves around me. It was Jolu! They were both there. He whispered, "You're safe, bro," in my ear and hugged me even tighter than Vanessa had.

When he let go, I looked around. "Where's Darryl?" I asked.

They both looked at each other. "Maybe he's still in the truck," Jolu said.

We turned and looked at the truck at the alley's end. It was a nondescript white 18-wheeler. Someone had already brought the little folding staircase inside. The rear lights glowed red, and the truck rolled backwards toward us, emitting a steady eep, eep, eep.

"Wait!" I shouted as it accelerated toward us. "Wait! What about Darryl?" The truck drew closer. I kept shouting. "What about Darryl?"

Jolu and Vanessa each had me by an arm and were dragging me away. I struggled against them, shouting. The truck pulled out of the alley's mouth and reversed into the street and pointed itself downhill and drove away. I tried to run after it, but Van and Jolu wouldn't let me go.

I sat down on the sidewalk and put my arms around my knees and cried. I cried and cried and cried, loud sobs of the sort I hadn't done since I was a little kid. They wouldn't stop coming. I couldn't stop shaking.

Vanessa and Jolu got me to my feet and moved me a little ways up the street. There was a Muni bus stop with a bench and they sat me on it. They were both crying, too, and we held each other for a while, and I knew we were crying for Darryl, whom none of us ever expected to see again.

We were north of Chinatown, at the part where it starts to become North Beach, a neighborhood with a bunch of neon strip clubs and the legendary City Lights counterculture bookstore, where the Beat poetry movement had been founded back in the 1950s.

I knew this part of town well. My parents' favorite Italian restaurant was here and they liked to take me here for big plates of linguine and huge Italian ice cream mountains with candied figs and lethal little espressos afterward.

Now it was a different place, a place where I was tasting freedom for the first time in what seemed like an enternity.

We checked our pockets and found enough money to get a table at one of the Italian restaurants, out on the sidewalk, under an awning. The pretty waitress lighted a gas heater with a barbecue lighter, took our orders and went inside. The sensation of giving orders, of controlling my destiny, was the most amazing thing I'd ever felt.

"How long were we in there?" I asked.

"Six days," Vanessa said.

"I got five," Jolu said.

"I didn't count."

"What did they do to you?" Vanessa said. I didn't want to talk about it, but they were both looking at me. Once I started, I couldn't stop. I told them everything, even when I'd been forced to piss myself, and they took it all in silently. I paused when the waitress delivered our sodas and waited until she got out of earshot, then finished. In the telling, it receded into the distance. By the end of it, I couldn't tell if I was embroidering the truth or if I was making it all seem *less* bad. My memories swam like little fish that I snatched at, and sometimes they wriggled out of my grasp.

Jolu shook his head. "They were hard on you, dude," he said. He told us about his stay there. They'd questioned him, mostly about me, and he'd kept on telling them the truth, sticking to a plain telling of the facts about that day and about our friendship. They had gotten him to repeat it over and over again, but they hadn't played games with his head the way they had with me. He'd eaten his meals in a mess hall with a bunch of other people, and been given time in a TV room where they were shown last year's blockbusters on video.

Vanessa's story was only slightly different. After she'd gotten them angry by talking to me, they'd taken away her clothes and made her wear a set of orange prison coveralls. She'd been left in her cell for two days without contact, though she'd been fed regularly. But mostly it was the same as Jolu: the same questions, repeated again and again.

"They really hated you," Jolu said. "Really had it in for you. Why?"

I couldn't imagine why. Then I remembered.

You can cooperate, or you can be very, very sorry.

"It was because I wouldn't unlock my phone for them, that first night. That's why they singled me out." I couldn't believe it, but there was no other explanation. It had been sheer vindictiveness. My mind reeled at the thought. They had done all that as a mere punishment for defying their authority.

I had been scared. Now I was angry. "Those bastards," I said, softly. "They did it to get back at me for mouthing off."

Jolu swore and then Vanessa cut loose in Korean, something she only did when she was really, really angry.

"I'm going to get them," I whispered, staring at my soda. "I'm going to get them."

Jolu shook his head. "You can't, you know. You can't fight back against that."

None of us much wanted to talk about revenge then. Instead, we talked about what we would do next. We had to go home. Our phones' batteries were dead and it had been years since this neighborhood had any pay phones. We just needed to go home. I even thought about taking a taxi, but there wasn't enough money between us to make that possible.

So we walked. On the corner, we pumped some quarters into

a *San Francisco Chronicle* newspaper box and stopped to read the front section. It had been five days since the bombs went off, but it was still all over the front cover.

Severe haircut woman had talked about "the bridge" blowing up, and I'd just assumed that she was talking about the Golden Gate bridge, but I was wrong. The terrorists had blown up the *Bay Bridge.*

"Why the hell would they blow up the Bay Bridge?" I said. "The Golden Gate is the one on all the postcards." Even if you've never been to San Francisco, chances are you know what the Golden Gate looks like: it's that big orange suspension bridge that swoops dramatically from the old military base called the Presidio to Sausalito, where all the cutesy wine-country towns are with their scented candle shops and art galleries. It's picturesque as hell, and it's practically the symbol for the state of California. If you go to the Disneyland California Adventure park, there's a replica of it just past the gates, with a monorail running over it.

So naturally I assumed that if you were going to blow up a bridge in San Francisco, that's the one you'd blow.

"They probably got scared off by all the cameras and stuff," Jolu said. "The National Guard's always checking cars at both ends and there's all those suicide fences and junk all along it." People have been jumping off the Golden Gate since it opened in 1937—they stopped counting after the thousandth suicide in 1995.

"Yeah," Vanessa said. "Plus the Bay Bridge actually goes somewhere." The Bay Bridge goes from downtown San Francisco to Oakland and thence to Berkeley, the East Bay townships that are home to many of the people who live and work in town. It's one of the only parts of the Bay Area where a normal person can afford a house big enough to really stretch out in, and there's also the university and a bunch of light industry over there. The BART goes under the Bay and connects the two cities, too, but it's the Bay Bridge that sees most of the traffic. The Golden Gate was a nice bridge if you were a tourist or a rich retiree living out in wine country, but it was mostly ornamental. The Bay Bridge is—was—San Francisco's workhorse bridge.

I thought about it for a minute. "You guys are right," I said. "But I don't think that's all of it. We keep acting like terrorists attack landmarks because they hate landmarks. Terrorists don't hate landmarks or bridges or airplanes. They just want to screw stuff up and make people scared. To make terror. So of course they went after the Bay Bridge after the Golden Gate got all those cameras—after airplanes got all metal-detectored and X-rayed." I thought about it some more, staring blankly at the cars rolling down the street, at the people walking down the sidewalks, at the city all around me. "Terrorists don't hate airplanes or bridges. They love terror." It was so obvious I couldn't believe I'd never thought of it before. I guess that being treated like a terrorist for a few days was enough to clarify my thinking.

The other two were staring at me. "I'm right, aren't I? All this crap, all the X-rays and ID checks, they're all useless, aren't they?"

They nodded slowly.

"Worse than useless," I said, my voice going up and cracking. "Because they ended up with us in prison, with Darryl—" I hadn't thought of Darryl since we sat down and now it came back to me: my friend, missing, disappeared. I stopped talking and ground my jaws together.

"We have to tell our parents," Jolu said.

"We should get a lawyer," Vanessa said.

I thought of telling my story. Of telling the world what had become of me. Of the videos that would no doubt come out, of me weeping, reduced to a groveling animal.

"We can't tell them anything," I said, without thinking.

"What do you mean?" Van said.

"We can't tell them anything," I repeated. "You heard her. If we talk, they'll come back for us. They'll do to us what they did to Darryl."

"You're joking," Jolu said. "You want us to—"

"I want us to fight back," I said. "I want to stay free so that I can do that. If we go out there and blab, they'll just say that we're kids, making it up. We don't even know where we were held! No one will believe us. Then, one day, they'll come for us.

"I'm telling my parents that I was in one of those camps on the other side of the Bay. I came over to meet you guys there and we got stranded, and just got loose today. They said in the papers that people were still wandering home from them."

"I can't do that," Vanessa said. "After what they did to you, how can you even think of doing that?"

"It happened to *me*, that's the point. This is me and them, now. I'll beat them, I'll get Darryl. I'm not going to take this lying down. But once our parents are involved, that's it for us. No one will believe us and no one will care. If we do it my way, people will care."

"What's your way?" Jolu said. "What's your plan?"

"I don't know yet," I admitted. "Give me until tomorrow morning, give me that, at least." I knew that once they'd kept it a secret for a day, it would have to be a secret forever. Our parents would be even more skeptical if we suddenly "remembered" that we'd been held in a secret prison instead of taken care of in a refugee camp.

Van and Jolu looked at each other.

"I'm just asking for a chance," I said. "We'll work out the story on the way, get it straight. Give me one day, just one day."

The other two nodded glumly and we set off downhill again, heading back toward home. I lived on Potrero Hill, Vanessa lived in the North Mission and Jolu lived in Noe Valley—three wildly different neighborhoods just a few minutes' walk from one another.

We turned onto Market Street and stopped dead. The street was barricaded at every corner, the cross streets reduced to a single lane, and parked down the whole length of Market Street were big, nondescript 18-wheelers like the one that had carried us, hooded, away from the ship's docks and to Chinatown.

Each one had three steel steps leading down from the back and they buzzed with activity as soldiers, people in suits and cops went in and out of them. The suits wore little badges on their lapels and the soldiers scanned them as they went in and out—wireless authorization badges. As we walked past one, I got a look at it, and saw the familiar logo: Department of Homeland Security. The soldier saw me staring and stared back hard, glaring at me.

I got the message and moved on. I peeled away from the gang at

Van Ness. We clung to each other and cried and promised to call each other.

The walk back to Potrero Hill has an easy route and a hard route, the latter taking you over some of the steepest hills in the city, the kind of thing that you see car chases on in action movies, with cars catching air as they soar over the zenith. I always take the hard way home. It's all residential streets, and the old Victorian houses they call "painted ladies" for their gaudy, elaborate paint jobs, and front gardens with scented flowers and tall grasses. Housecats stare at you from hedges, and there are hardly any homeless.

It was so quiet on those streets that it made me wish I'd taken the *other* route, through the Mission, which is . . . *raucous* is probably the best word for it. Loud and vibrant. Lots of rowdy drunks and angry crackheads and unconscious junkies, and also lots of families with strollers, old ladies gossiping on stoops, lowriders with boom-cars going thumpa-thumpa-thumpa down the streets. There were hipsters and mopey emo art students and even a couple old-school punk rockers, old guys with pot bellies bulging out beneath their Dead Kennedys shirts. Also drag queens, angry gang kids, graffiti artists and bewildered gentrifiers trying not to get killed while their real estate investments matured.

I went up Goat Hill and walked past Goat Hill Pizza, which made me think of the jail I'd been held in, and I had to sit down on the bench out in front of the restaurant until my shakes passed. Then I noticed the truck up the hill from me, a nondescript 18-wheeler with three metal steps coming down from the back end. I got up and got moving. I felt the eyes watching me from all directions.

I hurried the rest of the way home. I didn't look at the painted ladies or the gardens or the housecats. I kept my eyes down.

Both my parents' cars were in the driveway, even though it was the middle of the day. Of course. Dad works in the East Bay, so he'd be stuck at home while they worked on the bridge. Mom—well, who knew why Mom was home.

They were home for me.

Even before I'd finished unlocking the door it had been jerked out of my hand and flung wide. There were both of my parents, looking gray and haggard, bug-eyed and staring at me. We stood there in frozen tableau for a moment, then they both rushed forward and dragged me into the house, nearly tripping me up. They were both talking so loud and fast all I could hear was a wordless, roaring gabble and they both hugged me and cried and I cried, too, and we just stood there like that in the little foyer, crying and making almost-words until we ran out of steam and went into the kitchen.

I did what I always did when I came home: got myself a glass of water from the filter in the fridge and dug a couple cookies out of the "biscuit barrel" that Mom's sister had sent us from England. The normalcy of this made my heart stop hammering, my heart catching up with my brain, and soon we were all sitting at the table.

"Where have you been?" they both said, more or less in unison.

I had given this some thought on the way home. "I got trapped," I said. "In Oakland. I was there with some friends, doing a project, and we were all quarantined."

"For five days?"

"Yeah," I said. "Yeah. It was really bad." I'd read about the quarantines in the *Chronicle* and I cribbed shamelessly from the quotes they'd published. "Yeah. Everyone who got caught in the cloud. They thought we had been attacked with some kind of superbug and they packed us into shipping containers in the docklands, like sardines. It was really hot and sticky. Not much food, either."

"Christ," Dad said, his fists balling up on the table. Dad teaches in Berkeley three days a week, working with a few grad students in the library science program. The rest of the time he consults for clients in the city and down the Peninsula, third-wave dotcoms that are doing various things with archives. He's a mild-mannered librarian by profession, but he'd been a real radical in the sixties and wrestled a little in high school. I'd seen him get crazy angry now and again—I'd even made him that angry now and again— and he could seriously lose it when he was Hulking out. He once threw a swing-set from Ikea across my granddad's whole lawn when it fell apart for the fiftieth time while he was assembling it.

"Barbarians," Mom said. She's been living in America since she was a teenager, but she still comes over all British when she encounters American cops, health care, airport security or homelessness. Then the word is "barbarians," and her accent comes back strong. We'd been to London twice to see her family and I can't say as it felt any more civilized than San Francisco, just more cramped.

"But they let us go, and ferried us over today." I was improvising now.

"Are you hurt?" Mom said. "Hungry?"

"Sleepy?"

"Yeah, a little of all that. Also Dopey, Doc, Sneezy and Bashful." We had a family tradition of Seven Dwarfs jokes. They both smiled a little, but their eyes were still wet. I felt really bad for them. They must have been out of their minds with worry. I was glad for a chance to change the subject. "I'd totally love to eat."

"I'll order a pizza from Goat Hill," Dad said.

"No, not that," I said. They both looked at me like I'd sprouted antennas. I normally have a thing about Goat Hill Pizza—as in, I can normally eat it like a goldfish eats his food, gobbling until it either runs out or I pop. I tried to smile. "I just don't feel like pizza," I said, lamely. "Let's order some curry, okay?" Thank heaven that San Francisco is take-out central.

Mom went to the drawer of take-out menus (more normalcy, feeling like a drink of water on a dry, sore throat) and riffled through them. We spent a couple of distracting minutes going through the menu from the halal Pakistani place on Valencia. I settled on a mixed tandoori grill and creamed spinach with farmer's cheese, a salted mango lassi (much better than it sounds) and little fried pastries in sugar syrup.

Once the food was ordered, the questions started again. They'd heard from Van's, Jolu's and Darryl's families (of course) and had tried to report us missing. The police were taking names, but there were so many "displaced persons" that they weren't going to open files on anyone unless they were still missing after seven days.

Meanwhile, millions of have-you-seen sites had popped up on the net. A couple of the sites were old MySpace clones that had run out of money and saw a new lease on life from all the attention.

After all, some venture capitalists had missing family in the Bay Area. Maybe if they were recovered, the site would attract some new investment. I grabbed Dad's laptop and looked through them. They were plastered with advertising, of course, and pictures of missing people, mostly grad photos, wedding pictures and that sort of thing. It was pretty ghoulish.

I found my pic and saw that it was linked to Van's, Jolu's and Darryl's. There was a little form for marking people found and another one for writing up notes about other missing people. I filled in the fields for me and Jolu and Van, and left Darryl blank.

"You forgot Darryl," Dad said. He didn't like Darryl much— once he'd figured out that a couple inches were missing out of one of the bottles in his liquor cabinet, and to my enduring shame I'd blamed it on Darryl. In truth, of course, it had been both of us, just fooling around, trying out vodka-and-Cokes during an all-night gaming session.

"He wasn't with us," I said. The lie tasted bitter in my mouth.

"Oh my God," my mom said. She squeezed her hands together. "We just assumed when you came home that you'd all been together."

"No," I said, the lie growing. "No, he was supposed to meet us but we never met up. He's probably just stuck over in Berkeley. He was going to take the BART over."

Mom made a whimpering sound. Dad shook his head and closed his eyes. "Don't you know about the BART?" he said.

I shook my head. I could see where this was going. I felt like the ground was rushing up to me.

"They blew it up," Dad said. "The bastards blew it up at the same time as the bridge."

That hadn't been on the front page of the *Chronicle*, but then, a BART blowout under the water wouldn't be nearly as picturesque as the images of the bridge hanging in tatters and pieces over the Bay. The BART tunnel from the Embarcadero in San Francisco to the West Oakland station was submerged.

I went back to Dad's computer and surfed the headlines. No one was sure, but the body count was in the thousands. Between the cars that plummeted 191 feet to the sea and the people drowned in the trains, the deaths were mounting. One reporter claimed to have interviewed an "identity counterfeiter" who'd helped "dozens" of people walk away from their old lives by simply vanishing after the attacks, getting new ID made up and slipping away from bad marriages, bad debts and bad lives.

Dad actually got tears in his eyes, and Mom was openly crying. They each hugged me again, patting me with their hands as if to assure themselves that I was really there. They kept telling me they loved me. I told them I loved them, too.

We had a weepy dinner and Mom and Dad had each had a couple glasses of wine, which was a lot for them. I told them that I was getting sleepy, which was true, and mooched up to my room. I wasn't going to bed, though. I needed to get online and find out what was going on. I needed to talk to Jolu and Vanessa. I needed to get working on finding Darryl.

I crept up to my room and opened the door. I hadn't seen my old bed in what felt like a thousand years. I lay down on it and reached over to my bedstand to grab my laptop. I must have not plugged it in all the way—the electrical adapter needed to be jiggled just right—so it had slowly discharged while I was away. I plugged it back in and gave it a minute or two to charge up before trying to power it up again. I used the time to get undressed and throw my clothes in the trash—I never wanted to see them again—and put on a clean pair of boxers and a fresh T-shirt. The fresh-laundered clothes, straight out of my drawers, felt so familiar and comfortable, like getting hugged by my parents.

I powered up my laptop and punched a bunch of pillows into place behind me at the top of the bed. I scooched back and opened my computer's lid and settled it onto my thighs. It was still booting, and man, those icons creeping across the screen looked *good*. It came all the way up and then it started giving me more low-power warnings. I checked the power cable again and wiggled it and they went away. The power jack was really flaking out.

In fact, it was so bad that I couldn't actually get anything done. Every time I took my hand off the power cable it lost contact and the computer started to complain about its battery. I took a closer look at it.

The whole case of my computer was slightly misaligned, the seam split in an angular gape that started narrow and widened toward the back.

Sometimes you look at a piece of equipment and discover something like this and you wonder, *Was it always like that?* Maybe you just never noticed.

But with my laptop, that wasn't possible. You see, I built it. After the Board of Ed issued us all SchoolBooks, there was no way my parents were going to buy me a computer of my own, even though technically the SchoolBook didn't belong to me, and I wasn't supposed to install software on it or mod it.

I had some money saved—odd jobs, Christmases and birthdays, a little bit of judicious ebaying. Put it all together and I had enough money to buy a totally crappy, five-year-old machine.

So Darryl and I built one instead. You can buy laptop cases just like you can buy cases for desktop PCs, though they're a little more specialized than plain old PCs. I'd built a couple PCs with Darryl over the years, scavenging parts from Craigslist and garage sales and ordering stuff from cheap Taiwanese vendors we found on the net. I figured that building a laptop would be the best way to get the power I wanted at the price I could afford.

To build your own laptop, you start by ordering a "barebook"—a machine with just a little hardware in it and all the right slots. The good news was, once I was done, I had a machine that was a whole pound lighter than the Dell I'd had my eye on, ran faster and cost a third of what I would have paid Dell. The bad news was that assembling a laptop is like building one of those ships in a bottle. It's all finicky work with tweezers and magnifying glasses, trying to get everything to fit in that little case. Unlike a full-sized PC—which is mostly air—every cubic millimeter of space in a laptop is spoken for. Every time I thought I had it, I'd go to screw the thing back together and find that something was keeping the case from closing all the way, and it'd be back to the drawing board.

So I knew *exactly* how the seam on my laptop was supposed to look when the thing was closed, and it was *not* supposed to look like this.

I kept jiggling the power adapter, but it was hopeless. There was no way I was going to get the thing to boot without taking it apart. I groaned and put it beside the bed. I'd deal with it in the morning.

That was the theory, anyway. Two hours later, I was still staring at the ceiling, playing back movies in my head of what they'd done to me, what I should have done, all regrets and *esprit d'escalier.*

I rolled out of bed. It had gone midnight and I'd heard my parents hit the sack at eleven. I grabbed the laptop and cleared some space on my desk and clipped the little LED lamps to the temples of my magnifying glasses and pulled out a set of little precision screwdrivers. A minute later, I had the case open and the keyboard removed and I was staring at the guts of my laptop. I got a can of compressed air and blew out the dust that the fan had sucked in and looked things over.

Something wasn't right. I couldn't put my finger on it, but then it had been months since I'd had the lid off this thing. Luckily, the third time I'd had to open it up and struggle to close it again, I'd gotten smart: I'd taken a photo of the guts with everything in place. I hadn't been totally smart: at first, I'd just left that pic on my hard drive, and naturally I couldn't get to it when I had the laptop in parts. But then I'd printed it out and stuck it in my messy drawer of papers, the dead-tree graveyard where I kept all the warranty cards and pin-out diagrams. I shuffled them—they seemed messier than I remembered—and brought out my photo. I set it down next to the computer and kind of unfocused my eyes, trying to find things that looked out of place.

Then I spotted it. The ribbon cable that connected the keyboard to the logic board wasn't connected right. That was a weird one. There was no torque on that part, nothing to dislodge it in the course of normal operations. I tried to press it back down again and discovered that the plug wasn't just badly mounted—there was something between it and the board. I tweezed it out and shone my light on it.

There was something new in my keyboard. It was a little chunk of hardware, only a sixteenth of an inch thick, with no markings.

The keyboard was plugged into it, and it was plugged into the board. It other words, it was perfectly situated to capture all the keystrokes I made while I typed on my machine.

It was a bug.

My heart thudded in my ears. It was dark and quiet in the house, but it wasn't a comforting dark. There were eyes out there, eyes and ears, and they were watching me. Surveilling me. The surveillance I faced at school had followed me home, but this time, it wasn't just the Board of Education looking over my shoulder: the Department of Homeland Security had joined them.

I almost took the bug out. Then I figured that whoever put it there would know that it was gone. I left it in. It made me sick to do it.

I looked around for more tampering. I couldn't find any, but did that mean there hadn't been any? Someone had broken into my room and planted this device—had disassembled my laptop and reassembled it. There were lots of other ways to wiretap a computer. I could never find them all.

I put the machine together with numb fingers. This time, the case wouldn't snap shut just right, but the power cable stayed in. I booted it up and set my fingers on the keyboard, thinking that I would run some diagnostics and see what was what.

But I couldn't do it.

Hell, maybe my room was wiretapped. Maybe there was a camera spying on me now.

I'd been feeling paranoid when I got home. Now I was nearly out of my skin. It felt like I was back in jail, back in the interrogation room, stalked by entities who had me utterly in their power. It made me want to cry.

Only one thing for it.

I went into the bathroom and took off the toilet paper roll and replaced it with a fresh one. Luckily, it was almost empty already. I unrolled the rest of the paper and dug through my parts box until I found a little plastic envelope full of ultrabright white LEDs I'd scavenged out of a dead bike lamp. I punched their leads through the cardboard tube carefully, using a pin to make the holes, then got out some wire and connected them all in series with little metal clips. I twisted the wires into the leads for a nine-volt battery and connected the battery. Now I had a tube ringed with ultra-bright, directional LEDs, and I could hold it up to my eye and look through it.

I'd built one of these last year as a science fair project and had been thrown out of the fair once I showed that there were hidden cameras in half the classrooms at Chavez High. Pinhead video cameras cost less than a good restaurant dinner these days, so they're showing up everywhere. Sneaky store clerks put them in changing rooms or tanning salons and get pervy with the hidden footage they get from their customers—sometimes they just put it on the net. Knowing how to turn a toilet paper roll and three bucks' worth of parts into a camera-detector is just good sense.

This is the simplest way to catch a spy-cam. They have tiny lenses, but they reflect light like the dickens. It works best in a dim room: stare through the tube and slowly scan all the walls and other places someone might have put a camera until you see the glint of a reflection. If the reflection stays still as you move around, that's a lens.

There wasn't a camera in my room—not one I could detect, anyway. There might have been audio bugs, of course. Or better cameras. Or nothing at all. Can you blame me for feeling paranoid?

I loved that laptop. I called it the Salmagundi, which means anything made out of spare parts.

Once you get to naming your laptop, you know that you're really having a deep relationship with it. Now, though, I felt like I didn't want to ever touch it again. I wanted to throw it out the window. Who knew what they'd done to it? Who knew how it had been tapped?

I put it in a drawer with the lid shut and looked at the ceiling. It was late and I should have been in bed. There was no way I was going to sleep now, though. I was tapped. Everyone might be tapped. The world had changed forever.

"I'll find a way to get them," I said. It was a vow, I knew it when I heard it, though I'd never made a vow before.

I couldn't sleep after that. And besides, I had an idea.

Somewhere in my closet was a shrink-wrapped box containing one still-sealed, mint-in-package Xbox Universal. Every Xbox has been sold way below cost—Microsoft makes most of its money charging games companies money for the right to put out Xbox games—but the Universal was the first Xbox that Microsoft decided to give away entirely for free.

Last Christmas season, there'd been poor losers on every corner dressed as warriors from the Halo series, handing out bags of these game machines as fast as they could. I guess it worked—everyone says they sold a whole butt-load of games. Naturally, there were countermeasures to make sure you only played games from companies that had bought licenses from Microsoft to make them.

Hackers blow through those countermeasures. The Xbox was cracked by a kid from MIT who wrote a best-selling book about it, and then the 360 went down, and then the short-lived Xbox Portable (which we all called the "luggable"—it weighed three pounds!) succumbed. The Universal was supposed to be totally bulletproof. The high school kids who broke it were Brazilian Linux hackers who lived in a *favela*—a kind of squatter's slum.

Never underestimate the determination of a kid who is time-rich and cash-poor.

Once the Brazilians published their crack, we all went nuts on it. Soon there were dozens of alternate operating systems for the Xbox Universal. My favorite was ParanoidXbox, a flavor of Paranoid-Linux. ParanoidLinux is an operating system that assumes that its operator is under assault from the government (it was intended for use by Chinese and Syrian dissidents), and it does everything it can to keep your communications and documents a secret. It even throws up a bunch of "chaff" communications that are supposed to disguise the fact that you're doing anything covert. So while you're receiving a political message one character at a time, ParanoidLinux is pretending to surf the Web and fill in questionnaires and flirt in chat rooms. Meanwhile, one in every five hundred characters you receive is your real message, a needle buried in a huge haystack.

I'd burned a ParanoidXbox DVD when they first appeared, but I'd never gotten around to unpacking the Xbox in my closet, finding a TV to hook it up to and so on. My room is crowded enough as it is without letting Microsoft crashware eat up valuable workspace.

Tonight, I'd make the sacrifice. It took about twenty minutes to get up and running. Not having a TV was the hardest part, but eventually I remembered that I had a little overhead LCD projector that had standard TV RCA connectors on the back. I connected it to the Xbox and shone it on the back of my door and got Paranoid-Linux installed.

Now I was up and running, and ParanoidLinux was looking for other Xbox Universals to talk to. Every Xbox Universal comes with built-in wireless for multiplayer gaming. You can connect to your neighbors on the wireless link and to the Internet, if you have a wireless Internet connection. I found three different sets of neighbors in range. Two of them had their Xbox Universals also connected to the Internet. ParanoidXbox loved that configuration: it could siphon off some of my neighbors' Internet connections and use them to get online through the gaming network. The neighbors would never miss the packets: they were paying for flat-rate Internet connections, and they weren't exactly doing a lot of surfing at 2 A.M.

The best part of all of this is how it made me *feel*: in control. My technology was working for me, serving me, protecting me. It wasn't spying on me. This is why I loved technology: if you used it right, it could give you power and privacy.

My brain was really going now, running like sixty. There were lots of reasons to run ParanoidXbox—the best one was that anyone could write games for it. Already there was a port of MAME, the Multiple Arcade Machine Emulator, so you could play practically any game that had ever been written, all the way back to Pong— games for the Apple][+ and games for the Colecovision, games for the NES and the Dreamcast, and so on.

Even better were all the cool multiplayer games being built specifically for ParanoidXbox—totally free hobbyist games that anyone could run. When you combined it all, you had a free console full of free games that could get you free Internet access.

And the best part—as far as I was concerned—was that Paranoid-Xbox was *paranoid*. Every bit that went over the air was scrambled to within an inch of its life. You could wiretap it all you wanted, but you'd never figure out who was talking, what they were talking about or who they were talking to. Anonymous Web, email and IM. Just what I needed.

All I had to do now was convince everyone I knew to use it, too.

chapter 6

Believe it or not, my parents made me go to school the next day. I'd only fallen into feverish sleep at three in the morning, but at seven the next day, my dad was standing at the foot of my bed, threatening to drag me out by the ankles. I managed to get up—something had died in my mouth after painting my eyelids shut—and into the shower.

I let my mom force a piece of toast and a banana into me, wishing fervently that my parents would let me drink coffee at home. I could sneak one on the way to school, but watching them sip down their black gold while I was drag-assing around the house, getting dressed and putting my books in my bag—it was awful.

I've walked to school a thousand times, but today it was different. I went up and over the hills to get down into the Mission, and everywhere there were trucks. I saw new sensors and traffic cameras installed at many of the stop signs. Someone had a lot of surveillance gear lying around, waiting to be installed at the first opportunity. The attack on the Bay Bridge had been just what they needed.

It all made the city seem more subdued, like being inside an elevator, embarrassed by the close scrutiny of your neighbors and the ubiquitous cameras.

The Turkish coffee shop on 24th Street fixed me up good with a go-cup of Turkish coffee. Basically, Turkish coffee is mud, pretending to be coffee. It's thick enough to stand a spoon up in, and it has way more caffeine than the kiddee-pops like Red Bull. Take it from someone who's read the Wikipedia entry: this is how the Ottoman Empire was won: maddened horsemen fueled by lethal jet-black coffee-mud.

I pulled out my debit card to pay and he made a face. "No more debit," he said.

"Huh? Why not?" I'd paid for my coffee habit on my card for years at the Turk's. He used to hassle me all the time, telling me I was too young to drink the stuff, and he still refused to serve me at all during school hours, convinced that I was skipping class. But over the years, the Turk and me have developed a kind of gruff understanding.

He shook his head sadly. "You wouldn't understand. Go to school, kid."

There's no surer way to make me want to understand than to tell me I won't. I wheedled him, demanding that he tell me. He looked like he was going to throw me out, but when I asked him if he thought I wasn't good enough to shop there, he opened up.

"The security," he said, looking around his little shop with its tubs of dried beans and seeds, its shelves of Turkish groceries. "The government. They monitor it all now, it was in the papers. PATRIOT Act II, the Congress passed it yesterday. Now they can monitor every time you use your card. I say no. I say my shop will not help them spy on my customers."

My jaw dropped.

"You think it's no big deal maybe? What is the problem with government knowing when you buy coffee? Because it's one way they know where you are, where you been. Why you think I left Turkey? Where you have government always spying on the people, is no good. I move here twenty years ago for freedom—I no help them take freedom away."

"You're going to lose so many sales," I blurted. I wanted to tell him he was a hero and shake his hand, but that was what came out. "Everyone uses debit cards."

"Maybe not so much anymore. Maybe my customers come here because they know I love freedom, too. I am making sign for window. Maybe other stores do the same. I hear the ACLU will sue them for this."

"You've got all my business from now on," I said. I meant it. I reached into my pocket. "Um, I don't have any cash, though."

He pursed his lips and nodded. "Many peoples say the same thing. Is okay. You give today's money to the ACLU."

In two minutes, the Turk and I had exchanged more words

than we had in all the time I'd been coming to his shop. I had no idea he had all these passions. I just thought of him as my friendly neighborhood caffeine dealer. Now I shook his hand and when I left his store, I felt like he and I had joined a team. A secret team.

I'd missed two days of school but it seemed like I hadn't missed much class. They'd shut the school on one of those days while the city scrambled to recover. The next day had been devoted, it seemed, to mourning those missing and presumed dead. The newspapers published biographies of the lost, personal memorials. The Web was filled with these capsule obituaries, thousands of them.

Embarrassingly, I was one of those people. I stepped into the schoolyard, not knowing this, and then there was a shout and a moment later there were a hundred people around me, pounding me on the back, shaking my hand. A couple girls I didn't even know kissed me, and they were more than friendly kisses. I felt like a rock star.

My teachers were only a little more subdued. Ms. Galvez cried as much as my mother had and hugged me three times before she let me go to my desk and sit down. There was something new at the front of the classroom. A camera. Ms. Galvez caught me staring at it and handed me a permission slip on smeary xeroxed school letterhead.

The Board of the San Francisco Unified School District had held an emergency session over the weekend and unanimously voted to ask the parents of every kid in the city for permission to put closed circuit television cameras in every classroom and corridor. The law said they couldn't force us to go to school with cameras all over the place, but it didn't say anything about us *volunteering* to give up our Constitutional rights. The letter said that the Board was sure that they would get complete compliance from the city's parents, but that they would make arrangements to teach those kids whose parents objected in a separate set of "unprotected" classrooms.

Why did we have cameras in our classrooms now? Terrorists. Of course. Because by blowing up a bridge, terrorists had indicated that schools were next. Somehow that was the conclusion that the Board had reached anyway.

I read this note three times and then I stuck my hand up.

"Yes, Marcus?"

"Ms. Galvez, about this note?"

"Yes, Marcus."

"Isn't the point of terrorism to make us afraid? That's why it's called *terror*ism, right?"

"I suppose so." The class was staring at me. I wasn't the best student in school, but I did like a good in-class debate. They were waiting to hear what I'd say next.

"So aren't we doing what the terrorists want from us? Don't they win if we act all afraid and put cameras in the classrooms and all of that?"

There was some nervous tittering. One of the others put his hand up. It was Charles. Ms. Galvez called on him.

"Putting cameras in makes us safe, which makes us less afraid."

"Safe from what?" I said, without waiting to be called on.

"Terrorism," Charles said. The others were nodding their heads.

"How do they do that? If a suicide bomber rushed in here and blew us all up—"

"Ms. Galvez, Marcus is violating school policy. We're not supposed to make jokes about terrorist attacks—"

"Who's making jokes?"

"Thank you, both of you," Ms. Galvez said. She looked really unhappy. I felt kind of bad for hijacking her class. "I think that this is a really interesting discussion, but I'd like to hold it over for a future class. I think that these issues may be too emotional for us to have a discussion about them today. Now, let's get back to the suffragists, shall we?"

So we spent the rest of the hour talking about suffragists and the new lobbying strategies they'd devised for getting four women into every congresscritter's office to lean on him and let him know what it would mean for his political future if he kept on denying women the vote. It was normally the kind of thing I really liked— little guys making the big and powerful be honest. But today I couldn't concentrate. It must have been Darryl's absence. We both liked Social Studies and we would have had our SchoolBooks out and an IM session up seconds after sitting down, a back channel for talking about the lesson.

I'd burned twenty ParanoidXbox discs the night before and I had them all in my bag. I handed them out to people I knew were really, really into gaming. They'd all gotten an Xbox Universal or two the year before, but most of them had stopped using them. The games were really expensive and not a lot of fun. I took them aside between periods, at lunch and study hall, and sang the praises of the ParanoidXbox games to the sky. Free and fun—addictive social games with lots of cool people playing them from all over the world.

Giving away one thing to sell another is what they call a "razor blade business"—companies like Gillette give you free razor blade handles and then stiff you by charging you a small fortune for the blades. Printer cartridges are the worst for that—the most expensive champagne in the world is cheap when compared with inkjet ink, which costs all of a penny a gallon to make wholesale.

Razor blade businesses depend on you not being able to get the "blades" from someone else. After all, if Gillette can make nine bucks on a ten-dollar replacement blade, why not start a competitor that makes only four bucks selling an identical blade: an 80 percent profit margin is the kind of thing that makes your average businessguy go all drooly and round-eyed.

So razor blade companies like Microsoft pour a lot of effort into making it hard and/or illegal to compete with them on the blades. In Microsoft's case, every Xbox has had countermeasures to keep you from running software that was released by people who didn't pay the Microsoft blood money for the right to sell Xbox programs.

The people I met didn't think much about this stuff. They perked up when I told them that the games were unmonitored. These days, any online game you play is filled with all kinds of unsavory sorts. First there are the pervs who try to get you to come out to some remote location so they can go all weird and Silence of the Lambs on you. Then there are the cops, who are pretending to be gullible kids so they can bust the pervs. Worst of all, though, are the monitors who spend all their time spying on our discussions and snitching on us for violating their Terms of Service, which say no flirting, no cussing and no "clear or masked language which insultingly refers to any aspect of sexual orientation or sexuality."

I'm no 24/7 horn-dog, but I'm a seventeen-year-old boy. Sex does come up in conversation every now and again. But God help you if it came up in chat while you were gaming. It was a real buzz-kill. No one monitored the ParanoidXbox games, because they weren't run by a company: they were just games that hackers had written for the hell of it.

So these game-kids loved the story. They took the discs greedily, and promised to burn copies for all their friends—after all, games are most fun when you're playing them with your buddies.

When I got home, I read that a group of parents was suing the school board over the surveillance cameras in the classrooms, but that they'd already lost their bid to get a preliminary injunction against them.

I don't know who came up with the name Xnet, but it stuck. You'd hear people talking about it on the Muni. Van called me up to ask me if I'd heard of it and I nearly choked once I figured out what she was talking about: the discs I'd started distributing last week had been sneakernetted and copied all the way to Oakland in the space of two weeks. It made me look over my shoulder—like I'd broken a rule and now the DHS would come and take me away forever.

They'd been hard weeks. The BART had completely abandoned cash fares now, switching them for arphid "contactless" cards that you waved at the turnstiles to go through. They were cool and convenient, but every time I used one, I thought about how I was being tracked. Someone on Xnet posted a link to an Electronic Frontier Foundation white paper on the ways that these things could be used to track people, and the paper had tiny stories about little groups of people that had protested at the BART stations.

I used the Xnet for almost everything now. I'd set up a fake email address through the Pirate Party, a Swedish political party that hated Internet surveillance and promised to keep their mail accounts a secret from everyone, even the cops. I accessed it strictly via Xnet, hopping from one neighbor's Internet connection to the next, staying anonymous—I hoped—all the way to Sweden. I wasn't using w1n5t0n anymore. If Benson could figure it out, anyone could. My new handle, come up with on the spur of the moment, was M1k3y, and I got a *lot* of email from people who heard in chat rooms and message boards that I could help them troubleshoot their Xnet configurations and connections.

I missed Harajuku Fun Madness. The company had suspended the game indefinitely. They said that for "security reasons" they didn't think it would be a good idea to hide things and then send people off to find them. What if someone thought it was a bomb? What if someone put a bomb in the same spot?

What if I got hit by lightning while walking with an umbrella? Ban umbrellas! Fight the menace of lightning!

I kept on using my laptop, though I got a skin-crawly feeling when I used it. Whoever had wiretapped it would wonder why I didn't use it. I figured I'd just do some random surfing with it every day, a little less each day, so that anyone watching would see me slowly changing my habits, not doing a sudden reversal. Mostly I read those creepy obits—all those thousands of my friends and neighbors dead at the bottom of the Bay.

Truth be told, I *was* doing less and less homework every day. I had business elsewhere. I burned new stacks of ParanoidXbox every day, fifty or sixty, and took them around the city to people I'd heard were willing to burn sixty of their own and hand them out to their friends.

I wasn't too worried about getting caught doing this, because I had good crypto on my side. Crypto is cryptography, or "secret writing," and it's been around since Roman times (literally: Augustus Caesar was a big fan and liked to invent his own codes, some of which we use today for scrambling joke punch lines in email).

Crypto is math. Hard math. I'm not going to try to explain it in detail because I don't have the math to really get my head around it, either—look it up on Wikipedia if you really want.

But here's the Cliff's Notes version: Some kinds of mathematical functions are really easy to do in one direction and really hard to do in the other direction. It's easy to multiply two big prime numbers together and make a giant number. It's really, really hard to take any given giant number and figure out which primes multiply together to give you that number.

That means that if you can come up with a way of scrambling something based on multiplying large primes, unscrambling it without knowing those primes will be hard. Wicked hard. Like, a trillion years of all the computers ever invented working 24/7 won't be able to do it.

There are four parts to any crypto message: the original message, called the "cleartext." The scrambled message, called the "ciphertext." The scrambling system, called the "cipher." And finally there's the key: secret stuff you feed into the cipher along with the cleartext to make ciphertext.

It used to be that crypto people tried to keep all of this a secret. Every agency and government had its own ciphers *and* its own keys. The Nazis and the Allies didn't want the other guys to know how they scrambled their messages, let alone the keys that they could use to descramble them. That sounds like a good idea, right? Wrong.

The first time anyone told me about all this prime factoring stuff, I immediately said, "No way, that's BS. I mean, *sure* it's hard to do this prime factorization stuff, whatever you say it is. But it used to be impossible to fly or go to the moon or get a hard drive with more than a few kilobytes of storage. Someone *must* have invented a way of descrambling the messages." I had visions of a hollow mountain full of National Security Agency mathematicians reading every email in the world and snickering.

In fact, that's pretty much what happened during World War II. That's the reason that life isn't more like Castle Wolfenstein, where I've spent many days hunting Nazis.

The thing is, ciphers are hard to keep secret. There's a lot of math that goes into one, and if they're widely used, then everyone who uses them has to keep them a secret, too, and if someone changes sides, you have to find a new cipher.

The Nazi cipher was called Enigma, and they used a little mechanical computer called an Enigma Machine to scramble and unscramble the messages they got. Every sub and boat and station needed one of these, so it was inevitable that eventually the Allies would get their hands on one.

When they did, they cracked it. That work was led by my personal all-time hero, a guy named Alan Turing, who pretty much invented computers as we know them today. Unfortunately for him, he was gay, so after the war ended, the stupid British government forced him to get shot up with hormones to "cure" his homosexuality and he killed himself. Darryl gave me a biography of Turing for my fourteenth birthday—wrapped in twenty layers of paper and in a recycled Batmobile toy, he was like that with presents—and I've been a Turing junkie ever since.

Now the Allies had the Enigma Machine, and they could intercept lots of Nazi radio messages, which shouldn't have been that big a deal, since every captain had his own secret key. Since the Allies didn't have the keys, having the machine shouldn't have helped.

Here's where secrecy hurts crypto. The Enigma cipher was flawed. Once Turing looked hard at it, he figured out that the Nazi cryptographers had made a mathematical mistake. By getting his hands on an Enigma Machine, Turing could figure out how to crack *any* Nazi message, no matter what key it used.

That cost the Nazis the war. I mean, don't get me wrong. That's good news. Take it from a Castle Wolfenstein veteran. You wouldn't want the Nazis running the country.

After the war, cryptographers spent a lot of time thinking about this. The problem had been that Turing was smarter than the guy who thought up Enigma. Any time you had a cipher, you were vulnerable to someone smarter than you coming up with a way of breaking it.

And the more they thought about it, the more they realized that *anyone* can come up with a security system that he can't figure out how to break. But *no one* can figure out what a smarter person might do.

You have to publish a cipher to know that it works. You have to tell *as many people as possible* how it works, so that they can thwack on it with everything they have, testing its security. The longer you go without anyone finding a flaw, the more secure you are.

Which is how it stands today. If you want to be safe, you don't use crypto that some genius thought of last week. You use the stuff that people have been using for as long as possible without anyone figuring out how to break them. Whether you're a bank, a terrorist, a government or a teenager, you use the same ciphers.

If you tried to use your own cipher, there'd be the chance that someone out there had found a flaw you missed and was doing a Turing on your butt, deciphering all your "secret" messages and chuckling at your dumb gossip, financial transactions and military secrets.

So I knew that crypto would keep me safe from eavesdroppers, but I wasn't ready to deal with histograms.

I got off the BART and waved my card over the turnstile as I headed up to the 24th Street station. As usual, there were lots of weirdos hanging out in the station, drunks and Jesus freaks and intense Mexican men staring at the ground and a few gang kids. I looked straight past them as I hit the stairs and jogged up to the surface. My bag was empty now, no longer bulging with the ParanoidXbox discs I'd been distributing, and it made my shoulders feel light and put a spring in my step as I came up the street. The preachers were at work still, exhorting in Spanish and English about Jesus and so on.

The counterfeit sunglass sellers were gone, but they'd been replaced by guys selling robot dogs that barked the national anthem and would lift their legs if you showed them a picture of Osama bin Laden. There was probably some cool stuff going on in their little brains and I made a mental note to pick a couple of them up and take them apart later. Face-recognition was pretty new in toys, having only recently made the leap from the military to casinos trying to find cheats to law-enforcement.

I started down 24th Street toward Potrero Hill and home, rolling my shoulders and smelling the burrito smells wafting out of the restaurants and thinking about dinner.

I don't know why I happened to glance back over my shoulder, but I did. Maybe it was a little bit of subconscious sixth sense stuff. I knew I was being followed.

They were two beefy white guys with little mustaches that made me think of either cops or the gay bikers who rode up and down the Castro, but gay guys usually had better haircuts. They had on windbreakers the color of old cement and blue jeans, with their waistbands concealed. I thought of all the things a cop might wear on his waistband, of the utility belt that DHS guy in the truck had worn. Both guys were wearing Bluetooth headsets.

I kept walking, my heart thumping in my chest. I'd been expecting this since I started. I'd been expecting the DHS to figure out what I was doing. I took every precaution, but severe haircut lady had told me that she'd be watching me. She'd told me I was a marked man. I realized that I'd been waiting to get picked up and taken back to jail. Why not? Why should Darryl be in jail and not me? What did I have going for me? I hadn't even had the guts to tell my parents—or his—what had really happened to us.

I quickened my step and took a mental inventory. I didn't have anything incriminating in my bag. Not too incriminating, anyway. My SchoolBook was running the crack that let me IM and stuff, but half the people in school had that. I'd changed the way I encrypted the stuff on my phone—now I *did* have a fake partition that I could turn back into cleartext with one password, but all the good stuff was hidden, and needed another password to open up. That hidden section looked just like random junk—when you encrypt data, it becomes indistinguishable from random noise—and they'd never even know it was there.

There were no discs in my bag. My laptop was free of incriminating evidence. Of course, if they thought to look hard at my Xbox, it was game over. So to speak.

I stopped where I was standing. I'd done as good a job as I could of covering myself. It was time to face my fate. I stepped into the nearest burrito joint and ordered one with carnitas—shredded pork—and extra salsa. Might as well go down with a full stomach. I got a bucket of horchata, too, an ice-cold rice drink that's like watery, semisweet rice pudding (better than it sounds).

I sat down to eat, and a profound calm fell over me. I was about to go to jail for my "crimes," or I wasn't. My freedom since they'd taken me in had been just a temporary holiday. My country was not my friend anymore: we were now on different sides and I'd known I could never win.

The two guys came into the restaurant as I was finishing the burrito and going up to order some churros—deep-fried dough with cinnamon sugar—for dessert. I guess they'd been waiting outside and got tired of my dawdling.

They stood behind me at the counter, boxing me in. I took my churro from the pretty granny and paid her, taking a couple of quick bites of the dough before I turned around. I wanted to eat at least a little of my dessert. It might be the last dessert I got for a long, long time.

Then I turned around. They were both so close I could see the zit on the cheek of the one on the left, the little booger up the nose of the other.

"'Scuse me," I said, trying to push past them. The one with the booger moved to block me.

"Sir," he said, "can you step over here with us?" He gestured toward the restaurant's door.

"Sorry, I'm eating," I said and moved again. This time he put his hand on my chest. He was breathing fast through his nose, making the booger wiggle. I think I was breathing hard, too, but it was hard to tell over the hammering of my heart.

The other one flipped down a flap on the front of his windbreaker to reveal an SFPD insignia. "Police," he said. "Please come with us."

"Let me just get my stuff," I said.

"We'll take care of that," he said. The booger one stepped right up close to me, his foot on the inside of mine. You do that in some martial arts, too. It lets you feel if the other guy is shifting his weight, getting ready to move.

I wasn't going to run, though. I knew I couldn't outrun fate.

They took me outside and around the corner to a waiting unmarked police car. It wasn't like anyone in that neighborhood would have had a hard time figuring out that it was a cop car, though. Only police drove big Crown Victorias now that gas had hit seven bucks a gallon. What's more, only cops could double-park in the middle of Van Ness Street without getting towed by the schools of predatory tow operators that circled endlessly, ready to enforce San Francisco's incomprehensible parking regulations and collect a bounty for kidnapping your car.

Booger blew his nose. I was sitting in the back seat, and so was he. His partner was sitting in the front, typing with one finger on an ancient, ruggedized laptop that looked like Fred Flintstone had been its original owner.

Booger looked closely at my ID again. "We just want to ask you a few routine questions."

"Can I see your badges?" I said. These guys were clearly cops, but it couldn't hurt to let them know I knew my rights.

Booger flashed his badge at me too fast for me to get a good look at it, but Zit in the front seat gave me a long look at his. I got their division number and memorized the four-digit badge number. It was easy: 1337 is also the way hackers write "leet," or "elite."

They were both being very polite and neither of them was trying to intimidate me the way that the DHS had done when I was in their custody.

"Am I under arrest?"

"You've been momentarily detained so that we can ensure your safety and the general public safety," Booger said.

He passed my driver's license to Zit, who pecked it slowly into his computer. I saw him make a typo and almost corrected him, but figured it was better to just keep my mouth shut.

"Is there anything you want to tell me, Marcus? Do they call you Marc?"

"Marcus is fine," I said. Booger looked like he might be a nice guy. Except for the part about kidnapping me into his car, of course.

"Marcus. Anything you want to tell me?"

"Like what? Am I under arrest?"

"You're not under arrest right now," Booger said. "Would you like to be?"

"No," I said.

"Good. We've been watching you since you left the BART. Your Fast Pass says that you've been riding to a lot of strange places at a lot of funny hours."

I felt something let go inside my chest. This wasn't about the Xnet at all, then, not really. They'd been watching my subway use and wanted to know why it had been so freaky lately. How totally stupid.

"So you guys follow everyone who comes out of the BART station with a funny ride history? You must be busy."

"Not everyone, Marcus. We get an alert when anyone with an uncommon ride profile comes out and that helps us assess whether we want to investigate. In your case, we came along because we wanted to know why a smart-looking kid like you had such a funny ride profile."

Now that I knew I wasn't about to go to jail, I was getting pissed. These guys had no business spying on me—Christ, the BART had no business *helping* them to spy on me. Where the hell did my subway pass get off on finking me out for having a "nonstandard ride pattern"?

"I think I'd like to be arrested now," I said.

Booger sat back and raised his eyebrow at me.

"Really? On what charge?"

"Oh, you mean riding public transit in a nonstandard way isn't a crime?"

Zit closed his eyes and scrubbed them with his thumbs.

Booger sighed a put-upon sigh. "Look, Marcus, we're on your side here. We use this system to catch bad guys. To catch terrorists and drug dealers. Maybe you're a drug dealer yourself. Pretty good way to get around the city, a Fast Pass. Anonymous."

"What's wrong with anonymous? It was good enough for Thomas Jefferson. And by the way, am I under arrest?"

"Let's take him home," Zit said. "We can talk to his parents."

"I think that's a great idea," I said. "I'm sure my parents will be anxious to hear how their tax dollars are being spent—"

I'd pushed it too far. Booger had been reaching for the door handle but now he whirled on me, all Hulked out and throbbing veins. "Why don't you shut up right now, while it's still an option? After everything that's happened in the past two weeks, it wouldn't kill you to cooperate with us. You know what, maybe we *should* arrest you. You can spend a day or two in jail while your lawyer looks for you. A lot can happen in that time. A *lot*. How'd you like that?"

I didn't say anything. I'd been giddy and angry. Now I was scared witless.

"I'm sorry," I managed, hating myself again for saying it.

Booger got in the front seat and Zit put the car in gear, cruising up 24th Street and over Potrero Hill. They had my address from my ID.

Mom answered the door after they rang the bell, leaving the chain on. She peeked around it, saw me and said, "Marcus? Who are these men?"

"Police," Booger said. He showed her his badge, letting her get a good look at it—not whipping it away the way he had with me. "Can we come in?"

Mom closed the door and took the chain off and let them in. They brought me in and Mom gave the three of us one of her looks.

"What's this about?"

Booger pointed at me. "We wanted to ask your son some routine questions about his movements, but he declined to answer them. We felt it might be best to bring him here."

"Is he under arrest?" Mom's accent was coming on strong. Good old Mom.

"Are you a United States citizen, ma'am?" Zit said.

She gave him a look that could have stripped paint. "I shore am, hyuck," she said, in a broad southern accent. "Am *I* under arrest?"

The two cops exchanged a look.

Zit took the fore. "We seem to have gotten off to a bad start. We identified your son as someone with a nonstandard public transit usage pattern, as part of a new proactive enforcement program. When we spot people whose travels are unusual, or that match a suspicious profile, we investigate further."

"Wait," Mom said. "How do you know how my son uses the Muni?"

"The Fast Pass," he said. "It tracks voyages."

"I see," Mom said, folding her arms. Folding her arms was a bad sign. It was bad enough she hadn't offered them a cup of tea—in Mom-land, that was practically like making them shout through the mail slot—but once she folded her arms, it was not going to end well for them. At that moment, I wanted to go and buy her a big bunch of flowers.

"Marcus here declined to tell us why his movements had been what they were."

"Are you saying you think my son is a terrorist because of how he rides the bus?"

"Terrorists aren't the only bad guys we catch this way," Zit said. "Drug dealers. Gang kids. Even shoplifters smart enough to hit a different neighborhood with every run."

"You think my son is a drug dealer?"

"We're not saying that—" Zit began. Mom clapped her hands at him to shut him up.

"Marcus, please pass me your backpack."

I did.

Mom unzipped it and looked through it, turning her back to us first.

"Officers, I can now affirm that there are no narcotics, explosives or shoplifted gewgaws in my son's bag. I think we're done here. I would like your badge numbers before you go, please."

Booger sneered at her. "Lady, the ACLU is suing three hundred cops on the SFPD, you're going to have to get in line."

Mom made me a cup of tea and then chewed me out for eating dinner when I knew that she'd been making falafel. Dad came home while we were still at the table and Mom and I took turns telling him the story. He shook his head.

"Lillian, they were just doing their jobs." He was still wearing the blue blazer and khakis he wore on the days that he was consulting in Silicon Valley. "The world isn't the same place it was last week."

Mom set down her teacup. "Drew, you're being ridiculous. Your son is not a terrorist. His use of the public transit system is not cause for a police investigation."

Dad took off his blazer. "We do this all the time at my work. It's how computers can be used to find all kinds of errors, anomalies and outcomes. You ask the computer to create a profile of an average record in a database and then ask it to find out which records in the database are furthest away from average. It's part of something called Bayesian analysis and it's been around for centuries now. Without it, we couldn't do spam-filtering—"

"So you're saying that you think the police should suck as hard as my spam filter?" I said.

Dad never got angry at me for arguing with him, but tonight I could see the strain was running high in him. Still, I couldn't resist. My own father, taking the police's side!

"I'm saying that it's perfectly reasonable for the police to conduct their investigations by starting with data-mining, and then following it up with legwork where a human being actually intervenes to see why the abnormality exists. I don't think that a computer should be telling the police whom to arrest, just helping them sort through the haystack to find a needle."

"But by taking in all that data from the transit system, they're *creating the haystack*," I said. "That's a gigantic mountain of data and there's almost nothing worth looking at there, from the police's point of view. It's a total waste."

"I understand that you don't like that this system caused you some inconvenience, Marcus. But you of all people should appreciate the gravity of the situation. There was no harm done, was there? They even gave you a ride home."

They threatened to send me to jail, I thought, but I could see there was no point in saying it.

"Besides, you still haven't told us where the blazing hells you've been to create such an unusual traffic pattern."

That brought me up short.

"I thought you relied on my judgment, that you didn't want to spy on me." He'd said this often enough. "Do you really want me to account for every trip I've ever taken?"

I hooked up my Xbox as soon as I got to my room. I'd bolted the projector to the ceiling so that it could shine on the wall over my bed (I'd had to take down my awesome mural of punk rock hand-bills I'd taken down off telephone poles and glued to big sheets of white paper).

I powered up the Xbox and watched as it came onto the screen. I was going to email Van and Jolu to tell them about the hassle with the cops, but as I put my fingers to the keyboard, I stopped again.

A feeling crept over me, one not unlike the feeling I'd had when I realized that they'd turned poor old Salmagundi into a traitor. This time, it was the feeling that my beloved Xnet might be broadcasting the location of every one of its users to the DHS.

It was what Dad had said: *You ask the computer to create a profile of an average record in a database and then ask it to find out which records in the database are furthest away from average.*

The Xnet was secure because its users weren't directly connected to the Internet. They hopped from Xbox to Xbox until they found one that was connected to the Internet, then they injected their material as undecipherable, encrypted data. No one could tell which of the Internet's packets were Xnet and which ones were just plain old banking and e-commerce and other encrypted communication. You couldn't find out who was tying the Xnet, let alone who was using the Xnet.

But what about Dad's "Bayesian statistics"? I'd played with Bayesian math before. Darryl and I once tried to write our own better spam filter and when you filter spam, you need Bayesian math. Thomas Bayes was an 18th-century British mathematician that no one cared about until a couple hundred years after he died, when computer scientists realized that his technique for statistically analyzing mountains of data would be super-useful for the modern world's info-Himalayas.

Here's some of how Bayesian stats work. Say you've got a bunch of spam. You take every word that's in the spam and count how many times it appears. This is called a "word-frequency histogram" and it tells you what the probability is that any bag of words is likely to be spam. Now, take a ton of email that's not spam—in the biz, they call that "ham"—and do the same.

Wait until a new email arrives and count the words that appear in it. Then use the word-frequency histogram in the candidate message to calculate the probability that it belongs in the "spam" pile or the "ham" pile. If it turns out to be spam, you adjust the "spam" histogram accordingly. There are lots of ways to refine the technique—looking at words in pairs, throwing away old data—but this is how it works at core. It's one of those great, simple ideas that seems obvious after you hear about it.

It's got lots of applications—you can ask a computer to count the lines in a picture and see if it's more like a "dog" line-frequency histogram or a "cat" line-frequency histogram. It can find porn, bank fraud and flamewars. Useful stuff.

And it was bad news for the Xnet. Say you had the whole Internet wiretapped—which, of course, the DHS has. You can't tell who's passing Xnet packets by looking at the contents of those packets, thanks to crypto.

What you *can* do is find out who is sending way, way more encrypted traffic out than everyone else. For a normal Internet surfer, a session online is probably about 95 percent cleartext, 5 percent ciphertext. If someone is sending out 95 percent ciphertext, maybe you could dispatch the computer-savvy equivalents of Booger and Zit to ask them if they're terrorist drug dealer Xnet users.

This happens all the time in China. Some smart dissident will get the idea of getting around the Great Firewall of China, which is used to censor the whole country's Internet connection, by using an encrypted connection to a computer in some other country. Now, the Party there can't tell what the dissident is surfing: maybe it's porn, or bomb-making instructions, or dirty letters from his girlfriend in the Philippines, or political material, or good news about Scientology. They don't have to know. All they have to know is that this guy gets way more encrypted traffic than his neighbors. At that point, they send him to a forced labor camp just to set an example so that everyone can see what happens to smart-asses.

So far, I was willing to bet that the Xnet was under the DHS's radar, but it wouldn't be the case forever. And after tonight, I wasn't sure that I was in any better shape than a Chinese dissident. I was putting all the people who signed onto the Xnet in jeopardy. The law didn't care if you were actually doing anything bad; they were willing to put you under the microscope just for being statistically abnormal. And I couldn't even stop it—now that the Xnet was running, it had a life of its own.

I was going to have to fix it some other way.

I wished I could talk to Jolu about this. He worked at an Internet Service Provider called Pigspleen Net that had hired him when he was twelve, and he knew way more about the net than I did. If anyone knew how to keep our butts out of jail, it would be him.

Luckily, Van and Jolu and I were planning to meet for coffee the next night at our favorite place in the Mission after school. Officially, it was our weekly Harajuku Fun Madness team meeting, but with the game canceled and Darryl gone, it was pretty much just a weekly weepfest, supplemented by about six phone calls and IMs a day that went, "Are you okay? Did it really happen?" It would be good to have something else to talk about.

"You're out of your mind," Vanessa said. "Are you actually, totally, really, for-real crazy or what?"

She had shown up in her girl's school uniform because she'd been stuck going the long way home, all the way down to the San Mateo bridge then back up into the city, on a shuttle bus service that her school was operating. She hated being seen in public in her gear, which was totally Sailor Moon—a pleated skirt and a tunic and kneesocks. She'd been in a bad mood ever since she turned up at the cafe, which was full of older, cooler, mopey emo art students who snickered into their lattes when she turned up.

"What do you want me to do, Van?" I said. I was getting exasperated myself. School was unbearable now that the game wasn't on, now that Darryl was missing. All day long, in my classes, I consoled myself with the thought of seeing my team, what was left of it. Now we were fighting.

"I want you to stop putting yourself at risk, M1k3y." The hairs on the back of my neck stood up. Sure, we always used our team handles at team meetings, but now that my handle was also associated with my Xnet use, it scared me to hear it said aloud in a public place.

"Don't use that name in public anymore," I snapped.

Van shook her head. "That's just what I'm talking about. You could end up going to jail for this, Marcus, and not just you. Lots of people. After what happened to Darryl—"

"I'm doing this for Darryl!" Art students swiveled to look at us and I lowered my voice. "I'm doing this because the alternative is to let them get away with it all."

"You think you're going to stop them? You're out of your mind. They're the government."

"It's still our country," I said. "We still have the right to do this."

Van looked like she was going to cry. She took a couple of deep breaths and stood up. "I can't do it, I'm sorry. I can't watch you do this. It's like watching a car wreck in slow motion. You're going to destroy yourself, and I love you too much to watch it happen."

She bent down and gave me a fierce hug and a hard kiss on the cheek that caught the edge of my mouth. "Take care of yourself, Marcus," she said. My mouth burned where her lips had pressed it. She gave Jolu the same treatment, but square on the cheek. Then she left.

Jolu and I stared at each other after she'd gone.

I put my face in my hands. "Dammit," I said, finally.

Jolu patted me on the back and ordered me another latte. "It'll be okay," he said.

"You'd think Van, of all people, would understand." Van's parents were North Korean refugees. They'd lived under a crazy dictator for decades before escaping to America, determined to give their daughter a better life.

Jolu shrugged. "Maybe that's why she's so freaked out. Because she knows how dangerous it can get."

I knew what he was talking about. Two of Van's uncles had gone to jail after her parents got out and had never reappeared.

"Yeah," I said.

"So how come you weren't on Xnet last night?"

I was grateful for the distraction. I explained it all to him, the Bayesian stuff and my fear that we couldn't go on using Xnet the way we had been without getting nabbed. He listened thoughtfully.

"I see what you're saying. The problem is that if there's too much crypto in someone's Internet connection, they'll stand out as unusual. But if you don't encrypt, you'll make it easy for the bad guys to wiretap you."

"Yeah," I said. "I've been trying to figure it out all day. Maybe we could slow the connection down, spread it out over more peoples' accounts—"

"Won't work," he said. "To get it slow enough to vanish into the noise, you'd have to basically shut down the network, which isn't an option."

"You're right," I said. "But what else can we do?"

"What if we changed the definition of normal?"

And that was why Jolu got hired to work at Pigspleen when he was twelve. Give him a problem with two bad solutions and he'd figure out a third totally different solution based on throwing away all your assumptions. I nodded vigorously. "Go on, tell me."

"What if the average San Francisco Internet user had a *lot* more crypto in his average day on the Internet? If we could change the split so it's more like fifty-fifty cleartext to ciphertext, then the users that supply the Xnet would just look like normal."

"But how do we do that? People just don't care enough about their privacy to surf the net through an encrypted link. They don't see why it matters if eavesdroppers know what they're googling for."

"Yeah, but Web pages are small amounts of traffic. If we got people to routinely download a few giant encrypted files every day, that would create as much ciphertext as thousands of Web pages."

"You're talking about indienet," I said.

"You got it," he said.

indienet—all lower case, always—was the thing that made Pigspleen Net into one of the most successful independent ISPs in the world. Back when the major record labels started suing their fans for downloading their music, a lot of the independent labels and their artists were aghast. How can you make money by suing your customers?

Pigspleen's founder had the answer: she opened up a deal for any act that wanted to work with their fans instead of fighting them. Give Pigspleen a license to distribute your music to its customers and it would give you a share of the subscription fees based on how popular your music was. For an indie artist, the big problem isn't piracy, it's obscurity: no one even cares enough about your tunes to steal 'em.

It worked. Hundreds of independent acts and labels signed up with Pigspleen, and the more music there was, the more fans switched to getting their Internet service from Pigspleen, and the more money there was for the artists. Inside of a year, the ISP had a hundred thousand new customers and now it had a million—more than half the broadband connections in the city.

"An overhaul of the indienet code has been on my plate for months now," Jolu said. "The original programs were written really fast and dirty and they could be made a lot more efficient with a little work. But I just haven't had the time. One of the high-marked to-do items has been to encrypt the connections, just because Trudy likes it that way." Trudy Doo was the founder of Pigspleen. She was an old-time San Francisco punk legend, the singer/frontwoman of the anarcho-feminist band Speedwhores, and she was crazy about privacy. I could totally believe that she'd want her music service encrypted on general principles.

"Will it be hard? I mean, how long would it take?"

"Well, there's tons of crypto code for free online, of course," Jolu said. He was doing the thing he did when he was digging into a meaty code problem—getting that faraway look, drumming his fingers on the table, making the coffee slosh into the saucers. I wanted to laugh—everything might be destroyed and crap and scary, but Jolu would write that code.

"Can I help?"

He looked at me. "What, you don't think I can manage it?"

"What?"

"I mean, you did this whole Xnet thing without even telling me. Without talking to me. I kind of thought that you didn't need my help with this stuff."

I was brought up short. "What?" I said again. Jolu was looking really steamed now. It was clear that this had been eating at him for a long time. "Jolu—"

He looked at me and I could see that he was furious. How had I missed this? God, I was such an idiot sometimes. "Look dude, it's not a big deal"—by which he clearly meant that it was a really big deal—"it's just that you know, you never even *asked*. I hate the DHS. Darryl was my friend, too. I could have really helped with it."

I wanted to stick my head between my knees. "Listen Jolu, that was really stupid of me. I did it at like two in the morning. I was just crazy when it was happening. I—" I couldn't explain it. Yeah, he was right, and that was the problem. It had been two in the morning but I could have talked to Jolu about it the next day or the next. I hadn't because I'd known what he'd say—that it was an ugly hack, that I needed to think it through better. Jolu was always figuring out how to turn my 2 A.M. ideas into real code, but the stuff that he came out with was always a little different from what I'd come up with. I'd wanted the project for myself. I'd gotten totally into being M1k3y.

"I'm sorry," I said at last. "I'm really, really sorry. You're totally right. I just got freaked out and did something stupid. I really need your help. I can't make this work without you."

"You mean it?"

"Of course I mean it," I said. "You're the best coder I know. You're a goddamned genius, Jolu. I would be honored if you'd help me with this."

He drummed his fingers some more. "It's just— You know. You're the leader. Van's the smart one. Darryl was . . . He was your second-in-command, the guy who had it all organized, who watched the details. Being the programmer, that was *my* thing. It felt like you were saying you didn't need me."

"Oh man, I am such an idiot. Jolu, you're the best-qualified person I know to do this. I'm really, really, really—"

"All right, already. Stop. Fine. I believe you. We're all really screwed up right now. So yeah, of course you can help. We can probably even pay you—I've got a little budget for contract programmers."

"Really?" No one had ever paid me for writing code.

"Sure. You're probably good enough to be worth it." He grinned and slugged me in the shoulder. Jolu's really easygoing most of the time, which is why he'd freaked me out so much.

I paid for the coffees and we went out. I called my parents and let them know what I was doing. Jolu's mom insisted on making us sandwiches. We locked ourselves in his room with his computer and the code for indienet and we embarked on one of the great all-time marathon programming sessions. Once Jolu's family went to bed around 11:30, we were able to kidnap the coffee machine up to his room and go IV with our magic coffee bean supply.

If you've never programmed a computer, you should. There's nothing like it in the whole world. When you program a computer, it does *exactly* what you tell it to do. It's like designing a machine— any machine, like a car, like a faucet, like a gas hinge for a door— using math and instructions. It's awesome in the truest sense: it can fill you with awe.

A computer is the most complicated machine you'll ever use. It's made of billions of microminiaturized transistors that can be configured to run any program you can imagine. But when you sit down at the keyboard and write a line of code, those transistors do what you tell them to.

Most of us will never build a car. Pretty much none of us will ever create an aviation system. Design a building. Lay out a city.

Those are complicated machines, those things, and they're off-limits to the likes of you and me. But a computer is like, ten times more complicated, and it will dance to any tune you play. You can learn to write simple code in an afternoon. Start with a language like Python, which was written to give nonprogrammers an easier way to make the machine dance to their tune. Even if you only write code for one day, one afternoon, you have to do it. Computers can control you or they can lighten your work—if you want to be in charge of your machines, you have to learn to write code.

We wrote a lot of code that night.

chapter 8

I wasn't the only one who got screwed up by the histograms. There are lots of people who have abnormal traffic patterns, abnormal usage patterns. Abnormal is so common, it's practically normal.

The Xnet was full of these stories, and so were the newspapers and the TV news. Husbands were caught cheating on their wives; wives were caught cheating on their husbands; kids were caught sneaking out with illicit girlfriends and boyfriends. A kid who hadn't told his parents he had AIDS got caught going to the clinic for his drugs.

Those were the people with something to hide—not guilty people, but people with secrets. There were even more people with nothing to hide at all, but who nevertheless resented being picked up and questioned. Imagine if someone locked you in the back of a police car and demanded that you prove that you're *not* a terrorist.

It wasn't just public transit. Most drivers in the Bay Area have a FasTrak pass clipped to their sun-visors. This is a little radio-based "wallet" that pays your tolls for you when you cross the bridges, saving you the hassle of sitting in a line for hours at the toll plazas. They'd tripled the cost of using cash to get across the bridge (though they always fudged this, saying that FasTrak was cheaper, not that anonymous cash was more expensive). Whatever holdouts were left afterward disappeared after the number of cash lanes was reduced to just one per bridgehead, so that the cash lines were even longer.

So if you're a local, or if you're driving a rental car from a local agency, you've got a FasTrak. It turns out that toll plazas aren't the only place that your FasTrak gets read, though. The DHS had put FasTrak readers all over town—when you drove past them, they logged the time and your ID number, building an ever more perfect picture of who went where and when, in a database that was augmented by "speeding cameras," "red light cameras" and all the other license plate cameras that had popped up like mushrooms.

No one had given it much thought. And now that people were paying attention, we were all starting to notice little things, like the fact that the FasTrak doesn't have an off switch.

So if you drove a car, you were just as likely to be pulled over by an SFPD cruiser that wanted to know why you were taking so many trips to the Home Depot lately, and what was that midnight drive up to Sonoma last week about?

The little demonstrations around town on the weekend were growing. Fifty thousand people marched down Market Street after a week of this monitoring. I couldn't care less. The people who'd occupied my city didn't care what the natives wanted. They were a conquering army. They knew how we felt about that.

One morning I came down to breakfast just in time to hear Dad tell Mom that the two biggest taxi companies were going to give a "discount" to people who used special cards to pay their fares, supposedly to make drivers safer by reducing the amount of cash they carried. I wondered what would happen to the information about who took which cabs where.

I realized how close I'd come. The new indienet client had been pushed out as an automatic update just as this stuff started to get bad, and Jolu told me that 80 percent of the traffic he saw at Pigspleen was now encrypted. The Xnet just might have been saved.

Dad was driving me nuts, though.

"You're being paranoid, Marcus," he told me over breakfast one day as I told him about the guys I'd seen the cops shaking down on the BART the day before.

"Dad, it's ridiculous. They're not catching any terrorists, are they? It's just making people scared."

"They may not have caught any terrorists yet, but they're sure getting a lot of scumbags off the streets. Look at the drug dealers—it says they've put dozens of them away since this all started. Remember when those druggies robbed you? If we don't bust their dealers, it'll only get worse." I'd been mugged the year before. They'd been pretty civilized about it. One skinny guy who smelled bad told me he had a gun, the other one asked me for my wallet. They even let me keep my ID, though they got my debit card and Fast Pass. It had still scared me witless and left me paranoid and checking my shoulder for weeks.

"But most of the people they hold up aren't doing anything wrong, Dad," I said. This was getting to me. My own father! "It's crazy. For every guilty person they catch, they have to punish thousands of innocent people. That's just not good."

"Innocent? Guys cheating on their wives? Drug dealers? You're defending them, but what about all the people who died? If you don't have anything to hide—"

"So you wouldn't mind if they pulled *you* over?" My dad's histograms had proven to be depressingly normal so far.

"I'd consider it my duty," he said. "I'd be proud. It would make me feel safer."

Easy for him to say.

Vanessa didn't like me talking about this stuff, but she was too smart about it for me to stay away from the subject for long. We'd get together all the time and talk about the weather and school and stuff, and then, somehow, I'd be back on this subject. Vanessa was cool when it happened—she didn't Hulk out on me again—but I could see it upset her.

Still.

"So my dad says, 'I'd consider it my duty.' Can you freaking *believe* it? I mean, God! I almost told him then about going to jail, asking him if he thought that was our 'duty'!"

We were sitting in the grass in Dolores Park after school, watching the dogs chase frisbees.

Van had stopped at home and changed into an old T-shirt for one of her favorite Brazilian tecno-brega bands, Carioca Probidão—the forbidden guy from Rio. She'd gotten the shirt at a live show we'd all gone to two years before, sneaking out for a grand adventure down at the Cow Palace, and she'd sprouted an inch or two since, so it was tight and rode up her tummy, showing her flat little belly button.

She lay back in the weak sun with her eyes closed behind her shades, her toes wiggling in her flip-flops. I'd known Van since forever, and when I thought of her, I usually saw the little kid I'd known with hundreds of jangly bracelets made out of sliced-up soda cans, who played the piano and couldn't dance to save her life. Sitting out there in Dolores Park, I suddenly saw her as she was.

She was totally h4wt—that is to say, hot. It was like looking at that picture of a vase and noticing that it was also two faces. I could see that Van was just Van, but I could also see that she was hella pretty, something I'd never noticed.

Of course, Darryl had known it all along, and don't think that I wasn't bummed out anew when I realized this.

"You can't tell your dad, you know," she said. "You'd put us all at risk." Her eyes were closed and her chest was rising up and down with her breath, which was distracting in a really embarrassing way.

"Yeah," I said, glumly. "But the problem is that I know he's just totally full of it. If you pulled my dad over and made him prove he wasn't a child-molesting, drug-dealing terrorist, he'd go berserk. Totally off the rails. He hates being put on hold when he calls about his credit card bill. Being locked in the back of a car and questioned for an hour would give him an aneurism."

"They only get away with it because the normals feel smug compared to the abnormals. If everyone was getting pulled over, it'd be a disaster. No one would ever get anywhere, they'd all be waiting to get questioned by the cops. Total gridlock."

Whoa.

"Van, you are a total genius," I said.

"Tell me about it," she said. She had a lazy smile and she looked at me through half-lidded eyes, almost romantic.

"Seriously. We can do this. We can mess up the profiles easily. Getting people pulled over is easy."

She sat up and pushed her hair off her face and looked at me. I felt a little flip in my stomach, thinking that she was really impressed with me.

"It's the arphid cloners," I said. "They're totally easy to make. Just flash the firmware on a ten-dollar Radio Shack reader/writer and you're done. What we do is go around and randomly swap the tags on people, overwriting their Fast Passes and FasTraks with other people's codes. That'll make *everyone* skew all weird and screwy, and make everyone look guilty. Then: total gridlock."

Van pursed her lips and lowered her shades and I realized she was so angry she couldn't speak.

"Good-bye, Marcus," she said, and got to her feet. Before I knew it, she was walking away so fast she was practically running.

"Van!" I called, getting to my feet and chasing after her. "Van! Wait!"

She picked up speed, making me run to catch up with her.

"Van, what the hell," I said, catching her arm. She jerked it away so hard I punched myself in the face.

"You're psycho, Marcus. You're going to put all your little Xnet buddies in danger for their lives, and on top of it, you're going to turn the whole city into terrorism suspects. Can't you stop before you hurt these people?"

I opened and closed my mouth a couple times. "Van, *I'm* not the problem, *they* are. I'm not arresting people, jailing them, making them disappear. The Department of Homeland Security are the ones doing that. I'm fighting back to make them stop."

"How, by making it worse?"

"Maybe it has to get worse to get better, Van. Isn't that what you were saying? If everyone was getting pulled over—"

"That's not what I meant. I didn't mean you should get everyone arrested. If you want to protest, join the protest movement. Do something positive. Didn't you learn *anything* from Darryl? *Anything?*"

"You're damned right I did," I said, losing my cool. "I learned that they can't be trusted. That if you're not fighting them, you're helping them. That they'll turn the country into a prison if we let them. What did you learn, Van? To be scared all the time, to sit tight and keep your head down and hope you don't get noticed? You think it's going to get better? If we don't do anything, this is as *good as it's going to get.* It will only get worse and worse from now on. You want to help Darryl? Help me bring them down!"

There it was again. My vow. Not to get Darryl free, but to bring down the entire DHS. That was crazy, even I knew it. But it was what I planned to do. No question about it.

Van shoved me hard with both hands. She was strong from school athletics—fencing, lacrosse, field hockey, all the girls-school sports—and I ended up on my ass on the disgusting San Francisco sidewalk. She took off and I didn't follow.

> The important thing about security systems isn't how they work, it's how they fail.

That was the first line of my first blog post on Open Revolt, my Xnet site. I was writing as M1k3y, and I was ready to go to war.

> Maybe all the automatic screening is supposed to catch terrorists. Maybe it will catch a terrorist sooner or later. The problem is that it catches _us_ too, even though we're not doing anything wrong.

> The more people it catches, the more brittle it gets. If it catches too many people, it dies.

> Get the idea?

I pasted in my HOWTO for building an arphid cloner, and some tips for getting close enough to people to read and write their tags. I put my own cloner in the pocket of my vintage black leather motocross jacket with the armored pockets and left for school. I managed to clone six tags between home and Chavez High.

It was war they wanted. It was war they'd get.

If you ever decide to do something as stupid as build an automatic terrorism detector, here's a math lesson you need to learn first. It's called "the paradox of the false positive," and it's a doozy.

Say you have a new disease, called Super-AIDS. Only one in a million people gets Super-AIDS. You develop a test for Super-AIDS that's 99 percent accurate. I mean, 99 percent of the time, it gives the correct result—true if the subject is infected, and false if the subject is healthy. You give the test to a million people.

One in a million people have Super-AIDS. One in a hundred people that you test will generate a "false positive"—the test will say he has Super-AIDS even though he doesn't. That's what "99 percent accurate" means: one percent wrong.

What's one percent of one million?

$1{,}000{,}000/100 = 10{,}000$.

One in a million people has Super-AIDS. If you test a million random people, you'll probably only find one case of real Super-AIDS. But your test won't identify *one* person as having Super-AIDS. It will identify *ten thousand* people as having it.

Your 99 percent accurate test will perform with 99.99 percent *inaccuracy*.

That's the paradox of the false positive. When you try to find something really rare, your test's accuracy has to match the rarity of the thing you're looking for. If you're trying to point at a single pixel on your screen, a sharp pencil is a good pointer: the pencil tip is a lot smaller (more accurate) than the pixels. But a pencil tip is no good at pointing at a single *atom* in your screen. For that, you need a pointer—a test—that's one atom wide or less at the tip.

This is the paradox of the false positive, and here's how it applies to terrorism:

Terrorists are really rare. In a city of twenty million like New York, there might be one or two terrorists. Maybe ten of them at the outside. $10/20{,}000{,}000 = 0.00005$ percent. One twenty-thousandth of a percent.

That's pretty rare all right. Now, say you've got some software that can sift through all the bank records, or toll pass records, or public transit records, or phone call records in the city and catch terrorists 99 percent of the time.

In a pool of twenty million people, a 99 percent accurate test will identify two hundred thousand people as being terrorists. But only ten of them are terrorists. To catch ten bad guys, you have to haul in and investigate two hundred thousand innocent people.

Guess what? Terrorism tests aren't anywhere *close* to 99 percent accurate. More like 60 percent accurate. Even 40 percent accurate, sometimes.

What this all meant was that the Department of Homeland Security had set itself up to fail badly. They were trying to spot incredibly rare events—a person is a terrorist—with inaccurate systems.

Is it any wonder we were able to make such a mess?

I stepped out the front door whistling on a Tuesday morning one week into Operation False Positive. I was rockin' out to some new music I'd downloaded from the Xnet the night before—lots of people sent M1k3y little digital gifts to say thank you for giving them hope.

I turned onto 23rd Street and carefully took the narrow stone steps cut into the side of the hill. As I descended, I passed Mr. Wiener Dog. I don't know Mr. Wiener Dog's real name, but I see him nearly every day, walking his three panting wiener dogs up the staircase to the little parkette. Squeezing past them all on the stairs is pretty much impossible and I always end up tangled in a leash, knocked into someone's front garden or perched on the bumper of one of the cars parked next to the curb.

Mr. Wiener Dog is clearly Someone Important, because he has a fancy watch and always wears a nice suit. I had mentally assumed that he worked down in the financial district.

Today as I brushed up against him, I triggered my arphid cloner, which was already loaded in the pocket of my leather jacket. The cloner sucked down the numbers off his credit cards and his car keys, his passport and the hundred-dollar bills in his wallet.

Even as it was doing that, it was flashing some of them with new numbers, taken from other people I'd brushed against. It was like switching the license plates on a bunch of cars, but invisible and instantaneous. I smiled apologetically at Mr. Wiener Dog and continued down the stairs. I stopped at three of the cars long enough to swap their FasTrak tags with numbers taken off cars I'd gone past the day before.

You might think I was being a little aggro here, but I was cautious and conservative compared to a lot of the Xnetters. A couple girls in the Chemical Engineering program at UC Berkeley had figured out how to make a harmless substance out of kitchen products that would trip an explosive sniffer. They'd had a merry time sprinkling it on their profs' briefcases and jackets, then hiding out and watching the same profs try to get into the auditoriums and libraries on campus, only to get flying-tackled by the new security squads that had sprung up everywhere.

Other people wanted to figure out how to dust envelopes with substances that would test positive for anthrax, but everyone else thought they were out of their minds. Luckily, it didn't seem like they'd be able to figure it out.

I passed by San Francisco General Hospital and nodded with satisfaction as I saw the huge lines at the front doors. They had a police checkpoint, too, of course, and there were enough Xnetters working as interns and cafeteria workers and whatnot there that everyone's badges had been snarled up and swapped around. I'd read the security checks had tacked an hour onto everyone's work day, and the unions were threatening to walk out unless the hospital did something about it.

A few blocks later, I saw an even longer line for the BART. Cops were walking up and down the line pointing people out and calling them aside for questioning, bag searches and pat downs. They kept getting sued for doing this, but it didn't seem to be slowing them down.

I got to school a little ahead of time and decided to walk down to 22nd Street to get a coffee—and I passed a police checkpoint where they were pulling over cars for secondary inspection.

School was no less wild—the security guards on the metal detectors were also wanding our school IDs and pulling out students with odd movements for questioning. Needless to say, we all had pretty weird movements. Needless to say, classes were starting an hour or more later.

Classes were crazy. I don't think anyone was able to concentrate. I overheard two teachers talking about how long it had taken them to get home from work the day before, and planning to sneak out early that day.

It was all I could do to keep from laughing. The paradox of the false positive strikes again!

Sure enough, they let us out of class early and I headed home the long way, circling through the Mission to see the havoc. Long lines of cars. BART stations lined up around the blocks. People swearing at ATMs that wouldn't dispense their money because they'd had their accounts frozen for suspicious activity (that's the danger of wiring your checking account straight into your FasTrak and Fast Pass!).

I got home and made myself a sandwich and logged into the Xnet. It had been a good day. People from all over town were crowing about their successes. We'd brought the city of San Francisco to a standstill. The news reports confirmed it—they were calling it the DHS gone haywire, blaming it all on the fake-ass "security" that was supposed to be protecting us from terrorism. The Business section of the San Francisco *Chronicle* gave its whole front page to an estimate of the economic cost of the DHS security resulting from missed work hours, meetings and so on. According to the *Chronicle*'s economist, a week of this crap would cost the city more than the Bay Bridge bombing had.

Mwa-ha-ha-ha.

The best part: Dad got home that night late. Very late. Three *hours* late. Why? Because he'd been pulled over, searched, questioned. Then it happened *again*. Twice.

Twice!

He was so angry I thought he was going to pop. You know I said I'd only seen him lose his cool rarely? That night, he lost it more than he ever had.

"You wouldn't believe it. This cop, he was like eighteen years old and he kept saying, 'But sir, why were you in Berkeley yesterday if your client is in Mountain View?' I kept explaining to him that I teach at Berkeley and then he'd say, 'I thought you were a consultant,' and we'd start over again. It was like some kind of sitcom where the cops have been taken over by the stupidity ray.

"What's worse was he kept insisting that I'd been in Berkeley today as well, and I kept saying no, I hadn't been, and he said I had been. Then he showed me my FasTrak billing and it said I'd driven the San Mateo bridge three times that day!

"That's not all," he said, and drew in a breath that let me know he was really steamed. "They had information about where I'd been, places that *didn't have a toll plaza.* They'd been polling my pass just on the street, at random. And it was *wrong*! Holy crap, I mean, they're spying on us all and they're not even competent!"

I'd drifted down into the kitchen as he railed there, and now I was watching him from the doorway. Mom met my eye and we both raised our eyebrows as if to say, *Who's going to say "I told you so" to him?* I nodded at her. She could use her spousular powers to nullify his rage in a way that was out of my reach as a mere filial unit.

"Drew," she said, and grabbed him by the arm to make him stop stalking back and forth in the kitchen, waving his arms like a street preacher.

"What?" he snapped.

"I think you owe Marcus an apology." She kept her voice even and level. Dad and I are the spazzes in the household—Mom's a total rock.

Dad looked at me. His eyes narrowed as he thought for a minute. "All right," he said at last. "You're right. I was talking about competent surveillance. These guys were total amateurs. I'm sorry, son," he said. "You were right. That was ridiculous." He stuck his hand out and shook my hand, then gave me a firm, unexpected hug.

"God, what are we doing to this country, Marcus? Your generation deserves to inherit something better than this." When he let me go, I could see the deep wrinkles in his face, lines I'd never noticed.

I went back up to my room and played some Xnet games. There was a good multiplayer thing, a clockwork pirate game where you had to quest every day or two to wind up your whole crew's mainsprings before you could go plundering and pillaging again. It was the kind of game I hated but couldn't stop playing: lots of repetitive quests that weren't all that satisfying to complete, a little bit of player-versus-player combat (scrapping to see who would captain the ship) and not that many cool puzzles that you had to figure out. Mostly, playing this kind of game made me homesick for Harajuku Fun Madness, which balanced out running around in the real world, figuring out online puzzles and strategizing with your team.

But today it was just what I needed. Mindless entertainment.

My poor dad.

I'd done that to him. He'd been happy before, confident that his tax dollars were being spent to keep him safe. I'd destroyed that confidence. It was false confidence, of course, but it had kept him going. Seeing him now, miserable and broken, I wondered if it was better to be clear-eyed and hopeless or to live in a fool's paradise. That shame—the shame I'd felt since I gave up my passwords, since they'd broken me—returned, leaving me listless and wanting to just get away from myself.

My character was a swabbie on the pirate ship *Zombie Charger*, and he'd wound down while I'd been offline. I had to IM all the other players on my ship until I found one willing to wind me up. That kept me occupied. I liked it, actually. There was something magic about a total stranger doing you a favor. And since it was the Xnet, I knew that all the strangers were friends, in some sense.

> Where u located?

The character who wound me up was called Lizanator, and it was female, though that didn't mean that it was a girl. Guys had some weird affinity for playing female characters.

> San Francisco

I said.

> No stupe, where you located in San Fran?

> Why, you a pervert?

That usually shut down that line of conversation. Of course every gamespace was full of pedos and pervs, and cops pretending to be pedo- and perv-bait (though I sure hoped there weren't any cops on the Xnet!). An accusation like that was enough to change the subject nine out of ten times.

> Mission? Potrero Hill? Noe? East Bay?

> Just wind me up k thx?

She stopped winding.

> You scared?

> Safe—why do you care?

> Just curious

I was getting a bad vibe off her. She was clearly more than just curious. Call it paranoia. I logged off and shut down my Xbox.

Dad looked at me over the table the next morning and said, "It looks like it's going to get better, at least." He handed me a copy of the *Chronicle* open to the third page.

A Department of Homeland Security spokesman has confirmed that the San Francisco office has requested a 300 percent budget and personnel increase from Washington, DC.

What?

Major General Graeme Sutherland, the commanding officer for Northern California DHS operations, confirmed the request at a press conference yesterday, noting that a spike in suspicious activity in the Bay Area prompted the request. "We are tracking a spike in underground chatter and activity and believe that saboteurs are deliberately manufacturing false security alerts to undermine our efforts."

My eyes crossed. No freaking way.

"These false alarms are potentially 'radar chaff' intended to disguise real attacks. The only effective way of combatting them is to step up staffing and analyst levels so that we can fully investigate every lead."

Sutherland noted the delays experienced all over the city were "unfortunate" and committed to eliminating them.

I had a vision of the city with four or five times as many DHS enforcers, brought in to make up for my own stupid ideas. Van was right. The more I fought them, the worse it was going to get.

Dad pointed at the paper. "These guys may be fools, but they're methodical fools. They'll just keep throwing resources at this problem until they solve it. It's tractable, you know. Mining all the data in the city, following up on every lead. They'll catch the terrorists."

I lost it. "Dad! Are you *listening to yourself*? They're talking about investigating practically every person in the city of San Francisco!"

"Yeah," he said, "that's right. They'll catch every alimony cheat, every dope dealer, every dirtbag and every terrorist. You just wait. This could be the best thing that ever happened to this country."

"Tell me you're joking," I said. "I beg you. You think that that's what they intended when they wrote the Constitution? What about the Bill of Rights?"

"The Bill of Rights was written before data-mining," he said. He was awesomely serene, convinced of his rightness. "The right to freedom of association is fine, but why shouldn't the cops be allowed to mine your social network to figure out if you're hanging out with gangbangers and terrorists?"

"Because it's an invasion of my privacy!" I said.

"What's the big deal? Would you rather have privacy or terrorists?"

Agh. I hated arguing with my dad like this. I needed a coffee. "Dad, come on. Taking away our privacy isn't catching terrorists: it's just inconveniencing normal people."

"How do you know it's not catching terrorists?"

"Where are the terrorists they've caught?"

"I'm sure we'll see arrests in good time. You just wait."

"Dad, what the hell has happened to you since last night? You were ready to go nuclear on the cops for pulling you over—"

"Don't use that tone with me, Marcus. What's happened since last night is that I've had the chance to think it over and to read *this*." He rattled his paper. "The reason they caught me is that the bad guys are actively jamming them. They need to adjust their techniques to overcome the jamming. But they'll get there. Meanwhile the occasional road stop is a small price to pay. This isn't the time to be playing lawyer about the Bill of Rights. This is the time to make some sacrifices to keep our city safe."

I couldn't finish my toast. I put the plate in the dishwasher and left for school. I had to get out of there.

The Xnetters weren't happy about the stepped-up police surveillance, but they weren't going to take it lying down. Someone called a phone-in show on KQED and told them that the police were wasting their time, that we could monkey-wrench the system faster than they could untangle it. The recording was a top Xnet download that night.

"This is California Live and we're talking to an anonymous caller at a pay phone in San Francisco. He has his own information about the slowdowns we've been facing around town this week. Caller, you're on the air."

"Yeah, yo, this is just the beginning, you know? I mean, like, we're just getting started. Let them hire a billion pigs and put a checkpoint on every corner. We'll jam them all! And like, all this crap about terrorists? We're not terrorists! Give me a break, I mean, really! We're jamming up the system because we hate the Homeland Security, and because we love our city. Terrorists? I can't even spell jihad. Peace out."

He sounded like an idiot. Not just the incoherent words, but also his gloating tone. He sounded like a kid who was indecently proud of himself. He *was* a kid who was indecently proud of himself.

The Xnet flamed out over this. Lots of people thought he was an idiot for calling in, while others thought he was a hero. I worried that there was probably a camera aimed at the pay phone he'd used. Or an arphid reader that might have sniffed his Fast Pass. I hoped he'd had the smarts to wipe his fingerprints off the quarter, keep his hood up and leave all his arphids at home. But I doubted it. I wondered if he'd get a knock on the door sometime soon.

The way I knew when something big had happened on Xnet was that I'd suddenly get a million emails from people who wanted M1k3y to know about the latest haps. It was just as I was reading about Mr. Can't-Spell-Jihad that my mailbox went crazy. Everyone had a message for me—a link to a LiveJournal on the Xnet—one of the many anonymous blogs that were based on the Freenet document publishing system that was also used by Chinese democracy advocates.

> Close call
> We were jamming at the Embarcadero tonite and goofing around giving everyone a new car key or door key or Fast Pass or FasTrak, tossing around a little fake gunpowder. There were cops everywhere but we were smarter than them; we're there pretty much every night and we never get caught.
> So we got caught tonight. It was a stupid mistake we got sloppy we got busted. It was an undercover who caught my pal and then got the rest of us. They'd been watching the crowd for a long time and they had one of those trucks nearby and they took four of us in but missed the rest.
> The truck was JAMMED like a can of sardines with every kind of person, old young black white rich poor all suspects, and there were two cops trying to ask us questions and the undercovers kept bringing in more of us. Most people were trying to get to the front of the line to get through questioning so we kept on moving back and it was like hours in there and really hot and it was getting more crowded not less.
> At like 8PM they changed shifts and two new cops came in and bawled out the two cops who were there all like wtf? aren't you doing anything here. They had a real fight and then the two old cops left and the new cops sat down at their desks and whispered to each other for a while.
> Then one cop stood up and started shouting EVERYONE JUST GO HOME

JESUS CHRIST WE'VE GOT BETTER THINGS TO DO THAN BOTHER YOU WITH
MORE QUESTIONS IF YOU'VE DONE SOMETHING WRONG JUST DON'T DO IT
AGAIN AND LET THIS BE A WARNING TO YOU ALL.

> A bunch of the suits got really pissed which was HILARIOUS because I
mean ten minutes before they were buggin about being held there and now they
were wicked pissed about being let go, like make up your minds!

> We split fast though and got out and came home to write this. There
are undercovers everywhere, believe. If you're jamming, be open-eyed and get
ready to run when problems happen. If you get caught try to wait it out they're
so busy they'll maybe just let you go.

> We made them that busy! All those people in that truck were there be-
cause we'd jammed them. So jam on!

I felt like I was going to throw up. Those four people—kids I'd
never met—they nearly went away forever because of something
I'd started.

Because of something I'd told them to do. I was no better than
a terrorist.

The DHS got their budget requisition approved. The president
went on TV with the governor to tell us that no price was too high
for security. We had to watch it the next day in school at assembly.
My dad cheered. He'd hated the president since the day he was
elected, saying he wasn't any better than the last guy and the last
guy had been a complete disaster, but now all he could do was talk
about how decisive and dynamic the new guy was.

"You have to take it easy on your father," Mom said to me one
night after I got home from school. She'd been working from home
as much as possible. Mom's a freelance relocation specialist who
helps British people get settled in in San Francisco. The UK High
Commission pays her to answer emails from mystified British people across the country who are totally confused by how freaky we
Americans are. She explains Americans for a living, and she said
that these days it was better to do that from home, where she didn't
have to actually see any Americans or talk to them.

I don't have any illusions about Britain. America may be willing
to trash its Constitution every time some jihadist looks cross-eyed

at us, but as I learned in my ninth-grade Social Studies independent project, the Brits don't even *have* a Constitution. They've got laws there that would curl the hair on your toes: they can put you in jail for an entire year if they're really sure that you're a terrorist but don't have enough evidence to prove it. Now, how sure can they be if they don't have enough evidence to prove it? How'd they get that sure? Did they see you committing terrorist acts in a really vivid dream?

And the surveillance in Britain makes America look like amateur hour. The average Londoner is photographed five hundred times a day, just walking around the streets. Every license plate is photographed at every corner in the country. Everyone from the banks to the public transit company is enthusiastic about tracking you and snitching on you if they think you're remotely suspicious.

But Mom didn't see it that way. She'd left Britain halfway through high school and she'd never felt at home here, no matter that she'd married a boy from Petaluma and raised a son here. To her, this was always the land of barbarians, and Britain would always be home.

"Mom, he's just wrong. You of all people should know that. Everything that makes this country great is being flushed down the toilet and he's going along with it. Have you noticed that they haven't *caught any terrorists*? Dad's all like, 'We need to be safe,' but he needs to know that most of us don't feel safe. We feel endangered all the time."

"I know this all, Marcus. Believe me, I'm not a fan of what's been happening to this country. But your father is—" She broke off. "When you didn't come home after the attacks, he thought—"

She got up and made herself a cup of tea, something she did whenever she was uncomfortable or disconcerted.

"Marcus," she said. "Marcus, we thought you were dead. Do you understand that? We were mourning you for days. We were imagining you blown to bits, at the bottom of the ocean. Dead because some bastard decided to kill hundreds of strangers to make some point."

That sank in slowly. I mean, I understood that they'd been worried. Lots of people died in the bombings—four thousand was the present estimate—and practically everyone knew someone who didn't come home that day. There were two people from my school who had disappeared.

"Your father was ready to kill someone. Anyone. He was out of his mind. You've never seen him like this. I've never seen him like it, either. He was out of his mind. He'd just sit at this table and curse and curse and curse. Vile words, words I'd never heard him say. One day—the third day—someone called and he was sure it was you, but it was a wrong number and he threw the phone so hard it disintegrated into thousands of pieces." I'd wondered about the new kitchen phone.

"Something broke in your father. He loves you. We both love you. You are the most important thing in our lives. I don't think you realize that. Do you remember when you were ten, when I went home to London for all that time? Do you remember?"

I nodded silently.

"We were ready to get a divorce, Marcus. Oh, it doesn't matter why anymore. It was just a bad patch, the kind of thing that happens when people who love each other stop paying attention for a few years. He came and got me and convinced me to come back for you. We couldn't bear the thought of doing that to you. We fell in love again for you. We're together today because of you."

I had a lump in my throat. I'd never known this. No one had ever told me.

"So your father is having a hard time right now. He's not in his right mind. It's going to take some time before he comes back to us, before he's the man I love again. We need to understand him until then."

She gave me a long hug, and I noticed how thin her arms had gotten, how saggy the skin on her neck was. I always thought of my mother as young, pale, rosy-cheeked and cheerful, peering shrewdly through her metal-rim glasses. Now she looked a little like an old woman. I had done that to her. The terrorists had done that to her. The Department of Homeland Security had done that to her. In a weird way, we were all on the same side, and Mom and Dad and all those people we'd spoofed were on the other side.

I couldn't sleep that night. Mom's words kept running through my head. Dad had been tense and quiet at dinner and we'd barely spoken, because I didn't trust myself not to say the wrong thing and because he was all wound up over the latest news, that Al Qaeda was definitely responsible for the bombing. Six different terrorist groups had claimed responsibility for the attack, but only Al Qaeda's Internet video disclosed information that the DHS said they hadn't disclosed to anyone.

I lay in bed and listened to a late-night call-in radio show. The topic was sex problems, with this gay guy who I normally loved to listen to, he would give people such raw advice, but good advice, and he was really funny and campy.

Tonight I couldn't laugh. Most of the callers wanted to ask what to do about the fact that they were having a hard time getting busy with their partners ever since the attack. Even on sex-talk radio, I couldn't get away from the topic.

I switched the radio off and heard a purring engine on the street below.

My bedroom is in the top floor of our house, one of the painted ladies. I have a sloping attic ceiling and windows on both sides— one overlooks the whole Mission, the other looks out into the street in front of our place. There were often cars cruising at all hours of the night, but there was something different about this engine noise.

I went to the street window and pulled up my blinds. Down on the street below me was a white, unmarked van whose roof was festooned with radio antennas, more antennas than I'd ever seen on a car. It was cruising very slowly down the street, a little dish on top spinning around and around.

As I watched, the van stopped and one of the back doors popped open. A guy in a DHS uniform—I could spot one from a hundred yards now—stepped out into the street. He had some kind of handheld device, and its blue glow lit his face. He paced back and forth, first scouting my neighbors, making notes on his device, then heading for me. There was something familiar in the way he walked, looking down—

He was using a wifinder! The DHS was scouting for Xnet nodes.

I let go of the blinds and dove across my room for my Xbox. I'd left it up while I downloaded some cool animations one of the Xnetters had made of the president's no-price-too-high speech. I yanked the plug out of the wall, then scurried back to the window and cracked the blind a fraction of an inch.

The guy was looking down into his wifinder again, walking back and forth in front of our house. A moment later, he got back into his van and drove away.

I got out my camera and took as many pictures as I could of the van and its antennas. Then I opened them in a free image-editor called the GIMP and edited out everything from the photo except the van, erasing my street and anything that might identify me.

I posted them to Xnet and wrote down everything I could about the vans. These guys were definitely looking for the Xnet, I could tell.

Now I really couldn't sleep.

Nothing for it but to play windup pirates. There'd be lots of players even at this hour. The real name for windup pirates was Clockwork Plunder, and it was a hobbyist project that had been created by teenaged death metal freaks from Finland. It was totally free to play, and offered just as much fun as any of the $15/month services like Ender's Universe and Middle Earth Quest and Discworld Dungeons.

I logged back in and there I was, still on the deck of the *Zombie Charger*, waiting for someone to wind me up. I hated this part of the game.

> Hey you

I typed to a passing pirate.

> Wind me up?

He paused and looked at me.

> y should i?

> We're on the same team. Plus you get experience points.

What a jerk.

> Where are you located?

> San Francisco

This was starting to feel familiar.

> Where in San Francisco?

I logged out. There was something weird going on in the game. I jumped onto the LiveJournals and began to crawl from blog to blog. I got through half a dozen before I found something that froze my blood.

LiveJournalers love quizzes. What kind of hobbit are you? Are you a great lover? What planet are you most like? Which character from some movie are you? What's your emotional type? They fill them in and their friends fill them in and everyone compares their results. Harmless fun.

But the quiz that had taken over the blogs of the Xnet that night was what scared me, because it was anything but harmless:

> _ What's your sex
> _ What grade are you in?
> _ What school do you go to?
> _ Where in the city do you live?

The quizzes plotted the results on a map with colored pushpins for schools and neighborhoods, and made lame recommendations for places to buy pizza and stuff.

But look at those questions. Think about my answers:

> _ Male
> _ 17
> _ Chavez High
> _ Potrero Hill

There were only two people in my whole school who matched that profile. Most schools it would be the same. If you wanted to figure out who the Xnetters were, you could use these quizzes to find them all.

That was bad enough, but what was worse was what it implied: someone from the DHS was using the Xnet to get at us. The Xnet was compromised by the DHS.

We had spies in our midst.

I'd given Xnet discs to hundreds of people, and they'd done the same. I knew the people I gave the discs to pretty well. Some of them I knew very well. I've lived in the same house all my life and I've made hundreds and hundreds of friends over the years, from people who went to day care with me to people I played soccer with, people who LARPed with me, people I met clubbing, people I knew from school. My ARG team were my closest friends, but there were plenty of people I knew and trusted enough to hand an Xnet disc to.

I needed them now.

I woke Jolu up by ringing his cell phone and hanging up after the first ring, three times in a row. A minute later, he was up on Xnet and we were able to have a secure chat. I pointed him to my blog-post on the radio vans and he came back a minute later all freaked out.

> You sure they're looking for us?

In response I sent him to the quiz.

> OMG we're doomed

> No it's not that bad but we need to figure out who we can trust

> How?

> That's what I wanted to ask you—how many people can you totally vouch for like trust them to the ends of the earth?

> Um 20 or 30 or so

> I want to get a bunch of really trustworthy people together and do a key-exchange web-of-trust thing

Web of trust is one of those cool crypto things that I'd read about but never tried. It was a nearly foolproof way to make sure that you could talk to the people you trusted, but that no one else could listen in. The problem is that it requires you to physically meet with the people in the Web at least once, just to get started.

> I get it sure. That's not bad. But how you going to get everyone together for the key-signing?

> That's what I wanted to ask you about—how can we do it without getting busted?

Jolu typed some words and erased them, typed more and erased them.

> Darryl would know

I typed.

> God, this was the stuff he was great at.

Jolu didn't type anything. Then,

> How about a party?

he typed.

> How about if we all get together somewhere like we're teenagers having a party and that way we'll have a ready-made excuse if anyone shows up asking us what we're doing there?

> That would totally work! You're a genius, Jolu.

> I know it. And you're going to love this: I know just where to do it, too

> Where?

> Sutro Baths!

What would you do if you found out you had a spy in your midst? You could denounce him, put him up against the wall and take him out. But then you might end up with another spy in your midst, and the new spy would be more careful than the last one and maybe not get caught quite so readily.

Here's a better idea: start intercepting the spy's communications and feed him and his masters misinformation. Say his masters instruct him to gather information on your movements. Let him follow you around and take all the notes he wants, but steam open the envelopes that he sends back to HQ and replace his account of your movements with a fictitious one. If you want, you can make him seem erratic and unreliable so they get rid of him. You can manufacture crises that might make one side or the other reveal the identities of other spies. In short, you own them.

This is called the man-in-the-middle attack and if you think about it, it's pretty scary. Someone who man-in-the-middles your communications can trick you in any of a thousand ways.

Of course, there's a great way to get around the man-in-the-middle attack: use crypto. With crypto, it doesn't matter if the enemy can see your messages, because he can't decipher them, change them and resend them. That's one of the main reasons to use crypto.

But remember: for crypto to work, you need to have keys for the people you want to talk to. You and your partner need to share a secret or two, some keys that you can use to encrypt and decrypt your messages so that men-in-the-middle get locked out.

That's where the idea of public keys comes in. This is a little hairy, but it's so unbelievably elegant, too.

In public-key crypto, each user gets two keys. They're long

strings of mathematical gibberish, and they have an almost magic property. Whatever you scramble with one key, the other will unlock, and vice versa. What's more, they're the *only* keys that can do this—if you can unscramble a message with one key, you *know* it was scrambled with the other (and vice versa).

So you take either one of these keys (it doesn't matter which one) and you just *publish* it. You make it a total *nonsecret*. You want anyone in the world to know what it is. For obvious reasons, they call this your "public key."

The other key, you hide in the darkest reaches of your mind. You protect it with your life. You never let anyone ever know what it is. That's called your "private key." (Duh.)

Now say you're a spy and you want to talk with your bosses. Their public key is known by everyone. Your public key is known by everyone. No one knows your private key but you. No one knows their private key but them.

You want to send them a message. First, you encrypt it with your private key. You could just send that message along, and it would work pretty well, since they would know when the message arrived that it came from you. How? Because if they can decrypt it with your public key, it can *only* have been encrypted with your private key. This is the equivalent of putting your seal or signature on the bottom of a message. It says, *I wrote this, and no one else. No one could have tampered with it or changed it.*

Unfortunately, this won't actually keep your message a *secret*. That's because your public key is really well known (it has to be, or you'll be limited to sending messages to those few people who have your public key). Anyone who intercepts the message can read it. They can't change it and make it seem like it came from you, but if you don't want people to know what you're saying, you need a better solution.

So instead of just encrypting the message with your private key, you *also* encrypt it with your boss's public key. Now it's been locked twice. The first lock—the boss's public key—only comes off when combined with your boss's private key. The second lock—your private key—only comes off with your public key. When your bosses receive the message, they unlock it with both keys and now they know for sure that: a) you wrote it, and b) only they can read it.

It's very cool. The day I discovered it, Darryl and I immediately exchanged keys and spent months cackling and rubbing our hands as we exchanged our military-grade secret messages about where to meet after school and whether Van would ever notice him.

But if you want to understand security, you need to consider the most paranoid possibilities. Like, what if I tricked you into thinking that *my* public key was your boss's public key? You'd encrypt the message with your private key and my public key. I'd decrypt it, read it, reencrypt it with your boss's *real* public key and send it on. As far as your boss knows, no one but you could have written the message and no one but him could have read it.

And I get to sit in the middle, like a fat spider in a web, and all your secrets belong to me.

Now, the easiest way to fix this is to really widely advertise your public key. If it's *really* easy for anyone to know what your real key is, man-in-the-middle gets harder and harder. But you know what? Making things well known is just as hard as keeping them secret. Think about it—how many billions of dollars are spent on shampoo ads and other crap, just to make sure that as many people know about something that some advertiser wants them to know?

There's a cheaper way of fixing man-in-the-middle: the web of trust. Say that before you leave HQ, you and your bosses sit down over coffee and actually tell each other your keys. No more man-in-the-middle! You're absolutely certain whose keys you have, because they were put into your own hands.

So far, so good. But there's a natural limit to this: how many people can you physically meet with and swap keys? How many hours in the day do you want to devote to the equivalent of writing your own phone book? How many of those people are willing to devote that kind of time to you?

Thinking about this like a phone book helps. The world was once a place with a lot of phone books, and when you needed a number, you could look it up in the book. But for many of the numbers that you wanted to refer to on a given day, you would either know it by heart or you'd be able to ask someone else. Even today, when I'm out with my cell phone, I'll ask Jolu or Darryl if they have a number I'm looking for. It's faster and easier than looking it up online and they're more reliable, too. If Jolu has a number, I trust him, so I trust the number, too. That's called "transitive trust"—trust that moves across the web of our relationships.

A web of trust is a bigger version of this. Say I meet Jolu and get his key. I can put it on my "keyring"—a list of keys that I've signed with my private key. That means you can unlock it with my public key and know for sure that me—or someone with my key, anyway—says that "this key belongs to this guy."

So I hand you my keyring and provided that you trust me to have actually met and verified all the keys on it, you can take it and add it to your keyring. Now, you meet someone else and you hand the whole ring to him. Bigger and bigger the ring grows, and provided that you trust the next guy in the chain, and he trusts the next guy in his chain and so on, you're pretty secure.

Which brings me to keysigning parties. These are *exactly* what they sound like: a party where everyone gets together and signs everyone else's keys. Darryl and I, when we traded keys, that was kind of a mini keysigning party, one with only two sad and geeky attendees. But with more people, you create the seed of the web of trust, and the web can expand from there. As everyone on your keyring goes out into the world and meets more people, they can add more and more names to the ring. You don't have to meet the new people, just trust that the signed key you get from the people in your web is valid.

So that's why web of trust and parties go together like peanut butter and chocolate.

"Just tell them it's a superprivate party, invitational only," I said. "Tell them not to bring anyone along or they won't be admitted."

Jolu looked at me over his coffee. "You're joking, right? You tell people that, and they'll bring *extra* friends."

"Argh," I said. I spent a night a week at Jolu's these days, keeping the code up to date on indienet. Pigspleen actually paid me a nonzero sum of money to do this, which was really weird. I never thought I'd be paid to write code.

"So what do we do? We only want people we really trust there, and we don't want to mention why until we've got everyone's keys and can send them messages in secret."

Jolu debugged and I watched over his shoulder. This used to be called "extreme programming," which was a little embarrassing. Now we just call it "programming." Two people are much better at spotting bugs than one. As the cliche goes, "With enough eyeballs, all bugs are shallow."

We were working our way through the bug reports and getting ready to push out the new rev. It all autoupdated in the background, so our users didn't really need to do anything, they just woke up once a week or so with a better program. It was pretty freaky to know that the code I wrote would be used by hundreds of thousands of people, *tomorrow!*

"What do we do? Man, I don't know. I think we just have to live with it."

I thought back to our Harajuku Fun Madness days. There were lots of social challenges involving large groups of people as part of that game.

"Okay, you're right. But let's at least try to keep this secret. Tell them that they can bring a maximum of one person, and it has to be someone they've known personally for a minimum of five years."

Jolu looked up from the screen. "Hey," he said. "Hey, that would totally work. I can really see it. I mean, if you told me not to bring anyone, I'd be all, 'Who the hell does he think he is?' But when you put it that way, it sounds like some awesome 007 stuff."

I found a bug. We drank some coffee. I went home and played a little Clockwork Plunder, trying not to think about key-winders with nosy questions, and slept like a baby.

Sutro Baths are San Francisco's authentic fake Roman ruins. When it opened in 1896, it was the largest indoor bathing house in the world, a huge Victorian glass solarium filled with pools and tubs and even an early water slide. It went downhill by the fifties, and the owners torched it for the insurance in 1966. All that's left is a labyrinth of weathered stone set into the sere cliff face at Ocean Beach. It looks for all the world like a Roman ruin, crumbled and mysterious, and just beyond it is a set of caves that let out into the sea. In rough tides, the waves rush through the caves and over the ruins—they've even been known to suck in and drown the occasional tourist.

Ocean Beach is way out past Golden Gate Park, a stark cliff lined with expensive, doomed houses, plunging down to a narrow beach studded with jellyfish and brave (insane) surfers. There's a giant white rock that juts out of the shallows off the shore. That's called Seal Rock, and it used to be the place where the sea lions congregated until they were relocated to the more tourist-friendly environs of Fisherman's Wharf.

After dark, there's hardly anyone out there. It gets very cold, with a salt spray that'll soak you to your bones if you let it. The rocks are sharp and there's broken glass and the occasional junkie needle.

It is an awesome place for a party.

Bringing along the tarpaulins and chemical glove-warmers was my idea. Jolu figured out where to get the beer—his older brother, Javier, had a buddy who actually operated a whole underage drinking service: pay him enough and he'd back up to your secluded party spot with ice chests and as many brews as you wanted. I blew a bunch of my indienet programming money, and the guy showed up right on time—8 P.M., a good hour after sunset—and lugged the six foam ice chests out of his pickup truck and down into the ruins of the baths. He even brought a spare chest for the empties.

"You kids play safe now," he said, tipping his cowboy hat. He was a fat Samoan guy with a huge smile, and a scary tank top that you could see his armpit- and belly- and shoulder-hair escaping from. I peeled twenties off my roll and handed them to him—his markup was 150 percent. Not a bad racket.

He looked at my roll. "You know, I could just take that from you," he said, still smiling. "I'm a criminal, after all."

I put my roll in my pocket and looked him levelly in the eye.

I'd been stupid to show him what I was carrying, but I knew that there were times when you should just stand your ground.

"I'm just messing with you," he said, at last. "But you be careful with that money. Don't go showing it around."

"Thanks," I said. "Homeland Security'll get my back though."

His smile got even bigger. "Ha! They're not even real five-oh. Those peckerwoods don't know nothin'."

I looked over at his truck. Prominently displayed in his windscreen was a FasTrak. I wondered how long it would be until he got busted.

"You got girls coming tonight? That why you got all the beer?"

I smiled and waved at him as though he was walking back to his truck, which he should have been doing. He eventually got the hint and drove away. His smile never faltered.

Jolu helped me hide the coolers in the rubble, working with little white LED torches on headbands. Once the coolers were in place, we threw little white LED keychains into each one, so it would glow when you took the styrofoam lid off, making it easier to see what you were doing.

It was a moonless night and overcast, and the distant streetlights barely illuminated us. I knew we'd stand out like blazes on an infrared scope, but there was no chance that we'd be able to get a bunch of people together without being observed. I'd settle for being dismissed as a little drunken beach party.

I don't really drink much. There's been beer and pot and ecstasy at the parties I've been going to since I was fourteen, but I hated smoking (though I'm quite partial to a hash brownie every now and again), ecstasy took too long—who's got a whole weekend to get high and come down—and beer, well, it was all right, but I didn't see what the big deal was. My favorite was big, elaborate cocktails, the kind of thing served in a ceramic volcano, with six layers, on fire, and a plastic monkey on the rim, but that was mostly for the theater of it all.

I actually like being drunk. I just don't like being hungover, and boy, do I ever get hungover. Though again, that might have to do with the kind of drinks that come in a ceramic volcano.

But you can't throw a party without putting a case or two of beer on ice. It's expected. It loosens things up. People do stupid things after too many beers, but it's not like my friends are the kind of people who have cars. And people do stupid things no matter what—beer or grass or whatever are all incidental to that central fact.

Jolu and I each cracked beers—Anchor Steam for him, a Bud Light for me—and clinked the bottles together, sitting down on a rock.

"You told them nine P.M.?"

"Yeah," he said.

"Me too."

We drank in silence. The Bud Light was the least alcoholic thing in the ice chest. I'd need a clear head later.

"You ever get scared?" I said, finally.

He turned to me. "No man, I don't get scared. I'm always scared. I've been scared since the minute the explosions happened. I'm so scared sometimes, I don't want to get out of bed."

"Then why do you do it?"

He smiled. "About that," he said. "Maybe I won't, not for much longer. I mean, it's been great helping you. Great. Really excellent. I don't know when I've done anything so important. But Marcus, bro, I have to say . . ." He trailed off.

"What?" I said, though I knew what was coming next.

"I can't do it forever," he said at last. "Maybe not even for another month. I think I'm through. It's too much risk. The DHS, you can't go to war on them. It's crazy. Really actually crazy."

"You sound like Van," I said. My voice was much more bitter than I'd intended.

"I'm not criticizing you, man. I think it's great that you've got the bravery to do this all the time. But I haven't got it. I can't live my life in perpetual terror."

"What are you saying?"

"I'm saying I'm out. I'm going to be one of those people who acts like it's all okay, like it'll all go back to normal some day. I'm going to use the Internet like I always did, and only use the Xnet to play games. I'm going to get out is what I'm saying. I won't be a part of your plans anymore."

I didn't say anything.

"I know that's leaving you on your own. I don't want that, believe me. I'd much rather you give up with me. You can't declare war on the government of the USA. It's not a fight you're going to win. Watching you try is like watching a bird fly into a window again and again."

He wanted me to say something. What I wanted to say was, *Jesus Jolu, thanks so very much for abandoning me! Do you forget what it was like when they took us away? Do you forget what the country used to be like before they took it over?* But that's not what he wanted me to say. What he wanted me to say was:

I understand, Jolu. I respect your choice.

He drank the rest of his beer and pulled out another one and twisted off the cap.

"There's something else," he said.

"What?"

"I wasn't going to mention it, but I want you to understand why I have to do this."

"Jesus, Jolu, *what*?"

"I hate to say it, but you're *white*. I'm not. White people get caught with cocaine and do a little rehab time. Brown people get caught with crack and go to prison for twenty years. White people see cops on the street and feel safer. Brown people see cops on the street and wonder if they're about to get searched. The way the DHS is treating you? The law in this country has always been like that for us."

It was so unfair. I didn't ask to be white. I didn't think I was being braver just because I'm white. But I knew what Jolu was saying. If the cops stopped someone in the Mission and asked to see some ID, chances were that person wasn't white. Whatever risk I ran, Jolu ran more. Whatever penalty I'd pay, Jolu would pay more.

"I don't know what to say," I said.

"You don't have to say anything," he said. "I just wanted you to know, so you could understand."

I could see people walking down the side trail toward us. They were friends of Jolu's, two Mexican guys and a girl I knew from around, short and geeky, always wearing cute black Buddy Holly glasses that made her look like the outcast art student in a teen movie who comes back as the big success.

Jolu introduced me and gave them beers. The girl didn't take one, but instead produced a small silver flask of vodka from her purse and offered me a drink. I took a swallow—warm vodka must be an acquired taste—and complimented her on the flask, which was embossed with a repeating motif of PaRappa the Rapper characters.

"It's Japanese," she said as I played another LED keyring over it. "They have all these great booze-toys based on kids' games. Totally twisted."

I introduced myself and she introduced herself. "Ange," she said, and shook my hand with hers—dry, warm, with short nails. Jolu introduced me to his pals, whom he'd known since computer camp in the fourth grade. More people showed up—five, then ten, then twenty. It was a seriously big group now.

We'd told people to arrive by 9:30 sharp, and we gave it until 9:45 to see who all would show up. About three quarters were Jolu's friends. I'd invited all the people I really trusted. Either I was more discriminating than Jolu or less popular. Now that he'd told me he was quitting, it made me think that he was less discriminating. I was really pissed at him, but trying not to let it show by concentrating on socializing with other people. But he wasn't stupid. He knew what was going on. I could see that he was really bummed. Good.

"Okay," I said, climbing up on a ruin. "Okay, hey, hello?" A few people nearby paid attention to me, but the ones in the back kept on chatting. I put my arms in the air like a referee, but it was too dark. Eventually I hit on the idea of turning my LED keychain on and pointing it at each of the talkers in turn, then at me. Gradually, the crowd fell quiet.

I welcomed them and thanked them all for coming, then asked them to close in so I could explain why we were there. I could tell they were into the secrecy of it all, intrigued and a little warmed up by the beer.

"So here it is. You all use the Xnet. It's no coincidence that the Xnet was created right after the DHS took over the city. The people who did that are an organization devoted to personal liberty, who created the network to keep us safe from DHS spooks and enforcers." Jolu and I had worked this out in advance. We weren't going to cop to being behind it all, not to anyone. It was way too risky. Instead, we'd put it out that we were merely lieutenants in "M1k3y"'s army, acting to organize the local resistance.

"The Xnet isn't pure," I said. "It can be used by the other side just as readily as by us. We know that there are DHS spies who use it now. They use social engineering hacks to try to get us to reveal ourselves so that they can bust us. If the Xnet is going to succeed, we need to figure out how to keep them from spying on us. We need a network within the network."

I paused and let this sink in. Jolu had suggested that this might be a little heavy—learning that you're about to be brought into a revolutionary cell.

"Now, I'm not here to ask you to do anything active. You don't have to go out jamming or anything. You've been brought here because we know you're cool, we know you're trustworthy. It's that trustworthiness I want to get you to contribute tonight. Some of you will already be familiar with the web of trust and keysigning parties, but for the rest of you, I'll run it down quickly—" Which I did.

"Now what I want from you tonight is to meet the people here and figure out how much you can trust them. We're going to help you generate key-pairs and share them with each other."

This part was tricky. Asking people to bring their own laptops wouldn't have worked out, but we still needed to do something hella complicated that wouldn't exactly work with paper and pencil.

I held up a laptop Jolu and I had rebuilt the night before, from the ground up. "I trust this machine. Every component in it was laid by our own hands. It's running a fresh-out-of-the-box version of ParanoidLinux, booted off of the DVD. If there's a trustworthy computer left anywhere in the world, this might well be it.

"I've got a key-generator loaded here. You come up here and give it some random input—mash the keys, wiggle the mouse—and it will use that as the seed to create a random public and private key for you, which it will display on the screen. You can take a picture of the private key with your phone, and hit any key to make it go away forever—it's not stored on the disc at all. Then it will show you your public key. At that point, you call over all the people here you trust and who trust you, and *they* take a picture of the screen with you standing next to it, so they know whose key it is.

"When you get home, you have to convert the photos to keys. This is going to be a lot of work, I'm afraid, but you'll only have to do it once. You have to be super-careful about typing these in— one mistake and you're screwed. Luckily, we've got a way to tell if you've got it right: beneath the key will be a much shorter number, called the 'fingerprint.' Once you've typed in the key, you can generate a fingerprint from it and compare it to the fingerprint, and if they match, you've got it right."

They all boggled at me. Okay, so I'd asked them to do something pretty weird, it's true, but still.

chapter 11

Jolu stood up.

"This is where it starts, guys. This is how we know which side you're on. You might not be willing to take to the streets and get busted for your beliefs, but if you *have* beliefs, this will let us know it. This will create the web of trust that tells us who's in and who's out. If we're ever going to get our country back, we need to do this. We need to do something like this."

Someone in the audience—it was Ange—had a hand up, holding a beer bottle.

"So call me stupid but I don't understand this at all. Why do you want us to do this?"

Jolu looked at me, and I looked back at him. It had all seemed so obvious when we were organizing it. "The Xnet isn't just a way to play free games. It's the last open communications network in America. It's the last way to communicate without being snooped on by the DHS. For it to work we need to know that the person we're talking to isn't a snoop. That means that we need to know that the people we're sending messages to are the people we think they are.

"That's where you come in. You're all here because we trust you. I mean, really trust you. Trust you with our lives."

Some of the people groaned. It sounded melodramatic and stupid.

I got back to my feet.

"When the bombs went off," I said, and then something welled up in my chest, something painful. "When the bombs went off, there were four of us caught up by Market Street. For whatever reason, the DHS decided that made us suspicious. They put bags over our heads, put us on a ship and interrogated us for days. They humiliated us. Played games with our minds. Then they let us go.

144 | **cory doctorow**

"All except one person. My best friend. He was with us when they picked us up. He'd been hurt and he needed medical care. He never came out again. They say they never saw him. They say that if we ever tell anyone about this, they'll arrest us and make us disappear.

"Forever."

I was shaking. The shame. The goddamned shame. Jolu had the light on me.

"Oh Christ," I said. "You people are the first ones I've told. If this story gets around, you can bet they'll know who leaked it. You can bet they'll come knocking on my door." I took some more deep breaths. "That's why I volunteered on the Xnet. That's why my life, from now on, is about fighting the DHS. With every breath. Every day. Until we're free again. Any one of you could put me in jail now, if you wanted to."

Ange put her hand up again. "We're not going to rat on you," she said. "No way. I know pretty much everyone here and I can promise you that. I don't know how to know who to trust, but I know who *not* to trust: old people. Our parents. Grown-ups. When they think of someone being spied on, they think of someone *else*, a bad guy. When they think of someone being caught and sent to a secret prison, it's someone *else*—someone brown, someone young, someone foreign.

"They forget what it's like to be our age. To be the object of suspicion *all the time*! How many times have you gotten on the bus and had every person on it give you a look like you'd been gargling turds and skinning puppies?

"What's worse, they're turning into adults younger and younger out there. Back in the day, they used to say, 'Never trust anyone over 30.' I say, 'Don't trust any bastard over 25!'"

That got a laugh, and she laughed, too. She was pretty, in a weird, horsey way, with a long face and a long jaw. "I'm not really kidding, you know? I mean, think about it. Who elected these ass-clowns? Who let them invade our city? Who voted to put the cameras in our classrooms and follow us around with creepy spyware chips in our transit passes and cars? It wasn't a sixteen-year-old. We may be dumb, we may be young, but we're not scum."

"I want that on a T-shirt," I said.

"It would be a good one," she said. We smiled at each other.

"Where do I go to get my keys?" she said, and pulled out her phone.

"We'll do it over there, in the secluded spot by the caves. I'll take you in there and set you up, then you do your thing and take the machine around to your friends to get photos of your public key so they can sign it when they get home."

I raised my voice. "Oh! One more thing! Jesus, I can't believe I forgot this. *Delete those photos once you've typed in the keys!* The last thing we want is a Flickr stream full of pictures of all of us conspiring together."

There was some good-natured, nervous chuckling, then Jolu turned out the light and in the sudden darkness I could see nothing. Gradually, my eyes adjusted and I set off for the cave. Someone was walking behind me. Ange. I turned and smiled at her, and she smiled back, luminous teeth in the dark.

"Thanks for that," I said. "You were great."

"You mean what you said about the bag on your head and everything?"

"I meant it," I said. "It happened. I never told anyone, but it happened." I thought about it for a moment. "You know, with all the time that went by since, without saying anything, it started to feel like a bad dream. It was real though." I stopped and climbed up into the cave. "I'm glad I finally told people. Any longer and I might have started to doubt my own sanity."

I set up the laptop on a dry bit of rock and booted it from the DVD with her watching. "I'm going to reboot it for every person. This is a standard ParanoidLinux disc, though I guess you'd have to take my word for it."

"Hell," she said. "This is all about trust, right?"

"Yeah," I said. "Trust."

I retreated some distance as she ran the key-generator, listening to her typing and mousing to create randomness, listening to the crash of the surf, listening to the party noises from over where the beer was.

She stepped out of the cave, carrying the laptop. On it, in huge white luminous letters, were her public key and her fingerprint and email address. She held the screen up beside her face and waited while I got my phone out.

"Cheese," she said. I snapped her pic and dropped the camera back in my pocket. She wandered off to the revelers and let them each get pics of her and the screen. It was festive. Fun. She really had a lot of charisma—you didn't want to laugh at her, you just wanted to laugh *with* her. And hell, it *was* funny! We were declaring a secret war on the secret police. Who the hell did we think we were?

So it went, through the next hour or so, everyone taking pictures and making keys. I got to meet everyone there. I knew a lot of them—some were my invitees—and the others were friends of my pals or my pals' pals. We should all be buddies. We were, by the time the night was out. They were all good people.

Once everyone was done, Jolu went to make a key, and then turned away, giving me a sheepish grin. I was past my anger with him, though. He was doing what he had to do. I knew that no matter what he said, he'd always be there for me. And we'd been through the DHS jail together. Van, too. No matter what, that would bind us together forever.

I did my key and did the perp-walk around the gang, letting everyone snap a pic. Then I climbed up on the high spot I'd spoken from earlier and called for everyone's attention.

"So a lot of you have noted that there's a vital flaw in this procedure: What if this laptop can't be trusted? What if it's secretly recording our instructions? What if it's spying on us? What if Jose-Luis and I can't be trusted?"

More good-natured chuckles. A little warmer than before, more beery.

"I mean it," I said. "If we were on the wrong side, this could get all of us—all of *you*—into a heap of trouble. Jail, maybe."

The chuckles turned more nervous.

"So that's why I'm going to do this," I said, and picked up a hammer I'd brought from my dad's toolkit. I set the laptop down beside me on the rock and swung the hammer, Jolu following the swing with his keychain light. Crash—I'd always dreamt of killing a laptop with a hammer, and here I was doing it. It felt pornographically good. And bad.

Smash! The screen-panel fell off, shattered into millions of pieces, exposing the keyboard. I kept hitting it, until the keyboard fell off, exposing the motherboard and the hard drive. Crash! I aimed square for the hard drive, hitting it with everything I had. It took three blows before the case split, exposing the fragile media inside. I kept hitting it until there was nothing bigger than a cigarette lighter, then I put it all in a garbage bag. The crowd was cheering wildly—loud enough that I actually got worried that someone far above us might hear over the surf and call the law.

"All right!" I called. "Now, if you'd like to accompany me, I'm going to march this down to the sea and soak it in salt water for ten minutes."

I didn't have any takers at first, but then Ange came forward and took my arm in her warm hand and said, "That was beautiful," in my ear and we marched down to the sea together.

It was perfectly dark by the sea, and treacherous, even with our keychain lights. Slippery, sharp rocks that were difficult enough to walk on even without trying to balance six pounds of smashed electronics in a plastic bag. I slipped once and thought I was going to cut myself up, but Ange caught me with a surprisingly strong grip and kept me upright. I was pulled in right close to her, close enough to smell her perfume, which smelled like new cars. I love that smell.

"Thanks," I managed, looking into the big eyes that were further magnified by her mannish, black-rimmed glasses. I couldn't tell what color they were in the dark, but I guessed something dark, based on her dark hair and olive complexion. She looked Mediterranean, maybe Greek or Spanish or Italian.

I crouched down and dipped the bag in the sea, letting it fill with salt water. I managed to slip a little and soak my shoe, and I swore and she laughed. We'd hardly said a word since we lit out for the ocean. There was something magical in our wordless silence.

At that point, I had kissed a total of three girls in my life, not counting that moment when I went back to school and got a hero's welcome. That's not a gigantic number, but it's not a minuscule one, either. I have reasonable girl radar, and I think I could have kissed her. She wasn't h4wt in the traditional sense, but there's something about a girl and a night and a beach, plus she was smart and passionate and committed.

But I didn't kiss her, or take her hand. Instead we had a moment that I can only describe as spiritual. The surf, the night, the sea and the rocks, and our breathing. The moment stretched. I sighed. This had been quite a ride. I had a lot of typing to do tonight, putting all those keys into my keychain, signing them and publishing the signed keys. Starting the web of trust.

She sighed, too.

"Let's go," I said.

"Yeah," she said.

Back we went. It was a good night, that night.

Jolu waited after for his brother's friend to come by and pick up his coolers. I walked with everyone else up the road to the nearest Muni stop and got on board. Of course, none of us was using an is-sued Muni pass. By that point, Xnetters habitually cloned someone else's Muni pass three or four times a day, assuming a new identity for every ride.

It was hard to stay cool on the bus. We were all a little drunk, and looking at our faces under the bright bus lights was kind of hilarious. We got pretty loud and the driver used his intercom to tell us to keep it down twice, then told us to shut up right now or he'd call the cops.

That set us to giggling again and we disembarked in a mass before he did call the cops. We were in North Beach now, and there were lots of buses, taxis, the BART at Market Street, neon-lit clubs and cafes to pull apart our grouping, so we drifted away.

I got home and fired up my Xbox and started typing in keys from my phone's screen. It was dull, hypnotic work. I was a little drunk, and it lulled me into a half-sleep.

I was about ready to nod off when a new IM window popped up.

> herro!

I didn't recognize the handle—spexgril—but I had an idea who might be behind it.

> hi

I typed, cautiously.

> it's me, from tonight

Then she paste-bombed a block of crypto. I'd already entered her public key into my keychain, so I told the IM client to try decrypting the code with the key.

> it's me, from tonight

It was her!

> Fancy meeting you here

I typed, then encrypted it to my public key and mailed it off.

> It was great meeting you

I typed.

> You too. I don't meet too many smart guys who are also cute and also socially aware. Good god, man, you don't give a girl much of a chance.

My heart hammered in my chest.

> Hello? Tap tap? This thing on? I wasn't born here folks, but I'm sure dying here. Don't forget to tip your waitresses, they work hard. I'm here all week.

I laughed aloud.

> Im here, I'm here. Laughing too hard to type is all

> Well at least my IM comedy-fu is still mighty

Um.

> It was really great to meet you too

> Yeah, it usually is. Where are you taking me?

> Taking you?

> On our next adventure?

> I didnt really have anything planned

> Oki—then I'll take YOU. Saturday. Dolores Park. Illegal open air concert. Be there or be a dodecahedron

> Wait what?

> Dont you even read Xnet? Its all over the place. You ever hear of the Speedwhores?

I nearly choked. That was Trudy Doo's band—as in Trudy Doo, the woman who had paid me and Jolu to update the indienet code.

> Yeah Ive heard of them

> They're putting on a huge show and they've got like fifty bands signed to play the bill, going to set up on the tennis courts and bring out their own amp trucks and rock out all night

I felt like I'd been living under a rock. How had I missed that? There was an anarchist bookstore on Valencia that I sometimes passed on the way to school that had a poster of an old revolutionary named Emma Goldman with the caption "If I can't dance, I don't want to be a part of your revolution." I'd been spending all my energies on figuring out how to use the Xnet to organize dedicated fighters so they could jam the DHS, but this was so much cooler. A big concert—I had no idea how to do one of those, but I was glad someone did.

And now that I thought of it, I was damned proud that they were using the Xnet to do it.

The next day I was a zombie. Ange and I had chatted—flirted—until 4 A.M. Lucky for me, it was a Saturday and I was able to sleep in, but between the hangover and the sleep-dep, I could barely put two thoughts together.

By lunchtime, I managed to get up and get my ass out onto the streets. I staggered down toward the Turk's to buy my coffee—these days, if I was alone, I always bought my coffee there, like the Turk and I were part of a secret club.

On the way, I passed a lot of fresh graffiti. I liked Mission graffiti; a lot of the times, it came in huge, luscious murals, or sarcastic art-student stencils. I liked that the Mission's taggers kept right on going, under the nose of the DHS. Another kind of Xnet, I supposed—they must have all kinds of ways of knowing what was going on, where to get paint, what cameras worked. Some of the cameras had been spray-painted over, I noticed.

Maybe they used Xnet!

Painted in ten-foot-high letters on the side of an auto yard's fence were the drippy words: DON'T TRUST ANYONE OVER 25.

I stopped. Had someone left my "party" last night and come here with a can of paint? A lot of those people lived in the neighborhood.

I got my coffee and had a little wander around town. I kept

thinking I should be calling someone, seeing if they wanted to get a movie or something. That's how it used to be on a lazy Saturday like this. But who was I going to call? Van wasn't talking to me, I didn't think I was ready to talk to Jolu, and Darryl—

Well, I couldn't call Darryl.

I got my coffee and went home and did a little searching around on the Xnet's blogs. These anonablogs were untraceable to any author—unless that author was stupid enough to put her name on it—and there were a lot of them. Most of them were apolitical, but a lot of them weren't. They talked about schools and the unfairness there. They talked about the cops. Tagging.

Turned out there'd been plans for the concert in the park for weeks. It had hopped from blog to blog, turning into a full-blown movement without my noticing. And the concert was called "DON'T TRUST ANYONE OVER 25."

Well, that explained where Ange got it. It was a good slogan.

Monday morning, I decided I wanted to check out that anarchist bookstore again, see about getting one of those Emma Goldman posters. I needed the reminder.

I detoured down to 16th and Mission on my way to school, then up to Valencia and across. The store was shut, but I got the hours off the door and made sure they still had that poster up.

As I walked down Valencia, I was amazed to see how much of the DON'T TRUST ANYONE OVER 25 stuff there was. Half the shops had DON'T TRUST merch in the windows: lunchboxes, babydoll tees, pencil boxes, trucker hats. The hipster stores have been getting faster and faster, of course. As new memes sweep the net in the course of a day or two, stores have gotten better at putting merch in the windows to match. Some funny little youtube of a guy launching himself with jet-packs made of carbonated water would land in your inbox on Monday and by Tuesday you'd be able to buy T-shirts with stills from the video on it.

But it was amazing to see something make the leap from Xnet to the head shops. Distressed designer jeans with the slogan written in careful high school ballpoint ink. Embroidered patches.

Good news travels fast.

It was written on the blackboard when I got to Ms. Galvez's Social Studies class. We all sat at our desks, smiling at it. It seemed to smile back. There was something profoundly cheering about the idea that we could all trust each other, that the enemy could be identified. I knew it wasn't entirely true, but it wasn't entirely false, either.

Ms. Galvez came in and patted her hair and set down her SchoolBook on her desk and powered it up. She picked up her chalk and turned around to face the board. We all laughed. Good-naturedly, but we laughed.

She turned around and was laughing, too. "Inflation has hit the nation's slogan-writers, it seems. How many of you know where this phrase comes from?"

We looked at each other. "Hippies?" someone said, and we laughed. Hippies are all over San Francisco, both the old stoner kinds with giant skanky beards and tie-dyes, and the new kind, who are more into dress-up and maybe playing Hacky Sack than protesting anything.

"Well, yes, hippies. But when we think of hippies these days, we just think of the clothes and the music. Clothes and music were incidental to the main part of what made that era, the sixties, important.

"You've heard about the civil rights movement to end segregation, white and black kids like you riding buses into the South to sign up black voters and protest against official state racism. California was one of the main places where the civil rights leaders came from. We've always been a little more political than the rest of the country, and this is also a part of the country where black people have been able to get the same union factory jobs as white people, so they were a little better off than their cousins in the Southland.

"The students at Berkeley sent a steady stream of freedom riders south, and they recruited them from information tables on campus, at Bancroft and Telegraph Avenue. You've probably seen that there are still tables there to this day.

"Well, the campus tried to shut them down. The president of the university banned political organizing on campus, but the civil rights kids wouldn't stop. The police tried to arrest a guy who was handing out literature from one of these tables, and they put him in a van, but three thousand students surrounded the van and refused to let it budge. They wouldn't let them take this kid to jail. They stood on top of the van and gave speeches about the First Amendment and Free Speech.

"That galvanized the Free Speech Movement. That was the start of the hippies, but it was also where more radical student movements came from. Black power groups like the Black Panthers—and later gay rights groups like the Pink Panthers, too. Radical women's groups, even 'lesbian separatists' who wanted to abolish men altogether! And the Yippies. Anyone ever hear of the Yippies?"

"Didn't they levitate the Pentagon?" I said. I'd once seen a documentary about this.

She laughed. "I forgot about that, but yes, that was them! Yippies were like very political hippies, but they weren't serious the way we think of politics these days. They were very playful. Pranksters. They threw money into the New York Stock Exchange. They circled the Pentagon with hundreds of protesters and said a magic spell that was supposed to levitate it. They invented a fictional kind of LSD that you could spray onto people with squirt guns and shot each other with it and pretended to be stoned. They were funny and they made great TV—one Yippie, a clown called Wavy Gravy, used to get hundreds of protesters to dress up like Santa Claus so that the cameras would show police officers arresting and dragging away Santa on the news that night—and they mobilized a lot of people.

"Their big moment was the Democratic National Convention in 1968, where they called for demonstrations to protest the Vietnam War. Thousands of demonstrators poured into Chicago, slept in the parks, and picketed every day. They had lots of bizarre stunts that year, like running a pig called Pigasus for the presidential nomination. The police and the demonstrators fought in the streets—they'd done that many times before, but the Chicago cops didn't have the smarts to leave the reporters alone. They beat up the reporters, and the reporters retaliated by finally showing what really went on at these demonstrations, so the whole country watched their kids being really savagely beaten down by the Chicago police. They called it a 'police riot.'

"The Yippies loved to say, 'Never trust anyone over thirty.' They meant that people who were born before a certain time, when America had been fighting enemies like the Nazis, could never understand what it meant to love your country enough to refuse to fight the Vietnamese. They thought that by the time you hit thirty, your attitudes would be frozen and you couldn't ever understand why the kids of the day were taking to the streets, dropping out, freaking out.

"San Francisco was ground zero for this. Revolutionary armies were founded here. Some of them blew up buildings or robbed banks for their cause. A lot of those kids grew up to be more or less normal, while others ended up in jail. Some of the university dropouts did amazing things—for example, Steve Jobs and Steve Wozniak, who founded Apple Computers and invented the PC."

I was really getting into this. I knew a little of it, but I'd never heard it told like this. Or maybe it had never mattered as much as it did now. Suddenly, those lame, solemn, grown-up street demonstrations didn't seem so lame after all. Maybe there was room for that kind of action in the Xnet movement.

I put my hand up. "Did they win? Did the Yippies win?"

She gave me a long look, like she was thinking it over. No one said a word. We all wanted to hear the answer.

"They didn't lose," she said. "They kind of imploded a little. Some of them went to jail for drugs or other things. Some of them changed their tunes and became yuppies and went on the lecture circuit telling everyone how stupid they'd been, talking about how good greed was and how dumb they'd been.

"But they did change the world. The war in Vietnam ended, and the kind of conformity and unquestioning obedience that people had called patriotism went out of style in a big way. Black rights, women's rights and gay rights came a long way. Chicano rights, rights for disabled people, the whole tradition of civil liberties was created or strengthened by these people. Today's protest movement is the direct descendant of those struggles."

"I can't believe you're talking about them like this," Charles said. He was leaning so far out of his seat he was half standing, and his sharp, skinny face had gone red. He had wet, large eyes and big lips, and when he got excited he looked a little like a fish.

Ms. Galvez stiffened a little, then said, "Go on, Charles."

"You've just described terrorists. Actual terrorists. They blew up buildings, you said. They tried to destroy the stock exchange. They beat up cops, and stopped cops from arresting people who were breaking the law. They attacked us!"

Ms. Galvez nodded slowly. I could tell she was trying to figure out how to handle Charles, who really seemed like he was ready to pop. "Charles raises a good point. The Yippies weren't foreign agents, they were American citizens. When you say 'They attacked us,' you need to figure out who 'they' and 'us' are. When it's your fellow countrymen—"

"Crap!" he shouted. He was on his feet now. "We were at war then. These guys were giving aid and comfort to the enemy. It's easy to tell who's us and who's them: if you support America, you're us. If you support the people who are shooting at Americans, you're *them*."

"Does anyone else want to comment on this?"

Several hands shot up. Ms. Galvez called on them. Some people pointed out that the reason that the Vietnamese were shooting at Americans is that the Americans had flown to Vietnam and started running around the jungle with guns. Others thought that Charles had a point, that people shouldn't be allowed to do illegal things.

Everyone had a good debate except Charles, who just shouted at people, interrupting them when they tried to get their points out. Ms. Galvez tried to get him to wait for his turn a couple times, but he wasn't having any of it.

I was looking something up on my SchoolBook, something I knew I'd read.

I found it. I stood up. Ms. Galvez looked expectantly at me. The other people followed her gaze and went quiet. Even Charles looked at me after a while, his big wet eyes burning with hatred for me.

"I wanted to read something," I said. "It's short. 'Governments are instituted among men, deriving their just powers from the consent of the governed, that whenever any form of government becomes destructive of these ends, it is the right of the people to alter or abolish it, and to institute new government, laying its foundation on such principles, and organizing its powers in such form, as to them shall seem most likely to effect their safety and happiness.'"

chapter 12

Ms. Galvez's smile was wide.

"Does anyone know what that comes from?"

A bunch of people chorused, "The Declaration of Independence."

I nodded.

"Why did you read that to us, Marcus?"

"Because it seems to me that the founders of this country said that governments should only last for so long as we believe that they're working for us, and if we stop believing in them, we should overthrow them. That's what it says, right?"

Charles shook his head. "That was hundreds of years ago!" he said. "Things are different now!"

"What's different?"

"Well, for one thing, we don't have a king anymore. They were talking about a government that existed because some old jerk's great-great-great-grandfather believed that God put him in charge and killed everyone who disagreed with him. We have a democratically elected government—"

"I didn't vote for them," I said.

"So that gives you the right to blow up a building?"

"What? Who said anything about blowing up a building? The Yippies and hippies and all those people believed that the government no longer listened to them—look at the way people who tried to sign up voters in the South were treated! They were beaten up, arrested—"

"Some of them were killed," Ms. Galvez said. She held up her hands and waited for Charles and me to sit down. "We're almost out of time for today, but I want to commend you all on one of the most interesting classes I've ever taught. This has been an excellent discussion and I've learned much from you all. I hope you've learned from each other, too. Thank you all for your contributions.

"I have an extra-credit assignment for those of you who want a little challenge. I'd like you to write up a paper comparing the political response to the antiwar and civil rights movements in the Bay Area to the present day civil rights responses to the War on Terror. Three pages minimum, but take as long as you'd like. I'm interested to see what you come up with."

The bell rang a moment later and everyone filed out of the class. I hung back and waited for Ms. Galvez to notice me.

"Yes, Marcus?"

"That was amazing," I said. "I never knew all that stuff about the sixties."

"The seventies, too. This place has always been an exciting place to live in politically charged times. I really liked your reference to the Declaration—that was very clever."

"Thanks," I said. "It just came to me. I never really appreciated what those words all meant before today."

"Well, those are the words every teacher loves to hear, Marcus," she said, and shook my hand. "I can't wait to read your paper."

I bought the Emma Goldman poster on the way home and stuck it up over my desk, tacked over a vintage blacklight poster. I also bought a NEVER TRUST T-shirt that had a photoshop of Grover and Elmo kicking the grown-ups Gordon and Susan off Sesame Street. It made me laugh. I later found out that there had already been about six photoshop contests for the slogan online in places like Fark and Worth1000 and B3ta and there were hundreds of readymade pics floating around to go on whatever merch someone churned out.

Mom raised an eyebrow at the shirt, and Dad shook his head and lectured me about not looking for trouble. I felt a little vindicated by his reaction.

Ange found me online again and we IM-flirted until late at night again. The white van with the antennas came back and I switched off my Xbox until it had passed. We'd all gotten used to doing that.

Ange was really excited by this party. It looked like it was going to be monster. There were so many bands signed up they were talking about setting up a B-stage for the secondary acts.

> How'd they get a permit to blast sound all night in that park? There's houses all around there

> Per-mit? What is "per-mit"? Tell me more of your hu-man per-mit.

> Woah, it's illegal?

> Um, hello? _You're_ worried about breaking the law?

> Fair point

> LOL

I felt a little premonition of nervousness though. I mean, I was taking this perfectly awesome girl out on a date that weekend—well, she was taking me, technically—to an illegal rave being held in the middle of a busy neighborhood.

It was bound to be interesting at least.

Interesting.

People started to drift into Dolores Park through the long Saturday afternoon, showing up among the ultimate frisbee players and the dog-walkers. Some of them played frisbee or walked dogs. It wasn't really clear how the concert was going to work, but there were a lot of cops and undercovers hanging around. You could tell the undercovers because, like Zit and Booger, they had Castro haircuts and Nebraska physiques: tubby guys with short hair and untidy mustaches. They drifted around, looking awkward and uncomfortable in their giant shorts and loose-fitting shirts that no doubt hung down to cover the chandelier of gear hung around their midriffs.

Dolores Park is pretty and sunny, with palm trees, tennis courts and lots of hills and regular trees to run around on, or hang out on. Homeless people sleep there at night, but that's true everywhere in San Francisco.

I met Ange down the street at the anarchist bookstore. That had been my suggestion. In hindsight, it was a totally transparent move to seem cool and edgy to this girl, but at the time I would have sworn that I picked it because it was a convenient place to meet up. She was reading a book called *Up Against the Wall Motherf___er* when I got there.

"Nice," I said. "You kiss your mother with that mouth?"

"Your mama don't complain," she said. "Actually, it's a history of a group of people like the Yippies, but from New York. They all used that word as their last names, like 'Ben M-F.' The idea was to have a group out there, making news, but with a totally unprintable name. Just to screw around with the news media. Pretty funny, really." She put the book back on the shelf and now I wondered if I should hug her. People in California hug to say hello and good-bye all the time. Except when they don't. And sometimes they kiss on the cheek. It's all very confusing.

She settled it for me by grabbing me in a hug and tugging my head down to her, kissing me hard on the cheek, then blowing a fart on my neck. I laughed and pushed her away.

"You want a burrito?" I asked.

"Is that a question or a statement of the obvious?"

"Neither. It's an order."

I bought some funny stickers that said THIS PHONE IS TAPPED which were the right size to put on the receivers on the pay phones that still lined the streets of the Mission, it being the kind of neighborhood where you got people who couldn't necessarily afford a cell phone.

We walked out into the night air. I told Ange about the scene at the park when I left.

"I bet they have a hundred of those trucks parked around the block," she said. "The better to bust you with."

"Um." I looked around. "I sort of hoped that you would say something like, 'Aw, there's no chance they'll do anything about it.'"

"I don't think that's really the idea. The idea is to put a lot of civilians in a position where the cops have to decide, are we going to treat these ordinary people like terrorists? It's a little like the jamming, but with music instead of gadgets. You jam, right?"

Sometimes I forget that all my friends don't know that Marcus and M1k3y are the same person. "Yeah, a little," I said.

"This is like jamming with a bunch of awesome bands."

"I see."

Mission burritos are an institution. They are cheap, giant and delicious. Imagine a tube the size of a bazooka shell, filled with spicy grilled meat, guacamole, salsa, tomatoes, refried beans, rice, onions and cilantro. It has the same relationship to Taco Bell that a Lamborghini has to a Hot Wheels car.

There are about two hundred Mission burrito joints. They're all heroically ugly, with uncomfortable seats, minimal decor—faded Mexican tourist office posters and electrified framed Jesus and Mary holograms—and loud mariachi music. The thing that distinguishes them, mostly, is what kind of exotic meat they fill their wares with. The really authentic places have brains and tongue, which I never order, but it's nice to know it's there.

The place we went to had both brains and tongue, which we didn't order. I got carne asada and she got shredded chicken and we each got a big cup of horchata.

As soon as we sat down, she unrolled her burrito and took a little bottle out of her purse. It was a little stainless steel aerosol canister that looked for all the world like a pepper spray self-defense unit. She aimed it at her burrito's exposed guts and misted them with a fine red oily spray. I caught a whiff of it and my throat closed and my eyes watered.

"What the hell are you doing to that poor, defenseless burrito?"

She gave me a wicked smile. "I'm a spicy food addict," she said. "This is capsaicin oil in a mister."

"Capsaicin—"

"Yeah, the stuff in pepper spray. This is like pepper spray but slightly more dilute. And way more delicious. Think of it as Spicy Cajun Visine if it helps."

My eyes burned just thinking of it.

"You're kidding," I said. "You are so not going to eat that."

Her eyebrows shot up. "That sounds like a challenge, sonny. You just watch me."

She rolled the burrito up as carefully as a stoner rolling up a joint, tucking the ends in, then rewrapping it in the tinfoil. She peeled off one end and brought it up to her mouth, poised with it just before her lips.

Right up to the time she bit into it, I couldn't believe that she was going to do it. I mean, that was basically an antipersonnel weapon she'd just slathered on her dinner.

162 | **cory doctorow**

She bit into it. Chewed. Swallowed. Gave every impression of having a delicious dinner.

"Want a bite?" she said, innocently.

"Yeah," I said. I like spicy food. I always order the curries with four chilies next to them on the menu at the Pakistani places.

I peeled back more foil and took a big bite.

Big mistake.

You know that feeling you get when you take a big bite of horseradish or wasabi or whatever, and it feels like your sinuses are closing at the same time as your windpipe, filling your head with trapped, nuclear-hot air that tries to batter its way out through your watering eyes and nostrils? That feeling like steam is about to pour out of your ears like a cartoon character?

This was a lot worse.

This was like putting your hand on a hot stove, only it's not your hand, it's the entire inside of your head, and your esophagus all the way down to your stomach. My entire body sprang out in a sweat and I choked and choked.

Wordlessly, she passed me my horchata and I managed to get the straw into my mouth and suck hard on it, gulping down half of it in one go.

"So there's a scale, the Scoville scale, that we chili-fanciers use to talk about how spicy a pepper is. Pure capsaicin is about fifteen million Scovilles. Tabasco is about fifty thousand. Pepper spray is a healthy three million. This stuff is a puny two hundred thousand, about as hot as a mild Scotch bonnet pepper. I worked up to it in about a year. Some of the real hardcore can get up to a million or so, twenty times hotter than Tabasco. That's pretty freaking hot. At Scoville temperatures like that, your brain gets totally awash in endorphins. It's a better body-stone than hash. And it's good for you."

I was getting my sinuses back now, able to breathe without gasping.

"Of course, you get a ferocious ring of fire when you go to the john," she said, winking at me.

Yowch.

"You are insane," I said.

"Fine talk from a man whose hobby is building and smashing laptops," she said.

"Touché," I said and touched my forehead.

"Want some?" She held out her mister.

"Pass," I said, quickly enough that we both laughed.

When we left the restaurant and headed for Dolores Park, she put her arm around my waist and I found that she was just the right height for me to put my arm around her shoulders. That was new. I'd never been a tall guy, and the girls I'd dated had all been my height—teenaged girls grow faster than guys, which is a cruel trick of nature. It was nice. It felt nice.

We turned the corner on 20th Street and walked up toward Dolores. Before we'd taken a single step, we could feel the buzz. It was like the hum of a million bees. There were lots of people streaming toward the park, and when I looked toward it, I saw that it was about a hundred times more crowded than it had been when I went to meet Ange.

That sight made my blood run hot. It was a beautiful cool night and we were about to party, really party, party like there was no tomorrow. "Eat, drink and be merry, for tomorrow we die."

Without saying anything we both broke into a trot. There were lots of cops, with tense faces, but what the hell were they going to do? There were a *lot* of people in the park. I'm not so good at counting crowds. The papers later quoted organizers as saying there were 20,000 people; the cops said 5,000. Maybe that means there were 12,500.

Whatever. It was more people than I'd ever stood among, as part of an unscheduled, unsanctioned, *illegal* event.

We were among them in an instant. I can't swear to it, but I don't think there was anyone over twenty-five in that press of bodies. Everyone was smiling. Some young kids were there, ten or twelve, and that made me feel better. No one would do anything too stupid with kids that little in the crowd. No one wanted to see little kids get hurt. This was just going to be a glorious spring night of celebration.

I figured the thing to do was push in toward the tennis courts. We threaded our way through the crowd, and to stay together we took each other's hands. Only staying together didn't require us to intertwine fingers. That was strictly for pleasure. It was very pleasurable.

The bands were all inside the tennis courts, with their guitars and mixers and keyboards and even a drum kit. Later, on Xnet, I found a Flickr stream of them smuggling all this stuff in, piece by piece, in gym bags and under their coats. Along with it all were huge speakers, the kind you see in automotive supply places, and among them, a stack of . . . car batteries. I laughed. Genius! That was how they were going to power their stacks. From where I stood, I could see that they were cells from a hybrid car, a Prius. Someone had gutted an eco-mobile to power the night's entertainment. The batteries continued outside the courts, stacked up against the fence, tethered to the main stack by wires threaded through the chain-link. I counted two hundred batteries! Christ! Those things weighed a ton, too.

There's no way they organized this without email and wikis and mailing lists. And there's no way people this smart would have done that on the public Internet. This had all taken place on the Xnet, I'd bet my boots on it.

We just kind of bounced around in the crowd for a while as the bands tuned up and conferred with one another. I saw Trudy Doo from a distance, in the tennis courts. She looked like she was in a cage, like a pro wrestler. She was wearing a torn wife-beater and her hair was in long, fluorescent pink dreads down to her waist. She was wearing army camouflage pants and giant gothy boots with steel over-toes. As I watched, she picked up a heavy motorcycle jacket, as worn as a catcher's mitt, and put it on like armor. It probably was armor, I realized.

I tried to wave to her, to impress Ange I guess, but she didn't see me and I kind of looked like a spazz so I stopped. The energy in the crowd was amazing. You hear people talk about "vibes" and "energy" for big groups of people, but until you've experienced it, you probably think it's just a figure of speech.

It's not. It's the smiles, infectious and big as watermelons, on every face. Everyone bopping a little to an unheard rhythm, shoulders rocking. Rolling walks. Jokes and laughs. The tone of every voice tight and excited, like a firework about to go off. And you can't help but be a part of it. Because you are.

By the time the bands kicked off, I was utterly stoned on crowd-vibe. The opening act was some kind of Serbian turbo-folk, which I couldn't figure out how to dance to. I know how to dance to exactly two kinds of music: trance (shuffle around and let the music move you) and punk (bash around and mosh until you get hurt or exhausted or both). The next act was Oakland hip-hoppers, backed by a thrash metal band, which is better than it sounds. Then some bubblegum pop. Then Speedwhores took the stage, and Trudy Doo stepped up to the mic.

"My name is Trudy Doo and you're an idiot if you trust me. I'm thirty-two and it's too late for me. I'm lost. I'm stuck in the old way of thinking. I still take my freedom for granted and let other people take it away from me. You're the first generation to grow up in Gulag America, and you know what your freedom is worth to the last goddamned cent!"

The crowd roared. She was playing fast little skittery nervous chords on her guitar and her bass player, a huge fat girl with a dykey haircut and even bigger boots and a smile you could open beer bottles with was laying it down fast and hard already. I wanted to bounce. I bounced. Ange bounced with me. We were sweating freely in the evening, which reeked of perspiration and pot smoke. Warm bodies crushed in on all sides of us. They bounced, too.

"Don't trust anyone over 25!" she shouted.

We roared. We were one big animal throat, roaring.

"Don't trust anyone over 25!"

"Don't trust anyone over 25!"

"Don't trust anyone over 25!"

"Don't trust anyone over 25!"

"Don't trust anyone over 25!"

"Don't trust anyone over 25!"

She banged some hard chords on her guitar and the other guitarist, a little pixie of a girl whose face bristled with piercings, jammed in, going wheedle-dee-wheedle-dee-dee up high, past the twelfth fret.

"It's our goddamned city! It's our goddamned country. No

terrorist can take it from us for so long as we're free. Once we're not free, the terrorists win! Take it back! Take it back! You're young enough and stupid enough not to know that you can't possibly win, so you're the only ones who can lead us to victory! *Take it back!*"

"TAKE IT BACK!" we roared. She jammed down hard on her guitar. We roared the note back and then it got really really LOUD.

I danced until I was so tired I couldn't dance another step. Ange danced alongside me. Technically, we were rubbing our sweaty bodies against each other for several hours, but believe or not, I totally wasn't being a horn-dog about it. We were dancing, lost in the godbeat and the thrash and the screaming—TAKE IT BACK! TAKE IT BACK!

When I couldn't dance anymore, I grabbed her hand and she squeezed mine like I was keeping her from falling off a building. She dragged me toward the edge of the crowd, where it got thinner and cooler. Out there, on the edge of Dolores Park, we were in the cool air and the sweat on our bodies went instantly icy. We shivered and she threw her arms around my waist. "Warm me," she commanded. I didn't need a hint. I hugged her back. Her heart was an echo of the fast beats from the stage—break beats now, fast and furious and wordless.

She smelled of sweat, a sharp tang that smelled great. I knew I smelled of sweat, too. My nose was pointed into the top of her head, and her face was right at my collarbone. She moved her hands to my neck and tugged.

"Get down here, I didn't bring a stepladder," is what she said and I tried to smile, but it's hard to smile when you're kissing.

Like I said, I'd kissed three girls in my life. Two of them had never kissed anyone before. One had been dating since she was twelve. She had issues.

None of them kissed like Ange. She made her whole mouth soft, like the inside of a ripe piece of fruit, and she didn't jam her tongue in my mouth, but slid it in there, and sucked my lips into her mouth at the same time, so it was like my mouth and hers were merging. I heard myself moan and I grabbed her and squeezed her harder.

Slowly, gently, we lowered ourselves to the grass. We lay on our sides and clutched each other, kissing and kissing. The world disappeared so there was only the kiss.

My hands found her butt, her waist. The edge of her T-shirt. Her warm tummy, her soft navel. They inched higher. She moaned, too.

"Not here," she said. "Let's move over there." She pointed across the street at the big white church that gives Mission Dolores Park and the Mission its name. Holding hands, moving quickly, we crossed to the church. It had big pillars in front of it. She put my back up against one of them and pulled my face down to hers again. My hands went quickly and boldly back to her shirt. I slipped them up her front.

"It undoes in the back," she whispered into my mouth. I had a boner that could cut glass. I moved my hands around to her back, which was strong and broad, and found the hook with my fingers, which were trembling. I fumbled for a while, thinking of all those jokes about how bad guys are at undoing bras. I was bad at it. Then the hook sprang free. She gasped into my mouth. I slipped my hands around, feeling the wetness of her armpits—which was sexy and not at all gross for some reason—and then brushed the sides of her breasts.

That's when the sirens started.

They were louder than anything I'd ever heard. A sound like a physical sensation, like something blowing you off your feet. A sound as loud as your ears could process, and then louder.

"DISPERSE IMMEDIATELY," a voice said, like God rattling in my skull.

"THIS IS AN ILLEGAL GATHERING. DISPERSE IMMEDI-ATELY."

The band had stopped playing. The noise of the crowd across the street changed. It got scared. Angry.

I heard a click as the PA system of car speakers and car batteries in the tennis courts powered up.

"TAKE IT BACK!"

It was a defiant yell, like a sound shouted into the surf or screamed off a cliff.

"TAKE IT BACK!"

The crowd *growled,* a sound that made the hairs on the back of my neck stand up. *"TAKE IT BACK!"* they chanted. "TAKE IT BACK TAKE IT BACK TAKE IT BACK!"

The police moved in in lines, carrying plastic shields, wearing Darth Vader helmets that covered their faces. Each one had a black truncheon and infrared goggles. They looked like soldiers out of some futuristic war movie. They took a step forward in unison and every one of them banged his truncheon on his shield, a cracking noise like the earth splitting. Another step, another crack. They were all around the park and closing in now.

"DISPERSE IMMEDIATELY," the voice of God said again. There were helicopters overhead now. No floodlights, though. The infrared goggles, right. Of course. They'd have infrared scopes in the sky, too. I pulled Ange back against the doorway of the church, tucking us back from the cops and the choppers.

"TAKE IT BACK!" the PA roared. It was Trudy Doo's rebel yell and I heard her guitar thrash out some chords, then her drummer playing, then that big deep bass.

"TAKE IT BACK!" the crowd answered, and they boiled out of the park at the police lines.

I've never been in a war, but now I think I know what it must be like. What it must be like when scared kids charge across a field at an opposing force, knowing what's coming, running anyway, screaming, hollering.

"DISPERSE IMMEDIATELY," the voice of God said. It was coming from trucks parked all around the park, trucks that had swung into place in the last few seconds.

That's when the mist fell. It came out of the choppers, and we just caught the edge of it. It made the top of my head feel like it was going to come off. It made my sinuses feel like they were being punctured with ice picks. It made my eyes swell and water, and my throat close.

Pepper spray. Not a hundred thousand Scovilles. A million and a half. They'd gassed the crowd.

I didn't see what happened next, but I heard it, over the sound of both me and Ange choking and holding each other. First the choking, retching sounds. The guitar and drums and bass crashed to a halt. Then coughing.

Then screaming.

The screaming went on for a long time. When I could see again, the cops had their scopes up on their foreheads and the choppers were flooding Dolores Park with so much light it looked like daylight. Everyone was looking at the park, which was good news, because when the lights went up like that, we were totally visible.

"What do we do?" Ange said. Her voice was tight, scared. I didn't trust myself to speak for a moment. I swallowed a few times.

"We walk away," I said. "That's all we can do. Walk away. Like we were just passing by. Down to Dolores and turn left and up toward 16th Street. Like we're just passing by. Like this is none of our business."

"That'll never work," she said.

"It's all I've got."

"You don't think we should try to run for it?"

"No," I said. "If we run, they'll chase us. Maybe if we walk, they'll figure we haven't done anything and let us alone. They have a lot of arrests to make. They'll be busy for a long time."

The park was rolling with bodies, people and adults clawing at their faces and gasping. The cops dragged them by the armpits, then lashed their wrists with plastic cuffs and tossed them into the trucks like rag dolls.

"Okay?" I said.

"Okay," she said.

And that's just what we did. Walked, holding hands, quickly and businesslike, like two people wanting to avoid whatever trouble someone else was making. The kind of walk you adopt when you want to pretend you can't see a panhandler, or don't want to get involved in a street fight.

It worked.

We reached the corner and turned and kept going. Neither of us dared to speak for two blocks. Then I let out a gasp of air I hadn't known I'd been holding in.

We came to 16th Street and turned down toward Mission Street.

Normally that's a pretty scary neighborhood at 2 A.M. on a Saturday night. That night it was a relief—same old druggies and hookers and dealers and drunks. No cops with truncheons, no gas.

"Um," I said as we breathed in the night air. "Coffee?"

"Home," she said. "I think home for now. Coffee later."

"Yeah," I agreed. She lived up in Hayes Valley. I spotted a taxi rolling by and I hailed it. That was a small miracle—there are hardly any cabs when you need them in San Francisco.

"Have you got cab fare home?"

"Yeah," she said. The cabdriver looked at us through his window. I opened the back door so he wouldn't take off.

"Good night," I said.

She put her hands behind my head and pulled my face toward her. She kissed me hard on the mouth, nothing sexual in it, but somehow more intimate for that.

"Good night," she whispered in my ear, and slipped into the taxi.

Head swimming, eyes running, a burning shame for having left all those Xnetters to the tender mercies of the DHS and the SFPD, I set off for home.

Monday morning, Fred Benson was standing behind Ms. Galvez's desk.

"Ms. Galvez will no longer be teaching this class," he said, once we'd taken our seats. His voice had a self-satisfied note that I recognized immediately. On a hunch, I checked out Charles. He was smiling like it was his birthday and he'd been given the best present in the world.

I put my hand up.

"Why not?"

"It's Board policy not to discuss employee matters with anyone except the employee and the disciplinary committee," he said, without even bothering to hide how much he enjoyed saying it.

"We'll be beginning a new unit today, on national security. Your SchoolBooks have the new texts. Please open them and turn to the first screen."

The opening screen was emblazoned with a DHS logo and the title: WHAT EVERY AMERICAN SHOULD KNOW ABOUT HOMELAND SECURITY.

I wanted to throw my SchoolBook on the floor.

I'd made arrangements to meet Ange at a cafe in her neighborhood after school. I jumped on the BART and found myself sitting behind two guys in suits. They were looking at the *San Francisco Chronicle,* which featured a full-page postmortem on the "youth riot" in Mission Dolores Park. They were tutting and clucking over it. Then one said to the other, "It's like they're brainwashed or something. Christ, were we ever that stupid?"

I got up and moved to another seat.

chapter 13

"They're total whores," Ange said, spitting the word out. "In fact, that's an insult to hardworking whores everywhere. They're, they're *profiteers*."

We were looking at a stack of newspapers we'd picked up and brought to the cafe. They all contained "reporting" on the party in Dolores Park and to a one, they made it sound like a drunken, druggy orgy of kids who'd attacked the cops. *USA Today* described the cost of the "riot" and included the cost of washing away the pepper spray residue from the gas-bombing, the rash of asthma attacks that clogged the city's emergency rooms and the cost of processing the eight hundred arrested "rioters."

No one was telling our side.

"Well, the Xnet got it right, anyway," I said. I'd saved a bunch of the blogs and videos and photostreams to my phone and I showed them to her. They were firsthand accounts from people who'd been gassed and beaten up. The video showed us all dancing, having fun, showed the peaceful political speeches and the chant of "Take It Back" and Trudy Doo talking about us being the only generation that could believe in fighting for our freedoms.

"We need to make people know about this," she said.

"Yeah," I said, glumly. "That's a nice theory."

"Well, why do you think the press doesn't ever publish our side?"

"You said it, they're whores."

"Yeah, but whores do it for the money. They could sell more papers and commercials if they had a controversy. All they have now is a crime—controversy is much bigger."

"Okay, point taken. So why don't they do it? Well, reporters can barely search regular blogs, let alone keep track of the Xnet. It's not as if that's a real adult-friendly place to be."

"Yeah," she said. "Well, we can fix that, right?"

"Huh?"

"Write it all up. Put it in one place, with all the links. A single place where you can go that's intended for the press to find it and get the whole picture. Link it to the HOWTOs for Xnet. Internet users can get to the Xnet, provided they don't care about the DHS finding out what they've been surfing."

"You think it'll work?"

"Well, even if it doesn't, it's something positive to do."

"Why would they listen to us, anyway?"

"Who wouldn't listen to M1k3y?"

I put down my coffee. I picked up my phone and slipped it into my pocket. I stood up, turned on my heel and walked out of the cafe. I picked a direction at random and kept going. My face felt tight, the blood gone into my stomach, which churned.

They know who you are, I thought. *They know who M1k3y is.* That was it. If Ange had figured it out, the DHS had, too. I was doomed. I had known that since they let me go from the DHS truck, that someday they'd come and arrest me and put me away forever, send me to wherever Darryl had gone.

It was all over.

She nearly tackled me as I reached Market Street. She was out of breath and looked furious.

"What the *hell* is your problem, mister?"

I shook her off and kept walking. It was all over.

She grabbed me again. "Stop it, Marcus, you're scaring me. Come on, talk to me."

I stopped and looked at her. She blurred before my eyes. I couldn't focus on anything. I had a mad desire to jump into the path of a Muni trolley as it tore past us, down the middle of the road. Better to die than to go back.

"Marcus!" She did something I'd only seen people do in the movies. She slapped me, a hard crack across the face. "Talk to me, dammit!"

I looked at her, and put my hand to my face, which was stinging hard.

"No one is supposed to know who I am," I said. "I can't put

it any more simply. If you know, it's all over. Once other people know, it's all over."

"Oh God, I'm sorry. Look, I only know because, well, because I blackmailed Jolu. After the party I stalked you a little, trying to figure out if you were the nice guy you seemed to be or a secret axe-murderer. I've known Jolu for a long time and when I asked him about you, he gushed like you were the Second Coming or something, but I could hear that there was something he wasn't telling me. I've known Jolu for a long time. He dated my sister at computer camp when he was a kid. I have some really good dirt on him. I told him I'd go public with it if he didn't tell me."

"So he told you."

"No," she said. "He told me to go to hell. Then I told him something about me. Something I'd never told anyone else."

"What?"

She looked at me. Looked around. Looked back at me. "Okay. I won't swear you to secrecy because what's the point? Either I can trust you or I can't.

"Last year, I—" she broke off. "Last year, I stole the standardized tests and published them on the net. It was just a lark. I happened to be walking past the principal's office and I saw them in his safe, and the door was hanging open. I ducked into his office—there were six sets of copies and I just put one into my bag and took off again. When I got home, I scanned them all and put them up on a Pirate Party server in Denmark."

"That was *you*?" I said.

She blushed. "Um. Yeah."

"Holy crap!" I said. It had been huge news. The Board of Education said that its No Child Left Behind tests had cost tens of millions of dollars to produce and that they'd have to spend it all over again now that they'd had the leak. They called it "edu-terrorism." The news had speculated endlessly about the political motivations of the leaker, wondering if it was a teacher's protest, or a student, or a thief, or a disgruntled government contractor.

"That was YOU?"

"It was me," she said.

"And you told Jolu this—"

"Because I wanted him to be sure that I would keep the secret. If he knew *my* secret, then he'd have something he could use to put me in jail if I opened my trap. Give a little, get a little. Quid pro quo, like in Silence of the Lambs."

"And he told you."

"No," she said. "He didn't."

"But—"

"Then I told him how into you I was. How I was planning to totally make an idiot of myself and throw myself at you. *Then* he told me."

I couldn't think of anything to say then. I looked down at my toes. She grabbed my hands and squeezed them.

"I'm sorry I squeezed it out of him. It was your decision to tell me, if you were going to tell me at all. I had no business—"

"No," I said. Now that I knew how she'd found out, I was starting to calm down. "No, it's good you know. *You.*"

"Me," she said. "Li'l ol' me."

"Okay, I can live with this. But there's one other thing."

"What?"

"There's no way to say this without sounding like a jerk, so I'll just say it. People who date each other—or whatever it is we're doing now—they split up. When they split up, they get angry at each other. Sometimes even hate each other. It's really cold to think about that happening between us, but you know, we've got to think about it."

"I solemnly promise that there is nothing you could ever do to me that would cause me to betray your secret. Nothing. Screw a dozen cheerleaders in my bed while my mother watches. Make me listen to Britney Spears. Rip off my laptop, smash it with hammers and soak it in seawater. I promise. Nothing. Ever."

I whooshed out some air.

"Um," I said.

"Now would be a good time to kiss me," she said, and turned her face up.

M1k3y's next big project on the Xnet was putting together the ultimate roundup of reports of the DON'T TRUST party at Dolores

Park. I put together the biggest, most badass site I could, with sections showing the action by location, by time, by category—police violence, dancing, aftermath, singing. I uploaded the whole concert.

It was pretty much all I worked on for the rest of the night. And the next night. And the next.

My mailbox overflowed with suggestions from people. They sent me dumps off their phones and their pocket cameras. Then I got an email from a name I recognized—Dr Eeevil (three "e"s), one of the prime maintainers of ParanoidLinux.

> M1k3y
> I have been watching your Xnet experiment with great interest. Here in Germany, we have much experience with what happens with a government that gets out of control.
> One thing you should know is that every camera has a unique "noise signature" that can be used to later connect a picture with a camera. That means that the photos you're republishing on your site could potentially be used to identify the photographers, should they later be picked up for something else.
> Luckily, it's not hard to strip out the signatures, if you care to. There's a utility on the ParanoidLinux distro you're using that does this—it's called photonomous, and you'll find it in /usr/bin. Just read the man pages for documentation. It's simple though.
> Good luck with what you're doing. Don't get caught. Stay free. Stay paranoid.
> Dr Eeevil

I defingerprintized all the photos I'd posted and put them back up, along with a note explaining what Dr Eeevil had told me, warning everyone else to do the same. We all had the same basic Paranoid-Xbox install, so we could all anonymize our pictures. There wasn't anything I could do about the photos that had already been downloaded and cached, but from now on we'd be smarter.

That was all the thought I gave the matter that night, until I got down to breakfast the next morning and Mom had the radio on, playing the NPR morning news.

"Arabic news agency Al-Jazeera is running pictures, video and firsthand accounts of last weekend's youth riot in Mission Dolores Park," the announcer said as I was drinking a glass of orange juice. I managed not to spray it across the room, but I *did* choke a little.

"Al-Jazeera reporters claim that these accounts were published on the so-called 'Xnet,' a clandestine network used by students and Al Qaeda sympathizers in the Bay Area. This network's existence has long been rumored, but today marks its first mainstream mention."

Mom shook her head. "Just what we need," she said. "As if the police weren't bad enough. Kids running around, pretending to be guerillas and giving them the excuse to really crack down."

"The Xnet weblogs have carried hundreds of reports and multimedia files from young people who attended the riot and allege that they were gathered peacefully until the police attacked *them*. Here is one of those accounts.

"'All we were doing was dancing. I brought my little brother. Bands played and we talked about freedom, about how we were losing it to these jerks who say they hate terrorists but who attack us though we're not terrorists we're Americans. I think they hate freedom, not us.

"'We danced and the bands played and it was all fun and good and then the cops started shouting at us to disperse. We all shouted take it back! Meaning take America back. The cops gassed us with pepper spray. My little brother is twelve. He missed three days of school. My stupid parents say it was my fault. How about the police? We pay them and they're supposed to protect us but they gassed us for no good reason, gassed us like they gas enemy soldiers.'

"Similar accounts, including audio and video, can be found on Al-Jazeera's website and on the Xnet. You can find directions for accessing this Xnet on NPR's homepage."

Dad came down.

"Do you use the Xnet?" he said. He looked intensely at my face. I felt myself squirm.

"It's for video games," I said. "That's what most people use it for. It's just a wireless network. It's what everyone did with those free Xboxes they gave away last year."

He glowered at me. "Games? Marcus, you don't realize it, but you're providing cover for people who plan on attacking and destroying this country. I don't want to see you using this Xnet. Not anymore. Do I make myself clear?"

I wanted to argue. Hell, I wanted to shake him by the shoulders. But I didn't. I looked away. I said, "Sure, Dad." I went to school.

At first I was relieved when I discovered that they weren't going to leave Mr. Benson in charge of my social studies class. But the woman they found to replace him was my worst nightmare.

She was young, just about twenty-eight or twenty-nine, and pretty, in a wholesome kind of way. She was blonde and spoke with a soft southern accent when she introduced herself to us as Mrs. Andersen. That set off alarm bells right away. I didn't know *any* women under the age of sixty that called themselves "Mrs."

But I was prepared to overlook it. She was young, pretty, she sounded nice. She would be okay.

She wasn't okay.

"Under what circumstances should the federal government be prepared to suspend the Bill of Rights?" she said, turning to the blackboard and writing down a row of numbers, one through ten.

"Never," I said, not waiting to be called on. This was easy. "Constitutional rights are absolute."

"That's not a very sophisticated view." She looked at her seating plan. "Marcus. For example, say a policeman conducts an improper search—he goes beyond the stuff specified in his warrant. He discovers compelling evidence that a bad guy killed your father. It's the only evidence that exists. Should the bad guy go free?"

I knew the answer to this, but I couldn't really explain it. "Yes," I said, finally. "But the police shouldn't conduct improper searches—"

"Wrong," she said. "The proper response to police misconduct is disciplinary action against the police, not punishing all of society for one cop's mistake." She wrote "Criminal guilt" under point one on the board.

"Other ways in which the Bill of Rights can be superseded?"

Charles put his hand up. "Shouting fire in a crowded theater?"

"Very good"—she consulted the seating plan—"Charles. There are many instances in which the First Amendment is not absolute. Let's list some more of those."

Charles put his hand up again. "Endangering a law-enforcement officer."

"Yes, disclosing the identity of an undercover policeman or intelligence officer. Very good." She wrote it down. "Others?"

"National security," Charles said, not waiting for her to call on him again. "Libel. Obscenity. Corruption of minors. Child porn. Bomb-making recipes." Mrs. Andersen wrote these down fast, but stopped at child porn. "Child porn is just a form of obscenity."

I was feeling sick. This was not what I'd learned or believed about my country. I put my hand up.

"Yes, Marcus?"

"I don't get it. You're making it sound like the Bill of Rights is optional. It's the Constitution. We're supposed to follow it absolutely."

"That's a common oversimplification," she said, giving me a fake smile. "But the fact of the matter is that the framers of the Constitution intended it to be a living document that was revised over time. They understood that the Republic wouldn't be able to last forever if the government of the day couldn't govern according to the needs of the day. They never intended the Constitution to be looked on like religious doctrine. After all, they came here fleeing religious doctrine."

I shook my head. "What? No. They were merchants and artisans who were loyal to the king until he instituted policies that were against their interests and enforced them brutally. The religious refugees were way earlier."

"Some of the framers were descended from religious refugees," she said.

"And the Bill of Rights isn't supposed to be something you pick and choose from. What the framers hated was tyranny. That's what the Bill of Rights is supposed to prevent. They were a revolutionary army and they wanted a set of principles that everyone could agree to. Life, liberty and the pursuit of happiness. The right of people to throw off their oppressors."

"Yes, yes," she said, waving at me. "They believed in the right of people to get rid of their kings, but—" Charles was grinning and when she said that, he smiled even wider.

"—they set out the Bill of Rights because they thought that

having absolute rights was better than the risk that someone would take them away. Like the First Amendment: it's supposed to protect us by preventing the government from creating two kinds of speech, allowed speech and criminal speech. They didn't want to face the risk that some jerk would decide that the things that he found unpleasant were illegal."

She turned and wrote, "Life, liberty and the pursuit of happiness" on the board.

"We're getting a little ahead of the lesson, but you seem like an advanced group." The others laughed at this, nervously.

"The role of government is to secure for citizens the rights of life, liberty and the pursuit of happiness. In that order. It's like a filter. If the government wants to do something that makes us a little unhappy, or takes away some of our liberty, it's okay, providing they're doing it to save our lives. That's why the cops can lock you up if they think you're a danger to yourself or others. You lose your liberty and happiness to protect life. If you've got life, you might get liberty and happiness later."

Some of the others had their hands up. "Doesn't that mean that they can do anything they want, if they say it's to stop someone from hurting us in the future?"

"Yeah," another kid said. "This sounds like you're saying that national security is more important than the Constitution."

I was so proud of my fellow students then. I said, "How can you protect freedom by suspending the Bill of Rights?"

She shook her head at us like we were being very stupid. "The 'revolutionary' founding fathers *shot traitors* and spies. They didn't believe in absolute freedom, not when it threatened the Republic. Now you take these Xnet people—"

I tried hard not to stiffen.

"—these so-called jammers who were on the news this morning. After this city was attacked by people who've declared war on this country, they set about sabotaging the security measures set up to catch the bad guys and prevent them from doing it again. They did this by endangering and inconveniencing their fellow citizens—"

"They did it to show that our rights were being taken away in the name of protecting them!" I said. Okay, I shouted. God, she had me so steamed. "They did it because the government was treating *everyone* like a suspected terrorist."

"So they wanted to prove that they shouldn't be treated like terrorists," Charles shouted back, "so they acted like terrorists? So they committed terrorism?"

I boiled.

"Oh for Christ's sake. Committed terrorism? They showed that universal surveillance was more dangerous than terrorism. Look at what happened in the park last weekend. Those people were dancing and listening to music. How is *that* terrorism?"

The teacher crossed the room and stood before me, looming over me until I shut up. "Marcus, you seem to think that nothing has changed in this country. You need to understand that the bombing of the Bay Bridge changed everything. Thousands of our friends and relatives lie dead at the bottom of the Bay. This is a time for national unity in the face of the violent insult our country has suffered—"

I stood up. I'd had enough of this "everything has changed" crapola. "National unity? The whole point of America is that we're the country where dissent is welcome. We're a country of dissidents and fighters and university dropouts and free speech people."

I thought of Ms. Galvez's last lesson and the thousands of Berkeley students who'd surrounded the police van when they tried to arrest a guy for distributing civil rights literature. No one tried to stop those trucks when they drove away with all the people who'd been dancing in the park. I didn't try. I was running away.

Maybe everything *had* changed.

"I believe you know where Mr. Benson's office is," she said to me. "You are to present yourself to him immediately. I will *not* have my classes disrupted by disrespectful behavior. For someone who claims to love freedom of speech, you're certainly willing to shout down anyone who disagrees with you."

I picked up my SchoolBook and my bag and stormed out. The door had a gas-lift, so it was impossible to slam or I would have slammed it.

I went fast to Mr. Benson's office. Cameras filmed me as I went. My gait was recorded. The arphids in my student ID broadcast my identity to sensors in the hallway. It was like being in jail.

"Close the door, Marcus," Mr. Benson said. He turned his screen around so that I could see the video feed from the social studies classroom. He'd been watching.

"What do you have to say for yourself?"

"That wasn't teaching, it was *propaganda*. She told us that the Constitution didn't matter!"

"No, she said it wasn't religious doctrine. And you attacked her like some kind of fundamentalist, proving her point. Marcus, you of all people should understand that everything changed when the bridge was bombed. Your friend Darryl—"

"Don't you say a goddamned word about him," I said, the anger bubbling over. "You're not fit to talk about him. Yeah, I understand that everything's different now. We used to be a free country. Now we're not."

"Marcus, do you know what 'zero tolerance' means?"

I backed down. He could expel me for "threatening behavior." It was supposed to be used against gang kids who tried to intimidate their teachers. But of course he wouldn't have any compunction about using it on me.

"Yes," I said. "I know what it means."

"I think you owe me an apology," he said.

I looked at him. He was barely suppressing his sadistic smile. A part of me wanted to grovel. It wanted to beg for his forgiveness for all my shame. I tamped that part down and decided that I would rather get kicked out than apologize.

"Governments are instituted among men, deriving their just powers from the consent of the governed, that whenever any form of government becomes destructive of these ends, it is the right of the people to alter or abolish it, and to institute new government, laying its foundation on such principles, and organizing its powers in such form, as to them shall seem most likely to effect their safety and happiness." I remembered it word for word.

He shook his head. "Remembering things isn't the same as understanding them, sonny." He bent over his computer and made some clicks. His printer purred. He handed me a sheet of warm Board letterhead that said I'd been suspended for two weeks.

"I'll email your parents now. If you are still on school property in thirty minutes, you'll be arrested for trespassing."

I looked at him.

"You don't want to declare war on me in my own school," he said. "You can't win that war. GO!"

I left.

The Xnet wasn't much fun in the middle of the school day, when all the people who used it were in school. I had the piece of paper folded in the back pocket of my jeans, and I threw it on the kitchen table when I got home. I sat down in the living room and switched on the TV. I never watched it, but I knew that my parents did. The TV and the radio and the newspapers were where they got all their ideas about the world.

The news was terrible. There were so many reasons to be scared. American soldiers were dying all over the world. Not just soldiers, either. National guardsmen, who thought they were signing up to help rescue people from hurricanes, stationed overseas for years and years of a long and endless war.

I flipped around the 24-hour news networks, one after another, a parade of officials telling us why we should be scared. A parade of photos of bombs going off around the world.

I kept flipping and found myself looking at a familiar face. It was the guy who had come into the truck and spoken to severe haircut lady when I was chained up in the back. Wearing a military uniform. The caption identified him as Major General Graeme Sutherland, Regional Commander, DHS.

"I hold in my hands actual literature on offer at the so-called concert in Dolores Park last weekend." He held up a stack of pamphlets. There'd been lots of pamphleteers there, I remembered. Wherever you got a group of people in San Francisco, you got pamphlets.

"I want you to look at these for a moment. Let me read you their titles. 'Without the Consent of the Governed: A Citizen's Guide to Overthrowing the State.' Here's one: 'Did the September 11th Bombings Really Happen?' And another: 'How To Use Their Security

Against Them.' This literature shows us the true purpose of the illegal gathering on Saturday night. This wasn't merely an unsafe gathering of thousands of people without proper precaution, or even toilets. It was a recruiting rally for the enemy. It was an attempt to corrupt children into embracing the idea that America shouldn't protect herself.

"Take this slogan: 'Don't Trust Anyone Over 25.' What better way to ensure that no considered, balanced, adult discussion is ever injected into your pro-terrorist message than to exclude adults, limiting your group to impressionable young people?

"When police came on the scene, they found a recruitment rally for America's enemies in progress. The gathering had already disrupted the nights of hundreds of residents in the area, none of whom had been consulted in the planning of this all-night rave party.

"They ordered these people to disperse—that much is visible on all the video—and when the revelers turned to attack them, egged on by the musicians on stage, the police subdued them using nonlethal crowd control techniques.

"The arrestees were ringleaders and provocateurs who had led the thousands of impressionistic young people there to charge the police lines. Eight hundred and twenty-seven of them were taken into custody. Many of these people had prior offenses. More than a hundred of them had outstanding warrants. They are still in custody.

"Ladies and gentlemen, America is fighting a war on many fronts, but nowhere is she in more grave danger than she is here, at home. Whether we are being attacked by terrorists or those who sympathize with them."

A reporter held up a hand and said, "General Sutherland, surely you're not saying that these children were terrorist sympathizers for attending a party in a park?"

"Of course not. But when young people are brought under the influence of our country's enemies, it's easy for them to end up over their heads. Terrorists would love to recruit a fifth column to fight the war on the home front for them. If these were my children, I'd be gravely concerned."

Another reporter chimed in. "Surely this is just an open air concert, General? They were hardly drilling with rifles."

The general produced a stack of photos and began to hold them up. "These are pictures that officers took with infrared cameras before moving in." He held them next to his face and paged through them one at a time. They showed people dancing really rough, some people getting crushed or stepped on. Then they moved into sex stuff by the trees, a girl with three guys, two guys necking together. "There were children as young as ten years old at this event. A deadly cocktail of drugs, propaganda and music resulted in dozens of injuries. It's a wonder there weren't any deaths."

I switched the TV off. They made it look like it had been a riot. If my parents thought I'd been there, they'd have strapped me to my bed for a month and only let me out afterward wearing a tracking collar.

Speaking of which, they were going to be *pissed* when they found out I'd been suspended.

They didn't take it well. Dad wanted to ground me, but Mom and I talked him out of it.

"You know that vice principal has had it in for Marcus for years," Mom said. "The last time we met him you cursed him for an hour afterward. I think the word 'asshole' was mentioned repeatedly."

Dad shook his head. "Disrupting a class to argue against the Department of Homeland Security—"

"It's a social studies class, Dad," I said. I was beyond caring anymore, but I felt like if Mom was going to stick up for me, I should help her out. "We were talking about the DHS. Isn't debate supposed to be healthy?"

"Look, son," he said. He'd taken to calling me "son" a lot. It made me feel like he'd stopped thinking of me as a person and switched to thinking of me as a kind of half-formed larva that needed to be guided out of adolescence. I hated it. "You're going to have to learn to live with the fact that we live in a different world today. You have every right to speak your mind of course, but you have to be prepared for the consequences of doing so. You have to face the fact that there are people who are hurting, who aren't going to want to argue the finer points of Constitutional law when their lives are at stake. We're in a lifeboat now, and once you're in the lifeboat, no one wants to hear about how mean the captain is being."

I barely restrained myself from rolling my eyes.

"I've been assigned two weeks of independent study, writing one paper for each of my subjects, using the city for my background—a history paper, a social studies paper, an English paper, a physics paper. It beats sitting around at home watching television."

Dad looked hard at me, like he suspected I was up to something, then nodded. I said good night to them and went up to my room. I fired up my Xbox and opened a word processor and started to brainstorm ideas for my papers. Why not? It really was better than sitting around at home.

I ended up IMing with Ange for quite a while that night. She was sympathetic about everything and told me she'd help me with my papers if I wanted to meet her after school the next night. I knew where her school was—she went to the same school as Van—and it was all the way over in the East Bay, where I hadn't visited since the bombs went.

I was really excited at the prospect of seeing her again. Every night since the party, I'd gone to bed thinking of two things: the sight of the crowd charging the police lines and the feeling of the side of her breast under her shirt as we leaned against the pillar. She was amazing. I'd never been with a girl as . . . aggressive as her before. It had always been me putting the moves on and them pushing me away. I got the feeling that Ange was as much of a horn-dog as I was. It was a tantalizing notion.

I slept soundly that night, with exciting dreams of me and Ange and what we might do if we found ourselves in a secluded spot somewhere.

The next day, I set out to work on my papers. San Francisco is a good place to write about. History? Sure, it's there, from the Gold Rush to the World War Two shipyards, the Japanese internment camps, the invention of the PC. Physics? The Exploratorium has the coolest exhibits of any museum I've ever been to. I took a perverse satisfaction in the exhibits on soil liquefaction during big quakes. English? Jack London, Beat Poets, science fiction writers like Pat Murphy and Rudy Rucker. Social studies? The Free Speech Movement, Cesar Chavez, gay rights, feminism, the antiwar movement. . . .

I've always loved just learning stuff for its own sake. Just to be smarter about the world around me. I could do that just by walking around the city. I decided I'd do an English paper about the Beats first. City Lights books had a great library in an upstairs room where Allen Ginsberg and his buddies had created their radical druggy poetry. The one we'd read in English class was *Howl* and I would never forget the opening lines, they gave me shivers down my back:

> I saw the best minds of my generation destroyed by
>   madness, starving hysterical naked,
> dragging themselves through the negro streets at dawn
>   looking for an angry fix,
> angelheaded hipsters burning for the ancient heavenly
>   connection to the starry dynamo in the machinery of
>   night. . . .

I liked the way he ran those words all together, "starving hysterical naked." I knew how that felt. And "best minds of my generation" made me think hard, too. It made me remember the park and the police and the gas falling. They busted Ginsberg for obscenity over *Howl*—all about a line about gay sex that would hardly have caused us to blink an eye today. It made me happy somehow, knowing that we'd made some progress. That things had been even more restrictive than this before.

I lost myself in the library, reading these beautiful old editions of the books. I got lost in Jack Kerouac's *On the Road*, a novel I'd been meaning to read for a long time, and a clerk who came up to check on me nodded approvingly and found me a cheap edition that he sold me for six bucks.

I walked into Chinatown and had dim sum buns and noodles

with hot sauce that I had previously considered to be pretty hot, but which would never seem anything like hot ever again, not now that I'd had an Ange special.

As the day wore on toward afternoon, I got on the BART and switched to a San Mateo bridge shuttle bus to bring me around to the East Bay. I read my copy of *On the Road* and dug the scenery whizzing past. *On the Road* is a semiautobiographical novel about Jack Kerouac, a druggy, hard-drinking writer who goes hitchhiking around America, working crummy jobs, howling through the streets at night, meeting people and parting ways. Hipsters, sad-faced hobos, con men, muggers, scumbags and angels. There's not really a plot—Kerouac supposedly wrote it in three weeks on a long roll of paper, stoned out of his mind—only a bunch of amazing things, one thing happening after another. He makes friends with self-destructing people like Dean Moriarty, who get him involved in weird schemes that never really work out, but still it works out, if you know what I mean.

There was a rhythm to the words, it was luscious, I could hear it being read aloud in my head. It made me want to lie down in the bed of a pickup truck and wake up in a dusty little town somewhere in the central valley on the way to LA, one of those places with a gas station and a diner, and just walk out into the fields and meet people and see stuff and do stuff.

It was a long bus ride and I must have dozed off a little—staying up late IMing with Ange was hard on my sleep schedule, since Mom still expected me down for breakfast. I woke up and changed buses and before long, I was at Ange's school.

She came bounding out of the gates in her uniform—I'd never seen her in it before, it was kind of cute in a weird way, and reminded me of Van in her uniform. She gave me a long hug and a hard kiss on the cheek.

"Hello you!" she said.

"Hiya!"

"Whatcha reading?"

I'd been waiting for this. I'd marked the passage with a finger. "Listen: 'They danced down the streets like dingledodies, and I shambled after as I've been doing all my life after people who interest me, because the only people for me are the mad ones, the ones who are mad to live, mad to talk, mad to be saved, desirous of everything at the same time, the ones that never yawn or say a commonplace thing, but burn, burn, burn like fabulous yellow roman candles exploding like spiders across the stars and in the middle you see the blue centerlight pop and everybody goes "A-www!"'"

She took the book and read the passage again for herself. "Wow, dingledodies! I love it! Is it all like this?"

I told her about the parts I'd read, walking slowly down the sidewalk back toward the bus stop. Once we turned the corner, she put her arm around my waist and I slung mine around her shoulder. Walking down the street with a girl—my girlfriend? Sure, why not?—talking about this cool book. It was heaven. Made me forget my troubles for a little while.

"Marcus?"

I turned around. It was Van. In my subconscious I'd expected this. I knew because my conscious mind wasn't remotely surprised. It wasn't a big school, and they all got out at the same time. I hadn't spoken to Van in weeks, and those weeks felt like months. We used to talk every day.

"Hey, Van," I said. I suppressed the urge to take my arm off of Ange's shoulders. Van seemed surprised, but not angry; more ashen, shaken. She looked closely at the two of us.

"Angela?"

"Hey, Vanessa," Ange said.

"What are you doing here?" Van asked me.

"I came out to get Ange," I said, trying to keep my tone neutral. I was suddenly embarrassed to be seen with another girl.

"Oh," Van said. "Well, it was nice to see you."

"Nice to see you, too, Vanessa," Ange said, swinging me around, marching me back toward the bus stop.

"You know her?" Ange said.

"Yeah, since forever."

"Was she your girlfriend?"

"What? No! No way! We were just friends."

"You *were* friends?"

I felt like Van was walking right behind us, listening in, though at the pace we were walking, she would have to be jogging to keep up. I resisted the temptation to look over my shoulder for as long as possible, then I did. There were lots of girls from the school behind us, but no Van.

"She was with me and Jose-Luis and Darryl when we were arrested. We used to ARG together. The four of us, we were kind of best friends."

"And what happened?"

I dropped my voice. "She didn't like the Xnet," I said. "She thought we would get into trouble. That I'd get other people into trouble."

"And that's why you stopped being friends?"

"We just drifted apart."

We walked a few steps. "You weren't, you know, boyfriend/girl-friend friends?"

"No!" I said. My face was hot. I felt like I sounded like I was lying, even though I was telling the truth.

Ange jerked us to a halt and studied my face.

"Were you?"

"No! Seriously! Just friends. Darryl and her—well, not quite, but Darryl was so into her. There was no way—"

"But if Darryl hadn't been into her, you would have, huh?"

"No, Ange, no. Please, just believe me and let it go. Vanessa was a good friend and we're not anymore, and that upsets me, but I was never into her that way, all right?"

She slumped a little. "Okay, okay. I'm sorry. I don't really get along with her is all. We've never gotten along in all the years we've known each other."

Oh ho, I thought. This would be how it came to be that Jolu knew her for so long and I never met her; she had some kind of thing with Van and he didn't want to bring her around.

She gave me a long hug and we kissed, and a bunch of girls passed us going *woooo* and we straightened up and headed for the bus stop. Ahead of us walked Van, who must have gone past while we were kissing. I felt like a complete jerk.

Of course, she was at the stop and on the bus and we didn't say a word to each other, and I tried to make conversation with Ange all the way, but it was awkward.

The plan was to stop for a coffee and head to Ange's place to hang out and "study," i.e. take turns on her Xbox looking at the Xnet. Ange's mom got home late on Tuesdays, which was her night for yoga class and dinner with her girls, and Ange's sister was going out with her boyfriend, so we'd have the place to ourselves. I'd been having pervy thoughts about it ever since we'd made the plan.

We got to her place and went straight to her room and shut the door. Her room was kind of a disaster, covered with layers of clothes and notebooks and parts of PCs that would dig into your stocking feet like caltrops. Her desk was worse than the floor, piled high with books and comics, so we ended up sitting on her bed, which was okay by me.

The awkwardness from seeing Van had gone away somewhat and we got her Xbox up and running. It was in the center of a nest of wires, some going to a wireless antenna she'd hacked into it and stuck to the window so she could tune in the neighbors' WiFi. Some went to a couple of old laptop screens she'd turned into stand-alone monitors, balanced on stands and bristling with exposed electronics. The screens were on both bedside tables, which was an excellent setup for watching movies or IMing from bed—she could turn the monitors sidewise and lie on her side and they'd be right side up, no matter which side she lay on.

We both knew what we were really there for, sitting side by side propped against the bedside table. I was trembling a little and su-perconscious of the warmth of her leg and shoulder against mine, but I needed to go through the motions of logging into Xnet and seeing what email I'd gotten and so on.

There was an email from a kid who liked to send in funny phone-cam videos of the DHS being really crazy—the last one had been of them disassembling a baby's stroller after a bomb-sniffing dog had shown an interest in it, taking it apart with screwdrivers right on the street in the Marina while all these rich people walked past, staring at them and marveling at how weird it was.

I'd linked to the video and it had been downloaded like crazy. He'd hosted it on the Internet Archive's Alexandria mirror in

Egypt, where they'd host anything for free so long as you'd put it under the Creative Commons license, which let anyone remix it and share it. The U.S. archive—which was down in the Presidio, only a few minutes away—had been forced to take down all those videos in the name of national security, but the Alexandria archive had split away into its own organization and was hosting anything that embarrassed the USA.

This kid—his handle was Kameraspie—had sent me an even better video this time around. It was at the doorway to City Hall in Civic Center, a huge wedding cake of a building covered with statues in little archways and gilt leaves and trim. The DHS had a secure perimeter around the building, and Kameraspie's video showed a great shot of their checkpoint as a guy in an officer's uniform approached and showed his ID and put his briefcase on the X-ray belt.

It was all okay until one of the DHS people saw something he didn't like on the X-ray. He questioned the general, who rolled his eyes and said something inaudible (the video had been shot from across the street, apparently with a homemade concealed zoom lens, so the audio was mostly of people walking past and traffic noises).

The general and the DHS guy got into an argument, and the longer they argued, the more DHS guys gathered around them. Finally, the general shook his head angrily and waved his finger at the DHS guy's chest and picked up his briefcase and started to walk away. The DHS guys shouted at him, but he didn't slow. His body language really said, *I am totally, utterly pissed.*

Then it happened. The DHS guys ran after the general. Kameraspie slowed the video down here, so we could see, in frame by frame slo-mo, the general half-turning, his face all like, *No freaking way are you about to tackle me,* then changing to horror as three of the giant DHS guards slammed into him, knocking him sideways, then catching him at the middle, like a career-ending football tackle. The general—middle-aged, steely gray hair, lined and dignified face—went down like a sack of potatoes and bounced twice, his face slamming off the sidewalk and blood starting out of his nose.

The DHS hog-tied the general, strapping him at the ankles and wrists. The general was shouting now, really shouting, his face purpling under the blood streaming from his nose. Legs swished by in the tight zoom. Passing pedestrians looked at this guy in his uniform getting tied up, and you could see from his face that this was the worst part, this was the ritual humiliation, the removal of dignity. The clip ended.

"Oh my dear sweet Buddha," I said, looking at the screen as it faded to black, starting the video again. I nudged Ange and showed her the clip. She watched wordless, jaw hanging down to her chest.

"Post that," she said. "Post that post that post that post that!"

I posted it. I could barely type as I wrote it up, describing what I'd seen, adding a note to see if anyone could identify the military man in the video, if anyone knew anything about this.

I hit publish.

We watched the video. We watched it again.

My email pinged.

> I totally recognize that dude—you can find his bio on Wikipedia. He's General Claude Geist. He commanded the joint UN peacekeeping mission in Haiti.

I checked the bio. There was a picture of the general at a press conference, and notes about his role in the difficult Haiti mission. It was clearly the same guy.

I updated the post.

Theoretically, this was Ange's and my chance to make out, but that wasn't what we ended up doing. We crawled the Xnet blogs, looking for more accounts of the DHS searching people, tackling people, invading them. This was a familiar task, the same thing I'd done with all the footage and accounts from the riots in the park. I started a new category on my blog for this, AbusesOfAuthority, and filed them away. Ange kept coming up with new search terms for me to try and by the time her mom got home, my new category had seventy posts, headlined by General Geist's City Hall takedown.

I worked on my Beat paper all the next day at home, reading Kerouac and surfing the Xnet. I was planning on meeting Ange at school, but I totally wimped out at the thought of seeing Van again, so I texted her an excuse about working on the paper.

There were all kinds of great suggestions for AbusesOfAuthority coming in; hundreds of little and big ones, pictures and audio. The meme was spreading.

It spread. The next morning there were even more. Someone started a new blog also called AbusesOfAuthority that collected hundreds more. The pile grew. We competed to find the juiciest stories, the craziest pictures.

The deal with my parents was that I'd eat breakfast with them every morning and talk about the projects I was doing. They liked that I was reading Kerouac. It had been a favorite book of both of theirs and it turned out there was already a copy on the bookcase in my parents' room. My dad brought it down and I flipped through it. There were passages marked up with pen, dog-eared pages, notes in the margin. My dad had really loved this book.

It made me remember a better time, when my dad and I had been able to talk for five minutes without shouting at each other about terrorism, and we had a great breakfast talking about the way that the novel was plotted, all the crazy adventures.

But the next morning at breakfast they were both glued to the radio.

"Abuses of Authority—it's the latest craze on San Francisco's notorious Xnet, and it's captured the world's attention. Called A-oh-A, the movement is composed of 'Little Brothers' who watch back against the Department of Homeland Security's antiterrorism measures, documenting the failures and excesses. The rallying cry is a popular viral video clip of a General Claude Geist, a retired three-star general, being tackled by DHS officers on the sidewalk in front of City Hall. Geist hasn't made a statement on the incident, but commentary from young people who are upset with their own treatment has been fast and furious.

"Most notable has been the global attention the movement has received. Stills from the Geist video have appeared on the front pages of newspapers in Korea, Great Britain, Germany, Egypt and Japan, and broadcasters around the world have aired the clip on prime-time news. The issue came to a head last night, when the

British Broadcasting Corporation's National News Evening program ran a special report on the fact that no American broadcaster or news agency has covered this story. Commenters on the BBC's website noted that BBC America's version of the news did not carry the report."

They brought on a couple of interviews: British media watchdogs, a Swedish Pirate Party kid who made jeering remarks about America's corrupt press, a retired American newscaster living in Tokyo; then they aired a short clip from Al-Jazeera, comparing the American press record and the record of the national news media in Syria.

I felt like my parents were staring at me, that they knew what I was doing. But when I cleared away my dishes, I saw that they were looking at each other.

Dad was holding his coffee cup so hard his hands were shaking. Mom was looking at him.

"They're trying to discredit us," Dad said finally. "They're trying to sabotage the efforts to keep us safe."

I opened my mouth, but my mom caught my eye and shook her head. Instead I went up to my room and worked on my Kerouac paper. Once I'd heard the door slam twice, I fired up my Xbox and got online.

> Hello M1k3y. This is Colin Brown. I'm a producer with the Canadian Broadcasting Corporation's news programme The National. We're doing a story on Xnet and have sent a reporter to San Francisco to cover it from there. Would you be interested in doing an interview to discuss your group and its actions?

I stared at the screen. Jesus. They wanted to *interview* me about "my group"?

> Um thanks no. I'm all about privacy. And it's not "my group." But thanks for doing the story!

A minute later, another email.

> We can mask you and ensure your anonymity. You know that the Department of Homeland Security will be happy to provide their own spokesperson. I'm interested in getting your side.

I filed the email. He was right, but I'd be crazy to do this. For all I knew, he *was* the DHS.

I picked up more Kerouac. Another email came in. Same request, different news agency: KQED wanted to meet me and record a radio interview. A station in Brazil. The Australian Broadcasting Corporation. Deutsche Welle. All day, the press requests came in. All day, I politely turned them down.

I didn't get much Kerouac read that day.

"Hold a press conference," is what Ange said as we sat in the cafe near her place that evening. I wasn't keen on going out to her school anymore, getting stuck on a bus with Van again.

"What? Are you crazy?"

"Do it in Clockwork Plunder. Just pick a trading post where there's no PvP allowed and name a time. You can login from here."

PvP is player-versus-player combat. Parts of Clockwork Plunder were neutral ground, which meant that we could theoretically bring in a ton of noob reporters without worrying about gamers killing them in the middle of the press conference.

"I don't know anything about press conferences."

"Oh, just google it. I'm sure someone's written an article on holding a successful one. I mean, if the president can manage it, I'm sure you can. He looks like he can barely tie his shoes without help."

We ordered more coffee.

"You are a very smart woman," I said.

"And I'm beautiful," she said.

"That, too," I said.

chapter 15

I'd blogged the press conference even before I'd sent out the invitations to the press. I could tell that all these writers wanted to make me into a leader or a general or a supreme guerrilla commandant, and I figured one way of solving that would be to have a bunch of Xnetters running around answering questions, too.

Then I emailed the press. The responses ranged from puzzled to enthusiastic—only the Fox reporter was "outraged" that I had the gall to ask her to play a game in order to appear on her TV show. The rest of them seemed to think that it would make a pretty cool story, though plenty of them wanted lots of tech support for signing onto the game.

I picked 8 P.M., after dinner. Mom had been bugging me about all the evenings I'd been spending out of the house until I finally spilled the beans about Ange, whereupon she came over all misty and kept looking at me like, *my-little-boy's-growing-up*. She wanted to meet Ange, and I used that as leverage, promising to bring her over the next night if I could "go to the movies" with Ange tonight.

Ange's mom and sister were out again—they weren't real stay-at-homes—which left me and Ange alone in her room with her Xbox and mine. I unplugged one of her bedside screens and attached my Xbox to it so that we could both login at once.

Both Xboxes were idle, logged into Clockwork Plunder. I was pacing.

"It's going to be fine," she said. She glanced at her screen. "Patcheye Pete's Market has six hundred players in it now!" We'd picked Patcheye Pete's because it was the market closest to the village square where new players spawned. If the reporters weren't already Clockwork Plunder players—ha!—then that's where they'd show up. In my blog post I'd asked people generally to hang out on the route between Patcheye Pete's and the spawn-gate and direct anyone who looked like a disoriented reporter over to Pete's.

"What the hell am I going to tell them?"

"You just answer their questions—and if you don't like a question, ignore it. Someone else can answer it. It'll be fine."

"This is insane."

"This is perfect, Marcus. If you want to really screw the DHS, you have to embarrass them. It's not like you're going to be able to outshoot them. Your only weapon is your ability to make them look like morons."

I flopped on the bed and she pulled my head into her lap and stroked my hair. I'd been playing around with different haircuts before the bombing, dying it all kinds of funny colors, but since I'd gotten out of jail I couldn't be bothered. It had gotten long and stupid and shaggy and I'd gone into the bathroom and grabbed my clippers and buzzed it down to half an inch all around, which took zero effort to take care of and helped me to be invisible when I was out jamming and cloning arphids.

I opened my eyes and stared into her big brown eyes behind her glasses. They were round and liquid and expressive. She could make them bug out when she wanted to make me laugh, or make them soft and sad, or lazy and sleepy in a way that made me melt into a puddle of horniness.

That's what she was doing right now.

I sat up slowly and hugged her. She hugged me back. We kissed. She was an amazing kisser. I know I've already said that, but it bears repeating. We kissed a lot, but for one reason or another we always stopped before it got too heavy.

Now I wanted to go further. I found the hem of her T-shirt and tugged. She put her hands over her head and pulled back a few inches. I knew that she'd do that. I'd known since the night in the park. Maybe that's why we hadn't gone further—I knew I couldn't rely on her to back off, which scared me a little.

But I wasn't scared then. The impending press conference, the fights with my parents, the international attention, the sense that there was a movement that was careening around the city like a wild pinball—it made my skin tingle and my blood sing.

And she was beautiful, and smart, and clever and funny, and I was falling in love with her.

Her shirt slid off. She arched her back to help me get it over her shoulders. She reached behind her and did something and her bra fell away. I stared goggle-eyed, motionless and breathless, and then she grabbed *my* shirt and pulled it over my head, grabbing me and pulling my bare chest to hers.

We rolled on the bed and touched each other and ground our bodies together and groaned. She kissed all over my chest and I did the same to her. I couldn't breathe, I couldn't think, I could only move and kiss and lick and touch.

We dared each other to go forward. I undid her jeans. She undid mine. I lowered her zipper, she did mine, and tugged my jeans off. I tugged off hers. A moment later we were both naked, except for my socks, which I peeled off with my toes.

It was then that I caught sight of the bedside clock, which had long ago rolled onto the floor and lay there, glowing up at us.

"Crap!" I yelped. "It starts in two minutes!" I couldn't freaking believe that I was about to stop what I was about to stop doing, when I was about to stop doing it. I mean, if you'd asked me, "Marcus, you are about to get laid for the firstest time EVAR, will you stop if I let off this nuclear bomb in the same room as you?" the answer would have been a resounding and unequivical *NO*.

And yet we stopped for this.

She grabbed me and pulled my face to hers and kissed me until I thought I would pass out, then we both grabbed our clothes and more or less dressed, grabbing our keyboards and mice and heading for Patcheye Pete's.

You could easily tell who the press were: they were the noobs who played their characters like staggering drunks, weaving back and forth and up and down, trying to get the hang of it all, occasionally hitting the wrong key and offering strangers all or part of their inventory, or giving them accidental hugs and kicks.

The Xnetters were easy to spot, too: we all played Clockwork Plunder whenever we had some spare time (or didn't feel like doing our homework), and we had pretty tricked-out characters with cool weapons and booby traps on the keys sticking out of our backs that would cream anyone who tried to snatch them and leave us to wind down.

When I appeared, a system status message displayed M1K3Y HAS ENTERED PATCHEYE PETE'S—WELCOME SWABBIE WE OFFER FAIR TRADE FOR FINE BOOTY. All the players on the screen froze, then they crowded around me. The chat exploded. I thought about turning on my voice-paging and grabbing a headset, but seeing how many people were trying to talk at once, I realized how confusing that would be. Text was much easier to follow and they couldn't misquote me (heh heh).

I'd scouted the location before with Ange—it was great campaigning with her, since we could both keep each other wound up. There was a high spot on a pile of boxes of salt rations that I could stand on and be seen from anywhere in the market.

> Good evening and thank you all for coming. My name is M1k3y and I'm not the leader of anything. All around you are Xnetters who have as much to say about why we're here as I do. I use the Xnet because I believe in freedom and the Constitution of the United States of America. I use Xnet because the DHS has turned my city into a police-state where we're all suspected terrorists. I use Xnet because I think you can't defend freedom by tearing up the Bill of Rights. I learned about the Constitution in a California school and I was raised to love my country for its freedom. If I have a philosophy, it is this:

> Governments are instituted among men, deriving their just powers from the consent of the governed, that whenever any form of government becomes destructive of these ends, it is the right of the people to alter or abolish it, and to institute new government, laying its foundation on such principles, and organizing its powers in such form, as to them shall seem most likely to effect their safety and happiness.

> I didn't write that, but I believe it. The DHS does not govern with my consent.

> Thank you

I'd written this the day before, bouncing drafts back and forth with Ange. Pasting it in only took a second, though it took everyone in the game a moment to read it. A lot of the Xnetters cheered, big showy pirate "Hurrah"s with raised sabers and pet parrots squawking and flying overhead.

Gradually, the journalists digested it, too. The chat was running past fast, so fast you could barely read it, lots of Xnetters saying things like "Right on" and "America, love it or leave it" and "DHS go home" and "America out of San Francisco," all slogans that had been big on the Xnet blogosphere.

> M1k3y, this is Priya Rajneesh from the BBC. You say you're not the leader of any movement, but do you believe there is a movement? Is it called the Xnet?

Lots of answers. Some people said there wasn't a movement, some said there was and lots of people had ideas about what it was called: Xnet, Little Brothers, Little Sisters and my personal favorite, the United States of America.

They were really cooking. I let them go, thinking of what I could say. Once I had it, I typed,

> I think that kind of answers your question, doesn't it? There may be one or more movements and they may be called Xnet or not.

> M1k3y, I'm Doug Christensen from the Washington Internet Daily. What do you think the DHS should be doing to prevent another attack on San Francisco, if what they're doing isn't successful.

More chatter. Lots of people said that the terrorists and the government were the same—either literally, or just meaning that they were equally bad. Some said the government knew how to catch terrorists but preferred not to because "war presidents" got reelected.

> I don't know

I typed finally.

> I really don't. I ask myself this question a lot because I don't want to get blown up and I don't want my city to get blown up. Here's what I've figured out, though: if it's the DHS's job to keep us safe, they're failing. All the crap they've done, none of it would stop the bridge from being blown up again. Tracing us around the city? Taking away our freedom? Making us suspicious of each other, turning us against each other? Calling dissenters traitors? The point of terrorism is to terrify us. The DHS terrifies me.

> I don't have any say in what the terrorists do to me, but if this is a free country then I should be able to at least say what my own cops do to me. I should be able to keep them from terrorizing me.

> I know that's not a good answer. Sorry.

> What do you mean when you say that the DHS wouldn't stop terrorists? How do you know?

> Who are you?

> I'm with the Sydney Morning Herald.

> I'm 17 years old. I'm not a straight-A student or anything. Even so, I figured out how to make an Internet that they can't wiretap. I figured out how to jam their person-tracking technology. I can turn innocent people into suspects and turn guilty people into innocents in their eyes. I could get metal onto an airplane or beat a no-fly list. I figured this stuff out by looking at the web and by thinking about it. If I can do it, terrorists can do it. They told us they took away our freedom to make us safe. Do you feel safe?

> In Australia? Why yes I do

The pirates all laughed.

More journalists asked questions. Some were sympathetic, some were hostile. When I got tired, I handed my keyboard to Ange and let her be M1k3y for a while. It didn't really feel like M1k3y and me were the same person anymore anyway. M1k3y was the kind of kid who talked to international journalists and inspired a movement. Marcus got suspended from school and fought with his dad and wondered if he was good enough for his kick-ass girlfriend.

By 11 P.M. I'd had enough. Besides, my parents would be expecting me home soon. I logged out of the game and so did Ange and we lay there for a moment. I took her hand and she squeezed hard. We hugged.

She kissed my neck and murmured something.

"What?"

"I said I love you," she said. "What, you want me to send you a telegram?"

"Wow," I said.

"You're that surprised, huh?"

"No. Um. It's just—I was going to say that to you."

"Sure you were," she said, and bit the tip of my nose.

"It's just that I've never said it before," I said. "So I was working up to it."

"You still haven't said it, you know. Don't think I haven't noticed. We girls pick up on these things."

"I love you, Ange Carvelli," I said.

"I love you too, Marcus Yallow."

We kissed and nuzzled and I started to breathe hard and so did she. That's when her mom knocked on the door.

"Angela," she said, "I think it's time your friend went home, don't you?"

"Yes, Mother," she said, and mimed swinging an axe. As I put my socks and shoes on, she muttered, "They'll say, that Angela, she was such a good girl, who would have thought it, all the time she was in the backyard, helping her mother out by sharpening that hatchet."

I laughed. "You don't know how easy you have it. There is *no way* my folks would leave us alone in my bedroom until 11 o'clock."

"11:45," she said, checking her clock.

"Crap!" I yelped and tied my shoes.

"Go," she said, "run and be free! Look both ways before crossing the road! Write if you get work! Don't even stop for a hug! If you're not out of here by the count of ten, there's going to be *trouble,* mister. One. Two. Three."

I shut her up by leaping onto the bed, landing on her and kissing her until she stopped trying to count. Satisfied with my victory, I pounded down the stairs, my Xbox under my arm.

Her mom was at the foot of the stairs. We'd only met a couple times. She looked like an older, taller version of Ange—Ange said her father was the short one—with contacts instead of glasses. She seemed to have tentatively classed me as a good guy, I and appreciated it.

"Good night, Mrs. Carvelli," I said.

"Good night, Mr. Yallow," she said. It was one of our little rituals, ever since I'd called her Mrs. Carvelli when we first met.

I found myself standing awkwardly by the door.

"Yes?" she said.

"Um," I said. "Thanks for having me over."

"You're always welcome in our home, young man," she said.

"And thanks for Ange," I said finally, hating how lame it sounded. But she smiled broadly and gave me a brief hug.

"You're very welcome," she said.

The whole bus ride home, I thought over the press conference, thought about Ange naked and writhing with me on her bed, thought about her mother smiling and showing me the door.

My mom was waiting up for me. She asked me about the movie and I gave her the response I'd worked out in advance, cribbing from the review it had gotten in the *Bay Guardian*.

As I fell asleep, the press conference came back. I was really proud of it. It had been so cool, to have all these big-shot journos show up in the game, to have them listen to me and to have them listen to all the people who believed in the same things as me. I dropped off with a smile on my lips.

I should have known better.

Xnet Leader: I Could Get Metal Onto An Airplane
DHS Doesn't Have My Consent To Govern
Xnet Kids: USA Out Of San Francisco

Those were the *good* headlines. Everyone sent me the articles to blog, but it was the last thing I wanted to do.

I'd blown it, somehow. The press had come to my press conference and concluded that we were terrorists or terrorist dupes. The worst was the reporter on Fox News, who had apparently shown up anyway, and who devoted a ten-minute commentary to us, talking about our "criminal treason." Her killer line, repeated on every news outlet I found, was:

"They say they don't have a name. I've got one for them. Let's call these spoiled children Cal Qaeda. They do the terrorists' work on the home front. When—not if, but when—California gets attacked again, these brats will be as much to blame as the House of Saud."

Leaders of the antiwar movement denounced us as fringe elements. One guy went on TV to say that he believed we had been fabricated by the DHS to discredit them.

The DHS had their own press conference announcing that they would double the security in San Francisco. They held up an arphid cloner they'd found somewhere and demonstrated it in action, using it to stage a car theft, and warned everyone to be on the alert for young people behaving suspiciously, especially those whose hands were out of sight.

They weren't kidding. I finished my Kerouac paper and started in on a paper about the Summer of Love, the summer of 1967 when the antiwar movement and the hippies converged on San Francisco. The guys who founded Ben and Jerry's—old hippies themselves—had founded a hippie museum in the Haight, and there were other archives and exhibits to see around town.

But it wasn't easy getting around. By the end of the week, I was getting frisked an average of four times a day. Cops checked my ID and questioned me about why I was out in the street, carefully eyeballing the letter from Chavez saying that I was suspended.

I got lucky. No one arrested me. But the rest of the Xnet weren't so lucky. Every night the DHS announced more arrests, "ringleaders" and "operatives" of Xnet, people I didn't know and had never heard of, paraded on TV along with the arphid sniffers and other devices that had been in their pockets. They announced that the people were "naming names," compromising the "Xnet network" and that more arrests were expected soon. The name "M1k3y" was often heard.

Dad loved this. He and I watched the news together, him gloating, me shrinking away, quietly freaking out. "You should see the stuff they're going to use on these kids," Dad said. "I've seen it in action. They'll get a couple of these kids and check out their friends lists on IM and the speed-dials on their phones, look for names that come up over and over, look for patterns, bringing in more kids. They're going to unravel them like an old sweater."

I canceled Ange's dinner at our place and started spending even more time there. Ange's little sister Tina started to call me "the houseguest," as in "is the houseguest eating dinner with me tonight?" I liked Tina. All she cared about was going out and partying and meeting guys, but she was funny and utterly devoted to Ange. One night as we were doing the dishes, she dried her hands and said, conversationally, "You know, you seem like a nice guy, Marcus. My sister's just crazy about you and I like you, too. But

I have to tell you something: if you break her heart, I will track you down and pull your scrotum over your head. It's not a pretty sight."

I assured her that I would sooner pull my own scrotum over my head than break Ange's heart and she nodded. "So long as we're clear on that."

"Your sister is a nut," I said as we lay on Ange's bed again, looking at Xnet blogs. That is pretty much all we did: fool around and read Xnet.

"Did she use the scrotum line on you? I hate it when she does that. She just loves the word 'scrotum,' you know. It's nothing personal."

I kissed her. We read some more.

"Listen to this," she said. "Police project four to six *hundred* arrests this weekend in what they say will be the largest coordinated raid on Xnet dissidents to date."

I felt like throwing up.

"We've got to stop this," I said. "You know there are people who are doing *more* jamming to show that they're not intimidated? Isn't that just *crazy*?"

"I think it's brave," she said. "We can't let them scare us into submission."

"What? No, Ange, no. We can't let hundreds of people go to *jail*. You haven't been there. I have. It's worse than you think. It's worse than you can imagine."

"I have a pretty fertile imagination," she said.

"Stop it, okay? Be serious for a second. I won't do this. I won't send those people to jail. If I do, I'm the guy that Van thinks I am."

"Marcus, I'm being serious. You think that these people don't know they could go to jail? They believe in the cause. You believe in it, too. Give them the credit to know what they're getting into. It's not up to you to decide what risks they can or can't take."

"It's my responsibility because if I tell them to stop, they'll stop."

"I thought you weren't the leader?"

"I'm not, of course I'm not. But I can't help it if they look to me for guidance. And so long as they do, I have a responsibility to help them stay safe. You see that, right?"

"All I see is you getting ready to cut and run at the first sign of trouble. I think you're afraid they're going to figure out who *you* are. I think you're afraid for *you*."

"That's not fair," I said, sitting up, pulling away from her.

"Really? Who's the guy who nearly had a heart attack when he thought that his secret identity was out?"

"That was different," I said. "This isn't about me. You know it isn't. Why are you being like this?"

"Why are *you* like this?" she said. "Why aren't *you* willing to be the guy who was brave enough to get all this started?"

"This isn't brave, it's suicide."

"Cheap teenage melodrama, M1k3y."

"Don't call me that!"

"What, 'M1k3y'? Why not, *M1k3y*?"

I put my shoes on. I picked up my bag. I walked home.

> Why I'm not jamming

> I won't tell anyone else what to do, because I'm not anyone's leader, no matter what Fox News thinks.

> But I am going to tell you what _I_ plan on doing. If you think that's the right thing to do, maybe you'll do it too.

> I'm not jamming. Not this week. Maybe not next. It's not because I'm scared. It's because I'm smart enough to know that I'm better free than in prison. They figured out how to stop our tactic, so we need to come up with a new tactic. I don't care what the tactic is, but I want it to work. It's _stupid_ to get arrested. It's only jamming if you get away with it.

> There's another reason not to jam. If you get caught, they might use you to catch your friends, and their friends, and their friends. They might bust your friends even if they're not on Xnet, because the DHS is like a maddened bull and they don't exactly worry if they've got the right guy.

> I'm not telling you what to do.

> But the DHS is dumb and we're smart. Jamming proves that they can't fight terrorism because it proves that they can't even stop a bunch of kids. If you get caught, it makes them look like they're smarter than us.

> THEY AREN'T SMARTER THAN US! We are smarter than them. Let's be smart. Let's figure out how to jam them, no matter how many goons they put on the streets of our city.

I posted it. I went to bed.

I missed Ange.

Ange and I didn't speak for the next four days, including the week-end, and then it was time to go back to school. I'd almost called her a million times, written a thousand unsent emails and IMs.

Now I was back in Social Studies class, and Mrs. Andersen greeted me with voluble, sarcastic courtesy, asking me sweetly how my "holiday" had been. I sat down and mumbled nothing. I could hear Charles snicker.

She taught us a class on Manifest Destiny, the idea that the Americans were destined to take over the whole world (or at least that's how she made it seem) and seemed to be trying to provoke me into saying something so she could throw me out.

I felt the eyes of the class on me, and it reminded me of M1k3y and the people who looked up to him. I was sick of being looked up to. I missed Ange.

I got through the rest of the day without anything making any kind of mark on me. I don't think I said eight words.

Finally it was over and I hit the doors, heading for the gates and the stupid Mission and my pointless house.

I was barely out the gate when someone crashed into me. He was a young homeless guy, maybe my age, maybe a little older. He wore a long, greasy overcoat, a pair of baggy jeans and rotting sneakers that looked like they'd been through a wood chipper. His long hair hung over his face, and he had a pubic beard that straggled down his throat into the collar of a no-color knit sweater.

I took this all in as we lay next to each other on the sidewalk, people passing us and giving us weird looks. It seemed that he'd crashed into me while hurrying down Valencia, bent over with the burden of a split backpack that lay beside him on the pavement, covered in tight geometric doodles in Magic Marker.

He got to his knees and rocked back and forth, like he was drunk or had hit his head.

"Sorry buddy," he said. "Didn't see you. You hurt?"

I sat up, too. Nothing felt hurt.

"Um. No, it's okay."

He stood up and smiled. His teeth were shockingly white and straight, like an ad for an orthodontic clinic. He held his hand out to me and his grip was strong and firm.

"I'm really sorry." His voice was also clear and intelligent. I'd expected him to sound like the drunks who talked to themselves as they roamed the Mission late at night, but he sounded like a knowledgeable bookstore clerk.

"It's no problem," I said.

He stuck out his hand again.

"Zeb," he said.

"Marcus," I said.

"A pleasure, Marcus," he said. "Hope to run into you again sometime!"

Laughing, he picked up his backpack, turned on his heel and hurried away.

I walked the rest of the way home in a bemused fog. Mom was at the kitchen table and we had a little chat about nothing at all, the way we used to do, before everything changed.

I took the stairs up to my room and flopped down in my chair. For once, I didn't want to log in to the Xnet. I'd checked in that morning before school to discover that my note had created a gigantic controversy among people who agreed with me and people who were righteously pissed that I was telling them to back off from their beloved sport.

I had three thousand projects I'd been in the middle of when it had all started. I was building a pinhole camera out of legos, I'd been playing with aerial kite photography using an old digital camera with a trigger hacked out of silly putty that was stretched out at launch and slowly snapped back to its original shape, triggering the shutter at regular intervals. I had a vacuum tube amp I'd been building into an ancient, rusted, dented olive oil tin that looked like an archaeological find—once it was done, I'd planned to build in a dock for my phone and a set of 5.1 surround-sound speakers out of tuna fish cans.

I looked over my workbench and finally picked up the pinhole camera. Methodically snapping legos together was just about my speed.

I took off my watch and the chunky silver two-finger ring that showed a monkey and a ninja squaring off to fight and dropped them into the little box I used for all the crap I load into my pockets and around my neck before stepping out for the day: phone, wallet, keys, wifinder, change, batteries, retractable cables . . . I dumped it all out into the box, and found myself holding something I didn't remember putting in there in the first place.

It was a piece of paper, gray and soft as flannel, furry at the edges where it had been torn away from some larger piece of paper. It was covered in the tiniest, most careful handwriting I'd ever seen. I unfolded it and held it up. The writing covered both sides, running down from the top left corner of one side to a crabbed signature at the bottom right corner of the other side.

The signature read, simply: ZEB.

I picked it up and started to read.

Dear Marcus

You don't know me but I know you. For the past three months, since the Bay Bridge was blown up, I have been imprisoned on Treasure Island. I was in the yard on the day you talked to that Asian girl and got tackled. You were brave. Good on you.

I had a burst appendix the day afterward and ended up in the infirmary. In the next bed was a guy named Darryl. We were both in recovery for a long time and by the time we got well, we were too much of an embarrassment to them to let go.

So they decided we must really be guilty. They questioned us every day. You've been through their questioning, I know. Imagine it for months. Darryl and I ended up cell-mates. We knew we were bugged, so we only talked about inconsequentialities. But at night, when we were in our cots, we would softly tap out messages to each other in Morse code (I knew my HAM radio days would come in useful sometime).

At first, their questions to us were just the same crap as ever, who did it, how'd they do it. But after a little while, they switched to asking us about the Xnet. Of course, we'd never heard of it. That didn't stop them asking.

Darryl told me that they brought him arphid cloners,

Xboxes, all kinds of technology and demanded that he tell them who used them, where they learned to mod them. Darryl told me about your games and the things you learned.

Especially: The DHS asked us about our friends. Who did we know? What were they like? Did they have political feelings? Had they been in trouble at school? With the law?

We call the prison Gitmo-by-the-Bay. It's been a week since I got out and I don't think that anyone knows that their sons and daughters are imprisoned in the middle of the Bay. At night we could hear people laughing and partying on the mainland.

I got out last week. I won't tell you how, in case this falls into the wrong hands. Maybe others will take my route.

Darryl told me how to find you and made me promise to tell you what I knew when I got back. Now that I've done that I'm out of here like last year. One way or another, I'm leaving this country. Screw America.

Stay strong. They're scared of you. Kick them for me. Don't get caught.

Zeb

There were tears in my eyes as I finished the note. I had a disposable lighter somewhere on my desk that I sometimes used to melt the insulation off of wires, and I dug it out and held it to the note. I knew I owed it to Zeb to destroy it and make sure no one else ever saw it, in case it might lead them back to him, wherever he was going.

I held the flame and the note, but I couldn't do it.

Darryl.

With all the crap with the Xnet and Ange and the DHS, I'd almost forgotten he existed. He'd become a ghost, like an old friend who'd moved away or gone on an exchange program. All that time, they'd been questioning him, demanding that he rat me out, explain the Xnet, the jammers. He'd been on Treasure Island, the abandoned military base that was halfway along the demolished span of the Bay Bridge. He'd been so close I could have swam to him.

I put the lighter down and reread the note. By the time it was done, I was weeping, sobbing. It all came back to me, the lady with the severe haircut and the questions she'd asked and the reek of piss and the stiffness of my pants as the urine dried them into coarse canvas.

"Marcus?"

My door was ajar and my mother was standing in it, watching me with a worried look. How long had she been there?

I armed the tears away from my face and snorted up the snot. "Mom," I said. "Hi."

She came into my room and hugged me. "What is it? Do you need to talk?"

The note lay on the table.

"Is that from your girlfriend? Is everything all right?"

She'd given me an out. I could just blame it all on problems with Ange and she'd leave my room and leave me alone. I opened my mouth to do just that, and then this came out:

"I was in jail. After the bridge blew. I was in jail for that whole time."

The sobs that came then didn't sound like my voice. They sounded like an animal noise, maybe a donkey or some kind of big cat noise in the night. I sobbed so my throat burned and ached with it, so my chest heaved.

Mom took me in her arms, the way she used to when I was a little boy, and she stroked my hair, and she murmured in my ear, and rocked me, and gradually, slowly, the sobs dissipated.

I took a deep breath and Mom got me a glass of water. I sat on the edge of my bed and she sat in my desk chair and I told her everything.

Everything.

Well, most of it.

chapter **16**

At first Mom looked shocked, then outraged, and finally she gave up altogether and just let her jaw hang open as I took her through the interrogation, pissing myself, the bag over my head, Darryl. I showed her the note.

"Why—?"

In that single syllable, every recrimination I'd dealt myself in the night, every moment that I'd lacked the bravery to tell the world what it was really about, why I was really fighting, what had really inspired the Xnet.

I sucked in a breath.

"They told me I'd go to jail if I talked about it. Not just for a few days. Forever. I was—I was scared."

Mom sat with me for a long time, not saying anything. Then, "What about Darryl's father?"

She might as well have stuck a knitting needle in my chest. Darryl's father. He must have assumed that Darryl was dead, long dead.

And wasn't he? After the DHS has held you illegally for three months, would they ever let you go?

But Zeb got out. Maybe Darryl would get out. Maybe me and the Xnet could help get Darryl out.

"I haven't told him," I said.

Now Mom was crying. She didn't cry easily. It was a British thing. It made her little hiccoughing sobs much worse to hear.

"You will tell him," she managed. "You will."

"I will."

"But first we have to tell your father."

Dad no longer had any regular time when he came home. Between his consulting clients—who had lots of work now that the DHS was shopping for data-mining start-ups on the peninsula—and the long commute to Berkeley, he might get home any time between 6 P.M. and midnight.

Tonight Mom called him and told him he was coming home *right now*. He said something and she just repeated it: *right now*.

When he got there, we had arranged ourselves in the living room with the note between us on the coffee table.

It was easier to tell, the second time. The secret was getting lighter. I didn't embellish, I didn't hide anything. I came clean.

I'd heard of coming clean before but I'd never understood what it meant until I did it. Holding in the secret had dirtied me, soiled my spirit. It had made me afraid and ashamed. It had made me into all the things that Ange said I was.

Dad sat stiff as a ramrod the whole time, his face carved of stone. When I handed him the note, he read it twice and then set it down carefully.

He shook his head and stood up and headed for the front door.

"Where are you going?" Mom asked, alarmed.

"I need a walk," was all he managed to gasp, his voice breaking.

We stared awkwardly at each other, Mom and me, and waited for him to come home. I tried to imagine what was going on in his head. He'd been such a different man after the bombings and I knew from Mom that what had changed him were the days of thinking I was dead. He'd come to believe that the terrorists had nearly killed his son and it had made him crazy.

Crazy enough to do whatever the DHS asked, to line up like a good little sheep and let them control him, drive him.

Now he knew that it was the DHS that had imprisoned me, the DHS that had taken San Francisco's children hostage in Gitmo-by-the-Bay. It made perfect sense, now that I thought of it. Of course it had been Treasure Island where I'd been kept. Where else was a ten-minute boat ride from San Francisco?

When Dad came back, he looked angrier than he ever had in his life.

"You should have told me!" he roared.

Mom interposed herself between him and me. "You're blaming

216 | **cory doctorow**

the wrong person," she said. "It wasn't Marcus who did the kidnapping and the intimidation."

He shook his head and stamped. "I'm not blaming Marcus. I know *exactly* who's to blame. Me. Me and the stupid DHS. Get your shoes on, grab your coats."

"Where are we going?"

"To see Darryl's father. Then we're going to Barbara Stratford's place."

I knew the name Barbara Stratford from somewhere, but I couldn't remember where. I thought that maybe she was an old friend of my parents', but I couldn't exactly place her.

Meantime, I was headed for Darryl's father's place. I'd never really felt comfortable around the old man, who'd been a Navy radio operator and ran his household like a tight ship. He'd taught Darryl Morse code when he was a kid, which I'd always thought was cool. It was one of the ways I knew that I could trust Zeb's letter. But for every cool thing like Morse code, Darryl's father had some crazy military discipline that seemed to be for its own sake, like insisting on hospital corners on the beds and shaving twice a day. It drove Darryl up the wall.

Darryl's mother hadn't liked it much, either, and had taken off back to her family in Minnesota when Darryl was ten—Darryl spent his summers and Christmases there.

I was sitting in the back of the car, and I could see the back of Dad's head as he drove. The muscles in his neck were tense and kept jumping around as he ground his jaws.

Mom kept her hand on his arm, but no one was around to comfort me. If only I could call Ange. Or Jolu. Or Van. Maybe I would when the day was done.

"He must have buried his son in his mind," Dad said, as we whipped up through the hairpin curves leading up Twin Peaks to the little cottage that Darryl and his father shared. The fog was on Twin Peaks, the way it often was at night in San Francisco, making the headlamps reflect back on us. Each time we swung around a corner, I saw the valleys of the city laid out below us, bowls of twinkling lights that shifted in the mist.

"Is this the one?"

"Yes," I said. "This is it." I hadn't been to Darryl's in months, but I'd spent enough time here over the years to recognize it right off.

The three of us stood around the car for a long moment, waiting to see who would go and ring the doorbell. To my surprise, it was me.

I rang it and we all waited in held-breath silence for a minute. I rang it again. Darryl's father's car was in the driveway, and we'd seen a light burning in the living room. I was about to ring a third time when the door opened.

"Marcus?" Darryl's father wasn't anything like I remembered him. Unshaven, in a housecoat and bare feet, with long toenails and red eyes. He'd gained weight, and a soft extra chin wobbled beneath the firm military jaw. His thin hair was wispy and disordered.

"Mr. Glover," I said. My parents crowded into the door behind me.

"Hello, Ron," my mother said.

"Ron," my father said.

"You, too? What's going on?"

"Can we come in?"

His living room looked like one of those news segments they show about abandoned kids who spend a month locked in before they're rescued by the neighbors: frozen meal boxes, empty beer cans and juice bottles, moldy cereal bowls and piles of newspapers. There was a reek of cat piss and litter crunched underneath our feet. Even without the cat piss, the smell was incredible, like a bus station toilet.

The couch was made up with a grimy sheet and a couple of greasy pillows and the cushions had a dented, much-slept-upon look.

We all stood there for a long silent moment, embarrassment overwhelming every other emotion. Darryl's father looked like he wanted to die.

Slowly, he moved aside the sheet from the sofa and cleared the stacked, greasy food trays off of a couple of the chairs, carrying them into the kitchen, and, from the sound of it, tossing them on the floor.

We sat gingerly in the places he'd cleared, and then he came back and sat down, too.

"I'm sorry," he said vaguely. "I don't really have any coffee to offer you. I'm having more groceries delivered tomorrow so I'm running low—"

"Ron," my father said. "Listen to us. We have something to tell you, and it's not going to be easy to hear."

He sat like a statue as I talked. He glanced down at the note, read it without seeming to understand it, then read it again. He handed it back to me.

He was trembling.

"He's—"

"Darryl is alive," I said. "Darryl is alive and being held prisoner on Treasure Island."

He stuffed his fist in his mouth and made a horrible groaning sound.

"We have a friend," my father said. "She writes for the *Bay Guardian*. An investigative reporter."

That's where I knew the name from. The free weekly *Guardian* often lost its reporters to bigger daily papers and the Internet, but Barbara Stratford had been there forever. I had a dim memory of having dinner with her when I was a kid.

"We're going there now," my mother said. "Will you come with us, Ron? Will you tell her Darryl's story?"

He put his face in his hands and breathed deeply. Dad tried to put his hand on his shoulders, but Mr. Glover shook it off violently.

"I need to clean myself up," he said. "Give me a minute."

Mr. Glover came back downstairs a changed man. He'd shaved and gelled his hair back, and had put on a crisp military dress uniform with a row of campaign ribbons on the breast. He stopped at the foot of the stairs and kind of gestured at it.

"I don't have much clean stuff that's presentable at the moment. And this seemed appropriate. You know, if she wanted to take pictures."

He and Dad rode up front and I got in the back, behind him. Up close, he smelled a little of beer, like it was coming through his pores.

It was midnight by the time we rolled into Barbara Stratford's driveway. She lived out of town, down in Mountain View, and as we sped down the 101, none of us said a word. The high-tech buildings alongside the highway streamed past us.

This was a different Bay Area to the one I lived in, more like the suburban America I sometimes saw on TV. Lots of freeways and subdivisions of identical houses, towns where there weren't any homeless people pushing shopping carts down the sidewalk—there weren't even sidewalks!

Mom had phoned Barbara Stratford while we were waiting for Mr. Glover to come downstairs. The journalist had been sleeping, but Mom had been so wound up she forgot to be all British and embarrassed about waking her up. Instead, she just told her, tensely, that she had something to talk about and that it had to be in person.

When we rolled up to Barbara Stratford's house, my first thought was of the Brady Bunch place—a low ranch house with a brick baffle in front of it and a neat, perfectly square lawn. There was a kind of abstract tile pattern on the baffle, and an old-fashioned UHF TV antenna rising from behind it. We wandered around to the entrance and saw that there were lights on inside already.

The writer opened the door before we had a chance to ring the bell. She was about my parents' age, a tall thin woman with a hawklike nose and shrewd eyes with a lot of laugh lines. She was wearing a pair of jeans that were hip enough to be seen at one of the boutiques on Valencia Street, and a loose Indian cotton blouse that hung down to her thighs. She had small round glasses that flashed in her hallway light.

She smiled a tight little smile at us.

"You brought the whole clan, I see," she said.

Mom nodded. "You'll understand why in a minute," she said. Mr. Glover stepped from behind Dad.

"And you called in the Navy?"

"All in good time."

We were introduced one at a time to her. She had a firm hand-shake and long fingers.

Her place was furnished in Japanese minimalist style, just a few precisely proportioned, low pieces of furniture, large clay pots of bamboo that brushed the ceiling, and what looked like a large, rusted piece of a diesel engine perched on top of a polished marble plinth. I decided I liked it. The floors were old wood, sanded and stained, but not filled, so you could see cracks and pits underneath the varnish. I *really* liked that, especially as I walked over it in my stocking feet.

"I have coffee on," she said. "Who wants some?"

We all put up our hands. I glared defiantly at my parents.

"Right," she said.

She disappeared into another room and came back a moment later bearing a rough bamboo tray with a half-gallon thermos jug and six cups of precise design but with rough, sloppy decorations. I liked those, too.

"Now," she said, once she'd poured and served. "It's very good to see you all again. Marcus, I think the last time I saw you, you were maybe seven years old. As I recall, you were very excited about your new video games, which you showed me."

I didn't remember it at all, but that sounded like what I'd been into at seven. I guessed it was my Sega Dreamcast.

She produced a tape recorder and a yellow pad and a pen, and twirled the pen. "I'm here to listen to whatever you tell me, and I can promise you that I'll take it all in confidence. But I can't prom-ise that I'll do anything with it, or that it's going to get published." The way she said it made me realize that my mom had called in a pretty big favor getting this lady out of bed, friend or no friend. It must be kind of a pain in the ass to be a big-shot investigative reporter. There were probably a million people who would have liked her to take up their cause.

Mom nodded at me. Even though I'd told the story three times that night, I found myself tongue-tied. This was different from tell-ing my parents. Different from telling Darryl's father. This—this would start a new move in the game.

I started slowly, and watched Barbara take notes. I drank a whole cup of coffee just explaining what ARGing was and how I got out of school to play. Mom and Dad and Mr. Glover all listened intently to this part. I poured myself another cup and drank it on the way to explaining how we were taken in. By the time I'd run through the whole story, I'd drained the pot and I needed to piss like a racehorse.

Her bathroom was just as stark as the living room, with a brown, organic soap that smelled like clean mud. I came back in and found the adults quietly watching me.

Mr. Glover told his story next. He didn't have anything to say about what had happened, but he explained that he was a veteran and that his son was a good kid. He talked about what it felt like to believe that his son had died, about how his ex-wife had had a collapse when she found out and ended up in the hospital. He cried a little, unashamed, the tears streaming down his lined face and darkening the collar of his dress uniform.

When it was all done, Barbara went into a different room and came back with a bottle of Irish whiskey. "It's a Bushmills fifteen-year-old rum-cask aged blend," she said, setting down four small cups. None for me. "It hasn't been sold in ten years. I think this is probably an appropriate time to break it out."

She poured them each a small glass of the liquor, then raised hers and sipped at it, draining half the cup. The rest of the adults followed suit. They drank again, and finished the cups. She poured them new shots.

"All right," she said. "Here's what I can tell you right now. I believe you. Not just because I know you, Lillian. The story sounds right, and it ties in with other rumors I've heard. But I'm not going to be able to just take your word for it. I'm going to have to investigate every aspect of this, and every element of your lives and stories. I need to know if there's anything you're not telling me, anything that could be used to discredit you after this comes to light. I need everything. It could take weeks before I'm ready to publish.

"You also need to think about your safety and this Darryl's safety. If he's really an 'unperson' then bringing pressure to bear on the DHS could cause them to move him somewhere much farther away. Think Syria. They could also do something much worse." She let that hang in the air. I knew she meant that they might kill him.

"I'm going to take this letter and scan it now. I want pictures of all of you, now and later—we can send out a photographer, but I want to document this as thoroughly as I can tonight, too."

I went with her into her office to do the scan. I'd expected a stylish, low-powered computer that fit in with her decor, but instead, her spare bedroom/office was crammed with top-of-the-line PCs, big flat-panel monitors, and a scanner big enough to lay a whole sheet of newsprint on. She was fast with it all, too. I noted with some approval that she was running ParanoidLinux. This lady took her job seriously.

The computers' fans set up an effective white noise shield, but even so, I closed the door and moved in close to her.

"Um, Barbara?"

"Yes?"

"About what you said, about what might be used to discredit me?"

"Yes?"

"What I tell you, you can't be forced to tell anyone else, right?"

"In theory. Let me put it this way. I've gone to jail twice rather than rat out a source."

"Okay, okay. Good. Wow. Jail. Wow. Okay." I took a deep breath. "You've heard of Xnet? Of M1k3y?"

"Yes?"

"I'm M1k3y."

"Oh," she said. She worked the scanner and flipped the note over to get the reverse. She was scanning at some unbelievable resolution, 10,000 dots per inch or higher, and on-screen it was like the output of an electron-tunneling microscope.

"Well, that does put a different complexion on this."

"Yeah," I said. "I guess it does."

"Your parents don't know."

"Nope. And I don't know if I want them to."

"That's something you're going to have to work out. I need to think about this. Can you come by my office? I'd like to talk to you about what this means, exactly."

"Do you have an Xbox Universal? I could bring over an installer."

"Yes, I'm sure that can be arranged. When you come by, tell the receptionist that you're Mr. Brown, to see me. They know what that means. No note will be taken of you coming, and all the security camera footage for the day will be automatically scrubbed and the cameras deactivated until you leave."

"Wow," I said. "You think like I do."

She smiled and socked me in the shoulder. "Kiddo, I've been at this game for a hell of a long time. So far, I've managed to spend more time free than behind bars. Paranoia is my friend."

I was like a zombie the next day in school. I'd totaled about three hours of sleep, and even three cups of the Turk's caffeine mud failed to jump-start my brain. The problem with caffeine is that it's too easy to get acclimated to it, so you have to take higher and higher doses just to get above normal.

I'd spent the night thinking over what I had to do. It was like running through a maze of twisty little passages, all alike, every one leading to the same dead end. When I went to Barbara, it would be over for me. That was the outcome, no matter how I thought about it.

By the time the school day was over, all I wanted was to go home and crawl into bed. But I had an appointment at the *Bay Guardian,* down on the waterfront. I kept my eyes on my feet as I wobbled out the gate, and as I turned into 24th Street, another pair of feet fell into step with me. I recognized the shoes and stopped.

"Ange?"

She looked like I felt. Sleep-deprived and raccoon-eyed, with sad brackets in the corners of her mouth.

"Hi there," she said. "Surprise. I gave myself French Leave from school. I couldn't concentrate anyway."

"Um," I said.

"Shut up and give me a hug, you idiot."

I did. It felt good. Better than good. It felt like I'd amputated part of myself and it had been reattached.

"I love you, Marcus Yallow."

"I love you, Angela Carvelli."

"Okay," she said breaking it off. "I liked your post about why you're not jamming. I can respect it. What have you done about finding a way to jam them without getting caught?"

"I'm on my way to meet an investigative journalist who's going to publish a story about how I got sent to jail, how I started Xnet and how Darryl is being illegally held by the DHS at a secret prison on Treasure Island."

"Oh." She looked around for a moment. "Couldn't you think of anything, you know, ambitious?"

"Want to come?"

"I am coming, yes. And I would like you to explain this in detail if you don't mind."

After all the retellings, this one, told as we walked to Potrero Avenue and down to 15th Street, was the easiest. She held my hand and squeezed it often.

We took the stairs up to the *Bay Guardian*'s offices two at a time. My heart was pounding. I got to the reception desk and told the bored girl behind it, "I'm here to see Barbara Stratford. My name is Mr. Green."

"I think you mean Mr. Brown?"

"Yeah," I said, and blushed. "Mr. Brown."

She did something at her computer, then said, "Have a seat. Barbara will be out in a minute. Can I get you anything?"

"Coffee," we both said in unison. Another reason to love Ange: we were addicted to the same drug.

The receptionist—a pretty Latina woman only a few years older than us, dressed in Gap styles so old they were actually kind of hipster-retro—nodded and stepped out and came back with a couple of cups bearing the newspaper's masthead.

We sipped in silence, watching visitors and reporters come and go. Finally, Barbara came to get us. She was wearing practically the same thing as the night before. It suited her. She quirked an eyebrow at me when she saw that I'd brought a date.

"Hello," I said. "Um, this is—"

"Ms. Brown," Ange said, extending a hand. Oh, yeah, right, our identities were supposed to be a secret. "I work with Mr. Green." She elbowed me lightly.

"Let's go then," Barbara said, and led us back to a board room with long glass walls with their blinds drawn shut. She set down a tray of Whole Foods organic Oreo clones, a digital recorder and another yellow pad.

"Do you want to record this, too?" she asked.

Hadn't actually thought of that. I could see why it would be useful if I wanted to dispute what Barbara printed, though. Still, if I couldn't trust her to do right by me, I was doomed anyway.

"No, that's okay," I said.

"Right, let's go. Young lady, my name is Barbara Stratford and I'm an investigative reporter. I gather you know why I'm here, and I'm curious to know why you're here."

"I work with Marcus on the Xnet," she said. "Do you need to know my name?"

"Not right now, I don't," Barbara said. "You can be anonymous if you'd like. Marcus, I asked you to tell me this story because I need to know how it plays with the story you told me about your friend Darryl and the note you showed me. I can see how it would be a good adjunct; I could pitch this as the origin of the Xnet. 'They made an enemy they'll never forget,' that sort of thing. But to be honest, I'd rather not have to tell that story if I don't have to.

"I'd rather have a nice clean tale about the secret prison on our doorstep, without having to argue about whether the prisoners there are the sort of people likely to walk out the doors and establish an underground movement bent on destabilizing the federal government. I'm sure you can understand that."

I did. If the Xnet was part of the story, some people would say, see, they need to put guys like that in jail or they'll start a riot.

"This is your show," I said. "I think you need to tell the world about Darryl. When you do that, it's going to tell the DHS that I've gone public and they're going to go after me. Maybe they'll figure out then that I'm involved with the Xnet. Maybe they'll connect me to M1k3y. I guess what I'm saying is, once you publish about

226 | cory doctorow

Darryl, it's all over for me no matter what. I've made my peace with that."

"As good be hanged for a sheep as a lamb," she said. "Right. Well, that's settled. I want the two of you to tell me everything you can about the founding and operation of the Xnet, and then I want a demonstration. What do you use it for? Who else uses it? How did it spread? Who wrote the software? Everything."

"This'll take a while," Ange said.

"I've got a while," Barbara said. She drank some coffee and ate a fake Oreo. "This could be the most important story of the War on Terror. This could be the story that topples the government. When you have a story like this, you take it very carefully."

chapter 17

So we told her. I found it really fun, actually. Teaching people how to use technology is always exciting. It's so cool to watch people figure out how the technology around them can be used to make their lives better. Ange was great, too—we made an excellent team. We'd trade off explaining how it all worked. Barbara was pretty good at this stuff to begin with, of course.

It turned out that she'd covered the crypto wars, the period in the early nineties when civil liberties groups like the Electronic Frontier Foundation fought for the right of Americans to use strong crypto. I dimly knew about that period, but Barbara explained it in a way that made me get goose pimples.

It's unbelievable today, but there was a time when the government classed crypto as a munition and made it illegal for anyone to export or use it on national security grounds. Get that? We used to have illegal *math* in this country.

The National Security Agency were the real movers behind the ban. They had a crypto standard that they said was strong enough for bankers and their customers to use, but not so strong that the mafia would be able to keep its books secret from them. The standard, DES-56, was said to be practically unbreakable. Then one of EFF's millionaire cofounders built a $250,000 DES-56 cracker that could break the cipher in two hours.

Still the NSA argued that it should be able to keep American citizens from possessing secrets it couldn't pry into. Then EFF dealt its death blow. In 1995, they represented a Berkeley mathematics grad student called Dan Bernstein in court. Bernstein had written a crypto tutorial that contained computer code that could be used to make a cipher stronger than DES-56. Millions of times stronger. As far as the NSA was concerned, that made his article into a weapon, and therefore unpublishable.

Well, it may be hard to get a judge to understand crypto and what it means, but it turned out that the average Appeals Court judge isn't real enthusiastic about telling grad students what kind of scholarly articles they're allowed to write. The crypto wars ended with a victory for the good guys when the 9th Circuit Appellate Division Court ruled that code was a form of expression protected under the First Amendment—"Congress shall make no law abridging the freedom of speech." If you've ever bought something on the Internet, or sent a secret message, or checked your bank balance, you used crypto that EFF legalized. Good thing, too: the NSA just isn't that smart. Anything they know how to crack, you can be sure that terrorists and mobsters can get around, too.

Barbara had been one of the reporters who'd made her reputation from covering the issue. She'd cut her teeth covering the tail end of the civil rights movement in San Francisco, and she recognized the similarity between the fight for the Constitution in the real world and the fight in cyberspace.

So she got it. I don't think I could have explained this stuff to my parents, but with Barbara it was easy. She asked smart questions about our cryptographic protocols and security procedures, sometimes asking stuff I didn't know the answer to—sometimes pointing out potential breaks in our procedure.

We plugged in the Xbox and got it online. There were four open WiFi nodes visible from the board room and I told it to change between them at random intervals. She got this, too—once you were actually plugged into the Xnet, it was just like being on the Internet, only some stuff was a little slower, and it was all anonymous and unsniffable.

"So now what?" I said as we wound down. I'd talked myself dry and I had a terrible acid feeling from the coffee. Besides, Ange kept squeezing my hand under the table in a way that made me want to break away and find somewhere private to finish making up for our first fight.

"Now I do journalism. You go away and I research all the things you've told me and try to confirm them to the extent that I can. I'll let you see what I'm going to publish and I'll let you know when it's going to go live. I'd prefer that you *not* talk about this with anyone else now, because I want the scoop and because I want to make sure that I get the story before it goes all muddy from press speculation and DHS spin.

"I *will* have to call the DHS for comment before I go to press, but I'll do that in a way that protects you to whatever extent possible. I'll also be sure to let you know before that happens.

"One thing I need to be clear on: this isn't your story anymore. It's mine. You were very generous to give it to me and I'll try to repay the gift, but you don't get the right to edit anything out, to change it or to stop me. This is now in motion and it won't stop. Do you understand that?"

I hadn't thought about it in those terms but once she said it, it was obvious. It meant that I had launched and I wouldn't be able to recall the rocket. It was going to fall where it was aimed, or it would go off course, but it was in the air and couldn't be changed now. Sometime in the near future, I would stop being Marcus—I would be a public figure. I'd be the guy who blew the whistle on the DHS.

I'd be a dead man walking.

I guess Ange was thinking along the same lines, because she'd gone a color between white and green.

"Let's get out of here," she said.

Ange's mom and sister were out again, which made it easy to decide where we were going for the evening. It was past supper time, but my parents had known that I was meeting with Barbara and wouldn't give me any grief if I came home late.

When we got to Ange's, I had no urge to plug in my Xbox. I had had all the Xnet I could handle for one day. All I could think about was Ange, Ange, Ange. Living without Ange. Knowing Ange was angry with me. Ange never going to talk to me again. Ange never going to kiss me again.

She'd been thinking the same. I could see it in her eyes as we shut the door to her bedroom and looked at each other. I was hungry for her, like you'd hunger for dinner after not eating for days. Like you'd thirst for a glass of water after playing soccer for three hours straight.

Like none of that. It was more. It was something I'd never felt before. I wanted to eat her whole, devour her.

Up until now, she'd been the sexual one in our relationship. I'd let her set and control the pace. It was amazingly erotic to have *her* grab *me* and take off my shirt, drag my face to hers.

But tonight I couldn't hold back. I wouldn't hold back.

The door clicked shut and I reached for the hem of her T-shirt and yanked, barely giving her time to lift her arms as I pulled it over her head. I tore my own shirt over my head, listening to the cotton crackle as the stitches came loose.

Her eyes were shining, her mouth open, her breathing fast and shallow. Mine was, too, my breath and my heart and my blood all roaring in my ears.

I took off the rest of our clothes with equal zest, throwing them into the piles of dirty and clean laundry on the floor. There were books and papers all over the bed and I swept them aside. We landed on the unmade bedclothes a second later, arms around one another, squeezing like we would pull ourselves right through one another. She moaned into my mouth and I made the sound back, and I felt her voice buzz in my vocal chords, a feeling more intimate than anything I'd ever felt before.

She broke away and reached for the bedstand. She yanked open the drawer and threw a white pharmacy bag on the bed before me. I looked inside. Condoms. Trojans. One dozen spermicidal. Still sealed. I smiled at her and she smiled back and I opened the box.

I'd thought about what it would be like for years. A hundred times a day I'd imagined it. Some days, I'd thought of practically nothing else.

It was nothing like I expected. Parts of it were better. Parts of it were lots worse. While it was going on, it felt like an eternity. Afterward, it seemed to be over in the blink of an eye.

Afterward, I felt the same. But I also felt different. Something had changed between us.

It was weird. We were both shy as we put our clothes on and puttered around the room, looking away, not meeting each other's eyes. I wrapped the condom in a kleenex from a box beside the bed and took it into the bathroom and wound it with toilet paper and stuck it deep into the trash can.

When I came back in, Ange was sitting up in bed and playing with her Xbox. I sat down carefully beside her and took her hand. She turned to face me and smiled. We were both worn out, trembly.

"Thanks," I said.

She didn't say anything. She turned her face to me. She was grinning hugely, but fat tears were rolling down her cheeks.

I hugged her and she grabbed tightly onto me. "You're a good man, Marcus Yallow," she whispered. "Thank you."

I didn't know what to say, but I squeezed her back. Finally, we parted. She wasn't crying anymore, but she was still smiling.

She pointed at my Xbox, on the floor beside the bed. I took the hint. I picked it up and plugged it in and logged in.

Same old same old. Lots of email. The new posts on the blogs I read streamed in. Spam. God did I get a lot of spam. My Swedish mailbox was repeatedly joe-jobbed—used as the return address for spams sent to hundreds of millions of Internet accounts, so that all the bounces and angry messages came back to me. I didn't know who was behind it. Maybe the DHS trying to overwhelm my mailbox. Maybe it was just people pranking. The Pirate Party had pretty good filters, though, and they gave anyone who wanted it five hundred gigabytes of email storage, so I wasn't likely to be drowned any time soon.

I filtered it all out, hammering on the delete key. I had a separate mailbox for stuff that came in encrypted to my public key, since that was likely to be Xnet-related and possibly sensitive. Spammers hadn't figured out that using public keys would make their junk mail more plausible yet, so for now this worked well.

There were a couple dozen encrypted messages from people in the web of trust. I skimmed them—links to videos and pics of new abuses from the DHS, horror stories about near-escapes, rants about stuff I'd blogged. The usual.

Then I came to one that was only encrypted to my public key.

That meant that no one else could read it, but I had no idea who had written it. It said it came from Masha, which could either be a handle or a name—I couldn't tell which.

> M1k3y

> You don't know me, but I know you.

> I was arrested the day that the bridge blew. They questioned me. They decided I was innocent. They offered me a job: help them hunt down the terrorists who'd killed my neighbors.

> It sounded like a good deal at the time. Little did I realize that my actual job would turn out to be spying on kids who resented their city being turned into a police state.

> I infiltrated Xnet on the day it launched. I am in your web of trust. If I wanted to spill my identity, I could send you email from an address you'd trust. Three addresses, actually. I'm totally inside your network as only another 17-year-old can be. Some of the email you've gotten has been carefully chosen misinformation from me and my handlers.

> They don't know who you are, but they're coming close. They continue to turn people, to compromise them. They mine the social network sites and use threats to turn kids into informants. There are hundreds of people working for the DHS on Xnet right now. I have their names, handles and keys. Private and public.

> Within days of the Xnet launch, we went to work on exploiting Paranoid-Linux. The exploits so far have been small and insubstantial, but a break is inevitable. Once we have a zero-day break, you're dead.

> I think it's safe to say that if my handlers knew that I was typing this, my ass would be stuck in Gitmo-by-the-Bay until I was an old woman.

> Even if they don't break ParanoidLinux, there are poisoned ParanoidXbox distros floating around. They don't match the checksums, but how many people look at the checksums? Besides me and you? Plenty of kids are already dead, though they don't know it.

> All that remains is for my handlers to figure out the best time to bust you to make the biggest impact in the media. That time will be sooner, not later. Believe.

> You're probably wondering why I'm telling you this.

> I am too.

> Here's where I come from. I signed up to fight terrorists. Instead, I'm spy-

ing on Americans who believe things that the DHS doesn't like. Not people who plan on blowing up bridges, but protesters. I can't do it anymore.

> But neither can you, whether or not you know it. Like I say, it's only a matter of time until you're in chains on Treasure Island. That's not if, that's when.

> So I'm through here. Down in Los Angeles, there are some people. They say they can keep me safe if I want to get out.

> I want to get out.

> I will take you with me, if you want to come. Better to be a fighter than a martyr. If you come with me, we can figure out how to win together. I'm as smart as you. Believe.

> What do you say?

> Here's my public key.

> Masha

When in trouble or in doubt, run in circles, scream and shout.

Ever hear that rhyme? It's not good advice, but at least it's easy to follow. I leapt off the bed and paced back and forth. My heart thudded and my blood sang in a cruel parody of the way I'd felt when we got home. This wasn't sexual excitement, it was raw terror.

"What?" Ange said. "What?"

I pointed at the screen on my side of the bed. She rolled over and grabbed my keyboard and scribed on the touchpad with her fingertip. She read in silence.

I paced.

"This has to be lies," she said. "The DHS is playing games with your head."

I looked at her. She was biting her lip. She didn't look like she believed it.

"You think?"

"Sure. They can't beat you, so they're coming after you using Xnet."

"Yeah."

I sat back down on the bed. I was breathing fast again.

"Chill out," she said. "It's just head games. Here."

She never took my keyboard from me before, but now there was a new intimacy between us. She hit reply and typed,

234 | **cory doctorow**

> Nice try.

She was writing as M1k3y now, too. We were together in a way that was different from before.

"Go ahead and sign it. We'll see what she says."

I didn't know if that was the best idea, but I didn't have any better ones. I signed it and encrypted it with my private key and the public key Masha had provided.

The reply was instant.

> I thought you'd say something like that.

> Here's a hack you haven't thought of. I can anonymously tunnel video over DNS. Here are some links to clips you might want to look at before you decide I'm full of it. These people are all recording each other, all the time, as insurance against a back-stab. It's pretty easy to snoop on them as they snoop on each other.

> Masha

Attached was source code for a little program that appeared to do exactly what Masha claimed: pull video over the Domain Name Service protocol.

Let me back up a moment here and explain something. At the end of the day, every Internet protocol is just a sequence of text sent back and forth in a prescribed order. It's kind of like getting a truck and putting a car in it, then putting a motorcycle in the car's trunk, then attaching a bicycle to the back of the motorcycle, then hanging a pair of Rollerblades on the back of the bike. Except that then, if you want, you can attach the truck to the Rollerblades.

For example, take Simple Mail Transport Protocol, or SMTP, which is used for sending email.

Here's a sample conversation between me and my mail server, sending a message to myself:

> HELO littlebrother.com.se
250 mail.pirateparty.org.se Hello mail.pirateparty.org.se, pleased to meet you
> MAIL FROM:m1k3y@littlebrother.com.se
250 2.1.0 m1k3y@littlebrother.com.se . . . Sender ok
> RCPT TO:m1k3y@littlebrother.com.se
250 2.1.5 m1k3y@littlebrother.com.se . . . Recipient ok

```
> DATA
354 Enter mail, end with "." on a line by itself
> When in trouble or in doubt, run in circles, scream and shout
> .
250 2.0.0 k5SMW0xQ006174 Message accepted for delivery
QUIT
221 2.0.0 mail.pirateparty.org.se closing connection
Connection closed by foreign host.
```

This conversation's grammar was defined in 1982 by Jon Postel, one of the Internet's heroic forefathers, who used to literally run the most important servers on the net under his desk at the University of Southern California, back in the paleolithic era.

Now, imagine that you hooked up a mail server to an IM session. You could send an IM to the server that said "HELO littlebrother.com.se" and it would reply with "250 mail.pirateparty. org.se Hello mail.pirateparty.org.se, pleased to meet you." In other words, you could have the same conversation over IM as you do over SMTP. With the right tweaks, the whole mail server business could take place inside of a chat. Or a web session. Or anything else.

This is called "tunneling." You put the SMTP inside a chat "tunnel." You could then put the chat back into an SMTP tunnel if you wanted to be really weird, tunneling the tunnel in another tunnel.

In fact, every Internet protocol is susceptible to this process. It's cool, because it means that if you're on a network with only web access, you can tunnel your mail over it. You can tunnel your favorite P2P over it. You can even tunnel Xnet—which itself is a tunnel for dozens of protocols—over it.

Domain Name Service is an interesting and ancient Internet protocol, dating back to 1983. It's the way your computer converts a computer's name—like pirateparty.org.se—to the IP number that computers actually use to talk to each other over the net, like 204.11.50.136. It generally works like magic, even though it's got millions of moving parts—every ISP runs a DNS server, as do most governments and lots of private operators. These DNS boxes all talk to each other all the time, making and filling requests to each other so no matter how obscure the name is you feed to your computer, it will be able to turn it into a number.

Before DNS, there was the HOSTS file. Believe it or not, this was a single document that listed the name and address of *every single computer* connected to the Internet. Every computer had a copy of it. This file was eventually too big to move around, so DNS was invented, and ran on a server that used to live under Jon Postel's desk. If the cleaners knocked out the plug, the entire Internet lost its ability to find itself. Seriously.

The thing about DNS today is that it's everywhere. Every network has a DNS server living on it, and all those servers are configured to talk to each other and to random people all over the Internet.

What Masha had done was figure out a way to tunnel a video-streaming system over DNS. She was breaking up the video into billions of pieces and hiding each of them in a normal message to a DNS server. By running her code, I was able to pull the video from all those DNS servers, all over the Internet, at incredible speed. It must have looked bizarre on the network histograms, like I was looking up the address of every computer in the world.

But it had two advantages I appreciated at once: I was able to get the video with blinding speed—as soon as I clicked the first link, I started to receive full-screen pictures, without any jitter or stuttering—and I had no idea where it was hosted. It was totally anonymous.

At first I didn't even clock the content of the video. I was totally floored by the cleverness of this hack. Streaming video from DNS? That was so smart and weird, it was practically *perverted*.

Gradually, what I was seeing began to sink in.

It was a board room table in a small room with a mirror down one wall. I knew that room. I'd sat in that room, while severe haircut lady had made me speak my password aloud. There were five comfortable chairs around the table, each with a comfortable person, all in DHS uniform. I recognized Major General Graeme Sutherland, the DHS Bay Area commander, along with Severe Haircut. The others were new to me. They all watched a video screen at the end of the table, on which there was an infinitely more familiar face.

Kurt Rooney was known nationally as the president's chief strategist, the man who returned the party for its third term, and who was steaming toward a fourth. They called him "Ruthless" and I'd seen a news report once about how tight a rein he kept his staffers on, calling them, IMing them, watching their every motion, controlling every step. He was old, with a lined face and pale gray eyes and a flat nose with broad, flared nostrils and thin lips, a man who looked like he was smelling something bad all the time.

He was the man on the screen. He was talking, and everyone else was focused on his screen, everyone taking notes as fast as they could type, trying to look smart.

"—say that they're angry with authority, but we need to show the country that it's terrorists, not the government, that they need to blame. Do you understand me? The nation does not love that city. As far as they're concerned, it is a Sodom and Gomorrah of fags and atheists who deserve to rot in hell. The only reason the country cares what they think in San Francisco is that they had the good fortune to have been blown to hell by some Islamic terrorists.

"These Xnet children are getting to the point where they might start to be useful to us. The more radical they get, the more the rest of the nation understands that there are threats everywhere."

His audience finished typing.

"We can control that, I think," Severe Haircut said. "Our people in the Xnet have built up a lot of influence. The Manchurian Bloggers are running as many as fifty blogs each, flooding the chat channels, linking to each other, mostly just taking the party line set by this M1k3y. But they've already shown that they can provoke radical action, even when M1k3y is putting the brakes on."

Major General Sutherland nodded. "We have been planning to leave them underground until about a month before the midterms." I guessed that meant the midterm elections, not my exams. "That's per the original plan. But it sounds like—"

"We've got another plan for the midterms," Rooney said. "Need-to-know, of course, but you should all probably not plan on traveling for the month before. Cut the Xnet loose now, as soon as you can. So long as they're moderates, they're a liability. Keep them radical."

The video cut off.

Ange and I sat on the edge of the bed, looking at the screen. Ange reached out and started the video again. We watched it. It was worse the second time.

I tossed the keyboard aside and got up.

"I am *so sick* of being scared," I said. "Let's take this to Barbara and have her publish it all. Put it all on the net. Let them take me away. At least I'll know what's going to happen then. At least then I'll have a little *certainty* in my life."

Ange grabbed me and hugged me, soothed me. "I know baby, I know. It's all terrible. But you're focusing on the bad stuff and ignoring the good stuff. You've created a movement. You've out-flanked the jerks in the White House, the crooks in DHS uniforms. You've put yourself in a position where you could be responsible for blowing the lid off of the entire rotten DHS thing.

"Sure they're out to get you. 'Course they are. Have you ever doubted it for a moment? I always figured they were. But Marcus, *they don't know who you are*. Think about that. All those people, money, guns and spies, and you, a seventeen-year-old high school kid—you're still beating them. They don't know about Barbara. They don't know about Zeb. You've jammed them in the streets of San Francisco and humiliated them before the world. So stop mop-ing, all right? You're winning."

"They're coming for me, though. You see that. They're going to put me in jail forever. Not even jail. I'll just disappear, like Darryl. Maybe worse. Maybe Syria. Why leave me in San Francisco? I'm a liability as long as I'm in the USA."

She sat down on the bed with me.

"Yeah," she said. "That."

"That."

"Well, you know what you have to do, right?"

"What?" She looked pointedly at my keyboard. I could see the tears rolling down her cheeks. "No! You're out of your mind. You think I'm going to run off with some nut off the Internet? Some spy?"

"You got a better idea?"

I kicked a pile of her laundry into the air. "Whatever. Fine. I'll talk to her some more."

"You talk to her," Ange said. "You tell her you and your girl-friend are getting out."

"What?"

"Shut up, dickhead. You think you're in danger? I'm in just as much danger, Marcus. It's called guilt by association. When you go, I go." She had her jaw thrust out at a mutinous angle. "You and I—we're together now. You have to understand that."

We sat down on the bed together.

"Unless you don't want me," she said, finally, in a small voice.

"You're kidding me, right?"

"Do I look like I'm kidding?"

"There's no way I would voluntarily go without you, Ange. I could never have asked you to come, but I'm ecstatic that you offered."

She smiled and tossed me my keyboard.

"Email this Masha creature. Let's see what this chick can do for us."

I emailed her, encrypting the message, waiting for a reply. Ange nuzzled me a little and I kissed her and we necked. Something about the danger and the pact to go together—it made me forget the awkwardness of having sex, made me freaking horny as hell.

We were half-naked again when Masha's email arrived.

> Two of you? Jesus, like it won't be hard enough already.

> I don't get to leave except to do field intelligence after a big Xnet hit. You get me? The handlers watch my every move, but I go off the leash when something big happens with Xnetters. I get sent into the field then.

> You do something big. I get sent to it. I get us both out. All three of us, if you insist.

> Make it fast, though. I can't send you a lot of email, understand? They watch me. They're closing in on you. You don't have a lot of time. Weeks? Maybe just days.

> I need you to get me out. That's why I'm doing this, in case you're wondering. I can't escape on my own. I need a big Xnet distraction. That's your department. Don't fail me, M1k3y, or we're both dead. Your girlie too.

> Masha

My phone rang, making us both jump. It was my mom wanting to know when I was coming home. I told her I was on my way. She didn't mention Barbara. We'd agreed that we wouldn't talk about any of this stuff on the phone. That was my dad's idea. He could be as paranoid as me.

"I have to go," I said.

"Our parents will be—"

"I know," I said. "I saw what happened to my parents when they thought I was dead. Knowing that I'm a fugitive isn't going to be much better. But they'd rather I be a fugitive than a prisoner. That's what I think. Anyway, once we disappear, Barbara can publish without worrying about getting us into trouble."

We kissed at the door of her room. Not one of the hot, sloppy numbers we usually did when parting ways. A sweet kiss this time. A slow kiss. A good-bye kind of kiss.

BART rides are introspective. When the train rocks back and forth and you try not to make eye contact with the other riders and you try not to read the ads for plastic surgery, bail bondsmen and AIDS testing, when you try to ignore the graffiti and not look too closely at the stuff in the carpeting. That's when your mind starts to really churn and churn.

You rock back and forth and your mind goes over all the things you've overlooked, plays back all the movies of your life where you're no hero, where you're a chump or a sucker.

Your brain comes up with theories like this one:

If the DHS wanted to catch M1k3y, what better way than to lure him into the open, panic him into leading some kind of big, public Xnet event? Wouldn't that be worth the chance of a compromising video leaking?

Your brain comes up with stuff like that even when the train ride only lasts two or three stops. When you get off, and you start moving, the blood gets running and sometimes your brain helps you out again.

Sometimes your brain gives you solutions in addition to problems.

chapter 18

There was a time when my favorite thing in the world was putting on a cape and hanging out in hotels, pretending to be an invisible vampire whom everyone stared at.

It's complicated, and not nearly as weird as it sounds. The Live Action Role Playing scene combines the best aspects of D&D with drama club with going to sci-fi cons.

I understand that this might not make it sound as appealing to you as it was to me when I was fourteen.

The best games were the ones at the scout camps out of town: a hundred teenagers, boys and girls, fighting the Friday night traffic, swapping stories, playing handheld games, showing off for hours. Then debarking to stand in the grass before a group of older men and women in badass, homemade armor, dented and scarred, like armor must have been in the old days, not like it's portrayed in the movies, but like a soldier's uniform after a month in the bush.

These people were nominally paid to run the games, but you didn't get the job unless you were the kind of person who'd do it for free. They'd have already divided us into teams based on the questionnaires we'd filled in beforehand, and we'd get our team assignments then, like being called up for baseball sides.

Then you'd get your briefing packages. These were like the briefings the spies get in the movies: here's your identity, here's your mission, here's the secrets you know about the group.

From there, it was time for dinner: roaring fires, meat popping on spits, tofu sizzling on skillets (it's northern California, a vegetarian option is not optional), and a style of eating and drinking that can only be described as quaffing.

Already, the keen kids would be getting into character. My first game, I was a wizard. I had a bag of beanbags that represented spells—when I threw one, I would shout the name of the spell I was casting—fireball, magic missile, cone of light—and the player or "monster" I threw it at would keel over if I connected. Or not—sometimes we had to call in a ref to mediate, but for the most part, we were all pretty good about playing fair. No one liked a dice lawyer.

By bedtime, we were all in character. At fourteen, I wasn't super-sure what a wizard was supposed to sound like, but I could take my cues from the movies and novels. I spoke in slow, measured tones, keeping my face composed in a suitably mystical expression, and thinking mystical thoughts.

The mission was complicated, retrieving a sacred relic that had been stolen by an ogre who was bent on subjugating the people of the land to his will. It didn't really matter a whole lot. What mattered was that I had a private mission, to capture a certain kind of imp to serve as my familiar, and that I had a secret nemesis, another player on the team who had taken part in a raid that killed my family when I was a boy, a player who didn't know that I'd come back, bent on revenge. Somewhere, of course, there was another player with a similar grudge against me, so that even as I was enjoying the camaraderie of the team, I'd always have to keep an eye open for a knife in the back, poison in the food.

For the next two days, we played it out. There were parts of the weekend that were like hide-and-seek, some that were like wilderness survival exercises, some that were like solving crossword puzzles. The game masters had done a great job. And you really got to be friends with the other people on the mission. Darryl was the target of my first murder, and I put my back into it, even though he was my pal. Nice guy. Shame I'd have to kill him.

I fireballed him as he was seeking out treasure after we wiped out a band of orcs, playing rock-paper-scissors with each orc to determine who would prevail in combat. This is a lot more exciting than it sounds.

It was like summer camp for drama geeks. We talked until late at night in tents, looked at the stars, jumped in the river when we got hot, slapped away mosquitos. Became best friends, or lifelong enemies.

I don't know why Charles's parents sent him LARPing. He wasn't the kind of kid who really enjoyed that kind of thing. He was more the pulling-wings-off-flies type. Oh, maybe not. But he just was not into being in costume in the woods. He spent the whole time mooching around, sneering at everyone and everything, trying to convince us all that we weren't having the good time we all felt like we were having. You've no doubt found that kind of person before, the kind of person who is compelled to ensure that everyone else has a rotten time.

The other thing about Charles was that he couldn't get the hang of simulated combat. Once you start running around the woods and playing these elaborate, semimilitary games, it's easy to get totally adrenalized to the point where you're ready to tear out someone's throat. This is not a good state to be in when you're carrying a prop sword, club, pike or other utensil. This is why no one is ever allowed to hit anyone, under any circumstances, in these games. Instead, when you get close enough to someone to fight, you play a quick couple rounds of rock-paper-scissors, with modifiers based on your experience, armaments and condition. The referees mediate disputes. It's quite civilized, and a little weird. You go running after someone through the woods, catch up with him, bare your teeth, and sit down to play a little roshambo. But it works—and it keeps everything safe and fun.

Charles couldn't really get the hang of this. I think he was perfectly capable of understanding that the rule was no contact, but he was simultaneously capable of deciding that the rule didn't matter, and that he wasn't going to abide by it. The refs called him on it a bunch of times over the weekend, and he kept on promising to stick by it, and kept on going back. He was one of the bigger kids there already, and he was fond of "accidentally" tackling you at the end of a chase. Not fun when you get tackled into the rocky forest floor.

I had just mightily smote Darryl in a little clearing where he'd been treasure-hunting, and we were having a little laugh over my extreme sneakiness. He was going to go monstering—killed players could switch to playing monsters, which meant that the longer the game wore on, the more monsters there were coming after you, meaning that everyone got to keep on playing and the game's battles just got more and more epic.

That was when Charles came out of the woods behind me and

tackled me, throwing me to the ground so hard that I couldn't breathe for a moment. "Gotcha!" he yelled. I only knew him slightly before this, and I'd never thought much of him, but now I was ready for murder. I climbed slowly to my feet and looked at him, his chest heaving, grinning. "You're so dead," he said. "I totally got you."

I smiled and something felt wrong and sore in my face. I touched my upper lip. It was bloody. My nose was bleeding and my lip was split, cut on a root I'd face-planted into when he tackled me.

I wiped the blood on my pants leg and smiled. I made like I thought that it was all in fun. I laughed a little. I moved toward him.

Charles wasn't fooled. He was already backing away, trying to fade into the woods. Darryl moved to flank him. I took the other flank. Abruptly, he turned and ran. Darryl's foot hooked his ankle and sent him sprawling. We rushed him, just in time to hear a ref's whistle.

The ref hadn't seen Charles foul me, but he'd seen Charles's play that weekend. He sent Charles back to the camp entrance and told him he was out of the game. Charles complained mightily, but to our satisfaction, the ref wasn't having any of it. Once Charles had gone, he gave *us* both a lecture, too, telling us that our retaliation was no more justified than Charles's attack.

It was okay. That night, once the games had ended, we all got hot showers in the scout dorms. Darryl and I stole Charles's clothes and towel. We tied them in knots and dropped them in the urinal. A lot of the boys were happy to contribute to the effort of soaking them. Charles had been very enthusiastic about his tackles.

I wish I could have watched him when he got out of his shower and discovered his clothes. It's a hard decision: do you run naked across the camp, or pick apart the tight, piss-soaked knots in your clothes and then put them on?

He chose nudity. I probably would have chosen the same. We lined up along the route from the showers to the shed where the packs were stored and applauded him. I was at the front of the line, leading the applause.

The Scout Camp weekends only came three or four times a year, which left Darryl and me—and lots of other LARPers—with a serious LARP deficiency in our lives.

Luckily, there were the Wretched Daylight games in the city hotels. Wretched Daylight is another LARP, rival vampire clans and vampire hunters, and it's got its own quirky rules. Players get cards to help them resolve combat skirmishes, so each skirmish involves playing a little hand of a strategic card game. Vampires can become invisible by cloaking themselves, crossing their arms over their chests, and all the other players have to pretend they don't see them, continuing with their conversations about their plans and so on. The true test of a good player is whether you're honest enough to go on spilling your secrets in front of an "invisible" rival without acting as though he was in the room.

There were a couple of big Wretched Daylight games every month. The organizers of the games had a good relationship with the city's hotels and they let it be known that they'd take ten unbooked rooms on Friday night and fill them with players who'd run around the hotel, playing low-key Wretched Daylight in the corridors, around the pool, and so on, eating at the hotel restaurant and paying for the hotel WiFi. They'd close the booking on Friday afternoon, email us, and we'd go straight from school to whichever hotel it was, bringing our knapsacks, sleeping six or eight to a room for the weekend, living on junk food, playing until 3 A.M. It was good, safe fun that our parents could get behind.

The organizers were a well known literacy charity that ran kids' writing workshops, drama workshops and so on. They had been running the games for ten years without incident. Everything was strictly booze and drug free, to keep the organizers from getting busted on some kind of corruption of minors rap. We'd draw between ten and a hundred players, depending on the weekend, and for the cost of a couple movies, you could have two and a half days' worth of solid fun.

One day, though, they lucked into a block of rooms at the Monaco, a hotel in the Tenderloin that catered to arty older tourists, the kind of place where every room came with a goldfish bowl, where the lobby was full of beautiful old people in fine clothes, showing off their plastic surgery results.

Normally, the mundanes—our word for nonplayers—just ignored us, figuring that we were skylarking kids. But that weekend there happened to be an editor for an Italian travel magazine stay-ing, and he took an interest in things. He cornered me as I skulked in the lobby, hoping to spot the clan-master of my rivals and swoop in on him and draw his blood. I was standing against the wall with my arms folded over my chest, being invisible, when he came up to me and asked me, in accented English, what me and my friends were doing in the hotel that weekend?

I tried to brush him off, but he wouldn't be put off. So I figured I'd just make something up and he'd go away.

I didn't imagine that he'd print it. I really didn't imagine that it would get picked up by the American press.

"We're here because our prince has died, and so we've had to come in search of a new ruler."

"A prince?"

"Yes," I said, getting into it. "We're the Old People. We came to America in the 16th century and have had our own royal family in the wilds of Pennsylvania ever since. We live simply in the woods. We don't use modern technology. But the prince was the last of the line and he died last week. Some terrible wasting disease took him. The young men of my clan have left to find the descendants of his great-uncle, who went away to join the modern people in the time of my grandfather. He is said to have multiplied, and we will find the last of his bloodline and bring them back to their rightful home."

I read a lot of fantasy novels. This kind of thing came easily to me.

"We found a woman who knew of these descendants. She told us one was staying in this hotel, and we've come to find him. But we've been tracked here by a rival clan who would keep us from bringing home our prince, to keep us weak and easy to dominate. Thus it is vital we keep to ourselves. We do not talk to the New People when we can help it. Talking to you now causes me great discomfort."

He was watching me shrewdly. I had uncrossed my arms, which meant that I was now "visible" to rival vampires, one of whom had been slowly sneaking up on us. At the last moment, I turned and saw her, arms spread, hissing at us, vamping it up in high style.

I threw my arms wide and hissed back at her, then pelted

through the lobby, hopping over a leather sofa and deking around a potted plant, making her chase me. I'd scouted an escape route down through the stairwell to the basement health club and I took it, shaking her off.

I didn't see him again that weekend, but I *did* relate the story to some of my fellow LARPers, who embroidered the tale and found lots of opportunities to tell it over the weekend.

The Italian magazine had a staffer who'd done her master's degree on Amish antitechnology communities in rural Pennsylvania, and she thought we sounded awfully interesting. Based on the notes and taped interviews of her boss from his trip to San Francisco, she wrote a fascinating, heart-wrenching article about these weird, juvenile cultists who were crisscrossing America in search of their "prince." Hell, people will print anything these days.

But the thing was, stories like that get picked up and republished. First it was Italian bloggers, then a few American bloggers. People across the country reported "sightings" of the Old People, though whether they were making it up, or whether others were playing the same game, I didn't know.

It worked its way up the media food chain all the way to the *New York Times,* who, unfortunately, have an unhealthy appetite for fact-checking. The reporter they put on the story eventually tracked it down to the Monaco Hotel, who put them in touch with the LARP organizers, who laughingly spilled the whole story.

Well, at that point, LARPing got a lot less cool. We became known as the nation's foremost hoaxers, as weird, pathological liars. The press who we'd inadvertently tricked into covering the story of the Old People were now interested in redeeming themselves by reporting on how unbelievably weird we LARPers were, and that was when Charles let everyone in school know that Darryl and I were the biggest LARPing weenies in the city.

That was not a good season. Some of the gang didn't mind, but we did. The teasing was merciless. Charles led it. I'd find plastic fangs in my bag, and kids I passed in the hall would go "bleh, bleh" like a cartoon vampire, or they'd talk with fake Transylvanian accents when I was around.

We switched to ARGing pretty soon afterward. It was more fun in some ways, and it was a lot less weird. Every now and again, though, I missed my cape and those weekends in the hotel.

The opposite of *esprit d'escalier* is the way that life's embarrassments come back to haunt us even after they're long past. I could remember every stupid thing I'd ever said or done, recall them with picture-perfect clarity. Any time I was feeling low, I'd naturally start to remember other times I felt that way, a hit parade of humiliations coming one after another to my mind.

As I tried to concentrate on Masha and my impending doom, the Old People incident kept coming back to haunt me. There'd been a similar, sick, sinking doomed feeling then, as more and more press outlets picked up the story, as the likelihood increased of someone figuring out that it had been me who'd sprung the story on the stupid Italian editor in the designer jeans with crooked seams, the starched collarless shirt and the oversized metal-rimmed glasses.

There's an alternative to dwelling on your mistakes. You can learn from them.

It's a good theory, anyway. Maybe the reason your subconscious dredges up all these miserable ghosts is that they need to get closure before they can rest peacefully in humiliation afterlife. My subconscious kept visiting me with ghosts in the hopes that I would do something to let them rest in peace.

All the way home, I turned over this memory and the thought of what I would do about "Masha," in case she was playing me. I needed some insurance.

And by the time I reached my house—to be swept up into melancholy hugs from Mom and Dad—I had it.

The trick was to time this so that it happened fast enough that the DHS couldn't prepare for it, but with a long enough lead time that the Xnet would have time to turn out in force.

The trick was to stage this so that there were too many present to arrest us all, but to put it somewhere that the press could see it and the grown-ups, so the DHS wouldn't just gas us again.

The trick was to come up with something with the media friendliness of the levitation of the Pentagon. The trick was to stage something that we could rally around, like three thousand Berkeley students refusing to let one of their number be taken away in a police van.

The trick was to put the press there, ready to say what the police did, the way they had in 1968 in Chicago.

It was going to be some trick.

I cut out of school an hour early the next day, using my customary techniques for getting out, not caring if it would trigger some kind of new DHS checker that would result in my parents getting a note.

One way or another, my parents' last problem after tomorrow would be whether I was in trouble at school.

I met Ange at her place. She'd had to cut out of school even earlier, but she'd just made a big deal out of her cramps and pretended she was going to keel over and they sent her home.

We started to spread the word on Xnet. We sent it in email to trusted friends, and IMed it to our buddy lists. We roamed the decks and towns of Clockwork Plunder and told our teammates. Giving everyone enough information to get them to show up but not so much as to tip our hand to the DHS was tricky, but I thought I had just the right balance:

> VAMPMOB TOMORROW

> If you're a goth, dress to impress. If you're not a goth, find a goth and borrow some clothes. Think vampire.

> The game starts at 8:00AM sharp. SHARP. Be there and ready to be divided into teams. The game lasts 30 minutes, so you'll have plenty of time to get to school afterward.

> Location will be revealed tomorrow. Email your public key to m1k3y@littlebrother.pirateparty.org.se and check your messages at 7AM for the update. If that's too early for you, stay up all night. That's what we're going to do.

> This is the most fun you will have all year, guaranteed.

> Believe.

> M1k3y

Then I sent a short message to Masha.

> Tomorrow

> M1k3y

A minute later, she emailed back:

> I thought so. VampMob, huh? You work fast. Wear a red hat. Travel light.

What do you bring along when you go fugitive? I'd carried enough heavy packs around enough scout camps to know that every ounce you add cuts into your shoulders with all the crushing force of gravity with every step you take—it's not just one ounce, it's one ounce that you carry for a million steps. It's a ton.

"Right," Ange said. "Smart. And you never take more than three days' worth of clothes, either. You can rinse stuff out in the sink. Better to have a spot on your T-shirt than a suitcase that's too big and heavy to stash under a plane seat."

She'd pulled out a ballistic nylon courier bag that went across her chest, between her breasts—something that made me get a little sweaty—and slung diagonally across her back. It was roomy inside, and she'd set it down on the bed. Now she was piling clothes next to it.

"I figure that three T-shirts, a pair of pants, a pair of shorts, three changes of underwear, three pairs of socks and a sweater will do it."

She dumped out her gym bag and picked out her toiletries. "I'll have to remember to stick my toothbrush in tomorrow morning before I head down to Civic Center."

Watching her pack was impressive. She was ruthless about it all. It was also freaky—it made me realize that the next day, I was going to go away. Maybe for a long time. Maybe forever.

"Do I bring my Xbox?" she asked. "I've got a ton of stuff on the hard drive, notes and sketches and email. I wouldn't want it to fall into the wrong hands."

"It's all encrypted," I said. "That's standard with ParanoidXbox. But leave the Xbox behind, there'll be plenty of them in LA. Just create a Pirate Party account and email an image of your hard drive to yourself. I'm going to do the same when I get home."

She did so, and queued up the email. It was going to take a couple hours for all the data to squeeze through her neighbor's WiFi network and wing its way to Sweden.

Then she closed the flap on the bag and tightened the compression straps. She had something the size of a soccer ball slung over her back now, and I stared admiringly at it. She could walk down the street with that under her shoulder and no one would look twice—she looked like she was on her way to school.

"One more thing," she said, and went to her bedside table and took out the condoms. She took the strips of rubbers out of the box and opened the bag and stuck them inside, then gave me a slap on the ass.

"Now what?" I said.

"Now we go to your place and do your stuff. It's time I met your parents, no?"

She left the bag amid the piles of clothes and junk all over the floor. She was ready to turn her back on all of it, walk away, just to be with me. Just to support the cause. It made me feel brave, too.

Mom was already home when I got there. She had her laptop open on the kitchen table and was answering email while talking into a headset connected to it, helping some poor Yorkshireman and his family acclimate to living in Louisiana.

I came through the door and Ange followed, grinning like mad, but holding my hand so tight I could feel the bones grinding together. I didn't know what she was so worried about. It wasn't like she was going to end up spending a lot of time hanging around with my parents after this, even if it went badly.

Mom hung up on the Yorkshireman when we got in.

"Hello, Marcus," she said, giving me a kiss on the cheek. "And who is this?"

"Mom, meet Ange. Ange, this is my mom, Louisa." Mom stood up and gave Ange a hug.

"It's very good to meet you, darling," she said, looking her over from top to bottom. Ange looked pretty acceptable, I think. She dressed well, and low-key, and you could tell how smart she was just by looking at her.

"A pleasure to meet you, Mrs. Yallow," she said. She sounded very confident and self-assured. Much better than I had when I'd met her mom.

"It's Lillian, love," she said. She was taking in every detail. "Are you staying for dinner?"

"I'd love that," she said.

"Do you eat meat?" Mom's pretty acclimated to living in California.

"I eat anything that doesn't eat me first," she said.

"She's a hot sauce junkie," I said. "You could serve her old tires and she'd eat 'em if she could smother them in salsa."

Ange socked me gently in the shoulder.

"I was going to order Thai," Mom said. "I'll add a couple of their five-chili dishes to the order."

Ange thanked her politely and Mom bustled around the kitchen, getting us glasses of juice and a plate of biscuits and asking three times if we wanted any tea. I squirmed a little.

"Thanks, Mom," I said. "We're going to go upstairs for a while."

Mom's eyes narrowed for a second, then she smiled again. "Of course," she said. "Your father will be home in an hour, we'll eat then."

I had my vampire stuff all stashed in the back of my closet. I let Ange sort through it while I went through my clothes. I was only going as far as LA. They had stores there, all the clothing I could need. I just needed to get together three or four favorite tees and a favorite pair of jeans, a tube of deodorant, a roll of dental floss.

"Money!" I said.

"Yeah," she said. "I was going to clean out my bank account on the way home at an ATM. I've got maybe fifteen hundred saved up."

"Really?"

"What am I going to spend it on?" she said. "Ever since the Xnet, I haven't had to even pay any service charges."

"I think I've got three hundred or so."

"Well, there you go. Grab it on the way to Civic Center in the morning."

I had a big book bag I used when I was hauling lots of gear around town. It was less conspicuous than my camping pack. Ange went through my piles mercilessly and culled them down to her favorites.

Once it was packed and under my bed, we both sat down.

"We're going to have to get up really early tomorrow," she said.

"Yeah, big day."

The plan was to get messages out with a bunch of fake Vamp-

Mob locations tomorrow, sending people out to secluded spots within a few minutes' walk of Civic Center. We'd cut out a spray-paint stencil that just said VAMPMOB CIVIC CENTER → → that we would spray-paint at those spots around 5 A.M. That would keep the DHS from locking down Civic Center before we got there. I had the mailbot ready to send out the messages at 7 A.M.—I'd just leave my Xbox running when I went out.

"How long . . ." She trailed off.

"That's what I've been wondering, too," I said. "It could be a long time, I suppose. But who knows? With Barbara's article coming out"—I'd queued an email to her for the next morning, too—"and all, maybe we'll be heroes in two weeks."

"Maybe," she said, and sighed.

I put my arm around her. Her shoulders were shaking.

"I'm terrified," I said. "I think that it would be crazy not to be terrified."

"Yeah," she said. "Yeah."

Mom called us to dinner. Dad shook Ange's hand. He looked unshaved and worried, the way he had since we'd gone to see Barbara, but on meeting Ange, a little of the old Dad came back. She kissed him on the cheek and he insisted that she call him Drew.

Dinner was actually really good. The ice broke when Ange took out her hot sauce mister and treated her plate, and explained about Scoville units. Dad tried a forkful of her food and went reeling into the kitchen to drink a gallon of milk. Believe it or not, Mom still tried it after that and gave every impression of loving it. Mom, it turned out, was an undiscovered spicy food prodigy, a natural.

Before she left, Ange pressed the hot sauce mister on Mom. "I have a spare at home," she said. I'd watched her pack it in her backpack. "You seem like the kind of woman who should have one of these."

chapter 19

Here's the email that went out at 7 A.M. the next day, while Ange and I were spray-painting VAMPMOB CIVIC CENTER → → at strategic locations around town.

> RULES FOR VAMPMOB

> You are part of a clan of daylight vampires. You've discovered the secret of surviving the terrible light of the sun. The secret was cannibalism: the blood of another vampire can give you the strength to walk among the living.

> You need to bite as many other vampires as you can in order to stay in the game. If one minute goes by without a bite, you're out. Once you're out, turn your shirt around backwards and go referee—watch two or three vamps to see if they're getting their bites in.

> To bite another vamp, you have to say "Bite!" five times before they do. So you run up to a vamp, make eye-contact and shout "bite bite bite bite bite!" and if you get it out before she does, you live and she crumbles to dust.

> You and the other vamps you meet at your rendezvous are a team. They are your clan. You derive no nourishment from their blood.

> You can "go invisible" by standing still and folding your arms over your chest. You can't bite invisible vamps, and they can't bite you.

> This game is played on the honor system. The point is to have fun and get your vamp on, not to win.

> There is an end-game that will be passed by word of mouth as winners begin to emerge. The game-masters will start a whisper campaign among the players when the time comes. Spread the whisper as quickly as you can and watch for the sign.

> M1k3y

> bite bite bite bite bite!

We'd hoped that a hundred people would be willing to play VampMob. We'd sent out about two hundred invites each. But when I sat bolt upright at 4 A.M. and grabbed my Xbox, there were four hundred replies there. Four *hundred*.

I fed the addresses to the bot and stole out of the house. I descended the stairs, listening to my father snore and my mom rolling over in their bed. I locked the door behind me.

At 4:15 A.M., Potrero Hill was as quiet as the countryside. There were some distant traffic rumbles, and once a car crawled past me. I stopped at an ATM and drew out $320 in twenties, rolled them up and put a rubber band around them, and stuck the roll in a zip-up pocket low on the thigh of my vampire pants.

I was wearing my cape again, and a ruffled shirt, and tuxedo pants that had been modded to have enough pockets to carry all my little bits and pieces. I had on pointed boots with silver-skull buckles, and I'd teased my hair into a black dandelion clock around my head. Ange was bringing the white makeup and had promised to do my eyeliner and black nail polish. Why the hell not? When was the next time I was going to get to play dress-up like this?

Ange met me in front of her house. She had her backpack on, too, and fishnet tights, a ruffled gothic lolita maid's dress, white face-paint, elaborate kabuki eye makeup, and her fingers and throat dripped with silver jewelry.

"You look *great!*" we said to each other in unison, then laughed quietly and stole off through the streets, spray-paint cans in our pockets.

As I surveyed Civic Center, I thought about what it would look like once four hundred VampMobbers converged on it. I expected them in ten minutes, out front of City Hall. Already the big plaza teemed with commuters who neatly sidestepped the homeless people begging there.

I've always hated Civic Center. It's a collection of huge wedding cake buildings: courthouses, museums and civic buildings like City Hall. The sidewalks are wide, the buildings are white. In the tourist guides to San Francisco, they manage to photograph it so that it looks like Epcot Center, futuristic and austere.

But on the ground, it's grimy and gross. Homeless people sleep on all the benches. The district is empty by 6 P.M. except for drunks and druggies, because with only one kind of building there, there's no legit reason for people to hang around after the sun goes down. It's more like a mall than a neighborhood, and the only businesses there are bail bondsmen and liquor stores, places that cater to the families of crooks on trial and the bums who make it their night-time home.

I really came to understand all this when I read an interview with an amazing old urban planner, a woman called Jane Jacobs who was the first person to really nail why it was wrong to slice cities up with freeways, stick all the poor people in housing proj-ects and use zoning laws to tightly control who got to do what where.

Jacobs explained that real cities are organic and they have a lot of variety—rich and poor, white and brown, Anglo and Mex, re-tail and residential and even industrial. A neighborhood like that has all kinds of people passing through it at all hours of the day or night, so you get businesses that cater to every need, you get people around all the time, acting like eyes on the street.

You've encountered this before. You go walking around some older part of some city and you find that it's full of the coolest looking stores, guys in suits and people in fashion-rags, upscale restaurants and funky cafes, a little movie theater maybe, houses with elaborate paint jobs. Sure, there might be a Starbucks, too, but there's also a neat-looking fruit market and a florist who ap-pears to be three hundred years old as she snips carefully at the flowers in her windows. It's the opposite of a planned space, like a mall. It feels like a wild garden or even a woods: like it *grew*.

You couldn't get any further from that than Civic Center. I read an interview with Jacobs where she talked about the great old neighborhood they knocked down to build it. It had been just that kind of neighborhood, the kind of place that happened without permission or rhyme or reason.

Jacobs said that she predicted that within a few years, Civic Center would be one of the worst neighborhoods in the city, a ghost town at night, a place that sustained a thin crop of weedy booze shops and flea-pit motels. In the interview, she didn't seem very glad to have been vindicated; she sounded like she was talking about a dead friend when she described what Civic Center had become.

Now it was rush hour and Civic Center was as busy at it could be. The Civic Center BART also serves as the major station for Muni trolley lines, and if you need to switch from one to another, that's where you do it. At 8 A.M. there were thousands of people coming up the stairs, going down the stairs, getting into and out of taxis and on and off buses. They got squeezed by DHS checkpoints by the different civic buildings, and routed around aggressive panhandlers. They all smelled like their shampoos and colognes, fresh out of the shower and armored in their work suits, swinging laptop bags and briefcases. At 8 A.M., Civic Center was business central.

And here came the vamps. A couple dozen coming down Van Ness, a couple dozen coming up Market. More coming from the other side of Market. More coming up from Van Ness. They slipped around the sides of the buildings, wearing the white face-paint and the black eyeliner, black clothes, leather jackets, huge stompy boots. Fishnet fingerless gloves.

They began to fill up the plaza. A few of the business people gave them passing glances and then looked away, not wanting to let these weirdos into their personal realities as they thought about whatever crap they were about to wade through for another eight hours. The vamps milled around, not sure when the game was on. They pooled together in large groups, like an oil spill in reverse, all this black gathering in one place. A lot of them sported old-timey hats, bowlers and toppers. Many of the girls were in full-on elegant gothic lolita maid costumes with huge platforms.

I tried to estimate the numbers. Two hundred. Then, five minutes later, it was three hundred. Four hundred. They were still streaming in. The vamps had brought friends.

Someone grabbed my ass. I spun around and saw Ange, laughing so hard she had to hold her thighs, bent double.

"Look at them all, man, look at them all!" she gasped. The square was twice as crowded as it had been a few minutes ago. I had no idea how many Xnetters there were, but easily a thousand of them had just showed up to my little party. Christ.

The DHS and SFPD cops were starting to mill around, talking into their radios and clustering together. I heard a faraway siren.

"All right," I said, shaking Ange by the arm. "All right, let's *go*."

We both slipped off into the crowd and as soon as we encountered our first vamp, we both said, loudly, "Bite bite bite bite bite!" My victim was a stunned—but cute—girl with spiderwebs drawn on her hands and smudged mascara running down her cheeks. She said, "Crap," and moved away, acknowledging that I'd gotten her.

The call of "bite bite bite bite bite" had scrambled the other nearby vamps. Some of them were attacking each other, others were moving for cover, hiding out. I had my victim for the minute, so I skulked away, using mundanes for cover. All around me, the cry of "bite bite bite bite bite!" and shouts and laughs and curses.

The sound spread like a virus through the crowd. All the vamps knew the game was on now, and the ones who were clustered together were dropping like flies. They laughed and cussed and moved away, clueing the still-in vamps that the game was on. And more vamps were arriving by the second.

8:16. It was time to bag another vamp. I crouched low and moved through the legs of the straights as they headed for the BART stairs. They jerked back with surprise and swerved to avoid me. I had my eyes laser-locked on a set of black platform boots with steel dragons over the toes, and so I wasn't expecting it when I came face to face with another vamp, a guy of about fifteen or sixteen, hair gelled straight back and wearing a PVC Marilyn Manson jacket draped with necklaces of fake tusks carved with intricate symbols.

"Bite bite bite—" he began, when one of the mundanes tripped over him and they both went sprawling. I leapt over to him and shouted "Bite bite bite bite bite!" before he could untangle himself again.

More vamps were arriving. The suits were really freaking out. The game overflowed the sidewalk and moved into Van Ness, spreading up toward Market Street. Drivers honked, the trolleys made angry *dings*. I heard more sirens, but now traffic was snarled in every direction.

It was freaking *glorious*.

BITE BITE BITE BITE BITE!

The sound came from all around me. There were so many vamps there, playing so furiously, it was like a roar. I risked standing up and looking around and found that I was right in the middle of a giant crowd of vamps that went as far as I could see in every direction.

BITE BITE BITE BITE BITE!

This was even better than the concert in Dolores Park. That had been angry and rockin', but this was—well, it was just *fun*. It was like going back to the playground, to the epic games of tag we'd play on lunch breaks when the sun was out, hundreds of people chasing each other around. The adults and the cars just made it more fun, more funny.

That's what it was: it was *funny*. We were all laughing now.

But the cops were really mobilizing now. I heard helicopters. Any second now, it would be over. Time for the endgame.

I grabbed a vamp.

"Endgame: when the cops order us to disperse, pretend you've been gassed. Pass it on. What did I just say?"

The vamp was a girl, tiny, so short I thought she was really young, but she must have been seventeen or eighteen from her face and the smile. "Oh, that's wicked," she said.

"What did I say?"

"Endgame: when the cops order us to disperse, pretend you've been gassed. Pass it on. What did I just say?"

"Right," I said. "Pass it on."

She melted into the crowd. I grabbed another vamp. I passed it on. He went off to pass it on.

Somewhere in the crowd, I knew Ange was doing this, too. Somewhere in the crowd, there might be infiltrators, fake Xnetters, but what could they do with this knowledge? It's not like the cops had a choice. They were going to order us to disperse. That was guaranteed.

I had to get to Ange. The plan was to meet at the Founders' Statue in the Plaza, but reaching it was going to be hard. The crowd wasn't moving anymore, it was *surging,* like the mob had in the way down to the BART station on the day the bombs went off. I struggled to make my way through it just as the PA underneath the helicopter switched on.

"THIS IS THE DEPARTMENT OF HOMELAND SECURITY. YOU ARE ORDERED TO DISPERSE IMMEDIATELY."

Around me, hundreds of vamps fell to the ground, clutching their throats, clawing at their eyes, gasping for breath. It was easy to fake being gassed, we'd all had plenty of time to study the footage of the partiers in Mission Dolores Park going down under the pepper spray clouds.

"DISPERSE IMMEDIATELY."

I fell to the ground, protecting my pack, reaching around to the red baseball hat folded into the waistband of my pants. I jammed it on my head and then grabbed my throat and made horrendous retching noises.

The only ones still standing were the mundanes, the salarymen who'd been just trying to get to their jobs. I looked around as best as I could at them as I choked and gasped.

"THIS IS THE DEPARTMENT OF HOMELAND SECURITY. YOU ARE ORDERED TO DISPERSE IMMEDIATELY. DISPERSE IMMEDIATELY." The voice of God made my bowels ache. I felt it in my molars and in my femurs and my spine.

The salarymen were scared. They were moving as fast as they could, but in no particular direction. The helicopters seemed to be directly overhead no matter where you stood. The cops were wading into the crowd now, and they'd put on their helmets. Some had shields. Some had gas masks. I gasped harder.

Then the salarymen were running. I probably would have run, too. I watched a guy whip a $500 jacket off and wrap it around his face before heading south toward Mission, only to trip and go sprawling. His curses joined the choking sounds.

This wasn't supposed to happen—the choking was just supposed to freak people out and get them confused, not panic them into a stampede.

There were screams now, screams I recognized all too well from the night in the park. That was the sound of people who were scared spitless, running into each other as they tried like hell to get away.

And then the air raid sirens began.

I hadn't heard that sound since the bombs went off, but I would never forget it. It sliced through me and went straight into my balls, turning my legs into jelly on the way. It made me want to run away in a panic. I got to my feet, red cap on my head, thinking of only one thing: Ange. Ange and the Founders' Statue.

Everyone was on their feet now, running in all directions, screaming. I pushed people out of my way, holding onto my pack and my hat, heading for Founders' Statue. Masha was looking for me, I was looking for Ange. Ange was out there.

I pushed and cursed. Elbowed someone. Someone came down on my foot so hard I felt something go *crunch* and I shoved him so he went down. He tried to get up and someone stepped on him. I shoved and pushed.

Then I reached out my arm to shove someone else and strong hands grabbed my wrist and my elbow in one fluid motion and brought my arm back around behind my back. It felt like my shoulder was about to wrench out of its socket, and I instantly doubled over, hollering, a sound that was barely audible over the din of the crowd, the thrum of the choppers, the wail of the sirens.

I was brought back upright by the strong hands behind me, which steered me like a marionette. The hold was so perfect I couldn't even think of squirming. I couldn't think of the noise or the helicopter or Ange. All I could think of was moving the way that the person who had me wanted me to move. I was brought around so that I was face to face with the person.

It was a girl whose face was sharp and rodentlike, half-hidden by a giant pair of sunglasses. Over the sunglasses, a mop of bright pink hair spiked out in all directions.

"You!" I said. I knew her. She'd taken a picture of me and threatened to rat me out to truant watch. That had been five minutes before the alarms started. She'd been the one, ruthless and cunning. We'd both run from that spot in the Tenderloin as the klaxon sounded behind us, and we'd both been picked up by the cops. I'd been hostile and they'd decided that I was an enemy.

She—Masha—became their ally.

"Hello, M1k3y," she hissed in my ear, close as a lover. A shiver went up my back. She let go of my arm and I shook it out.

"Christ," I said. "You!"

"Yes, me," she said. "The gas is gonna come down in about two minutes. Let's haul ass."

"Ange—my girlfriend—is by the Founders' Statue."

Masha looked over the crowd. "No chance," she said. "We try to make it there, we're doomed. The gas is coming down in two minutes, in case you missed it the first time."

I stopped moving. "I don't go without Ange," I said.

She shrugged. "Suit yourself," she shouted in my ear. "Your funeral."

She began to push through the crowd, moving away, north, toward downtown. I continued to push for the Founders' Statue. A second later, my arm was back in the terrible lock and I was being swung around and propelled forward.

"You know too much, jerk-off," she said. "You've seen my face. You're coming with me."

I screamed at her, struggled till it felt like my arm would break, but she was pushing me forward. My sore foot was agony with every step, my shoulder felt like it would break.

With her using me as a battering ram, we made good progress through the crowd. The whine of the helicopters changed and she gave me a harder push. "RUN!" she yelled. "Here comes the gas!"

The crowd noise changed, too. The choking sounds and scream sounds got much, much louder. I'd heard that pitch of sound before. We were back in the park. The gas was raining down. I held my breath and *ran*.

We cleared the crowd and she let go of my arm. I shook it out. I limped as fast as I could up the sidewalk as the crowd thinned and thinned. We were heading toward a group of DHS cops with riot shields and helmets and masks. As we drew near them, they moved to block us, but Masha held up a badge and they melted away like she was Obi-Wan Kenobi saying *These aren't the droids you're looking for.*

"You goddamned *bitch*," I said as we sped up Market Street. "We have to go back for Ange."

She pursed her lips and shook her head. "I feel for you, buddy. I haven't seen my boyfriend in months. He probably thinks I'm dead. Fortunes of war. We go back for your Ange, we're dead. If we push on, we have a chance. So long as we have a chance, she has a chance. Those kids aren't all going to Gitmo. They'll probably take a few hundred in for questioning and send the rest home."

We were moving up Market Street now, past the strip joints where the little encampments of bums and junkies sat, stinking like open toilets. Masha guided me to a little alcove in the shut door of one of the strip places. She stripped off her jacket and turned it inside out—the lining was a muted stripe pattern, and with the jacket's seams reversed, it hung differently. She produced a wool hat from her pocket and pulled it over her hair, letting it form a jaunty, off-center peak. Then she took out some makeup remover wipes and went to work on her face and fingernails. In a minute, she was a different woman.

"Wardrobe change," she said. "Now you. Lose the shoes, lose the jacket, lose the hat." I could see her point. The cops would be looking very carefully at anyone who looked like they'd been a part of the VampMob. I ditched the hat entirely—I'd never liked ball caps. Then I jammed the jacket into my pack and got out a long-sleeved tee with a picture of Rosa Luxemburg on it and pulled it over my black tee. I let Masha wipe my makeup off and clean my nails and a minute later, I was clean.

"Switch off your phone," she said. "You carrying any arphids?"

I had my student card, my ATM card, my Fast Pass. They all went into a silvered bag she held out, which I recognized as a radio-proof Faraday pouch. But as she put them in her pocket, I realized I'd just turned my ID over to her. If she was on the other side . . .

The magnitude of what had just happened began to sink in. In my mind, I'd pictured having Ange with me at this point. Ange would make it two against one. Ange would help me see if there was something amiss. If Masha wasn't all she said she was.

"Put these pebbles in your shoes before you put them on—"

"It's okay. I sprained my foot. No gait recognition program will spot me now."

She nodded once, one pro to another, and slung her pack. I picked up mine and we moved. The total time for the changeover was less than a minute. We looked and walked like two different people.

She looked at her watch and shook her head. "Come on," she said. "We have to make our rendezvous. Don't think of running, either. You've got two choices now. Me, or jail. They'll be analyzing the footage from that mob for days, but once they're done, every face in it will go in a database. Our departure will be noted. We are both wanted criminals now."

She got us off Market Street on the next block, swinging back into the Tenderloin. I knew this neighborhood. This was where we'd gone hunting for an open WiFi access point back on the day, playing Harajuku Fun Madness.

"Where are we going?" I said.

"We're about to catch a ride," she said. "Shut up and let me concentrate."

We moved fast, and sweat streamed down my face from under my hair, coursed down my back and slid down the crack of my ass and my thighs. My foot was *really* hurting and I was seeing the streets of San Francisco race by, maybe for the last time, ever.

It didn't help that we were plowing straight uphill, moving for the zone where the seedy Tenderloin gives way to the nosebleed real estate values of Nob Hill. My breath came in ragged gasps. She moved us mostly up narrow alleys, using the big streets just to get from one alley to the next.

We were just stepping into one such alley, Sabin Place, when someone fell in behind us and said, "Freeze right there." It was full of evil mirth. We stopped and turned around.

At the mouth of the alley stood Charles, wearing a halfhearted VampMob outfit of black T-shirt and jeans and white face-paint. "Hello, Marcus," he said. "You going somewhere?" He smiled a huge, wet grin. "Who's your girlfriend?"

"What do you want, Charles?"

"Well, I've been hanging out on that traitorous Xnet ever since I spotted you giving out DVDs at school. When I heard about your VampMob, I thought I'd go along and hang around the edges, just to see if you showed up and what you did. You know what I saw?"

I said nothing. He had his phone in his hand, pointed at us. Recording. Maybe ready to dial 911. Beside me, Masha had gone still as a board.

"I saw you *leading* the damned thing. And I *recorded* it, Marcus. So now I'm going to call the cops and we're going to wait right here for them. And then you're going to go to pound-you-in-the-ass prison, for a long, long time."

Masha stepped forward.

"Stop right there, chickie," he said. "I saw you get him away. I saw it all—"

She took another step forward and snatched the phone out of his hand, reaching behind her with her other hand and bringing it out holding a wallet open.

"DHS, dickhead," she said. "I'm DHS. I've been running this twerp back to his masters to see where he went. I *was* doing that. Now you've blown it. We have a name for that. We call it 'Obstruction of National Security.' You're about to hear that phrase a lot more often."

Charles took a step backwards, his hands held up in front of him. He'd gone even paler under his makeup. "What? No! I mean—I didn't know! I was trying to *help*!"

"The last thing we need is a bunch of high school Junior G-men 'helping' buddy. You can tell it to the judge."

He moved back again, but Masha was fast. She grabbed his wrist and twisted him into the same judo hold she'd had me in back at Civic Center. Her hand dipped back to her pockets and came out holding a strip of plastic, a handcuff strip, which she quickly wound around his wrists.

That was the last thing I saw as I took off running.

I made it as far as the other end of the alley before she caught up with me, tackling me from behind and sending me sprawling. I couldn't move very fast, not with my hurt foot and the weight of my pack. I went down in a hard face-plant and skidded, grinding my cheek into the grimy asphalt.

"Jesus," she said. "You're a goddamned idiot. You didn't *believe* that, did you?"

My heart thudded in my chest. She was on top of me and slowly she let me up.

"Do I need to cuff you, Marcus?"

I got to my feet. I hurt all over. I wanted to die.

"Come on," she said. "It's not far now."

"It" turned out to be a moving van on a Nob Hill side street, a 18-wheeler the size of one of the ubiquitous DHS trucks that still turned up on San Francisco's street corners, bristling with antennas.

This one, though, said "Three Guys and a Truck Moving" on the side, and the three guys were very much in evidence, trekking in and out of a tall apartment building with a green awning. They were carrying crated furniture, neatly labeled boxes, loading them one at a time onto the truck and carefully packing them there.

She walked us around the block once, apparently unsatisfied with something, then, on the next pass, she made eye contact with the man who was watching the van, an older black guy with a kidney-belt and heavy gloves. He had a kind face and he smiled at us as she led us quickly, casually up the truck's three stairs and into its depth. "Under the big table," he said. "We left you some space there."

The truck was more than half full, but there was a narrow corridor around a huge table with a quilted blanket thrown over it and bubble-wrap wound around its legs.

Masha pulled me under the table. It was stuffy and still and dusty under there, and I suppressed a sneeze as we scrunched in among the boxes. The space was so tight that we were on top of each other. I didn't think that Ange would have fit in there.

"Bitch," I said, looking at Masha.

"Shut up. You should be licking my boots, thanking me. You would have ended up in jail in a week, two tops. Not Gitmo-by-the-Bay. Syria, maybe. I think that's where they sent the ones they really wanted to disappear."

I put my head on my knees and tried to breathe deeply.

"Why would you do something so stupid as declaring war on the DHS anyway?"

I told her. I told her about being busted and I told her about Darryl.

She patted her pockets and came up with a phone. It was Charles's. "Wrong phone." She came up with another phone. She turned it on and the glow from its screen filled our little fort. After fiddling for a second, she showed it to me.

It was the picture she'd snapped of us, just before the bombs blew. It was the picture of Jolu and Van and me and—

Darryl.

I was holding in my hand proof that Darryl had been with us minutes before we'd all gone into DHS custody. Proof that he'd been alive and well and in our company.

"You need to give me a copy of this," I said. "I need it."

"When we get to LA," she said, snatching the phone back. "Once you've been briefed on how to be a fugitive without getting both our asses caught and shipped to Syria. I don't want you getting rescue ideas about this guy. He's safe enough where he is—for now."

I thought about trying to take it from her by force, but she'd already demonstrated her physical skill. She must have been a black belt or something.

We sat there in the dark, listening to the three guys load the truck with box after box, tying things down, grunting with the effort of it. I tried to sleep, but couldn't. Masha had no such problem. She snored.

There was still light shining through the narrow, obstructed corridor that led to the fresh air outside. I stared at it, through the gloom, and thought of Ange.

My Ange. Her hair brushing her shoulders as she turned her head from side to side, laughing at something I'd done. Her face when I'd seen her last, falling down in the crowd at VampMob. All those people at VampMob, like the people in the park, down and writhing, the DHS moving in with truncheons. The ones who disappeared.

Darryl. Stuck on Treasure Island, his side stitched up, taken out of his cell for endless rounds of questioning about the terrorists.

Darryl's father, ruined and boozy, unshaven. Washed up and in his uniform, "for the photos." Weeping like a little boy.

My own father, and the way that he had been changed by my disappearance to Treasure Island. He'd been just as broken as Darryl's father, but in his own way. And his face, when I told him where I'd been.

That was when I knew that I couldn't run.

That was when I knew that I had to stay and fight.

Masha's breathing was deep and regular, but when I reached with glacial slowness into her pocket for her phone, she snuffled a little and shifted. I froze and didn't even breathe for a full two minutes, counting one hippopotami, two hippopotami.

Slowly, her breath deepened again. I tugged the phone free of her jacket pocket one millimeter at a time, my fingers and arm trembling with the effort of moving so slowly.

Then I had it, a little candy bar shaped thing.

I turned to head for the light, when I had a flash of memory: Charles, holding out his phone, waggling it at us, taunting us. It had been a candy bar shaped phone, silver, plastered in the logos of a dozen companies that had subsidized the cost of the handset through the phone company. It was the kind of phone where you had to listen to a commercial every time you made a call.

It was too dim to see the phone clearly in the truck, but I could feel it. Were those company decals on its sides? Yes? Yes. I had just stolen *Charles's* phone from Masha.

I turned back around slowly, slowly, and slowly, slowly, *slowly,* I reached back into her pocket. *Her* phone was bigger and bulkier, with a better camera and who knew what else?

I'd been through this once before—that made it a little easier. Millimeter by millimeter again, I teased it free of her pocket, stopping twice when she snuffled and twitched.

I had the phone free of her pocket and I was beginning to back away when her hand shot out, fast as a snake, and grabbed my wrist, hard, fingertips grinding away at the small, tender bones below my hand.

I gasped and stared into Masha's wide-open, staring eyes.

"You are such an idiot," she said, conversationally, taking the phone from me, punching at its keypad with her other hand. "How did you plan on unlocking this again?"

I swallowed. I felt bones grind against each other in my wrist. I bit my lip to keep from crying out.

She continued to punch away with her other hand. "Is this what you thought you'd get away with?" She showed me the picture of all of us, Darryl and Jolu, Van and me. "This picture?"

I didn't say anything. My wrist felt like it would shatter.

"Maybe I should just delete it, take temptation out of your way." Her free hand moved some more. Her phone asked her if she was sure and she had to look at it to find the right button.

That's when I moved. I had Charles's phone in my other hand still, and I brought it down on her crushing hand as hard as I could, banging my knuckles on the table overhead. I hit her hand so hard the phone shattered and she yelped and her hand went slack. I was still moving, reaching for her other hand, for her now-unlocked phone with her thumb still poised over the okay key. Her fingers spasmed on the empty air as I snatched the phone out of her hand.

I moved down the narrow corridor on hands and knees, heading for the light. I felt her hands slap at my feet and ankles twice, and I had to shove aside some of the boxes that had walled us in like a Pharaoh in a tomb. A few of them fell down behind me, and I heard Masha grunt again.

The rolling truck door was open a crack and I dove for it,

270 | cory doctorow

slithering out under it. The steps had been removed and I found myself hanging over the road, sliding headfirst into it, clanging my head off the blacktop with a thump that rang my ears like a gong. I scrambled to my feet, holding the bumper, and desperately dragged down on the door handle, slamming it shut. Masha screamed inside—I must have caught her fingertips. I felt like throwing up, but I didn't.

I padlocked the truck instead.

chapter 20

None of the three guys were around at the moment, so I took off. My head hurt so much I thought I must be bleeding, but my hands came away dry. My twisted ankle had frozen up in the truck so that I ran like a broken marionette, and I stopped only once, to cancel the photo-deletion on Masha's phone. I turned off its radio—both to save the battery and to keep it from being used to track me—and set the sleep timer to two hours, the longest setting available. I tried to set it to not require a password to wake from sleep, but that required a password itself. I was just going to have to tap the keypad at least once every two hours until I could figure out how to get the photo off of the phone. I would need a charger, then.

I didn't have a plan. I needed one. I needed to sit down, to get online—to figure out what I was going to do next. I was sick of letting other people do my planning for me. I didn't want to be acting because of what Masha did, or because of the DHS, or because of my dad. Or because of Ange? Well, maybe I'd act because of Ange. That would be just fine, in fact.

I'd just been slipping downhill, taking alleys when I could, merging with the Tenderloin crowds. I didn't have any destination in mind. Every few minutes, I put my hand in my pocket and nudged one of the keys on Masha's phone to keep it from going asleep. It made an awkward bulge, unfolded there in my jacket.

I stopped and leaned against a building. My ankle was killing me. Where was I, anyway?

O'Farrell, at Hyde Street. In front of a dodgy "Asian Massage Parlor." My traitorous feet had taken me right back to the beginning—taken me back to where the photo on Masha's phone had been taken, seconds before the Bay Bridge blew, before my life changed forever.

I wanted to sit down on the sidewalk and bawl, but that wouldn't solve my problems. I had to call Barbara Stratford, tell her what had happened. Show her the photo of Darryl.

What was I thinking? I had to show her the video, the one that Masha had sent me—the one where the president's chief strategist gloated at the attacks on San Francisco and admitted that he knew when and where the next attacks would happen and that he wouldn't stop them because they'd help his man get reelected.

That was a plan, then: get in touch with Barbara, give her the documents and get them into print. The VampMob had to have really freaked people out, made them think that we really were a bunch of terrorists. Of course, when I'd been planning it, I had been thinking of how good a distraction it would be, not how it would look to some NASCAR Dad in Nebraska.

I'd call Barbara, and I'd do it smart, from a pay phone, putting my hood up so that the inevitable CCTV wouldn't get a photo of me. I dug a quarter out of my pocket and polished it on my shirttail, getting the fingerprints off it.

I headed downhill, down and down to the BART station and the pay phones there. I made it to the trolley car stop when I spotted the cover of the week's *Bay Guardian,* stacked in a high pile next to a homeless black guy who smiled at me. "Go ahead and read the cover, it's free—it'll cost you fifty cents to look inside, though."

The headline was set in the biggest type I'd seen since 9/11:

Inside Gitmo-by-the-Bay

Beneath it, in slightly smaller type:

"How the DHS has kept our children and friends in secret prisons on our doorstep.

"By Barbara Stratford, Special to the *Bay Guardian*"

The newspaper seller shook his head. "Can you believe that?" he said. "Right here in San Francisco. Man, the government *sucks.*"

Theoretically, the *Guardian* was free, but this guy appeared to have cornered the local market for copies of it. I had a quarter in my hand. I dropped it into his cup and fished for another one. I didn't bother polishing the fingerprints off it this time.

"We're told that the world changed forever when the Bay Bridge was blown up by parties unknown. Thousands of our friends and neighbors died on that day. Almost none of them have been recovered; their remains are presumed to be resting in the city's harbor.

"But an extraordinary story told to this reporter by a young man who was arrested by the DHS minutes after the explosion suggests that our own government has illegally held many of those thought dead on Treasure Island, which had been evacuated and declared off-limits to civilians shortly after the bombing . . ."

I sat down on a bench—the same bench, I noted with a prickly hair-up-the-neck feeling, where we'd rested Darryl after escaping from the BART station—and read the article all the way through. It took a huge effort not to burst into tears right there. Barbara had found some photos of me and Darryl goofing around together and they ran alongside the text. The photos were maybe a year old, but I looked so much *younger* in them, like I was ten or eleven. I'd done a lot of growing up in the past couple months.

The piece was beautifully written. I kept feeling outraged on behalf of the poor kids she was writing about, then remembering that she was writing about *me*. Zeb's note was there, his crabbed handwriting reproduced in large, a half-sheet of the newspaper. Barbara had dug up more info on other kids who were missing and presumed dead, a long list, and asked how many had been stuck there on the island, just a few miles from their parents' doorsteps.

I dug another quarter out of my pocket, then changed my mind. What was the chance that Barbara's phone wasn't tapped? There was no way I was going to be able to call her now, not directly. I needed some intermediary to get in touch with her and get her to meet me somewhere south. So much for plans.

What I really, really needed was the Xnet.

How the hell was I going to get online? My wifinder was blinking like crazy—there was wireless all around me, but I didn't have an Xbox and a TV and a ParanoidXbox DVD to boot from. WiFi, WiFi everywhere . . .

That's when I spotted them. Two kids, about my age, moving among the crowd at the top of the stairs down into the BART.

What caught my eye was the way they were moving, kind of

clumsy, nudging up against the commuters and the tourists. Each had a hand in his pocket, and whenever they met one another's eye, they snickered. They couldn't have been more obvious jammers, but the crowd was oblivious to them. Being down in that neighborhood, you expect to be dodging homeless people and crazies, so you don't make eye contact, don't look around at all if you can help it.

I sidled up to one. He seemed really young, but he couldn't have been any younger than me.

"Hey," I said. "Hey, can you guys come over here for a second?"

He pretended not to hear me. He looked right through me, the way you would a homeless person.

"Come on," I said. "I don't have a lot of time." I grabbed his shoulder and hissed in his ear. "The cops are after me. I'm from Xnet."

He looked scared now, like he wanted to run away, and his friend was moving toward us. "I'm serious," I said. "Just hear me out."

His friend came over. He was taller, and beefy—like Darryl. "Hey," he said. "Something wrong?"

His friend whispered in his ear. The two of them looked like they were going to bolt.

I grabbed my copy of the *Bay Guardian* from under my arm and rattled it in front of them. "Just turn to page five, okay?"

They did. They looked at the headline. The photo. Me.

"Oh, dude," the first one said. "We are *so* not worthy." He grinned at me like crazy, and the beefier one slapped me on the back.

"No *way*—" he said. "You're M—"

I put a hand over his mouth. "Come over here, okay?"

I brought them back to my bench. I noticed that there was something old and brown staining the sidewalk underneath it. Darryl's blood? It made my skin pucker up. We sat down.

"I'm Marcus," I said, swallowing hard as I gave my real name to these two who already knew me as M1k3y. I was blowing my cover, but the *Bay Guardian* had already made the connection for me.

"Nate," the small one said. "Liam," the bigger one said. "Dude, it is *such* an honor to meet you. You're like our all-time hero—"

"Don't say that," I said. "Don't say that. You two are like a flashing advertisement that says, 'I am jamming, please put my ass in Gitmo-by-the-Bay.' You couldn't be more obvious."

Liam looked like he might cry.

"Don't worry, you didn't get busted. I'll give you some tips, later." He brightened up again. What was becoming weirdly clear was that these two really *did* idolize M1k3y, and that they'd do anything I said. They were grinning like idiots. It made me uncomfortable, sick to my stomach.

"Listen, I need to get on Xnet, now, without going home or anywhere near home. Do you two live near here?"

"I do," Nate said. "Up at the top of California Street. It's a bit of a walk—steep hills." I'd just walked all the way down them. Masha was somewhere up there. But still, it was better than I had any right to expect.

"Let's go," I said.

Nate loaned me his baseball hat and traded jackets with me. I didn't have to worry about gait-recognition, not with my ankle throbbing the way it was—I limped like an extra in a cowboy movie.

Nate lived in a huge four-bedroom apartment at the top of Nob Hill. The building had a doorman, in a red overcoat with gold brocade, and he touched his cap and called Nate "Mr. Nate" and welcomed us all there. The place was spotless and smelled of furniture polish. I tried not to gawp at what must have been a couple million bucks' worth of condo.

"My dad," he explained. "He was an investment banker. Lots of life insurance. He died when I was fourteen and we got it all. They'd been divorced for years, but he left my mom as beneficiary."

From the floor-to-ceiling window, you could see a stunning view of the other side of Nob Hill, all the way down to Fisherman's Wharf, to the ugly stub of the Bay Bridge, the crowd of cranes and trucks. Through the mist, I could just make out Treasure Island. Looking down all that way, it gave me a crazy urge to jump.

I got online with his Xbox and a huge plasma screen in the living room. He showed me how many open WiFi networks were visible from his high vantage point—twenty, thirty of them. This was a good spot to be an Xnetter.

There was a *lot* of email in my M1k3y account. Twenty thousand new messages since Ange and I had left her place that morning. Lots of it was from the press, asking for follow-up interviews, but most of it was from the Xnetters, people who'd seen the *Guardian* story and wanted to tell me that they'd do anything to help me, anything I needed.

That did it. Tears started to roll down my cheeks.

Nate and Liam exchanged glances. I tried to stop, but it was no good. I was sobbing now. Nate went to an oak bookcase on one wall and swung a bar out of one of its shelves, revealing gleaming rows of bottles. He poured me a shot of something golden brown and brought it to me.

"Rare Irish whiskey," he said. "Mom's favorite."

It tasted like fire, like gold. I sipped at it, trying not to choke. I didn't really like hard liquor, but this was different. I took several deep breaths.

"Thanks, Nate," I said. He looked like I'd just pinned a medal on him. He was a good kid.

"All right," I said, and picked up the keyboard. The two boys watched in fascination as I paged through my mail on the gigantic screen.

What I was looking for, first and foremost, was email from Ange. There was a chance that she'd just gotten away. There was always that chance.

I was an idiot to even hope. There was nothing from her. I started going through the mail as fast as I could, picking apart the press requests, the fan mail, the hate mail, the spam . . .

And that's when I found it: a letter from Zeb.

> It wasn't nice to wake up this morning and find the letter that I thought you would destroy in the pages of the newspaper. Not nice at all. Made me feel . . . hunted.

> But I've come to understand why you did it. I don't know if I can approve of your tactics, but it's easy to see that your motives were sound.

> If you're reading this, that means that there's a good chance you've gone underground. It's not easy. I've been learning that. I've been learning a lot more.

> I can help you. I should do that for you. You're doing what you can for me. (Even if you're not doing it with my permission.)

> Reply if you get this, if you're on the run and alone. Or reply if you're in custody, being run by our friends on Gitmo, looking for a way to make the pain stop. If they've got you, you'll do what they tell you. I know that. I'll take that risk.

> For you, M1k3y.

"Whooooa," Liam breathed. "Duuuuuude." I wanted to smack him. I turned to say something awful and cutting to him, but he was staring at me with eyes as big as saucers, looking like he wanted to drop to his knees and worship me.

"Can I just say," Nate said, "can I just say that it is the biggest honor of my entire life to help you? Can I just say that?"

I was blushing now. There was nothing for it. These two were totally starstruck, even though I wasn't any kind of star, not in my own mind at least.

"Can you guys—" I swallowed. "Can I have some privacy here?"

They slunk out of the room like bad puppies and I felt like a tool. I typed fast.

"I got away, Zeb. And I'm on the run. I need all the help I can get. I want to end this now." I remembered to take Masha's phone out of my pocket and tickle it to keep it from going to sleep.

They let me use the shower, gave me a change of clothes, a new backpack with half their earthquake kit in it—energy bars, medicine, hot and cold packs and an old sleeping bag. They even slipped a spare Xbox Universal already loaded with ParanoidXbox on it into there. That was a nice touch. I had to draw the line at a flare gun.

I kept on checking my email to see if Zeb had replied. I answered the fan mail. I answered the mail from the press. I deleted the hate mail. I was half expecting to see something from Masha, but chances were she was halfway to LA by now, her fingers hurt, and in no position to type. I tickled her phone again.

They encouraged me to take a nap and for a brief, shameful moment, I got all paranoid like maybe these guys were thinking of turning me in once I was asleep. Which was idiotic—they could have turned me in just as easily when I was awake. I just couldn't compute the fact that they thought *so much* of me. I had known, intellectually, that there were people who would follow M1k3y. I'd met some of those people that morning, shouting BITE BITE BITE and vamping it up at Civic Center. But these two were more personal. They were just nice, goofy guys, they coulda been any of my friends back in the days before the Xnet, just two pals who palled around having teenage adventures. They'd volunteered to join an army, my army. I had a responsibility to them. Left to themselves, they'd get caught, it was only a matter of time. They were too trusting.

"Guys, listen to me for a second. I have something serious I need to talk to you about."

They almost stood at attention. It would have been funny if it wasn't so scary.

"Here's the thing. Now that you've helped me, it's really dangerous. If you get caught, I'll get caught. They'll get anything you know out of you—" I held up my hand to forestall their protests. "No, stop. You haven't been through it. Everyone talks. Everyone breaks. If you're ever caught, you tell them everything, right away, as fast as you can, as much as you can. They'll get it all eventually anyway. That's how they work.

"But you won't get caught, and here's why: you're not jammers anymore. You are retired from active duty. You're a"—I fished in my memory for vocabulary words culled from spy thrillers—"you're a sleeper cell. Stand down. Go back to being normal kids. One way or another, I'm going to break this thing, break it wide open, end it. Or it will get me, finally, do me in. If you don't hear from me within seventy-two hours, assume that they got me. Do whatever you want then. But for the next three days—and forever, if I do what I'm trying to do—stand down. Will you promise me that?"

They promised with all solemnity. I let them talk me into napping, but made them swear to rouse me once an hour. I'd have to tickle Masha's phone and I wanted to know as soon as Zeb got back in touch with me.

The rendezvous was on a BART car, which made me nervous. They're full of cameras. But Zeb knew what he was doing. He had me meet him in the last car of a certain train departing from Powell Street Station, at a time when that car was filled with the press of bodies. He sidled up to me in the crowd, and the good commuters of San Francisco cleared a space for him, the hollow that always surrounds homeless people.

"Nice to see you again," he muttered, facing into the doorway. Looking into the dark glass, I could see that there was no one close enough to eavesdrop—not without some kind of high-efficiency mic rig, and if they knew enough to show up here with one of those, we were dead anyway.

"You too, brother," I said. "I'm—I'm sorry, you know?"

"Shut up. Don't be sorry. You were braver than I am. Are you ready to go underground now? Ready to disappear?"

"About that."

"Yes?"

"That's not the plan."

"Oh," he said.

"Listen, okay? I have—I have pictures, video. Stuff that really *proves* something." I reached into my pocket and tickled Masha's phone. I'd bought a charger for it in Union Square on the way down, and had stopped and plugged it in at a cafe for long enough to get the battery up to four out of five bars. "I need to get it to Barbara Stratford, the woman from the *Guardian*. But they're going to be watching her—watching to see if I show up."

"You don't think that they'll be watching for me, too? If your plan involves me going within a mile of that woman's home or office—"

"I want you to get Van to come and meet me. Did Darryl ever tell you about Van? The girl—"

"He told me. Yes, he told me. You don't think they'll be watching her? All of you who were arrested?"

"I think they will. I don't think they'll be watching her as hard. And Van has totally clean hands. She never cooperated with any of my—" I swallowed. "With my projects. So they might be a little more relaxed about her. If she calls the *Bay Guardian* to make an appointment to explain why I'm just full of crap, maybe they'll let her keep it."

He stared at the door for a long time.

"You know what happens when they catch us again." It wasn't a question.

280 | cory doctorow

I nodded.

"Are you sure? Some of the people that were on Treasure Island with us got taken away in helicopters. They got taken *offshore*. There are countries where America can outsource its torture. Countries where you will rot forever. Countries where you wish they would just get it over with, have you dig a trench and then shoot you in the back of the head as you stand over it."

I swallowed and nodded.

"Is it worth the risk? We can go underground for a long, long time here. Someday we might get our country back. We can wait it out."

I shook my head. "You can't get anything done by doing nothing. It's our *country*. They've taken it from us. The terrorists who attack us are still free—but *we're not*. I can't go underground for a year, ten years, my whole life, waiting for freedom to be handed to me. Freedom is something you have to take for yourself."

That afternoon, Van left school as usual, sitting in the back of the bus with a tight knot of her friends, laughing and joking the way she always did. The other riders on the bus took special note of her, she was so loud, and besides, she was wearing that stupid, giant floppy hat, something that looked like a piece out of a school play about Renaissance sword fighters. At one point they all huddled together, then turned away to look out the back of the bus, pointing and giggling. The girl who wore the hat now was the same height as Van, and from behind, it could be her.

No one paid any attention to the mousy little Asian girl who got off a few stops before the BART. She was dressed in a plain old school uniform, and looking down shyly as she stepped off. Besides, at that moment, the loud Korean girl let out a whoop and her friends followed along, laughing so loudly that even the bus driver slowed down, twisted in his seat and gave them a dirty look.

Van hurried away down the street with her head down, her hair tied back and dropped down the collar of her out-of-style bubble jacket. She had slipped lifts into her shoes that made her two wobbly, awkward inches taller, and had taken her contacts out and put on her least-favored glasses, with huge lenses that took up half her face. Although I'd been waiting in the bus shelter for her and knew when to expect her, I hardly recognized her. I got up and walked along behind her, across the street, trailing by half a block.

The people who passed me looked away as quickly as possible. I looked like a homeless kid, with a grubby cardboard sign, street-grimy overcoat, huge, overstuffed knapsack with duct tape over its rips. No one wants to look at a street kid, because if you meet his eye, he might ask you for some spare change. I'd walked around Oakland all afternoon and the only people who'd spoken to me were a Jehovah's Witness and a Scientologist, both trying to convert me. It felt gross, like being hit on by a pervert.

Van followed the directions I'd written down carefully. Zeb had passed them to her the same way he'd given me the note outside school—bumping into her as she waited for the bus, apologizing profusely. I'd written the note plainly and simply, just laying it out for her: I know you don't approve. I understand. But this is it, this is the most important favor I've ever asked of you. Please. Please.

She'd come. I knew she would. We had a lot of history, Van and I. She didn't like what had happened to the world, either. Besides, an evil, chuckling voice in my head had pointed out, she was under suspicion now that Barbara's article was out.

We walked like that for six or seven blocks, looking at who was near us, what cars went past. Zeb told me about five-person trails, where five different undercovers traded off duties following you, making it nearly impossible to spot them. You had to go somewhere totally desolate, where anyone at all would stand out like a sore thumb.

The overpass for the 880 was just a few blocks from the Coliseum BART station, and even with all the circling Van did, it didn't take long to reach it. The noise from overhead was nearly deafening. No one else was around, not that I could tell. I'd visited the site before I suggested it to Van in the note, taking care to check for places where someone could hide. There weren't any.

Once she stopped at the appointed place, I moved quickly to catch up to her. She blinked owlishly at me from behind her glasses.

"Marcus," she breathed, and tears swam in her eyes. I found

282 | cory doctorow

that I was crying, too. I'd make a really rotten fugitive. Too senti-
mental.

She hugged me so hard I couldn't breathe. I hugged her back
even harder.

Then she kissed me.

Not on the cheek, not like a sister. Full on the lips, a hot, wet,
steamy kiss that seemed to go on forever. I was so overcome with
emotion—

No, that's bull. I knew exactly what I was doing. I kissed her
back.

Then I stopped and pulled away, nearly shoved her away. "Van,"
I gasped.

"Oops," she said.

"Van," I said again.

"Sorry," she said. "I—"

Something occurred to me just then, something I guess I should
have seen a long, long time before.

"You *like* me, don't you?"

She nodded miserably. "For years," she said.

Oh, God. Darryl, all these years, so in love with her, and the
whole time she was looking at me, secretly wanting me. And then I
ended up with Ange. Ange said that she'd always fought with Van.
And I was running around, getting into so much trouble.

"Van," I said. "Van, I'm so sorry."

"Forget it," she said, looking away. "I know it can't be. I just
wanted to do that once, just in case I never—" She bit down on the
words.

"Van, I need you to do something for me. Something important.
I need you to meet with the journalist from the *Bay Guardian,* Barbara Stratford, the one who wrote the article. I need you to give her
something." I explained about Masha's phone, told her about the
video that Masha had sent me.

"What good will this do, Marcus? What's the point?"

"Van, you were right, at least partly. We can't fix the world by
putting other people at risk. I need to solve the problem by telling
what I know. I should have done that from the start. Should have
walked straight out of their custody and to Darryl's father's house

and told him what I knew. Now, though, I have evidence. This stuff—it could change the world. This is my last hope. The only hope for getting Darryl out, for getting a life that I don't spend underground, hiding from the cops. And you're the only person I can trust to do this."

"Why me?"

"You're kidding, right? Look at how well you handled getting here. You're a pro. You're the best at this of any of us. You're the only one I can trust. That's why you."

"Why not your friend Ange?" She said the name without any inflection at all, like it was a block of cement.

I looked down. "I thought you knew. They arrested her. She's in Gitmo—on Treasure Island. She's been there for days now." I had been trying not to think about this, not to think about what might be happening to her. Now I couldn't stop myself and I started to sob. I felt a pain in my stomach, like I'd been kicked, and I pushed my hands into my middle to hold myself in. I folded there, and the next thing I knew, I was on my side in the rubble under the freeway, holding myself and crying.

Van knelt down by my side. "Give me the phone," she said, her voice an angry hiss. I fished it out of my pocket and passed it to her.

Embarrassed, I stopped crying and sat up. I knew that snot was running down my face. Van was giving me a look of pure revulsion. "You need to keep it from going to sleep," I said. "I have a charger here." I rummaged in my pack. I hadn't slept all the way through the night since I acquired it. I set the phone's alarm to go off every ninety minutes and wake me up so that I could keep it from going to sleep. "Don't fold it shut, either."

"And the video?"

"That's harder," I said. "I emailed a copy to myself, but I can't get onto the Xnet anymore." In a pinch, I could have gone back to Nate and Liam and used their Xbox again, but I didn't want to risk it. "Look, I'm going to give you my login and password for the Pirate Party's mail server. You'll have to use TOR to access it—Homeland Security is bound to be scanning for people logging into p-party mail."

"Your login and password," she said, looking a little surprised.

"I trust you, Van. I know I can trust you."

She shook her head. "You *never* give out your passwords, Marcus."

"I don't think it matters anymore. Either you succeed or I—or it's the end of Marcus Yallow. Maybe I'll get a new identity, but I don't think so. I think they'll catch me. I guess I've known all along that they'd catch me, some day."

She looked at me, furious now. "What a waste. What was it all for, anyway?"

Of all the things she could have said, nothing could have hurt me more. It was like another kick in the stomach. What a waste, all of it, futile. Darryl and Ange, gone. I might never see my family again. And still, Homeland Security had my city and my country caught in a massive, irrational shrieking freak-out where anything could be done in the name of stopping terrorism.

Van looked like she was waiting for me to say something, but I had nothing to say to that. She left me there.

Zeb had a pizza for me when I got back "home"—to the tent under a freeway overpass in the Mission that he'd staked out for the night. He had a pup tent, military surplus, stenciled with SAN FRANCISCO LOCAL HOMELESS COORDINATING BOARD.

The pizza was a Domino's, cold and clabbered, but delicious for all that. "You like pineapple on your pizza?"

Zeb smiled condescendingly at me. "Freegans can't be choosy," he said.

"Freegans?"

"Like vegans, but we only eat free food."

"Free food?"

He grinned again. "You know—*free* food. From the free food store?"

"You stole this?"

"No, dummy. It's from the other store. The little one out behind the store? Made of blue steel? Kind of funky smelling?"

"You got this out of the garbage?"

He flung his head back and cackled. "Yes indeedy. You should *see* your face. Dude, it's okay. It's not like it was rotten. It was fresh—just a screwed-up order. They threw it out in the box. They sprinkle rat poison over everything at closing time, but if you get there quick, you're okay. You should see what grocery stores throw out! Wait until breakfast. I'm going to make you a fruit salad you won't believe. As soon as one strawberry in the box goes a little green and fuzzy, the whole thing is out—"

I tuned him out. The pizza was fine. It wasn't as if sitting in the Dumpster would infect it or something. If it was gross, that was only because it came from Domino's—the worst pizza in town. I'd never liked their food, and I'd given it up altogether when I found out that they bankrolled a bunch of ultra-crazy politicians who thought that global warming and evolution were satanic plots.

It was hard to shake the feeling of grossness, though.

But there *was* another way to look at it. Zeb had showed me a secret, something I hadn't anticipated: there was a whole hidden world out there, a way of getting by without participating in the system.

"Freegans, huh?"

"Yogurt, too," he said, nodding vigorously. "For the fruit salad. They throw it out the day after the best-before date, but it's not as if it goes green at midnight. It's yogurt, I mean, it's basically just rotten milk to begin with."

I swallowed. The pizza tasted funny. Rat poison. Spoiled yogurt. Furry strawberries. This would take some getting used to.

I ate another bite. Actually, Domino's pizza sucked a little less when you got it for free.

Liam's sleeping bag was warm and welcoming after a long, emotionally exhausting day. Van would have made contact with Barbara by now. She'd have the video and the picture. I'd call her in the morning and find out what she thought I should do next. I'd have to come in once she published, to back it all up.

I thought about that as I closed my eyes, thought about what it would be like to turn myself in, the cameras all rolling, following the infamous M1k3y into one of those big, columnated buildings in Civic Center.

The sound of the cars screaming by overhead turned into a kind of ocean sound as I drifted away. There were other tents nearby, homeless people. I'd met a few of them that afternoon, before it got dark and we all retreated to huddle near our own tents. They were all older than me, rough looking and gruff. None of them looked crazy or violent, though. Just like people who'd had bad luck, or made bad decisions, or both.

I must have fallen asleep, because I don't remember anything else until a bright light was shined into my face, so bright it was blinding.

"That's him," said a voice behind the light.

"Bag him," said another voice, one I'd heard before, one I'd heard over and over again in my dreams, lecturing to me, demanding my passwords. Severe haircut woman.

The bag went over my head quickly and was cinched so tight at the throat that I choked and threw up my freegan pizza. As I spasmed and choked, hard hands bound my wrists, then my ankles. I was rolled onto a stretcher and hoisted, then carried into a vehicle, up a couple of clanging metal steps. They dropped me into a padded floor. There was no sound at all in the back of the vehicle once they closed the doors. The padding deadened everything except my own choking.

"Well, hello again," she said. I felt the van rock as she crawled in with me. I was still choking, trying to gasp in a breath. Vomit filled my mouth and trickled down my windpipe.

"We won't let you die," she said. "If you stop breathing, we'll make sure you start again. So don't worry about it."

I choked harder. I sipped at air. Some was getting through. Deep, wracking coughs shook my chest and back, dislodging some more of the puke. More breath.

"See?" she said. "Not so bad. Welcome home, M1k3y. We've got somewhere very special to take you."

I relaxed onto my back, feeling the van rock. The smell of used pizza was overwhelming at first, but as with all strong stimuli, my brain gradually grew accustomed to it, filtered it out until it was just a faint aroma. The rocking of the van was almost comforting.

That's when it happened. An incredible, deep calm that swept over me like I was lying on the beach and the ocean had swept in and lifted me as gently as a parent, held me aloft and swept me out onto a warm sea under a warm sun. After everything that had happened, I was caught, but it didn't matter. I had gotten the information to Barbara. I had organized the Xnet. I had won. And if I hadn't won, I had done everything I could have done. More than I ever thought I could do. I took a mental inventory as I rode, thinking of everything that I had accomplished, that *we* had accomplished. The city, the country, the world was full of people who wouldn't live the way DHS wanted us to live. We'd fight forever. They couldn't jail us all.

I sighed and smiled.

She'd been talking all along, I realized. I'd been so far into my happy place that she'd just gone away.

"—smart kid like you. You'd think that you'd know better than to mess with us. We've had an eye on you since the day you walked out. We would have caught you even if you hadn't gone crying to your lesbo journalist traitor. I just don't get it—we had an understanding, you and me. . . ."

We rumbled over a metal plate, the van's shocks rocking, and then the rocking changed. We were on water. Heading to Treasure Island. Hey, Ange was there. Darryl, too. Maybe.

The hood didn't come off until I was in my cell. They didn't bother with the cuffs at my wrists and ankles, just rolled me off the stretcher and onto the floor. It was dark, but by the moonlight from the single, tiny, high window, I could see that the mattress had been taken off the cot. The room contained me, a toilet, a bed frame and a sink, and nothing else.

I closed my eyes and let the ocean lift me. I floated away. Somewhere, far below me, was my body. I could tell what would happen next. I was being left to piss myself. Again. I knew what that was like. I'd pissed myself before. It smelled bad. It itched. It was humiliating, like being a baby.

But I'd survived it.

I laughed. The sound was weird, and it drew me back into my body, back to the present. I laughed and laughed. I'd had the worst that they could throw at me, and I'd survived it, and I'd *beaten them,* beaten them for months, showed them up as chumps and despots. I'd *won.*

I let my bladder cut loose. It was sore and full anyway, and no time like the present.

The ocean swept me away.

When morning came, two efficient, impersonal guards cut the bindings off my wrists and ankles. I still couldn't walk—when I stood, my legs gave way like a stringless marionette's. Too much time in one position. The guards pulled my arms over their shoulders and half dragged, half carried me down the familiar corridor. The bar codes on the doors were curling up and dangling now, attacked by the salt air.

I got an idea. "Ange!" I yelled. "Darryl!" I yelled. My guards yanked me along faster, clearly disturbed but not sure what to do about it. "Guys, it's me, Marcus! Stay free!"

Behind one of the doors, someone sobbed. Someone else cried out in what sounded like Arabic. Then it was cacophony, a thousand different shouting voices.

They brought me to a new room. It was an old shower room, with the showerheads still present in the mould tiles.

"Hello, M1k3y," Severe Haircut said. "You seem to have had an eventful morning." She wrinkled her nose pointedly.

"I pissed myself," I said, cheerfully. "You should try it."

"Maybe we should give you a bath, then," she said. She nodded, and my guards carried me to another stretcher. This one had restraining straps running its length. They dropped me onto it and it was ice-cold and soaked through. Before I knew it, they had the straps across my shoulders, hips and ankles. A minute later, three more straps were tied down. A man's hands grabbed the railings by my head and released some catches, and a moment later I was tilted down, my head below my feet.

"Let's start with something simple," she said. I craned my head to see her. She had turned to a desk with an Xbox on it, connected to an expensive-looking flat-panel TV. "I'd like you to tell me your login and password for your Pirate Party email, please?"

I closed my eyes and let the ocean carry me off the beach.

"Do you know what waterboarding is, M1k3y?" Her voice reeled me in. "You get strapped down like this, and we pour water over your head, up your nose and down your mouth. You can't suppress the gag reflex. They call it a simulated execution, and from what I can tell from this side of the room, that's a fair assessment. You won't be able to fight the feeling that you're dying."

I tried to go away. I'd heard of waterboarding. This was it, real torture. And this was just the beginning.

I couldn't go away. The ocean didn't sweep in and lift me. There was a tightness in my chest, my eyelids fluttered. I could feel clammy piss on my legs and clammy sweat in my hair. My skin itched from the dried puke.

She swam into view above me. "Let's start with the login," she said.

I closed my eyes, squeezed them shut.

"Give him a drink," she said.

I heard people moving. I took a deep breath and held it.

The water started as a trickle, a ladleful of water gently poured over my chin, my lips. Up my upturned nostrils. It went back into my throat, starting to choke me, but I wouldn't cough, wouldn't gasp and suck it into my lungs. I held onto my breath and squeezed my eyes harder.

There was a commotion from outside the room, a sound of chaotic boots stamping, angry, outraged shouts. The dipper was emptied into my face.

I heard her mutter something to someone in the room, then to me she said, "Just the login, Marcus. It's a simple request. What could I do with your login, anyway?"

This time, it was a bucket of water, all at once, a flood that didn't stop, it must have been gigantic. I couldn't help it. I gasped and aspirated the water into my lungs, coughed and took more water in. I knew they wouldn't kill me, but I couldn't convince my body of that. In every fiber of my being, I knew I was going to die. I couldn't even cry—the water was still pouring over me.

Then it stopped. I coughed and coughed and coughed, but at the angle I was at, the water I coughed up dribbled back into my nose and burned down my sinuses.

The coughs were so deep they hurt, hurt my ribs and my hips as I twisted against them. I hated how my body was betraying me,

how my mind couldn't control my body, but there was nothing for
it.

Finally, the coughing subsided enough for me to take in what
was going on around me. People were shouting and it sounded like
someone was scuffling, wrestling. I opened my eyes and blinked
into the bright light, then craned my neck, still coughing a little.

The room had a lot more people in it than it had had when we
started. Most of them seemed to be wearing body armor, helmets
and smoked-plastic visors. They were shouting at the Treasure Island guards, who were shouting back, necks corded with veins.

"Stand down!" one of the body armors said. "Stand down and
put your hands in the air. You are under arrest!"

Severe haircut woman was talking on her phone. One of the
body armors noticed her and he moved swiftly to her and batted
her phone away with a gloved hand. Everyone fell silent as it sailed
through the air in an arc that spanned the small room, clattering
to the ground in a shower of parts.

The silence broke and the body armors moved into the room.
Two grabbed each of my torturers. I almost managed a smile at the
look on Severe Haircut's face when two men grabbed her by the
shoulders, turned her around and yanked a set of plastic handcuffs
around her wrists.

One of the body armors moved forward from the doorway. He
had a video camera on his shoulder, a serious rig with blinding
white light. He got the whole room, circling me twice while he got
me. I found myself staying perfectly still, as though I was sitting
for a portrait.

It was ridiculous.

"Do you think you could get me off of this thing?" I managed to
get it all out with only a little choking.

Two more body armors moved up to me, one a woman, and began to unstrap me. They flipped their visors up and smiled at me.
They had red crosses on their shoulders and helmets.

Beneath the red crosses was another insignia: CHP. California
Highway Patrol. They were state troopers.

I started to ask what they were doing there, and that's when I
saw Barbara Stratford. She'd evidently been held back in the cor-

ridor, but now she came in pushing and shoving. "There you are," she said, kneeling beside me and grabbing me in the longest, hardest hug of my life.

That's when I knew it—Guantanamo-by-the-Bay was in the hands of its enemies. I was saved.

chapter 21

They left me and Barbara alone in the room then, and I used the working showerhead to rinse off—I was suddenly embarrassed to be covered in piss and barf. When I finished, Barbara was in tears.

"Your parents—" she began.

I felt like I might throw up again. God, my poor folks. What they must have gone through.

"Are they here?"

"No," she said. "It's complicated," she said.

"What?"

"You're still under arrest, Marcus. Everyone here is. They can't just sweep in and throw open the doors. Everyone here is going to have to be processed through the criminal justice system. It could take, well, it could take months."

"I'm going to have to stay here for *months*?"

She grabbed my hands. "No, I think we're going to be able to get you arraigned and released on bail pretty fast. But pretty fast is a relative term. I wouldn't expect anything to happen today. And it's not going to be like those people had it. It will be humane. There will be real food. No interrogations. Visits from your family.

"Just because the DHS is out, it doesn't mean that you get to just walk out of here. What's happened here is that we're getting rid of the bizarro-world version of the justice system they'd instituted and replacing it with the old system. The system with judges, open trials and lawyers.

"So we can try to get you transferred to a juvie facility on the mainland, but Marcus, those places can be really rough. Really, really rough. This might be the best place for you until we get you bailed out."

Bailed out. Of course. I was a criminal—I hadn't been charged yet, but there were bound to be plenty of charges they could think of. It was practically illegal just to think impure thoughts about the government.

She gave my hands another squeeze. "It sucks, but this is how it has to be. The point is, it's *over*. The governor has thrown the DHS out of the state, dismantled every checkpoint. The state Attorney General has issued warrants for any law-enforcement officers involved in 'stress interrogations' and secret imprisonments. They'll go to jail, Marcus, and it's because of what you did."

I was numb. I heard the words, but they hardly made sense. Somehow, it was over, but it wasn't over.

"Look," she said. "We probably have an hour or two before this all settles down, before they come back and put you away again. What do you want to do? Walk on the beach? Get a meal? These people had an incredible staff room—we raided it on the way in. Gourmet all the way."

At last a question I could answer. "I want to find Ange. I want to find Darryl."

I tried to use a computer I found to look up their cell numbers, but it wanted a password, so we were reduced to walking the corridors, calling out their names. Behind the cell doors, prisoners screamed back at us, or cried, or begged us to let them go. They didn't understand what had just happened, couldn't see their former guards being herded onto the docks in plastic handcuffs, taken away by California state SWAT teams.

"Ange!" I called over the din, "Ange Carvelli! Darryl Glover! It's Marcus!"

We'd walked the whole length of the cell block and they hadn't answered. I felt like crying. They'd been shipped overseas—they were in Syria or worse. I'd never see them again.

I sat down and leaned against the corridor wall and put my face in my hands. I saw severe haircut woman's face, saw her smirk as she asked me for my login. She had done this. She would go to jail for it, but that wasn't enough. I thought that when I saw her again, I might kill her. She deserved it.

"Come on," Barbara said. "Come on, Marcus. Don't give up. There's more around here, come on."

She was right. All the doors we'd passed in the cell block were old, rusting things that dated back to when the base was first built. But at the very end of the corridor, sagging open, was a new high-security door as thick as a dictionary. We pulled it open and ventured into the dark corridor within.

There were four more cell doors here, doors without bar codes. Each had a small electronic keypad mounted on it.

"Darryl?" I said. "Ange?"

"Marcus?"

It was Ange, calling out from behind the farthest door. Ange, my Ange, my angel.

"Ange!" I cried. "It's me, it's me!"

"Oh God, Marcus," she choked out, and then it was all sobs.

I pounded on the other doors. "Darryl! Darryl, are you here?"

"I'm here." The voice was very small, and very hoarse. "I'm here. I'm very, very sorry. Please. I'm very sorry."

He sounded . . . broken. Shattered.

"It's me, D," I said, leaning on his door. "It's Marcus. It's over—they arrested the guards. They kicked the Department of Homeland Security out. We're getting trials, open trials. And we get to testify against *them*."

"I'm sorry," he said. "Please, I'm so sorry."

The California patrolmen came to the door then. They still had their camera rolling. "Ms. Stratford?" one said. He had his faceplate up and he looked like any other cop, not like my savior. Like someone come to lock me up.

"Captain Sanchez," she said. "We've located two of the prisoners of interest here. I'd like to see them released and inspect them for myself."

"Ma'am, we don't have access codes for those doors yet," he said.

She held up her hand. "That wasn't the arrangement. I was to have complete access to this facility. That came direct from the governor, sir. We aren't budging until you open these cells." Her face was perfectly smooth, without a single hint of give or flex. She meant it.

The captain looked like he needed sleep. He grimaced. "I'll see what I can do," he said.

They did manage to open the cells, finally, about half an hour later. It took three tries, but they eventually got the right codes entered, matching them to the arphids on the ID badges they'd taken off the guards they'd arrested.

They got into Ange's cell first. She was dressed in a hospital gown, open at the back, and her cell was even more bare than mine had been—just padding all over, no sink or bed, no light. She emerged blinking into the corridor and the police camera was on her, its bright lights in her face. Barbara stepped protectively between us and it. Ange stepped tentatively out of her cell, shuffling a little. There was something wrong with her eyes, with her face. She was crying, but that wasn't it.

"They drugged me," she said. "When I wouldn't stop screaming for a lawyer."

That's when I hugged her. She sagged against me, but she squeezed back, too. She smelled stale and sweaty, and I smelled no better. I never wanted to let go.

That's when they opened Darryl's cell.

He had shredded his paper hospital gown. He was curled up, naked, in the back of the cell, shielding himself from the camera and our stares. I ran to him.

"D," I whispered in his ear. "D, it's me. It's Marcus. It's over. The guards have been arrested. We're going to get bail, we're going home."

He trembled and squeezed his eyes shut. "I'm sorry," he whispered, and turned his face away.

They took me away then, a cop in body armor and Barbara, took me back to my cell and locked the door, and that's where I spent the night.

I don't remember much about the trip to the courthouse. They had me chained to five other prisoners, all of whom had been in for a lot longer than me. One only spoke Arabic—he was an old man, and he trembled. The others were all young. I was the only white one. Once we had been gathered on the deck of the ferry, I saw that nearly everyone on Treasure Island had been one shade of brown or another.

I had only been inside for one night, but it was too long. There was a light drizzle coming down, normally the sort of thing that would make me hunch my shoulders and look down, but today I joined everyone else in craning my head back at the infinite gray sky, reveling in the stinging wet as we raced across the bay to the ferry docks.

They took us away in buses. The shackles made climbing into the buses awkward, and it took a long time for everyone to load. No one cared. When we weren't struggling to solve the geometry problem of six people, one chain, narrow bus aisle, we were just looking around at the city around us, up the hill at the buildings.

All I could think of was finding Darryl and Ange, but neither were in evidence. It was a big crowd and we weren't allowed to move freely through it. The state troopers who handled us were gentle enough, but they were still big, armored and armed. I kept thinking I saw Darryl in the crowd, but it was always someone else with that same beaten, hunched look that he'd had in his cell. He wasn't the only broken one.

At the courthouse, they marched us into interview rooms in our shackle group. An ACLU lawyer took our information and asked us a few questions—when she got to me, she smiled and greeted me by name—and then led us into the courtroom before the judge. He wore an actual robe, and seemed to be in a good mood.

The deal seemed to be that anyone who had a family member to post bail could go free, and everyone else got sent to prison. The ACLU lawyer did a lot of talking to the judge, asking for a few more hours while the prisoners' families were rounded up and brought to the courthouse. The judge was pretty good about it, but when I realized that some of these people had been locked up since the bridge blew, taken for dead by their families, without trial, subjected to interrogation, isolation, torture—I wanted to just break the chains myself and set everyone free.

When I was brought before the judge, he looked down at me

and took off his glasses. He looked tired. The ACLU lawyer looked tired. The bailiffs looked tired. Behind me, I could hear a sudden buzz of conversation as my name was called by the bailiff. The judge rapped his gavel once, without looking away from me. He scrubbed at his eyes.

"Mr. Yallow," he said, "the prosecution has identified you as a flight risk. I think they have a point. You certainly have more, shall we say, *history,* than the other people here. I am tempted to hold you over for trial, no matter how much bail your parents are prepared to post."

My lawyer started to say something, but the judge silenced her with a look. He scrubbed at his eyes.

"Do you have anything to say?"

"I had the chance to run," I said. "Last week. Someone offered to take me away, get me out of town, help me build a new identity. Instead I stole her phone, escaped from our truck and ran away. I turned over her phone—which had evidence about my friend, Darryl Glover, on it—to a journalist and hid out here, in town."

"You stole a phone?"

"I decided that I couldn't run. That I had to face justice—that my freedom wasn't worth anything if I was a wanted man, or if the city was still under the DHS. If my friends were still locked up. That freedom for me wasn't as important as a free country."

"But you did steal a phone."

I nodded. "I did. I plan on giving it back, if I ever find the young woman in question."

"Well, thank you for that speech, Mr. Yallow. You are a very well-spoken young man." He glared at the prosecutor. "Some would say a very brave man, too. There was a certain video on the news this morning. It suggested that you had some legitimate reason to evade the authorities. In light of that, and of your little speech here, I will grant bail, but I will also ask the prosecutor to add a charge of Misdemeanor Petty Theft to the count, as regards the matter of the phone. For this, I expect another $50,000 in bail."

He banged his gavel again, and my lawyer gave my hand a squeeze.

The judge looked down at me again and reseated his glasses.

He had dandruff, there on the shoulders of his robe. A little more rained down as his glasses touched his wiry, curly hair.

"You can go now, young man. Stay out of trouble."

I turned to go and someone tackled me. It was Dad. He literally lifted me off my feet, hugging me so hard my ribs creaked. He hugged me the way I remembered him hugging me when I was a little boy, when he'd spin me around and around in hilarious, vomitous games of airplane that ended with him tossing me in the air and catching me and squeezing me like that, so hard it almost hurt.

A set of softer hands pried me gently out of his arms. Mom. She held me at arm's-length for a moment, searching my face for something, not saying anything, tears streaming down her face. She smiled and it turned into a sob and then she was holding me, too, and Dad's arm encircled us both.

When they let go, I managed to finally say something. "Darryl?"

"His father met him somewhere else. He's in the hospital."

"When can I see him?"

"It's our next stop," Dad said. He was grim. "He doesn't—" He stopped. "They say he'll be okay," he said. His voice was choked.

"How about Ange?"

"Her mother took her home. She wanted to wait here for you, but . . ."

I understood. I felt full of understanding now, for how all the families of all the people who'd been locked away must feel. The courtroom was full of tears and hugs, and even the bailiffs couldn't stop it.

"Let's go see Darryl," I said. "And let me borrow your phone?"

I called Ange on the way to the hospital where they were keeping Darryl—San Francisco General, just down the street from our place—and arranged to see her after dinner. She talked in a hurried whisper. Her mom wasn't sure whether to punish her or not, but Ange didn't want to tempt fate.

There were two state troopers in the corridor where Darryl was being held. They were holding off a legion of reporters who stood on tiptoe to see around them and get pictures. The flashes popped in our eyes like strobes, and I shook my head to clear it. My parents had brought me clean clothes and I'd changed in the backseat, but I still felt gross, even after scrubbing myself in the courthouse bathrooms.

Some of the reporters called my name. Oh yeah, that's right, I was famous now. The state troopers gave me a look, too—either they'd recognized my face or my name when the reporters called it out.

Darryl's father met us at the door of his hospital room, speaking in a whisper too low for the reporters to hear. He was in civvies, the jeans and sweater I normally thought of him wearing, but he had his service ribbons pinned to his breast.

"He's sleeping," he said. "He woke up a little while ago and he started crying. He couldn't stop. They gave him something to help him sleep."

He led us in, and there was Darryl, his hair clean and combed, sleeping with his mouth open. There was white stuff at the corners of his mouth. He had a semiprivate room, and in the other bed there was an older Arab-looking guy, in his forties. I realized it was the guy I'd been chained to on the way off of Treasure Island. We exchanged embarrassed waves.

Then I turned back to Darryl. I took his hand. His nails had been chewed to the quick. He'd been a nail-biter when he was a kid, but he'd kicked the habit when we got to high school. I think Van talked him out of it, telling him how gross it was for him to have his fingers in his mouth all the time.

I heard my parents and Darryl's dad take a step away, drawing the curtains around us. I put my face down next to his on the pillow. He had a straggly, patchy beard that reminded me of Zeb.

"Hey, D," I said. "You made it. You're going to be okay."

He snored a little. I almost said, "I love you," a phrase I'd only said to one nonfamily member ever, a phrase that was weird to say to another guy. In the end, I just gave his hand another squeeze. Poor Darryl.

epilogue

Barbara called me at the office on July 4th weekend. I wasn't the only one who'd come into work on the holiday weekend, but I was the only one whose excuse was that my day-release program wouldn't let me leave town.

In the end, they convicted me of stealing Masha's phone. Can you believe that? The prosecution had done a deal with my lawyer to drop all charges related to "electronic terrorism" and "inciting riots" in exchange for my pleading guilty to the misdemeanor petty theft charge. I got three months in a day-release program with a halfway house for juvenile defenders in the Mission. I slept at the halfway house, sharing a dorm with a bunch of actual criminals, gang kids and druggie kids, a couple of real nuts. During the day, I was "free" to go out and work at my "job."

"Marcus, they're letting her go," she said.

"Who?"

"Johnstone, Carrie Johnstone," she said. "The closed military tribunal cleared her of any wrongdoing. The file is sealed. She's being returned to active duty. They're sending her to Iraq."

Carrie Johnstone was severe haircut woman's name. It came out in the preliminary hearings at the California Superior Court, but that was just about all that came out. She wouldn't say a word about who she took orders from, what she'd done, who had been imprisoned and why. She just sat, perfectly silent, day after day, in the courthouse.

The feds, meanwhile, had blustered and shouted about the governor's "unilateral, illegal" shutdown of the Treasure Island facility, and the Mayor's eviction of fed cops from San Francisco. A lot of those cops had ended up in state prisons, along with the guards from Gitmo-by-the Bay.

Then, one day, there was no statement from the White House, nothing from the state capitol. And the next day, there was a dry, tense press conference held jointly on the steps of the governor's mansion, where the head of the DHS and the governor announced their "understanding."

The DHS would hold a closed, military tribunal to investigate "possible errors in judgment" committed after the attack on the Bay Bridge. The tribunal would use every tool at its disposal to ensure that criminal acts were properly punished. In return, control over DHS operations in California would go through the State Senate, which would have the power to shut down, inspect or re-prioritize all homeland security in the state.

The roar of the reporters had been deafening and Barbara had gotten the first question in. "Mr. Governor, with all due respect: we have incontrovertible video evidence that Marcus Yallow, a citizen of this state, native-born, was subjected to a simulated execution by DHS officers, apparently acting on orders from the White House. Is the State really willing to abandon any pretense of justice for its citizens in the face of illegal, barbaric *torture*?" Her voice trembled, but didn't crack.

The governor spread his hands. "The military tribunals will accomplish justice. If Mr. Yallow—or any other person who has cause to fault the Department of Homeland Security—wants further justice, he is, of course, entitled to sue for such damages as may be owing to him from the federal government."

That's what I was doing. Over twenty thousand civil lawsuits were filed against the DHS in the week after the governor's announcement. Mine was being handled by the ACLU, and they'd filed motions to get at the results of the closed military tribunals. So far, the courts were pretty sympathetic to this.

But I hadn't expected this.

"She got off totally scot-free?"

"The press release doesn't say much. 'After a thorough examination of the events in San Francisco and in the special antiterror detention center on Treasure Island, it is the finding of this tribunal that Ms. Johnstone's actions do not warrant further discipline.' There's that word, 'further'—like they've already punished her."

I snorted. I'd dreamed of Carrie Johnstone nearly every night since I was released from Gitmo-by-the-Bay. I'd seen her face looming over mine, that little snarly smile as she told the man to give me a "drink."

"Marcus—" Barbara said, but I cut her off.

"It's fine. It's fine. I'm going to do a video about this. Get it out over the weekend. Mondays are big days for viral video. Everyone'll be coming back from the holiday weekend, looking for something funny to forward around school or the office."

I saw a shrink twice a week as part of my deal at the halfway house. Once I'd gotten over seeing that as some kind of punishment, it had been good. He'd helped me focus on doing constructive things when I was upset, instead of letting it eat me up. The videos helped.

"I have to go," I said, swallowing hard to keep the emotion out of my voice.

"Take care of yourself, Marcus," Barbara said.

Ange hugged me from behind as I hung up the phone. "I just read about it online," she said. She read a million newsfeeds, pulling them with a headline reader that sucked up stories as fast as they ended up on the wire. She was our official blogger, and she was good at it, snipping out the interesting stories and throwing them online like a short-order cook turning around breakfast orders.

I turned around in her arms so that I was hugging her from in front. Truth be told, we hadn't gotten a lot of work done that day. I wasn't allowed to be out of the halfway house after dinnertime, and she couldn't visit me there. We saw each other around the office, but there were usually a lot of other people around, which kind of put a crimp in our cuddling. Being alone in the office for a day was too much temptation. It was hot and sultry, too, which meant we were both in tank tops and shorts, a lot of skin-to-skin contact as we worked next to each other.

"I'm going to make a video," I said. "I want to release it today."

"Good," she said. "Let's do it."

Ange read the press release. I did a little monologue, synched over that famous footage of me on the waterboard, eyes wild in the harsh light of the camera, tears streaming down my face, hair matted and flecked with barf.

"This is me. I am on a waterboard. I am being tortured in a simulated execution. The torture is supervised by a woman called Carrie Johnstone. She works for the government. You might remember her from this video."

I cut in the video of Johnstone and Kurt Rooney. "That's Johnstone and Secretary of State Kurt Rooney, the president's chief strategist."

"The nation does not love that city. As far as they're concerned, it is a Sodom and Gomorrah of fags and atheists who deserve to rot in hell. The only reason the country cares what they think in San Francisco is that they had the good fortune to have been blown to hell by some Islamic terrorists."

"He's talking about the city where I live. At last count, four thousand two hundred fifteen of my neighbors were killed on the day he's talking about. But some of them may not have been killed. Some of them disappeared into the same prison where I was tortured. Some mothers and fathers, children and lovers, brothers and sisters will never see their loved ones again—because they were secretly imprisoned in an illegal jail right here in the San Francisco Bay. They were shipped overseas. The records were meticulous, but Carrie Johnstone has the encryption keys." I cut back to Carrie Johnstone, the footage of her sitting at the board table with Rooney, laughing.

I cut in the footage of Johnstone being arrested. "When they arrested her, I thought we'd get justice. All the people she broke and disappeared. But the president"—I cut to a still of him laughing and playing golf on one of his many holidays—"and chief strategist"—now a still of Rooney shaking hands with an infamous terrorist leader who used to be on "our side"—"intervened. They sent her to a secret military tribunal and now that tribunal has cleared her. Somehow, they saw nothing wrong with all of this."

I cut in a photomontage of the hundreds of shots of prisoners in their cells that Barbara had published on the *Bay Guardian*'s site the day we were released. "We elected these people. We pay their salaries. They're supposed to be on our side. They're supposed to defend our freedoms. But these people"—a series of shots of Johnstone and the others who'd been sent to the tribunal—"betrayed our trust. The election is four months away. That's a lot of time. Enough for you to go out and find five of your neighbors—five people who've given up on voting because their choice is 'none of the above.'

"Talk to your neighbors. Make them promise to vote. Make them promise to take the country back from the torturers and thugs. The people who laughed at my friends as they lay fresh in their graves at the bottom of the harbor. Make them promise to talk to their neighbors.

"Most of us choose none of the above. It's not working. You have to choose—choose freedom.

"My name is Marcus Yallow. I was tortured by my country, but I still love it here. I'm seventeen years old. I want to grow up in a free country. I want to live in a free country."

I faded out to the logo of the website. Ange had built it, with help from Jolu, who got us all the free hosting we could ever need on Pigspleen.

The office was an interesting place. Technically we were called Coalition of Voters for a Free America, but everyone called us the Xnetters. The organization—a charitable nonprofit—had been cofounded by Barbara and some of her lawyer friends right after the liberation of Treasure Island. The funding was kicked off by some tech millionaires who couldn't believe that a bunch of hacker kids had kicked the DHS's ass. Sometimes, they'd ask us to go down the peninsula to Sand Hill Road, where all the venture capitalists were, and give a little presentation on Xnet technology. There were about a zillion start-ups who were trying to make a buck on the Xnet.

Whatever—I didn't have to have anything to do with it, and I got a desk and an office with a storefront, right there on Valencia Street, where we gave away ParanoidXbox CDs and held workshops on building better WiFi antennas. A surprising number of average people dropped in to make personal donations, both of hardware (you can run ParanoidLinux on just about anything, not just Xbox Universals) and cash money. They loved us.

The big plan was to launch our own ARG in September, just in time for the election, and to really tie it in with signing up voters and getting them to the polls. Only 42 percent of Americans showed up at the polls for the last election—nonvoters had a huge majority. I kept trying to get Darryl and Van to one of our planning sessions, but they kept on declining. They were spending a lot of time together, and Van insisted that it was totally nonromantic. Darryl wouldn't talk to me much at all, though he sent me long emails about just about everything that wasn't about Van or terrorism or prison.

Ange squeezed my hand. "God, I hate that woman," she said.

I nodded. "Just one more rotten thing this country's done to Iraq," I said. "If they sent her to my town, I'd probably become a terrorist."

"You did become a terrorist when they sent her to your town."

"So I did," I said.

"Are you going to Ms. Galvez's hearing on Monday?"

"Totally." I'd introduced Ange to Ms. Galvez a couple weeks before, when my old teacher invited me over for dinner. The teacher's union had gotten a hearing for her before the board of the Unified School District to argue for getting her old job back. They said that Fred Benson was coming out of (early) retirement to testify against her. I was looking forward to seeing her again.

"Do you want to go get a burrito?"

"Totally."

"Let me get my hot sauce," she said.

I checked my email one more time—my Pirate Party email, which still got a dribble of messages from old Xnetters who hadn't found my Coalition of Voters address yet.

The latest message was from a throwaway email address from one of the new Brazilian anonymizers.

> **Found her, thanks. You didn't tell me she was so h4wt.**

"Who's *that* from?"

I laughed. "Zeb," I said. "Remember Zeb? I gave him Masha's email address. I figured, if they're both underground, might as well introduce them to one another."

"He thinks Masha is *cute*?"

306 | cory doctorow

"Give the guy a break, he's clearly had his mind warped by circumstances."

"And you?"

"Me?"

"Yeah—was your mind warped by circumstances?"

I held Ange out at arm's length and looked her up and down and up and down. I held her cheeks and stared through her thick-framed glasses into her big, mischievous tilted eyes. I ran my fingers through her hair.

"Ange, I've never thought more clearly in my whole life."

She kissed me then, and I kissed her back, and it was some time before we went out for that burrito.

afterword

by Bruce Schneier

I'm a security technologist. My job is making people secure.

I think about security systems and how to break them. Then, how to make them more secure. Computer security systems. Surveillance systems. Airplane security systems and voting machines and RFID chips and everything else.

Cory invited me into the last few pages of his book because he wanted me to tell you that security is fun. It's incredibly fun. It's cat and mouse, who can outsmart whom, hunter versus hunted fun. I think it's the most fun job you can possibly have. If you thought it was fun to read about Marcus outsmarting the gait-recognition cameras with rocks in his shoes, think of how much more fun it would be if you were the first person in the world to think of that.

Working in security means knowing a lot about technology. It might mean knowing about computers and networks, or cameras and how they work, or the chemistry of bomb detection. But really, security is a mindset. It's a way of thinking. Marcus is a great example of that way of thinking. He's always looking for ways a security system fails. I'll bet he couldn't walk into a store without figuring out a way to shoplift. Not that he'd do it—there's a difference between knowing how to defeat a security system and actually defeating it—but he'd know he could.

It's how security people think. We're constantly looking at security systems and how to get around them; we can't help it.

This kind of thinking is important no matter what side of security you're on. If you've been hired to build a shoplift-proof store, you'd better know how to shoplift. If you're designing a camera system that detects individual gaits, you'd better plan for people putting rocks in their shoes. Because if you don't, you're not going to design anything good.

So when you're wandering through your day, take a moment to look at the security systems around you. Look at the cameras in the stores you shop at. (Do they prevent crime, or just move it next door?) See how a restaurant operates. (If you pay after you eat, why don't more people just leave without paying?) Pay attention at airport security. (How could you get a weapon onto an airplane?) Watch what the teller does at a bank. (Bank security is designed to prevent tellers from stealing just as much as it is to prevent you from stealing.) Stare at an anthill. (Insects are all about security.) Read the Constitution, and notice all the ways it provides people with security against government. Look at traffic lights and door locks and all the security systems on television and in the movies. Figure out how they work, what threats they protect against and what threats they don't, how they fail, and how they can be exploited.

Spend enough time doing this, and you'll find yourself thinking differently about the world. You'll start noticing that many of the security systems out there don't actually do what they claim to, and that much of our national security is a waste of money. You'll understand privacy as essential to security, not in opposition. You'll stop worrying about things other people worry about, and start worrying about things other people don't even think about.

Sometimes you'll notice something about security that no one has ever thought about before. And maybe you'll figure out a new way to break a security system.

It was only a few years ago that someone invented phishing.

I'm frequently amazed how easy it is to break some pretty big-name security systems. There are a lot of reasons for this, but the big one is that it's impossible to prove that something is secure. All you can do is try to break it. If you fail, you know that it's secure enough to keep *you* out, but what about someone who's smarter than you? Anyone can design a security system so strong he himself can't break it.

Think about that for a second, because it's not obvious. No one is qualified to analyze their own security designs, because the designer and the analyzer will be the same person, with the same limits. Someone else has to analyze the security, because it has to be secure against things the designers didn't think of.

This means that all of us have to analyze the security that other people design. And surprisingly often, one of us breaks it. Marcus's exploits aren't far-fetched; that kind of thing happens all the time. Go onto the net and look up "bump key" or "Bic pen Kryptonite lock"; you'll find a couple of really interesting stories about seemingly strong security defeated by pretty basic technology.

And when that happens, be sure to publish it on the Internet somewhere. Secrecy and security aren't the same, even though it may seem that way. Only bad security relies on secrecy; good security works even if all the details of it are public.

And making vulnerabilities public forces security designers to design better security, and makes us all better consumers of security. If you buy a Kryptonite bike lock and it can be defeated with a Bic pen, you're not getting very good security for your money. And, likewise, if a bunch of smart kids can defeat the DHS's antiterrorist technologies, then it's not going to do a very good job against real terrorists.

Trading privacy for security is stupid enough; not getting any actual security in the bargain is even more stupid.

So close the book and go. The world is full of security systems. Hack one of them.

Bruce Schneier
www.schneier.com

bibliography

No writer creates from scratch—we all engage in what Isaac Newton called "standing on the shoulders of giants." We borrow, plunder and remix the art and culture created by those around us and by our literary forebears.

If you liked this book and want to learn more, there are plenty of sources to turn to, online and at your local library or bookstore.

Hacking is a great subject. All science relies on telling other people what you've done so that they can verify it, learn from it and improve on it, and hacking is all about that process, so there's plenty published on the subject.

Start with Andrew "bunnie" Huang's *Hacking the Xbox* (No Starch Press, 2003), a wonderful book that tells the story of how bunnie, then a student at MIT, reverse-engineered the Xbox's anti-tampering mechanisms and opened the way for all the subsequent cool hacks for the platform. In telling the story, bunnie has also created a kind of Bible for reverse engineering and hardware hacking.

Bruce Schneier's *Secrets and Lies* (Wiley, 2000) and *Beyond Fear* (Copernicus, 2003) are the definitive layperson's texts on understanding security and thinking critically about it, while his *Applied Cryptography* (Wiley, 1995) remains the authoritative source for understanding crypto. Bruce maintains an excellent blog and mailing list at schneier.com/blog. Crypto and security are the realm of the talented amateur, and the "cypherpunk" movement is full of kids, homemakers, parents, lawyers and every other stripe of person, hammering away on security protocols and ciphers.

There are several great magazines devoted to this subject, but the two best ones are *2600: The Hacker Quarterly,* which is full of pseudonymous, boasting accounts of hacks accomplished, and

O'Reilly's *MAKE* magazine, which features solid how-tos for making your own hardware projects at home.

The online world overflows with material on this subject, of course. Ed Felten and Alex J. Halderman's Freedom to Tinker (www.freedom-to-tinker.com) is a blog maintained by two fantastic Princeton engineering profs who write lucidly about security, wiretapping, anticopying technology and crypto.

Don't miss Natalie Jeremijenko's "Feral Robotics" at UC San Diego (xdesign.ucsd.edu/feralrobots/). Natalie and her students rewire toy robot dogs from Toys "R" Us and turn them into badass toxic waste detectors. They unleash them on public parks where big corporations have dumped their waste and demonstrate in media-friendly fashion how toxic the ground is.

Like many of the hacks in this book, the tunneling-over-DNS stuff is real. Dan Kaminsky, a tunneling expert of the first water, published details in 2004 (www.doxpara.com/bo2004.ppt).

The guru of "citizen journalism" is Dan Gillmor, who is presently running the Center for Citizen Media at Harvard and UC Berkeley—he also wrote a hell of a book on the subject, *We, the Media* (O'Reilly, 2004).

If you want to learn more about hacking arphids, start with Annalee Newitz's *Wired* article "The RFID Hacking Underground" (www.wirednews.com/wired/archive/14.05/rfid.html). Adam Greenfield's *Everyware* (New Riders Press, 2006) is a chilling look at the dangers of a world of arphids.

Neil Gershenfeld's Fab Lab at MIT (fab.cba.mit.edu) is hacking out the world's first real, cheap "3D printers" that can pump out any object you can dream of. This is documented in Gershenfeld's excellent book on the subject, *Fab* (Basic Books, 2005).

Bruce Sterling's *Shaping Things* (MIT Press, 2005) shows how arphids and fabs could be used to force companies to build products that don't poison the world.

Speaking of Bruce Sterling, he wrote the first great book on hackers and the law, *The Hacker Crackdown* (Bantam, 1993), which is also the first book published by a major publisher that was released on the Internet at the same time (copies abound; see stuff .mit.edu/hacker/hacker.html for one). It was reading this book that turned me on to the Electronic Frontier Foundation, where I was privileged to work for four years.

The Electronic Frontier Foundation (www.eff.org) is a charitable membership organization with a student rate. They spend the money that private individuals give them to keep the Internet safe for personal liberty, free speech, due process and the rest of the Bill of Rights. They're the Internet's most effective freedom fighters, and you can join the struggle just by signing up for their mailing list and writing to your elected officials when they're considering selling you out in the name of fighting terrorism, piracy, the mafia or whatever bogeyman has caught their attention today. EFF also helps maintain TOR, The Onion Router, which is a real technology you can use *right now* to get out of your government, school or library's censoring firewall (tor.eff.org).

EFF has a huge, deep website with amazing information aimed at a general audience, as do the American Civil Liberties Union (aclu.org), Public Knowledge (publicknowledge.org), FreeCulture (freeculture.org), Creative Commons (creativecommons.org)—all of which are also worthy of your support. FreeCulture is an international student movement that actively recruits kids to found their own local chapters at their high schools and universities. It's a great way to get involved and make a difference.

A lot of websites chronicle the fight for cyberliberties, but few go at it with the verve of Slashdot, "News for Nerds, Stuff That Matters" (slashdot.org).

And of course, you *have* to visit Wikipedia, the collaborative, net-authored encyclopedia that anyone can edit, with more than a million entries in English alone. Wikipedia covers hacking and counterculture in astonishing depth and with amazing, up-to-the-nanosecond currency. One caution: you can't just look at the entries in Wikipedia. It's really important to look at the "History" and "Discussion" links at the top of every Wikipedia page to see how the current version of the truth was arrived at, get an appreciation for the competing points of view there and decide for yourself whom you trust.

If you want to get at some *real* forbidden knowledge, have a skim around Cryptome (cryptome.org), the world's most amazing archive

of secret, suppressed and liberated information. Cryptome's brave
publishers collect and publish material that's been pried out of
the state by Freedom of Information Act requests, or leaked by
whistle-blowers.

The best fictional account of the history of crypto is, hands
down, Neal Stephenson's *Cryptonomicon* (Avon, 2002). Stephenson
tells the story of Alan Turing and the Nazi Enigma Machine, turning it into a gripping war novel that you won't be able to put down.

The Pirate Party mentioned in *Little Brother* is real and thriving
in Sweden (www.piratpartiet.se), Denmark, the USA and France at
the time of this writing (July, 2006). They're a little out there, but
a movement takes all kinds.

Speaking of out there, Abbie Hoffman and the Yippies did
indeed try to levitate the Pentagon, throw money into the stock
exchange and work with a group called the Up Against the Wall
Motherf___ers. Abbie Hoffman's classic book on ripping off the
system, *Steal This Book,* is back in print (Four Walls Eight Windows, 2002) and it's also online as a collaborative wiki for people
who want to try to update it (stealthiswiki.nine9pages.com).

Hoffman's autobiography, *Soon to Be a Major Motion Picture*
(also in print from Four Walls Eight Windows), is one of my favorite memoirs ever, even if it is highly fictionalized. Hoffman was an
incredible storyteller and had great activist instincts. If you want
to know how he really lived his life, though, try Larry Sloman's
Steal This Dream (Doubleday, 1998).

More counterculture fun: Jack Kerouac's *On the Road* can be
had in practically any used bookstore for a buck or two. Allen
Ginsberg's *HOWL* is online in many places, and you can hear him
read it if you search for the MP3 at archive.org. For bonus points,
track down the album *Tenderness Junction* by the Fugs, which in-
cludes the audio of Allen Ginsberg and Abbie Hoffman's levitation
ceremony at the Pentagon.

This book couldn't have been written if not for George Orwell's
magnificent, world-changing *Nineteen Eighty-Four,* the best novel
ever published on how societies go wrong. I read this book when
I was twelve and have read it thirty or forty times since, and
every time, I get something new out of it. Orwell was a master of

storytelling and was clearly sick over the totalitarian state that had emerged in the Soviet Union. *Nineteen Eighty-Four* holds up today as a genuinely frightening work of science fiction, and it is one of the novels that literally changed the world. Today, "Orwellian" is synonymous with a state of ubiquitous surveillance, doublethink and torture.

Many novelists have tackled parts of the story in *Little Brother*. Daniel Pinkwater's towering comic masterpiece, *Alan Mendelsohn: The Boy from Mars* (presently in print as part of the omnibus *5 Novels*, Farrar Straus Giroux, 1997) is a book that every geek needs to read. If you've ever felt like an outcast for being too smart or weird, READ THIS BOOK. It changed my life.

On a more contemporary front, there's Scott Westerfeld's *So Yesterday* (Razorbill, 2004), which follows the adventures of cool hunters and counterculture jammers. Scott and his wife, Justine Larbalestier, were my partial inspiration to write a book for young adults—as was Kathe Koja. Thanks, guys.

acknowledgments

This book owes a tremendous debt to many writers, friends, mentors and heroes who made it possible.

For the hackers and cypherpunks: Andrew "bunnie" Huang, Seth Schoen, Ed Felten, Alex Halderman, Gweeds, Natalie Jeremijenko, Emmanuel Goldstein, Aaron Swartz

For the heroes: Mitch Kapor, John Gilmore, John Perry Barlow, Larry Lessig, Shari Steele, Cindy Cohn, Fred von Lohmann, Jamie Boyle, George Orwell, Abbie Hoffman, Joe Trippi, Bruce Schneier, Ross Dowson, Harry Kopyto, Tim O'Reilly

For the writers: Bruce Sterling, Kathe Koja, Scott Westerfeld, Justine Larbalestier, Pat York, Annalee Newitz, Dan Gillmor, Daniel Pinkwater, Kevin Poulsen, Wendy Grossman, Jay Lake, Ben Rosenbaum

For the friends: Fiona Romeo, Quinn Norton, Danny O'Brien, Jon Gilbert, danah boyd, Zak Hanna, Emily Hurson, Grad Conn, John Henson, Amanda Foubister, Xeni Jardin, Mark Frauenfelder, David Pescovitz, John Battelle, Karl Levesque, Kate Miles, Neil and Tara-Lee Doctorow, Rael Dornfest, Ken Snider

For the mentors: Judy Merril, Roz and Gord Doctorow, Harriet Wolff, Jim Kelly, Damon Knight, Scott Edelman

Thank you all for giving me the tools to think and write about these ideas.

homeland

For Alice and Poesy, who make me whole

Attending Burning Man made me simultaneously one of the most photographed people on the planet and one of the least surveilled humans in the modern world.

I adjusted my burnoose, covering up my nose and mouth and tucking its edge into place under the lower rim of my big, scratched goggles. The sun was high, the temperature well over a hundred degrees, and breathing through the embroidered cotton scarf made it even more stifling. But the wind had just kicked up, and there was a lot of playa dust—fine gypsum sand, deceptively soft and powdery, but alkali enough to make your eyes burn and your skin crack—and after two days in the desert, I had learned that it was better to be hot than to choke.

Pretty much everyone was holding a camera of some kind— mostly phones, of course, but also big SLRs and even old-fashioned film cameras, including a genuine antique plate camera whose operator hid out from the dust under a huge black cloth that made me hot just to look at it. Everything was ruggedized for the fine, blowing dust, mostly through the simple expedient of sticking it in a Ziploc bag, which is what I'd done with my phone. I turned around slowly to get a panorama and saw that the man walking past me was holding the string for a gigantic helium balloon a hundred yards overhead, from which dangled a digital video camera. Also, the man holding the balloon was naked.

Well, not entirely. He was wearing shoes. I understood that: playa dust is hard on your feet. They call it playa-foot, when the alkali dust dries out your skin so much that it starts to crack and peel. Everyone agrees that playa-foot sucks.

Burning Man is a festival held every Labor Day weekend in the middle of Nevada's Black Rock Desert. Fifty thousand people show up in this incredibly harsh, hot, dusty environment and build a huge city—Black Rock City—and *participate*. "Spectator" is a vicious insult in Black Rock City. Everyone's supposed to be *doing* stuff and, yeah, also admiring everyone else's stuff (hence all the cameras). At Burning Man, everyone is the show.

I wasn't naked, but the parts of me that were showing *were* decorated with elaborate mandalas laid on with colored zinc. A lady as old as my mother, wearing a tie-dyed wedding dress, had offered to paint me that morning, and she'd done a great job. That's another thing about Burning Man: it runs on a gift economy, which means that you generally go around offering nice things to strangers a lot, which makes for a surprisingly pleasant environment. The designs the painter had laid down made me look *amazing,* and there were plenty of cameras aiming my way as I ambled across the open desert toward Nine O'Clock.

Black Rock City is a pretty modern city: it has public sanitation (portable chem-toilets decorated with raunchy poems reminding you not to put anything but toilet paper in them), electricity and Internet service (at Six O'Clock, the main plaza in the middle of the ring-shaped city), something like a government (the nonprofit that runs Burning Man), several local newspapers (all of them doing better than the newspapers in the real world!), a dozen radio stations, an all-volunteer police force (the Black Rock Rangers, who patrolled wearing tutus or parts of chicken suits or glitter paint), and many other amenities associated with the modern world.

But BRC has no official surveillance. There are no CCTVs, no checkpoints—at least not after the main gate, where tickets are collected—no ID checks at all, no bag searches, no RFID sniffers, no mobile phone companies logging your movements. There was also no mobile phone service. No one drives—except for the weird art cars registered with the Department of Mutant Vehicles—so there were no license plate cameras and no sniffers for your E-ZPasses. The WiFi was open and unlogged. Attendees at Burning Man agreed not to use their photos commercially without permission, and it was generally considered polite to ask people before taking their portraits.

So there I was, having my picture taken through the blowing

dust as I gulped down water from the water jug I kept clipped to my belt at all times, sucking at the stubby built-in straw under cover of the blue-and-silver burnoose, simultaneously observed and observer, simultaneously observed and unsurveilled, and it was *glorious*.

"Wahoo!" I shouted to the dust and the art cars and the naked people and the enormous wooden splay-armed effigy perched atop a pyramid straight ahead of me in the middle of the desert. This was The Man, and we'd burn him in three nights, and that's why it was called Burning Man. I couldn't wait.

"You're in a good mood," a jawa said from behind me. Even with the tone-shifter built into its dust mask, the cloaked sand-person had an awfully familiar voice.

"Ange?" I said. We'd been missing each other all that day, ever since I'd woken up an hour before her and snuck out of the tent to catch the sunrise (which was *awesome*), and we'd been leaving each other notes back at camp all day about where we were heading next. Ange had spent the summer spinning up the jawa robes, working with cooling towels that trapped sweat as it evaporated, channeling it back over her skin for extra evaporative cooling. She'd hand-dyed it a mottled brown, tailored it into the characteristic monkish robe shape, and added crossed bandoliers. These exaggerated her breasts, which made the whole thing entirely and totally *warsome*. She hadn't worn it out in public yet, and now, in the dust and the glare, she was undoubtedly the greatest sandperson I'd ever met. I hugged her and she hugged me back so hard it knocked the wind out of me, one of her trademarked wrestling-hold cuddles.

"I smudged your paint," she said through the voice-shifter after we unclinched.

"I got zinc on your robes," I said.

She shrugged. "Like it matters! We both look fabulous. Now, what have you seen and what have you done and where have you been, young man?"

"Where to start?" I said. I'd been wandering up and down the radial avenues that cut through the city, lined with big camps sporting odd exhibits—one camp where a line of people were efficiently making snow cones for anyone who wanted them, work-ing with huge blocks of ice and a vicious ice-shaver. Then a camp where someone had set up a tall, linoleum-covered slide that you could toboggan down on a plastic magic carpet, after first dump-ing a gallon of waste water over the lino to make it plenty slippery. It was a very clever way to get rid of gray water (that's water that you've showered in, or used to wash your dishes or hands—black water being water that's got poo or pee in it). One of the other Burn-ing Man rules was "leave no trace"—when we left, we'd take every scrap of Black Rock City with us, and that included all the gray wa-ter. But the slide made for a great gray water evaporator, and every drop of liquid that the sliders helped turn into vapor was a drop of liquid the camp wouldn't have to pack all the way back to Reno.

There'd been pervy camps where they were teaching couples to tie each other up; a "junk food glory hole" that you put your mouth over in order to receive a mysterious and unhealthy treat (I'd gotten a mouthful of some kind of super-sugary breakfast cereal studded with coconut "marshmallows" shaped like astrological symbols); a camp where they were offering free service for playa bikes (beater bikes caked with playa dust and decorated with glitter and fun fur and weird fetishes and bells); a tea-house camp where I'd been given a very precisely made cup of some kind of Japanese tea I'd never heard of that was delicious and sharp; camps full of whimsy; camps full of physics; camps full of optical illusions; camps full of men and women; a kids' camp full of screaming kids running around playing some kind of semisupervised outdoor game—things I'd never suspected existed.

And I'd only seen a tiny slice of Black Rock City.

I told Ange about as much as I could remember and she nod-ded or said "ooh," or "aah," or demanded to know where I'd seen things. Then she told me about the stuff she'd seen—a camp where topless women were painting one another's breasts; a camp where an entire brass band was performing; a camp where they'd built a medieval trebuchet that fired ancient, broken-down pianos down a firing range, the audience holding its breath in total silence while they waited for the glorious crash each piano made when it ex-ploded into flinders on the hardpack desert.

"Can you believe this place?" Ange said, jumping up and down on the spot in excitement, making her bandoliers jingle.

"I know—can you believe we almost didn't make it?"

I'd always sort of planned on going out to see The Man burn—after all, I grew up in San Francisco, the place with the largest concentration of burners in the world. But it took a lot of work to participate in Burning Man. First, there was the matter of packing for a camping trip in the middle of the desert where you had to pack in *everything*—including water—and then pack it all out again, everything you didn't leave behind in the porta-potties. And there were *very* strict rules about what could go in *those*. Then there was the gift economy: figuring out what I could bring to the desert that someone else might want. Plus the matter of costumes, cool art, and inventions to show off . . . every time I started to think about it, I just about had a nervous breakdown.

But this year, of all years, I'd made it. This was the year both my parents lost their jobs. The year I'd dropped out of college rather than take on any more student debt. The year I'd spent knocking on every door I could find, looking for paid work—*anything!*—without getting even a nibble.

"Never underestimate the determination of a kid who is cash-poor and time-rich," Ange said solemnly, pulling down her face mask with one hand and yanking me down to kiss me with the other.

"That's catchy," I said. "You should print T-shirts."

"Oh," she said. "That reminds me. I got a T-shirt!"

She threw open her robe to reveal a proud red tee that read MAKE BEAUTIFUL ART AND SET IT ON FIRE, laid out like those British KEEP CALM AND CARRY ON posters, with the Burning Man logo where the crown should be.

"Just in time, too," I said, holding my nose. I was only partly kidding. At the last minute, we'd both decided to ditch half the clothes we'd planned on bringing so that we could fit more parts for Secret Project X-1 into our backpacks. Between that and taking "bits and pits" baths by rubbing the worst of the dried sweat, body paint, sunscreen, and miscellaneous fluids off with baby wipes once a day, neither of us smelled very nice.

She shrugged. "The playa provides." It was one of the Burning Man mottoes we'd picked up on the first day, when we both realized that we thought the other one had brought the sunscreen, and just as we were about to get into an argument about it, we stumbled on Sunscreen Camp, where some nice people had slathered us all over with SPF 50 and given us some baggies to take with. "The playa provides!" they'd said, and wished us well.

I put my arm around her shoulders. She dramatically turned her nose up at my armpit, then made a big show of putting on her face mask.

"Come on," she said. "Let's go out to the temple."

The temple was a huge, two-story sprawling structure, dotted with high towers and flying buttresses. It was filled with robotic Tibetan gongs that played strange clanging tunes throughout the day. I'd seen it from a distance that morning while walking around the playa, watching the sun turn the dust rusty orange, but I hadn't been up close.

The outer wings of the temple were open to the sky, made of the same lumber as the rest of the whole elaborate curlicue structure. The walls were lined with benches and were inset with niches and nooks. And everywhere, every surface, was covered in writing and signs and posters and pictures.

And almost all of it was about dead people.

"Oh," Ange said to me, as we trailed along the walls, reading the memorials that had been inked or painted or stapled there. I was reading a handwritten thirty-page-long letter from an adult woman to her parents, about all the ways they'd hurt her and made her miserable and destroyed her life, about how she'd felt when they'd died, about how her marriages had been destroyed by the craziness they'd instilled in her. It veered from wild accusation to tender exasperation to anger to sorrow, like some kind of emotional roller coaster. I felt like I was spying on something I wasn't supposed to see, except that everything in the temple was there to be seen.

Every surface in the temple was a memorial to something or someone. There were baby shoes and pictures of grannies, a pair of crutches and a beat-up cowboy hat with a hatband woven from

homeland | 329

dead dried flowers. Burners—dressed and undressed like a circus from the end of the world—walked solemnly around these, reading them, more often than not with tears running down their faces. Pretty soon, I had tears running down my face. It moved me in a way that nothing had ever moved me before. Especially since it was all going to burn on Sunday night, before we tore down Black Rock City and went home.

Ange sat in the dust and began looking through a sketchbook whose pages were filled with dense, dark illustrations. I wandered into the main atrium of the temple, a tall, airy space whose walls were lined with gongs. Here, the floor was carpeted with people— sitting and lying down, eyes closed, soaking in the solemnity of the moment, some with small smiles, some weeping, some with expressions of utmost serenity.

I'd tried meditating once, during a drama class in high school. It hadn't worked very well. Some of the kids kept on giggling. There was some kind of shouting going on in the hallway outside the door. The clock on the wall ticked loudly, reminding me that at any moment, there'd be a loud buzzer and the roar and stamp of thousands of kids all trying to force their way through a throng to their next class. But I'd read a lot about meditation and how good it was supposed to be for you. In theory it was easy, too: just sit down and think of nothing.

So I did. I shifted my utility belt around so that I could sit down without it digging into my ass and waited until a patch of floor was vacated, then sat. There were streamers of sunlight piercing the high windows above, lancing down in gray-gold spikes that glittered with dancing dust. I looked into one of these, at the dancing motes, and then closed my eyes. I pictured a grid of four squares, featureless and white with thick black rims and sharp corners. In my mind's eye, I erased one square. Then another. Then another. Now there was just one square. I erased it.

There was nothing now. I was thinking of nothing, literally. Then I was thinking about the fact that I was thinking about nothing, mentally congratulating myself, and I realized that I was thinking of something again. I pictured my four squares and started over.

I don't know how long I sat there, but there were moments when the world seemed to both go away and be more present than it ever had been. I was living in that exact and very moment, not anticipating anything that might happen later, not thinking of anything that had just happened, just being *right there*. It only lasted for a fraction of a second each time, but each of those fragmentary moments were . . . well, they were something.

I opened my eyes. I was breathing in time with the gongs around me, a slow, steady cadence. There was something digging into my butt, a bit of my utility belt's strap or something. The girl in front of me had a complex equation branded into the skin of her shoulder blades, the burned skin curdled into deep, sharp-relief mathematical symbols and numbers. Someone smelled like weed. Someone was sobbing softly. Someone outside the temple called out to someone else. Someone laughed. Time was like molasses, flowing slowly and stickily around me. Nothing seemed important and everything seemed wonderful. That was what I'd been looking for, all my life, without ever knowing it. I smiled.

"Hello, M1k3y," a voice hissed in my ear, very soft and very close, lips brushing my lobe, breath tickling me. The voice tickled me, too, tickled my memory. I knew that voice, though I hadn't heard it in a very long time.

Slowly, as though I were a giraffe with a neck as tall as a tree, I turned my head to look around.

"Hello, Masha," I said, softly. "Fancy meeting you here."

Her hand was on my hand and I remembered the way she'd twisted my wrist around in some kind of martial arts hold the last time I'd seen her. I didn't think she'd be able to get away with bending my arm up behind my back and walking me out of the temple on my tiptoes. If I shouted for help, thousands of burners would . . . well, they wouldn't tear her limb from limb, but they'd do *something*. Kidnapping people on the playa was definitely against the rules. It was in the Ten Principles, I was nearly certain of it.

She tugged at my wrist. "Let's go," she said. "Come on."

I got to my feet and followed her, freely and of my own will, and even though I trembled with fear as I got up, there was a nugget of excitement in there, too. Of course this was happening now, at Burning Man. A couple years ago, I'd been in the midst of more excitement than anyone would or could want. I'd led a techno-guerrilla army against the Department of Homeland Security, met a girl and fell in love with her, been arrested and tortured, found celebrity, and sued the government. Since then, it had all gone downhill, in a weird way. Being waterboarded was terrible, awful, unimaginable—I still had nightmares—but it happened and then it *ended*. My parents' slow slide into bankruptcy, the hard, grinding reality of a city with no jobs for anyone, let alone a semiqualified college dropout like me, and the student debt that I *had* to pay every month. It was a pile of misery that I lived under every day, and it showed no sign of going away. It wasn't dramatic, dynamic trouble, the kind of thing you got war stories out of years after the fact. It was just, you know, reality.

And reality sucked.

So I went with Masha, because Masha had been living underground with Zeb for the better part of two years, and whatever else she was, she was someone whose life was generating a lot of exciting stories. Her reality might suck too, but it sucked in huge, showy, neon letters—not in the quiet, crabbed handwriting of a desperate and broke teenager scribbling in his diary.

I went with Masha, and she led me out of the temple. The wind was blowing worse than it had been before, real white-out conditions, and I pulled down my goggles and pulled up my scarf again. Even with them on, I could barely see, and each breath of air filled my mouth with the taste of dried saliva and powdery gypsum from my burnoose. Masha's hair wasn't bright pink anymore; it was a mousy blond-brown, turned gray with dust, cut into duckling fuzz all over, the kind of haircut you could maintain yourself with a clipper. I'd had that haircut, off and on, through much of my adolescence. Her skull bones were fine and fragile, her skin stretched like paper over her cheekbones. Her neck muscles corded and her jaw muscles jumped. She'd lost weight since I'd seen her last, and her skin had gone leathery brown, a color that was deeper than a mere summer tan.

We went all of ten steps out from the temple, but we might have been a mile from it—it was lost in the dust. There were people around, but I couldn't make out their words over the spooky moan of the wind blowing through the temple's windows. Bits of grit crept between my goggles and my sweaty cheeks and made my eyes and nose run.

"Far enough," she said, and let go of my wrist, holding her hands before her. I saw that the fingertips on her left hand were weirdly deformed and squashed and bent, and I had a vivid recollection of slamming the rolling door of a moving van down on her hand as she chased me. She'd been planning to semikidnap me at the time, and I was trying to get away with evidence that my best friend Darryl had been kidnapped by Homeland Security, but I still heard the surprised and pained shout she'd let out when the door crunched on her hand. She saw where I was looking and took her hand away, tucking it into the sleeve of the loose cotton shirt she wore.

"How's tricks, M1k3y?" she said.

"It's Marcus these days," I said. "Tricks have been better. How about you? Can't say I expected to see you again. Ever. Especially not at Burning Man."

Her eyes crinkled behind her goggles and her veil shifted and I knew she was smiling. "Why, M1k3y—*Marcus*—it was the easiest way for me to get to see *you*."

It wasn't exactly a secret that I was planning to come to Burning Man that year. I'd been posting desperate "Will trade work for a ride to the playa" and "Want to borrow your old camping gear" messages to Craigslist and the hackerspace mailing lists for months, trying to prove that the proverbial time-rich kid could out-determination cash-poorness. Anyone who was trying to figure out where I was going to be over Labor Day weekend could have googled my semiprecise location in about three seconds.

"Um," I said. "Um. Look, Masha, you know, you're kind of freaking me out. Are you here to kill me or something? Where's Zeb?"

She closed her eyes and the pale dust sifted down between us. "Zeb's off enjoying the playa. Last time I saw him, he was volunteering in the café and waiting to go to a yoga class. He's actually a pretty good barista—better than he is at being a yogi, anyway. And no, I'm not going to kill you. I'm going to give you something, and leave it up to you to decide what to do with it."

"You're going to give me something?"

"Yeah. It's a gift economy around here. Haven't you heard?"

"What, exactly, are you going to give me, Masha?"

She shook her head. "Better you don't know until we make the handoff. Technically, it would be better—for you, at least—if you *never* knew. But that's how it goes." She seemed to be talking to herself now. Being underground had changed her. She was, I don't know, *hinky*. Like something was wrong with her, like she was up to something, or like she could run at any second. She'd been so self-confident and decisive and unreadable. Now she seemed half crazy. Or maybe one-quarter crazy, and one-quarter terrified.

"Tonight," she said. "They're going to burn the Library of Al-exandria at 8 P.M. After that burn, walk out to the trash fence, di-rectly opposite Six O'Clock. Wait for me if I'm not there when you show up. I've got stuff to do first."

"Okay," I said. "I suppose I can do that. Will Zeb be there? I'd love to say hello to him again."

She rolled her eyes. "Zeb'll probably be there, but you might not see him. You come alone. And come out dark. No lights, got it?"

"No," I said. "Actually, no. I'm with Ange, as you must know, and I'm not going out there without her, assuming she wants to come. And no lights? You've got to be kidding me."

For a city of fifty thousand people involved with recreational substances, flaming art, and enormous, mutant machines, Black Rock has a remarkably low mortality rate. But in a city where they laughed at danger, walking after dark without lights—*lots* of lights, preferably—was considered borderline insane. One of the most dangerous things you could do at Burning Man was walk the playa at night without illumination: that made you a "darktard," and darktards were at risk of being run into by art bikes scream-ing over the dust in the inky night, they risked getting crushed by mammoth art cars, and they were certain to be tripped over and kicked and generally squashed. Burning Man's unofficial motto might have been "safety third," but no one liked a darktard.

She closed her eyes and stood statue-still. The wind was dying down a little, but I still felt like I'd just eaten a pound of talcum powder, and my eyes were stinging like I'd been pepper-sprayed.

"Bring your girly if you must. But no lights, not after you get out past the last art car. And if both of you end up in trouble because you wouldn't come out alone, you'll know whose fault it was."

She turned on her heel and walked off into the dust, and she was out of my sight in a minute. I hurried back to the temple to find Ange.

They burn a *lot* of stuff at Burning Man. Of course, there's the burning of The Man himself on Saturday night. I'd seen that on video a hundred times from a hundred angles, with many different Men (he is different every year). It's raucous and primal, and the explosives hidden in his base made huge mushroom clouds when they went off. The temple burn, on Sunday night, was as quiet and solemn as The Man's burn was insane and frenetic. But before either of them get burned, there are lots of "little" burns.

The night before, there'd been the burning of the regional art. Burner affinity groups from across America, Canada, and the rest of the world had designed and built beautiful wooden structures ranging from something the size of a park bench up to three-story-tall fanciful towers. These ringed the circle of open playa in the middle of Black Rock City, and we'd gone and seen all of them the day we arrived, because we'd been told that they'd burn first. And they did, all at once, more than any one person could see, each one burning in its own way as burners crowded around them, held at a safe distance by Black Rock Rangers until the fires collapsed into stable configurations, masses of burning lumber on burn-platforms over the playa. Anything that burned got burned on a platform, because "leave no trace" meant that you couldn't even leave behind *scorch marks*.

That had been pretty spectacular, but tonight they were going to burn the Library of Alexandria. Not the original, of course: Julius Caesar (or someone!) burned that one in 48 B.C., taking with it the largest collection of scrolls that had ever been assembled at that time. It wasn't the first library anyone had burned, and it wasn't the last, but it was the library that symbolized the wanton destruction of knowledge. The Burning Man Library of Alexandria was set on twenty-four great wheels on twelve great axles and it could be hauled across the playa by gangs of hundreds of volunteers who tugged at the ropes affixed to its front. Inside, the columned building was lined with nooks that were, in turn, stuffed with scrolls, each one handwritten, each a copy of some public domain book downloaded from Project Gutenberg and hand-transcribed onto long rolls of paper by volunteers who'd worked at the project all year. Fifty thousand books had been converted to scrolls in this fashion, and they would all burn. LIBRARIES BURN: it was the message stenciled at irregular intervals all over the Library of Alexandria and sported by the librarians who volunteered there, fetching you scrolls and helping you find the passages you were looking for. I'd gone in and read some Mark Twain, a funny story I remembered reading in school about when Twain had edited an agricultural newspaper. I'd been delighted to discover that someone had gone to the trouble of writing that one out, using rolled-up lined school notepaper and taping it together in a continuous scroll that went on for hundreds of yards.

As I helped the librarian roll up the scroll—she agreed that the Twain piece was really funny—and put it away, I'd said, unthinkingly, "It's such a shame that they're going to burn all these."

She'd smiled sadly and said, "Well, sure, but that's the point, isn't it? Ninety percent of the works in copyright are orphan works: no one knows who owns the rights to them, and no one can figure out how to put them back into print. Meanwhile, the copies of them that we do know about are disintegrating or getting lost. So there's a library out there, the biggest library ever, ninety percent of the stuff anyone's ever created, and it's burning, in slow motion. Libraries burn." She shrugged. "That's what they do. But maybe someday we'll figure out how to make so many copies of humanity's creative works that we'll save most of them from the fire."

And I read my Mark Twain and felt the library rock gently under me as the hundreds of rope-pullers out front dragged the Library of Alexandria from one side of the open playa to the other, inviting more patrons to get on board and have a ride and read a book before it all burned down. On the way out, the librarian gave me a thumbdrive: "It's a compressed copy of the Gutenberg archive. Fifty thousand books and counting. There's also a list of public domain books that we *don't* have, and a list of known libraries, by city, where they can be found. Feel free to get a copy and scan or retype it."

The little thumbdrive only weighed an ounce or two, but it felt as heavy as a mountain of books as I slipped it gravely into my pocket.

And now it was time to burn the Library of Alexandria. Again.

The Library had been hauled onto a burn-platform, and the hauling ropes were coiled neatly on its porch. Black Rock Rangers in their ranger hats and weird clothes surrounded it in a wide circle, sternly warning anyone who wandered too close to stay back. Ange and I stood on the front line, watching as a small swarm of Bureau of Land Management feds finished their inspection of the structure. I could see inside, see the incendiary charges that had been placed at careful intervals along the Library's length, see the rolled scrolls in their nooks. I felt weird tears in my eyes as I contemplated what was about to happen—tears of awe and sorrow and joy. Ange noticed and wiped the tears away, kissed my ear and whispered, "It's okay. Libraries burn."

Now three men stepped out of the crowd. One was dressed as Caesar in white Roman robes and crown, sneering magnificently. The next wore monkish robes and a pointed mitre with a large cross on it. He was meant to be Theophilus, Patriarch of Alexandria, another suspect in the burning of the Library. He looked beatifically on the crowd, then turned to Caesar. Finally, there was a man in a turban with a pointed beard—Caliph Omar, the final person usually accused of history's most notorious arson. The three shook hands, then each drew a torch out of his waistband and lit it from a firepot burning in the center of the Library's porch They paced off from one another and stationed themselves in the middle of the back and side walls and, as the audience shouted and roared, thrust their torches lovingly in little holes set at the bottom of the walls.

There must have been some kind of flash powder or some-thing in those nooks, because as each man scurried away, great arcs of flame shot out of them, up and out, scorching the Library walls. The walls burned merrily, and there was woodsmoke and gunpowder in the air now, the wind whipping it toward and past us, fanning the flames. The crowd noise increased, and I realized I was part of the chorus, making a kind of drawn-out, happy yelp.

Now the incendiary charges went, in near-perfect synch, a blos-som of fire that forced its way out between the Library's columns, the fire's tongues lashing at sizzling embers—fragments of paper, fragments of books—that chased high into the night's sky. The heat of the blast made us all step back from one another, and em-bers rained out of the sky, winking out as they fell around us like ashen rain. The crowd moved like a slow-motion wave, edging its way out of the direction of the prevailing wind and the rain of fire. I smelled singed hair and fun fur, and a tall man in a loincloth be-hind me smacked me between the shoulders, shouting, "You were on fire, sorry!" I gave him a friendly wave—it was getting too loud to shout any kind of words—and continued to work my way to the edge.

Now there were fireworks, and not like the fireworks I'd seen on countless Fourth of July nights, fireworks that were artfully ar-ranged to go off in orderly ranks, first one batch and then the next. These were fireworks with *tempo*, mortars screaming into the sky without pause, detonations so close together they were nearly one single explosion, a flaring, eye-watering series of booms that didn't let up, driven by the thundering, clashing music from the gigan-tic art cars behind the crowd, dubstep and funk and punk and some kind of up-tempo swing and even a gospel song all barely distinguishable. The crowd howled. I howled. The flames licked high and paper floated high on the thermals, burning bright in the desert night. The smoke was choking and there were bodies all around me, pressing in, dancing. I felt like I was part of some kind of mass organism with thousands of legs and eyes and throats and voices, and the flames went higher.

Soon the Library was just a skeleton of structural supports in

stark black, surrounded by fiery orange and red. The building tee-
tered, its roof shuddered, the columns rocked and shifted. Each
time it seemed the building was about to collapse, the crowd
gasped and held its breath, and each time it recovered its balance,
we made a disappointed "Aww."

And then one of the columns gave way, snapping in two, taking
the far corner of the roof with it, and the roof sheared downward
and pulled free of the other columns, and they fell, too, and the
whole thing collapsed in a crash and crackle, sending a fresh cloud
of burning paper up in its wake. The Black Rock Rangers pulled
back and we rushed forward, surrounding the wreckage, crowding
right up to the burning, crackling pile of lumber and paper and
ash. The music got a lot louder—the art cars were pulling in tight
now—and there was the occasional boom as a stray firework left
in the pile sent up a glowing mortar. It was glorious. It was insane.

It was over, and it was time to get moving.

"Let's go," I said to Ange. She'd taken the news about Masha
calmly, but she'd said, "There's no way I'm letting you go out there
alone," when I told her that Masha had insisted on meeting me.

"That's what I told her," I said, and Ange stood on tiptoes,
reached up, and patted me on the head.

"That's my boy," she said.

We threaded our way through the dancing, laughing crowd,
getting faceful of woodsmoke, pot smoke, sweat, patchouli (Ange
loved the smell, I hated it), ash, and playa dust. Soon we found
ourselves through the crowd of people and in a crowd of art cars.
It was an actual, no-fooling art car traffic jam: hundreds of mutant
vehicles in a state of pure higgeldy-piggeldy, so that a three-story
ghostly pirate ship (on wheels) found itself having to navigate
through the gap between a tank with the body of a '59 El Camino
on a crane arm that held it and its passengers ten feet off the
ground and a rocking, rolling electric elephant with ten big-eyed
weirdos riding on its howdah. Complicating things was the exodus
of playa bikes, ridden with joyous recklessness by laughing, calling, goggled cyclists and streaming off into the night, becoming
distant, erratic comets of bright LEDs, glowsticks, and electrolu-
minescent wire.

EL wire was Burning Man's must-have fashion accessory. It was cheap and came in many colors, and glowed brightly for as long as the batteries in its pack held out. You could braid it into your hair, pin or glue it to your clothes, or just dangle it from anything handy. Ange's jawa bandoliers were woven through and through with different colors of pulsing EL wire, and she'd carefully worked a strand into the edge of her hood and another down the hem of her robe, so she glowed like a line drawing of herself from a distance. All my EL wire had been gotten for free, by harvesting other peoples' dead EL wire and painstakingly fixing it, tracking down the shorts and faults and taping them up. I'd done my army surplus boots with EL laces, and wound it in coils around my utility belt. Both of us were visible from a good distance, but that didn't stop a few cyclists from nearly running us down. They were very polite and apologetic about it, of course, but they were distracted. "Distracted" is a permanent state of being on the playa.

But as we ventured deeper into the desert, the population thinned out. Black Rock City's perimeter is defined by the "trash fence" that rings the desert, not too far in from the mountain ranges that surround it. These fences catch any MOOP ("matter out of place") that blows out of peoples' camps, where it can be harvested and packed out—leave no trace—and all that. Between the trash fence and the center of the city is two miles of open playa, nearly featureless, dotted here and there with people, art, and assorted surprises. If Six O'Clock Plaza is the sun, and The Man and temple and the camps are the inner solar system, the trash fence is something like the asteroid belt, or Pluto (allow me to pause for a moment here and say, PLUTO IS TOO A PLANET!).

Now we were walking in what felt like the middle of nowhere. So long as we didn't look over our shoulders at the carnival happening behind us, we could pretend that we were the only people on Earth.

Well, almost. We pretty much tripped over a couple who were naked and squirming on a blanket, way out in the big empty. It was a dangerous way to get your jollies, but nookie was a moderately good excuse for being a darktard. And they were pretty good-natured about it, all things considered. "Sorry," I called over my shoulder as we moved past them. "Time to go dark ourselves," I said.

"Guess so," Ange said, and fiddled with the battery switch on her bandolier. A moment later, she winked out of existence. I did the same. The sudden dark was so profound that the night looked the same with my eyes open and shut.

"Look up," Ange said. I did.

"My God, it's full of stars," I said, which is the joke I always tell when there's a lot of stars in the sky (it's a killer line from the book *2001*, though the idiots left it out of the movie). But I'd never seen a sky full of stars like this. The Milky Way—usually a slightly whitish streak, even on clear, moonless nights—was a glowing silvery river that sliced across the sky. I'd looked at Mars through binox once or twice and seen that it was, indeed, a little more red than the other stuff in the sky. But that night, in the middle of the desert, with the playa dust settled for a moment, it glowed like a coal in the lone eye of a cyclopean demon.

I stood there with my head flung back, staring wordlessly at the night, until I heard a funny sound, like the patter of water on stone, or—

"Ange, are you *peeing*?"

She shushed me. "Just having a sneaky playa-pee—the portasans are all the way back there. It'll evaporate by morning. Chill."

One of the occupational hazards of drinking water all the time was that you had to pee all the time, too. Some lucky burners had RVs at their camps with nice private toilets, but the rest of us went to "pee camp" when we needed to go. Luckily, the bathroom poetry—"poo-etry"—taped up inside the stalls made for pretty good reading. Technically, you weren't supposed to pee on the playa, but way out here the chances of getting caught were basically zero, and it really was a long way back to the toilets. Listening to Ange go made me want to go, too, so we enjoyed a playa-pee together in the inky, warm dark.

Walking in the dark, it was impossible to tell how close we were to the trash fence; there was just black ahead of us, with the slightly blacker black of the mountains rising to the lighter black of the starry sky. But gradually, we were able to pick out some tiny, flickering lights—candle lights, I thought—up ahead of us, in a long, quavering row.

As we got closer, I saw that they were candles, candle lanterns, actually, made of tin and glass, each with a drippy candle in it. They were placed at regular intervals along a gigantic, formal dinner table long enough to seat fifty people at least, with precise place settings and wineglasses and linen napkins folded into tents at each setting. "WTF?" I said softly.

Ange giggled. "Someone's art project," she said. "A dinner table at the trash fence. Woah."

"Hi there," a voice said from the dark, and a shadow detached itself from the table and then lit up with EL wire, revealing itself to be a young woman with bright purple hair and a leather jacket cut down into a vest. "Welcome." Suddenly there were more shadows turning into people—three more young women, one with green hair, one with blue hair, and . . .

"Hello, Masha," I said.

She gave me a little salute. "Meet my campmates," she said. "You've met before, actually. The day the bridge went."

Right, of course. These were the girls who'd been playing on Masha's Harajuku Fun Madness team when we'd run into them in the Tenderloin, moments before the Bay Bridge had been blown up by parties unknown. What had I called them? *The Popsicle Squad.* Yeah. "Nice to see you again," I said. "This is Ange."

Masha inclined her chin in a minute acknowledgment. "They've been good enough to let us use their dinner table for a little conversation, but I don't want to spend too much time out here. Plenty of people looking for me."

"Is Zeb here?"

"He went for a pee," she said. "He'll be back soon. But let's get started, okay?"

"Let's do it," Ange said. She'd stiffened up beside me the minute I'd said hi to Masha, and I had an idea that maybe she wasn't as cool about this meeting as she'd been playing it. Why should she be?

Masha brought us down to the farthest end of the table, away from her friends. We seated ourselves, and I saw that what I'd thought were bread baskets were in fact laden with long-lasting hippie junk food: whole-wheat pop-tarts from Trader Joe's, organic beef jerky, baggies of what turned out to be homemade granola. High-energy food that wouldn't melt in the sun. Masha noticed me inspecting the goods and she said, "Go ahead, that's what it's there for, help yourself." I tore into a pack of jerky (stashing the wrapper in my utility belt to throw away later at camp—turning gift-economy snacks into MOOP was really bad manners) and Ange got herself a pop-tart, just as Masha leaned across the table, opened the little glass door in the candle lantern, and blew the candle out. Now we were just black blobs in the black night, far from the nearest human, invisible.

I felt a hand—Masha's hand—grab my arm in the dark and feel its way down to my hand and then push something small and hard into my fingers, then let go.

"That's a USB stick, a little one. It's a crypto key that will unlock a four-gigabyte torrent file that you can get with a torrent magnet file on The Pirate Bay and about ten other torrent sites. It's called insurancefile.masha.torrent, and the checksum's on the USB stick, too. I'd appreciate it if you would download and seed the file, and ask anyone you trust to do the same."

"So," I said, speaking into the dark toward where Masha was sitting. "There's this big torrent blob filled with encrypted *something* floating around on the net, and if something happens, you want me to release the key so that it can be decrypted, right?"

"Yes, that's about the size of things," Masha said. I tried to imagine what might be in the insurance file. Blackmail photos? Corporate secrets? Pictures of aliens at Area 51? Proof of Bigfoot's existence?

"What's on it?" Ange said. Her voice was a little tight and tense, and though she was trying to hide it, I could tell she was stressing.

"Are you sure you want to know that?" Masha said. Her voice was absolutely emotionless.

"If you want us to do something other than throw this memory stick into a fire, you're goddamned right we do. I can't think of any reason to trust you, not one."

Masha didn't say anything. She heaved a sigh, and I heard her unscrew a bottle and take a drink of something. I smelled whiskey.

"Look," she said. "Back when I was, you know, *inside* at the DHS, I got to know a lot of things. Got to see a lot of things. Got to know a lot of people. Some of those people, they've *stayed* in touch with me. Not everyone at DHS wants to see America turned into a police state. Some people, they're just doing their jobs, maybe trying to catch actual bad guys or fight actual crime or prevent actual disasters, but they get to see things as they do these jobs, things that they're not happy about. Eventually, you come across something so terrible, you can't look yourself in the mirror anymore unless you do something about it.

"So maybe you copy some files, pile up some evidence. You think to yourself, *Someday, someone will have the chance to speak out against this, and I'll quietly slip them these files, and my conscience will forgive me for being a part of an organization that's doing such rotten stuff.*

"So what happened is, someone you used to work with, someone who got a bad deal and has been underground and on the road, someone you trust, that person contacts you from deep underground and lets it be known that she'll hold on to all those docs for you, put them together with other peoples' docs, see if there are any interesting connections between them. That person will take them off your hands, launder them so no one will ever know where they came from, release them when the moment comes. This is quite a nice service to provide for tortured bureaucrats, you see, since it's the kind of thing that lets them sleep at night and still deposit their paychecks.

"Word gets around. Lots of people find it useful to outsource their conscience to a disgraced runaway outlaw, and, well, stuff does start to trickle in. Then pour in. Soon, you're sitting on gigabytes of that stuff."

"Four gigabytes, by any chance?" I said. I was feeling a little light-headed. Masha was giving me the keys to decode all the ugliest secrets of the American government, all the stuff that had so horrified loyal DHS employees that they'd felt the need to smuggle it out. Masha herself would be so hot that she was practically radioactive: I could hardly believe that space-lasers weren't beaming out of the sky to kill her where she sat. And me? Well, once I had the key, no one could be sure I hadn't downloaded the insurance file and had a look, so that meant I was, fundamentally, a dead man.

"About that," she said.

"Gee, thanks."

"You have no right to do this," Ange said. "Whatever you're up to, you're putting *us* in danger, without asking us, without us knowing anything about it. How *dare* you?"

Masha cut her off with a sharp "*Shh*" sound.

"Don't shush me—" Ange began, and I heard/felt/saw Masha grab her and squeeze.

"Shut *up*," she hissed.

Ange shut up. I held my breath. There was the distant *wub wub wub* of terrible dubstep playing from some faraway art car, the soughing of the wind blowing in the slats of the trash fence, and there—had I heard a footstep? Another footstep? Hesitant, stumbling, in the dark? A soft crunch, there it was again, *crunch, crunch,* closer now, and I felt Masha coil up, get ready to run, and I tasted the beef jerky again as it rose in my throat, buoyed up on a fountain of stomach acid. My ears hammered with my pulse and the sweat on the back of my neck dried to ice in an instant.

Crunch, crunch. The steps were practically upon us now, and there was a *bang* that made me jump as Masha leapt away from the table, knocked over her chair, and set off into the dark of the playa.

Then there was a blazing light, right in my face, blinding me, and a hand reaching out for me, and I scrambled away from it, grabbing for Ange, screaming something in wordless terror, Ange shouting, too, and then a voice said, "Hey, Marcus! Stop! It's me!"

I knew that voice, though I'd only heard it for an instant, long ago, on the street in front of Chavez High.

"Zeb?" I said.

"Dude!" he shouted, and I was grabbed up in a tight, somewhat

346 | cory doctorow

smelly hug, my face pressed against his whiskered cheek. His blazing headlamp blinded me, but from what I could feel, he'd grown a beard of the same size and composition as a large animal, a big cat or possibly a beaver. The terror drained out of me, but left behind all its nervous energy, and I found myself laughing uproariously.

Suddenly, small strong hands separated us and Zeb was rolling on the playa, tackled by Masha, who must have circled back and recognized his voice. She was calling him all sorts of names as she wrestled him to the ground, straddling his chest and pinning his arms under her elbows.

"Sorry, sorry!" he said, and he was laughing, too, and so was Masha, and so was Ange, for that matter. "Sorry, okay! I just didn't want to disturb you. The girls told me you were down here. Thought a light would kill the atmosphere."

Masha let him up and gave him a kiss in a spot on his cheek where his beard was a little thinner.

"You are *such* an idiot," she said. He laughed again and tousled her hair. Masha was a totally different person with Zeb, playful and younger and not so totally lethal. I liked her better.

"Ange, this is Zeb. Zeb, this is Ange." He shook her hand.

"I've heard of you," she said.

"And I've heard of you, too," he said.

"Okay, sit down, you idiots, and turn off that damned light, Zeb." Masha was getting her down-to-business voice back, and we did what she said.

I still felt angry at her for what she'd done to us, but after being scared witless and then let down an instant later, it was hard to get back to that angry feeling. All my adrenaline had been dumped into my bloodstream already, and it would take a while to manufacture some more, I guess. Still, things were far from settled. "Masha," I said, "you know that what you've done here is really unfair, right?"

I couldn't see or hear her in the dark, and the silence stretched on so long I thought maybe she'd fallen asleep or tiptoed away. Then, suddenly, she said, "God, you're still a kid, aren't you?"

The way she said it made me feel like I was about eight years old, like I was some kind of hayseed with cow crap between my

toes, and like she was some kind of world-traveling superspy underground fugitive ninja.

"Up yours," I said, trying to make it sound cynical and mean,
and not like I was a widdle kid with hurt feewings. I don't think I
was very successful.

She gave a mean laugh. "I mean it. 'Fair'? What's 'fair' got to do
with anything? There is stuff going on in the world, bad stuff, the
kind of stuff that ends up with dead people in shallow graves, and
you're either part of the solution or you're part of the problem. Is
it fair to all the people who risked everything to get me these docs
for you to walk away from them, because you don't want to have
your safe little life disrupted?

"Oh, M1k3y, you're *such a big hero*. After all you bravely, what,
bravely told *other people's stories* to a *reporter*? Because you held a
press conference? What a big, brave man." She spat loudly.

Yeah, it got me. Because you know what? She was right. Basically. Give or take. There'd been plenty of nights when I lay in
bed and stared at the ceiling and thought *exactly* these thoughts.
There'd been kids in the Xnet who did stuff that was way crazier
than anything I'd done, kids whose jamming had put them right
up against Homeland Security and the cops, kids who'd ended up
in jail for a long time, without any newspaper coverage advertising
their bravery. Some of them were probably still in there. The fact
that I didn't know for sure—didn't even know all their names, or
how many there were—was yet another reason that I didn't deserve anyone's admiration.

Every bit of clever, flashy wit ran and hid in the furthest corners of my mind. I heard Zeb shuffle his feet uncomfortably. No
one knew what to say.

Except Ange. "Well, I suppose not everyone can be a sellout,"
she said. "Not everyone can be a snitch who gets to sit in the hidden bunkers and spy on the ones who're getting beaten and jailed
and tortured and disappeared. Not everyone can draw a fat salary
for their trouble until the day comes that it's all too much for their
poor little conscience and they just have to go and run away to a
beach in Mexico somewhere, lying in the bed they made for themselves."

It made me smile, there in the dark. Go, Ange! Whatever my sins were, they were sins of omission: I could have done more. But Masha'd done the worst kind of evil: sins of commission. She'd done wrong. Really, really wrong. She'd tried to make up for it since. But *she* was in no position to shame *me*.

Another one of those long silences. I thought about dropping the USB stick in the dust and walking off in the dark. You know what stopped me?

Zeb.

Because Zeb *was* a hero. He'd broken out of Gitmo-by-the-Bay and instead of running, he'd come and found me at Chavez High so that he could pass on Darryl's note. He could have just hit the road, but he hadn't. And I'd told his secrets to the world, put him in harm's way. This wasn't just Masha's mission, this was Zeb's mission, too. They were a team. I owed him. We all did.

"Enough," I said, swallowing hard on all the stupid emotions, trying to find some of that Zen calm I'd attained at the temple. "Enough. Fine, it's not fair. Life's not fair. I've got this thing now. What do I do with it?"

"Keep it safe," Masha said, her voice back in that emotionless zone that I guessed she was good at finding when she needed it. "And if you ever hear that I've gone down, or Zeb's gone down, release it. Shout it from the mountaintops. If I ever ask you to release it, release it. And if you haven't heard from me by the Friday of the next Burning Man, one year from now, release it. Do you think you can do that?"

"Sounds like something I could manage," I said.

"I figure even you can't screw this up," she said, but I could tell she was just putting up her tough-chick front, and I didn't take it personally. "Okay, fine. I'm out of here. Don't screw up, all right?"

I heard her feet crunch away.

"See you at camp, babe!" Zeb called at her retreating back, and his headlamp came back on, dazzling me again. He grabbed a pop-tart from the basket and opened it, chewed at it enthusiastically. "I love that girl, honestly I do. But she is so *tightly wound*!"

It was so manifestly true that there was nothing for it but to laugh, and so we did, and it turned out that Zeb had some beer that he gift-economied to us, and I had some cold-brew coffee concentrate in a flask that we dipped into afterward, just to get us back up from the beer's mellow down, and then we all needed pee camp, and we went back into the night and the playa and the dust.

All day long, people had been telling me that the weather man said we were in for a dust storm, but I just assumed that "dust storm" meant that I'd have to tuck my scarf under the lower rim of my goggles, the way I had been doing every time it got windy on the playa.

But the dust storm that blew up after we left Zeb behind and returned to the nonstop circus was *insane.* The night turned white with flying dust, and our lights just bounced back in our faces, creating gloomy gray zones in front of us that seemed to go on forever. It reminded me of really bad fog, the kind of thing you get sometimes in San Francisco, usually in the middle of summer, reducing all the tourists in their shorts and T-shirts to hypothermia candidates. But fog made it hard to *see,* and the dust storm made it hard—nearly impossible—to breathe. Our eyes and noses streamed, our mouths were caked with dust, every breath triggered a coughing fit. We stumbled and staggered and clutched each other's hands because if we let go, we'd be swallowed by the storm.

Ange pulled my ear down to her mouth and shouted, "We have to get inside!"

"I know!" I said. "I'm just trying to figure out how to get back to camp; I think we're around Nine O'Clock and B." The ring roads that proceeded concentrically from center camp were lettered in alphabetical order. We were at Seven Fifteen and L, way out in the hinterlands. Without the dust, the walk would have taken fifteen minutes, and been altogether pleasant. With the dust . . . well, it felt like it might take *hours.*

"Screw that," Ange said. "We have to get inside somewhere *now.*" She started dragging me. I tripped over a piece of rebar hammered into the playa and topped with a punctured tennis ball—

someone's tent stake. Ange's iron grip kept me from falling, and she hauled me along.

Then we were at a structure—a hexayurt, made from triangular slabs of flat Styrofoam, duct-taped on its seams. The outside was covered with an insulating layer of silver-painted Bubble Wrap. We felt our way around to the "door" (a styro slab with a duct-tape hinge on one edge and a pull-loop). Ange was about to yank this open when I stopped her and knocked instead. Storm or no storm, it was weird and wrong to just walk into some stranger's home.

The wind howled. If someone was coming, I couldn't hear them over its terrible moaning whistle. I raised my hand to knock again, and the door swung open. A bearded face peered out at us and shouted, "Get in!"

We didn't need to be asked twice. We dove through the door and it shut behind us. I could still hardly see; my goggles were nearly opaque with caked-on dust, and the light in the hexayurt was dim, provided by LED lanterns draped with gauzy scarves.

"Look at what the storm blew in," said a gravelly, jovial voice from the yurt's shadows. "Better hose 'em off before you bring 'em over here, John, those two've got half the playa in their ears."

"Come on," said the bearded man. He was wearing tie-dyes and had beads braided into his long beard and what was left of his hair. He grinned at us from behind a pair of round John Lennon glasses. "Let's get you cleaned up. Shoes first, thanks."

Awkwardly, we bent down and unlaced our shoes. We *did* have half the playa in them. The other half was caught in the folds of our clothes and our hair and our ears.

"Can I get you two something to wear? We can beat the dust out of your clothes once the wind dies down."

My first instinct was to say no, because we hadn't even been introduced, plus it seemed like more hospitality than even the gift economy demanded. On the other hand, we weren't doing these people any kindness by crapping up their hexayurt. On the other other hand—

"That'd be so awesome," Ange said. "Thank you."

That's why she's my girlfriend. Left to my own devices, I'd be on-the-other-handing it until Labor Day. "Thanks," I said.

352 | **cory doctorow**

The man produced billowy bundles of bright silk. "They're salwar kameez," he said. "Indian clothes. Here, these are the pants, and you wrap the tops around like so." He demonstrated. "I get them on eBay from women's clothing collectives in India. Straight from the source. Very comfortable and practically one size fits all."

We stripped down to our underwear and wound the silk around us as best we could. We helped each other with the tricky bits, and our host helped, too. "That's better," he said, and gave us a package of baby wipes, which are the playa's answer to a shower. We went through a stack of them wiping the dust off each other's faces and out of each other's ears and cleaning our hands and bare feet—the dust had infiltrated our shoes and socks!

"And that's it," the man said, clasping his hands together and beaming. He had a soft, gentle way of talking, but you could tell by the twinkle of his eyes that he didn't miss anything and that something very interesting was churning away in his mind. Either he was a Zen master or an axe murderer—no one else was that calm and mirthful. "I'm John, by the way."

Ange shook his hand. "Ange," she said.

"Marcus," I said.

Lots of people used "playa names," cute pseudonyms that let them assume new identities while they were at Burning Man. I'd had enough of living with my notorious alter ego, M1k3y, and didn't feel the need to give myself another handle. I hadn't talked it over with Ange, but she, too, didn't seem to want or need a temporary name.

"Come on and meet the rest."

"The rest" turned out to be three more guys, sitting on low cushions around a coffee table that was littered with paper, dice, and meticulously painted lead figurines. We'd interrupted an old-school gaming session, the kind you play with a dungeon master and lots of role-playing. I'm hardly in any position to turn up my nose at someone else's amusements—after all, I spent years doing live-action role-play—but this was seriously nerdy. The fact that they were playing in the middle of a dust storm on the playa just made it more surreal.

"Hi!" Ange said. "That looks like fun!"

"It certainly is," said a gravelly voice, and I got a look at its owner. He had a lined and seamed face, kind eyes, and a slightly wild beard, and he was wearing a scarf around his neck with a turquoise pin holding it in place. "Are you initiated in the mysteries of this particular pursuit?"

I slipped my hand into Ange's and did my best not to be shy or awkward. "I've never played, but I'm willing to learn."

"An admirable sentiment," said another man. He was also in his fifties or sixties, with a neat gray Vandyke beard and dark rimmed glasses. "I'm Mitch, this is Barlow, and this is Wil, our dungeon master."

The last man was a lot younger than the other three—maybe a youthful forty—and clean-shaven, with apple cheeks and short hair. "Hey, folks," he said. "You're just in time. Are you going to sit in? I've got some pre-rolled characters you can play. We're just doing a minidungeon while we wait out the storm."

John brought us some cushions from the hexayurt's recesses and sat down with crossed legs and perfect, straight yoga posture. We settled down beside him. Wil gave us our character sheets—I was a half-elf mage, Ange was a human fighter with an enchanted sword—and dug around in a case until he found hand-painted figurines that matched the descriptions. "My son paints them," he said. "I used to help, but the kid's a machine—I can't keep up with him." I looked closely at the figs. They were, well, they were *beautiful*. They'd been painted in incredible detail, more than I could actually make out in the dim light of the yurt. My character's robes had been painted with mystical silver sigils, and Ange's character's chain mail had each ring picked out in tarnished silver, with tiny daubs of black paint in the center of each minute ring.

"These are amazing," I said. I'd always thought of tabletop RPGs as finicky and old-fashioned, but these figs had been painted by someone very talented who really loved the game, and if someone *that* talented thought this was worth his time, I'd give it a chance, too.

Wil was a great game master, spinning the story of our quest in a dramatic voice that sucked me right in. The other guys listened intently, though they interjected from time to time with funny quips that cracked one another up. I got the feeling they'd known one another for a long time, and when we took a break for fresh mint tea—these guys knew how to live!—I asked how they knew one another.

They all smiled kind of awkwardly at one another. "It's kind of a reunion," Mitch said. "We all worked together a long time ago."

"Did you do a start-up together?"

They laughed again. I could tell that I was missing something. Wil said, "You ever hear of the Electronic Frontier Foundation?" I sure had. I figured it out a second before he said it: "These guys founded it."

"Wait, wait," I said. "You're *John Perry Barlow*?" The guy in the kerchief nodded and grinned like a pirate. "And you're John Gilmore?" John shrugged and raised his eyebrows. "And *you're* Mitch Kapor?" The guy with the Vandyke gave a little wave. Ange was looking slightly left out. "Ange, *these guys founded EFF.* That one started the first ISP in San Francisco; that one commercialized spreadsheets; and that one wrote the Declaration of Independence of Cyberspace."

Barlow laughed like a cement mixer. "And turned teraliters of sewage into gigaliters of diesel fuel with tailored algae. I also wrote a song or two. Since we're on the subject."

"Oh yeah," I said. "Barlow also wrote songs for the Grateful Dead."

Ange shook her head. "You make them sound like the elder gods of the Internet."

"Enough with the 'elder' stuff," Mitch said, and sipped his tea. "You certainly seem to know your Internet trivia, young man."

I blushed. A couple of times on the playa, people had recognized me as M1k3y and come over to tell me how much they admired me and so on, and it had embarrassed me, but now I *wanted* these guys to know about that part of my life and I couldn't figure out how to get it out without sounding like I was boasting to three of the all-time heroes of the Internet. Again, Ange saved me. "Marcus and I worked with some EFF people a couple years ago. He started Xnet."

Wil laughed aloud at that. "That was *you*?" he said. He put on a hard-boiled detective voice: "Of all the yurts in all the playa, they had to walk into mine."

Mitch held out his hand. "It's an honor, sir," he said. I shook his hand, tongue-tied. The others followed suit. I was in a daze, and when John told me that he "really admired the work" I'd done, I thought I'd die from delight.

"Enough!" Ange said. "I won't be able to get his head out of the door if it gets any more swollen. Now, are we here to talk or to roll some goddamned dice?"

"I like your attitude," Wil said, and thumbed through his notebook and set down some terrain tiles on the graph paper in front of us. Ange turned out to be a master strategist—which didn't surprise me, but clearly impressed everyone else—and she arrayed our forces such that we sliced through the trash hordes, beat the minibosses, and made it to the final boss without suffering any major losses. She was a born tank, and loved bulling through our adversaries while directing our forces. Wil gave her tons of extra XP for doing it all in character—barbarian swordmistress came easily to her—and her example led us all, so by the time we got to the dragon empress in her cavern at the middle of the dungeon, we were all talking like a fantasy novel. Barlow was a master at this, improvising heroic poetry and delivering it in that whiskey voice of his. Meanwhile, Mitch and John kept catching little hints that Wil dropped in his narration, discovering traps and hidden treasures based on the most obscure clues. I can't remember when we'd had a better time.

Mitch and Barlow kept shifting on their cushions, and just as we broke through into the main cavern, they called for a stretch break, and got to their feet and rubbed vigorously at their lower backs, groaning. Wil stretched, too, and checked the yurt's door. "Storm's letting up," he called. It was coming on to midnight, and when Wil opened the door, a cool, refreshing breeze blew in, along with the sound of distant music.

Part of me wanted to rush back out into the night and find some music to dance to, and part of me wanted to stay in the yurt with my heroes, playing D&D. That was the thing about Burning Man—there was so *much* I wanted to do!

Wil came over and handed me another cup of mint tea, the leaves floating in the hot water. "Pretty awesome. Can't believe these guys let me DM their game. And I can't believe I ran into *you*." He shook his head. "This place is like nerdstock."

"Have you known them for long?"

"Not really. I met Barlow and Gilmore awhile back, when I did a fund-raiser for EFF. I ran into Gilmore at random today and I told him I'd brought my D&D stuff along and the next thing I knew, I was running a game for them."

"What kind of fund-raiser were you doing?" Wil looked familiar, but I couldn't quite place him.

"Oh," he said, and stuck his hands in his pockets. "They brought me in to pretend-fight a lawyer in a Barney the Purple Dinosaur costume. It was because the Barney people had been sending a lot of legal threats out to websites and EFF had been defending them, and, well, it was a lot of fun."

I knew him from *somewhere*. It was driving me crazy. "Look, do I know you? You look really familiar—"

"Ha!" he said. "I thought you knew. I made some movies when I was a kid, and I was on *Star Trek: The Next Generation*, and—"

My jaw dropped so low I felt like it was in danger of scraping my chest. "You're *Wil Wheaton*?"

He looked embarrassed. I've never been much of a Trek fan, but I'd seen a ton of the videos Wheaton had done with his comedy troupe, and of course, I knew about Wheaton's Law: *Don't be a dick*.

"That's me," he said.

"You were the first person I ever followed on Twitter!" I said. It was a weird thing to say, sure, but it was the first thing that came to mind. He was a *really* funny tweeter.

"Well, thank you!" he said. No wonder he was such a good narrator—he'd been acting since he was like seven years old. Being around all these people made me wish I had access to Wikipedia so I could look them all up.

We sat back down to play against the megaboss, the dragon empress. She had all kinds of fortifications, and a bunch of lethal attacks. I figured out how to use an illusion spell to trick her into moving into a side corridor that gave her less room to maneuver, and this made it possible for the fighters to attack her in waves while I used a digging spell to send chunks of the cave roof onto her head. This seemed like a good idea to me (and everyone else, I swear it!), right up to the time that I triggered a cave-in that killed us all.

But no one was too angry with me. We'd all cheered every time I rolled a fifteen or better and one of my spells brought some roof down on the dragon's head, and no one had bothered too much about all those dice rolls Wil was making behind his screen. Besides, it was nearly 1 A.M., and there was a party out there! We changed out of John's beautiful silk clothes and back into our stiff, dust-caked playa-wear and switched on all our EL wire and fit our goggles over our eyes and said a million thanks and shook everyone's hands and so on. Just as I was about to go, Mitch wrote an email address on my arm with a Sharpie (there was plenty of stuff there already—playa coordinates of parties and email addresses of people I planned on looking up).

"Ange tells me you're looking for a job. That's the campaign manager for Joseph Noss. I hear she's looking for a webmaster. Tell her I sent you."

I was speechless. After months of knocking on doors, sending in résumés, emailing and calling, an honest-to-goodness job—with a recommendation from an honest-to-goodness legend! I stammered out my thanks and as soon as we were outside, I kissed Ange and bounced up and down and dragged her off to the playa, nearly crashing into a guy on a dusty Segway tricked out with zebra-striped fun fur. He gave us a grin and a wave.

We didn't see Masha or Zeb again until the temple burn on Sunday night, the last night.

We'd burned The Man the night before, and it had been in-freaking-*sane*. Hundreds of fire-dancers executing precision maneuvers, tens of thousands of burners sitting in ranks on the playa, screaming our heads off as fireballs and mushroom clouds of flame rose out of The Man's pyramid, then the open-throated roar as it collapsed and the Rangers dropped their line and we all rushed forward to the fire, everyone helping everyone else along, like the world's most courteous stampede. I flashed on the crush of bodies in the BART station after the Bay Bridge blew, the horrible feeling of being forced by the mass of people to step on those who'd fallen, the sweat and the stink and the noise. Someone had *stabbed* Darryl in that crowd, given him the wound that started us on our awful adventure.

This crowd was nothing like that mob, but my internal organs didn't seem to know that, and they did slow flip-flops in my abdomen, and my legs turned to jelly, and I found myself slowly sliding to the playa. There were tears pouring down my face, and I felt like I was floating above my body as Ange grabbed me under my armpits, struggling to get me to my feet as she spoke urgent, soothing words into my ears. People stopped and helped, one tall woman steering traffic around us, a small older man grabbing me beneath my armpits with strong hands, pulling me upright.

I snapped back into my body, felt the jellylegged feeling recede, and blinked away the tears. "I'm sorry," I said. "Sorry." I was so embarrassed I felt like digging a hole and pulling the playa in over my head. But neither of the people who'd stopped to help seemed surprised. The woman told me where to find the nearest medical camp and the man gave me a hug and told me to take it easy.

Ange didn't say anything, just held me for a moment. She knew that I sometimes got a little wobbly in crowds, and she knew I didn't like to talk about it. We made our way to the fire and watched it for a moment, then went back out into the playa for the parties and the dancing and forgetting. I reminded myself that I was in love, at Burning Man, and that there might be a job waiting for me when I got back to San Francisco, and kicked myself in the ass every time I felt the bad feeling creeping up on me.

Temple burn was very different. We got there really early and sat down nearly at the front and watched the sun set and turn the temple's white walls orange, then red, then purple. Then the spotlights went up, and it turned blazing white again. The wind blew and I heard the rustle of all the paper remembrances fluttering in its nooks and on its walls.

We were sitting amid thousands of people, tens of thousands of people, but there was hardly a sound. When I closed my eyes, I could easily pretend that I was alone in the desert with the temple and all its memories and good-byes and sorrows. I felt the ghost of that feeling I'd had when I'd sat in the temple and tried to clear my mind, to be in the present and throw away all my distractions. The temple had an instantly calming effect on me, silenced all the chattering voices in the back of my head. I don't believe in spooks and ghosts and gods, and I don't think the temple had any *supernatural* effect, but it had an absolutely *natural* effect, made me sorrowful and hopeful and calm and, well, *soft-edged* all at once.

I wasn't the only one. We all sat and watched the temple, and people spoke in hushed tones, museum voices, church whispers. Time stretched. Sometimes I felt like I was dozing off. Other times I felt like I could feel every pore and every hair on my body. Ange stroked my back, and I squeezed her leg softly. I looked at the faces around me. Some were calm, some softly cried, some smiled in profound contentment. The wind ruffled my scarf.

And then I spotted them. Three rows back from us, holding hands: Masha and Zeb. I nearly didn't recognize them at first, because Masha had her head on Zeb's shoulder and wore an expression of utter vulnerability and sadness, absolutely unlike her normal display of half-angry, half-cocky impatience. I looked away before I caught her eye, feeling like I'd intruded on her privacy.

I turned back to the temple just in time to see the first flames lick at its insides, the paper crackling and my breath catching in my chest. Then a tremendous column of fire sprouted out of the central atrium, *whoosh*ing in a pillar a hundred yards tall, the heat and light so intense I had to turn my face away. The crowd *sighed*, a huge, soft sound, and I sighed with it.

There was someone walking through the crowd now, a compact woman in goggles and gray clothes in a cut that somehow felt military, though they didn't have any markings or insignia. She was moving with odd intensity, holding a small video camera up to one eye and peering through it. People muttered objections as she stepped on them or blocked their view, then spoke louder, saying "Sit down!" and "Down in front" and "Spectator!" This last with a vicious spin on it that was particularly apt, given her preoccupation with that camera.

I looked away from her and tried to put her out of my mind. The temple was burning along its length now, and someone near me drew a breath and let out a deep, bassy "Ommmmmm" that made my ears buzz. Another voice joined in, and then another, and then I joined in, the sound like a living thing that traveled up and down my chest and through my skull, suffusing me with calm. It was exactly what I needed, that sound, and as my voice twined with all those others, with Ange's, I felt like a part of something so much larger than myself.

A sharp pain in my thigh made me open my eyes. It was the lady with the camera, facing away from me, scanning the fire and the crowd with it, and she'd caught some of the meat of my thigh as she stepped past me. I looked up in annoyance, ready to say something *really* nasty, and found myself literally frozen in terror.

You see, I knew that face. I could never have forgotten it.

Her name was Carrie Johnstone. I'd called her "Severe Haircut Woman" before I learned it. The last time I'd seen her in person, she'd had me strapped to a board and ordered a soldier hardly older than me to waterboard me—to simulate my execution. To torture me.

For years, that face had haunted my nightmares, swimming out of the dark of my dreams to taunt me; to savage me with sharp, animal teeth; to choke me out with a tight bag over my face; to ask me relentless questions I couldn't answer and hit me when I said so.

A closed-door military tribunal had found her not guilty of any crime, and she'd been "transferred" to help wind down the Forward Operating Base in Tikrit, Iraq. I had a news alert for her, but no news of her ever appeared. As far as I could tell, she'd vanished.

It was like being back in my nightmares, one of those paralysis dreams where your legs and arms won't work. I wanted to shout and scream and run, but all I could do was sit as my heart thundered so loud that my pulse blotted out all the other sounds, even that all-consuming *Ommmm*.

Johnstone didn't even notice. She radiated an arrogant disregard for people, her face smooth and emotionless as the people around her asked her (or shouted at her) to move. She took another step past me and I stared at her back—tense beneath her jacket, coiled for action—as she strode back through the crowd, disappearing over the horizon, hair beneath a stocking cap that was the same desert no-color as her clothes.

Ange squeezed my hand. "What's wrong?" she asked.

I shook my head and squeezed back. I wasn't going to tell her I'd just seen the bogeywoman on the playa. Even if that *was* Johnstone, so what? Everyone came to Burning Man, it seemed—software pioneers, fugitives, poets, and me. I hadn't seen any rules against war criminals attending.

"It's nothing," I choked out. I looked over the crowd. Johnstone had disappeared. I turned back to the burning temple, tried to find the peace I'd felt a moment before.

By the time the temple burned down, I'd nearly convinced myself that I'd imagined Johnstone. After all, it had been dark, the only light the erratic flicker of the temple. The woman had held a camera to her face, obscuring it. And I'd seen her from below. I'd been visiting all my ghosts that night, seeing the faces of friends lost and betrayed and saved in the temple's fire. I'd only seen the face for a moment. What were the odds that *Carrie Johnstone* would be at *Burning Man*? It was like finding Attila the Hun at a yoga class. Like finding Darth Vader playing ultimate frisbee in the park. Like finding Megatron volunteering at a children's hospital. Like finding Nightmare Moon having a birthday party at Chuck E. Cheese.

Thinking up these analogies—and even dumber ones that I won't inflict upon you—helped me calm down as Ange and I walked slowly away from temple burn with the rest of the crowd, a solemn and quiet procession.

"Going home tomorrow," I said.

"Exodus," Ange said. That's what it was called at Burning Man, and it was supposed to be epic—thousands of cars and RVs stretching for miles, being released in "pulses" every hour so that the traffic didn't bunch up. We'd scored a ride back with Lemmy from Noisebridge, the hackerspace I hung around at in San Francisco. I didn't know him well, but we knew where he was camped and had arranged to meet him with our stuff at 7 A.M. to help him pack his car. Getting up that early would be tricky, but I had a secret weapon: my contribution to the Burning Man gift economy, aka cold-brew coffee.

You've had hot coffee before, and in the hands of a skilled maker, coffee can be *amazing*. But the fact is that coffee is one of the hardest things to get right in the world. Even with great beans and a great roast and great equipment, a little too much heat, the wrong grind, or letting things go on too long will produce a cup of bitterness. Coffee's full of different acids, and depending on the grind, temperature, roast, and method, you can "overextract" the acids from the beans, or overheat them and oxidize them, producing that awful taste you get at donut shops and Starbucks.

But there is Another Way. If you make coffee in *cold* water, you *only* extract the sweetest acids, the highly volatile flavors that hint at chocolate and caramel, the ones that boil away or turn to sourness under imperfect circumstances. Brewing coffee in cold water sounds weird, but in fact, it's just about the easiest way to make a cup (or a jar) of coffee.

Just grind coffee—keep it coarse, with grains about the size of sea salt—and combine it with twice as much water in an airtight jar. Give it a hard shake and stick it somewhere cool overnight (I used a cooler bag loaded with ice from ice camp and wrapped the whole thing in Bubble Wrap for insulation). In the morning, strain it through a colander and a paper coffee filter. What you've got now is coffee concentrate, which you can dilute with cold water to taste—I go about half and half. If you're feeling fancy, serve it over ice.

Here's the thing: cold-brew coffee tastes *amazing,* and it's practically impossible to screw it up. Unlike espresso, where all the grounds have to be about the same size so that the high-pressure water doesn't cause fracture lines in the "puck" of coffee that leave some of the coffee unextracted and the rest overextracted, cold-brew grounds can be just about any size. Seriously, you could grind it with a stone axe. Unlike drip coffee, which goes sour and bitter if you leave the grounds in contact with the water for too long, cold brew just gets yummier and yummier (and more and more caffeinated!) the longer the grounds sit in the water. Cold brewing in a jar is pretty much the easiest way to make coffee in the known universe—if you don't mind waiting overnight for the brew—and it produces the best-tasting, most potent coffee you've ever drunk. The only downside is that it's kind of a pain in the ass to clean up, but if you want to spend some more money, you can invest in various gadgets to make it easier to filter the grounds, from cheap little Toddy machines all the way up to hand-blown glass Kyoto drippers that look like something from a mad scientist's lab. But all you need to make a perfectly astounding cup of cold-brewed jet fuel is a mason jar, coffee, water, and something to strain it through. They've been making iced coffee this way in New Orleans for centuries, but for some unknown reason, it never seems to have caught on big-time.

All week, I'd been patrolling the playa armed with a big thermos bottle filled with cold-brew concentrate, pouring out cups to anyone who seemed nice or in need of a lift. Every single person I shared it with had been astounded at the flavor. It's funny watching someone take a sip of cold brew for the first time, because it looks and smells *strong,* and it is, and coffee drinkers have been trained to think that "strong" equals "bitter." The first mouthful washes over your tongue and the coffee flavor wafts up the back of your throat and fills up your sinus cavity and your nose is all, *THIS IS INCREDIBLY STRONG!* And the flavor *is* strong, but there isn't a *hint* of bitterness. It's like someone took a cup of coffee and subtracted everything that wasn't totally delicious, and what's left behind is a pure, powerful coffee liquor made up of all these subtle flavors: citrus and cocoa and a bit of maple syrup, all overlaid on the basic and powerful coffee taste you know and love.

I know I converted at least a dozen people to the cult of cold brew over the week, and the only challenge had been keeping Ange from drinking it all before I could give it away. But we'd have jet fuel in plenty for the morning's pack-up and Exodus. I'd put up *all* the leftover coffee to brew before we went to the temple burn, and if we drank even half of it, our ride would have to let us out of the car during the Exodus pulses to run laps around the playa and work off the excess energy.

Thinking about this, I took my thermos off my belt and gave it a shake. "Want some magic bean juice?" I asked.

"Yum," Ange said, and took the flask from me and swigged at it.

"Leave some for me," I said, and pried it out of her fingers and drank the last few swallows. The deep, trancelike experience of temple burn had left me feeling like I wanted to find someone's pillow camp and curl up on a mountain of cushions, but it was my last night on the playa, and I was going to *dance*, so I needed some rocket fuel.

Just as I lowered the flask, I spotted Masha and Zeb again, walking stiffly beside each other, faces set like stone, expressionless. They were at least fifty yards away from me, in the dark of night, and at first I thought they were just in some kind of deeply relaxed state from the extraordinary events of the night. But I soon saw that there was something definitely wrong. Walking *very* close behind them were a pair of large men in stocking caps just like the ones Carrie Johnstone—or her twin—had been wearing, and they had tight gray-black scarves pulled over their faces, though it wasn't blowing dust just then. The crowd parted a little and I saw that they were dressed as Carrie Johnstone had been, the same semimilitary jackets and baggy pants and big black boots. There was something wrong with them, and I couldn't place it for a moment, but then it hit me: they were darktards—no EL wire, no lights. And for that matter, Zeb and Masha had gone dark.

I saw all this in a second and mostly reconstructed it after the fact, because I was already moving. "This way," I said to Ange, and grabbed her hand and started to push through the crowd. There was something *really* wrong with that little scene, and Masha might not be my favorite person in the world, but whatever was going down with her and Zeb and those two guys, I wanted to find out about it.

Even as we pushed through the crowd, part of my brain was already telling me a little story about how it would all be okay: *It's probably not even them. Those two guys probably have EL wire all over their clothes, but they're saving battery. Boy, is Ange going to think I'm a paranoia case when I tell her what I thought I saw—*

The four were heading out into the dark of the open playa now, and there was someone bringing up the rear, emerging from the crowd behind them. It was Carrie Johnstone, and I saw her profile clearly now, silhouetted by the orange light of a flamethrower flaring a fireball into the night as a mutant vehicle zoomed past. There was no doubt at all in my mind now, this was *her*. She was sweeping her head from side to side in a smooth, alert rhythm, like the Secret Service bodyguards that shadowed the president when you saw him on TV.

Ange was saying something, but I couldn't hear her, and she was pulling on my hand, so I let go of her, because I *knew* it was Carrie Johnstone, and I *knew* that Zeb and Masha were under her power. I had been under her power. So had Ange. I knew what that meant, and I wasn't going to let her snatch anyone else.

All five of them were vanishing into the night and I began to push and shove my way through the crowd, not caring anymore if I stepped on someone's toes or bumped into them. People swore at me, but I barely heard them. My vision had shrunk to a narrow tunnel with Carrie Johnstone at the end of it. I patted at my utility belt and found my thermos, which was made of hard metal alloy. It didn't weigh much, but if you hit someone from behind with it, as hard as you could, they'd know they'd been hit. That's what I was going to do to Carrie Johnstone.

I was making a wordless noise. It started off quietly, under my breath, but it was quickly turning into a roar. No, not a roar, a *battle cry*. For years, this woman had haunted and hunted me in my dreams. She'd humiliated me, broken me—and now she was doing it again to someone else. And I had her in my sights and in my power.

Someone on a playa bike nearly ran me down but swerved at the last moment and fell over right in front of me, clipping my shin. I didn't even slow down. In fact, I sped up, leapt over the bike, and took off at a run.

I'd never run like that in my life, a flat-out sprint with my feet barely touching the ground. I was just taking another step when the whole night turned hellish orange around me, and then there was a terrible *whoomph* sound, and a blast of heat and noise and wind lifted me off my feet and threw me face-first into the dust.

I was dazed for a moment—we all were—and then I rolled over and picked myself up. My nose was bleeding, and when I put my hand up to it, it brushed against my lip and it felt *weird*, numb and wet, and I thought, in a distant, abstract way, *I've really done a number on my face, I guess.* That same part of me quietly chided myself for violating first-aid protocol by moving around after an injury. Even if I didn't have a spinal injury or a concussion, I might have broken some small bone that hadn't had a chance to start sending pain signals to my brain yet, might be mashing that broken bone under all my weight as I climbed to my feet.

I told the voice to shut up. I remember that very clearly, actually thinking, *Shut up, you, I'm busy,* like you'd do to a yappy dog. Because whatever had turned the sky orange, whatever had sent that gust of heat and wind and sound through the night, *Carrie Johnstone had been responsible for it, and it had been part of her plan to take Zeb and Masha out.* I knew it. Not in the way I knew what my address was, but in the way that I knew that a ball thrown straight into the air would come straight back again. A logical certainty.

I set off back in the direction that Masha and Zeb and Johnstone and her goons had been heading, out into the darkness, limping a little now as my right knee started to complain, loudly. I told it to shut up, too.

They were gone. Of course they were. Unlit, moving fast, out there on the playa, they could have disappeared just by moving off a hundred yards in nearly any direction. They probably had night-scopes and all sorts of clever little asshole-ninja superspy gadgets that they could use to avoid me if they wanted to.

If she wanted to. Carrie Johnstone probably could have killed me without breaking a sweat, and I'm sure her goons could have done the same. They were some sort of soldiers, while I was a scrawny nineteen-year-old from San Francisco whose last fight had been settled in Mrs. Bapuji's day care with a firm admonishment to share the Elmo doll with little Manny Hernandez.

But I didn't care. I was on a mission. I wasn't a coward. I wasn't going to sit back and wait for other people to do all the work. So I lurched into the dark.

There was no sign of them. I called out their names, screaming myself hoarse, running this way and that, and I was still running when Ange caught up with me, grabbed my arm, and pulled me bodily back to the infirmary tent. There were a lot of us there, waiting to be seen by the paramedics, nurses, EMTs, and doctors who streamed from across the playa to help with the aftermath of the worst disaster in the history of Burning Man.

Octotank, the art car that exploded, had started out life as a ditch digger, and it retained the huge, powerful tank treads and chassis. A maker collective working out of a warehouse in San Bernardino had removed everything else and meticulously mounted an ancient Octopus carnival ride atop it. You've seen Octopus rides, though your local version might have been called "the Spider," "the Schwarzkopf Monster," or "the Polyp." They've got six or more articulated arms, each one ending in a ride seat, sometimes just a chair with a lap bar and sometimes a full cage.

Now, that would have been cool enough, but then the mutant vehicle designers had mounted a flamethrower to the roof of each of Octotank's cars and hooked them up to an Arduino controller that caused them to fire in breathtaking sequences. They all drew their fuel from the same massive reservoir mounted to one side of Octotank's body, but each one had a mechanism that injected the fuel with different metal salts, and these impurities all burned with different bright colors. When Octotank was in motion, all eight cars swinging around in the night as it trundled across the playa, shooting tall pillars of multicolored flame into the sky from the swirling mandalas of its cars, well, it was magnificent.

Right up to the moment it exploded, of course.

The fuel reservoir was already half empty, thankfully, otherwise it would have done more than knock me (and about a hundred other people) on my face—it would have incinerated us.

Miraculously, no one *was* incinerated, though a couple dozen were burned badly enough that they were airlifted to Reno. Octotank had been built by careful, thoughtful makers, and they'd put in triple fail-safes, the final measure being that the reservoir had been built with its thinnest wall on the outer, lower edge, so if it ever did blow, it would direct its force into the ground and not the driver or the riders. The force of the blast had knocked Octotank over, snapping off two of its arms, but the riders had been strapped down by their lap belts and had rolled with the vast, broken mechanisms, getting scrapes and a few broken bones.

As for me, my nose was broken, I had a pretty ugly cut to my forehead, and I'd bitten partway through my lip and needed three stitches. I had a sprained knee and a headache that could have been used to jackhammer concrete. But compared to a lot of the people who crowded in—and around—the infirmary camp that night, I'd gotten off light.

Ange and I sat with our backs against an RV in the infirmary camp. A woman in a pink furry cowboy hat and a glittering corset who'd identified herself as a nurse asked me to stick close so that they could watch for signs of a concussion. I didn't want to sit still, but Ange made me and called me an idiot when I argued.

We didn't find out what had happened right away, couldn't have. We weren't looking at Octotank when it blew. Ange, being short, had been lost in a forest of taller bodies, trying to catch up to me (one of the reasons she didn't get hurt is that she was in among everyone else, and found herself in the middle of a pile of people—once she was sure that the people on the bottom were being seen to, she'd taken off again after me). I'd been running around in the dark, looking everywhere for Masha, Zeb, and the goon squad.

So we got the story secondhand and thirdhand from people in the infirmary. There were lots of wild theories, and everyone was buzzing about the Department of Mutant Vehicles, which certified all the art cars on the playa, and which was staffed with legendary mechanics and pyrotechnicians. Could they have missed some critical flaw in Octotank's build?

I didn't think so.

chapter 4

I convinced Ange to let me go and get some water from the infirmary's big cooler—"My butt's getting numb"—and took the chance to survey the human wreckage. It was terrible, and I thought I knew what had caused it.

When I got back to Ange, I handed her my water bottle and watched her drink, then said, "Ange, if I told you something crazy, would you listen?"

She rolled her eyes. "Marcus Yallow, you've been telling me crazy things since the night I met you. Have I ever not listened?"

She had a point. "Sorry," I said. I leaned in close to her. "Back at the temple burn, do you remember a woman walking around with a camera, right in front?"

She shrugged. "Not really. Maybe?"

I swallowed. What I was about to say sounded crazy in my head, and it was going to sound crazier out in the air, and it was just for starters. "It was Carrie Johnstone," I said.

Ange looked puzzled for a moment, like she was trying to place the name.

"Wait, *Carrie Johnstone*? *The* Carrie Johnstone?"

I nodded. "I got a couple of good looks at her. I'm sure." I didn't sound sure. "I'm pretty sure."

"So she's a burner now? That's weird."

"I don't think she's a burner, Ange. I think she was here to kidnap Masha and Zeb."

"Uh-huh," Ange said. "Marcus—"

"Dammit," I said, "you *said you'd listen!*"

She shut her mouth, opened it, shut it. "I did. Sorry. Go on."

So I told her about what I'd seen, Zeb and Masha and the goons, and my stupid, half-baked attempt to catch them as they'd marched into the night.

"So what are you saying?"

"What do you *think* I'm saying, Ange?"

"It sounds like you think that Johnstone and her pals kidnapped Masha and Zeb."

I didn't say anything. Of *course* that's what I was thinking, but that was just for starters. I had another idea, one that was even more crazy-sounding. I wanted to know—*had* to know—whether it would occur to Ange, too, or whether I'd just had my brains rattled when I face-planted into the gypsum flats of Black Rock Desert.

"What?" she said. Then she opened her eyes a little wider. "You think that Johnstone blew up Octotank to . . . what, to cover her getaway?"

I closed my eyes. I couldn't bear to look at Ange, because she was staring at me like I was nuts.

"Look at it this way: they've been driving fire-breathing art cars around the desert for decades now, without a single major mishap. The first time one goes boom, it happens *just* as Carrie Johnstone, a war criminal with a history of ruthless disregard for human life, is in the middle of kidnapping a rogue agent who has been trafficking in giant troves of secret documents. The timing of the explosion is perfect, and a hundred percent of the attention on the playa is occupied for the next several hours. Meanwhile, they could get away in a million ways—hell, they could just stroll over to the trash fence and hop over it and leg it out over the mountains, or jump into a waiting car. The Black Rock Rangers will all be scrambling to help the wounded, not patrolling with nightscopes for people trying to sneak in without a ticket."

"Yeah," Ange said. "I suppose." She squeezed my hand again. "Or: people have been driving homemade flamethrowermobiles around the desert for decades, and it was only a matter of time until one blew up. And you saw someone, in the dark, do something that looked like a kidnapping, but at a distance, and right before you had your head knocked around and broke your nose, after a week's worth of sleep deprivation, recreational chemical use, and caffeine abuse." She said it calmly and evenly, and kept hold of my hand as I struggled to go.

"Marcus," she said, grabbing my chin and forcing me to look into her eyes. I winced as she put pressure on the sutures in my lip, but she didn't loosen her grip. "*Marcus*, I know what you've been through. I went through it, too; some of it, at least. I know that improbable things happen sometimes. I was there when Masha gave you her key. You have the right to believe what you believe."

"But," I said. I could hear there was a *but* coming.

"Occam's razor," she said.

Occam's razor: the rule that says that when you're confronted with a lot of explanations for a given phenomenon, the least complicated one is the one that is most likely to be right. Maybe your parents won't let you into the locked drawer in their bedroom because they're secret spies and they don't want you finding their cyanide capsules and blowdart rigs. Or maybe that's just where they keep their (eww) sex toys. Given that you know that your parents have had sex at least once, and given that (in San Francisco, at least) odds are good they've bought the odd dildo or two over the years, the superspy hypothesis has to be shuffled to the bottom of the pile. Or, to put it another way, "Extraordinary claims require extraordinary evidence."

"I like Occam's Razor," I said. "It's a useful thinking tool. But it's not a *law*. Sometimes, the unlikely happens. It's happened to both of us. I saw what I saw, and I saw it just a few days after I saw Masha, who *is* mixed up in all kinds of espionage stuff, and who was acting paranoid as hell. Maybe she had a good reason for that."

"Yeah. And maybe all that stuff primed you to interpret anything that happened in the days that followed in dramatic and scary ways." She let go of me and looked away at the crowds of people. "Marcus, if you think you know what happened, you know what you should do. Masha *told* you what to do."

If you ever hear that I've gone down, or Zeb's gone down, release it. Shout it from the mountaintops.

You know what? I hadn't even thought of that. I'd been so fixated on rescuing Masha, or proving I wasn't losing my mind, I'd totally forgotten that I was her insurance policy, that she'd fully expected that she might "go down" and that she'd entrusted me with her personal countermeasure.

Now that I thought of it, I found that the idea terrified me.

"I don't know what's in her insurance file," I said, "but I've got an idea that if we were to make it public, it'd make some very powerful people *very* angry at us." I flashed on how I'd felt when Johnstone had been standing right over me, that paralyzing horror that started somewhere at the bottom of my spine and froze me to the spot. I believed that Johnstone had kidnapped Masha to keep the contents of that file a secret. What would she do to me if *I* released it?

Worse: what would she do if Masha told her *I* had the insurance file?

"Oh, crap," I said. "Oh, Ange, what'll we do?"

We both agreed that we didn't have to do *anything* that night. I was injured, we were in the middle of the playa without functional laptops, and, to be honest, we were both scared witless about the insurance file and what might happen if we were to go public with it. I still had the USB stick with me—I'd kept it in my utility belt, in its little secure zip-up money belt section. I kept compulsively checking it until Ange made me stop. After a few hours, we decided that I didn't have a concussion and snuck away before anyone could disagree with us. We caught a few precious hours' sleep in the tent, holding tight to each other, before the alarm on Ange's cheap, rugged plastic watch went off, *weep-weep-weep,* and we got up to break camp and start Exodus.

We'd slept in our clothes—it got cold at night in the desert, even with our sleeping bags zipped together for shared warmth— and when we got outside the tent and stood, I saw that my burnoose and the front of my T-shirt were crusted with dried blood from my broken nose and swollen lip. My nose and lip felt like they'd ballooned to elephantine proportions in the night, though when I brushed the dust off a nearby car's side mirror and checked my reflection, I saw that they were merely double their normal size. I looked like I'd been run over by a tank, one of my eyes blackened, my mouth distorted in a weird, pouty sneer, my taped-up nose misshapen and bulbous.

"Groagh," I said, and my lip split again and began to seep blood. My face *hurt*. They'd given me some Tylenol 3s at the infirmary and I took two of them, washing them down with cold brew, undiluted straight from the mason jar, then kept on swigging at the bean juice. I needed energy if I was going to help Ange break down our camp and lug our gear across Black Rock City to the camp where the guy who was giving us our ride had been staying.

Ange said, "You just sit down, Marcus, I got this."

I shook my head and said, "Nogh," a painful syllable that made my face bleed some more.

"Forget it, sit down."

I shook my head again.

"God, you're stubborn," she said. "Fine, kill yourself. Don't come running to me when you're dead."

I waved at her and handed her the cold-brew jar. She made a face. "There's blood in that one." I looked at the rim and saw it was smeared with red from my lip. I dug another jar out of the ice chest and passed it to her. She went to work on it. "Got to drink plenty of water, too," she said. "Remember, this stuff is a diuretic."

She was right. I alternated two swigs of water for every swig of cold brew at regular intervals over the next forty-five minutes as I crammed, jammed, piled, and mashed our stuff into our bags. The biggest item to pack, by far, was Secret Project X-1 and all its assorted bits and pieces.

When I joined Noisebridge, I hadn't really known what I wanted to do. All I knew was that these maker-types had set up a hackerspace in the Mission, filled it with lathes and laser cutters and workbenches and drill presses, and that anyone could join and use the gear to make, well, anything. I'd hung around for a month or two, dropping by after classes to just sit on the sofa and see what people were up to, bringing along my laptop and schoolbooks and studying in between watching as my fellow Noisebridgers invented every mad and amazing thing under the sun.

Noisebridge was a fantastic place. It had its own *space program*. Seriously. Almost every month, they launched homebrew weather balloons crammed with cameras and instrument packages to heights of seventy thousand feet and more and retrieved them.

There were people hacking robots, cars, clocks, pet doors, toys, and rollerblades—not to mention video-game consoles, server hardware, autonomous flying drones, and so on and so on.

And they had *3D printers,* devices that could produce actual physical objects on demand, based on 3D files they made or downloaded from the net. Most of these had started off life as Maker-Bots, an amazing and popular open-source 3D printer kit that you assembled yourself. MakerBots printed in plastic, using spools of cheap plastic wire, and the results were pretty amazing, especially considering that the kits cost less than a thousand dollars, and you could make one for less if you scrounged around for the parts in surplus catalogs and the prodigious bins of spare electronics at Noisebridge.

Being open source, MakerBots were a hacker's paradise, and people all over the world had modified their printers to do extraordinary and amazing things. The big excitement when I joined Noisebridge was a successful conversion to laser-based powder printing, which involved using an apparatus to spread a thin layer of plastic powder on the printing surface, then melting it into specific forms with a laser, then adding another layer of powder and melting it again with the laser, over and over, until you'd built up the whole solid shape.

Powder-based printers cost a *lot* more than MakerBots—like $500,000 or more—and they were all locked up in a complicated set of patents that meant that only a few companies could make and sell them. But patents didn't stop *people* from modding their MakerBots to do powder, and once they started, it became the most popular form of MakerBot modding in the world. Naturally it was: the objects that came out of a powder printer were much smoother and more detailed than the stuff that came out of a plastic wire printer, and with a powerful enough laser, you could use metallic powders and produce precisely made objects in stainless steel, brass, silver—whatever you wanted.

But what interested me wasn't printing in steel: it was printing in *sand.* There were lots of people around the world who were experimenting with alternatives to plastic or metal powder as a printing medium, because, well, anything you could melt with a laser could be fed into a printer. You could print the most wonderful stuff with sugar or make brittle, tragically short-lived stuff out of the whey powder they sold in bulk for bodybuilding. But like I say, *sand* was the stuff that caught my imagination. When you melt sand, you get *glass,* and a beautiful, streaky kind of glass it was, and every day brought more amazing sculptures and jewelry and action figures and, well, *everything* made of melted sand. As a printing material, sand was as cheap as it got, cheaper even than whey powder.

But there wasn't any sand on the playa. What we had instead was *dust.* Gypsum dust, the stuff that they make drywall out of. In other words, stuff that you could (theoretically) make some wicked structures out of.

That was *my* plan, anyway. I made my own MakerBot, downloading the plans from their site, laser-cutting the balsa wood, building the Arduino-based controller, scrounging parts when I could, buying them when I absolutely couldn't find them, but only through surplus stores. In the end, it cost me less than $200, and took me about two months, and it worked *beautifully.* As soon as I got it working, I promptly broke it (of course) and tried to get it running as a powder printer. That was a *lot* more complicated, and the powerful laser it required cost as much as the rest of the printer. But I got it working, too.

And while I was gutting through that breakdown/upgrade/fix cycle, I hated every minute of it, felt like the world's biggest idiot for not being able to do something that everyone else (for some extremely specialized definition of "everyone else") seemed able to pull off. But you know what? I couldn't stop. Because whenever something went wrong, it always seemed like the solution was tantalizingly within reach, and if I just did *one more thing* I'd have it all working. One more thing and one more thing and one more thing again, and then, miraculously, *it worked!* I went from nearly comatose to elated beyond all reason in one millionth of a second, as the air above my workbench was filled with the sweet, toxic smell of melting sand and a bead of glass formed on the build platform.

The bead took form, and my calibration testfile, a block with several holes in it that were sized to snugly fit a collection of standard bolts I kept in my pocket for testing, began to take shape.

I didn't need to use them. I could *see* that it was working. I'd taken that stupid printer apart and put it back together hundreds of times. I knew its movements like the movements of my own hands and its sounds like I knew the sound of my own heart. I laughed and danced on the spot, for real, and watched it go through its paces for a few minutes, before the excitement got to me and I raced out onto Mission Street, ready to grab the first person I could lay hands on and drag them back to Noisebridge to see *my machine working*! Of course, as soon as I got out the door, I realized it was three in the morning, and there was no one to be seen.

So that was my MakerBot, and the plan had been—what else—to mod it to print in playa dust, using melted sugar as a fuser. Sugar's *strong*—melt some caramels and brush them onto a 2×4 and clamp another 2×4 to the spot overnight while the "glue" sets and you'll get a joint that's so strong the wood will tear apart before the glue gives. But sugar is also water-soluble, so when I was done, my playa-dust prints could be dissolved in water. "Leave no trace," just like Burning Man principle eight says. I did some test runs, using powdered drywall that I ground up in an old hand-cranked coffee grinder, and I had it working pretty well when I disassembled the MakerBot and packed it up to take to the playa.

That was Secret Project X-1, and I *swear* it worked like a charm when I left San Francisco. I have no idea why it failed so miserably when we got to Black Rock City. The solar panels tested out good, and I borrowed a multimeter from another camp and checked every circuit and contact, and everything seemed to be in working order. But the stubborn, evil bastard refused to even turn on.

Even bloodied and bruised and traumatized and terrorized, I still felt a pang when I packed away X-1 again. I had this incredible plan to 3D print the most amazing shapes and objects out of playa dust—fanciful animals, busts of famous monsters, all the best junk from Thingiverse, the online library of free 3D forms. I was going to be the best, coolest, cleverest burner in the history of the playa. A legend. Instead, I was the guy who sweated and swore

at his invention for twenty-four hours straight before his girlfriend
went upside his head and told him to stop swearing at his printer
and *get out there* and enjoy Burning Man. She was totally right, and
everyone liked my cold brew, but man, it hurt to pack away X-1
without having printed a single widget.

"You'll get it working next year," Ange said. "Don't worry." She
looked off at the cloud of dust rising from the playa as fifty thousand burners packed up and got ready to turn Black Rock City
back into Black Rock Desert (though there'd be cleanup teams
staying behind for a few months going over the whole desert, erasing the final signs of human occupation). "We have to go."

We hardly spoke on the long drive home. Our ride, Lemmy—a guy in his forties who had been coming to Burning Man for twenty years—told us that Exodus was usually like a party, with people getting out of their vehicles between pulses and hanging out, dancing, chatting. But after the night's explosion and injuries, no one wanted to party down. The hourly pulse of cars released onto the winding road to Reno was like a funeral procession, and it was no better once we got to the little Indian reservation towns on the way to Reno and stopped for gas.

That matched my mood perfectly, to tell the truth. I was all beat up, and the painkillers made me groggy, while the jerking and jouncing of the car on the roads kept me from sleeping. Ange took over the driving in Reno, and I finally found my way into sleep, waking up briefly when we gassed up again in Sacramento, and then the next thing I knew, I was back home on Potrero Hill, at my parents' front door.

I kissed Ange good-bye and dragged my knapsack and duffel bag to the front door, fumbling my key into the lock. I had planned on calling my parents from Reno to let them know I was on the way, but sleep had taken precedence, and now I was heading home with a face that looked like it had been through a meat grinder and a pocket full of government secrets that were being hunted by a ruthless torturer. *Hey Mom, hey Dad! Funny thing, you'll never guess what happened to me while I was out in the middle of the desert.* Yay, this was going to be f-u-n.

The house was a mess. That was the new normal. It started when Dad lost his job and started spending a lot of time at home. Who knew he was such a slob? Mom refused to pick up after him (yay, Mom!), but she also turned out to have a high grodiness tolerance. By the time she lost *her* job, well, the place was already a pit. And it didn't get better after that.

I stepped over the scatter of shoes by the front door and dragged my junk through a pile of old newspapers, knocking them over and sending them slithering to the floor. "Hi, guys," I said. I wished that I'd be able to get my butt upstairs and into bed before I had to hold down a conversation, but I knew it wasn't very likely.

"Marcus!" Mom called from the living room. "We were so worried!" And one second later, there she was in the hallway, and gasping at my face. "Oh my word," she said, her British accent and funny little Britishisms ramping up the way they did when she was stressing.

"It's okay, Mom," I said. "There was an accident at Burning Man and—"

"We heard all about it," she said.

Duh. It hadn't even occurred to me that the stuff that happened at Burning Man would be news in the rest of the world. San Francisco was the birthplace of Burning Man, so of *course* they'd heard. And then they hadn't heard from me. Christ, I was a rotten son.

"I'm sorry," I said. "Really. It's better than it looks. I just had some painkillers before we left and fell asleep or I would have called—"

Now Dad was in the hallway, too. "God, Marcus, what happened?"

I closed my eyes, took a deep breath. "Can I make you a deal? How about if I tell you what happened really quickly, then I go have a shower and sleep, and then we can talk it over?"

This is what I love about my parents: they both looked at each other with their eyebrows up, like, *That sounds reasonable to me,* and nodded, and said, "Okay," and then gave me a crushing hug that felt *so* good, even if I was so tired I could barely stay vertical.

I unlaced my boots—bending over caused a fresh headache to blossom right behind my eyes—and kicked them off with two little puffs of playa dust. Dad cleared a pile of books off the sofa while Mom made tea for me and her and coffee for Dad (I'm embarrassed to say that despite all my efforts to educate him, Dad still drank—*ugh*—instant). I told them the story as quickly as I could, leaving out the part about Masha and Zeb and Carrie Johnstone. Here, back in San Francisco, it all seemed, I don't know, remote? Like something that happened to someone else, or something I'd read about in a book. Maybe it was the painkillers, or Ange's (understandable) skepticism, but I found myself questioning my own memories.

"Oh," I said, as I was finishing up. "Someone offered me a job, too! Someone running for senator who needs a new webmaster or something. I'm going to drop them a line in the morning."

"That's fantastic, sweetie," Mom said, looking like she meant it. Dad said some nice things, too, but I could tell that he was thinking about the job he *didn't* have. After my trial and conviction—for stealing Masha's phone, of all things—he "mysteriously" found that he couldn't get his security clearance renewed. So that meant that a lot of his consulting gigs dried up. We'd been worried, but not totally freaked, because at least he had his adjunct professorship at UC Berkeley. But then California went broke—really, really broke, not like all the other times it had gone broke as I was growing up—and the UC system got its budgets slashed to practically nothing. Adjuncts had been the first to go. And of course, when he lost his job, I lost my discount on tuition, and started piling up the student debt. That's right: my Xnet stuff cost my dad his job, and that cost me my college education. I think that's called "the law of unintended consequences," but I just like to think of it as FAIL.

"Okay, shower now," I said, having a sip of my tea. It was milky and sugary and strong, the way Mom liked it, and it was the taste of my childhood, the flavor of the sick days when Mom had taken care of me while I lay in bed with the flu or a stomachache. I decided to take it up with me, to finish after I showered. But I didn't make it into the shower. I didn't even undress. I flopped down on my bed amid the piles of clothes I'd pulled out of my bag while I was repacking the week before to make room for X-1, and I was snoring in seconds.

When I woke up the sky was dark and my tea was cold. I finally had that shower, staying under the hot water until it ran ice cold, scrubbing the dust out of my pores. Then I went into my room and started piling up laundry and separating out gear that needed to be hosed down outside in the driveway or wiped down on my workbench. Finally, I unpacked my utility belt and found myself holding on to a dusty USB stick.

Normally I'm pretty careful with my data. That means that I don't leave anything important on a USB stick. People lose those things all the time. The first thing to do with something important is to stick it in a computer—my latest frankenbook, a hand-built laptop called Lurching Abomination that was the distant descendant of Salmagundi, the first laptop I ever built for myself. Lurching Abomination had a whopper of a hard drive, two terabytes, and I used TrueCrypt to give myself a "plausible deniability" partition, so that if you just turned it on and entered a crypto key, you'd get what looked like a normal ParanoidLinux installation with a browser and an email client that was hooked up to my public email addresses and Xnet accounts, where I got all the spam and friend requests from strangers and bots and stuff.

But if you—or if *I*—entered *another* password when starting up the machine, there was *another* ParanoidLinux instance hiding on that monster disk, and this one was only hooked up to my private accounts, my private bookmarks, my private calendars, my private social nets, and so on. With a little bit of monkeying, I could boot into the secure, secret version of my computer, fire up a virtual computer in a window, and put the plausible deniability version in that.

Next to Lurching Abomination was a stand-alone hard drive, and Lurch was smart enough to check every few minutes and see if the disk was connected, and if it was, to back itself up. That disk was also encrypted (duh—what would the point of doing all the crazy stuff with Lurch's disk be if I was going to make an unscrambled copy of all the data and leave it on my *desk*?). The disk's enclosure had enough smarts to try to periodically hook up to one of the big servers at Noisebridge and try to make a copy of itself there.

This all more or less worked, most of the time, and it meant that within a few minutes of copying any files onto my laptop, they would be encrypted, copied to my desktop drive, and copied again

382 | cory doctorow

to Noisebridge's array. *That* server was synched up with a massive storage farm run by and for hackspaces, located in an old nuclear fallout shelter somewhere in England (seriously!). So yeah, do your worst, steal my laptop, burn down my house, nuke San Francisco, and I'll *still* have a backup. Mwa-ha-ha. Yeah, it's crazy-paranoid, but: a) I'd been through some paranoid stuff, and b) it wasn't much harder than just using a commercial backup program, only my solution was safer and more robust and cheaper.

My hand hovered over the USB port. The USB stick was a no-name version, squarish and cheap looking, its case glued shut unevenly by some fifteen-year-old chained to a machine in China. You saw them lying smashed on the sidewalk, and people advertising banks or soda pop pressed them into your hands when you came out of the BART station. There was no way to tell if it was a 4GB stick or 500GB. It could hold all the books ever written or a video of someone's cat chasing a laser pointer or a buttload of ugly pornography.

Or it could contain the key to a trove of military and state secrets so hot that Carrie Johnstone would come out of the night and kidnap you to get them back. Only one way to find out.

The keyfile was less than 5K. It was just a long string of random numbers, and somewhere out there was the torrent file that they'd decrypt. But the keyfile itself was so small that I could have read it aloud to Ange on the phone, if I didn't mind reciting stuff like "I_?4Wac0'5_9'Ym4|PL" for an hour or so, and if Ange was willing to write it all down without getting a single letter, number, or weird piece of punctuation wrong.

Once I'd copied the key to my computer, I found myself sweating, my heart thundering in my chest. My hands shook as I typed the command that forced an immediate backup—I didn't want to wait ten minutes for the next scheduled backup. I didn't want to risk having Carrie Johnstone and her goons break down the door and stick a bag over my head and shove me into a waiting helicopter headed straight to Iraq. Of course, the *next* thing I did was start to download the torrent file.

If you haven't been paying close attention, you might just think BitTorrent = "pirate movie download," but there's plenty of cleverness in the way it works. Files are broken up into thousands of little pieces, and you can request any of the pieces you're missing from anyone who's got it. As you get more and more pieces of the file, you start to get requests from others, too—the whole thing is called a "swarm" and as you can see, the more people who are downloading, the faster the download gets. That's pretty cool, since in the physical world, the more people there are trying to get something, the harder all of them have to try to get at it. Imagine if food was like BitTorrent: every time you ate a meal, there'd be more food left over for everyone else to eat.

Of course, the downside of BitTorrent is that if only a few people have copies of a file, then there are only a few people who can share it with you. I typed "insurancefile.masha.torrent" into the search fields for a dozen BitTorrent search engines starting with The Pirate Bay, the biggest of them all. There were about ten "seeders"—computers that had whole copies of the file—out there on the net, and two other machines downloading it. That was interesting. Maybe they were evil government spooks who wanted to try to crack the files and find out what Masha had. Or maybe they were just random copyright-enforcement bots that downloaded *everything* and checked to see whether it contained anything worth suing over.

Either way, I wasn't going to use *my* IP address to download that file. My parents got their Internet through AT&T, a scumbag phone company with a track record of handing over their customers' data to the cops without court orders. Grabbing sensitive files off the net through them was like calling up the director of the DHS and saying, "Hey, are you missing any sensitive data? Because I'm small, defenseless, and unarmed, and I got 'em. Want my address?"

Which is why, no matter what, I always scraped up the money to pay for a subscription to IPredator, the proxy service operated by the Pirate Bay folks. IPredator was specifically designed to make it impossible for anyone else to tell what you've been downloading. It ping-ponged your data between Copenhagen and Stockholm, across an international border, and kept no logs or records of who was doing what. It was blazing fast—for a proxy, which are never as fast as a naked net connection—and it was run by some of the world's baddest-ass hacker antiauthoritarians, people who made me look like a goody-two-shoes obedient toddler who could barely turn on a computer. If anyone could make my download anonymous, it was those cats.

While the file trickled in, I hit my email. I've never been much of an email user—it's not like my friends and I used it to figure out when to hook up, we all used Twitter and Xnet's Facebook overlay (which scrambled our updates and messages)—but all my profs had used it while I was at Berkeley, and then everyone I was hitting up for work expected me to give them an email address. God, but email was *tedious*. People expected you to answer all of it, and there was: So. Much. Spam. When it came to Twitter and Xnet, I could just take everything that had come in while I was at Burning Man and mark it as read, and no one would get pissed off at me. But people who sent you email took it personally if you didn't reply. It was just how email worked. Even I felt put out if someone didn't reply to my email.

Download download download. Spam spam spam. Delete delete delete. The stupid email ritual, so beloved of my parents. So boring. When I finally whittled down the huge log of crap to a little toothpick of actual mail, my eye jumped to one sent by "Joseph Noss." Of course, it was probably a fund-raising appeal, since my email address seemed to have found its way into the mailing lists of every political candidate in the state. But in my notebook, there was the email address for Joseph Noss's campaign manager, carefully copied after Mitch Kapor had written it on my arm with his Sharpie. The coincidence was . . . interesting.

I opened it.

> From: Joseph Noss <joe@joenossforsenate.com>
> To: Marcus Yallow <myallow271828183@gmail.com>
> Subject: Webmaster
> Dear Marcus,
> My campaign manager, Flor, tells me she heard from Mitch Kapor that you were thinking of coming on board to be our webmaster. Your name sounded familiar so I looked you up, and, well, you know what I found. From what I can see, you would be absolutely perfect for the job. Can you give me a call when

you get this? We really need to make this happen, like, YESTERDAY. My personal cellular number is 510-314-1592.

> Joe

I read it twice and reached for my phone, everything else forgotten. After all these months of searching and begging, someone was *offering* me a job, and it was someone so cool his phone number was the first seven digits of pi. I mean, *woah*.

I dialed his number without having to look back at the screen—seriously, that was the coolest phone number I'd ever seen—and listened as the phone rang. Just before he picked up, I looked at the clock on my computer and realized it was nearly 11 P.M. on Monday night. I fought the reflex to hang up the phone as he answered.

"Joseph Noss speaking," he said, and, yup, that was him all right. I'd heard his voice on TV and YouTube enough to recognize it instantly, a deep growly sound like the "This is CNN" guy or an old soul singer.

"Um," I said, and pinched my leg to make myself stop saying *Um*, which is a trick Ange taught me. "Hello, sir, this is Marcus Yallow. You sent me an email? I hope it's not too late—"

"Not at all, Marcus, I was up late working. Sorry to say it, but 11 P.M. is prime time for me."

"Me, too," I said. "I've always been a night owl."

It's funny, but I liked him right off. Something in that voice—he sounded like someone who thought hard about things, and who was listening hard to everything he heard.

"I'm glad you called me, Marcus. I know you've been involved in little-p politics before, but as far as I can tell, you don't have any experience with the big-P kind, the kind that involves elections and so on. Is that right?"

"That's right, sir." I thought, *Ah well, it was worth a shot.* I didn't have the experience he was looking for after all.

But he said, "That's fine. We've got lots of experience with that sort of thing around here. Listen, Marcus, I want to give you a sense of the challenge we're up against here, and then maybe you can tell me whether you think you're the right sort of person to help us out.

"Now, California's got a reputation for being a little crazy, but we're trying to do something that's crazy even by California standards. You know I'm an independent candidate, right?"

"Yes," I said.

"The received wisdom here is that 'independent' is a synonym for 'unelectable.' The Dems and the Republicans have got all the major donors sewn up, they've got efficient machines, they've got close friends at every TV and radio station and newspaper in the state, and they've got national organizations they can draw on. Independents start with a huge disadvantage, and it only gets worse when push comes to shove, because if we gain even a little ground, well, the big boys bring in *their* big boys and crush us like bugs.

"I could have gotten the Democratic nomination. They know me from my days at City Hall, they know that this district is one where African-American candidates generally do well, and I'm thought of as a decent sort who can be relied upon to raise a decent amount of cash *and* stay honest and sober once he gets elected, which puts me far ahead of most of the jokers around these parts.

"I could have had the nomination. Between you and me, they asked, several times, and in several ways. They seemed pretty sure that a campaign for Joe Noss would be something of a sure bet. But the more I thought about this, the more I realized that I didn't *want* the nomination. I've seen what it means to be elected with major party support: it means that you have to toe the line. By which I mean, when there is a vote where your conscience tells you to go one way and party discipline tells you to go the other way, well, you'd best tell your conscience to sit that one out.

"That wouldn't be so bad if you could trust the party, but I can't say I trust either party in this country. You've got 'progressive' Democratic presidents who believe it's legal to assassinate American citizens overseas, who think that we should be spying on phone calls and email without warrants—well, I could go on, but I think you know what I mean."

"I do," I blurted. Maybe it was all the weird events of the past week, but listening to Joe talk made me excited, made me want to go out and man a barricade for him or something. It was the way he talked, even over the phone; it made you feel like whatever this guy was doing, it was going to work, and that if you were lucky, you'd get to be a part of it.

"I believe you do, Marcus! But it's not just the Dems, of course. I know many Republicans who are honorable, generous, thoughtful people. My father was one such Republican. But there are power brokers in the Republican party who are *insane*. I don't say that as a figure of speech. I mean it literally. There are important movers and shakers in the RNC who believe that the Earth is five thousand years old. And these are people who made their fortunes pumping sweet crude in Texas! You think they tell their geoengineers to only pump oil in places that accord with the Young Earth theory of creation? Now, those people are hardly the worst—there's plenty who think that torturing isn't just something you have to do when there's no alternative, but something you should do all the time. People who believe that anyone with ten million dollars is, by definition, good, and anyone without ten cents to his name is, by definition, a criminal. The thought of being beholden to these—well, let's use the word my daddy liked, because Daddy was a polite, well-spoken man, and he'd have called these people *dunces*—these *dunces*, well, I never even considered it for a moment.

"No, I thought to myself, Joe, there's some smart people who think you could win this election with their help. Maybe you could win it *without* their help. Maybe if you took up positions that people believed in, positions that were grounded in evidence and compassion, not ideology or lining your pockets, you'd be able to beat the all-powerful party machines and show up in the Senate without a single corporate logo sewn onto your suit jacket.

"Of course, there was no way I'd be able to do this using the old-fashioned methods—all the tactics we developed to win elections in the last century. I knew that this campaign would rise or fall on the strength of our technology use.

"Now, I might be over twenty-five"—he chuckled, a sound as deep as the ocean—"but I know a thing or two about technology. Enough, at least, to know how much I *don't* know. Finding the right tech people has been my top priority since I started this thing, and I think I've found some good people who can do top-level strategy and such. But I haven't found anyone to be my special forces commando, if you will. A *doer*, not just a *thinker*. So when your name came up, well, it made me excited, Marcus. I think you could be the delta force ninja of our technology team. Does that sound like your sort of thing?"

My mouth was so dry I could barely talk and my palms were so sweaty I could barely hold the phone, but I managed to blurt out, "Yes, absolutely, that sounds like my *dream* job!"

"I was hoping you'd say that. Now, it's not my job to hire you, that's my campaign manager's job. But my recommendations do carry a *little* weight around here. I'm looking at her diary right now, and it looks like she's free tomorrow morning at 8:30 A.M. That's a little early for a night owl, I know, but if I were to put a meeting with you in her calendar, do you think you could make it?"

"Even if I have to stay up all night, Mr. Noss."

"Call me Joe. And I hope that won't be necessary. Get yourself some sleep and set an alarm. I'll tell Flor to expect you at 8:30. That's Flor Prentice Y Diaz. Let me spell it for you."

"It's okay, I've just googled her," I said.

"Of course you have," he said. "Do your research now, then get yourself into bed and don't forget the alarm!"

"I won't," I said.

I spent the next twenty minutes poring over everything I could find about Flor Prentice Y Diaz—parents were Guatemalan refugees, raised in the Bay Area, master's in public policy from Stanford, former executive director of a big homelessness charity. A photo showed a handsome but severe Hispanic woman in her fifties, wrinkles around her eyes and deep lines around her mouth, big dark eyes that seemed to bore straight through me. Then I noticed where the photo had come from: a profile in the *Bay Guardian* by Barbara Stratford. I checked the time in my menubar. It was coming up on midnight, which was probably too late to call Barbara and ask her to put in a good word for me. But I *did* send her an email asking her to drop my name to Flor Prentice Y Diaz if she got a chance. Email did have its uses.

I checked the status of my big torrent download. The file was halfway down, and there were eight more downloaders in the swarm. I wondered how many of them worked for three-letter spy agencies in the DC area.

There was a soft knock at my door. I opened it. It was Mom.

"Hey, you," she said. "How long have you been up?"

"A couple hours, I guess," I said. "I'm sorry I didn't come downstairs, but when I checked my email, I found a message from Joseph Noss asking me to call him about the job, so I called him and he wants me to go in tomorrow morning to meet with his campaign manager at 8:30 A.M. I think I've found a job!"

Mom smiled and reached out and stroked my hair, the way she used to do when I was a kid. It was a tell she had, whenever she was feeling especially proud of me. It made me happy all over. "That's wonderful news, love. How are you feeling, though?" Tentatively, she touched the tape over my nose. I flinched a little. The painkillers had worn off.

"Well, my nose is still broken, but my headache is gone. Apart from that, I feel fine. It looks much worse than it is. And it could have been a *lot* worse. As it was, I basically tripped and fell on my face." I shook my head. "There were lots of people who got hurt worse than me, caught right in the explosion."

She took her hand away. "I wish you'd called. We were—well, we were worried, Marcus." She didn't say anything about the *other* times I'd gone missing, like after the Bay Bridge blew up, when I was being held and humiliated on Treasure Island by Carrie Johnstone and her jolly friends from the DHS; or when I'd gone underground, run away with Zeb only to be caught by Johnstone again, this time for a round of simulated execution on her waterboard. Neither of those incidents had been very pleasant for me, but they'd been hell on my parents, too. I was a jerk.

"I'm sorry," I said. "I was fast asleep by the time we got back into cell-phone range. But yeah, you're right, I should have called."

We sat there silently for a little while, each of us remembering the bad times before. "How's *your* job search going, Mom?"

"Oh," she said, "oh, don't worry about me. There's little bits of contract work coming in all the time. Nothing earth-shaking, just a little freelance editing and such. But between that and the savings and Dad's severance, we're getting by."

I didn't bother to ask what they would do when Dad's severance ran out. I'd overheard them talking about that enough times to know that it was a sensitive subject—and the fact that they always shut up about it when I entered the room told me that they didn't want me to worry about it. Dad had sold his car the month before and they'd listed the parking spot in our driveway for rent on Craigslist, which I thought was pretty clever, even if it would be weird to have some stranger using our driveway. But yeah, I could see what they could see: first you lose your job, then your car, then what? Mom had torn up her flowerbeds in the backyard and planted vegetables, which tasted great, but I knew that taste had less to do with things than the grocery bill did. The drawer full of takeout menus hadn't been opened in months, and Mom and Dad had a tendency to disappear on the bus whenever Safeway had a big sale on meat, coming back with huge bags full for the freezer. I didn't have anything against saving money, but I couldn't help but wonder where it might all end. There were a lot of FOR SALE signs on our block, and one or two empty places with foreclosure notices taped to the door.

"Well," I said. "Got to get up early tomorrow!"

"Are you going to wear a suit?" Mom said. "I could get something out of your father's closet."

"*Mom*," I said, "they're hiring me to be their *webmaster*—I'm pretty sure they don't want a dweeb in a suit."

She opened her mouth like she wanted to argue with me, then shut it again. "I'm sure you know what you're talking about," she said. "But just be sure to dress up smart, all right? No one likes a slob, even if he *is* the webmaster."

"Good night, Mom."

"I love you, Marcus."

"Love you, too."

Good thing I set three alarms. I managed to switch off both my phone and my alarm clock without even waking, but the raging music blaring out of Lurching Abomination's external speakers—Trudy Doo and the Speedwhores performing "Break It Off," which features some of the craziest death-metal screaming ever to be com-

mitted to MP3 by an all-girl post-punk anarcho-queer power-trio—
was impossible to sleep through. It was 7:15.

I showered and peeled off the tape over my nose and grimaced
at my beat-up face. Oh well, nothing to be done about it. Thinking
of my mother's advice, I dug through my closet and found a white
button-up shirt that I'd last worn to my graduation, and the gray
wool slacks I'd worn at the same event. I even found the brown
leather shoes that went with the outfit, and gave them a vigorous
wipe with an old sock, bringing out a bit of a shine. As I buttoned
up the shirt and tucked it in and got the line of buttons even with
my fly, I found myself growing excited. Mom was right (as usual):
dressing up made me *feel* competent, like the kind of guy you'd
want to hire.

Dad was already at the kitchen table, eating oatmeal with sliced
bananas and strawberries.

"Woah! You're looking suave, son," he said. I saw that he'd
shaved off the stubble he'd sported the night before, and was
dressed in his workout clothes.

"You going to the gym?" I said.

"Jogging," he said. "Just started. We're not using the gym anymore." *Translation: we can't afford the gym anymore.*

"That's great," I said.

"Yeah," he said, and I wished I hadn't said anything, because
he looked embarrassed, which wasn't usual for him. "Your mother
told me about your big interview. There's more oatmeal on the
stove and there's sliced fruit in that bowl."

Dad hadn't made me breakfast since I was thirteen years old,
when I started insisting that I was too old to have breakfast prepared for me and switched to grabbing some toast on my way out
the door. I realized he must have gotten up early just to make sure
that I went off to Joe's office with a full tummy. It made me want to
hug him, but something held me back, like acknowledging what a
big deal this was would have spoiled the illusion of normalcy.

I hadn't seen 8 A.M. in the Mission since I dropped out of school. I
stopped in at the Turk's for a lethally strong pour-over and let him
fuss over me when I told him I was going in for a job interview.

The Mission's always been a place with a lot of homelessness, but it seemed like things were worse than they'd ever been. At least, I couldn't remember seeing quite so many people sleeping on the edge of the sidewalk or in the doorways of boarded-up stores. I couldn't remember smelling quite so much pungent human pee-stink from the curbs.

I finished my coffee just as I reached Joseph Noss's campaign headquarters, between 22nd and 23rd on Mission, in a storefront that had been a huge discount furniture place for most of my life, but which had shut down the year before and had been sitting empty until now.

The big windows were plastered with orange and brown NOSS FOR STATE SENATE signs, neither Democrat blue nor Republican red. I checked my phone: 8:20. I was early. I tried the door, but it was locked. I rapped on the glass and peered in, trying to see if there was anyone inside. It was dark, and no one answered. I knocked again. Nothing. Oh, well. I stood by the door and waited for Flor Prentice Y Diaz, trying to project an air of employability.

She arrived at exactly 8:29, wearing blue jeans, a nice blouse, and a kerchief over her hair, and carrying a takeout cup from the Turk's. She had a serious, almost angry face on as she walked down the street, like there was a lot on her mind, but when she saw me, she smiled, then frowned as she took in my battered face. "Marcus?" she said.

I smiled back and extended my hand. "Hi there! Sorry about this—" I scrunched up my face. "I was at Burning Man last weekend and, well, a car exploded at me. It looks a lot worse than it is, really."

She shook my hand. Her grip was gentle, dry and warm. "I heard about that," she said. "Are you sure you're okay to be here? If you want to reschedule—"

I waved my hands. "No, no! Honestly, I'm fine. Besides, Joe—Mr. Noss—said that he was in a hurry, right?"

"Well, that's very true. All right then, let's get inside, shall we?"

She dug a big key ring out of her handbag and opened the doors, reaching out with one hand to hit a light switch. The fluorescents flickered on all around the cavernous space, revealing trestle-table desks with snarls of power strips beneath them. There were still signs advertising cheap sofas on some of the walls, and a long checkout counter that was now covered with silk-screening stuff. Someone had installed a big extractor fan over the table, but I could still smell the paint-y smell of the silk-screening station. Clotheslines hanging from the stained old drop ceiling were draped with shirts and posters in the campaign's orange and brown.

"This is where the magic happens," she said, crossing to a desk right in the middle of the floor. It had more papers on it than most, and a big external monitor. She slid a laptop out of her purse and connected its power cable and monitor cable and woke it up and entered her password. I politely looked away as she typed it, but I could hear that it was admirably long and complex—there was also the telltale sound of a shift key being depressed and several of those unmistakable spacebar *bangs*.

"Sounds like a good password," I said.

"Oh yes," she said. "Ever since I had my Yahoo mail compromised a few years ago and everyone I knew got an email saying I was stranded in London after being mugged and asking for them to wire money to help me out. I expect you've got your own little security rituals, right?"

I nodded. "Just a few. But as soon as you start looking into security, you discover that there's always more you could be doing."

She was staring intently at her screen as her email streamed in. I noticed she wasn't breathing, which was something I'd read about: email apnea. People unconsciously hold their breath when they're looking at their inboxes. I made a mental note to mention it to her later if I got the job.

"I like your taste in coffee," I said, as she slumped back and gasped for air. "The Turk is awesome."

"He's one of a kind," she said, sipping. She'd pulled some papers from her purse. I recognized my résumé. She tapped my address "You live pretty close to here, huh?"

"Oh yeah," I said. "I went to Chavez High, just up the street."

"I sent my kids there, too. But that would have been before your time."

I was feeling good about the interview. We were bonding. We

had all this stuff in common—Chavez High, the Turk . . . We hadn't even talked about Barbara Stratford.

She set the résumé down on her desk. "You seem like a very nice person, Marcus." Suddenly, I was a lot less confident. Her expression had turned into a professional mask. "But you don't exactly have a lot of work experience, do you?"

I felt my cheeks burning. "No," I said. "I mean—" I took a deep breath. "My dad got laid off from UC Berkeley last year and I had to drop out. No more discount tuition. So I've been looking for work ever since. But I've had some campaign experience, the Coalition of Voters for a Free America for two summers."

"Yes," she said. "Volunteer experience, right?"

"Right," I said. "We were all volunteers. But I'm very responsible. And I believe in Joe, and I believe that the Internet can change politics for the better—make it more accountable, more transparent. That's why I want to work here."

As I said it, it felt like exactly the right sort of thing to be saying. But when I was done, her expression was harder than ever. "Yes," she said. "I've heard all that before. I've been hearing it for twenty years now. But the fact is that elections are won by a lot of shoe leather and a lot of money and a lot of handshakes, the way they always have been. I know that Joe has lots of pie-in-the-sky ideas about reinventing elections *and* reforming politics, but I run the campaign and I think that reforming politics will be a big enough job to get through, and maybe we can leave the reinventing stuff for the next candidate."

I didn't know what to say to that. Some innate, primitive sense of organizational politics told me I should just keep my mouth shut.

"We've got a lot of people around here with big ideas about how the world should be run. That's fine. That goes with the territory when you're running as an independent—you get independent-minded people working for you. But the bottom line is that this is a *campaign* to *elect* a *candidate*. It's not a lab for egalitarian, consensus-based organizational reform. It's not a high-tech start-up.

"Right now, this campaign needs a *webmaster*. That's someone who'll put up a website that doesn't get hacked the minute we stick it online. That website's got to help us raise money, it's got to help us mobilize voters, and it's got to help us win an election. I want to make myself clear on this point, because I've hired a few web-masters in my day, and I know a thing or two about some of the problems endemic to the trade. I'm looking for a website that gets the job done: nothing more and nothing less. I don't want it to be one micron prettier than it needs to be. I don't want it to be one quantum more technically elegant than it needs to be. And be-cause our webmaster is also going to be our IT department, I need someone who can keep us all reasonably secure, keep our comput-ers backed up, and keep the network up. Someone who's available on-call twenty-four-seven right up to election day.

"So, now that you've heard my little speech, I need to ask you, does that sound like you, Marcus?"

But Joe said he wanted a delta force ninja, is what I didn't say. I had already figured out enough to know that what Joe wanted and what Joe got was filtered through his campaign manager, who held the decision to hire me in her hands.

"I have done all those things in the past," I said. "I'm reliable. I'm a fast learner. I believe in Joseph Noss. I may not have had much work experience, but that's only because no one's given me the chance. There are lots of people in San Francisco who could be your webmaster, but how many of them have helped run an underground network that beat back the DHS and restored the Bill of Rights to San Francisco?" I spent most of my life telling people that M1k3y was just part of a movement, scuffing my toe when people told me how much they admired me. But something told me that this wasn't the right time to be humble.

Her smile came back. "Okay, that was well said." She finished off the Turk's coffee. "I've asked around about you. Barbara Strat-ford called me as I was on my way in to work this morning to put in a good word for you. There are lots of people who think the world of you as a leader and a techno-guerrilla. But none of them have ever employed you, and we have more than enough 'leaders' around here. Have you ever read *The Time Machine*, Marcus?"

"Yeah," I said. "I wrote a paper on it in AP English."

"Then you'll remember the Eloi and the Morlocks. The Eloi

were the privileged surface dwellers, enjoying a life of high-tech sophistication and ease. But under the ground, there was an army of Morlocks, toiling away night and day in the subterranean engine rooms, making sure that everything was humming along tickedy-boo."

"You want Morlocks, not Eloi, right?"

She smiled. "Bright boy. Yes, exactly. It's not a glamorous job, but it's the job that needs doing. What I'm asking you to do now is look inside yourself and ask, 'Do I want to do the job that needs doing, even if it's boring and workaday and merely necessary and not at all exciting?' You say you believe in Joe—do you support him enough to join his army as a grunt and not a general?"

I could see why she was the campaign manager, and not Joe. Joe had made me want to take to the streets, but she made me want to prove I could get the job done. They must make a great team.

Which is not to say that I wasn't disappointed. I *had* hoped that I'd be greeted as a revolutionary hero and given a squadron of tough info-commandos to boss through a series of action-hero adventures. But the way that Flor Prentice Y Diaz pushed at me, implying that I was just a kid who wanted the spotlight more than he wanted to help, it was like a set of spurs in the belly. So even as I was thinking, *Man, that's an effective motivational technique,* I was also thinking, *I'll show her!*

I made a showy salute. "Yes ma'am, general, ma'am."

Her smile got wider. "All right, all right. I'm giving you a hard time this morning, because you come with a lot of advance recommendations, but there are also lots of warning flags. You're a bright young man, and bright young men are nice to have around, but in my experience, they need quite a lot of adult supervision. So I intend on *supervising* you very closely until I'm convinced that you have learned the difference between what we need and what you'd like us to have."

I blinked and replayed what she just said. "Does that mean I'm hired?"

She waved off the question. "Oh, Marcus, you've been hired since we sat down here. Joe loves you, or at least he loves your reputation, and he's as excited as a puppy about having you around here. But I needed to make sure you understood what working here entails."

I couldn't stop myself, I held my arms over my head like a quarterback after a touchdown: "All *right!*" I shouted.

She laughed at me. "Down, boy. Yes, you've got a j-o-b. Marian, our HR person, will talk over your pay and such with you later. But before we get started, there's one thing we need to discuss, and that's all this hacker business."

I composed myself. "Yes?"

"Don't. Do. It. You've done all sorts of clever things with computers, no doubt. You've outsmarted the feds and raided their data, you've gone wandering around computer systems where you had no business being. It's all in the grand old tradition of the Bay Area, but it has no place here. The first time I catch so much as a *whiff* of anything illegal, immoral, dangerous or 'leet'"—she made finger quotes—"I will personally bounce your ass to the curb before you have a chance to zip your fly. Do I make myself crystal clear?"

"You can really turn on and off the scary voice at will, huh?"

"I can. I find it's a useful way of indicating to my colleagues when I expect to be taken seriously."

"And you can do this really kind of stone-faced, severe facial expression, too. That's really amazing." What can I say? I'd just gotten a job. The joy was bringing out my inner weisenheimer.

"This face? This isn't my severe face. This is about gale force one. You do *not* want to be around for a force five."

"I'll keep that in mind."

chapter 6

I spent the rest of the morning jumping straight into the work with both feet. The previous webmaster, a volunteer, had just gone back to school at Brown, but she'd left behind a neat sheet of passwords and configuration data, as well as information on our network contracts. I figured the thing to do was to conduct an audit of everything I'd be in charge of, checking that it was all where it was supposed to be, doing what it was supposed to be doing. I grabbed a stack of one-side-printed paper out of a recycling box and three-hole punched it, then snapped it into a used three-ring binder I found in a supply closet. I could have used Lurch to take notes—I'd brought it in, booted into its plausible deniability partition, with all that deadly secret stuff locked away on disk sectors that were indistinguishable from random noise. But I needed to be able to walk and write, sitting down at peoples' desks and getting their names and copying down their network cards' MAC addresses and such, and paper is just easier for that sort of thing. I'd type it all in later.

Every so often I'd look up and see Flor watching me from her desk in the middle of the room. She'd catch my eye and then nod in satisfaction—at my hustle, I assumed. It made me feel good—like someone was noticing how I was busting my butt to make a good impression on my first day. I may be a Morlock, but it was nice to know the Eloi were looking on in approval. After talking with Flor, I'd remembered that the Morlocks ate the Eloi, which made the whole analogy a little weird. I wondered if she'd intended that, and if so, what it was supposed to mean.

Joe had swept in around 10 A.M. with one phone pressed to his head and another in his hand and had been swarmed by about a dozen staffers and volunteers with urgent questions. He clamped one phone between his ear and shoulder and used his free hand to point at people in the mob and then at places they were to wait for him, all the while without losing his place in the animated conversation he was having. As the crowd dispersed, he said his good-byes and dropped his phone into one pocket, then did the same with the other one.

He was a tall, broad-shouldered black guy with his graying hair cropped short. His skin was somewhere between an americano and a macchiato, a few shades darker than the high-necked sweater he wore over comfortable-looking blue jeans and black Converse. I decided I could dress down for work the next day.

I was in the middle of going through every line of the WiFi router's configuration file, plugged straight into it at the very back of the room. Much as I wanted to jump up and introduce myself, I decided to play it Morlock and let him get on with all the urgent stuff he needed to do and try to find a quiet moment later to say hello.

But Joe scouted around the room, spotted me, and said, loudly, "Marcus, all right!" and half jogged straight to me, hand already out.

"Hello, sir," I said.

"Marcus, I can't *tell* you how glad I am that you're joining us. Flor tells me she's very impressed with you. I'm not surprised. I imagine you've got plenty to do to get up to speed, but please ask Flor to put you in my diary for tomorrow, whenever she can squeeze you in, so we can talk about strategy, all right?"

"All right," I said, making an effort not to stammer. In person, Joseph Noss just radiated charisma, and it made me tongue-tied. Here was a guy who just felt, I don't know, *important* and *smart*, and I wanted to impress him, but everything I could think of to say felt too boring to burden him with.

"Good man," he said, and slapped my shoulder before turning on his heel to jog back to Flor's desk, pointing at the staffers he was ready to hear from as he went. They converged in a huddle at Flor's desk and I went back to work.

"Marcus?" someone said from behind me, a few minutes later.

I looked up, and into a semi-familiar face. It was a guy about my age, or maybe a little younger, with a scruffy beard, and he was grinning so widely I thought his head would fall off. I recognized him from somewhere, but I couldn't think where. I decided I'd try to fake it. I stood up and shook his hand. "Hey, man!" I said. "Great to see you again!"

He clapped in uncontainable delight. "Dude, I can't *believe* it's you. Are *you* the new webmaster? Really?"

"Yup," I said. "Sweet gig, huh?"

He shook his head furiously. "No. Way. I can't believe it! Marcus Yallow is our *webmaster*? Oh *man*!"

This was more familiar territory—someone going all gushy and me not knowing what to say in response. Been there, done that, still don't know what to do when it happens. "So, uh, what have you been up to?"

"I'm the swag barista," he said, thumping his chest. He was wearing a SAN FRANCISCO NEEDS NOSS shirt, done like an old-timey sci-fi movie poster, with a giant Joe standing astride the Golden Gate bridge. "I design the T-shirts and posters. I try to do a new one every couple days, and screen them on demand. Keep it fresh, mix it up, you know? One thing I wanted to ask you about was whether you could put up a Threadless clone for the website so I could do a little shirt-community for all the Nossers out there?"

"Uh," I said, "yeah. Sure, why not?" We were running the site on OpenCampaign, which was a free mod of WordPress designed for election campaigns. It could run WordPress plugins with no additional work, and the one that was based on the Threadless user-generated T-shirt site was one I'd looked at before. It didn't seem like it'd be too hard to run.

"You are such a dude. God, I can't believe this! Wait until I tell Nate. He is going to flip out."

And that's when I remembered him. "Liam?" I said.

"Yeah, of course! Liam! I've been volunteering here all summer! Ever since I saw Joe's July Fourth video. That stuff was straight-up inspiring, yo."

I had friends who ended their sentences with "yo," but always ironically, making fun of the people who were trying to talk all "street" and badass. Liam wasn't being ironic. He really did end his sentences with "yo."

"Yo," I said, then felt mean about it and gave him a friendly slug on the shoulder. "Liam, man, I didn't recognize you at first with the beard and all. How cool that we're going to be working together?"

"Me too. Look, do you have lunch plans? Want to get a burrito? I know a great place up on Valencia—"

"Sure, burritos sound great," I said. I hefted my notebook and said, "I'd better get back to work if I'm going to get time for a lunch break, then."

He did a couple of dance steps on the spot, then gave me a surprise hug, a real crusher that involved lifting me a couple inches off the floor. "See you at lunch!"

Once upon a time, I'd been part of a tight foursome of awesomely close friends. Darryl, Jolu, Van, and I had done everything together since we'd been little kids. But after the whole Xnet thing, well, one thing happened and then another. Van and Darryl started dating, and Van didn't like Ange at all (and there was all the weirdness about the fact that she'd been secretly crushing on me, which loomed up like an invisible wall whenever we saw each other). Darryl went off to Berkeley, and we'd seen each other a little at first, but between classes, Van, and his psychotherapy for all the crazy nightmares and freak-outs he still had thanks to the horrors of Gitmo-by-the-Bay, we barely had time to say hi. Jolu, meanwhile, had graduated from his job at Pigspleen to a sweet gig as a programmer on a start-up that was commercializing municipal data, cranking out services based on the feeds put out by City Hall. He had a ton of new friends, including a bunch of intimidatingly smart civic hackers, and when they were all really going at it, I could only understand about half of what they said. We didn't see much of each other.

And then there was Ange, who was the world's most perfect girlfriend: funny, smart, exciting. She liked the same movies and games that I did, liked the same books and music, and was always up for keeping me company when she wasn't at school—she'd gotten into SFSU for communications studies and was acing her courses. So even though I missed my friends, it wasn't like I was actually *lonely* or anything—so somehow I never got around to calling them or IMing them or poking them and seeing how they were doing.

But it had been a long time since I'd had a regular gang of friends, a little posse of my own. And I missed that.

Liam's friend Nate joined us for lunch, taking BART down from his mom's place downtown. He, too, gave me a crushing hug, and then he and Liam exchanged one of the same. These guys were as Californian as they came, and they *loved* their physical contact. I'd been born and raised in San Francisco, but my mom was British, and so I just hadn't gotten into the whole super-huggy scene ever.

We ended up at my favorite burrito joint, and I got tongue, which Ange had convinced me to try and which turned out to be amazingly tasty, provided you didn't think too hard about the fact that you were, you know, *eating a tongue*. Liam ordered one, too, and raved about how good it tasted and how he wished he'd tried it sooner.

"I still can't believe you're our *webmaster*," Liam said. "That's like, I don't know, Bruce Lee being your bouncer or something."

"Or Jack Daniels being your bartender," Nate said. He had the same beard as Liam.

"I think Jack Daniels is dead, or made up," Liam said.

"Okay, it's like Steve Wozniak fixing your PC," Nate said.

"Dude, old school," Liam said. "Woz is the guy who built the first Apple computers," he said to me.

"Yeah," I said. "I know."

"Oh," Liam said. "Yeah! Of course you do! Listen to me, huh?"

I wanted to find some way to politely say, *Hey, Liam, don't worry about impressing me, okay? I already like you, and all this stuff is just making you sound kind of desperate.* But every way I could think of saying that would make Liam feel like a loser and make me sound like a dick.

"What are you up to, Nate?" I said, pointedly changing the subject.

He shrugged. "Being unemployed. Polishing my nonexistent résumé." Another shrug.

"I know how that feels," I said. "I was unemployed until this morning."

They both boggled at me.

"No way," Liam said. "How could *you* be out of work? I assumed they'd poached you from some rad start-up or Google or something."

Now it was *my* turn to shrug. It seemed like unemployment talk always involved a fair bit of shrugging and looking away. "Dunno," I said. "I dropped out of school months ago, couldn't afford it anymore, and I've been looking ever since."

"Man," Nate said. "That's crazy. If you couldn't find work, what hope do *I* have?"

I didn't have an answer for him. I was starting to actually feel guilty about having a job, and I'd been employed for less than a day.

We finished our awkward lunch and went back to work, and I went back to mapping out the network and figuring out what needed fixing and what didn't, and I didn't even think about the torrent I'd downloaded the night before until I got home and rebooted my computer into my secret partition and the machine reconnected to IPredator and started seeding the file again.

The torrent contained a huge—HUGE—ZIP file that was encrypted. Of course, I had the key. And somewhere out there, Masha was being held captive—or worse—and I was pretty sure that she wanted me to dump the file *and* the key now.

I really wanted to talk this over with someone. Ange, of course. But she was still in class and wouldn't be out for hours. And this wasn't the kind of subject I wanted to talk about over the phone or email or IM or—well, I kind of felt like we should talk about it in a soundproofed room at the bottom of a mineshaft, but I didn't have either of those things.

I had been avoiding thinking about this for nearly thirty-six hours now. I'd had good excuses: I'd been blown up. I'd been doped up. I'd been asleep. I'd gotten a job. I'd had my first day at work. But I'd run out of excuses for inaction.

But wait! I just thought of a new excuse: it would be *insane* to have the decrypted file sitting on my drive, even on a secret partition. I couldn't get over the thought that a snatch team could break down my door at any time and haul me away. If I was loaded up on my "secret" partition at that point, it'd be easy for them to see what I was up to.

I decided I needed to build a few more layers of security into the system before I started to handle this info-plutonium.

First things first: go shopping for a virtual machine. Let me explain that, because VMs had become my best friends lately.

You can write a program that works just like your computer's microprocessor. You designate a file to act as your virtual computer's hard drive, and then you load it up with an operating system and any programs you want to run. When you "turn on the computer"—that is, when you run the program—it looks at the virtual drive and loads in the virtual operating system and follows all the instructions it finds there, passing them on to your *real* computer, which is running underneath all this.

It used to be that the main use for VMs was to simulate old computers on new ones—so you could simulate some ancient game console, an old Game Boy or whatever, and play all the vintage games. There's a megahuge games VM called MAME, the Multiple Arcade Machine Emulator, that can play pretty much every old game, ever.

The key word here is "old." That's because running a pretend computer inside a real computer is slow. But computers double in speed every eighteen months or so—this is called Moore's Law, for Gordon Moore, who helped start Intel. That means a brand-new computer will be about sixty-four times faster than a computer you could buy for the same money six years ago, which means that so long as you're working with old VMs, you probably won't even notice the speed lag.

But lately, computer manufacturers have been figuring out how to design chips to run VMs more efficiently, so the gap between a VM and the real computer it runs on keeps shrinking. This means that it's easier than ever to try out new operating systems and new programs. If there's something you're *really* paranoid about, you can just run a free VM program, install a free OS on it, and run anything you want in that little sandbox. Nothing that happens in that VM can affect your real computer—not unless you give it privileges to see your real hard drive and real files. The VM is like a head in a jar, and you can tell it anything you want about what's going on in the world and it'll have to believe you.

You can download hundreds—thousands!—of VMs from the Internet and just fire them up as you need them. Want to turn an old computer into a router or a file server for an hour or a day or a year? Various sysadmins have bottled up perfectly tuned VMs that run any specialized function like that out of the box. There are even user reviews to help you figure out which ones are the good ones. And since it's all built on open, free code like Linux, anyone can modify, improve, and redistribute them.

I went hunting for an extra paranoid VM, and I found one. It started with a copy of ParanoidLinux, my own favorite distro, and nuked any programs and services you didn't need, to make it all the more bulletproof. ParanoidVM also stored its user files in TrueCrypt plausible deniability chunks, so there was no way to tell from the forensic examination of the disk how many users there were and how many files they had.

That was good for starters, but I wanted a dead man's switch: something that would cause the whole thing to lock itself and shut down if I didn't do something every fifteen minutes. So I wrote a little script that hit me up for a password every quarter hour. If I didn't enter it, it would issue a system-wide command to kill any VMs that were running, then erase itself. So if a snatch squad *were* to nab me, all the work I'd done on the files would disappear unless they could torture the password out of me in a quarter of an hour.

They'd still have the key and the torrent file, but they wouldn't know whom I'd shown anything to or what we'd talked about. All

406 | **cory doctorow**

I'd have to do is key in my password every fifteen minutes, and not
go off to the toilet or forget and go to dinner, or I'd lose everything
I'd worked on up to the last save point.

There's a technical term for this kind of security work: yak-
shaving—wasting time doing silly chores to avoid something
harder and more important. There was an old essay I liked about
working for Google by a hacker called Dhanji Prasanna, which
talked about "shaving the entire yak pen at the zoo, and pretty
soon traveling to Tibet to shave foreign yaks you've never seen before and whose barbering you know little about."

That's the territory I was heading into. It was time to decrypt
the file.

It had been a while since I'd decrypted an encrypted ZIP file with a
very long password. There was a specialized command you could
use to specify that the password was in a file, and I couldn't remember it at first. I looked up how to do it. I did it. The list of files
scrolled past faster than my eye could follow. Lots of files. *LOTS
AND LOTS* of files.

810,097 files.

What had Masha said? *Eventually, you come across something so
terrible, you can't look yourself in the mirror anymore unless you do
something about it.*

That was a lot of dirty laundry, yo.

I could tell at a glance that they had human-generated file
names—weird punctuation, weird capitalization, and both were
all over the place. Computers might do weird capitalization, but
every file would have been weird in the same way. Some had pretty
descriptive names like "bribes paid to senate Def Cttee.doc" and
others were more cryptic, like "HumIntAfgh32533." There was a
file called "WATERBOARDING.PPT," a set of PowerPoint slides.
My stomach curdled into a hard ball just looking at it.

I double clicked it. The first slide was just a title: "STRESS IN-
TERROGATION SEMINAR 4320." The next slide was a long con-
fidentiality notice, naming a bunch of private military contractors
who, apparently, had been involved in producing this presentation. And the next slide—

—showed a boy, about my age, restrained in padded cuffs at the ankles, wrists, and chest, strapped to an angled wooden board that held his head lower than his feet, mouth covered tightly in Saran Wrap, having water poured down his nose in a splashing stream out of a bucket with a spout, held by two large, clean, white hands. The boy's body was arched up like a bow, straining against his restraints, pulling so hard that every muscle in his body stood out. He looked like an anatomical illustration.

No.

He looked like a torture victim.

The Saran Wrap was an evil touch. The water is poured down the nose, but it can't go into the lungs, because the body is tilted backwards. *His* body is tilted backwards. The body—*his body*—knows that there's water going into the windpipe and it's desperate for air. His mouth gasps, but the Saran Wrap only lets the air go out, because every time he tries to suck air *in,* the plastic makes a tight seal. The only place air could enter is his nose, and the water is pouring into his nose and so he can't breathe that way.

Eventually, his lungs empty out entirely, collapse like spent balloons, shrivel like raisins. His brain, starved of oxygen, begins to die. He may pull his bonds so hard he breaks his bones.

The government likes to call waterboarding a "simulated execution." It's not a simulation, though. They nearly kill you. If they don't stop, they will kill you.

One of the men at Guantánamo Bay, America's secret prison, was waterboarded more than 180 times. Nearly died 180 times. They say he planned 9/11. Maybe he did. But whatever he told them, they'd be crazy to trust it. When you're being slowly murdered, you will say anything and everything to get loose.

But I wasn't thinking about that. I was hypnotized by that boy, by the expression on his face, the veins standing out in his forehead, the terror in his eyes. I'd been there. I'd had that look in my eyes.

Time stopped.

And then the image disappeared. The window it was in disappeared. The VM that was in disappeared. My dead man's switch had been prompting me for a password, had run out of time, and had killed the VM and deleted itself like a good boy. I hadn't even noticed the password prompt. I'd been staring at that picture.

That picture was only one slide, from one file, out of more than 800,000 files. This was going to take a while.

Ange rang the bell around dinnertime, and my mom sent her up to my room. She let herself in and snuck up on me and put her arms around my neck and kissed the top of my head. I pretended I didn't hear her or see her reflection in my screen. It was a game we played. We were adorable.

"Hey there, workin' man, how was your first big day at the office?"

"Pretty much like I said in my texts; I'm mostly trying to figure out what the job will entail, trying to get a handle on everything. I told you about that Liam guy, too, right?"

"Yeah, how weird is that? Small world, but I wouldn't want to paint it."

"Well, he got less sweaty about things by the end of the day, came by for a real chat, and it turns out he knows his stuff pretty well and had lots of good ideas for me, some authentication ideas I hadn't thought of for managing guest laptops."

"I think it's adorable that you've got a little groupie," she said, pulling up my spare chair and transferring the clutter of MakerBot parts to my bed before sitting down.

"It's embarrassing," I said. "How was class?"

She crossed her eyes. "I thought that after high school I'd get to start learning like an *adult,* without everything being about how many factoids I can regurgitate on cue during exams. But pretty much all of my courses give seventy-five percent of the grade based on exams."

"Well, you could always leak the exams," I said, and her hands were over my mouth before I'd gotten the words out.

"Don't. Even. Joke," she said.

Ange's deep, dark secret is that she stole and published the No Child Left Behind tests when she was in the eleventh grade, along with the answer sheets. The school board never figured out who was responsible for it, and they claimed that the stunt had cost millions. Served 'em right.

"Sorry," I said. "But there's worse ideas. And who better to do it?"

"Tell you what, let's figure out what to do about Masha's little bombshell first. We can recycle anything we come up with for any final exams I should happen to find myself in possession of."

"That's why I love you; you're always thinking."

We joked a lot about love, but the truth was, I *did* love her, with a weird, scary kind of intensity. It probably had to do with drifting away from my gang of friends and dropping out of school—Ange was pretty much the only person I saw on a regular basis who wasn't a parent of mine. Every now and then, this freaked me out a little. I think it freaked her out, too—I was looking forward to getting a little more balance in my life from having a job with co-workers.

"So, what have you got?"

I felt that little paranoid shiver. You could eavesdrop on a room by bouncing a laser off the glass. The sound waves from the voices in the room made the glass vibrate, and the laser picked up the vibrations. I'd seen a demo of this in a YouTube video of a presentation from DEFCON, the big hacker conference in Vegas. The sound wasn't perfect, but it was pretty good. Good enough to pick out every word and recognize the speakers' voices.

"Um," I said. "Give me a sec, okay?"

I plugged a set of speakers into my laptop and then stretched out their wires until I could press them on the window glass. Then I used my computer's random-number generator, /dev/random, and requested some random white noise. The speakers began to hiss with staticky sound. I cranked them up to the point where I couldn't stand it, then turned them down a notch or two. I made sure the blinds were seated over the speakers again. Maybe a laser could pick up on the sound in the room, but I couldn't think of any way to subtract random noise from the audio signal. That didn't mean it was impossible, but at least we couldn't be eavesdropped on by anyone stupider than me.

"Huh," Ange said, observing this ritual. "Well, that's pretty intense."

"Yeah," I said. "It sure is." We moved the chairs so we could both see my laptop and I showed her my VM and the dead man's switch.

"Not bad," she said. "Okay, you've convinced me that you're worried about this stuff. Which, I suppose, means that you're sure that you saw Masha and Zeb get taken off the playa, and that means you think the explosion was deliberate." She closed her eyes and took a deep breath. "Back down the rabbit hole, here we go."

"Wait till you see." I brought up the VM, brought up the directory listing. Sat back.

"What is this? I don't even . . ." she said, staring wide-eyed at the listing. I handed her the mouse. She started clicking, beginning from the top. The first item was "budget_8B5S.xls." It turned out to be a spreadsheet listing income and outgo. The titles down the left side were peoples' names. Across the top was a list of companies with bland names like "Holdings import/export" and "Property Management Ltd" and in the middle were dollar figures. None of them were very big—$1,001, $5,100—the biggest was $7,111.

"A lot of ones in those figures," I said.

Ange nodded. "Yeah. That's interesting, isn't it?" She stared at them for a while longer and got out her laptop. "You still like IPredator for anonymity?"

"Generally. But why don't you run it through Tor after IPredator." Tor—The Onion Router—would bounce the browser requests through a bunch of random computers, and none of those computers would know where the request came from and where it was going. It was slow—slower than IPredator, which was slower than the raw network connection. But there's a time to be paranoid, and this was it.

I stared at the mysterious spreadsheet for a while. The dead man's switch asked for a password and I entered it.

"There you go. I knew I'd read about this. The number one appears more frequently than other numbers in financial data."

"What? Why?"

She showed me the article, a summary of a paper at a security conference. "A lot more stuff costs between $10 and $19 or $100 and $199 than $20 and up, or $200 and up. Retail psychology: people are more likely to buy stuff that costs $9 than $10; it's a big jump. Ninety-nine dollars has less psychological weight than $100, but $999 is a lot less crazy than $1,000. So you get a lot of clusters of numbers with ones in them. But when people make up numbers, faking their finances or cheating on their taxes, you get a much more even distribution of numbers. It's one of the ways the IRS looks for tax cheats. I read about it in a book on data-journalism—tried to get my section's TA to read it last year but she said she had to get us ready for the exams and to show it to her again afterward.

"So all these ones, they're inserted by someone who knows he's making up numbers and wants to be sure that there's plenty of extra ones to make the statistical distribution look right. Someone who doesn't expect a human being to look at these numbers closely, but worried that a computer might spot them."

She peered at my spreadsheet and started to type again, but the dead man's switch wanted a password again and I didn't grab the computer in time to enter it. The VM disappeared.

"That's frustrating," she said.

"I'll teach you the password."

"What if you set the timeout to longer? Thirty minutes?"

I shook my head. "I think I could probably hold out against someone who wanted my password for fifteen minutes, especially if they were on a snatch team that broke the door down and didn't have any time to prepare. Thirty minutes, though . . ."

"Oh," she said.

"There's a presentation in there on how to do waterboarding. A PowerPoint. It's got bar graphs showing the time to brain damage based on age and general health."

"Oh," she said again. She knew that there were times when showering would give me uncontrollable shakes. Being executed will do that to you.

I brought up the VM and opened the spreadsheet again. Ange started to enter the names.

"They're all staffers for Illinois State Assemblyman Bedfellow.

The logical next step is to look up which committees that Assemblyman is on, and what all he voted on. Data Journalism 101—or it would be, if there was a Data Journalism course in my program."

"Let's do it," I said.

"No," she said. "That's just one file. There's 800,000 more. We can't do this retail. We have to find a wholesale approach."

"We need Jolu," I said. "This is his thing."

We'd been brainstorming for hours. Ange was even more paranoid than I was. She had me clone the VM—easy, just copy the data file—and then set up a new TrueCrypt file that had one copy of the VM in its regular storage, and another copy in a hidden plausible deniability partition.

"Here's how it'll work: the snatch squad comes in, bags and tags you and grabs the computer. They start looking around, but before they can get very far, there's a password prompt. They start to rubber-hose you for the password, but you gut it out. *Whoosh,* the dead man's switch trips, the VM takes itself down, the data is scrambled.

"But *then* what happens?"

I chewed my lip. I had thought through this far before and hadn't liked what came next. "They try to get the password out of me to decrypt the file."

"Right."

I said, "And if you're here, they can work on you, too."

"Which is why we're doing this. Because right away we can give them a password, and that password will unlock this copy of the VM. It's got a full set of the leaks. But that's not the copy we work with. That's the one we hide in the plausible deniability partition. And that's where we keep all our notes, any mailing lists of people who know about this and work on it with us. We never give them that password. Our story is, we kept the leaks on this encrypted VM, and we didn't keep notes on them. We didn't know what to do about them. It's believable. I mean, we *don't* know what to do with them."

We did that. We came up with two long, crazy passwords and

practiced them on each other until we had them memorized. Then we stared at each other.

"Now what?"

"We need Jolu," I said again. "He's all about wholesale data these days."

Ange nuked the VMs, turning them back into random-seeming gibberish. "Those speakers are driving me crazy," she said. "Are you sure they'll stop this laser-listener stuff?"

I shook my head.

"Fine," she said. "Let's turn them down for a while, anyway."

"So, Jolu. You know that bringing Jolu into this is pretty much the same kind of dick move that Masha pulled when she brought *you* into it."

"I know. But it's different with Jolu. He's my friend. One of my best friends."

She chewed on some words for a while. "Marcus, no offense, but is that still true? When was the last time you guys actually hung out? When was the last time you even *talked*?"

I squirmed. She was right. "Okay, point taken, but that doesn't mean we're not still friends. We don't dislike each other, we're just, you know, busy with our own things. I've known Jolu for most of my life, since I was a little kid. He's the right guy for this."

"I don't mean to make you all defensive, all right? It's just that you're about to put Jolu into a really hard spot, and it's the kind of thing that you should be really, really sure about before you do it."

"Jolu wouldn't turn me down. This is *important*."

Ange gave me a long, long look. Here's what she wasn't saying: *If this is so important, why didn't you drop everything to do something about it? Why didn't you go to the cops, or the press? Why are you screwing around with a new job instead of making this your top priority?*

It was a thought that I kept having, too, and of course, I knew the answer, and so did Ange. I was too scared to go public. The last time I spilled everything to the press, I'd ended up in a torture chamber. The stuff Masha had dumped on me was a *lot* more important and scarier than what I'd had to say that time, too, if our small samples were anything to go by.

Besides, Masha hadn't told me to rescue her. She'd told me to get the material out. I would. Maybe if the material was out there, Carrie Johnstone would realize that snatching Masha would do no good and let her and Zeb go.

Maybe.

I've always done my best work at night, and I knew all the tricks—combining careful doses of coffee, catnaps, and showers to get my tortured, sleep-deprived brain to perform during daylight, while still cranking away through the vampire hours, where inspiration lurked in every shadow.

Jolu was the same, and that was one reason we got along so well. I can't count how many 3 A.M.s I'd shared with him over Skype or IM, or in person as we snuck out of the house to go dingledo-die around the streets of San Francisco. So even though it was 8 P.M. when Ange and I finally finished arguing, I didn't worry about whether he'd be free for the evening.

Though I *did* feel a little weird as my finger hovered over his icon in my speed dial. That thing, you know it: you haven't called someone in a long time, so it's weird to call them, so you don't call them, and more time goes by, and it gets weirder . . .

"Marcus!" he said. There was a lot of noise in the background, clinking bottles and glasses and loud talk.

"Jolu!" I said. "Look, man, I'm sorry to call you out of the blue—"

"One sec," he said. "Let me go somewhere quieter." I heard him navigate what sounded like a busy party. "Hey dude! Long time no speak!"

"I'm sorry to call you out of the blue—"

"No, no, it's cool. It's great, actually! Nice to hear from you."

Wonder if you'll feel the same way after I turn your life upside down.

"Can I meet you somewhere? It's important."

"Marcus?" he said. "Important how?"

"Important important. The kind of important I don't want to talk about on the phone."

I distinctly heard him say *Oh shit* under his breath. "Of course," he said. "Right now?"

"Yeah, now would be good."

"Um." A long pause. "What about the place where you met Ange?"

"You mean—" I stopped myself. Good old Jolu. Anyone listening in wouldn't know where I met Ange. He was more paranoid than I was, and that was *before* I told him what was up. He really was the right man for the job. "Okay, when?"

"Give me an hour?"

"Okay," I said. "And Jolu? Thanks."

I heard him snort, and I could totally picture the half smile that went with it, one bushy eyebrow raised in a quizzical expression. "No need. Anytime for you, man. You know that."

Friends. Nothing like them.

I met Ange at a key-signing party Jolu and I threw at Sutro Baths on Ocean Beach. The weird old/new ruins were spooky and dramatic, and the night was burned into my memory forever. Ange laughed when I told her where we were headed. She'd taken me there again on our first anniversary, with a picnic supper, and we'd watched the sun go down and necked on the blanket before we got too cold.

"I think we should switch off our phones," Ange said.

"Yeah," I said. That's the thing about paranoia—it's catching. But she was right—our phones would send our location to the phone companies, and if someone really wanted to snoop on us, it was always possible that they could find some way to tap into the GPSs on them. Then there'd be this really clear data trail: Marcus called Jolu, then Ange, Marcus, and Jolu all met up at Ocean Beach. Might as well get reflective orange vests and stencil COCONSPIRATOR on them. I took the battery out of my phone for good measure.

We were a quarter of an hour early—the buses were with us— and Jolu was ten minutes early. He hugged us both tightly, and Ange kissed him on the cheek. It had been months since I'd seen him—he'd dropped in on an open data lecture at Noisebridge—

and he looked different. He'd grown a tidy little mustache and pointed sideburns, and had his hair styled in a short razor-cut that looked somehow grown-up, cool, and businesslike all at once. He'd always been better dressed than the rest of us, but he was particularly natty that night in a button-up shirt with slightly wiggly stripes that made my eyes cross when I stared at them, heavy old denim jeans with big rivets, and elaborate leather shoes. I was in my old thrift-store jeans, beat-up motorcycle boots caked with playa dust, and a hoodie, and I felt like a slob.

He had wine on his breath. "I hope it wasn't a totally excellent party," I said.

"Just a release party for a new traffic-predicting app," he said, shrugging. "We get users' anonymized GPS data at different times on different roads and try to predict traffic jams ahead of time, also looking at all the planned road maintenance and anything realtime from the DOT. You share your calendar with us and we look at where you're going and use that to give you advice on what roads to avoid to get there on time."

"Woah, creepy," Ange said. I'd been thinking it, but hadn't wanted to say anything.

Jolu wasn't offended, though. He just grinned. "Yeah, it is. I mean, everyone is opt-in, and we anonymize the data when we get it so we don't know where *you've* been, just that *someone* has been there. But yeah, if we had a data leak, there'd be an awful lot of stuff there you might not want the world to know." He sat down on a rock and fished some gum out of his pockets, offered it around. It was black licorice gum, his favorite, the kind that turned your tongue and spit disgusting black. Just the smell of it made me smile and sent me spinning back in time to the old days.

"Or if the police seized your servers," Ange said. "It's so weird that we do all this Xnet stuff to keep our personal information from being captured by the government, but we give it to companies and the cops can just waltz in to their data centers whenever they want and just take it all."

"You don't know the half of it," Jolu said. "Get me to tell you about the lawful intercept stuff sometime, okay? It'll curl the hair on your toes."

418 | **cory doctorow**

"So, speaking of the police and servers," I said. "I've got an interesting technical problem I wanted to talk to you about."

"I figured you might."

"Before I start—is your phone on by any chance?"

He pulled it out of his pocket and removed the back, showed me the missing battery. "Dude, *estoy aqui por loco, no por pendejo*," which was the punch line to the funniest Spanish joke I knew. Okay, the only one. Google it.

Jolu listened attentively, asking a few questions as we told the story. I put in my theory about the explosion on the playa, and Ange didn't say anything about not believing me. When we were done, we both looked at him across the darkness and the gray no-color of the light leaking from the streetlamps on the cliff above us.

"So what do we do now?" he said.

"We?"

He shook his head. "Duh. Yes, 'we.' Did you think I wouldn't get involved?"

"The last time you sat where you're sitting and I sat where I'm sitting, you told me that it was different for you. You told me that the risk was bigger if you're brown than if you're white."

"Yeah, I said that. It's every bit as true today as it was then, too."

"But you're in."

He looked out into the darkness and didn't say anything. I smelled his gum.

"Marcus," he said. "Have you noticed how *messed up* everything is today? How we put a 'good' president in the White House and he kept right on torturing and bombing and running secret prisons? How every time we turn around, someone's trying to take away the Internet from us, make it into some kind of giant stupid shopping mall where the rent-a-cops can kick you out if they don't like your clothes? Have you noticed how much money the one percent have? How we're putting more people in jail every day, and more people are unemployed every day, and more people are losing their houses every day?"

"I've noticed," I said. "But haven't things always been screwed up? I mean, doesn't everyone assume that their generation has the most special, most awful problems?"

"Yeah," Ange said. "But not every generation has had the net."

"Bingo," Jolu said. "I'm not saying it wasn't terrible in the Great Depression or whatever. But we've got the power to *organize* like we've never had before. And the creeps and the spooks have the power to spy on us more than ever before, to control us and censor us and find us and snatch us."

"Who's going to win?" I said. "I mean, I used to think that we'd win, because we understand computers and they don't."

"Oh, they understand computers. And they're doing everything they can to invent new ways to mess you up with them. But if we leave the field, it'll just be *them*. People who want everything, want to be in charge of everyone."

"So we're going to win?"

Jolu laughed. "There's no winning or losing, Marcus. There's only doing."

"Man, I leave you alone for a couple of months and you turn into *Yoda*."

"So what do we do?" Ange asked again.

"Well, we're not going to be able to look at 800,000 of these."

"810,097," I said.

"That. I think we need to build some kind of site for these things, something secure and private, where we can run searches on them, try to find the good stuff, leave notes for each other."

"And then what do we do with them?"

"We release them."

"Duh," Ange said. "But how do you think we'll do that? How do you put the information in a place where people will see it and care about it, but not a place that can be traced back to us?"

Jolu shrugged and stared at the ruins. "I don't know I guess it depends on the kind of stuff we find. Maybe we google journalists who sound like they'd be interested in the story and email the docs to them from throwaway accounts. Something else, maybe. I don't know. But when you've got a problem that has two parts, and one part comes first, and you know how to solve that part, the best thing to do is solve that part and see if a solution to the rest suggests itself while you're working."

"That sounds right," I said.

"I suppose," Ange said. "But, Marcus, what about Zeb and Masha?"

"Yeah. Well, I don't know how we work that out. Maybe releasing the material will put them in more danger. Maybe it'll take them out of danger. We know who took them: Carrie Johnstone. That's got to be part of the story, however we release it."

"You're sure it was her?" Jolu asked.

"There are some faces I'll never, ever forget. Hers is one of them. It was *her*."

"Okay, okay. Let's talk about forward secrecy," he said.

It turned out Jolu had been hanging out with some heavy Tor dudes who were working on "darknet sites"—"hidden services" that could host files and message boards, sites that anyone could reach, providing they knew the address. But these were unlike regular sites: even if you knew the address, you couldn't figure out where the physical computer it led to was, who was running it, what server you'd have to seize to shut it down. Darknet sites were places you could visit but couldn't shut down.

"So you've got these rendezvous points, they're servers that know some other servers that know some other servers that know the way to reach the darknet site. You ask a rendezvous site to introduce you to the server and it does this dance with the other servers down the line, and creates a temporary circuit that bounces your connection through a one-off route to the darknet machine, so every time you visit the site, there's a different, random way to reach it.

"What I want to do is grab a cheapo server-on-demand VM and slap a ParanoidLinux install on it—nothing unencrypted, ever. Then we slap a copy of your data on it, and a clone of Google Spreadsheets. Grab a doc, put its title in the first field, a description in the next field, and a place where you can put some keywords. Smack together a script that runs every couple of minutes and searches for those keywords in the uncategorized documents, and automatically suggests possibly related ones."

"And then what? We look at 800,000 documents, us three?" I figured I might be able to do a hundred docs a night, depending on how complicated they were. At that rate, it'd take us three a year or so to get through them all. Too slow.

"No, not us three. With enough eyeballs, all bugs are shallow. We've got to bring more people in. People we can trust."

Jolu said, "Yeah, I know a few of those."

I was almost late for work the next day. After coming home, I'd stayed up for hours banging away at the document dump. I hadn't meant to, but Jolu's idea of searching for words in the dump gave me some ideas.

The first thing I searched for was "Masha" and "Zeb." I got a few documents with "zebra" and "mashallah," but nothing else. I tried "Marcus" and "Yallow." There were five Marcuses but none of them were me.

Then I tried "Carrie Johnstone" and hit the jackpot.

Carrie Johnstone had been a busy little soldier in Iraq. There were more than four hundred documents that mentioned her by name. I went after them alphabetically at first, but it was all confusing, until I had the bright idea of sorting them by date and starting with the oldest and reading toward the newest—a document that was just over a month old.

Reading those four hundred documents—some very short, some very long—kept me up to three in the morning, and the more I read, the more I learned about Carrie Johnstone's weird and terrible career in and out of the U.S. military.

The first documents dated from Johnstone's career at FOB Tikrit, Saddam Hussein's old palace. There was a memo she'd written describing the handover of a bunch of Iraqi prisoners to the Iraqi police. I didn't see at first why anyone would bother to save the document, but the next memo explained it. It was a memo explaining why they hadn't told the Red Cross about the transfer of prisoners, and hadn't gotten any kind of chain-of-custody receipts from the Iraqi cops. A little googling and I figured out what that meant: fifty-one men, women, and children had vanished into the custody of Iraq's police force, and no one knew whatever became of them. They had been arrested after anonymous tips, or snatched off the street for "suspicious behavior." And for all anyone knew, they were nameless and rotting in a jail somewhere, while their families wrote them off for dead. Or maybe they were dead, dumped in a mass grave.

Then she'd ended up at FOB Grizzly, working as an "intelligence officer" alongside the military police. She'd been reprimanded for unauthorized "stress interrogations" of suspected terrorists and had overseen an arrest sweep that brought in more than five hundred suspects, all of whom had been released over the coming months as it emerged that they had nothing to do with terrorism.

It was around then that she left the military, and though she'd written a letter of resignation, there was also a memo from a commanding officer to Army Human Resources Command saying that she'd been "shown the door" after an "incident" involving "materiel." Another memo was more explicit—she'd been involved in a plan that delivered American guns and ammo to private mercenaries working for a military contractor, and those guns and that ammo had been part of a massacre that killed over a hundred people.

From there, she'd gone private, working for the military "contractor"—hired killers, according to a quick search—and had distinguished herself with a very lucrative bid to take over the management contract for the FOB she'd been fired from.

It was ugly.

As I lay in bed with my thoughts swirling, I wondered if Carrie Johnstone had snatched Masha because the leaks file had so much embarrassing material about her, personally, or whether she'd been hired to retrieve them for the U.S. government. How could the Army fire her one day and then rehire her to do the same job at ten times her old salary a month later? Were they on crazy pills?

I couldn't afford to drag my ass around work the next day, so I didn't. I pounded the Turk's coffee and munched chocolate espresso beans and finished my inventory and network map. Joe surprised me by scheduling me for lunch. The first I heard of it was when he showed up at my desk at 12:30 and stood over it, smiling expectantly at me.

"Hi, Joe," I said.

"Lunchtime, Marcus?"

We went to a nice veggie place where they knew him by name and seated us right away. He knew their names, too, and greeted everyone from the waiter to the guy who filled up our water glasses personally, switching to Spanish as necessary and asking sincere, friendly questions about their wives and husbands and kids and health.

The sincere part was the weirdest thing. When I was really on fire and feeling very, very sociable, I might remember half of the names of the people I saw. I just sucked at names. And when people told me about their kids or parents or siblings or whatever, I tried to be interested, but I mean, how interested can you really be in the lives of people you barely know or have never met at all?

But Joe had the uncanny ability to seem really, genuinely interested in people. When he talked to you, you felt like he was also *listening* to you, carefully, thoughtfully, and not waiting for you to finish talking so that he could say whatever he was going to say next. It made him seem, I don't know, *holy* or something, like one of those people out of a religious story who overflows with love for his fellow man.

And the weirdest part? He didn't make me feel like a dick for not being that interested myself. Instead, he made me want to try to be more like him, more caring.

After our water glasses were full and we'd put in our orders, he said, "Thank you for making the time to see me today. I know you must be busy."

If it was anyone else, I'd have thought he was blowing smoke up my ass, but he really sounded like he thought being the webmaster/sysadmin/net guy was the hardest job in the world and he felt lucky that all he had to do was run around and try to get elected.

"You're welcome—I mean, it's a pleasure. I mean, it's wonderful. I'm so glad to have a job, and it's such a cool job, too. Everyone's really nice and interesting and I really believe in your platform, so,

424 | cory doctorow

well, it's just great." I was babbling like an idiot and I couldn't seem to stop—and he didn't seem to notice.

"You remember when I spoke to you on the phone the other night, I mentioned how my campaign would need great technology to be successful. And I'm sure that when you and Flor chatted she had some pointed opinions about that and what her side of the campaign needed from you. You might be wondering who wins in a little struggle like that. I wanted to give you some context to help you resolve that.

"Flor is your boss—and she's my boss, too. She's in charge of the campaign from top to bottom, and I'm familiar with her ideas about what campaigns need vis-à-vis boots on the ground, knocking on doors, and raising money. She's right as far as she goes, and that's why I let her be my boss.

"But I'm the candidate, and I have some additional priorities. I say 'additional'—not 'different.' Flor is right about needing money, boots, and door-knocking. But once you've got all that running to the best of your ability, there's more that I want you to get thinking about. I want you to tell me how technology can help me reach people who would otherwise be beyond my reach. I want you to tell me how technology can transform the way that voters and their representatives collaborate to produce good, accountable government. Every wave of technology, from newspapers to radio to TV, has transformed politics, and not always for the better. Some people think that the Internet is a tool for politicians to raise money or coordinate volunteers, but I don't think that's even one percent of what technology can do for politics. I want you to help me figure out the other ninety-nine percent."

Woah. "Okay," I said. "Do you want, what, an essay or a website or something?"

He smiled. "Let's start with a chat, like this one, tomorrow at the end of the day. I'll have Flor put it in both of our schedules."

It made me feel good and a little scared—I really didn't want to let him down, but all I could think of was darknet sites and leaked docs. I wondered what he would say if I told him that I was sitting on more than 800,000 confidential, compromising government memos. But I also remembered what Flor had said: *The first time I catch so much as a whiff of anything illegal, immoral, dangerous, or 'leet' I will personally bounce your ass to the curb before you have a chance to zip your fly.*

I went over to Ange's after work. Jolu had already set up our darknet site and grabbed a copy of the docs off BitTorrent. I'd handed him a USB stick with the key on it, and by the time I got my computer up into a secure mode with a dead man's switch and an anonymized, private network connection, the site was ready to go.

In fact, it was already going. Jolu had met with Van on his lunch break, and she'd plowed through more than fifty docs while I'd been bringing the Joe for Senate servers' patch levels up to date. I wondered whether Van had had a chance to talk to Darryl. He'd been my best friend, as tight as a brother, but I hadn't seen him in months. It was all too weird between us—the fact that he was with Van and that Van had confessed that she'd once had a crush on me; the unwordly fragility of his mind after his time in Gitmo-by-the-Bay; his constant struggle to keep up with even a half-time course load at Berkeley. I thought of what seeing that nasty little waterboarding PowerPoint would do to Darryl.

It wasn't just Van working on the docs, either. Jolu had enlisted some of his other trusted friends, people with cryptic handles like Left-Handed Mutant and Endless Vegetables. I hoped Jolu was right to trust them. I hoped he'd been cagey about where the docs had actually come from. Out of curiosity, I googled the strangers' handles and confirmed to my satisfaction that they didn't appear to have been used before. It would have been such a basic mistake to recycle a nickname that you'd already used someplace that could be linked to your real identity.

Endless Vegetables was working his (or her) way through a gigantic pile of documents on student loans, judging from the tags and summaries. I vaguely knew that the government guaranteed student loans made by universities, which were sold to banks that collected on them. The darknet docs went into disgusting details—like a series of jokey emails between a congressman who'd gotten a tearful letter from a constituent who'd been hit with crazy penalties that turned her $20,000 loan into a $180,000 loan and an executive at the bank who'd assessed the penalties. The congressman sounded like he was pretty good friends with the banker, and they made it sound like this girl's problem was hilarious.

Jolu had added an "I'm feeling lucky" button to the spreadsheet that would bring up a random, uncataloged doc. I hit it and found myself looking at a cryptic set of numbers and acronyms. I tried to google the search terms but found myself getting nowhere, so I grabbed another, and then another. It was mesmerizing, like channel surfing on a massive cable network that only got heavy, strange programs about corruption, murder, and sleaze.

"Jeebus H. Christmas," Ange said. "Have a look at the doc I just checked in."

I re-sorted the spreadsheet by author and found Ange's latest contribution, loaded it up. It was an instruction manual for a "lawful intercept" network appliance sold to cops and governments for installation at an Internet Service Provider. The appliance monitored all incoming requests for updates to Android phones, and checked to see if the phone's owner was on a list of targets. If they were, the appliance took over the network session and sent a fake update to the phone that gave spies and spooks the power to secretly turn on the phone's GPS, camera, and mic. I stared in mounting horror at the phone on the bed next to me, then flipped it over and took out the battery.

"Keep reading," Ange said. She'd been following the autolinked documents and found a bunch of captured emails and phone sessions. One was a complaint from a DHS field operative about a target who'd installed "ParanoidAndroid" on his phone and couldn't be gotten at.

"What's ParanoidAndroid?" I asked.

"I'm reading up on that now," Ange said. "Looks like it's a fork from the CyanogenMod." I knew about Cyanogen, of course— hackers had taken the source code for Google's Android operating system and made a fully free and open version that could do all kinds of cool tricks. "It doesn't accept updates unless their checksums match with other users and the official releases. Lets you tell whether an update is real or a spoof."

"Well, what are we waiting for? Let's install it!"

Ange pointed at her phone, which was already cabled to her laptop. "What do you think I'm doing?"

"Do mine next?"

"Duh."

There was more. Other lawful intercept appliances would disguise themselves as iTunes updates for Macs and PCs, and another one worked by sending fake updates to your browser. Then there were the saved emails between a senior DHS IT manager who'd worked at one of these companies before going to Homeland Security. His old boss was explaining how they were using a shell company in Equatorial Guinea—a country I'd never even heard of!—to market their products in China, Iran, and other countries.

It just got worse. Logs of law-enforcement requests to install spyware bugs on people involved in peaceful protest groups. Reports of break-ins by suspected criminals who'd used the systems to spy on their victims.

I was trying to figure out how all this stuff could possibly work. After all, software updates usually went over SSL, which used cryptographic certificates to verify the identity of the sender. How were they spoofing connections from Apple and Google and Microsoft and Mozilla?

Oh, that's how. A search on "certificates lawful intercept" brought up another email exchange, this one with a huge American security company that had one of the "signing certificates" that were trusted by all browsers and operating systems. They'd been supplying blank certificates to the DHS for years, it seemed—certificates that would give the government the power to undetectably impersonate your bank or your company, or Apple, Microsoft, and Google.

Ange and I split up the remaining lawful intercept docs, getting deeper and deeper into the terrifying secrets of snoops and spies. Before I knew it, it was 2 A.M. and I could barely keep my eyes open.

"Want to stay over?" Ange said as I yawned for the tenth time in five minutes.

"I think I already have," I said. We'd started staying over at each

428 | **cory doctorow**

other's houses that summer, and while it had been weird at first (especially over breakfast with the parents!), everyone had gotten used to it. My parents had more important stuff to worry about, and Ange's mom was just one of those cool grown-ups who seemed to have an instinctive grasp of what mattered and what didn't.

chapter 8

Once upon a time, terrorists blew up a bridge in my city and killed over four thousand people. They told me everything changed. They told me that we didn't have the same rights we used to, because catching terrorists was more important than our little freedoms.

They say they caught the terrorists. One of the guys, who had been killed by a drone in Yemen, supposedly thought the whole thing up. I guess I'm okay with him being dead if that's the case. I hope it's the case. No one would show us the proof, of course, because of "national security."

But "everything is different" turned out to be a demand and not a description. It pretended to describe what the new reality was, but instead it demanded that everyone accept a new reality, one where we could be spied on and arrested and even tortured.

A few years later, everything changed again. It seemed like overnight, no one had jobs anymore, no one had money anymore, and people started to lose their houses. It was weird, because now that it was *obvious* that everything had changed, no one wanted to talk about how everything had changed.

When the streets are full of armed cops and soldiers telling you that everything is different, everyone can point at one thing, a thing with a human face, and agree, "It's different, it's different."

But when some mysterious social/financial/political *force* upends the world and changes everything—when "everything is different now" is a description and not a demand—somehow, it gets much harder to agree on whether things were different and what we needed to do about it.

It was one thing to demand that the armed guards leave our

streets. It was another to figure out how to demand that the silent red overdue bills and sneaky process servers with their eviction notices go away.

I was nearly late getting to work the next day, but I just squeaked in. I'd stolen back one of my T-shirts from Ange's laundry pile (she liked to steal mine and sleep in them), and it smelled wonderfully of her and put me in a good mood as I came through the door and made a beeline for my desk.

"Dude!" Liam said, practically bouncing in place by my chair. "Can you believe it?"

"What?" I said.

"You know! The darknet stuff!"

All the blood rushed out of my head and into my gut and swirled there like a stormy ocean. My ears throbbed with my pulse. "What?" I said.

"You didn't see?"

He leaned over me and moused to my browser, went to the front page of Reddit, a site where you could submit and vote on news stories. Every item on the front page talked about darknet leaks. Feeling like I was in a horror movie, I clicked one of them. It was a story on wired.com about a file that had been anonymously dumped into pastebin.com, instructions for using a lawful intercept appliance to take over Android phones and work their cameras. Whoever had dumped the file had sent an email to a reporter at wired.com saying that there were more than 800,000 documents like it on a darknet site and that volunteers were combing through them, and there was a lot more to come. It didn't say where they'd come from or who the volunteers were.

I went back to Reddit and checked the others. How many darknet docs had leaked? It seemed like everyone had the same story, in different variants—800,000 docs, darknet, more to come, but nothing more. I started to calm down.

"You've got an Android phone, right?" Liam said.

"Yeah," I said. "I do. But I run ParanoidAndroid—it's an alternate OS that resists that kind of spyware."

"Really?" Joe said. He'd walked up on us on cat's-paw feet while we were talking, and I jumped in my seat. "Woah, sorry, calm down there, Marcus. I've got an Android phone, too. Tell you what, I'll order in pizza for lunch if you'll give us a workshop on keeping our phones secure. Sounds like the kind of thing we should all know about."

"Yeah, sure," I said. "Of course." Though as soon as I saw the *Wired* story, I'd started scheming to take lunch off and find a WiFi network with weak, crackable WEP security so that I could hop on, tunnel into the darknet, and try to figure out what had just happened. I mean, I knew better than anyone that there was no such thing as perfect security, and I understood that it was likely that someone, someday, would get a look at the darknet docs whom we hadn't invited in. But I didn't think that day would be the day after we set up the darknet!

But I couldn't screw up my job. I'd been desperate for work for so long, and it was such a cool job. The fact that I might now be the target of a ruthless mercenary army didn't mean that I didn't have to help Joe get elected.

So I did my job, and when the pizza came, I stood with a slice in one hand and a whiteboard pen in the other and sketched out a little flowchart of how your phone could be taken over, and what could be done with your phone after it was pwned.

Joe munched thoughtfully at a slice, wiped his fingers and his mouth, and put up his hand. "So you're saying that the police could take over our phones?"

"No!" Liam said, vibrating in his chair. "He's saying *anyone* could—"

I put up my hands and Liam calmed down. "What I mean is, once the intercept appliance is installed at the phone company's data center, anyone who has a login and password for it could use it."

"But who has that login and password? The police, yes?"

"Probably not, actually. The leaks suggested that these appliances were managed by the phone company or ISP. So a police officer calls up the lawful intercept technicians and they set it up for him. So the list of anyone who could break into the ISP's network, anyone who could bribe or blackmail someone at the ISP, anyone who can convincingly pretend to be a police officer to the

ISP, anyone who can get a *real* police officer to give him access, or anyone who can pay someone to do any of the above."

"So you're saying that turning anyone's phone into a superbug is as easy as fixing a parking ticket?"

"I've never fixed a parking ticket," I said. "I don't drive. Is it hard to fix a parking ticket?"

Joe drummed his fingers on the table. "Not if you're rich or well connected. Or so I'm told."

"Yeah," I said, "rich or well-connected people could turn any phone into a mobile bug. In theory there's no reason this is limited to Android phones. It could work by pushing out updates to iTunes, or Firefox, or any app. They'd just need a signing certificate and—" I stopped talking, because I'd just remembered that there hadn't been anything about the signing certificates in the leak. "And things like that. So theoretically, any computer, any phone, anything that updates itself automatically could be turned into a bug once these things are installed."

My hands were sweating. Joe and the rest of the office may not know what a "signing certificate" was, but Liam did, and he looked like he was committing every word I uttered to memory. "Uh," I said. "Also, once your computer is infected with this stuff, it's possible that people other than the police or whoever bugged you will start to watch what you do."

Joe put his hand up again. "Explain?" he said.

"Oh, well, here's how it would work. Say I pay someone to bug your computer. Now your computer has some malicious software on it that can, I don't know, look out your camera, listen to your mic, watch your keystrokes, snatch files off your hard drive, the whole thing. The bug will have some kind of control software, a program that I run to access your computer. Maybe that program lives on a server somewhere else, in which case anyone who breaks into that server can then break into all the infected computers and phones and stuff. Or maybe it lives on your computer, so if I take over your computer, I can jump from it to all the infected computers. But also, if someone figures out that your computer is running the bug, maybe they can connect directly to your computer—like they could hang around outside your house and crack your WiFi password and wait for your computer to log on, and then snag it, or maybe they don't know who you are and they just sit at Starbucks all day waiting for *anyone* with the bug to join the network and then they grab the computer's controls."

Flor put up her hand. "How realistic is this? I mean, this all sounds pretty scary, but can you give me an idea of how many computers have been infected this way? In the real world, is this something I need to worry about? Or is it like being struck by lightning?"

I shrugged. "I guess I'm the wrong guy to ask about that. I've never used this stuff, never shelled out a hundred grand for one of these boxes. I'm guessing if the police buy them, they must use them. I mean, you could think of this as HIV. Your computer has an immune system, all the passwords and so forth that stop it from being taken over by parasites. Once it's bugged, it's got a compromised immune system. So parasites can come in and infect it." I thought a moment. I was calming down. No, that's not right, I was just excited now, and not scared, because it was kind of cool that everyone in the office was hanging on my every word. It made me feel important and smart. "Actually, it's like the *network* has an immune system, including things like Internet Service Providers who don't conspire to trick your computer into downloading malicious software. When your ISP's router tells you a file is coming from Google or Apple or Mozilla, your computer assumes that that's where the packets are coming from. But once you start monkeying with that, once you create a procedure that tells ISPs to start secretly lying to their customers, well, it seems to me like you can expect that to start happening."

"So what do we do?"

"Oh," I said. "Well, for Android, that's easy. It's open and free, which means Google has to publish the source code for the operating system. A group of privacy hackers have created an alternate version called ParanoidAndroid that checks a bunch of places every time it gets an update and tries to figure out how trustworthy it is. It used to be really hard to install, but it keeps on getting easier. I've made up a little installer script that you can download from the intranet that makes it even simpler. Just plug in your Android phone and run the script and it should just work. Let me know if it doesn't."

"But how do we know we can trust your script?" Flor said. "Maybe you're bugging us all."

Liam practically leapt to his feet: "Marcus would *never* do that—"

I had to laugh. "No, she's right. You're right, Flor. You've got no reason to trust me. I've only been here a couple of days. I mean, you guys asked me to work here, so it's not likely that I'd have planned to take over this place with malicious software, but maybe I'm the kind of guy who goes around doing it all the time." I thought about it. "So, you could google everything I just told you and download ParanoidAndroid yourself—but maybe I planted all that information there for Google to find. I guess it all depends on how paranoid you're feeling."

"I'm feeling moderately paranoid, with a side of prudence and common sense," Joe announced, getting a laugh. "I'll install it. Then what do I do?"

"Nothing, unless your phone throws a warning about an update. Then you can google it or ask me, or rely on your own judgment. There's a paranoia flag for Ubuntu Linux, too, if any of you are running that—it'll tell you if an update doesn't match up with the fingerprints on the public servers. Sorry, but I don't know about anything comparable for Mac or Windows." I stood with my hands folded again. "Is there any more pizza?"

Jolu threw a little instant browser chat app up on darknet for us, and started it off with

> ALL RIGHT, WHO SPILLED THE BEANS? FIRST RULE OF DARKNET IS NO ONE TALKS ABOUT DARKNET —Swollen Rabbit

"Swollen Rabbit" was the handle he'd chosen for himself—he'd also put up a nickname generator to help us all choose random, single-use, cool-sounding handles for the system.

I felt like he wasn't taking this very seriously—all those caps and the jokey tone. We were dealing with a plutonium spill and he was treating it like a minor nuisance.

> This is serious folks. Swollen Rabbit, are you sure it was a leak from one of us and not a break-in? —Nasty Locomotive

> it's impossible to be sure but yeah. I've been over the logs and I don't see anyone except us. Maybe someone's got a screenlogger infection or something? —Swollen Rabbit

Oh yeah, of course. Maybe *we* were bugged. That'd be a weird form of humor: to use a bug to spy on someone who'd found a leak about bugs and then leak the leak to the press using the bug. . . . It was weird enough that it made me feel dizzy if I thought about it enough. I decided to fall back on Occam's Razor. The idea that someone blabbed was a *lot* simpler.

> I know I can trust you and the rest of our crew and Tasty Ducks

—that was Ange—

> but what about all your friends? —Nasty Locomotive

> Wait why should we trust YOUR crew? Who died and made you infallible? —Restless Agent

That was one of the people Jolu had brought in, though I didn't know anything else about him (or her). Jolu and I had decided it'd be better if we kept everything on a need-to-know basis. I didn't need to know who Restless Agent was, just that the handle represented someone Jolu trusted utterly.

But Jolu or no, I found myself getting ready to clobber this Restless Agent person. How *dare* anyone call Darryl and Van and Ange and me into question? Ange, meanwhile, had already read the message on her screen. She was sitting cross-legged on my bed, hair in her eyes, bent over her laptop. As soon as my fingers began to pound angrily on the keyboard, she said, "Woah there, hoss. Calm down."

"But—" I said.

"I know, I know. Someone is wrong on the Internet. Count to ten. In ternary."

"But—"

"Do it."

"One. Two. Ten. Eleven. Twelve. Twenty. Twenty-one. Twenty-two. One hundred. One oh one. One oh two." I stopped. "Wait, I lost count. Is one oh two ten or eleven?" I could count in binary when I was angry, but counting in ternary—base three—took too much concentration. "Fine, you win. I'm calm."

436 | cory doctorow

> You're right, you can't. —Tasty Ducks

> You don't know us and we don't know you. And we can't keep this up if someone here is showing off by letting blabby writers into the darknet. So what do we do? Shut it down? —Tasty Ducks

> I could turn on logging and make it visible to everyone. Then we'd know who got to see every document. If a doc leaked we'd have the list of everyone who saw it. If enough docs leaked we'll be able to narrow down the list and find the one person who saw everything —Swollen Rabbit

> Assuming only one person is blabbing —Nasty Locomotive

> Yeah maybe we're all running our mouths —Poseidon Snake

That was another of Jolu's buddies.

> Logging sounds like a good plan. If we can all see what everyone's done, it'll keep us all honest —Nasty Locomotive

> Unless I'm the rat in which case I could be editing the logs and you suckers would never know —Swollen Rabbit

> Ell Oh Ell. You're such a comedian. If you're the rat we're all dead meat. Don't be the rat, dude —Tasty Ducks

"All right, fine, that's settled for now," I said. "Thanks for keeping me from turning into Angry Internet Man."

"Any time. It was kind of weak for you to just say 'how can we trust your friends' where everyone could see it."

I wanted to argue, but it wasn't really an arguable point. After all, I'd lost my cool when Restless Agent did exactly the same thing.

"Yeah, okay, fine." I paged up and down through the monster spreadsheet with its 800,000-plus rows. "So what are we going to read through today, anyway?"

"More of the lawful intercept stuff, I guess. There's hundreds more suggested docs. Since the story's out there, it'd make sense to find out more."

"Okay," I said. "You take suggested docs from the first half, I'll take the ones from 400,000 onward. My mom says you're welcome to stay for dinner, by the way."

"Deal," she said, and we got to work.

One thing about the darknet docs I should probably mention: they were mostly unbelievably boring. Rows of numbers. Indecipherable memos written in bureaucratic jargon, laden with acronyms and names of people and agencies I'd never heard of. It was tempting to skip over these and look for juicy ones—or at least ones I could understand—but every so often I'd find something that made some other doc make sense, a piece of the puzzle falling into place, and I'd be glad I'd read it.

For example, there was a list from the San Francisco Unified School Board about schools that had participated in a "laptop anti-theft trial" that had run the year before. It used some kind of phone-home software on all the school-issued laptops that checked in with the school district every day or two. The district used it to track down stolen laptops—getting IP addresses from the software and turning them over to the cops. I noted without much interest that Chavez High was on the list of trial sites, the name standing out immediately, seeing as how I'd carried a backpack with the school's name through four years of attendance.

But ten or fifteen documents later, I found myself looking at a brochure for a product called LaptopLock, which was the product used in the trials. I wondered why Jolu's algorithm had tagged this stuff as relevant to the lawful intercept documents—which keywords had made it jump out. It turned out that the matching words were "covert activation" and "webcam." "Covert activation" was self-explanatory—if you had software that phoned home after a laptop was stolen, you wouldn't want it to advertise that that was what it was doing. "Attention thief: I am about to tell the police your IP address. Do you want me to continue? [OK] [CANCEL]."

But why would you want to activate the webcam on a stolen laptop? I paged through the brochure. Oh, right, to take pictures of the thief. The software could covertly activate the webcam—turn it on without turning on the little "camera on" light—take a pic and silently send it back to the school board. Well that *was* creepy. I wondered if any students had ever found a password and login and used that little "feature" to spy on other students. My laptop sat open on my desk all the time—when I was sleeping, when I was getting dressed, when Ange and I were—

Yikes.

So then I went digging for more docs. I had a product name

now, something I could use to search on, and hoo-boy were there a *lot* of hits for LaptopLock in the darknet docs. I did my sort-by-date trick and found myself reading through emails from a worried IT manager at the San Francisco Unified to her boss about the fact that there was a principal who was using LaptopLock's administrative interface to watch students—not laptop thieves—at all sorts of hours, including early in the morning (when they might be getting dressed) and late at night (when they might be sleeping).

The IT manager had looked at the principal's shared-drive folder and found thousands of pics of students and their families, sometimes naked, sometimes asleep. There was also audio and video of students and their parents having private conversations. The IT manager's boss was furious—because the IT manager wasn't supposed to be "snooping" on school principals. The argument got more and more vicious, as the IT manager pointed out that her snooping was nothing compared to this principal, and ended with the IT manager's resignation letter. I felt bad for her—she was an honorable geek, and it wasn't easy to find new jobs in this bad old modern world of ours.

It wasn't just the San Francisco Unified School District where a principal got a little power-crazy with the old LaptopLock control panel. It turns out that pretty much every school district had someone (or a few people) in positions of power who felt that spying on students was part of their job. But in the case of the San Francisco Unified School District, that someone was a certain school board member named Fred Benson.

Once upon a time, Fred had been a vice principal at Chavez High, and from that lordly height, he'd presided like a warden or a king, doling out harsh justice against anyone who offended his delicate sense of conservative morality.

Such as, ahem, me.

But old Fred had "retired" when it became clear that San Francisco and California were no longer going to put up with a city occupied by the forces of "law and order"—that is, the torturing, kidnapping, lying paramilitary who'd taken the city hostage in the name of "protecting us from terrorism." It had been *so* sad to see him pack up his desk and hit the bricks, just another casualty of the war on the war on terror.

But Fred was a retired athlete, the kind of thrusting, vigorous guy who just can't take it easy. He'd run for the school board—unopposed, except for a crank candidate who'd been convicted of three counts of felony fraud in a real estate swindle, who nevertheless got nearly half the vote—and had been collecting a tidy public salary and enjoying his ascent to the exalted pinnacle of the education system by bossing around teachers and trying to impose his "leadership style" on the whole school district.

In case you didn't catch it, I don't like this guy.

But even I was surprised to discover that old Fred was such a prolific user of the district's LaptopLock system. After all, he wasn't responsible for students at all, but look at that, he requested so many specific LaptopLock activations that the district's IT department had given him his own login, to save on work. Someone in that department wasn't happy about it, and that person had helpfully logged Fred's many, many, *many* uses of the system.

Did I say uses? I mean *abuses*.

"Come on, we've *got* to leak this," I said. "I mean, come *on*, Ange. Seriously? You don't think I should go public with this?"

"No, Marcus, I think it's a really stupid idea. You've just got through yelling at everyone about a leak. Once you do it, everyone'll do it. We agreed that we'd catalog the whole dump, decide on the highest priority stuff, then publish it in a way that kept us all safe. If you get us all busted tomorrow, Masha and Zeb are doomed. Hell, *we're* doomed. You don't have any right to put us all in jeopardy just to settle a score with some vice principal you have a hate-on for."

"He's a Peeping Tom! It's not just a personal vendetta. People have the right to know that this guy is spying on their kids. That could have been me, Ange. I've still got friends at Chavez High, kids that Benson *hates*—you can bet he's all over them, night and day."

"You're just picturing him sitting in his house and rubbing his hands and getting off on all his power and secrecy, admit it. Benson's not the worst monster in these files. Look at what the others have been up to. Look at 439,412."

I scrolled to the line, read the summary:

STATE DEPARTMENT BILL OF LADING. FREIGHT FOR-WARDING FOR LAWFUL INTERCEPT APPLIANCE TO SYRIA. SEE 298,120

And 298,120:

EMBASSY STAFF INTELLIGENCE REPORT ON TORTURE-MURDER OF DISSIDENTS CAUGHT WITH LAWFUL INTER-CEPT APPLIANCE

"Oh," I said.

"Yeah," she said. "Oh. So cut it out. Maintain discipline. This isn't kid's stuff, it's the big leagues."

And before I had a chance to get angry with her—really angry, the kind of angry you get when you've been totally wrong and someone calls you out and you don't have any excuse so you get mad instead—my mom called up the stairs, "Marcus, Ange, time for supper!"

There'd been a time when we'd had "family dinner" practically every night—either something that my mom or dad cooked in a huge frenzy of pots, pans, clatter, and smells, or, if everyone was too tired, something from a delivery restaurant. I'd even been known to cook from time to time, and I liked it, though it took a lot of energy to get started. Facing down the empty kitchen always seemed like a major chore. But I made a mean rack of lamb, and when I cooked pizza, there weren't ever any leftovers, no matter how much I made.

Family dinners had evaporated along with my parents' jobs. The contract work they got in pieces sometimes kept one or another away at suppertime, but the real reason was that they were trapped in the house together all day, and half the time I was there with them, and so no one much wanted to spend an hour at the table playing pass-the-peas. There just wasn't much small talk available to us. "How was your day?" was a painfully stupid question when the farthest apart you've been since getting up is about five yards.

But everyone put in an effort when Ange came over. My parents really liked her. Hey, so did I. Plus it was fun to watch her eat.

"Smells great!" she said as she came into the kitchen, as she always did. She already had her mister in her hand. When I'd met her, she was mixing up her chili oil at about 200,000 Scovilles, as hot as a mild Scotch Bonnet Pepper. But she was always in training, working her way up to higher heights of culinary daring. She mixed up a new batch of oil once a month, starting with a lethal, tight-stoppered bottle of crushed Red Savina Habanero in a few ounces of oil. She diluted this a little less every month, playing with the levels until it was just right. For Ange, "just right" was the temperature that made sweat appear on her upper lip within a minute of putting a drop of oil on her tongue.

A couple times a year, she'd actually taken the temperature of her oil, mixing a little alcohol in with her month's dose, then progressively diluting it in sugar water until she could barely taste the heat. The last time she checked, she'd been up to 320,000 Scovilles. It was around then that I started insisting that she brush her teeth between her eating and us kissing. I was starting to get chemical burns on my lips.

"It's just chips and sausages," Mom said. "Proper British comfort food, you know."

"Cooked by an American, no less," Dad said from the stove.

"Oi! *I* put the chips in the oven, didn't I?" Mom said. When Mom says "chips," she's speaking British and means "fries"—specifically the sweet potato oven fries she makes herself and freezes. I have to admit, they're pretty awesome.

"Yes, my dear, you certainly did. Plus, you supervised."

Dad set down the platter of faintly sizzling meat on the table. He once did some freelance work helping an organic meat cooperative with its data mining and ecommerce tuning, and when he'd written to them asking if they had anything else for him, they'd taken pity on him and offered to sell him some meat at employee rates. So we had all the emu, venison, and buffalo sausage we could want, as often as we wanted. I especially liked the venison, which tasted very good, assuming you didn't think too much about Bambi while you ate it.

Dad went back to turn off the stove's extractor fan, which had been humming loudly while it sucked out all the delicious meaty smoke and steam. Then he smacked himself in the forehead. "Wait, Ange, you're a vegetarian, aren't you?"

I hid a smile. Ange had gone veggie at the start of the summer, but Burning Man had brought out her inner carnivore—especially the trips to camps where they were handing out kick-ass barbecue.

"It's okay," Ange said. "Beef is just a highly processed form of vegetable matter."

"Riiiight," Dad said, and forked a couple of sausages onto her plate before sitting down himself.

It felt curiously wonderful to be having dinner as a family again, with a big plateful of food in front of me and my parents making bright conversation as though they weren't in a mild, continuous panic about the mortgage and the grocery bill.

But it couldn't last. I had to say something stupid.

"I saw the coolest thing the other day," I said. "It was from a history of crypto in World War II and there was this chapter on the history of cipher machines—Enigmas and such—at Bletchley Park, in England."

"Which ones were they again?" Mom said.

"The ones the Nazis used to scramble their messages," Dad said. "Even I know that."

"Sorry," Mom said. "I'm a little rusty on my Nazi gadgets."

"Actually," Ange said, swallowing a huge mouthful of buffalo sausage, "the Enigmas weren't exactly 'Nazi.' They were developed in the Netherlands, and sold as a commercial product to help bankers scramble their telegrams."

"Right," I said. "And all the Axis powers used them. So the first generations of these were, you know, *beautiful*. Just really well made by some totally badass engineers, copying the Dutch models, but after adding a bunch of cool tricks so they'd produce harder-to-break ciphers. There were about ten iterations of these things, the Enigma and its successors, and they kept on adding rotors and doing other stuff to make them stronger. But at the same time, they were using up all their best raw materials on killing people. So by the end of the war, you've got this box with twelve rotors, up from the original three, but it's made of sandwich metal and looks, I don't know, boringly functional, without any of that flair and craftsmanship of the first generation. I guess they were in a pretty bad mood by then. They probably spent half their time over-seeing slave labor or tending the death-camp adding machines. So, basically, everything elegant and beautiful in these things was just sucked out by the war, until all that was left was something you wouldn't call 'beautiful' unless you were totally insane."

"Woah," Ange said. "Symbolic."

I play-punched her in the shoulder. "It *was*, doofus. It was like a little illustration of the collapse of everything good in a society. I'll show you the pictures later. Those first-gen machines were *awe-some*, just amazingly made. They were like works of art. The last versions looked like they'd been built by someone who was absolutely miserable. You'll see."

Mom and Dad didn't say anything. I didn't think much of it, then I saw a silent tear slip down Dad's cheek. I felt weirdly ashamed and embarrassed. Dad got up wordlessly from the table and went to the bathroom, came back a few minutes later. None of us said anything while he was gone, and the silence continued after he got back, his face freshly washed and still slightly damp.

He ate a few mouthfuls and said, quietly, "Amazing how a soci-ety can just slide into the crapper, huh?"

Mom gave a brittle laugh. "I don't think it's as bad as all that, Drew."

He put his fork down and chewed and chewed and chewed at his food, chewed like he was angry at it. The words that came out after he swallowed had a choked, tight feel. "Isn't it? There were three more foreclosures on our street today, Lillian. *Today*. And as for slave labor, just think about how much of what we own is stamped 'Made in China,' and how much of our 'Made in the USA' came out of a prison somewhere."

"Drew—" Mom said.

"Marcus, Ange, I'm very sorry," he said.

"It's okay, Dad," I began.

"No, I mean I'm *sorry* that you've inherited such a miserable, collapsing old country. A place where rich bankers own everything, where you've got to be grateful for a part-time job with no benefits and no retirement plan, where the most health insurance you can afford is being careful and hoping you don't get sick, where—"

He clamped his lips shut and looked away. I'd seen a bill on Mom's desk from a health insurance company warning us that we'd lose our coverage if we didn't make a payment. I'd tried not to think too hard about it.

"It's okay, Dad," I said again. His skin had gone pale beneath his beard, and it made the wrinkles at the corners of his eyes and in his neck stand out. He looked twenty years older than he had at the start of dinner.

"Cheer up, Drew," Mom said. "Honestly, it could be much worse. There's plenty who'd be grateful for our problems. Let's have a glass of wine and watch *The Daily Show,* all right? I PVRed it." When my parents got rid of their cable box, I'd built them a cheapie PVR using MythTV and an old PC. It only worked with the few HD broadcast channels that aired in San Francisco, but it automatically converted the files so they could play on our phones and laptops, and snipped out all the commercials.

Dad looked down and didn't say anything.

"Come on, Ange," I said. We were pretty much through with dinner anyway. And there were darknet docs to plow through.

If you ever want to blow your own mind, sit down and think hard about what "randomness" means.

I mean, take pi, the ratio of a circle's circumference to its diameter. Everyone who's passed sixth-grade math knows that pi is an "irrational" number. It has no end, and it never repeats (as far as we know):

3.14159265358979323846264338327950288419716939937510 58209749445923078164062862089986280348253421170679821 4 80865132823066470938446095505822317253594081284811174 5 028410270193852110555964462294895493038196442881097566 59334461284756482337867831652712019091456485669234603 4 86104543266482133936072602491412737245870066063155881 7 48815209209628292540917153643678925903600113305305488 2 04665213841469519415116 09 . . .

And so on. With a short computer program, you can compute pi all day long. Hell, you can compute it to the heat-death of the universe.

You can grab any thousand digits of pi and about a hundred of them will be 1s, a hundred will be 2s, and so on. But there's no pattern within those digits. Pick any digit of pi—digit 2,670, which happens to be 0. The next digit happens to be 4, then 7, then 7, then two 5s. If you were rolling a ten-sided dice and you got these outcomes, you'd call it random. But if you know that 047755 are the values for the 2670th–2675th digits of pi, then you'd know that the next "dice roll" would be 5 (again!). Then 1. Then 3. Then 2.

This isn't "random." It's *predictable*. You may not know exactly what "random" means (I certainly don't!), but whatever "random" means, it *doesn't* mean "predictable," right?

So it would be crazy to call pi a "random number," even though it has a bunch of random-like characteristics.

So what about some other number? What if you asked your computer to use some kind of pseudorandom algorithm to spit up some grotendous number like this: 27182818284590452353360287 471352662497757. Is that random?

Well, not really. That *also* happens to be a number called "e," which is sometimes called "Napier's constant." Never mind what "e" means, it's complicated. The point is that e is a number like pi. Every digit in it can be predicted.

How about if your random-number generator gave you this number:
2222222222222222222222222222222222222222222222222222
2222222222222222222222222222222222222222222222222222
2222222222222222222222222222222222222222222222222222
2222222222222222222222222222222222222222222222222222
2222222222222222222222222222222222222222222222222222
2222222222222222222222222222222222222222222222222222
2222222222222222222222222222222222222222222222222222
2222222222222222222222222222222222222222222222222222
2222222222222222222222222222222222222222222222222222
2222222222222222222222222222222222222222222222222222
2222222222222222222222222222222222222222222222222222
2222222222222222222222222222222222222222222222222222
2222222222222222222222222

Is that random?

Well, duh. No.

Why isn't it random? Because if I said, "What's the one hundredth digit of a number that consists of a thousand twos?" you'd know the answer. You wouldn't be *surprised*.

It turns out a lot of people have spent a lot of time trying to come up with a decent definition of "random." One of the best definitions anyone's ever come up with is "A number is random if the simplest way to express it is by writing it down."

If you just went lolwut, don't panic. This is hard, but cool. So, take our friend pi again. You could write a program to print out pi in, like two hundred characters. Maybe less. Pi itself is infinite, which is a lot more than two hundred characters long. So the simplest way to express pi is definitely to write the "print out pi program" and not to write out all the infinite digits of pi.

And if pi is easy, "2222222222222222222222222222222222 2222222222" and so on is really easy. In python, it'd be: "print ".join(['2']*42)." Perl's more compact: "print 2×42." But even in verbose old BASIC, a programming language that's so flowery and ornate it's practically Shakespearean, it's:

10 PRINT "2" 20 GOTO 10 30 END

That's thirty characters, which is shorter than 2222222222222 22222222222222222222222222222 to infinity. A lot shorter. So if we mean a random number is a surprising one—one that has no easily expressed pattern or structure, then we can say that:

A number is "random" if the shortest program you can write to print that number out is longer than the number itself.

This has a neat compactness to it, the ring of a good rule: short, punchy, and to the point. A guy named Gregory Chaitin came up with this neat rule, then he came up with a hell of a twist on it. He was so proud of this feat that he mailed a paper to one of math's great mad geniuses, a guy called Kurt Gödel (pronounced "Girdle," more or less) and messed everything up by asking, "How do you know whether you've come up with the shortest program for printing out a number?"

Which was a good point. Programmers are always coming up with novel ways of solving problems, after all. And there may be some hidden pattern to a number you didn't even realize was there. Say I asked you to write a program to print out this number:

6464126002437968454377733902647251281941632007684873625176406596754069362175887930785591647877274739272002910342949562447661308200729250734529170764226621047673037863169954237455117456522022783324096803524667663190861011206745856287317413511162292078865132941244815471628182079877168346341322362234117788231027659825109358892359162055108763298087993165172528938001237817434896832151590562493347370206832232100118637395770567473867102173212375224325241626358034376253606808669163571594551527817803921774322823436633772811186390511893075901666

50742952758384008544635419317190531363659724905158409106582201814734799022359067138146905116051922301269482316113417439944714833040862484269139502336713412425123864026657258130943967621939655407386524229897879782198637918299709557924747320303239116410445906907977862315518349593035305923789817515891457650408025109479123421758482841881950138546165680301755035580054944894884871351605375593402345748979516602442338321406030005937105588457052515704266284600035

Look all you want, you probably won't find any pattern at all (if you do, it's a product of your imagination). So is it random? Nope. It's part of pi: digits 100,000–101,000, to be specific. *Now* you can write a *very* short program to print out that number: just add a line to the "print out pi" program that says, "Only start printing when you get to the 100,000th digit, and stop 1,000 digits later."

What Chaitin realized was that no one could ever know for sure whether a sufficiently long, interesting number could be printed out with a program shorter than it. That is, you could never tell whether *any* big number was random or not. In fact, maybe there were *no* random numbers. He called this "incompleteness," as in "You can never be completely sure you know if a number is random."

Gödel was already famous for the idea of "incompleteness," the idea that mathematical systems couldn't prove themselves. Chaitin saw incompleteness in the way we thought about random numbers, too.

As far as anyone knows, he was right. We basically can never know whether something is random or totally predictable. He is one of mathematics' great smartasses.

Fun fact: Gödel went crazy at the end of his life and became convinced that someone was trying to poison him. He refused to eat and ended up starving himself to death. No one knows exactly why he went crazy, but I sometimes wonder if all that uncertainty drove him around the bend.

I didn't leak the docs on LaptopLock. Neither did Ange. Neither did Jolu. According to the logs, we were the only ones that had touched them.

But they leaked anyway.

Of course, Liam knew about it before I did. He pretty much *ran* over to my desk as soon as he saw the story on Reddit. "You went to Chavez High, right?"

"Uh, yeah?"

"Did you know this Fred Benson skeeze?"

He didn't have to say anything else, really. By that point, I knew exactly what this had to be about. But it was worse than that. The pastebin dumps of the stuff about LaptopLock were all headed "DARKNET DOC ———" with the number of the document. The highest numbered LaptopLock document happened to be 745,120, and several people had already noted this and concluded that somewhere out there, there was a site called "darknet docs" with at least 745,120 documents on it.

We were blown.

"It's amazing, right? I mean, can you believe it? I wonder what else they've got?"

"Yeah," I said. "Huh. Wow."

Liam dragged a chair over to my desk. He put his head close to mine. He smelled of Axe body spray, which may just be the most disgusting scent known to humankind.

"Marcus," he said, in a low voice, "dude. You remember yesterday, when you were talking about root certs and stuff? It sounded like maybe you knew more about the subject than you were letting on."

"Did it."

"I mean, look, you're *Marcus Yallow*. If there's a darknet, you've gotta be all over that shit, yo. I mean, seriously, dude." He seemed to be waiting for me to say something. I never knew what to say when someone ended a sentence with *yo*. They always seemed to be acting out some script for a bromance comedy movie that I hadn't had a chance to see. But Liam was so excited he was shaking a little. "Come on, hook me up, man."

Ah, there it was. Liam wasn't stupid. He was enthusiastic and a little immature, but he listened carefully and knew that 10 plus 10 equaled 100 (in binary, at least). His heart was in the right place. And Jolu had brought his friends into the darknet clubhouse. But

I couldn't just randomly start signing up overenthusiastic puppies like Liam without talking to everyone else. Especially as there appeared to be someone in our base possibly killing our doodz.

"Liam, I seriously, totally, honestly have no idea what you're talking about. This is the first I've heard of it."

"Really? Like pinky-swear really?"

"Cross my eyes and hope to fry. I don't even have a Reddit account. I can't believe how much stuff they've dug up on the administrators who were using LaptopLock."

"Oh, that's nothing," Liam said, already forgetting his conviction that I was the ringleader of some leak-gang in his excitement at the awesome power of the Internet hivemind. "You should see what happens when Anon d0xxes someone."

I knew about Anonymous—the weird nongroup that was an offshoot of /b/, the messageboard on 4chan where everyone was anonymous and the name of the game was to be as humorously offensive as possible. I knew that they kept spinning out these subgroups that did something brave or stupid or vicious (or all three), like getting thousands of people to knock PayPal offline in protest of PayPal cutting off WikiLeaks. I knew that they had some incredibly badass hackers in their orbit, as well as plenty of kids who drifted in and out without knowing much about computers or politics, but who liked the camaraderie or the power or the lulz (or all three).

But I can't say as I spent a lot of time on them. I'd had my time in the cyberguerrilla underground and I had decided I didn't want any more to do with it, especially when it came to crazy, impossible-to-describe "movements" that spent as much time squabbling among themselves as they did fighting for freedom and lulz.

"D0xxes," I said, trying to remember what it meant.

"Yeah, they get really righteously pissed at someone and they d0x them, dig up all the documents they can about them that they can find—court records, property records, marriage, birth and death, school records, home address, work address, phone number, news dumps . . . everything. It's insane, like the DHS turned inside out, all that weird crap all the different agencies and companies and search engines know about you, just, like, *hanging out there,* all of it where the search engines can find it, forever. The stuff they found about your douchey old vice principal is *nothing,* man. If Anon gets on this tip, *bam,* it's going to be *sick."*

Now I remembered what d0xxing meant. Yikes. "Do you ever wonder if there's anyone else who can do that sort of thing?"

"What do you mean? Like the cops or the FBI or something?"

"Well, I mean, sure, yeah, of course they can do all this stuff." *And more,* I thought, imagining what you might dig up with a lawful intercept appliance. "But what about, I don't know, some CEO? Or a private military contractor?"

"You mean, is there someone like Anonymous out there, but doing it for the money instead of the lulz? Like hackers for hire or whatever? Oh, man, I'm totally sure there are. It's not like you have to be an angel or a genius to learn how to do an SQL injection or crack a crappy password file. I bet you half the creeps who used to give me noogies at recess are laughing it up at private intelligence outfits these days."

"Yeah," I said. I wondered how many of those particular kinds of creeps were drawing a paycheck from Carrie Johnstone and whether any of them might be hanging out in our darknet, messing with our heads.

I took a long lunch (feeling like a total slacker for grabbing extra time off on my third day at work) and asked Ange and Jolu to meet me in South Park, which was about the same distance from Ange's school and Jolu's and my offices. It was a slightly scuzzy little park right in the middle of SoMa—south of Market—but it had been ground zero for a whole ton of dotcom start-ups and tech companies and it was always full of the right kind of nerds. I felt comfortable there.

Jolu arrived first, looking cool and grown-up as usual. A couple of the people eating their lunches on the benches around us recognized him and waved at him.

"How do you do it?" I said when he sat down.

"What?" he said, smiling like he and I were in on some enormous joke together.

"I don't know; how are you so cool? I'm crapping myself over

452 | **cory doctorow**

this darknet stuff, I look like I dressed myself in the dark, I can't figure out how to cut my hair so I don't look fifteen years old, and you, you're so totally, I don't know, you know, *styling*."

He gave me that easy smile again. "I don't know, Marcus. I used to be kind of anxious all the time, did I look 'cool,' was I going to get in trouble, was the world going to end or whatever? And then one day, I just thought, *You know, whatever's happening, I'm not going to improve it by having a total spaz attack.* So I decided to just *stop*. And I did."

"You're a Zen master, you know that?"

"You should try it, pal. You're looking a little freaked out, if you don't mind my saying so."

"Well, you know: 'When in trouble or in doubt, run in circles, scream and shout.'"

"Yeah, I've heard you say that before. I guess what I'm asking is, how's that working out for you?"

I closed my eyes and rubbed my hands on my jeans. "Not so good."

"Why don't you try just cooling it down for a minute or two, see if you can't get your head right before this all kicks off?"

If it had been anyone except Jolu, I might have been offended, but I'd known Jolu forever, and he knew me as well as anyone in the world. I remembered that feeling I'd had in the temple that time I'd lain in the dust among the gongs and the Omm, the total peace and calm that had washed over me like a warm bath. I could *remember* how that felt, but I couldn't *feel* it—the harder I chased it, the more elusive it felt.

Jolu put his hand on my shoulder and gave me a gentle shake. "Easy there, hoss. Don't sprain anything. You look like you're getting ready to kung-fu my ass. This is about relaxing, not stressing out. If it's hard, you're doing something wrong."

I actually felt really bad, like I'd failed at something. To cover up for it, I kind of hammed it up, putting my face in my hands and acting like I was experiencing some kind of artistic torment.

"Don't sweat it, Marcus. Just something to keep in mind, all right? There's the stuff that's happening out there in the world, which we only have limited control over, and the stuff that's happening in our heads, which we can have total control over—in theory, at least. I've noticed that you spend a lot of time trying to change the outside world, but not much energy on changing how the outside world makes your inside world feel. I'm not saying you should give up on changing the world, but you might try doing a little of both for a while, see what happens."

He was smiling when he said it, and I knew he wasn't trying to be a dick, but it still made me feel ashamed. I guess because I knew he was right. All my life, people had been telling me to chill out, calm down, take it easy, but for some reason, taking it easy was *hard,* while freaking out came naturally.

He looked worried now. "Okay, forget I said anything. I only brought it up because you asked. Let's talk about the current situation, right? As in, what the hell's going on with the darknet? Who's reading over our shoulders? What are they up to?"

"Good," I said. I was relieved by the change of subject.

"Start with the process of elimination, because we need to start somewhere. The logs say no one but me, you, and Ange accessed those docs. Are you *sure* Ange didn't leak them? Don't get mad, okay? It's just about covering all the bases."

"Yeah, I get that. No, I can't imagine why Ange would do that. She practically tore my throat out when I suggested that we should go public with the stuff about Benson."

"So *you* wanted to leak them?"

"What? No. I mean, yeah, of course my first reaction was to nail all those bastards to a wall, but Ange told me not to be an idiot and I reconsidered it. Besides, all I wanted to do was talk to everyone else about it, not go rogue and do it myself. I don't even know how I'd leak it if I wanted to—whoever's doing it is good. They stick it up on pastebin, and Reddit goes crazy and the press follows."

Ange arrived then, looking absolutely beautiful in a chunky black sweater with a pixel-art Mario/Cthulhu mashup worked into the front, black-and-white striped tights, and a red skirt. She topped it off with ancient, cracked motorcycle boots the color of old cement and a 3D-printed plastic bracelet on each wrist. Ange was basically the most perfect woman I'd ever known, and my best friend in the whole world, and every now and again I'd see her coming down the street or walking through the park and I'd realize that I was pretty much the luckiest man that ever lived.

There's no way Ange had been leaking stuff behind our backs.

She gave Jolu a warm hug and then gave me a warmer one, with a big long kiss that ended with me burying my face in her neck and breathing in the heavenly smell of her collarbones.

"Hey, guys, so have you solved all our problems yet?"

"Not yet, but we're working on it."

We unpacked our lunches. I'd made myself a sack of PB&Js and thrown in an apple, some cookies, and a little bottle of cold brew before leaving the house that morning. I'd realized I'd need to start brown-bagging it when I started thinking about how little of my paycheck would be left over if I blew eight bucks every day on coffee, a burrito, and horchata. Ange, like always, had made herself a perfect and awesomely cute bento box with rice and vegetables and cold tofu and beef arranged in precise, colorful patterns. Jolu had one of his badass homemade energy bars, big as a 2 × 4 and twice as dense with all kinds of nuts and seeds, studded with bits of smoked bacon and dusted with his secret mix of spices. I'd seen him live off one of those for a whole day while on a camping trip, having a casual gnaw at it whenever he got a little peckish.

"Before we go any further," Ange said, around a dainty mouthful of rice and marinated eggplant, "Jolu, you're not the leak, are you? I mean, no offense, but—"

He laughed. "Yeah, I know. You should have seen Marcus here when I asked if he thought it could be you."

"Well, you've got to start somewhere. I'm not the leak, for what it's worth. I wish I was, because it would mean that no one was inside our security, messing with us. But Jolu, you haven't answered the question yet—are *you* the leak?"

"No, Ange. I wish I was, for the same reason. Because I don't like the alternative, either. I mean, either someone's really seriously compromised the security of my server, which would be pretty goddamned hard because there isn't a single byte of cleartext going in or out of that box, or—"

"Or someone's rooted your computer, or mine, or Ange's."

"Yeah."

That was the possibility that had been going through my head all morning. Someone with total control over my computer, someone with the power to light up the camera and the mic, to grab text off my screen or files off my hard drive. It wasn't a possibility I liked to think about. The darknet docs showed that Fred Benson had grabbed over eight thousand photos of *one* student alone, some poor kid the old bastard had a hate-on for.

How many times had my computer been compromised? Zero? Or eight thousand?

And more important: if my computer *had* been pwned, had it been "random"—someone scanning for vulnerabilities discovering my computer in a rare, unpatched moment and grabbing control over it—or had it been "special"? That is, had someone targeted me? Like Gödel, I wasn't sure I knew the difference between random and special anymore.

I don't know what Jolu told Restless Agent and the rest of his buddies, but there was no darknet chat accusing me or Ange of being the leak. I still didn't know who Jolu's people were, and didn't want to know, but I kind of assumed that they were people he worked with and that he'd gone back from lunch and had a little chat with them—hopefully away from any computers that might be covertly running their mics and cameras.

But of course, no one wanted to do much chatting at all on darknet, not without knowing who and how someone or someones were eavesdropping on us.

Long after the last person—Liam—had left Joe's campaign office, I sat at my desk, staring at my computer like it might have a live, venomous snake hiding inside it. I had stayed late at my desk, theoretically to finish up the day's work and make up for my little lunchtime face-to-face meeting, but also because I didn't want to try to deworm my laptop at home, not when I had an office filled with so many spare and useful computers lying around.

In theory, it should be easy to secure (or resecure) my laptop. Find another hard drive and create an encrypted filesystem on it. Boot up my computer—or any computer!—with a boot disk downloaded fresh from the Internet, after carefully validating the checksum to make absolutely, positively certain that I was using a clean, uninfected, pristine version of ParanoidLinux. Then I'd install a fresh build of ParanoidLinux on the new drive, copy over the user data from my old disk to the new one, and I'd essentially have given my computer a fresh brain with all the memories of the old one, but with a high degree of certainty about the brain's reliability and trustworthiness. It all worked best if you had a couple of spare laptops and hard drives lying around, which the Joe campaign had—old laptops are one of those things that no one really wants to throw away, so we'd accumulated a lot of semiantique machines that had been donated by Joe's supporters.

Figuring out whether the old machine had been infected at all was a harder, more subtle problem. If someone had infected the machine and altered the kernel—the nugget at the middle of the operating system where you'd hide the most vicious spyware—I'd either have to go through it line-by-line looking for something out of place (which might take a hundred years or so), or try to build an identical kernel from known good sources and compare the checksums and see if there was any obvious dissimilarity. The problem was that I'd patched and tweaked my kernel so many times over the years that if the new one didn't match, it would almost certainly be because I'd built the new one wrong, not because I'd been taken over. At the very least, I wouldn't be able to tell the difference.

My computer sat there, staring at me from its little webcam, a ring the size of a grain of rice. The mic was a pinhole-sized hole set into the screen's frame. The first thing I'd done after getting back to the office was grab a roll of duct tape from the supply cupboard, thinking I'd tape over the camera and mic.

But I hadn't done it. It felt paranoid. I *was* paranoid. If there was someone inside my computer, that person knew more about me than anyone. But so far, all that person had done was carefully, effectively release docs that I'd been planning to leak. Maybe that person wasn't a bad guy (or girl). Maybe that person was on my side, in some twisted way. I found myself imagining the snoop: a seventeen-year-old like me a couple years ago, glorying in the thrill of being where he shouldn't be. Or maybe an old, crusty FBI agent, sitting in a cubicle in Quantico, making careful notes on my facial expressions and my kissing techniques with Ange. Or some thick-necked mercenary saving screengrabs of the most embarrassing moments so that Carrie Johnstone could laugh at them later.

It was eerily silent inside Joe's office. The street noises were washed out by the air-conditioning's hum. I looked straight into the webcam and started talking: "You're in there, aren't you? I think it's pretty creepy, I have to say. If you think you're helping me, let me tell you, you're freaking me out instead. I'd much rather that you *talk* to me than sneak around spying on me. And if you're one of the bad guys, well, screw you. Nothing you do to me now will stop the darknet docs from going public, and if I get scared enough or disappear altogether, I'll just dump the whole goddamned pile. Do you hear me? Are you there?"

Boy, did I feel stupid and awkward. It was like the one time I'd tried praying by my bed, when I was about ten or eleven and I'd been seized by a weird, sudden terror that if there was a God, He'd be really pissed off at me and my family for our total disbelief in Him. I didn't actually *believe* in God, but I had this wobbly cost-benefit analysis moment that went like this: *It costs nothing to believe in God. If the tiny likelihood of the existence of God turns out to be the truth, then He'll punish a failure of belief with eternal damnation. The consequences are terrible, but the risk is low. Wouldn't it make sense to take out some sort of insurance policy to protect against this tiny possibility?* My dad had just changed our household insurer and an adjuster had come over to look at the house and talk about whether we'd need flood and fire and lightning and earthquake insurance, and how much, and Dad and I had geeked out on the math together, which had been codified by Richard Price, a British mathematician who had been the patron of Thomas Bayes, my dad's all-time math hero. So I had insurance on the brain.

That was weird enough—but the really weird part was that once I got this idea, it got me, too. I couldn't let go of the feeling that I hadn't bought the right kind of insurance—I was believing in the wrong God—or that I wasn't sending my premiums to the right place—I wasn't praying right. I spent about a week in a low-grade panic about my religious incompetence, and it was always worse at night, when I was lying in bed, waiting for sleep to come.

So one night, I'd gotten out of bed and, feeling incredibly dumb and self-conscious, I'd gotten down on my knees beside the bed, folded my hands together, bowed my head, and closed my eyes. I'd seen kids praying this way in old cartoons—I think Donald Duck made his nephews do it, or maybe that was Popeye—though I'd never done it myself.

I had searched for the words. "Please, God," is what came out. "Please, God, please don't kill us. Please make us happy and healthy. Please tell Darryl's dad to let him have a sleepover with me this weekend. Please help me do good on my history assignment—" Once I started going, it turned out that there was a whole litany of stuff I hadn't known that I was worried about, things that I wanted some invisible, all-powerful sky-daddy to solve for me. It came pouring out. I started out in a low conversational tone, but I dropped to a whisper, and then just moved my lips, the way I did when making a birthday-candle wish.

And then, after I'd run out and said, "Amen," I opened my eyes. My knees hurt. It had felt good to unburden myself of all those worries, and it had been surprising to discover them there, but at the same time, I couldn't help but feel absolutely, totally ridiculous. If there was a God, why would He care about whether I had a sleepover that weekend?

But what cinched it was the absence of any feeling of a *reply*. I'd spoken all my secret fears and worries, words so secret I hadn't even known they were inside me. I'd sent them into the air and into the sky, and the words had floated away, but no words had come back. No feeling of presence. No feeling of being listened to, or heard, or understood. I had spoken to the universe, and the universe hadn't given a damn. I stopped worrying about my "insurance premiums" that night, lost the nagging worry that I was meant to be praying to Allah or preparing for my bar mitzvah or joining the Hare Krishnas. In the space of an hour, I went from an anxious agnostic to a carefree atheist, and I'd stayed that way forever after.

That night, in Joe's office, I spoke words again into the air, sent them out to the universe.

That night, the universe answered.

> ooohhh busted

Unseen hands had dragged my computer's mouse pointer to the dock and clicked on the LibreOffice icon, making a new text document window appear on my screen with an inaudible mouse click. It was so spooky that the hairs on the back of my neck actually all stood up, and I shivered down my spine. I tried to keep a poker face, staring into the eye of the camera over my screen as one of my biggest fears in the world came to life before me.

I tried to think of something to say or do, but my mouth felt like it was full of ashes and my hands were trembling on the desk in front of me.

> you worry too much dude

With a deliberate effort, I got my arms to move, got my hands onto the lid of my laptop. I slammed it down, then I stood up so fast that my chair went over backwards. I found myself standing in the middle of Joe's office, shaking and goosepimply, and all I could see were the other screens in the room, with their webcam eyes, and imagine the ghostly, distant eyes staring out of them.

Willing myself not to run, I brisk-walked back to the wiring closet, seized with an animalistic need to tear the building's Internet connection out of the physical router, to turn us into a little lightless island of no-man's-land in the great glowing spiderweb of the planetary network. But once I got back into the humming, air-conditioned room with its server rack and its router and network switches and blocky uninterruptable power supplies, I found myself calming down, catching my breath. This room was full of computers, sure, but they didn't have cameras and mics. There was only one keyboard, a little clickety number that sounded like machine gun fire when you rattled out commands on it for checking or rebooting routers. There was one screen, a nine-inch flat panel with burned-in text from the password prompt for one of the routers. Everything in this room was familiar, and safe, and reassuringly technological. In this room, I was invisible to webcams, and in this room, I could program my routers to generate enormous, voluminous logs, whole libraries' worth of data about every packet in or out of the building. From this room, I might be able to set a trap.

———

The laptop sat back on my desk, the document window staring me in the face:

> you worry too much dude

"Are you there?"

Are you there, God? It's me, Marcus. A hysterical giggle welled up in my throat and I swallowed it.

Nothing. The air-conditioning hummed. Back in the wiring closet, the router was streaming a few extra million bits into its solid-state storage, the work of it all creating a tiny bit more heat than usual, making the air conditioner work just a tiny little bit harder. A puff of extra carbon wafted into the atmosphere.

I stared into the beady glass eye of the webcam, thinking of the unknown party or parties who may or may not be watching on the other end. I wondered how the bug worked. Did it phone home every time I signed on to a network, telling the snoops that I was online and available for watching and spying? Did it store up pictures of me and logs of my keystrokes when I was offline, waiting for an opportune moment to dump all this stuff?

Did someone's phone just get a discreet SMS? "MARCUS ON-LINE NOW" and a cheerful ringtone? Maybe "La Cucaracha"?

"Hello? Anyone home?"

Nothing.

"Come on, you chickenshits, I know you're out there." Now I had the paranoid sensation that I was being recorded, that anything I said or did might end up on YouTube in ten minutes. I tried to butch it up, be as tough and cool as a superspy so that I'd be able to stand tall when the world saw how I reacted to the news that I was on candid webcam. "There's no point in hiding now. I know you've got root. I'll be shutting down this machine and reinstalling the OS just as soon as I'm done. Last chance to chat before I patch your back door."

I stared at the screen. It stared back.

"Fine," I said, and reached up to close the lid. For a second, I felt like I might be insane, like I might have hallucinated the whole thing. Just as my hand reached the lid, a word appeared on the screen:

> wait

I sat back.

"Nice to see you again. Do you have something you'd like to say?"

> were on ur side dude

"You've been spying on me," I said. I heard the tremor in my voice.

> privacys dead get over it

I felt the tremor now. These bastards had been spying on me and they had the nerve to tell me to "get over it"?

"You're not—" My voice caught. I swallowed and took a couple of breaths. "You're not on my side if you believe that. Do you have any idea how totally evil it is to do what you're doing?"

> what a homo

> shut up

> felch me dickcheese

> ur sister said you like that

I started to get offended, and then I noticed something. This wasn't a string of insults directed at *me*. Two or more people were arguing in my text window. One was a much faster typist than the other, and smoother.

"Are you like twelve years old or something?" I said. "That's it, isn't it? You're children, right?"

> born same year as you marcus edward yallow 1320 rhode island drive san francisco ca 94107 . . . . hey were both aquariuses. . . . . fish in tha hizouse"

Hizouse was right up there with ending sentences with *yo* on my list of linguistic crimes. These *were* kids, even if Mr. Aquarius wasn't lying about his age. Emotionally, at least, these guys were children.

"I just want you to know that there's two people who might die because of what you've done. Those docs were given to me by someone who's been kidnapped since. You might have gotten some lulz out of it, but you've seriously screwed up the work we were doing to help our friends."

> we did it 4 zeb/masha you fag////// got tired of waiting around for you

For a second I thought they must be part of Masha's group,

maybe her multicolored-hair friends. But then—Occam's Razor—I figured they must have learned about Masha and Zeb by eavesdropping on me.

"That wasn't your call to make."

> no? oppps. our bad. now what?

"What do you mean?"

> now what are you going to do? the docs are getting out there. you can't change that. are you going 2 help or wot?

"Am *I* going to help? What do you think I've been doing all this time? I mean, when I wasn't running around trying to figure out how all the leaks got out. When I wasn't wasting time on you pindicks."

> flattery will get you nowhere

> sorry d00d it needed doing

> you r soooooooooooooooooo slow

> what u waiting 4? carrie johnstone is pure evil

> btw u shld c wot we got on johnstone

> shes a very naughty girl

> worse than youd imagine from ur little docs diving

> the kind of person makes you want to believe in 92nd term abortion

> she will be fun to destroy

> bet she goes total apeshirt

> apeshirt

> apeshirt

> eff you eff ay gee ess

> marcus

"Yes?" I'd been watching the typing. I thought there were three of them. Maybe four.

> u need 2 dump everything now now now what u waiting for a rainy day? What you think masha/zeb are doing right now? enjoying a beach holiday? smokin fatties in a hot club? more like experiencing batteries strapped to their nipples

With normal chat, you get the whole message in a blip—there's a pause, then some text. But this was different. I could watch the typist on the other end typing, the hesitations and the backspaces, even a couple spots where another mysterious typist broke in and tried to interrupt, only to be furiously deleted. There was a lot of *texture* in this text, and it made it somehow less spooky. These were squabbling people, not all-powerful gods, and the fact that they'd pwned me wasn't an indication of their omnipotence or their moral superiority.

"I want to dump it all, but I don't want to go to jail. And I want it to make a difference, to put it into stories that people can make sense out of and care about. You've been watching what we're doing, you know why we're doing it." My fear was turning into anger. "What's more, we'd be a lot further along if we weren't screwing around trying to do damage control after you decided to start posting without talking to us."

> srsly? yr pissed that we leaked yr leaks? weak

> masha trusted u, u didnt have da stones. we do. suck it.

"So, what, you just happened to root my computer just in time to get on this little campaign? You only started spying on me at the very second that I started doing something you disapprove of?"

> when we pwned u is irrelevant. stop changing the subject. u r 2 scared 2 do what needs doing. time 2 man up

"Or what? I make one call and all the darknet passwords'll be changed. Give me an hour, I'll have my computers cleaned off. You've got nothing, you little pricks, and without my cooperation, you'll have nothing."

> thats what you think.

I kept my face as still and expressionless as I could. Of course they didn't have "nothing"—in some sense, they had *everything*. Depending on how much they'd been logging, they'd have my passwords, my email, video of me, audio . . . and they'd have Ange, too—her name, her discussing the leaks with me, our makeout sessions.

"Yeah, you could ruin my life, but then no one will be in a position to help Masha. Is that what you want?"

I had the sense that there was just one person typing now, someone I started to think of as Final Boss, the über snoop in this little posse.

"We're going nowhere with this. I'm going now, going to rebuild everything, change all the passwords. You want to talk to me like people instead of stalkers, you know where I am."

> we certainly do

It took two hours to rebuild Lurching Abomination, almost all of it consisting of painfully slow file transfers from my backups and tedious verification of checksums as I downloaded my OS and all my apps all over again, making sure each time that I had clean copies that hadn't had a single byte changed.

I dragged a chair into the wiring closet and did the rebuild there. That gave me direct access to the router and its voluminous, verbose logs. I'd grabbed every packet going in and out of the building's network, a senseless tsunami, a packetstorm, a flood. Trying to make sense of the raw feed would be as pointless and brutal as trying to make sense of every mote of dust floating in the air. But dust is analog, and packets are digital. The router couldn't do much by way of large-scale statistical analysis, but it didn't need to—that wasn't its job.

VMWare had a fine catalog of virtual machines, preconfigured for heavy data crunching. With two clicks, I loaded one onto a cloud VM loaded on Amazon S3, ticking off the "private/encrypted" box. I booted the VM with another click, then switched to VNC, a screen-sharing app, and now I was looking at the desktop of my virtual machine on that little flatscreen with its burned-in ghost characters. I had the router throw its monster logfile at the machine, and in about two minutes, I had all the pretty charts and graphs you could ever want, courtesy of hadoop, a free data-munging package that did to large blobs of data what Photoshop did to graphics.

I knew just enough hadoop to be a danger to myself and those around me, but by mousing around a lot, I managed to pare away all the traffic except for the streams that were being used to snoop on my laptop. It was hard to tell from a single session, but it looked like the spyware waited a short interval after the machine found a new network, then sent out a little encrypted blip that I figured meant *Here I am*. A few milliseconds later, my computer got some bits back (*I see you*). Then, blam, an encrypted stream erupted from the machine. It was encrypted, so I didn't know what it was, technically, though I was moderately certain it was a feed from my screen, my camera, and my mic.

Hadoop had a handy traffic-analysis library that went further, hazarding a guess that some of the packets were from Kphone, a free Skype-style phone app that did video, and the rest were from VNC, the same program I was using. Which all made sense: if you were going to put together a trojan to take over peoples' computers, your fastest and most reliable method would be to just smush together a bunch of highly reliable, well-tested, best-of-breed apps. You could even keep it up to date with the bug fixes the apps released, piggybacking on their development, leaving you with more time to get on with invading peoples' privacy. I'd be willing to bet that the lawful intercept stuff detailed in the darknet dumps did exactly the same thing. Cops and robbers all using the same screwdrivers, and civilians in the middle, getting screwed.

Then I noticed something I should have seen from the start: the *I see you* message, the screengrabs, and the camera feed were all going to different IP addresses. I punched each one into Google and, of course, they were Tor exit nodes. My snoops weren't just encrypting the traffic from my machine, they were bouncing it all over the Internet so that I couldn't see where it was going. Somewhere out there was a server like our darknet dump except it had buttons labeled "View from Marcus's camera" and "Sound from Marcus's mic" and "Marcus's screen" and "Marcus's hard drive."

In other words, they'd taken the technology I used to protect my privacy on the net and used it to protect *their* privacy while they snooped on me. The irony, it burns.

That wasn't going to get me anywhere. Meanwhile, Lurch was back up to nominal. I'd even nuked its BIOS, the part of the computer that tells the rest of the computer how to turn on; a tedious process, but I felt like I'd be nuts not to do it. It was considered insanely hard to poison a computer's BIOS remotely, but if I was going to rebuild a computer that had been fatally pwned, ignoring the BIOS would be like changing all your house locks after losing your keys but leaving all the windows unlocked.

BIOS flashed, computer restored, trolls locked out, I shut off all the lights at Joe for Senate, shrugged on my jacket, set the burglar alarm, and stepped out into the cool night of the Mission.

466 | **cory doctorow**

And straight into the arms of the goons who'd been waiting for me in the parked car across the street.

I've been snatched twice. This was not the roughest of the lot (that would be when the DHS grabbed us off Market Street the day the Bay Bridge blew and clubbed us in the head when we asked what the hell was going on), nor was it the scariest (that would be when I puked into the bag Carrie Johnstone's squad cinched around my neck, convinced I was going to choke to death on Dumpster-dived pizza). It was so smooth and professional, I would have given them a customer service award if I wasn't so busy freaking out.

They stepped out of the car in perfect synchrony just as I came through the door. Two guys, big and beefy, with the "cop" vibe that always made my neck muscles go as tight as a tennis racket. One of them stood at the curb, covering me and watching who was around with a regular, predatory head swivel. The other closed the distance between me and him in three quick steps, coming right into my personal space, flipping a laminated DHS ID out of his pocket. Before I could look at it, he'd put it back in his pocket, as neat as a magician vanishing a card.

"Marcus," he said. "We'd like to talk to you for a moment."

When in trouble or in doubt . . .

"I'd like to have a lawyer present," I said.

"You won't need a lawyer, it's just an informal chat." He smelled like Axe body spray. It was the perfect gag-worthy aroma for a huge, looming goon.

"I would like to see your badge again," I said.

"You don't need to see my badge again. Let's go."

Run in circles . . .

I took one step up Mission Street, away from the goon, already looking around for passersby to call out to. A hand like a bar of iron wrapped itself around my bicep and *lifted,* and I felt like my shoulder might separate as my toes dangled over the pavement.

Scream and shout . . .

"FIRE!" I screamed. No one in the Mission is going to come running if you scream "Help!" but everyone likes to get a good look at a fire. That was the theory, anyway—what they told you in self-defense classes. "FIRE!" I screamed again.

The goon's other hand covered my mouth and nose with an airtight seal, his thumb hooked under my chin, clamping my jaw shut.

Maybe I should have tried "HELP!"

They did that cop thing when they put me in the car, pushing my head down with that weird rough/tender gesture so that I wouldn't brain myself on the door frame. But I was 110 percent certain that these two were not cops, or DHS, or anyone else on a government payroll. It was the gear in the car: none of your scarred, scratched, rubberized cop laptops like you got in the SFPD cruisers I'd been handcuffed in. These guys had computers that screamed "tactical," that matte black finish and those rugged matte black steel corner reinforcements, screens fitted with polarized privacy filters that made them appear black unless you were sitting right in front of them. They looked like they'd been designed by someone who'd never seen a modern computer, but had had one described to him by someone who spent a lot of time in muscle cars or Hummers.

They didn't just have a GPS: they had a crazy militarized one, with a hedgehog bristle of stubby, rubberized antennae and a street map display that showed the familiar streets of the Mission using blocky, eight-bit-style graphics that looked nothing at all like any commercial GPS or Google Maps. They had these crazy armored USB ports set right into the dashboard, each with a pair of LEDs set under hardened glass. There was a strong new-car smell, like they'd ordered some kind of fresh spookmobile that morning to stalk me with, something they could douse in gasoline and roll off a cliff when they were through with it.

These guys looked like they had money, a lot of it, and weren't afraid to spend it. They didn't look like the sort of people who had to fill in a lot of crazy paperwork to get reimbursed, the way my dad had had to do for the books he'd bought for his department at UC Berkeley. The guy who'd been on lookout slid into the back seat with me—I noticed that there were no door handles on the inside of the back doors and wondered how he'd get back out again when he was through with me. This was a distracting thing to wonder about. It took my mind off what "through with me" might mean.

"Hi there, Marcus," the man in the back said. He *also* smelled like Axe body spray, which must be the national scent of Douchesylvania. He had a disarmingly friendly look: his tight, smooth-shaved face had all kinds of smile lines and wrinkles around his eyes. He projected this air of total relaxation and confidence, like the grown-up version of the Most Popular Kid on the Football Team character from a bad teen movie. "You can call me Timmy." If we were about to play good cop/bad cop, Timmy was most definitely the good cop.

"I'd like to consult an attorney," I said.

He smiled wider. "I like that," he said. "That's exactly what she said he'd say, isn't it? She even got the voice down. Man, she really knows you well." "She" must be Carrie Johnstone, squirreled away in some lair somewhere, eating popcorn and regaling her underlings with stories of my weakness and patheticness.

These guys were here to shake me up, get me to say or do something, give them something: the names of the people who had access to the leaks, the passwords or keys, the locations of all the copies. They wanted to scare me. They *had* scared me. I felt like I could throw up at any second. I felt like I could piss myself.

No. You know what I felt like? I felt like I was *drowning*. Like I'd been strapped to a board, tilted backwards with Saran Wrap over my mouth, and had water ladled down my nose, so that it filled my windpipe. My choke reflex had come to life, sucking hard to try to bring air into my lungs. Each time I coughed, the Saran Wrap belled out, pushing out some of the precious sips of air left in my lungs. Each time I breathed in, the Saran Wrap formed a tight seal around my mouth, and the suction drew more water down my windpipe. My lungs began to empty and collapse. My brain began a kind of awful fireworks display, the last lights and noises of a panicked organ about to wither and die and rot.

That.

I was sweating now, all over my body, and had the feeling of a terrible weight on my chest. It was the weight of the knowledge that I was in the power of someone who believed that he could do anything he wanted to me and never pay a single consequence.

"Marcus, buddy, calm down, all right? We're not here to hurt you."

I hated myself for the weakness I was showing. I'd once slept badly, pinching a nerve or a vein or something in my leg, and when I'd stood up in the morning, my leg had given way like it was made of wood, and I'd pitched forward on my face. Now I felt like something else—my inner strength, the place I'd gone to that moment on the playa at the temple—had let me down when I least expected it.

"I would like," I said, voice a gasp, "to consult—"

He slapped me. Not hard. In fact, he was almost gentle. But he was *fast,* so fast I didn't even see his hand move, and had to reconstruct what had just happened from the way that his body shifted, leaning forward a little, then relaxing back, his arm a blur in between. My face stung, but didn't hurt.

"Marcus," he said, and now his voice was stern and paternal. "Enough of that. We're not here to hurt you." *But you slapped me, didn't you?* Of course, he hadn't slapped me hard. And I had no doubt that he could have, had he chosen to. He was a good six inches taller than me, broad-shouldered, and the muscles on his forearms and wrists stood out in cords and masses like a superhero drawing. "We just want to talk to you. If you want to get this over with, you should listen to what we have to say."

I stared fixedly ahead of me.

"There's something you have, Marcus. Something important. Something that you've been gossiping about to certain urinalists in the big old world.

"The thing you have, it's not yours. It's our job to get it back. Once we're confident that we have secured it, there will be no further need for us to communicate with you and no further need for you to communicate with us."

I thought about asking for a lawyer again, but couldn't see the point. I kept up my fixed staring.

"I understand that a certain party has asked you to publish this material." *What? Oh, right, Masha.* "That party has changed her mind."

I was trying to keep my poker face on, but I suck at poker faces. He saw something change in my expression.

"You think that we beat her up or something? Forced her to change her mind?" He laughed (a full-throated laugh, like someone hearing a funny joke) and his friend in the front seat laughed, too (a mean little bark of a laugh, like someone enjoying the sight of a stranger tripping and falling painfully). "Marcus, buddy. That little girl was plain worn-out from all her rough travel. She was tired of living on tortillas and beans, tired of hiding out in the badlands. She wanted what she'd had before, three hots and a cot, a big-screen TV and a minifridge full of Twinkies, all the luxury stuff. Living large. She didn't want to spend the rest of her life as a refugee, sleeping under a newspaper and eating out of the trash. And hey, we need people like her. Our group, we know her, some of us have worked with her before. We like what she does. She's good at it. We didn't beat her up, we didn't pull out her fingernails or drip candle wax on her skin. We just *offered her a job* and she took it."

This was so obvious a lie I nearly laughed myself. Whatever else Masha was, there was no way she'd sell out to these sick assholes.

But, well, how well did I know Masha, really? I'd only met her three times, after all. Only knew her by reputation, mostly, and it wasn't like her reputation was particularly spotless.

Zeb, though. No way Zeb would have gone for it. And I'd seen Masha and Zeb together. They were a unit. Or they seemed like it, at least.

"That little old man of hers," said Timmy, reading my mind—or my crappy poker face—again. "He doesn't really have much we need. We told her we'd keep him around though, if she wanted him. It's not like he takes up a lot of room or eats a lot of chow. Everyone's entitled to a pet. But she was through with him, not that I was privy to the, you know, intimate details. But they had words, is what I'm saying, and he went his way."

"I bet you think we're the bad guys. We're not, though. We're no monsters. We're good guys, Marcus."

Yeah, because good guys do a lot of kidnapping. Good guys blow up art cars in the middle of the desert and put a whole load of people in the hospital. You're a pack of angels. Thinking it, but not saying it.

"What if we take you to see her? We could do that, you know. It's a bit of traveling, though. Could take a while."

"You got all your shots?" said the guy in the front seat with a voice full of morbid cheer. "You don't wanna go there without all your shots, Marcus."

"That's very true. But if that's what it'll take to convince you, we'd be happy to. Who knows, maybe there'd be something you could do for us, too. Kid like you, you're at least half smart, which is smarter than most of the sheep out here. But I don't think you wanna go on a long trip right now, do you?"

The guy in front started the car and eased out onto Mission, and the guy in back put a gentle hand on my chest before I'd had a chance to move. A pane of opaque glass slid up between the front and back seats, and something happened to the rear windows, rendering them black. The only light came from the little dome light on the car's ceiling.

"Where are we going?" I said, and I sounded like a scared little kid, which was exactly what I felt like.

"Just somewhere more private, Marcus. Glad to hear you're up for a little chat, though. So, let's talk."

If I were a superspy, I'd have spent the ride counting hills and listening for the telltale cues of San Francisco traffic and figured out exactly where we were headed. But San Francisco is full of hills, and if you can tell one from the other while you're scared to death in a blacked-out box, you're a truer San Franciscan than I am.

Timmy hummed softly to himself while we drove. He had taken my jacket and bag and he methodically went through the pockets of both, taking out every bit of electronics—laptop, phone, e-reader, a little circuit tester I had stuck in my pocket so I could check on the Ethernet wiring in the office—and removed the battery from each device, then put the device and its battery in a heavy-duty freezer bag and set it to one side. Everything else got a fast but thorough examination and then went back into the bag, except for my multitool, a cool little Leatherman Skeletool that I'd coated in candy apple–red enamel using the gear at Noisebridge. He turned that over a few times, brought out the blade and tested it on his thumb—I kept it razor-sharp—and smiled and nodded approvingly. "Nice," he said, and I felt stupid pride that this bad-ass ninja goon approved of my knife. Maybe that's the feeling that Masha had felt when she went to work for the DHS the first time around, or when she joined up with Carrie Johnstone and tossed out Zeb—if that's what she'd actually done.

The knife went into a baggie on the seat beside him, with the electronics. He felt carefully around the seams and edges of my bags, and I realized that he was doing the kind of bag search that you would get at the airport if the people at the airport actually gave a crap about finding stuff, instead of putting on a little puppet show about security.

The car came to a stop. We'd been driving for a few minutes, or a hundred years, take your pick. The divider between the front and the back of the car slid down with that kind of purring near-silence of a really well-engineered mechanism. The guy in the front, whose ultrashort hair revealed a gnarly knob of scar tissue that ran from the crown of his head to the tendons standing out in the back of his neck, turned around to look at us. I looked past him, trying to figure out where we'd come. There was water, some dark shapes that might be boats, some industrial-looking build-ings. I thought it must be China Basin, a landfill neighborhood that was a mix of abandoned warehouses and factories and trendy condos and offices built into former abandoned warehouses and factories. Judging from the boarded-up windows and the plastic bags and other ancient trash caught in the trees, this was the ac-tual abandoned part.

"Well, here we are," Timmy said, and rubbed his hands to-gether. He and the other man exchanged a long look. "Marcus," Timmy said, turning back to me. "You know what the deal is now. We need what you've got back. We'll take whatever steps you make us take to convince you that that's the right thing to do. If you need us to take you to where your little friend is so she can explain the facts of life to you, that's what we'll do.

"I don't think you want that, do you? I think you'd like to have this unpleasantness behind you quickly and with a minimum of mess."

The other man twisted his face into an ugly smile. "You don't want a mess, buddy. You *really* don't want a mess."

I knew he was saying it to intimidate me.

But it worked.

"On the other hand," Timmy said, accepting a little bottle of mineral water from his friend and sucking back half of it in one go, "you could just give us what we want and we'll give you a ride to anywhere you'd like to go. You'd be out of this business, we'd get to knock off early and hit the strip bars, and you'd even get a free taxi ride out of it. It's up to you. Are you a smart guy, Marcus, or are you a stupid guy?"

I tried to find peace and calm, but it wouldn't come. So I looked for anger, which is an easy place to get to from scared, and yeah, there it was. "You guys are so full of it," I said. "You must think I'm a complete tard. I open up my laptop and nuke the file, and then what, you believe that's my only copy and you let me go? Please. If that file is so important to you, you're never going to trust me."

Timmy laughed and thumped the car door. "Oh, Marcus. Come on, we're pros. We know how to do this kind of thing. We don't want to take you along with us if we don't have to. Where we're headed, it's a nice place, it's a reward and an honor to get assigned there. The people there, they're elite. You wouldn't fit in. If we have any choice in the matter, we'll leave you right where we found you."

I tried again for a poker face. Yeah, sure they'd leave me. In a garbage bag at the bottom of the San Francisco Bay.

"Or maybe you think we want to off you? Now *that* wouldn't make any sense. Smart guy like you, you'd have lots of copies where we couldn't find them, but where they'd be sure to come to light some day if you weren't around. We want your cooperation, and we can only get that for so long as you're alive."

"And so long as you've got something to lose," the other guy said. Bad cop.

"Show him," Timmy said. The guy in the front seat got out and walked around the car, closing the door behind him with another well-engineered *thunk*. The car rocked a little on its suspension as he opened it and got something out. His shoes crunched softly on the ground as he came back around and opened the passenger-side door and slid in. He was holding a heavy-duty ballistic plastic equipment case, another tactical black number, with big, chunky latches that had worn away a little to show glints of silver metal beneath the matte black paint. He thumbed the latches and opened the case, which made a little gasketty, rubbery sound as it opened. It had been filled with foam rubber with precise cutouts to accommodate a little black box, some wires, assorted discs of plastic and clips.

"Polygraph," the man said. It was such a pleasant surprise that I found myself on the verge of laughter.

"Polygraph" is the fancy, semiscientific name for a "lie detector," a machine that's supposed to be able to tell whether you're fibbing by measuring things like "galvanic skin response" (another science-y word, meaning "sweatiness") and your heart rate. They were invented in 1921, and, like many science-y things, people decided they were so complicated that they must work. This, of course, is an insane reason to believe something.

Lie detectors are crap. What they tell you is whether the person they've been hooked up to is sweaty, or whether his pulse has gone up, but that doesn't mean he's lying. Courts don't admit lie detector evidence for a reason.

But they're still made and they're still used—for much the same reason that people still wear crystals around their necks to cure their diseases or buy "homeopathic remedies" to get better. It's a combination of two distinct flavors of stupidity. I call the first one "It's better than nothing." I call the second one "It worked for me."

These delusions are why many big corporations, the U.S. military, and the FBI subject their people to lie detectors. Imagine that you're some kind of millionaire big-shot company executive, the founder of a chain of successful convenience stores. You need to hire a regional manager, and if you hire the wrong person, he or she might rob you blind and ruin you. You need to get this right.

So you pay some expensive "executive recruiting" company to find the right person. They have a big sales pitch: we're smart, we've been doing this for years, and best of all, we're *scientific*. We have "scientific personality tests" we'll administer to make sure you're getting the right person. And before you hire that person, we'll wire her up to our lie detector and ask her some important questions, like "Are you planning on robbing the company?" and "Are you a secret drug user?" and so on.

Science is awesome, right? A scientific recruiting company's going to be totally badass at finding you the right person, using the science of hiring-ology, and their science lab must have a bunch of Ph.D. hire-ologists. But you've heard that the polygraph is, you know, kind of sketchy. Does it really work?

"Oh, sure," the consultants tell you. "Not perfectly, of course. But nothing's perfect. Polygraphs, though, *sometimes* tell you when someone is lying, and isn't that better than nothing?"

(The correct answer is "probably not." Flipping a coin or sacrificing a goat would "sometimes" tell you if someone was lying, if you had enough lies and enough goats and you did it for long enough.)

Now, imagine you're a section chief at the FBI. You got your job by passing a lie detector test. You'd been wired up, you'd been asked if you were a secret communist islamofascist terrorist dope-fiend. You'd said "no," and the machine agreed. It works! Now, some people out there say that the machine's a piece of crap, but what do they know? After all, it not only worked on you, it worked on everyone you work with!

(Of course, everyone it didn't work on wasn't hired, or was hired even though they're snorting lines of meth through rolled up pages of *The Communist Manifesto* while they strap on their suicide bombs.)

The world is full of science-y crap. You probably know someone who wears a copper bracelet to "help with arthritis." They might as well burn a witch or cover themselves in blue mud and dance widdershins under a full moon. There's a chance either of those things will make them feel better, because of the placebo effect (when your brain convinces itself to stop feeling bad), but there are an alarming number of people who insist that because something "works" it must not be a placebo, it must be "real."

These guys wanted to wire me up to a lie detector and sacrifice a goat and figure out if I'd lied to them. They were big and tough and rich, they were faster than I was and infinitely better armed, but they'd let a witch doctor sell them a magical lie-catching talisman, and so I was going to absolutely pwn them.

They were total dicks about it, too. They watched me enter my password on my computer, making a show of recording it with yet another black rubber tactical gizmo (it was like these guys had an infinite supply of grown-up Tonka toys): a webcam with a white LED that lit my fingers with harsh, uncompromising light as I entered it. They watched as I fired up TrueCrypt and brought up my hidden partition, watched as I did a directory listing and showed them the files, watched as I nuked them.

"Okay, that's fine. But what about your backups, Marcus?"

Maybe they weren't totally stupid.

"I've got a lot of backups," I admitted. "But I think I can solve that problem for you."

"Yeah? Tell me." Timmy was smiling again, all his smile lines crinkling, making him look like he was really enjoying himself and wanted me to enjoy myself, too. I started to get the feeling that Timmy might wear exactly that smile if he was cutting off my fingers or taping electrical wires to my nuts.

"Well, I encrypt all my backups, of course."

"Of course."

"And I need a key to get at the backups, right?"

"Sure."

"So what if I delete the key?"

"Haven't you backed up the key?"

"Yeah," I said. "I'll need to get online and erase it in a few places. But once it's gone, everything is gone. It might as well be random noise."

The other guy—Knothead—was holding the webcam with its bright light shining at me, and I couldn't make out his face. But when Timmy shifted his attention to him, he lowered the light and I saw he was wearing a (tactical) earpiece. I wondered how many times these guys dropped something small and important on the floor and lost it forever as its black paint job rendered it invisible. I wondered if any of them had been goths in an earlier life.

Probably not.

Knothead raised one thick finger. He was listening to someone on the earpiece. So the webcam must be streaming over the net to someone else, a technical expert who was watching everything I did, helping them figure out what to do. He nodded twice, said, "Check that," and turned to us. "Do it," he said. "We'll polygraph him later."

Timmy said, "I'm about to give you a WiFi password for the car. You're going to get a chance to do what you say you're doing. We're going to see what you do. We're going to verify what you do. If we can verify it, you get to go home. It's that simple. Do we have a deal?"

Before I'd been afraid. Now I was afraid they'd see how happy I was. That was important, because what I was about to do depended on them believing that I was very, very nervous.

I keyed in the WiFi password and waited while I connected. I wondered what sort of link I was on. I figured if I were them, I'd be running everything through an SSL tunnel to a Tor router somewhere on the net, so that everything came through nicely anonymized. Why not? If it was good enough for paranoid freaks like me, it'd suit them just fine. That was the thing about this stuff. It worked equally well for everyone—people who had leaks, people who worried about leaks, people who leaked leaks. We were all smart enough to keep our paranoid packets bouncing around the net like hyperactive superballs.

Certainly, the connection was slow enough. I waited interminably as my computer logged in to the backup at home. "This is my home drive," I said. I typed in the passphrase that unlocked the key on my hard drive and caused it to be sent to the disk on my desk at home. I let the camera see my fingers enter the commands to securely delete the leaks files from my primary backup drive, overwriting them with three successive passes of random (or "random") data, then did a search on the drive to show that that was the only copy. "That drive synchs up to one at the hackerspace, Noisebridge." I logged out and logged in to Noisebridge's open shell, pwny, the connection crawling over its layers of misdirection and encryption. "I'm nuking it here." I did. "Noisebridge backs up to the cloud. It's not a drive I can control, but Noisebridge resynchs every five minutes, and here's where the process logs."

I opened the logfile with the "tail -f" command, which let us see new lines as they were being written to it. We waited in stuffy silence for the next synch, then watched as the log showed the Noisebridge server being compared to the remote copy, noticing that I'd deleted the leaks files and keys, and instructing that they be deleted on the other side as well.

I logged out. "Done."

"Do we believe him, Timmy?" said Knothead, in a teasing, mean way.

"Oh, I believe him, but you know what they say: 'Trust, but verify.' Your turn, buddy."

Knothead came around and opened the back door and swapped places with Timmy. He brought out each piece of his high-technology lie detector, examining it minutely, making sure I saw him do it. Back in the days of the Spanish Inquisition, the torturers had a thing called "showing the implements" where they showed the heretic the weird cutlery they had on hand to lift, separate, and disconnect all the moist, tender, painful places in his body. Knothead would have made a great inquisitor, and he even had the science background for it. It's a shame he was born five hundred years too late to get the job.

He fitted me with a blood-pressure cuff—yeah, it was a tactical cuff, which clearly made this guy as happy as a pig in shit—and then started in with the electrodes. He had a lot of electrodes and he was going to use 'em all, that much was clear. Each one went in over a smear of conductive jelly that came out of a disposable packet, like the ketchup packets you get at McDonald's. These, at least, were nontactical, emblazoned instead with German writing and an unfamiliar logo.

That was when I started puckering and unpuckering my anus.

Yes, you read that right. Here's the thing about lie detectors: they work by measuring the signs of nervousness, like increases in pulse, respiration, and yeah, sweatiness. The theory is that people get more nervous when they're lying, and that nervousness can be measured by the gadget.

This doesn't work so well. There's plenty of cool customers who're capable of lying without any outward signs of anxiety, because they're not feeling any anxiety. That's pretty much the definition of a sociopath, in fact: someone who doesn't have any reaction to a lie. So lie detectors work great, except when it comes to the most dangerous liars in the world. That's the "It's better than nothing" stupidity I mentioned before, remember?

But there're plenty of people who start off nervous—say, people who're nervous because they're taking a lie detector test on which depends their job or their freedom. Or someone who's been kidnapped by a couple of private mercenaries who've threatened to take him to their hideout if he doesn't cooperate.

But sometimes, lie detectors *can* tell the difference between normal nervousness and lying nervousness. Which is why it's useful to inject a few little extra signs of anxiety into the process. There are lots of ways to do this. Supposedly, spies used to keep a thumbtack in their shoe and they could wiggle their toes against it to make their nervous systems do the Charleston at just the right moment to make their "calm" state seem pretty damned nervous. So when they told a lie, any additional nervousness would be swamped by the crazy parasympathetic nervous system jitterbug their bodies were jangling through.

Thumbtacks in your shoe are overkill, though. They're fine for supermacho superspies for whom a punctured toe is a badge of honor. But if you ever need to beat a polygraph, just pucker up— your butt, that is.

Squeezing and releasing your butthole recruits many major muscle and nerve groups, gets a lot of blood flowing, and makes you look like you're at least as nervous as a liar, when all you're doing are some rhythmic bum-squeezes. As a side bonus, do it enough and you will have BUNS OF STEEL.

One of the reasons Noisebridge is such a cool place is that people experimented with stuff like this all the time. Someone heard about the butt-squeezing attack for polygraphs and told someone else, and before you knew it, we'd found a couple models cheap on eBay and were merrily hooking them up to one another and squeezing. You'd think that you could tell if the person you were talking to was clenching, but you'd be wrong. A little bit of practice and you can be a perfectly covert anus flexer.

480 | cory doctorow

"What day is it?" Knothead said.

"Wednesday," I said, clenching. This was how you started a lie detector session, by getting the answers to a bunch of questions you knew the answer to, so you could see what the normal, nonlying state looked like.

"Is your name Marcus Yallow?"

Clench. "Yes." Clench.

"Am I wearing a black jacket?"

Squeeze, squeeze. "Yes." *And a black shirt and black pants and black socks and a black belt.* Clench, clench.

"Were you given the tools to download and decrypt a file containing confidential documents by a confederate at the Burning Man festival in Nevada?"

"Yes." Squeeze. I was going to have an ass you could bounce quarters off of by the time this was done.

"Were you born in San Francisco?"

Clench. "Yes."

"Do you speak Latin?"

"No." Clench.

Knothead went on in this vein for quite some time. It was clear that he was going to be ultra-sure that he had precisely calibrated his gizmo before he got to the good stuff.

Then: "Did you delete your copies of this file?"

Squeeze. "Yes."

"Have you got any remaining copies of this file?"

"No." Clench.

"Is there any way for you to retrieve a copy of this file or its decrypted components?"

"Yes. Some of them have been published already. I can access those."

He snarled, but Timmy laughed. "He's got you there, buddy."

"Excluding the documents that are already in the public's hands, is there any way for you to retrieve a copy of this file or its decrypted components?"

"Yes. I assume I can still download the encrypted torrent file."

Knothead jabbed a finger that was as hard as a steel rod into a spot below my ribs and a scorching ball of pain radiated outward from the spot and I pitched forward, gasping, gagging, feeling like I'd puke.

"Puke on me and I'll twist your head off and shove it down your neck," Knothead said, in an absolutely conversational tone.

I kept gasping, but the air didn't want to come back in. Sip by sip, I refilled my lungs. I hadn't thrown up.

"Is that going to decalibrate the polygraph?" Timmy said, sounding slightly irritated at the thought. I didn't for a second think that he was irritated with his partner for hurting me.

"Nope," said Knothead. "Watch." He reached out and gave me a firm, but not hard, smack across the face. "Hey, Marcus, you ready for more questions?"

"Yes," I said, and squeezed automatically.

"Are you sorry you were such a smartdick?"

"Yes." Squeeze.

"Have you deleted all the copies you possess of the documents you were leaked?"

"Yes." Squeeze.

"Do you still have access to the keys to decrypt any other copies you might find?"

"No." Squeeze.

"Have you told anyone else about these documents, or given copies of them to anyone else?"

"No." I squeezed. This was the big one. This was the one that determined whether they hunted down Ange or Jolu or my other friends and gave them the same treatment I got—and did to them whatever would be done to me. I kept squeezing and releasing.

He showed Timmy the screen. Timmy cocked his head and listened to the voice in his headset briefly. "Roger," he said. Knothead turned off the gadget. "It's all good, buddy. Nice work. Let's take our little pal here where he wants to go. Where you want to go, Marcus? The malt shop? The drive-in? You got a Bible-study class we could take you to? Eagle scouts?"

"I can walk from here," I said. I was bathed in sweat, and wanted desperately to get out of the car. My eyes kept darting back to the handleless doors, my brain kept thinking, *This isn't a car, it's a rolling prison.* I was half certain that they were still planning to fill my pockets with rocks and chuck me into the Bay. That's what mercenaries did, right? Kill people.

"Now, don't be like that, sweetie pie," Timmy said. "We were friendly enough, weren't we? We're just guys with a job to do. And by the way, that job is protecting your butt from some really bad guys who'd love to blow up your house and put your mama in a burka. You've done your country a service tonight. You should be proud of yourself."

I didn't say anything. Everything I could think of saying was the sort of thing that would earn me another slap, another punch. Maybe worse.

"Where are we taking you, Marcus? Want to come to the titty bar with us?"

"I'll get out here."

He looked disgusted. "Suit yourself," he said.

Knothead ripped the electrodes off me and popped the door. I began to repack my bag, just throwing things in. As I reached for my multitool, Timmy snatched it up and dangled it. "You don't mind if I keep this, do you? As a memento, you know? Of our time campaigning together for truth and justice?" His eyes glittered with lunatic merriment and he suddenly looked more dangerous than Knothead. I shook my head.

"Keep it."

"Gosh, that's very nice of you, Marcus," he said. "Isn't that nice of him?"

Knothead laughed. I grabbed my bag and zipped it up, then shrugged into my jacket and set out walking. I didn't know exactly where I was, but it wasn't hard to figure out that walking away from the water would take me toward SoMa, and from there I could find Mission Street and walk all the way home, or catch a bus, or hop on BART. I got about twenty steps before I heard the car's big engine gun, and then I jumped to one side as the car roared past me, nearly clipping me. It was a final dick-move screw-you from Knothead and Timmy, a last reminder that I was a little pussy and they were big, tough guys. It was so petty it should have been laughable, but if it was so funny, why did I start crying?

Real, big, wet sobs, too, and snot running down my face. My

hands were shaking, and my legs wobbled under me. I felt like my backpack weighed a million pounds, and I slipped out of it and let it drop to the ground, not caring about my laptop.

I felt . . . *beaten*. Like I counted for nothing. Like I *was* nothing. I tried to comfort myself with the fact that they were stupid enough to believe a lie detector, the fact that I'd outsmarted them. It didn't matter. They were bigger, stronger, better funded. They believed in lie detectors because they'd taken lie detector tests and so had everyone they knew, so they "knew" that the tests worked. It was no different from people who believed in astrology or faith healing because everyone they knew believed, too. It didn't stop these guys from being more powerful and stronger than me.

I made myself stop crying, squeezed my eyes shut, and tried to get rid of that scratchy, weepy feeling. I shouldered my bag again. I started walking. I needed to get home, get in touch with Ange and Jolu, tell them about this. Tell them about *everything*. My broken nose ached. It was nearly midnight and I was supposed to be at work in a few hours, with a proposal for turning Joe's campaign into "Election 2.0." I had no idea what I was going to tell him.

Maybe I'd just tell him the mercenaries ate my homework.

I didn't make it home. Halfway to Mission Street, I kept going to Market, kept walking to Hayes Valley and Ange's place. I stood at her door, dithering. It was late and every light was off in the house, and the battery on my phone was dead so I couldn't even call. I was going to have to ring the bell and wake up the whole house. Or I was going to have to go home and spend the night alone. I couldn't face that.

I realized I could sit down on the front step, get out my laptop, log on to Ange's WiFi, and use Skype to call her phone and wake her up. It was a perverse way of making a phone call to a person who was about ten yards away from me, but it was also how I made my cell phone ring when I couldn't remember where I put it. Ange's window must have been open a crack because as the Skype call rang, I could hear her ringtone—the *Doctor Who* Tardis *whoosh-whoosh* sound—floating out over the street.

"Who is this?" Skype calls came up UNKNOWN NUMBER.

"It's me. I'm downstairs. Let me in."

"Downstairs where?"

"Downstairs here. Like, right below you." I heard movement over my computer's speakers and through the window and the bones of the house: Ange getting on a bathrobe and coming down the stairs. A moment later, the chain scraped on the door and the dead bolts snapped open and the door opened and there was Ange. My computer started to play a feedback squeal as Ange's phone got too close to it and I flipped the lid shut as she stabbed at her phone's screen with a finger to hang it up.

"Marcus?"

"Let me in, okay?"

I love Ange. She kissed me hard on the mouth, grabbed my hand, and pulled me inside the house. We went upstairs together, tiptoeing, and before I went into her room, I whispered, "Is your computer on?"

She cocked her head at me. "Yeah."

"Go shut it off, okay?"

I waited outside her door while she went into her room and moved around. She opened her door, holding her laptop in one hand and its battery in the other.

"I think you'd better tell me what's going on."

I thought I'd have the biggest news of the night, but I was wrong.

"How sure are you that your computer is safe?" Ange said, when I was finished telling her my story. It wasn't exactly what I was expecting her to say at that juncture.

"Yes, I'm fine, just a little shaken up, thank you for asking," I said.

"Forget that for now. Do you think your computer is clean? Do you trust it enough to get into the darknet?"

Only now did I notice what I should have seen right away. Ange was freaked out, too, and not just because of what I had to tell her.

"What is it?"

"Do. You. Trust. Your. Computer—"

"Yes, yes," I said. I woke it up and started typing and clicking.

"Search the database," she said. "Look for Zyz. That's zee-why-zee."

"What's a 'zyz'?"

She gave me a *don't ask stupid questions* look. I typed.

Zyz wasn't always called Zyz. It was once called Fireguard Security, and it was founded by an exec at Halliburton, a giant military contractor that sucked a bazillion dollars out of America's bank accounts selling pricey, underperforming military services to our troops all over the world, then followed up by helping to build a couple of semidefective, way-over-budget oil wells, including one that may yet be responsible for the sterilization of the Gulf of Mexico.

Halliburton had a "dynamic, thrusting young VP" (seriously, that's what *Fortune* magazine called him) named Chambers Martin, who quit the company in 2008 to found Fireguard, which immediately began to make major bank by taking U.S. Army contracts to guard Halliburton supply convoys in Iraq and Afghanistan.

So far, so normal. There are plenty of companies who bled out the taxpayer by providing bloodthirsty mercs. They guarded truckloads of Twinkies around Kandahar Province and Fallujah to restock the Forward Operating Bases that were a cross between an armed fortress and a minimall. The Army paid them enormous fees to have soldiers' clothes laundered and to supply Internet access and Pizza Hut.

But Fireguard had bigger plans. Rather than simply sucking up tax dollars for substandard services, they decided to become . . . a bank. Specifically, they began to issue bonds based on their anticipated future U.S. government contracts. The simplest bonds are basically loans: I sell you a bond for $100 with a five percent return and then I pay you $5 a year over the term of the bond (say, five years), and when the bond runs out its term, say, five years, we're done. Of course, if I go broke before the bond runs out, I go bankrupt and you're screwed.

Fireguard was selling its debt left, right, and center, paying top interest rates, telling everyone that the gravy train could never end, because every year they were taking in bigger military contracts, which meant that every year, they'd have more money on hand to make their bonds' payouts. It worked great, until the military drawdowns started to reduce their annual revenues, and they needed to branch out.

So they started trading bonds, instead of just issuing them, beginning with bonds issued on student loan debt. It turned out that every dollar I borrowed to go to Berkeley got turned into a bond—someone with money bought the right to get paid every time I made a payment on my debt. This made big bucks for Berkeley and for other universities and companies that "gave" students the loans they needed to get their magic diploma paper. Student debt bonds are even better than skeezy military contractor debt bonds because a skeezy military contractor can go bankrupt, but students can't.

Bet you didn't know that, huh? If you borrowed money to go to college and you someday find yourself so flat broke that you have to go bankrupt, all your debts will be wiped off the books—credit cards, car notes—but your student debts are immortal. And whenever you miss a payment, the scuzzy finance companies that buy the debts from universities are allowed to jack your debt up with monster fees and penalties, so if you owe $30,000 for college and $50,000 in credit card debt and you go bankrupt, you'll find the credit card debt reduced or eliminated, but your student debt might grow to *$150,000* after all the missed-payment fees are tacked on. The way student debt bankruptcy laws are set up, they can take money out of your *Social Security check* to pay the student loans you took out as a teenager, even if you've already paid *millions* in fees and penalties.

Zyz liked the sound of this. So they took the money that was coming in from the sale of their bonds and started buying up student debt. But not just any student debt: desperate, miserable student debt. Debt carried by the poorest people in America, who had put themselves into permanent hock just to try to get a better job than their parents had by getting a degree.

These people were in trouble. Getting a college degree (or, ahem, dropping out of college) hadn't led to them getting great jobs. They were unemployed, or working a ton of crappy part-time jobs to make rent, and they were missing payments like crazy. They had debts that they could never, ever pay off.

Enter Zyz. They had a dynamic, thrusting plan to get people to pay: straight-up thuggery. Zyz knew a lot about scaring, hurting, and chasing people. They had deep connections with Homeland Security, which meant access to databases of who lived where, who they were related to, what their tax returns said, how much income their parents, ex-spouses, grandparents, cousins, and school pals made. Zyz was . . . aggressive . . . about using this information. Thrusting, even.

So far, so sleazy. But it got worse. People who owed money to Zyz started to do things that were pretty out of character for them: a couple armed robberies, some burglaries, a little blackmail. A bunch of them joined the military, only to be discharged for being grossly unfit for service.

Why were they doing this? Because Zyz was providing them with "financial advice." As in "You'd better find some way to pay your bills, pal, or things could get very, very bad for you and the people you love." Zyz wasn't just a private military service, and they weren't just high-flying financial engineers: they were the mafia.

All this was contained in a series of memos, including a bunch of letters from attorneys general and district attorneys who'd gotten complaints from Zyz's "clients." Zyz, of course, denied everything, while simultaneously getting friends of theirs in state and national government, law-enforcement, and the DHS itself to keep everything calm and easy.

The most damning memo came from a San Francisco city attorney who'd heard too many nearly identical stories from Zyz clients, and had painstakingly built a case against them, with mountains of supporting documents (all also included in the docs), only to have her boss tell her to forget about it because "there wasn't sufficient evidence to justify an additional investigation at this time."

Well, this lady—I cheered her on as I read—wasn't going to take this lying down. She continued to collect stories from Zyz's victims, and to pick away at Zyz's finances, trying to find the "sufficient evidence" that would convince her boss. This continued right up to the time that her bank foreclosed on her house, citing payments in arrears. Being woken up at 6 A.M. and thrown out of her house with her husband and two small children turned her into a full-time, professional prisoner of a bureaucratic nightmare, trying to clear her name and credit and get her house back.

That's where her story ended, but not Zyz's. Zyz had hired lobbyists in every state capital in America—which must have cost a fortune, and gave me an idea of the kind of money they were sucking in from buying and selling their dirty bonds—to push for legislation that allowed them "greater leeway" in going after the assets of parents and even grandparents of ex-students who owed money, especially when the ex-students were living at home. Translation: if you owed for your student loans and were so broke you had to live with your parents (ahem), they wanted to go after your folks' house, their wages, and their pension. They didn't just want to wait to raid *your* Social Security check; they wanted to raid your grandma's Social Security.

These lobbyists had been busy everywhere, but especially in California, where youth unemployment was leading the country, and where, thanks to skyrocketing tuition in the UC state system, there were also record numbers of dropouts like me, whose student debts had come due early, and Zyz wanted our parents' dough.

Now that elections were coming up, Zyz was spreading around a lot of money. They had dozens of subsidiaries for doing this, but once again, some hardworking whistle-blower (his or her name was scrubbed out of the memo) had compiled a list of them and pointed out that they had donated to every "serious" candidate in every race, often backing opposing candidates—anyone who stood a chance of ending up on an important committee if she or he won the election.

Once the darknet team had known to search for Zyz, they'd

uncovered a *mountain* of stuff like this. Including something that jumped out at me: Zyz had hired a top-notch head of security with years of DHS and military experience: Carrie Johnstone.

"Holy crap," I said.

"Yeah," Ange said. "This is why they're so freaked out. This is their big push. They've been buying up all this debt—cheap bonds backed by student loans from really broke-ass kids. If they can go after those kids' families' houses, they'll make millions—hundreds of millions."

"So what happens if we go public?"

"*If* we go public? What do you mean, 'if'?" She was looking at me like I'd grown another head.

"Ange," I said, putting up my hands. "You know. These guys, you've read about them. They know who I am. They know I'm the guy who got the leaks from Masha. If this stuff gets out, they'll—"

"What? Marcus, they're insane criminals. You're not going to keep yourself safe by going along with them. If it suits them, they'll come after you again. And what about Masha? Those hacker creeps might've been total dicks, but they're right about her. She trusted you to be her insurance policy and instead you've spent your time cataloging the evidence—"

"Wait, what? I've spent my time? You've spent your time, too, Ange. We all agreed that we needed to go through the darknet docs before we put them out, find out what we had, decide on a strategy—"

"Marcus, that's what *you* wanted, so that's what we did. There was no reason you couldn't have just tweeted the torrent name and the key and said, 'DOWNLOAD THIS NOW. IT'S FULL OF CRIMINAL STUFF.' You've got what, ten thousand followers? Once you did that, the file would be unkillable."

"Masha's not unkillable," I shot back.

"You don't even know if she's working with those creeps—"

"Ange, come on, you're not making sense. A second ago, you were telling me how evil I was because I hadn't released the docs to save Masha. Now you're saying it doesn't matter if we put Masha in danger because *she* might be evil? Which one is it?"

Ange shook her head. "It doesn't matter. What matters is that you could be doing something here, and instead you're doing your run-in-circles-scream-and-shout act."

"I just want to have a *plan* before I do something, Ange. What's wrong with that?"

"I've got a plan for you, Marcus. Step one: tell everyone how to get to the docs. Step two: there is no step two."

I felt trapped. Our voices kept getting louder, and I was worried that we'd wake up Ange's mom and sister. If we'd been arguing in public—in a park or something—I might have gotten up and walked away to cool off. But it was going on 2 A.M. Where was I going to go? And of course, all this only made me *more* angry.

"Sure, it's that easy. Especially if you're not the one getting kidnapped and threatened."

She was ready for that one. "You don't think they've figured out who I am? You don't think I'm next on the list if we publish this stuff? Marcus, I don't *care* what happens to me. This is too important to let my safety come first. This is bigger than me."

"Nice of you to volunteer me to give up my safety, too."

"I didn't think I had to volunteer you, Marcus. I thought that M1k3y would be right there, ready to fight for what was right, rather than screwing around with getting everything perfectly organized and *safe* before he took action."

There it was. Pretty much everything I'd been afraid of, laid out by the one person I loved, trusted, and needed more than anyone else in the world. There's only one thing worse than being shredded unfairly by someone like that: being shredded when you deserve it.

"Ange—" I began.

"Forget it," she said. "Let's just go to sleep."

We lay in bed next to each other, like two marble statues, rigid, not touching. I kept replaying the discussions I'd had that day and that night, the anonymous hackers who'd been in my computer, the thugs from Zyz, and Ange, furious and disappointed with me. Around and around they went, a chorus of shame and accusations.

When they got too loud, I stood up and started putting on my clothes, fumbling in the dark. I heard Ange hold her breath, expel it, start to say something, stop.

Half-dressed, shoes undone, my bag hastily restuffed with my crap, I stepped out of Ange's room and let myself down the stairs and out the front door.

At least I'd had the foresight to charge my phone. I scrolled through the speed dial. I suppose I could have called my parents, but what could I say to them? How could they help?

There were two people in my speed dial I hadn't called in months and months. They'd been autosorted to the bottom of the list. Only the fact that I'd manually favorited them kept them from being dropped altogether.

Darryl and Van.

I let my thumb hover over Darryl's picture for a long second as I walked down toward Market Street, thinking of how awkward it had been to talk with him, knowing that Van had confessed her crush on me and not knowing whether Darryl knew it, knowing that Van and Ange had hated each other for years and that this couldn't have made it any better, wondering all the time whether Darryl hated me for being his rival or hated my girlfriend for whatever grievance Van held. The days between our talks had turned to weeks, the weeks to months. The longer the gap between conversations and meetings, the weirder and more uncomfortable it would be to get back in touch—the more it would seem like some special occasion.

It was cold now, and I was shivering, and once I started shivering, it felt like something inside me was giving way and then I was shivering for reasons other than the cold, and I pressed the button. It was after three in the morning. It rang and rang.

"Hi, this is Darryl. Leave a message, or better yet, send me a text or an email."

I hung up.

It was funny how I could feel all alone and under surveillance at the same time. I had ParanoidAndroid installed, but that didn't mean that my phone wasn't rooted—just that it would be harder to root. Had it been in my line of sight the whole time I'd been in the car with Knothead and Timmy had control over it? Had the creeps who'd taken over my laptop taken a run or two at my phone?

It was all for the best. Waking someone up at three in the morning while you're having a meltdown is no way to restart a friendship—

My phone rang. Darryl.

"Hey, man."

"Are you okay, Marcus?" He sounded so genuinely concerned I wanted to cry again.

Sorry, dude, just pressed the wrong button—butt-dialing. Sorry. Go back to sleep. The words were on the tip of my tongue. They wouldn't come.

"No," I said. "No, I'm not." A siren screamed past me, a fire engine, and I jumped and gave a little squeak.

"Where are you?" he said.

I looked up at the street signs. "Market and Guerrero."

"Stay there," he said. "Be there in fifteen."

Friends.

Darryl's dad hadn't lost his job in the Berkeley layoffs, though he'd taken a "voluntary" pay cut. But things weren't so bad that they'd sold their car, a ten-year-old Honda that Darryl had his own keys for. It was fugly and held together with bondo and good thoughts, but it was a car, and capable of getting from Twin Peaks to downtown in fifteen minutes at 3 A.M., though I'm guessing that Darryl blew through a few yellow lights and maybe a red or two to make that time.

It pulled up to the curb and the locks popped, and I opened the door and slid in, my nose filling with the familiar smell of the car, which I'd ridden in a million times before: old coffee, a hint of McDonald's breakfast sandwich, the baked/mildewed smell of a vehicle that had spent a lot of time with its windows rolled up in the alternating scorching heat and misty cool of the Berkeley campus.

He was wearing track pants and a T-shirt, and his feet were bare in his unlaced Converse, big toe poking through a hole in the right one. Darryl had humongous feet, and his shoes were always going out at the toes.

The first words he said weren't "What's wrong?" or "Do you know what time it is?" or "You owe me, buddy, big time."

The first words he said were, "It's great to see you again, bud."

It was the best thing he could have said. "Yeah," I said. "Yeah, it's great to see you, too."

I tried to find some words, some place to start the story. He knew about the darknet, had been going through the docs. Presumably, he'd seen the Zyz docs, helped to assemble them. But there was so much to say, and I couldn't figure out where to begin. I closed my eyes to think and the next thing I knew, he was shaking me awake. I ungummed my eyelids and looked around. We were outside his dad's place, which had once been as familiar to me as my own home.

"Come on, bud," he said, "up you go."

I stumbled after him, scuffing my boots on the ground, kicking them off in the doorway, trailing after him up to the bedroom.

I barely registered that Van was in his bed, sitting up in the dark, wearing a T-shirt, hair in a crazy anime-spray. "Hey, Van," I said, as Darryl steered me to the narrow camping mattress that was already laid out at the foot of the bed. I flopped down on it, eyes closing before my head hit the pillow. Someone—Darryl—tried to make me roll off the bed so that he could pull the spare blanket out from under me and cover me with it, but I wasn't budging. I was made of lead. My body knew that it was somewhere safe, with people I could trust, and it was not going to allow me to keep it awake one second longer. A half-formed thought about setting an alarm so I wouldn't be late for work crossed my mind, but my hands were as heavy as cinder blocks, and my phone was a million miles away in my pocket. Besides, I was already asleep.

I woke to the smells of bacon and eggs and toast and, most of all, coffee. The bedroom was empty, filled with gray light filtering through the heavy blinds. I pulled them aside and saw that it was broad daylight. I checked my phone, noting the ache as I pulled it out—I'd slept on it—and saw that it was 11:24. I was incredibly late for work. My adrenals tried to fire and fill me with panic, but I was empty. Instead, I felt a kind of low-grade anxiety as I had a quick pee and headed downstairs into the sunny kitchen.

The light dazzled me and I shaded my eyes, provoking laughter from Darryl and Van, who were dancing around the kitchen in a clatter of pans and plates and glasses and mugs.

"Told you that'd get him up," Darryl said. "The boy thinks with his stomach."

Van giggled. "That's a good six inches higher than most boys' thought-centers." They smooched. Were Ange and I this sickening? Probably, I decided.

"Guys," I said. "I really, really owe you, but I can't stay for breakfast. I'm late—"

"For work," Darryl said. "I know. Which is why I called your mom and she called your boss and told him you were feeling poorly and would work from home for the morning and try to come in this afternoon. You're covered, bro. Sit and eat."

Friends! Did it get any better? I poked my nose toward the stove where a little caffettiera was starting to bubble. If you have to make coffee, a caffettiera isn't the worst way to do it, but they're tricky to get right. They're basically a double boiler: you fill the bottom part with water, the top with ground coffee, and you put it straight on the stove. The water heats up and expands and the pressure forces it through the coffee and into the top of the pot. But they have a tendency to get too hot, and the superhot water extracts all the worst, most bitter acids, making a cup of strong, nasty coffee that needs a gallon of milk and a pound of sugar to drown out the ick.

"Let me in," I said, twisting the burner off, grabbing a kitchen towel and running it under the cold tap and then wrapping it around the boiler, cooling down the water and stopping the extraction. I gave it a three-count, then unscrewed the top section. Ideally, you'd want to cool it all off even faster, but caffettiera have a tendency to crack if they change temperature too fast. I'd found that out the hard way in an adventure involving a bowl full of ice water, a caffettiera, and a mess that took most of the day to clean up. At least I didn't blow my hand off when the cast-iron boiler shattered.

"Marcus," Darryl said, "it's only coffee."

"Yeah," I said. "It's only coffee. What's your point?" I reached for the cupboard where the little espresso cups I'd given Darryl for Christmas years ago were kept, automatically remembering which cupboard that was, and I fished down three cups and poured out the coffee. I tasted mine. It wasn't terrible. It was almost good.

Darryl grabbed another and had a sip, then nodded. "Okay, that's better than anything I make."

Van tried hers. "Darryl, that's *amazing*. Come on, give the man credit where credit's due."

Darryl faked a little bow at me. "Sir, you astound me with your coffee prowess. Prithee, place thine butt in yonder chair so that I might proffer you a repast of finest fried victuals."

Van swatted him on the ass and I sat down and food appeared before me, with knife and fork and Tabasco—which reminded me of Ange and sent a knife through my heart—and even a multivitamin.

Darryl and Van sat, too, and we turned food into dirty dishes and then I turned the dirty dishes into clean ones while Darryl found some tunes and put them on and Van had a shower, coming back down with her hair wrapped in a towel, dressed in a little skirt and a loose, floppy cotton top that hung down as low as the skirt. She looked amazing, and I found myself staring for longer than was polite. She caught me at it and gave me a weird look and I looked away.

"You ready to talk about it?" Darryl said.

"Not really," I said. "But I guess I'd better."

Telling it again, the day after, with a full stomach, felt a little like I was recounting the plot of a movie I'd seen and less like I was telling the story of something that had happened to *me*. I found myself discoursing on weird details I'd noticed, like the Zyz guys' tactical gear obsession, which provoked comforting hoots of laughter from Van, making it all seem more like a well-worn story of my life, rather than a source of imminent doom. Darryl and Van knew about Zyz, so I was able to skip over that part of my talk with Ange, which left me with the part where she'd told me I was a coward and a jerk for not putting my life at risk. Or at least, that's how it came out.

They made sympathetic faces and noises, and I felt better in a way that was also kind of bad. Like I knew that I'd made myself to be the hero of a story that I didn't deserve to be the hero of.

"Jesus, Marcus, what a frigging *nightmare*," Van said.

"So what are you going to do?" Darryl said.

Van gave him an impatient look. "What do you think? He's going to walk away from this. He's right: this is too risky for him. It's not his fight."

Darryl had been holding her hand, and he let go of it. "Come on, he can't do that. For one thing, there's other people involved now. Even if he stops, they won't."

Van folded her arms. "Jolu will shut it down if Marcus tells him to. Problem solved."

It was amazing. They'd gone from being a cuddly couple to furious in seconds. It made me realize how infrequently I bickered with Ange, and how little I knew about their relationship. I tried to say something, but Darryl was already speaking.

"No, he won't. He can't and he shouldn't. The stuff about Zyz, all that other stuff, it *needs* to come out."

"Oh really? And why does it *need* to come out? Is it going to solve anything? Don't you think that everyone already knows that the whole system is rotten? Do you think a bunch of anonymous, unverified Internet rumors are going to make people rise up and take action? Throw off their chains and free the world? Come on, Darryl. After everything you've been through—"

Darryl stood up abruptly. "Going for a walk," he said. He was out the door before I could say anything. Darryl had had it worse than me, had been in Gitmo-by-the-Bay for *months*. They'd held him in solitary, messed with his mind, hurt him in ways that showed and ways that didn't. He'd spent a month in the hospital under observation before they let him out. No one ever said it out loud, but I knew they'd had him on suicide watch.

Van had tears in her eyes. "He is such an idiot sometimes," she said. "What's wrong with wanting to be safe? Where does he get off making *you* take the risk for someone else's principles?"

I didn't have anything to say to that. Of course, they weren't someone else's principles, they were mine. Or they had been, before

I'd had the principles terrorized out of me. How was it that Darryl had gone through so much more than I had but had emerged so fearless? Was he the broken one, or was I?

Van was crying now. I gave her a half-assed hug and she put her face on my shoulder and really cried, hard. She'd kissed me, just once, hard on the mouth, when she'd come through for me and helped me get a message through to Barbara Stratford at the *Bay Guardian*. That's when she'd confessed to me that she had a thing for me, and we'd never spoken about it since. At that moment, it was all I could think about. Between the fight with Ange and the events of the past few days and the strain, I felt like I was about to do something really, really stupid, like kiss her again.

I let go of her and stood up. My shoulder was wet with her tears. She looked up at me, tears streaking her face. I felt like I might cry, too. "I'm going to go find Darryl," I said. "He shouldn't be alone."

It was only once I was out the door that I wondered how Van felt about being alone.

I found Darryl exactly where I expected to find him: a little dog run up the hill from his house that had a commanding view of a valley bowl that swept back up the hills on the other side, to more hills, set below the weird semihuman shape of Sutro Tower, the broadcast antenna that looked like an alien with its hands held up in surrender. It's where we'd always snuck off to when we were up to no good—a covert joint or an illicit bottle of something, even a couple of epic firecracker experiments, which had miraculously failed to blind or maim us. Judging by the number of times we'd found roaches, bottles, and used-up firecrackers up there, we were hardly the only ones.

Darryl was sitting on the graffiti-carved bench looking down at the valley and the cars below, staring into the middle distance and seeing nothing, I guessed. I sat down next to him.

"I don't know how you can be so brave," I said. "I really don't. I wish I could do it."

He made a noise that sounded a bit like a laugh, but with no humor in it. "Brave? Marcus, I'm not brave. I'm *pissed*. All the time, do you understand that? A hundred times a day, I feel like I could beat someone's head in. Mostly *hers*." I didn't have to ask who "her" was—Carrie Johnstone, the woman of my nightmares. Darryl's, too. "I get *so* angry, so *fast*. It's like I'm watching myself from outside myself.

"You got to *do* something. I was locked away. I couldn't do anything. I couldn't help spread the Xnet, or go to big demonstrations, or jam with the other Xnetters. I sat in that room, naked, alone, for hours and hours and hours, nothing in there but my thoughts, my voices."

I'd never really thought of myself as *lucky* for being where I had been after the DHS took over San Francisco, but now that I looked at it from Darryl's point of view, I had to admit that yeah, it could have been a lot worse. I tried to imagine what it would have been like to be totally helpless and alone, instead of with all these amazing friends and people who looked up to me and hailed me.

"I'm sorry, D," I said.

"It's not your fault," he said. "I don't want to put this on you. It's my own damned problem." He swallowed a couple times. "It's partly why I hadn't been around much for you lately. Didn't want to say something, you know, ugly. Because I know you did what you did for me." Had I? Maybe a little. But I also did it for me, for the humiliation and suffering and fear, to try and get past all that. "But when Jolu told me about the darknet, when I saw those documents, I felt, like, all right, now it's my turn. Now I can finally *do* something about all the nastiness and corruption and evil in the world.

"But Van, she's not down for that. She just wants me to be safe. I get that. But she doesn't understand how being 'safe' means that I can't be *whole* again, can't get demons out of my head. I need to make something right, I need to be the star of my own movie for a change."

"Jeez, D, man—" I couldn't really find the words. I guess I'd suspected some of this, but I don't think I'd ever imagined that Darryl would ever say these words to me. It wasn't the kind of thing that guys said to each other—not even guys who were as close as brothers, the way we had been.

"Yeah," he said. "It sure is a bitch, isn't it?"

"So what do you want to do?" I said.

"What do *I* want to do?"

"Yeah," I said. "Yeah. What do *you* want to do? Not 'What do you think I should do?' or 'What do you think is the safest thing to do?' What does Darryl Glover want to do, right now, today?"

He looked down at his hands. His fingernails were chewed ragged, his cuticles dotted with little scabs from where he'd chewed them bloody. He'd done that as a kid, but he'd stopped when we were both fourteen. I didn't know he'd started again.

"I want to release the whole thing. Today. Now."

"Yeah," I said. "Yeah, that sounds about right. Let's fucking do it."

Van didn't like it, but she got in the car with us. Darryl drove carefully and slowly, but I was in the passenger seat and I could see how his hands were shaking. We snarled in traffic in SoMa, and Darryl showed off his encyclopedic knowledge of the alleyways of the neighborhood to beat it, popping out on Market Street from an alleyway that was so narrow we scraped up a couple of plastic recycling wheelie-bins on our way out. He was in Hayes Valley a few minutes later, pulling up in front of Ange's house. I knew she didn't have any classes that afternoon, but she hadn't answered her phone when I called her. I thumped on her door.

She came down in track pants and the T-shirt she'd slept in the night before, her eyes swollen and red. She folded her arms when she saw me and glared. "Get dressed, okay?" I said. "You can be pissed at me later. Get dressed." She looked over my shoulder at Darryl, who waved at her. Van gave a half-assed, unenthusiastic wave, too.

"You're kidding me," she said.

"Get dressed," I said. "It's happening."

She gave me a long, searching look. I looked back at her, thinking, *Come on, Ange, argue later, do this now before I lose my nerve.* My heart was fluttering in my chest like a pigeon trapped in a store, beating against the windows and trying to break out.

She turned on her heel and disappeared into the house. I heard her run up the stairs to her room. A minute later, her little sister, Tina, appeared in the hallway. "You remember when I told you if you broke her heart I'd pull your scrotum over your head?" She was two years younger than Ange, and tall and skinny where Ange was short and curvy, but they were unmistakably sisters, with nearly the same voice and facial expressions.

"I remember, Tina. Can we save the scrotal reconfiguration for later? We're kind of into something more important than me or Ange or any of us."

She cocked her head. "I'll think about it."

Ange came pelting down the stairs, toothpaste on the corner of her mouth. She was wearing a long electric-blue raincoat I loved and hand-painted Keds and huge, squarish Japanese pants she'd sewn herself from a pattern, all clothes that had been strewn on the floor of her room the last time I'd been in it, a hundred years ago, the night before.

"Tina, enough with the scrotums, already," Ange said as she reached us. Tina made an exaggerated, monkeylike face at her and then gave her a kiss on the cheek. "Come on," Ange said to me, whisking past me toward Darryl's car, hesitating for a second before yanking open the back door and sliding into the seat next to Van. I brought up the rear and got into the passenger seat, checking out whether Van and Ange were ready to kill each other while trying to look like I wasn't checking it out at all.

Inside the car, the tension was as thick as the fog on a wet night on Twin Peaks.

"You know where Jolu's office is, right?" I said to Darryl.

"We're going to see Jolu?" Ange said.

"I told you," I said. "It's happening. And if it's going to happen, we should all be there, in person. Better than worrying about our computers or phones being tapped."

Ange took her phone out of her purse and switched it off. I did the same, and so did Van. Darryl dug his phone out and handed it to me, and I did the same for him.

"Okay," Ange said.

Darryl said, "Yeah, I know where he works." We were halfway there already. Darryl had an almost mystical knack for beating San Francisco traffic. He could have been the world's greatest cab driver or getaway man.

"What's the plan?" Ange said as we got closer.

Van said, "They don't have a *plan*. They just got in the car and started driving."

I looked over my shoulder at Ange, who was nodding. "Yeah," she said. "That sounds like them."

The two women looked at each other for a moment. I tried not to hold my breath. They'd disliked each other since eighth grade, and while I'd never gotten the whole story, I assumed that it was one of those old grievances that takes on a life of its own, so that the reason you don't get along is that you don't get along.

They stopped looking. I turned back around. A few seconds later, Van said, conversationally, "You got a lawyer?"

Ange said, "Not really. There was the public defender and that guy from the ACLU, back in the Gitmo-by-the-Bay days, but no one who's really *my* lawyer."

"Yeah," Van said. "Did you have the woman from ACLU, or the guy?"

"Both. But the woman really seemed like she knew her stuff. What was her name?"

"Alyssa? Alanna?"

"Elana," Ange said. "She was great."

"So I was thinking we should write a lawyer's number on our arms, you know, just in case. One phone call, right? Don't want to waste it calling directory assistance."

"I'm pretty sure I've got her number in my email." I heard Ange open her computer, enter her password.

"Here's a Sharpie."

There was some mutual arm-scribbling.

"Not so big," Ange said.

"If I write it this big, the rest of us will be able to read it from across the room, even if ours has been washed off or, you know, whatever."

"Good point," Ange said. "Here, roll up your sleeve."

"You really think if we get busted anyone's going to let us talk to a lawyer?" I asked, secretly pleased at how civilized the two of them were being to each other.

"You shut up," Ange said. "Wouldn't you feel like a total moron if we *did* get a phone call and you didn't have a number? Idiot."

"Yeah, dude," Darryl said.

"You shut up, too," Van said. "And hold your arm out at the next red light."

I rolled up my sleeve and twisted to stick my arm into the back seat. Ange's fingers grabbed around my wrist and yanked painfully. I yelped, and she made a disgusted noise. "Silence," she said, and I felt the tickle of the Sharpie moving over my arm. It seemed to be taking an awfully long time. When I finally got my arm back, I saw that she'd made sour faces of the 0s and skulls out of the 8s. I decided that this was a gesture of affection. At least, it comforted me to think of it that way.

Jolu's little startup was three guys and a woman sharing two desks in the back of a bigger, richer startup, crammed together with four broken-down Aeron chairs that looked like they'd been in continuous use since the dot-com boom of the last century, more duct tape than original mesh. Jolu noticed us as we threaded our way down the office, past the desks of people from the bigger startup—some kind of analytics company that I'd vaguely heard of—toward him. He took a moment to assess the fact that all four of us were together, and quietly tapped one of his coworkers, the woman, on the shoulder, stood and moved to intercept us.

"Let's go to the meeting room," he said, pointing back the way we'd come.

The meeting room was barely big enough for all of us to fit in, and the meeting table was a converted ping-pong table (there was a net and paddles tucked onto one of the room's crowded shelves). But it had a door, and Jolu closed it.

"Everyone, this is Kylie Deveau," he said, pointing to his coworker, a pretty black woman a little older than us, with short hair and red-framed round-lensed wire-rim glasses. She smiled and shook hands all around.

"You must be the darknet," she said. "Pleased to meet you in the flesh."

"Kylie started the company," Jolu said. "I couldn't do darknet without letting her in on it."

"Yeah," I said. "I guess it wouldn't be fair."

"No," Jolu said. "Well, yeah. But I told Kylie because I figured that she was smarter than the rest of us put together." Kylie made a small pretend-bow. "She's the one who found the Zyz stuff in the first place. I assume that's why you are all here, right? Or is there some other enormous, terrible conspiracy I'm about to expose that I should know about?"

"No," I said. "Just that one. Nice to meet you, Kylie. Let me tell you about some people I ran into last night. Well, I say people, but the first batch could have been ghosts or super-intelligent LOLCats for all I know, and the second batch were more like gorillas or possibly hyenas."

"I can tell this is going to be good," Jolu said, and sat down.

Kylie said, "Well, I can see why you want to get this out now."

Darryl said, "You do? Because I keep feeling like it's suicidal." I winced when he used the word, thinking of all the shrinks who'd felt the need to keep Darryl under observation for all that time.

Kylie smiled. "It just might be. But doing nothing is entirely suicidal, isn't it? It's not like these characters are going to ignore the fact that you're still out here, not forever. I'm guessing that they only let you go because they'd had to act fast and hadn't had a chance to figure out how to put you away without sticking out their own necks. But from what we've seen, they've got a lot of juice with a lot of different agencies, enough to take away city attorneys' houses, anyway. I don't suppose it'd be hard for them to figure out a way to get the police to take a special interest in you."

"You know," I said, "I hadn't even thought about that until now. I'd only gotten as far as them putting a bag over my head and sticking me in a plane to Yemen or something."

Kylie said, "That sounds expensive. You know what jet fuel costs, these days? Much cheaper to get someone else to bear the expense. These guys are the world's biggest welfare queens, after all—suck up government money in military contracts, use it to issue bonds, get the government to pass laws that make your bonds into safer bets, then go after even bigger and better laws. I'm guessing they never spend a penny if they can get Uncle Sucker to foot the bill.

"No, I bet last night was all about making sure that if they *did* send the law after you that you wouldn't somehow get out of it, say, by revealing a giant trove of documents about all kinds of illegal activity. Which is why I think it's right for you to act now, because the next thing that's going to happen, I bet, is that someone from some law-enforcement agency is going to get an important phone call, maybe just about you, or maybe about you and all your friends, because they *know* who your friends are from last time around, and when that happens, it's going to be much harder for you to get the truth out there—"

I put my hands up. "I get the picture." I looked around at my friends—my oldest, best friends. Ange was looking a little pale, her hands clasped in front of her on the table, white-knuckled, the lawyer's number written in Van's familiar handwriting on her arm. Darryl, too, was looking sick and scared. Jolu, as always, was as cool as a movie star, though I could recognize the subtle signs around his eyes and the corners of his mouth, the vein that stood out faintly on his forehead and the pulse thudding in his throat. But Van—well, she looked grimly determined, and not at all scared. "So we'd better do it, right?" she said.

Jolu nodded. "It's time, all right. I wrote a script that would nuke our chats on the darknet site and erase all the logs and scrub our handles from the notes in the database."

"You wrote that script, huh?" Van said.

Jolu smiled his movie-star smile. "Yeah, the first night. I figured that there was a good chance we'd have to open up the site in a hurry, so I figured what the hell, better beat the rush. Stitch in time saves nine."

"That's a great motto, Jolu," Ange said. "Beats the shit out of 'When in trouble or in doubt, run in circles, scream and shout.'" I winced.

Jolu shrugged. "I don't want to get in the middle of whatever you two are into, Ange, but you know, there's a time and place for running in circles, too. We all got our own superpowers."

Darryl laughed nervously. "Yeah, he wouldn't be Marcus if he didn't do that scream-and-shout thing, right?"

"Guys," I said, "I'm here. I can hear you."

"Shut up, sweetheart," Ange said. But she leaned across the table and took my hand and gave it a squeeze. I squeezed back and she hauled back, dragging me across the table to her and she grabbed my head with her other hand and gave me a ferocious kiss. "You're an idiot," she said, when we were done. "But you're my idiot. Don't you ever run out on me after an argument again or I'm going to start sitting on you whenever you lose a fight until I'm sure you won't turn rabbit."

"*Daww,*" Jolu said. "Isn't young love *sweet*?"

"Actually," Van said, "it is." And Darryl got up and came around the table and wrapped her up in his long arms and hugged her so hard I heard her ribs creak.

Kylie said, "Children, love is sweet and important indeed, but we've got a job to do. Mr. Torrez, I believe you mentioned a script you have ready to run?"

Jolu thunked at his keyboard. "Done."

Darryl stuck his hand up. "So what I was thinking, you know, is that we should start by getting in touch with those weirdos who'd been spying on Marcus. They sure seemed to have a good idea about how to get people to notice what they had to say."

I bit my tongue. If I hadn't been kidnapped by two totally evil mercenaries after my run-in with the ghosts in my machine, I think my head would have exploded in rage at the suggestion that we should work with those total creeps. As it was, my creepiness scale had been radically recalibrated in the last day or so, and while the spooks who'd rooted my machine might have rated a nine the week before, now they were about a six, and falling fast.

Ange spoke up for me, though. "I don't think that's fair to Marcus, Darryl. They were spying on *him,* after all. They violated his privacy all the way, from asshole to appetite. I don't think that's the kind of people we want to work with."

I relaxed a little. Good old Ange.

"So what do you propose?" Darryl said. His body language was noticeably more on edge than it had been a second before. I remembered his confession in the park, his desire to get a chance to be the star of his own movie for a change. I'm sure it sucked to have someone else second-guess his awesome action-hero plan. But screw it, those guys were still creeps.

"We tell it to the press. Mail a link to Barbara Stratford, anonymously, tell her how to access the darknet. Of all the journalists in the world, she's probably the most likely to be able to figure out how to use a Tor darknet site. And if she can't figure it out, she'll know lots of hairfaces who can help her out." Barbara Stratford was a muckraking journo who wrote for the *Bay Guardian*. She was an old friend of my folks, and had led the effort to spring me from the clutches of Carrie Johnstone's torturers. But she was a traditional print journalist with a lot to lose, and she moved with a lot of plodding caution.

"That sounds *slow*," Darryl said. "What's she going to do, read all those docs, call up a second source to corroborate them, run it past legal, write a story, and file it for publication in next week's issue? We need this stuff to go live *now*."

Ange opened her mouth to argue, but Jolu held a hand up. "No reason we can't do both. We tell your reporter friend about it, but we also post the darknet address where anyone can find it."

"How?" I said. I'd been thinking about this. How do you publicize something while staying anonymous?

Jolu shrugged. "Create a new Twitter account, use it from behind IPredator. Create a new WordPress blog, do the same thing. Make a new Facebook identity, put it there, too."

I shook my head. "That'll never work. Who pays attention to a Twitter account that's just been created?"

"Well, you could retweet it, you've got thousands of followers. Or I could."

"Yeah, and I could just make a blinking EL wire sign that says 'That anonymous account? It's really me.'"

"Good point," Darryl said. "So we find someone we trust, and ask that person to ask *their* friends to big it up, link to it, retweet it, friend it, whatever. Make it hard to trace it back."

Now Jolu was shaking his head. "Sorry, dude. Remember that they'll be doing this on social networks—you know, places where they've conveniently laid out lists of all their friends for the whole world to see. All you do is, slurp up all those contacts, check to see which contact *they* have in common, and there you go, a convenient list of high-probability suspects to spy on or assassinate with your aerial drones."

Darryl shut up and glared at the table. Jolu stayed cool. "Sorry, man, but you know, it's just *reality*. It's not convenient, but it's real."

Through this all, Van had been hanging back a little, not really seeming to be engaged with us. Now she said, "Kylie, Jolu says you're the smartest person he knows, and he's a smart guy. So what do you think we should do?"

"Well, let me start by saying this is a hard problem. Maybe *the* hard problem today. You've got the same problem anyone who wants to attract attention to a product or a cause has. This is what every politician faces, everyone who makes soda pop or opens a restaurant, everyone who wants to sell a record or get people to come to their little league games. It's the reason that ad agencies and marketing companies exist, it's the basis for billions of dollars in business every year. And you've got the additional complications of wanting to make this stuff happen in a hurry, and of not wanting anyone to know who's behind it. What I mean to say here is, you're doing something *hard*.

"Now, all that said, there's at least two important things going for you here: first, you're *good*, you know a lot about computers and networks and people and technology. And second, you've got a great 'product' to 'sell'. I've been in those docs, I know the kind of dynamite you're sitting on. You're not trying to get people to give a damn about yet another flavor of sugar-water. You want to tell people about a trove of some genuinely explosive materiel, a pile of information plutonium that you've dug up in the government's backyard. There's a certain intrinsic interest in this stuff, you know, and it's the kind of thing that people might enjoy telling each other about.

"I think our best strategy is going to be sending out messages from our new account, messages to anyone we can think of with any political clout or a lot of followers or a big platform of some description. Your basic 'Hey mister, look what I've got' message.

Most of these people are going to ignore us, initially at least, because they get a bazillion of these every day, from con artists and spammers and PR people and nutcases. But we've got to think like dandelions here."

"What do you mean?" Van said. I could tell that she liked Kylie, saw her as a potential ally in her role as designated grown-up and worry-wart. I liked her, too—she talked like I wished I could talk, saying the stuff I thought better than I could.

"Well, we're mammals, so we tend to think of reproduction as being expensive and precious. When we want to copy ourselves, we take ourselves out of commission for months, then commit years of more-or-less full-time work to making sure our copies survive." I wasn't sure if I liked being talked about as a "copy" of my parents, but I couldn't deny the underlying truth. "But look at a dandelion: by the time it's seeding, it's made thousands of potential copies of itself, all those little bits of fluff that make up the puffball. When a gust of wind comes along, the dandelion doesn't follow all its children to make sure they get steered in the right direction and have their mittens and a packed lunch with them. Almost every seed a dandelion tosses into the wind is going to die without taking root, but that's not what matters to a dandelion. Dandelions don't care that every seed survives: they care that every opportunity to take root is exploited. A successful dandelion is one that colonizes every crack in the sidewalk, not one that successfully plants all its seeds.

"Sending out messages about the darknet shouldn't cost much. It's probably worth tailoring each message a little to the people we're spamming—put their name in the message, mention some kind of fit with what they do. But keep it down to less than a minute for each message, dandelion style. The important thing isn't to make sure that everyone we hit repeats the story, but rather to make sure that everyone who *might* give us a little signal boost knows that the story is out there to be boosted."

"And if that doesn't work?" I said. It all seemed a little too easy, too pat.

"We try something else," she said.

"And if a snatch squad takes us away and throws us in the

510 | cory doctorow

ocean with weights around our ankles before we can try something else?" Kylie gave me a look down her nose.

Van leapt in. "Marcus, I know you've got a reason to be worried, but honestly, what else can we do? It's not like you've got a better idea, right? You and Darryl decided it was time to do this, and we're all going along with it, but don't just shoot down everything—that's not fair."

I briefly reconsidered trying to get in touch with the creeps who'd been spying on me, but I didn't want to do that—and I didn't know how, either. Half of me wanted to just say screw it, and start shouting it all from the mountaintops, using my own accounts, which had plenty of followers. It'd probably cost me my job, but hell, if it was a race to make this well known before Zyz could come after me, that was more important than a paycheck I might never get to cash. The other half of me was, well, *scared*. The thing about Kylie's suggestion was that it sounded a lot safer.

"Fine," I said. "But when we all get sent to a secret prison in Afghanistan, don't come crying to me."

Darryl gave us a ride back to Ange's place. We flopped around her room as we had a million times before, perching with our computers on our laps, quickly researching people who might pick up our message, tailoring it for each one, and firing it out using the anonymous accounts that we'd cooked up at Jolu's office. We used both IPredator and Tor to do the research and messaging, which slowed us down somewhat—so to compensate we each targeted several people at once, using multiple tabs, cycling from one to the next. Jolu had offered to whip up *another* darknet site where we could all coordinate who we were spamming and what the response had been to avoid double-dipping, but Kylie had just said, "You're not thinking like a dandelion, Jolu," and he'd dropped the idea.

Ange and I had been on edge when we got back to her room, still smarting from the fight we'd had the night before, but we both quickly lost ourselves in the work and forgot about the fight. Soon we were joking and teasing the way we usually did—Ange started it when I got too engrossed in reading the bio of the Woz, the legendary engineering wizard who'd co-founded Apple, who had millions of Twitter followers. I was in a real Wikipedia clicktrance, following link after link to information about his achievements and career and all the awesome hacks he'd pulled off.

Ange threw a pencil at my head and said, "Hey, mister, I don't hear any typing. Are you thinking like a dandelion or a mammal?" I snorted and gave her the finger, but I also stopped screwing around and sent off the message.

We ate dinner in her room—PB&J sandwiches that we'd made together in the kitchen, and yeah, Ange even put hot sauce on that, which actually tasted pretty good, like Indonesian curry—and then she kicked me out. "You've got to go to work tomorrow," she said. "You can't afford to miss two days in a row."

I let myself be pushed out and spent the whole bus ride home reloading a search for links to our darknet site on my phone. There were a few, a couple dozen, but of course it was *hard* to figure out the darknet—you had to install Tor on your computer, and then you had to figure out how to use it, installing something like Tor-button in your browser. Even I forgot how to get it installed and had to look up the docs every time I set up a new computer. I swore to myself that if I made it out of this mess alive and intact, I'd throw myself into the work of the Noisebridge hackers who were always messing around with making Tor easier to use.

I was bone-tired. I'd hardly slept the night before, and my adrenals had been bashing my body around like a punching bag for the past seventy-two hours—plus I still had my stupid, aching broken nose and assorted bruises from Burning Man, not to mention the lasting effects of a week spent in the desert. It's a good thing Mom and Dad were so caught up in their own problems—if they'd been paying the kind of attention they used to give me back when I was sixteen, they'd have had a total freakout.

And yeah, that made me feel pretty rotten, too—lying there in my bed, setting the alarm on the glowing bedside nixie-tube clock I'd built, aching and stupid-feeling, and the stupid voices in my head kept whispering that my parents didn't even care enough about me to have a meltdown over my absence, which was as stupid as stupid could be.

It's a lucky thing I was so close to total exhaustion, because even the voices in my head couldn't fight the biological necessity of sleep and the next thing I knew, the alarm was yanking me back from murky dreams and I was staggering into the bathroom for a pee, a shower, and a tooth-brushing.

By the time I got out the door, I was half convinced that it was all over. After all, the last time I'd done this, Barbara Stratford had put my face on the cover of the *Bay Guardian,* and the events had more or less unfolded from there. The closer I got to the office, the more certain I was that I'd step through the door and the first thing anyone would say to me would be, *Man, can you believe all that darknet stuff? It's all anyone's talking about.*

But no one even looked up when I got in. No one seemed to know that the world had turned on its head. I sat down at my desk and tried to concentrate on putting together my briefing for Joe, who'd emailed me that he was sorry I was feeling under the weather but that he looked forward to hearing my ideas when I got back into the office.

I felt like I should be putting together some kind of PowerPoint presentation, but every time I loaded up LibreOffice Impress, the free equivalent, I felt like a total tool. I *hated* PowerPoint. Besides, all I could think about was the darknet.

I told myself I'd just spend a minute or two googling it and seeing what came up. Yeah, right.

An hour later, I was furious. Oh, there were a few prominent places that had published our link, some cracks in the sidewalk with dandelion stalks sprouting from them. But every single one of these was flooded with sarcastic, dismissive comments. Some people insisted it had to be a hoax. Others said there was nothing there. Hundreds claimed that it was impossible to reach and don't bother trying. All of these were from different IDs, and they all seemed to have been written by different people, but I found it hard to believe that everyone who looked at the darknet docs would be so convinced that there was nothing to them.

Worse: if *I* had just happened upon this stuff for the first time, I'd probably figure that anything that attracted all this negative attention and people saying "hoax" and "nothing to see here," was just junk. As Kylie pointed out, I spent most of my day trying to figure out what *not* to pay attention to, so that I could free up my attention for the good stuff, and one of the ways I figured out which stuff to ignore was by paying attention to what was said by the people who'd already gone and looked.

I dragged myself back to hopeless PowerPoint fiddling, and was incredibly relieved when Liam came by to pester me, thus putting me out of my misery.

"What do you think? Is the darknet stuff a hoax?"

I wasn't surprised that Liam had found out about it already. It would have been a surprise if he hadn't—this stuff was totally up his alley.

"Did you actually check it out?" I asked.

He looked a little embarrassed. "Naw," he said. "I mean, I used to have Tor on my machine, but then I upgraded the OS, and I hadn't gotten around to reinstalling it, and, well, with all those people saying it was a hoax . . ." He trailed off and shrugged.

"It's pretty weak to dismiss it as a hoax until you've seen it yourself, don't you think?" I said. "I mean, why would you take some random Internet idiot's word for it instead of checking it out with your own two eyes? Don't you have a brain? Don't you know how to *think*." Even as I said it, I knew how unfair it was, not least because Liam didn't make a secret of how much he looked up to me. He shrank as I pummeled him with words, looking like he wished the ground would open up and swallow him. The part of me that wasn't feeling like a total dick felt good about that, because he *deserved* to be humiliated and miserable for not going off and looking at the stuff we'd sweated so hard to make available to him. I mean, if *Liam* couldn't get worked up about the darknet docs, who would?

"So you've seen them?" he said in a small, hurt voice. "You think they're real?"

Yeah, I'm not just a dick, I'm an idiot. I hadn't planned on admitting that I'd seen the darknet docs to anyone, at least not until they were all over the front page and the evening news, because I didn't want to be known as a guy who was suspiciously interested in them. But now I couldn't say, *No dude, I didn't look either,* because that would make me look like even more of a dick.

"Yeah," I said, kicking myself. "I saw them. They're incredible. Explosive stuff. You should really, really have a look."

"Okay," he said. "Totally. You're right, I really should make up my mind for myself, not let other people tell me what to do."

And then he went off and did what I'd told him to do. I am a total dick.

chapter 11

What if you threw a blockbuster news event and no one showed up? We'd just dumped one of the biggest troves of leaked documents in the history of the human race all over the net, and no one really gave a crap. Some critical combination of the sheer size of the dump, our sketchy promotions strategy, the pain-in-the-ass nature of Tor, and the fact that the net was full of people saying that they were hoaxes and stupid and that there was nothing juicy there—it all added up to a big, fat yawn.

Joe finally came by my desk at 3:30, just as I was falling into the post-lunch slump, wherein my blood sugar troughed out so low that I felt like I could barely keep my eyes open—probably as a result of all the horchata I'd guzzled at lunch, the sugar sending my blood sugar spiking to infinity so it had nowhere to go but down.

"Hello, Marcus," he said. He was dressed in his campaigning uniform, a nicely tailored button-up sweater over a crisp white shirt, slacks that showed off the fact that although he was pushing fifty, he still had the waistline he'd had as a college varsity sprinter, a JOE FOR SENATE badge on his lapel. He had like eight of those sweaters, and he kept a spare in a dry-cleaning bag by his desk, just in case a car splattered him or a baby got sick on him between campaign stops.

"Joe," I said, feeling like I was about to be sick. "Look, I'm sorry I wasn't in yesterday, I was really under the weather. And well, today, you know, it's just been crazy. I've just about got the network here sorted out, but the website—" I waved my hands in a way that was meant to convey that it was a total disaster.

He looked grave. "I thought that the website was all in order. I remember you saying something to that effect. Or did I misunderstand?"

I was sinking lower with every utterance. "Well, yeah, it looked okay, but when I started doing a code-audit I found a bunch of potential code-injection vulnerabilities so I've been doing what I can to reduce the attack surface of the site, you know, so I can get it all down to a manageable scale, and—"

He held his hands up to stop my torrent of technobabble. "My, it certainly sounds like quite an undertaking. I really thought that Myra was better than that."

And now I *really* felt like a jerk. Myra, my predecessor, had done an awful lot with very little, and here I was, dumping all over her hard work to cover my own useless butt. "Well, yeah, I mean, she did, but things move really fast, and the patch levels were super lagged, and you know, the last thing we want is someone hijacking our donors' credit card numbers or passwords, or using our site to install malicious software on visitors' computers, and, well—"

"I get the picture. Well, you sound like you've got important things to do here, Marcus. But I want you to remember that this campaign needs you for more than your ability to patch our software and keep our computers running: we need fresh approaches, ways to reach people, motivate them, bring them out to the polls. I'm counting on you, Marcus. I think you're the right person for this job."

Well, I would be if I wasn't spending all my time trying to leak a mountain of confidential documents that contain the details of thousands of criminal conspiracies—while being kidnapped by mercenaries and spied on by weirdos who probably buy their Guy Fawkes masks by the crate.

"I won't let you down, Joe."

"I know you won't, Marcus. Remember: you're not here to be a grunt in the information troop, you're my delta force ninja. Get ninj-ing. In two months, we're going to have an election, and win or lose, that will be the end of the road for the Noss for Senate campaign, our sites, servers, and all the associated whatnot and foofaraw. We need technology that will last us until then and no further. Keep that in mind while you're managing your time, and

I'm sure you'll find room in your schedule to get past the station-keeping work and on to the important stuff. The *fun* stuff, right?"

"I'm sorry," I said. He was right. As important as the stuff I had been obsessed with was, I had taken a job, and I wasn't doing it. I could tell he was disappointed with me, and that was just a brutal feeling. I had a moment's premonition of what it would be like to get *fired* from this job, to go home and admit that to my parents. The world seemed to spin away from beneath me. "Tomorrow, okay? I promise."

He squeezed my shoulder. "You don't need to look so gutted, son. Remember, this is an *independent* campaign. We're *supposed* to be scrappy, exhausted, and overextended."

I smiled a little at that, and noticed that Joe had some pretty serious bags under his eyes. On impulse, I said, "Have you been getting enough sleep?"

He laughed again, that amazing, deep laugh that was his trademark. "You sound like Flor. And you look like you might be burning the candle at both ends, too. How much sleep did you get last night?"

"I decline to answer that question on the grounds that it might tend to incriminate me," I said.

"Spoken like a good civil libertarian. A good, *tired* civil libertarian. I tell you what, I'm damned busy tomorrow anyway. Take an extra day to get your thoughts in order. And get a good night's sleep. All right, Marcus?"

"It's a deal."

Have I mentioned that Joe was a really good guy and that he'd make a hell of a California senator?

When he left my desk, I found my spirits lifted. Knowing someone like Joe had confidence in me made me want to be a better person. And soon, ideas began to flow—not always good ones, but ideas. Stuff I'd seen done before, new things too. A way to use free voice-over-IP to let kids call their offline parents and grandparents to ask them to vote—"Have you called your mom today?" A browser plugin that would do a popup with the names of the large corporate donors to Joe's opponents, every time you loaded a page that mentioned their names, a reminder that the other guys were all bought and paid for.

And I had a killer idea. Or maybe a really stupid idea. I kept putting it out of my head, but it kept coming back and insisting that I put it down in the long file I was brainstorming into (ditching the PowerPoint was really helping, too). So I wrote it down and added THIS IS A KILLER STUPID IDEA right next to it, so I wouldn't forget.

At the end of the day, I caught Liam slinking out of the door, not making eye contact with me. God, I was such a dick sometimes.

I called out to him and dragged him back over by my desk and apologized, and before I knew it, I'd invited him out for a cup of coffee after work and I was shutting down my computer and throwing it in my bag and heading out the door with him.

On the way home, I passed a Guatemalan grocery with a bunch of mouth-watering fresh California produce out front. I had a few dollars in my pockets and I was suddenly seized with a desire to cook my family an amazing, fresh dinner, sit my mom and dad down at the table and have a rollicking discussion, the way we once had. I blew some money on the makings of a big salad and a fruit salad for dessert, then stopped in at a Vietnamese grocer for fresh noodles and some tofu and chicken for pho, the Vietnamese noodle soup. I'd only cooked it once before, but it wasn't that hard, and it was filling and cheap.

When I got home, I tied on an apron and googled some recipes and started washing the dishes and putting them away. Mom heard the rattle and clatter and came into the kitchen, carrying a mug of cold tea.

"Goodness, Marcus, have you contracted a brain fever?"

"Har. Har. You're not invited to dinner now. And it's going to be a good one. Pho."

"Fa?"

"Yes. Pho. It's pronounced 'fa.' Not 'foh.' Fun fact. And now you know."

"Indeed I do. What has precipitated this uncharacteristic burst of activity, dare I ask? I'm certain you haven't wrecked the car, as we no longer own one. Is there some sort of terrible news you plan on breaking to us? Are we to be grandparents?"

"Mom!"

"Inquiring minds want to know, Marcus."

"I just felt like a good supper, and thought you might enjoy one, too. And it's the least I could do, right? After you carried me about in your womb for nine months, endured the pain of childbirth, the long years of childrearing—"

"So you *were* listening all those times we explained the ways of the world to you."

"—I figure I'll make you some soup and salad and we can call it even, right?"

She picked up a soapy dishcloth from the counter and threw it at me, but it was a slow, easy toss and I caught it out of the air and wound up like a baseball pitcher, making her squeal and run out of the kitchen. "Dinner's in an hour!" I called after her. "Wear something nice, would you?"

She made a disgusted shriek and I heard her telling my dad about the weird thing their kid was doing now.

Yeah, I was in trouble, and it was only going to get worse. But in the previous week, I'd been blown up, had my nose broken, gotten a job, been kidnapped and freaked out, nearly broken up with the love of my life, and screwed up at the job I could hardly believe I'd landed.

I needed a night off. And I was going to enjoy it. I got one of my dad's beers out of the fridge and cracked it. Technically, I was still two years too young to be doing that, but screw it, it was time to unlax like a boss.

Mom treated me to a raised eyebrow as I set out the food and clicked my second beer in place in front of my plate. "Oh really?" she said.

"What, you want me to use a glass?"

Dad snorted. "Forget it, Lillian, it's not going to kill him. And if it does, we can collect on his life insurance policy."

And then there was no talking, only the sound of soup being

blown upon, the sound of noodles being slurped, the sound of Dad trying not to slurp his soup, Mom teasing him about eating like a barbarian. I couldn't remember the last time we'd eaten like this: normal and funny and not freaking out about, well, *everything*. It felt insanely great.

My phone rang while we were working our way through the fruit salad I'd made for dessert, garnishing it with chopped mint and drizzling it with spiced rum. I looked at the faceplate: 202-456-1414.

I knew that number, but I couldn't place it at first. 202 was Washington DC, right? Why was that number so familiar? The ringer went off again. Hum. Oh, yeah, right. It was the White House's main switchboard.

(Don't ask me how I knew that—just let it be said that I had friends who had weird ideas about what constituted a funny crank call in the eighth grade, which is how my junior high got a visit from the Secret Service: it had been scrawled on half the bathroom walls in school, with FOR A GOOD TIME CALL above it.)

"Excuse me," I said, getting up from the table so fast I nearly knocked over my chair, hustling up the stairs with my thumb over the green button. I pressed it as I passed into my room and closed the door.

"Hello?" I said.

There was a long, weird, flat silence, with a couple loud clicks.

"Hello?" I said again.

"Marcus?" It was a computer-generated voice, and not a very good one. Needless to say, it wasn't the president, or the White House. Spoofing caller ID was a pretty basic trick, a one-google query job.

"Yeah."

A little pause. Someone was typing. "You haven't been checking your email."

"What, in the last two hours? No. I haven't."

"And you're not on IM."

"No. I had dinner. Is there something you needed to say?"

"In the darknet docs, there's a procurement order and brochure for a product called 'Hearts and Minds.'" The text-to-speech en-

gine was stupid enough that "hearts" came out "heerts" and I had
to try to recalibrate my brain to understand what it meant.

"Okay, I'll take your word for it. What about it?"

"You should be checking your email." Somehow, the robot voice
managed to sound peeved. "It's all in the email."

"I'll check my email," I said. "But I've had a lot of IT crap to
wade through lately. Some total jackasses have been using my
computer to violate my privacy and creep me right the hell out. I
don't suppose you'd know anything about that, right?"

A pause. "Stop changing the subject."

"Look, I've got plenty of stuff I could be doing here. In case you
didn't notice, I released all the docs, just like you were whining at
me to do. For all the good it's done. No one gives a damn. In case
you didn't notice."

"Hearts and Minds"—*heerts and minds*—"just you have a look.
And check your email more often."

The line went dead. So much for my night off.

Zyz had its fingers in a lot of pies, and liked to spin off new di-
visions for each of its special projects. RedCoat was the name of
the "security software" contractor that did a lot of gross lawful
intercept work for various branches of the U.S. government, and
governments overseas.

Hearts and Minds was one of its flagship products, though it
didn't exactly show up on the company's website. But there it was
in the darknet docs, and the more I read about it, the angrier I
became.

It looked like Hearts and Minds started with a procurement
order from the United States Air Force Air Mobility Command,
which was looking for "persona management" software. What's
persona management? I didn't know either. It's the kind of weirdness you couldn't make up.

You've heard of "grassroots" political movements, right? That's
when ordinary people start to care about a political cause, and
start to demand justice and action.

The bizarro-world version of "grassroots" movements are "astroturf" movements. These are fake grassroots movements started

by political groups, governments, ad agencies, marketing companies, crooks, intelligence outfits. I wasn't sure at this point whether, practically speaking, there was any difference between these sorts of organizations. In astroturf movements, you get hundreds or even thousands of "ordinary" people writing letters to the editor, showing up for demonstrations, writing to their congresscritters or town assembly or school board, all the stuff that people do when they care about a cause. But in an astroturf movement, the "ordinary people" are, in fact, paid operatives—the cast of a giant theatrical production in which people are paid to pretend to be ordinary citizens who just happen to want to see a park turned into an oil field, for example.

Now, getting all those phonies to pretend to be real people with real passion costs a lot of money. A handy-dandy way to save on this unfortunate expense is to use "sock puppets"—that's when one person operates several online identities, each pretending to be a different person, each one vigorously agreeing with the rest. Sock puppetry can get seriously twisted—you can even create a sock puppet to *disagree* with your cause, but in such a disagreeable, stupid, oafish fashion that they make the other side look like dolts.

But being a sock puppeteer isn't easy. You've got to keep all your identities separate, remember what each one has said about its life and beliefs. The last thing you want is for your fake suburban housewife to start talking about the stuff that only your fake longhaul trucker should know.

If you want to run more than a couple fake people at a time, you need good tools to help you keep track of who's who in your imaginary world.

That tool is called "persona management."

Hearts and Minds was developed for the USAF, but RedCoat sold lots of copies elsewhere. The product brochure boasted that it was used by "reputation management" companies, "marketing and communications" and "strategic communications" outfits. It was clear from the testimonial quotes that these were all fancy names for companies that helped other companies discredit people who complained about their products and services online. If you were selling crappy food, or had rude staff, or if your strollers had a tendency to collapse and squish the babies inside them, it was cheaper to hire someone with a Hearts and Minds license to help "manage your reputation" by making your dissatisfied customers seem like lone whiners than it was to actually fix your shit.

The product literature boasted about how Hearts and Minds was more efficient than the 50 Cent Army, the name for the legion of fake commenters employed by the Chinese government to discredit anyone who complained about official corruption or crimes. They made fun of the crudeness of paying badly educated thugs 50 cents per post to smear their targets.

Hearts and Minds could let a single operator pretend to be dozens of people. All of a sudden, I had a pretty good idea where all those messages about how the darknet docs were just BS and hoaxes and irrelevant had come from. All of a sudden, I wondered how much of the stuff I thought to be "true" had been made true by some creep with a sock-puppet army and a copy of Hearts and Minds. It was an ugly feeling.

I did a lot of work on the darknet spreadsheet, unpicking the threads that documented Hearts and Minds (which I kept thinking of as "Heerts and Minds"), adding tags and cross references. Now that we'd told the world about the darknet docs, the spreadsheet was more important than ever, as it was the only index to the massive trove. We'd dropped signing our edits with individual IDs, and now we all shared a single admin account that let us all edit the sheet without letting the public vandalize it or add weird conspiracy theories to it (we had enough of those among ourselves). We'd indexed over 3,000 documents between us now, which only left, uh, well, basically 800,000 more to go. It was going to take a while.

When that was done, I dragged my exhausted ass into bed, barely getting my shoes off before I hit the sack. But a few hours later I woke up with a jolt from a claustrophobic dream, my mouth pasty and tasting of the ginger in the pho. I slopped into the bathroom and gulped a cup of water and swiped at my teeth with a toothbrush and at my face with a facecloth and went back to bed, put my head on the pillow, and closed my eyes. But now sleep wouldn't come. Why would anyone go to all that trouble to tell me about Hearts and Minds? It wasn't like I could do anything about it.

It was stupid, is what it was, and every time sleep stole over me, I'd feel a kind of full-body pucker of outrage that these dinks had made such a point of calling me up just to tell me that I was the target of powerful, highly resourced attackers who had me outgunned in every way. I mean, duh. I knew that already.

Not being able to sleep sucked mightily. I needed to sleep. I had a job to do tomorrow, and I needed a clear head, and it had been so long since I'd had a real night's sleep, it was starting to turn me into a member of the living dead. The more I worried about this, of course, the harder it was to find sleep. Finally I counted down slowly from one hundred, taking a breath at every number, trying to find that place I'd gone to in the temple on the playa, and I was just about there when a thought occurred to me:

If all the Hearts and Minds messages were being generated and managed by a single piece of software, maybe there was a way to automatically figure out whether someone was using Hearts and Minds to post—a fingerprint, a signature, a trademark. I had a moment's excitement at this, a sketch of a plan for a program to analyze Hearts and Minds messages and find the connection, and then sleep *did* come, and bash me over the head with a sledgehammer, knocking me into a deep, dark dreamless place that my alarm clock dragged me out of just a few short hours later.

I was at my desk when Liam came over, still looking a little wounded, but with that kind of worshipful look that made me so awesomely uncomfortable.

"So," he said, "uh, you going to go to lunch soon?"

I nodded. I'd packed another PB&J that morning before blearily going out the door, sprinkling a handful of chocolate espresso beans in the sandwich, which seemed like a good idea at the time but which I'd probably regret.

"'Cause I thought I might go to Civic Center for the occupation."

"Is there another one of those today?" It seemed like there were new occupations springing up every month, like putting up tents and taking over some public square had become the default way to show that you were pissed off about something. Sometimes they were huge, and sometimes they were just a few hardcore people, but I kind of felt like we'd all gotten to the point where news footage of pepper-spray-happy cops in Darth Vader suits waging chemical warfare on vomiting, weeping protesters had lost its shock value. I mean, I was sympathetic to the victims of course—I'd ridden the Scoville Express myself—but I just couldn't get as worked up as I'd been a couple years back when it all kicked off.

Liam's eyes bugged out, as though he couldn't believe that someone as amazingly cool as me didn't know about everything going on everywhere in the world. I always hated those people, people who always said, "Oh yeah, I heard about that," no matter what it was, even when you knew they were lying. The kind of people who'd never done anything for the first time. But hanging around Liam was going to turn me into one of them if I didn't watch it.

"It's *huge*, yo! A bunch of different Anons are way pissed about this darknet stuff, they want to get at Zyz." He put on a menacing robot voice. "We are Anonymous. We are legion. We don't forget. We don't forgive. Expect us." I squirmed. You used to hear a lot about Anonymous, a kind of tribe of Internet people who would pull off these daring raids and denial-of-service attacks. But then the price for botnets crashed and anyone could be a denial-of-service terrorist, and then there were a ton of big stupid Hollywood movies where the good guys or the bad guys or the serial killers or the stoners were running around in Guy Fawkes masks, and well, it just all got kind of lame and played out. There were still real anons out there, hanging out on places like 4chan and being deeply weird and offensive in the way that no Hollywood movie would dare to come close to, but the image of Anonymous has been turned into even more of a cartoon than it had been when they started. And as for this "We are legion" business, it had been the chorus of a summer pop song so awful you'd icepick your own ear to escape it. Any menace it had once held was now offset by the fact that it was the modern successor to La Macarena and the Chicken Dance.

"So it's a bunch of Anons in tents?"

"No, dude. Anons kicked it off, but it's, like, *everyone*. It's *huge*. There's students from all over the city, even high school kids playing hooky. Teachers, too! Even parents."

I dug around my bag for my sandwich and stuck it in my coat-pocket. "All right," I said. "You've convinced me." And truth be told, he *had*. Maybe the darknet docs weren't on the front page of every newspaper, but here was a bunch of people who were protesting because of them, sort-of-kind-of. If that was all I was going to get out of this, I'd take it. For now, anyway.

"We don't have to wear masks, do we?" Those plastic *V-for-Vendetta* masks were even more played out now. Plus the last thing I wanted was to be in a crowded, volatile situation with no peripheral vision.

"Naw," Liam said. "These are better." He reached into his pocket and pulled out a couple of worn black bandannas, screened with elaborate patterns. He shook one out and held it out. It was a cotton kerchief, silk-screened with the Guy Fawkes face right in the middle of it. "Watch," he said. He folded it in half diagonally, making it into a big triangle, and tied it around his neck like a cowboy. Then he pulled it like a bank robber, and the way he had it folded, his whole lower face was the Guy Fawkes face. Then he untied it and shook it out again and took off his baseball hat and fussed with the kerchief, tucking the top edge under the hat and then retying the corners at the back of his head, so that now it covered his whole face, with only his eyes looking out through the eyeholes he'd cut out of the cloth. "It's a transformer," he said, muffled by the cloth. "Choose your level of covertness and tie accordingly. Plus it's treated with stuff that's supposed to help with pepper spray. I got 'em from a guy on eBay. Want to take one? We could both wear them!"

He sounded so enthusiastic I wanted to hide in the toilet. One thing I did *not* want was to show up looking like the dork twins. "That's okay," I said. "I'll just keep it in my pocket, you know, in case."

"Cool," he said, crestfallen. I made a show of carefully folding the kerchief and tucking it into my pocket. Who knew, maybe I would need to blow my nose—or soak up some blood.

I heard the protest long before I saw it, the unmistakable drum-circle, whistle-blowing sound. It made something inside of me cramp up a little, a reminder of the Xnet concert in Mission Dolores park, the gassings and beatings that had followed it. But Liam was clearly energized by the noise, started to pogo a little as we came up out of the BART station and headed toward it. The streets were lined with SFPD cruisers, and the sidewalks were thronged with beefy SFPD officers, ostentatiously sporting thick bundles of zip tie handcuffs at their belts. They all had goggles pushed up on their foreheads, masks pulled down around their collars. For the gas, of course. And yeah, there were a couple officers wearing what looked like SCUBA tanks, except I knew they were filled with pepper spray, connected to spray-nozzle hoses that were clipped to their chests. I didn't make eye contact with them, but their body language told me they were paying plenty of attention to me and Liam. I wondered if it was the Guy Fawkes bandanna around Liam's neck.

The tents filled the area in front of City Hall, spray-painted with old slogans from old occupations. This left very little room for the demonstrators, so we spilled out into the street, holding hand-lettered signs about student debt, corrupt politics, joblessness. The news was always full of stories about homeless camps being moved along, and big lengths of Shotwell Street had turned into tent cities, the whole sidewalk full of tents and mattresses and piles of cardboard. There was a big billboard by the Powell Street BART advertising the services of a security-through-occupation company that would move its employees into abandoned or foreclosed houses to keep squatters out.

Off to one side, a woman had climbed up on the high concrete base of a lamp post. She had cut off her long, fluorescent pink dreads, and it made her seem a lot older and wiser, but I'd recognize Trudy Doo anywhere. The frontwoman for Speedwhores and founder of Pigspleen.net was a San Francisco icon, and she'd been

Jolu's boss until her ISP went out of business the year before. She shouted, "Mic check!"

Around her, people echoed the cry: "Mic check! Mic check!" This was the People's Mic, another fixture of occupy protests. At first, people did it because their cities wouldn't give them "amplification permits" to use megaphones, but even in cities where the authorities didn't play stupid amplification gotcha-games, the People's Mic was preferred. Something about having everyone cooperating to help each other be heard really felt *right*.

"We have the best government—"

She shouted with her gravelly punk-singer voice, making each word good and clear and loud. The crowd echoed it, with some grumbles. "We. Have. The. Best. Government," shouted the people around Trudy Doo. Then people around them repeated it. Then the people around them, and so on, in concentric circles that finally reached to the other side of Van Ness Ave, which was now thronged with people.

"Money can buy."

There was laughter near Trudy Doo, and it took a few moments before the laughter subsided enough for the people near her to repeat the punch line.

"I have been out at a million of these things.

"And we always say the same things.

"And sometimes it feels hopeless.

"But we keep coming out.

"Because the reasons we come out haven't changed.

"Because the corruption, the brutality, and the unemployment are still there.

"So we're still here."

There was applause here—occupy style, with hands in the air, fingers wiggling—but Trudy Doo wasn't done yet. She called out, "Mic check!" and everyone went silent.

"They tell us we overspent.

"They tell us we were greedy and we lied on our mortgage loans.

"They tell us it's a global world and we can't get paid more than they're paying in India or China.

"They tell us this is the new normal.

"No jobs.

"No schools.

"No libraries.

"No houses.

"No retirement.

"No health care.

"But somehow, there's enough money for wars.

"Somehow, there's enough money for banks and bonuses.

"Somehow, it makes economic sense to give war criminals the power to take our houses.

"But they haven't passed their dirty laws yet.

"Now we know about them, thanks to the darknet.

"And we know that any politician who votes for this is bought and paid for.

"So we're here.

"We're here to say that our country is no longer for sale.

"We're here to say we're watching."

She hopped nimbly off the base and people applauded again, both ways, and it turned into a chant, "We're watching, we're watching, we're watching." There were some people in Fawkes masks and they pointed to their eyes and then to City Hall, making a little dance out of it, shuffling back and forth funkily in their thrift-store three-piece suits. Liam was pretty much in heaven.

Trudy Doo was surrounded by a crowd, part of an intense discussion, explaining to people who hadn't heard of the darknet what it was. She spotted me and shouted, "Marcus, come here a sec!" Liam almost fangasmed right then. I admit I was a little bit pleased with myself to be called out by Trudy Doo.

But then she said, "Marcus, you've heard of the darknet docs, right?"

My mouth went dry. "Um, I guess," I said.

"Good. Gimme a sec."

She hopped nimbly back up on the base. "Mic check!" she bellowed, cupping her hands around her mouth.

"Mic check!" the crowd roared back.

"Listen up! Marcus here, some of you know him as M1k3y, right?"

All of a sudden, there were about a million pairs of eyes on me. I squirmed and made a half-assed wave.

"You want to know about darknet, right? He's the guy to ask.

"Get up here, Marcus!"

She hopped down off the base and there was a polite round of applause. She gave me a rough hug, smelling somehow of the power supply of an overheated computer, like she was wearing Eau du Server. "Knock 'em dead," she said, right in my ear, and gave me another squeeze, then shoved me toward the base. I hesitated a second by the base of the plinth and she grabbed me by the back of my jeans with one hand, put the other under my butt, and basically wedgied me up onto it.

I looked out at the crowd. They looked back. It wasn't all strangers. There were familiar faces there—people I knew from Noisebridge, a couple girls I'd seen around the Mission, some people I knew from high school. I even spotted John Gilmore, the EFF guy, wearing a tie-dyed shirt and flat cap, smiling impishly within his long beard, light glinting off his round glasses.

"Wow," I said, before I could stop myself. The crowd around me said, "Wow," People's Mic style, and there was laughter all round. Ah yes, the old "repeating stuff that wasn't meant to be said" gag. Har.

And now I had no choice: I was about to give a public lecture to a couple thousand people on my top-secret leaks site. Way to keep your cover, Marcus.

Once upon a time, I helped invent a network called Xnet, because we ran it on top of hacked Xbox Universals, a games console that Microsoft gave away for free one Christmas so that they could sell more software. Naturally, there'd been a lot of interest in figuring out how to get *other* games to play on the Xbox, so someone went out and hacked it to accept a new OS: GNU/Linux, the free operating system made out of free and open code that anyone could improve and republish. There are a zillion flavors of Linux, and one of them, ParanoidLinux, was the desktop equivalent of ParanoidAndroid: an OS that assumed you were being spied on and did everything it could to keep you private.

Jolu and I tweaked ParanoidLinux so that it was ready to crack other peoples' WiFi out of the box, and then share it around, so if one Xbox was within range of a cracked WiFi link, all the Xboxes in range of it could share its connection. We used ParanoidLinux's built-in Tor stuff to create our own secret servers, chat, and games, routing some of the trickier stuff through Pigspleen, Trudy Doo's old ISP.

By the time I got picked up by the DHS, Xnet was already showing its age. The ParanoidLinux project was always being patched as new security issues were found and clobbered, and keeping the Xnet version up to date was a lot of work for us. We handed over control of the project to a volunteer committee who ran it for a few more months before they folded it back in with Paranoid-Linux, which was, by this time, a boot-disk that set up Tor, secure versions of Firefox and a chat program called Pidgin, and other security tools right out of the box, so you just stuck it into any computer and rebooted it and you were locked down tight and se-cure, assuming you could manage all the complexity of your keys, and understood how darknet sites worked, and, well, a lot of other stuff that most of the world didn't get. Yet.

So the darknet was just the latest version of the Xnet—in the same way that humans were just the latest version of chimps. I could use it, sure, but could I even explain it anymore? I was about to find out.

"Darknet sites run on Tor.

"That's The Onion Router.

"It's a tool that bounces your traffic around the net.

"Making it harder to trace and censor you.

"A darknet site is a normal website.

"Except that your computer never knows its address.

"And it doesn't know your computer's address.

"There's a darknet site.

"It has over 800,000 leaked memos on it.

"No one knows who put them there.

"No one knows what's in them.

"But a few thousand have been cataloged.

"And they're scary as hell."

I took a deep breath.

"You probably saw a lot of comments.

"About how it's all BS.

"A hoax.

"Nothing there.

"Well, if you check the darknet.

"You'll find a ton of memos about something called Hearts and Minds." I managed not to pronounce it "heerts."

"That's a product developed by Zyz.

"To help them spam discussion forums.

"With fake people.

"And now there are a whole crapton of people.

"You've never heard of.

"Flooding message boards.

"Saying that the memos that show that Zyz is really evil.

"Are all BS.

"I think that's pretty suspicious."

Finger-wagging applause. That made me feel a little better about the fact that I was on the verge of outing myself as the darknet docs guy.

"The easiest way to get to the darknet.

"Is to install a free browser plugin called Torbutton.

"Then visit est5g5fuenqhqinx.onion.

"I know that's a long number to remember.

"I'll say it again."

A voice from the crowd—one of the Anonymous guys, muffled by his mask—said, "I have a bunch of flyers explaining all this with the address on it."

I waved at him. He waved back, all jaunty body language to match the wide, sardonic grin on his mask. "That guy has the address on flyers." He executed a showy bow over one leg.

"I hope you'll go and see the darknet docs yourself.

"And make up your own mind.

"Well, thanks, I guess," I finished, and hopped down off the base, my pulse going *whoosh-whoosh* in my ears. The crowd was clapping politely, which was more than I had any right to expect. It wasn't as if I'd riled them up, given them marching orders, and sent them to fight the powers of evil. I'd given them tech support. There'd been a million cameras on me, of course, and some of them would have been streaming live to the net, and the rest would be grabbing footage to upload to YouTube and whatnot later on. And then there were three clean-cut guys in blue SFPD windcheaters with little camcorders who circulated endlessly through the crowd, making sure to get long shots of every face, especially anyone standing on a piece of street furniture and yelling out instructions, like me. I swallowed. Well, they knew who I was already, right? I'd been gassed and busted by them before. As the old saying went, it was the equivalent of a formal introduction.

The Anon guy with the flyers came over and handed me one, then shook my hand. "Nice to meet you, sir," he said.

"You, too." He was about my age, as far as I could tell from his eyes and the way he held himself. I looked at the little quarter-sheet of paper in my hand, hastily sliced into an off-kilter rectangle. It had all the basic info: an address for downloading a ParanoidLinux disk image that would boot any computer, the darknet docs address, some URLs for tutorials. It was liberally decorated with Guy Fawkes masks and funny slogans, and it had a fingerprint you could use to verify that your ParanoidLinux disk image hadn't been interfered with during the download. For a second, I thought that the numeric address they'd listed was wrong, and I spun off on a paranoid fantasy that these guys were part of some kind of disinformation campaign and maybe the ParanoidLinux fingerprint was no good, maybe it went to a poisoned version that spied on everything you did? Then I realized I'd been reading the address wrong and decided I needed to calm the hell down. "This is good," I said. "Thanks for doing it."

The Anon cocked his mask at me. "No problem—it was the least I could do. Seemed like it needed doing. I jumped on the darknet docs as soon as I heard about 'em, saw that BS this morning about Hearts and Minds, figured people needed to know the truth, so I wrote it down and made some copies. That seems like the best way to do stuff these days: make a *lot* of copies."

He said it with such hilarity I had to laugh. "Works for the bacteria," I said.

"Yeah," he said. "You think we could get some biotech freak to encode it all in a bacteria? Leave it in a petri dish overnight, make a trillion copies?"

"Viral marketing," I said.

Liam said, "*Bacterial* marketing."

Anon guy laughed some more behind his mask. I wondered if it itched. "This is my friend Liam," I said. "He brought me here today." They shook, and the Anon guy fingered Liam's bandanna with admiration. Liam slipped it on and I could see he was grinning behind it.

"Dude," Anon guy said.

"I know, right?" Liam said.

Trudy Doo flung an arm around my shoulders from behind. "You look like you're doing good, Marcus," she said.

"I haven't slept properly in weeks, I broke my nose last week, and I'm kind of a nervous wreck, but that's nice of you to say," I said.

"Just like I said. Looks like you're keeping really busy, which means you're doing good. Better than being a tube-fed zombie waiting for the grave." She shook my shoulders.

"How are you doing?" It seemed like a rude thing to say to someone who'd just lost her company, but I didn't know what else to say, plus I was kind of basking in the envious looks I was getting from Liam and didn't want Trudy Doo to go away before I'd finished showing off how cool I was.

She shrugged. "Pissed off," she said. "Pissed off is *good*. I'd rather be pissed off than resigned and peaceful. All the stuff that's gone down, all the money the super-duper richie-richies took out of the economy, all the shenanigans from the big phone companies that nuked Pigspleen . . . Every bit of it's made me ready to fight and fight some more."

The Anons clustered around her as she spoke, clearly enjoying her rant. I wished I could talk like that.

I had another paranoid moment: maybe Anon guy was the person who'd been spying on me through my computer. Maybe he and his buddies were the ones who'd staged that ghostly argument in my word-processing window the other night. For some reason,

I'd pictured them living thousands of miles away, in a small town where there was a lot of spare time. But maybe they were practically my neighbors. Hell, maybe I hadn't flushed them out of my computer after all and they'd been watching me all along, had rushed down here when they saw Liam come and drag me off to the demonstration.

I couldn't go on like this. I was going to have to get my head straight. If I could only get a decent night's sleep, I could sort it all out. I'd felt that way for years, I realized. If I could only get a normal day, a day when my parents weren't freaking out about money and jobs, a day when I was just a regular student or a regular coder, or something else regular—

Was there ever going to be a "normal" again? Since we'd arrived, the crowd had been growing. And growing. And *growing*. I'd been in some big demonstrations in San Francisco before, but they were generally the kind that had permits and marshalls and were very orderly. This wasn't like that. I'd been vaguely aware all summer that occupy demonstrations had been growing, mobilizing more people each time. But I hadn't quite figured out what that meant, not until I realized that the nearly painful roaring in my ears was just thousands and thousands of people all *talking* in very close quarters.

"Holy crap," I said, and Liam grinned, looking around, then showed me his phone, which had a live feed off someone's UAV, one of several that were buzzing the demonstration. Some had police markings, others had news-crew logos, and some were more colorful, with rainbows and slogans and grinning skulls. But most of them were eerily blank, and could have belonged to anyone. The one that was feeding Liam's phone was flying a lazy figure-eight pattern over the crowd, which, I saw now, stretched all the way down to Grove Street and all the way up to Golden Gate Avenue, and there were people with homemade signs converging on the crowd from side streets.

Liam was practically dancing a jig, and he was showing his phone's display off to everyone else—Trudy Doo, the Anons, anyone who'd hold still. Meanwhile, I was fighting panic. There was one big, unscheduled crowd I'd been in, the thousands of people

536 | cory doctorow

who'd streamed into the Powell Street BART station when the air-raid sirens went off, a crowd so dense it had been like a living thing, a boa constrictor that strangled you, an enormous dray horse that trampled you to death. Someone in that crowd had stabbed Darryl, a random act of senseless violence that I had often laid awake at night wondering about. Had that person just freaked out? Or had they been secretly waiting for the day when the opportunity to stab strangers with impunity would arise?

The crowd pressed in on all sides of me, moving in little increments, a sixteenth of an inch at a time, but moving, and not stopping, and growing closer every moment. I tried to step backwards and landed on someone's toe. "Sorry!" I said, and it came out in a yelp.

"Um, Liam," I said, grabbing his arm.

"What is it?"

"I got a bad feeling, Liam. Can we go? Now? I want to get back to the office, and we're not going to do that if we go to jail." *Or if we get crushed to death.*

"It's cool," he said. "Don't worry about it."

"Liam, I'm *going*," I said. "I'll see you at Joe's."

"Wait," he said, grabbing hold of me. "I'll go." Then, "Wait. Shit."

"What?"

"Kettle."

I bit the inside of my cheek and swallowed hard against the rising knob of vomit coming up my throat. "Kettling" is when the police surround a protest in a cordon of cops with riot shields, face masks, batons, and helmets, and then *tighten* it, reducing the amount of space for the crowd, shoving them in together like frozen peas in a bag, often with nowhere to sit or lie down, with no food or water or toilets. Tens of thousands of people—kids, sick people, pregnant women, old people, people who needed to get back to work. For some reason, kettles had to be airtight—no one was allowed to get in or out until the police decided to let you dribble out in small numbers. Anyone who tried to get out was treated as a desperate criminal, which is why "kettle" had become synonymous with protesters on stretchers, blood streaming from their head wounds, eyes red with pepper spray, twitching with the effects of the gas and their injuries.

"Liam," I said. "We need to get out of here now." On his screen, I could see the skirmish line of SFPD officers with all their tactical crap, helmets and shields, like the wet dream of some Zyz mercenary or mall ninja. "Before they tighten the cordon."

To my amazement, he started *singing* and smiling. "Polly put the kettle on/Sukey take it off again!" Meanwhile, his fingers flew over his phone's screen. "Don't you know it?" he said, seeing my puzzlement.

"What?"

"Sukey? Like the old poem? 'Polly put the kettle on/Sukey take it off again'? No? It's a nursery rhyme. I thought everyone knew it!"

"I don't know this nursery rhyme, Liam. Why does it matter, precisely?" I was struggling not to bite his head off. No one should look that thrilled about being in a kettle.

"Sukey's an open source intelligence app. It gathers reports on kettles from people in the crowds, UAVs, webcams, SMSes, whatever, and overlays them on a U.S. Geographical Survey map, so that you can easily see what routes are still open. There's no way they could block *all* the side streets off in a space this big."

He handed me his phone and I peered intently at it. Angry, thick red lines denoted the police lines, with arrows showing the directions that reinforcements were arriving from. Thin green lines showed the escape routes.

"Dotted lines are unverified. Solid lines are verified, but they fade into unverified dots if they're not regularly refreshed. That one looks good." He pointed at a pedestrian walkway between two civic buildings, a few hundred yards down the street.

"That one's unverified," I said. "What about this one? It's verified and it's closer."

He shook his head. "Yeah, but someone needs to go verify that one. And if it's shut off, look, there's another verified route just past it. It'd be doing our part for the cause."

"I just want to *go*, Liam," I said.

He gave me a look of such utter disappointment that I was literally unable to set off, pinned in place by his gaze and the crush of bodies around me. The Anons had climbed up on the base and were impossible to read beneath their masks' gigantic grins. Trudy Doo had moved off into the crowd and I'd lost sight of her. But I felt like she was watching me, along with the Anons, and Liam, and the whole crowd, all watching "M1k3y" lose his nerve. Like they were already tweeting it.

"Forget it," I said. "Let's go check the Sukey route."

Liam smiled uncertainly and we set off. It was like walking through molasses, and while there was plenty of happy chanting and discussion, there were also far-off cries that might have been screams. I began to shiver as I inched through the press of bodies. But Sukey was right: the little walkway was unguarded, and people were slipping in and out of it. We followed them, going single file, and when we reached the end, Liam tapped his screen and verified the route. "Job done," he said, and we headed down Market Street. I made Liam take off his bandanna. We passed plenty of cops, both stationary and moving toward the demonstration. There were also plenty of demonstrators, and the police were stopping some of them, searching them and their bags. We passed a pair of girls about our age in plastic handcuffs, one looking furious, the other looking like she might cry any second, being led into a police cruiser. We hurried past.

We descended into the BART station and rode in uncomfortable silence. The oppressive feeling of being watched crowded in from all sides.

As we came up onto Mission, Liam said, "I can't believe how many people came out."

"Yeah."

"Like, no one wanted to come out until they found out that everyone else was. And once everyone started to come out, everyone else came out, too."

Unspoken, hanging in the air between us, was the question *So why aren't we there now?*

I finished the day at my desk, flipping back and forth from my work to newsfeeds and streams and tweets from the monster demonstration. According to Sukey, people were still escaping the kettle, but from what I could tell from the overhead shots, more people were joining the demo than were leaving. The UAV shots were like some kind of monster rock show. Ange texted me after class to say she was heading to one of the satellite demonstrations that had formed on the other side of the kettle, turning the police line into a stupid joke. Later, I found out that Jolu, Darryl, and Van had all been there separately. I didn't go back. Just before I fell asleep, I checked my phone and saw that the kettle had lifted and most of the demonstrators had gone home—except for the 600-plus who'd been hauled off to jail, and the couple dozen who'd gone to the hospital. I went to sleep.

I got up the next morning before my alarm sounded, lurching out of bed and into the bathroom in a mild panic over all the work I had to do that day. I pulled on a T-shirt that passed the sniff test (barely) and decided I could get away with the same socks I'd had on the day before. I was about to open my throat and tip a bowl of muesli down it when I saw the fat newspaper sitting on the kitchen table where my mom had left it. Thick as a hotel-room Bible: the *San Francisco Chronicle,* a newspaper that had thumped down on our doorstep every Saturday morning since time began.

Every *Saturday* morning. I put down my muesli mid-guzzle and flumpfed into a kitchen chair, all the get-out-of-the-house adrenaline leaving my body with an almost audible *whoosh.*

Five minutes later, I was still sitting there, contemplating the question of what I should do with my weekend. The last time I'd had a real *weekend* was back in high school, and even then I'd had all that homework. I decided it'd be good to make a big ole weekend brunch, something for Mom and Dad, with proper coffee (not the swill they normally drank) brewed up with my little AeroPress. Then I could have a leisurely shower, tidy up my room, stick a load of laundry in the machine, and meander down to Noisebridge and dust off Secret Project X-1 and see about getting my 3D printer going in time for *next year's* Burning Man.

It was the best plan I could have made—for a change. I did crazy-ass 3D pancake sculptures (I cook a mean pancake AT-AT), and the coffee was "brilliant" (a direct quote from my mom). The parents were duly impressed with my room-cleaning, and by the time I shoved Lurch into my backpack and jumped on my bike, I was feeling like maybe I'd found some of that "normal" I'd been missing.

There weren't too many Noisebridgers around by the time I rolled in at 10:30. I went to my shelf and grabbed down my box-o'-stuff, making puffs of playa dust rise off all the broken crap I'd brought back from Burning Man. I found a free workbench and nodded at the girl with the shaved head who was teaching her little sister how to solder at the next bench over. I got a can of compressed air and some soft cloths and started blowing out the dust and getting ready to wrestle with my printer anew. I slipped into an easy reverie, punctuated by Club-Mate breaks—this being the official drink of hackerspaces around the world, a sweet German soda laced with caffeine and maté tea extract, a jet fuel–grade stimulant.

When the cleaning was done, I grabbed a multimeter and started testing all the circuits in X-1, starting from the power supply and working my way through the system. Partway through my checks, I thought I found the problem, a spot where it looked like a stepper motor had been mounted backwards, so I grabbed Lurch and went hunting for a diagram to see if I was right, thinking, *Jeez, if it turns out that this was all that was wrong, I'm going to feel like a total derp.*

Of course, once my laptop was open on the workbench beside me, it was inevitable that I'd have a sneaky peek at my email—looking at my laptop without checking in would be like going to the cupboard and not snagging a cookie.

To: <marcusyallow@pirateparty.org.se>
From: Leaky McLeakerpants
Subject: carrie johnstone d0x
2 use as u see fit

It was signed with a little ASCII-art Guy Fawkes face made out of punctuation marks and letters, and attached to the email was a gigantic ZIP file.

I had a pretty good idea what that was: every single fact and fantasy that could be had about Carrie Johnstone and what she was up to. I'd seen d0xxes that went back to second-grade report cards, ones that included the subjects' kids' medical records, everything. Nothing was off limits when you were being d0xxed.

I closed my laptop's lid and closed my eyes.

A big part of me didn't want to see the docs in that folder. I had plenty of secret docs in my life already. And I knew what it was like to be totally, absolutely invaded. Carrie Johnstone had done it to me. So had the jerks who'd rooted my laptop. Somewhere in the world, someone might be staring at an email whose subject line was "Marcus Yallow d0x."

The thing was, I *knew* I was going to open that ZIP file. Of course I was. Who wouldn't? Carrie Johnstone was a monster: kidnapper, torturer, murderer. War criminal. Power-tripping mercenary. Scumbag and commander of scumbags. She was hunting me, too. Let's not forget that. Now that the story was out, wouldn't Zyz be back? How long until I met Timmy and Knothead again? Would I end up at the bottom of the Bay this time?

I *had* to open it. It was self-defense. In fact, I'd bet the only reason Carrie Johnstone hadn't had me whisked away to some private torture chamber was that she assumed that I'd been sneaky enough to gather this kind of dossier and had it ready to dump, on a dead man's switch, if I got disappeared. People like Carrie Johnstone always assume everyone else thinks like them. Not like people like me. People like me are good people. We deserve to read other peoples' dirty laundry. Especially bad people.

I was such a coward.

I unpacked the folder and started browsing the docs.

You would have done it, too.

"Marcus?" a voice said, some eternity later. It was Lemmy, the Noisebridger who'd given me and Ange our ride back from Burning Man. He was in his forties, an old ex-punk with stretched-out ear piercings and blurred tattoos up and down his arms. He was a demon in the machine shop, and was the first person I'd ask any time I had a question about something big, fast-moving, and lethal. I always got the impression that he thought my little electronics projects were cute toys, fun, but not serious like a giant piece of precision-machined metal.

I had the feeling he'd been talking to me for a little while, and that I hadn't heard him.

"Sorry," I said. "Engrossing reading, is all."

He smiled. "Look, I was going to go join the rest down at the big demonstration, bring some UAVs along. Want to come along and be my crew?"

"There's a big demonstration?"

He laughed. "Come on, buddy, take a break every now and then, will you? You know that big one that happened yesterday? Well, it looks like everyone who went yesterday's come back again, and they brought all their friends. Downtown's *shut down*. I've been playing with my quadcopters, think I can get them to produce some killer footage. They're all rigged to act as WiFi bridges, too, each on a different 4G network, so we should be able to supply some free connectivity to the crowd. I've also got a software-defined radio rig in three of them that can triangulate on police and emergency bands. I think I've got it set so they'll home in on any clusters of dense police-radio chatter, which should be pretty interesting. But you know, I'm not really much of a coder, so I thought I could use a pit crew to help me debug the code on the fly during the inaugural flight."

Lemmy was also a UAV nut, though, again, I think he'd have preferred unmanned autonomous tanks or ATVs, anything with a lot of shiny, heavy metal. I looked at my screen, and my screen looked back at me, with everything I could have ever wanted to know about Carrie Johnstone and a lot more.

I couldn't stop looking at it, but I didn't want to keep looking at it.

"Let's go," I said, putting my lid down and sticking Lurch in my bag. "You can't write code for shit, dude."

"Yeah," he said, cheerfully. "Code's just *details*. I'm a big-picture kind of guy."

Lemmy wanted to drive—it being hard to carry four miniature quadcopters the couple of miles to the periphery of the demonstration—but we probably could have crawled in less time than it took to beat the frozen traffic leading up to the march. I spent the time getting familiar with Lemmy's control software, which built on some standard libraries I was already familiar with: systems for steering UAVs and for running software-defined radios, mostly.

Software-defined radio is hot stuff, and it's kind of snuck up on the world without us noticing much. Old-fashioned radios work with a little quartz crystal, like the one in an electrical watch. Quartz vibrates, buzzing back and forth at a rate that's determined at the time that it's manufactured. You choose a crystal, build a circuit around it, and the radio is done—it can tune in to any signals that are inside the vibrational frequency of the crystal. One radio works for tuning in to GPS satellites, another to CDMA cellular phone signals, another for FM radio, and so on.

But SDR is *programmable* radio. Instead of a crystal, it uses a fast analog-to-digital converter, a little electronic gizmo that takes any analog signal off a sensor (say, light patterns off an electric eye, or sound patterns off a microphone) and turns it into ones and zeros. You connect the converter to a radio antenna and tell it what band to listen in on, and then you use standard software to make sense of what it receives.

What this means is that the same box can be used to read air-traffic signals, police band, CB radio, analog TV, digital TV, AM radio, FM radio, satellite radio, GPS, baby monitors, eleven flavors of WiFi, and every cellular phone standard ever invented, *all at once,* provided the converter is fast enough, the antenna is big enough, and the software is smart enough. It's the radio-wave equivalent of inventing a car that can turn itself into a bicycle, a jumbo jet, a zeppelin, an ocean liner, or a performance motorcycle just by loading different code into its computer. It's badass.

Lemmy's UAVs had some off-the-shelf SDRs he'd bought from an open-source hardware company called Adafruit in New York. Adafruit sells electronics that come with full source code and schematics, complete road maps for remaking them to do your bidding. Everyone at Noisebridge loved their SDRs and other gear. And since there were thousands of hackers and tinkerers around the world who worked with the Adafruit SDRs (and all the other versions that Adafruit's competition made from the same plans), there was a lot of very clean, very well-documented code for talking to them.

I dove into this in the passenger seat, vaguely aware that the car was lurching from stop to start, turning corner after corner, as Lemmy sought out a spot close to the protest.

"What's the verdict, doc?" he said, as he engaged the parking brake. "Is my code going to live?"

I shrugged. "Looks about right to me. Am I right in thinking you've just pasted in the code examples from the tutorials with a couple of lines tying each module in with the last?"

He grinned. "Yup. I treat writing code like making a cake from a cake mix: pour it into a bowl, add an egg and a cup of water, stir, and throw it in the oven. It's not always pretty, but it's always a cake."

"Well, let's see if we've got a cake, then."

I got out of the car, a tricky feat since we were parked on the upslope of a steep hill. I didn't immediately recognize the neighborhood, but when I did, I was surprised. "Are we on the *other side* of Nob Hill?"

"Yup. It's the closest I could get to the protest. That thing is *huge*."

"But we must be, I don't know, a mile away?"

"Oh, less than that. Plus the protest is getting bigger, from what I can tell. It might reach here before the day's out. Something's *happening*. People are *pissed*. I've been living here since the eighties and I've never seen anything on this scale."

He dug around in the trunk and pulled out his quadcopters. Each one was an X of light, flexible plastic, with helicopter rotors at the end of each leg of the X. A round pod in the middle carried the battery and the electronics, radios, and control systems. Without the battery, each one weighed less than a pound, but the batteries doubled their weight. He handed me two of them, and I held one in each hand, awkwardly fitting my fingers around the sensors and antennae in the center disc, trying not to bend anything or smudge any of the lens covers.

Then he handed me one more, being much rougher with it than I'd dared to be (but then, it was his quadcopter to break, not mine). I stuck it awkwardly under one arm. He perched the remaining one on his hand and thumbed at his phone with his other hand. The four rotors spun up with a dragonfly whirring, the quadcopter wobbled twice on his palm, then lifted off straight into the sky in a vertical takeoff that was so fast it seemed like the quadcopter had simply vanished like a special effect.

He took back the extra copter from me and showed me his phone, which was showing the view from the copter's lower camera, a receding landscape with the tops of our heads in the middle of it, shrinking to two little dots as the copter clawed at the air and pulled itself into the sky.

"Well, that works," he said. "Thought it'd be useful to have a little overview as we got close. Here, I'm going to webcast the feed." He thumbed some more buttons.

"Nice," I said. This was exactly what I loved about technology: when it just *worked* and turned individuals into forces of nature. We'd just put an eye in the sky that anyone could tune in to. "What's the link?"

"It automatically tweets the URL from my account when I start it up. Do you follow me?"

"Yeah," I said. I got out my phone and punched up the Twitter client, found the tweet with the link, and retweeted it, tapping in, "Heading to the #sanfrancisco #occupy #protest. Bringing quadcopters. Aerial video here."

We walked laboriously uphill to the top of Nob Hill, the copter hovering a hundred feet above us, high enough to be clear of any overhead wires or trees. From Lemmy's phone screen, we could see the hairy edges of the protest, where people were still arriving. Farther in, it looked almost like static, all these little dots—peoples' heads—moving in tiny, quick blips, packed as densely as oranges in an orange crate.

"Holy crap," I breathed, as the copter rose higher, revealing the size of the crowd, which spread from Fell Street to Market Street, spilling out over the side streets, filling them back for blocks and blocks.

"Day-umn," Lemmy agreed. "Want to buzz 'em?"

"Can you do that from here?"

"Yeah," he said. "It'll take the copter out of direct radio range, but we'll still get its feed off the net. And we can check out the software, see if it really works." I watched as he tapped out a flight pattern on his phone, tracing a zigzag over the crowd with his fingertip. Then he pressed GO. Over our heads, the copter zipped off toward the crowd, keeping its altitude for most of the journey, then gently descending to a mere five yards off the ground.

At this height, I could make out individual faces in the crowd, read the slogans on the signs. Then the flight path kicked in and the point of view swerved nauseously, tracing that zigzag with mathematical precision, sometimes shuddering as the copter got caught in a gust of wind. We stopped walking and just watched the feed for a while. I shouted "Look out!" at the phone's screen when the copter nearly collided with another UAV, this one covered in markings from MSNBC. Either it had some kind of automatic avoidance routine built into it, or there was a fast-fingered human operator nearby, because it banked hard and barely missed the midair collision.

"Uh, Lemmy, what happens if that thing crashes? I mean, I don't want to turn someone into hamburger."

"Well, yeah, me neither. In theory, any two rotors can give it enough lift to slow its descent, and it makes a lot of noise if it goes in for an emergency landing, which should help people get out of the way."

"Unless it's so noisy that they don't hear it."

"Yeah. Well, that's life in the big city."

I wasn't sure I agreed. Crashing the quadcopter into someone's head would really, really suck. On the other hand, the knowledge that this might happen certainly gave watching the footage an air of extreme danger, which made it that much more compelling. As if it wasn't compelling enough, watching the video of all those faces, thousands and thousands of them, ripping past at speed.

"Let's get down there," he said, and I agreed.

The demonstration was even louder than the one the day before, a roar like a PA stack that I could hear from two blocks away, over the honking horns of the cars trying to find their way around it. The sidewalk was too jammed with people to walk, so we joined the hundreds who were threading their way through the stuck cars, dodging the bikes and motorcycles that were doing the same. Soon we could barely move, and I realized we were now *in* the demonstration, even though there were stuck cars all around us. I looked in one, saw a harried-looking woman with two little kids in the back seat who were losing their minds, one hitting the other with a toy car, both of them screaming like banshees, silent gaping mouths through the closed windows.

I locked eyes with the driver, who was looking resigned and frazzled. I wondered about all the other people who were stuck around me, wanting to get home and feed the kids or get to work and not get docked for being late or wanting to get to the hospital or the airport. I entertained a brief fantasy of directing traffic, helping all those people get unstuck and turn around and head away from the protest, get moving again, but there was no way I could do that. (Later, I read reports of other people doing just that, and of the crowds making way to help this happen, and I felt both proud of my fellow human beings and ashamed of not having the guts to try it myself at the time.)

Now we couldn't move without a lot of "excuse me"s shouted into the ears of people who were shouting the same thing into the ears of the people ahead of them.

"This is insane," I said.

"Pretty amazing," Lemmy said, and smiled hugely.

Suddenly, it felt like the world was flipping upside down. It *was* amazing. Hundreds of thousands—millions?—of my neighbors and friends had taken over the city of San Francisco because they were pissed off about the same things I was pissed off about. They'd come and put their lives and liberty on the line because, well, because stuff was *messed up*. It wasn't just the darknet docs, it wasn't just the lobbying to make the deal over student loans even worse, it wasn't just the foreclosed houses and all the jobs that had vanished. It wasn't just the planetary devastation and global warming, it wasn't just the foreign dictators we'd propped up or the private prison industry we supported at home. It was *all of it*. It was the fact that there was all this *terrible stuff* and no one seemed to be able to do anything about it. Not our political leaders. Not our police. Not our army. Not our businesses. In fact, a lot of the time, it seemed like politicians, police, soldiers, and businesses were the ones *doing* the stuff we wanted to put a stop to, and they said things like "We don't like it either, but it has to be done, right?"

Here was a big slice of my city that had turned out to say *WRONG*. To say *STOP*. To say *ENOUGH*. I knew that these were all complicated problems that I couldn't grasp in their entirety, but I also knew that "It's complicated" was often an excuse, not an explanation. It was a way of copping out, saying that nothing further could be done, shrug, let's get back to business as usual.

I'd never seen this many people in one place. From the copters' point of view, it was like the city had come to life, the streets turning from lifeless stone and concrete into a living carpet of humanity that stretched on and on and on. It was scary, and I had no idea how it would turn out, but I didn't care. This was what I'd been waiting for, this was the thing that *had to happen*. No more business as usual. No more shrugging and saying, "What can you do?" From now on, we'd do *something*. Not "Run in circles, scream and shout," but "March together, demand a change."

I also realized that my stupid idea for what to do next for Joe's campaign wasn't so stupid after all.

Lemmy's copters just kept buzzing the crowd, and our Ustream channel kept picking up viewers, up to a couple thousand now. No doubt a lot of them were in that crowd, but plenty were from all over the world, to judge by the realtime stats.

Every so often, we'd deploy the three copters with the software-defined radio scanners to check for high concentrations of police-band chatter. The police had recently started to encrypt their signals, but that didn't matter: we didn't care *what* they were saying, we only wanted to detect places where a lot of police communications were taking place. In other words, we were interested in the fact that they were talking, not what they were talking about.

When the three detected police-band spikes, they sent the fourth copter to home in on it and take some video. That way, we caught a lot of footage of arriving convoys of militarized cops and then the National Guard. Hundreds of them, and dozens of police buses—the kind they took masses of prisoners away in—and even little clusters of police quadcopters that were sending their signals back and forth in the same encrypted band.

Two of these copters latched on to our scout and started to follow it around.

"Uh-oh," Lemmy said.

"Why uh-oh?"

"Well, even with these new power-cells, that little guy's going to run out of battery soon enough, and I'm going to have to bring him in for a fresh power pack, and they're going to know exactly who we are and where we are."

"Uh-oh," I agreed. "Is flying a UAV illegal?"

He shrugged. "Probably. I mean, no, not in general, but is there some kind of freaky, 'conspiracy to abet civil disorder' BS charge they could whomp up against anyone they don't like? I'm pretty sure there is."

"Uh-oh," I said again.

"I guess I'll just ditch it," he said. "Man, this sucks."

"How much time is on the power pack?"

He looked at the telemetry streaming off the scout. "Maybe twenty minutes."

"Can you tell it to land somewhere out of the way, maybe a rooftop, and we can try to collect it later?"

"Yeah," he said. "Good one."

I used Google Earth to scout out the nearby roofs and found a likely looking spot, which I showed to Lemmy, and he took over steering the scout to it—it was away from the main body of the protest, and who knows what the SFPD crew who were piloting our tails thought we were up to. I got to steer the remaining three, staying away from the police copters. Mostly, I just tried to zoom in on any place where things looked interesting. I found one spot, right by Civic Center, where a group of parents with small children had made a kind of kindergarten, an open circle of people with a bunch of playing kids in the middle. Boy, was that cool—made me think that my fellow humans were really basically great.

I got a call from Ange, who, of course, was already in the thick of the crowd, blocks away from me within the mass. I told her where I was and she told me to stay put and she'd come and meet me.

"Okay, we're down," Lemmy said. "You bookmarked that location, right?"

"Got it," I said.

"Roger that, mission control," he said.

"Yeah, that." I flicked from one copter feed to the next, watching as a cam soared over our heads and I saw that we weren't on the edge of the protest anymore—it now stretched for two blocks behind us, and there were lots of people still arriving.

I was still taking in this fact when a large, firm hand clamped my shoulder and I had a momentary panic, sure that this was someone from Zyz come to snatch me out of the crowd. Before I was even conscious of what I was doing, I had started to move into the thick of the crowd, turning sideways to eel my way through the small gaps between bodies. But then a familiar voice said, "Marcus!" and I stopped and turned around. It was Joe Noss, in his usual campaigning clothes, sweater and all. He was grinning like a bandit.

"Joe!" I said. "Sorry, you startled me!"

"Ah, I know no one wants to run into the boss on the weekend," he said. "Isn't this something, then?"

"It's amazing," I said, thinking as I said it that maybe he wasn't someone who supported this kind of thing and wondering if I'd said the wrong thing. "I mean, I think it's incredible, right?"

"Marcus, in all my life I've never seen anything like this. If there was ever a time to be an independent candidate, it's now. These people are just plain *fed up* with the way things work in government. And so am I; so there we are, all in this together."

"Preach, brother!" Lemmy said, and Joe smiled his thousand-watt smile at him.

"Hello there," he said. "I'm Joseph Noss."

"Oh, I know it! I'm Lemmy."

"Lemmy's a friend of mine. From the hackerspace."

Joe shook his hand. "What a treat. Marcus has told me about your space. It sounds, well, extraordinary. Like you're some kind of superheroes of science. From what he tells me, you folks can build just about anything you set your mind to."

Lemmy nodded vigorously. "Yeah, pretty much. And if we can't

552 | **cory doctorow**

build it, someone at some other makerspace or hackerspace will help us out. We have a Friday night drop-in—you should come by and see what we're up to."

"I'd love that, though perhaps I might have to wait until after election day, as I'm a little preoccupied." He scanned the crowd again. "I can't get over this," he said. "All these people."

"Look at this," Lemmy said, and showed him his screen.

"Is that from one of the news networks?" Joe asked.

Lemmy laughed. "Yeah, HNN, Hackerspace News Network. It's coming off some unmanned quadcopters I built. Up there." He pointed at the sky. Joe looked up, looked back at him.

"You're joking. You're flying *helicopters* by remote control?"

"Oh, they only weigh a couple pounds and they're the size of dinner plates. Little guys, nothing fancy. Maybe fifty bucks' worth of parts in each of them. Most expensive thing in them are the batteries, and I hand-built them from salvaged cell-phone battery packs."

Joe put his hands on his hips and cocked his head at Lemmy, as if wondering whether he was pulling his leg. Then he shook his head in admiration. "Incredible," he said. "Just amazing."

"Want to fly one?" Lemmy said, tapping at his screen. "There's about fifteen thousand people watching the feed off this one, go nuts. Just use the keypad."

Joe looked at the phone in his hand as if it were radioactive. "I don't think I'm qualified to operate an aircraft."

"Oh, you're not *operating* it. It operates itself. You just tell it where to go."

I thought Joe was going to balk, but he prodded tentatively at the screen, then more forcefully. "Amazing," he said, after a little time. "Just . . . *amazing.* What's this red icon flashing for, though?"

Lemmy took the phone. "Low battery," he said. "Better bring the gang in for a battery swap. Luckily I brought a ton of charged spares."

He disappeared down the rabbit hole, all his attention focused on his phone, doing that classic nerd-focus thing, radiating a cone of *I'm busy, don't bug me* as his fingers danced.

There was something I wanted to tell Joe, but I was scared to.

My mouth had dried up, but my palms were wet. The crowd noise around us was loud, but I could still hear my heart in my ears.

"Joe," I said. He looked at me with those eyes that seemed to bore straight into my soul.

"Yes, Marcus?" he said. His whole body language shifted into a posture of thoughtful listening, one of those politician magic tricks that seemed to set him apart from the rest of us. Part of my mind wondered if he even knew he was doing it, while the rest of my mind was calming down and responding to it. Minds are weird.

"I think I've got an idea for your campaign. It's a bit, um, ambitious, though."

"Ambitious is good. I like ambitious."

"What if we give our supporters a vote-finding machine, a little app they can run on their PCs? First it goes through your contacts lists on Facebook, Twitter, email, and whatever, and gives you a one-click way to send a message to each person in your neighborhood who you think you could recruit to support your campaign. We could give them some checkboxes for issues that they think each contact cares about, and automatically create a pitch note with your positions on each. Every new supporter is then asked to do the same thing with *their* contacts list. Then we go after everyone in the local campaign donor records, cross-checking to see if any existing supporters have a connection to them that we can use to pitch them for money. And then it moves on to voters and people you could register to vote.

"But we don't just use a static pitch. We start with what we think our best talking points are, write several variations, and test them to see which ones perform best. A/B testing—is this one or that one more effective? We can tweak the pitch several times a day, if we get enough volume, all through the campaign, like polling but *fast*. And anyone who recruits a friend gets points, and we do leaderboards, and invite the best performers every week to a big beer-and-pizza party at HQ, make it all into a game, a championship.

"Meanwhile, we use mapping software that knows where every voter is to calculate the optimal places to hold events around the state. The press database is blasting them out—and the press is coming, because they're actually fun. Instead of sober speeches about random words, they're much more like stand-up or *The Daily Show*—full of great, witty sound bites that work perfectly in an evening newscast or a newspaper story. And because they're so entertaining and always a little different, they bring quite a following; they become events."

Joe's eyes were wide. "You can build this?"

I shrugged. "Probably. I mean, most of it sounds like it's just a quick tweak of some of the free/open campaignware out there. But I don't think anyone's done it for elections yet. I could build something, get it running."

"So if you could build it, then my opponents could, too?"

"Can't see why not. But that sounds like a reason for you to build it first."

He laughed. I had an idea, though.

"So, but I've also been thinking of ways you can use the net that your opponents can't."

"Go on."

The same remote part of my mind wondered why he didn't say, "Can't this wait until Monday?" But then, he was Joe. He was the candidate. He didn't get weekends. He was here, with one of his campaign workers, and that meant that he was, fundamentally, *at work*.

"You know the darknet docs, right?" It took everything in me not to look around at that moment to see if anyone was watching.

"I'm familiar with them," he said. His face was unreadable, the same mask of *listening* he'd slipped into when I started talking.

"Well, they're hard to get at right now. You have to do a lot of stuff with Tor, which is this anonymizing technology that's kind of tricky. On the plus side, it's really hard to take them down or even figure out where they are. On the other hand, they're hard for normal people to go and see. That's because no one's hosting them on a regular, boring old Internet site, as a collection of documents that anyone with a web browser can see and link to."

"Yes," he said. "I think that's right. The main reason *I* didn't go and look at them myself is that it seemed altogether too complicated for someone who wasn't a dedicated techno-ninja."

I started to say, *It's not that hard*—and was about to launch into a little tutorial about how to use Tor, but I stopped myself. It didn't matter, and besides, if Joe *felt* like it was too complicated, it was important to acknowledge that he had the right to feel that way.

"Well, I *have* looked at these documents, and from what I've seen of them, they're full of corruption, crime, and sleaze. And by and large, this corruption, crime, and sleaze has been committed by the big parties and their pals. So it seems to me that if you want to convince people that they should risk voting for an independent candidate, it'd help if you could show people that they're not 'wasting their votes' when they vote for you, because any other vote is going to give power to the same dirtbags who did all this bad stuff."

"You think we should host all the darknet documents," he said. He didn't look like he thought it was the worst idea in the world, but he also didn't throw his arms up and give me a bear hug and shout, *Marcus, you've done it!*

"Yeah."

"From what I understand, only a small percentage of these documents have been examined. What if we put all this stuff on our site and it turns out that its full of lies or dirty jokes or peoples' bank details?"

Damn, I liked Joe. That was a really good question. "Well, there's the darknet spreadsheet, and that lists all the docs that have been combed over by the darknet team, whoever they are"—I made a conscious effort not to look guilty—"so we could just slurp those in. I could write a script that checks the spreadsheet several times a day and grabs anything that's been described."

He looked thoughtful. "Well, that's better than putting it all up, but, Marcus, we don't know who these darknet people are. What you're talking about is fundamentally giving them the ability to put anything they want on the Joe Noss campaign website, just by adding it to their spreadsheet. That seems like a big step to me. And a big risk."

That was frustratingly true. I hate it when people are right at me. "Um," I said. "Well, what if we set up a requirement that everything has to be looked at by a human in our office before it goes live?" I thought for a moment longer. "I could put up all the titles of the docs that we haven't approved yet, and let visitors to the site vote for which ones they want reviewed first. So if they started pouring in by the thousands, we'd prioritize the ones that Joe Noss supporters were most interested in."

He started nodding midway through this, and by the time I finished, he was smiling. "That's a very interesting idea. Not at all what I had in mind, I have to say, but it's pretty interesting. Being the best place in the world to find out about the corruption of traditional politics is a smart move for a reforming, independent political candidate. And you think you could build this?"

I thought about it for a moment or two, mentally sketching out the way I'd stitch together off-the-shelf parts from various software libraries that already existed for Drupal, the industrial-strength system we were using to manage our website. "Yeah," I said. "It should be pretty straightforward. I've done most of that stuff before, it's just a matter of doing it again, but gluing it together in a different way."

He nodded again. "Do it," he said. "Do both. Build me a demo and I'll show it to Flor and my advisory committee. I might get you in to help with that. If they sign off on it, we'll make it happen. Can you have something for Monday?"

It was Saturday. Theoretically, I could do this on Sunday. He'd said a demo, right? I could nail up a demo in a couple hours. "Yeah," I said. "I can do that."

"You are my delta force ninja, Marcus!"

Lemmy straightened up from his work on the quadcopters' batteries and laughed. "That sounds about right."

My phone rang then—it was Ange, lost in the crowd nearby, and I talked her in, waving my hands in the air so she could spot me. She gave me a giant hug, and I introduced her to Joe.

"Marcus thinks you're pretty awesome," she said to him, by way of hello.

"It's entirely mutual," he said, and the way he said it, it was like he meant it, not like a mere formality. I could actually feel my head swelling. "And I'm sure you're something special, given what I know about him. You should come by our office sometime and say hello, watch Marcus do his magic."

"I'd like that," Ange said, and I could tell she felt the same immediate trust and bond with Noss that I'd felt. It was like magic—scary and wonderful at once.

Ange crouched down to say hi to Lemmy and went to work with him getting the quadcopters ready to go again. She'd tuned in to our feed—following my tweet—and was itching to do some flying. I could tell that Lemmy would have a hard time getting the controller away from her.

"I imagine you go to these all the time," Joe said to me.

"Um," I said. "Not really. Liam and I went to one yesterday, but I have to admit I don't get down to protests very often."

"I see," he said. "When I was a young man, it seemed like all we did was protest—the Reagan years were pretty turbulent in San Francisco. Haven't been out to many since. I keep wondering when something's going to *happen,* though. We used to have speeches and such."

"Well," I said. "You can do a speech if you want. I think a lot of people would like to hear what you have to say." I told him about the People's Mic, which he'd heard of but never seen.

"It sounds like a microphone that only works if you can convince the people around you that you've got something to say," he said. "I like that."

"Want to try?" Having been shoved in front of the People's Mic the day before, I was eager to do it to someone else. After all, Joe was a real, no-fooling politician, with that spooky ability to make you trust him with a look and a few words.

He looked around at the crowd, considering it seriously. "I do believe I would," he said.

"Right now?"

He grinned. "Oh yes, certainly—before I lose my nerve and go home."

I put my hands around my mouth, and feeling a little self-conscious, hollered, "Mic check!"

A dozen or so people picked up the call. I repeated it, and again, until a few hundred people around us were saying "Mic check" and waiting for Joe to start.

Joe, meanwhile, had struck up a conversation with the driver of a nearby parked car, who had climbed out of the driver's seat and perched on the car's bumper. "This gentleman's volunteered the hood of his car for a stage," Joe said. The driver, an older Asian guy in a sportscoat and aviator shades, was looking interested and good-tempered. The whole thing was remarkably cheerful, really—for a gathering of hordes of pissed-off people, we were all in very good spirits. Must have been discovering how many of our neighbors felt the same way we did.

Joe stepped nimbly onto the car's hood, wobbled once, caught his balance.

"My name is Joe Noss and I'm running as an independent for the California senate, but that's not why I'm here today."

This was *waaay* too long for the People's Mic, and the words got jumbled in the repetition. Joe didn't look flustered, just did his thoughtful face again, and started over. "Sorry about that."

"*Sorry about that,*" the People's Mic said.

"My name is Joseph Noss.

"I'm running as an independent candidate.

"For the California senate.

"I could have had the party nomination from the Democrats.

"And probably from the Republicans.

"But I decided to go independent.

"Even though everyone says you can't win in this country.

"Unless you're part of a party.

"And they may be right.

"But I've been a Democrat all my life.

"And the spying, the wars, the banksterism.

"It's not the Democratic Party I joined.

"And the Republicans don't offer anything better.

"Because there's something *wrong* with our country.

"There's something wrong with our *world*.

"Somehow, the ideals of fairness, neighborliness, and justice have vanished.

"To be replaced by a cult of greed, shortsightedness, and whatever you can get away with."

He had the rolling tones of a preacher, and a voice like a bullhorn. He had to wait a long time between sentences, because there were rings and rings of people repeating his words, far down the street in every direction. The guy whose car he was standing on wasn't looking mildly amused anymore. He was looking enraptured. After every sentence, while he was waiting for the mic to finish, he had a look on his face of serene confidence.

"I don't have the answer.

"I don't think anyone has the answer.

"But I think we're only going to find the answer when we stop making it all worse.

"We need politicians who stand for people, not money.

"Which is what I have been.

"And what I plan on being.

"We have an office on Mission Street, right by 24th.

"It's open every weekday.

"You can drop in any time.

"Tell us what you hope for from your government.

"And we'll tell you what we plan on doing.

"And you can visit our website of course.

"Just google Joe Noss." He flashed me a smile. I'd noticed that he always made a point of spelling out double-you-double-you-double-you-dot-joseph-noss-for-california-senate-dot-org every time he finished his speeches, which made him sound like a time traveler from the 1990s, and I'd pointed out that he was the top three results for his own name on every search engine.

"Thank you."

He got a lot of People's Mic–style cheers, fingers wiggling in the air so as not to drown out the speaker, and people crushed in around him as he stepped down and thanked the guy whose car he'd been using. The guy gave him a surprise hug—this was California, after all!—and Joe took it like a pro and gave him a hearty, back-slapping bear hug in return.

"That was most remarkable, Marcus," he said. "Thank you for that opportunity."

"You did great," I said, feeling a little silly telling this guy who was a total pro that he'd done well by the lights of a pipsqueak like me, but he seemed genuinely happy.

We chatted a while longer, and then someone else stood up and did a People's Mic about her student debts, which had grown by over $200,000 in fines and penalties when the loan company lost one of her payments. There were a few more of these, and I was getting hungry. Ange had some cold pizza in tinfoil in her pack, so we moved off a ways and ate, and when we rejoined Lemmy, Joe was gone.

"Said he wanted to see what was happening elsewhere," Lemmy said. "Seems like a good guy."

"He is," I said, vicariously proud to have been the guy who introduced Joe to Lemmy.

Crowds have moods, like people, and these moods are more than the sum of the moods of everyone in the crowd. It's possible to be a happy person in an angry crowd—but not for long, because either you leave or you get angry yourself.

The mood of the crowd when we arrived had been happy, if a little nervous. As the day wore on and the crowds grew and grew, the mood got more excited, with tinges of holy-crap-can-you-believe-this and man-we-should-do-something and how-long-are-we-going-to-get-away-with-this.

The three of us—Lemmy, Ange, and me—moved around some, getting deeper into the crowd and then off into its sub-branches, using the copters to spot places where interesting stuff was happening. We visited a place where a marching band was playing ragtime and people were dancing and whooping; another where a gigantic group of drummers was beating out a wall of polyrhythmic sound; a few makeshift stages where People's Mic talks were going on. One was a really interesting talk about the Federal Reserve, the other an embarrassing conspiracy theory about the government being secretly behind the bombing of the Bay Bridge. The speaker claimed he'd worked on the rebuilding project and had been officially-secretly told not to save anything that might help figure out who was behind the attack.

I'd heard that theory a few times and it just didn't hang together—it seemed like the kind of thing you'd only believe in if you were looking for an excuse to distrust the government. I didn't need any excuse to distrust the government. I didn't need to speculate about the unlikely possibility that they'd blown up the Bay Bridge to find a reason to believe that there were people in power who were just *waiting* for the chance to set up a police state. I distrusted the government because when the Bay Bridge blew, the city of San Francisco became a police state in the space of hours. Either that meant that some evil genius had attacked the Bay Bridge in order to send in all his authoritarian thug henchmen, *or* it meant that there were people out there who were just *waiting* for *any* disaster, standing by with a whole well-developed plan for unleashing their goons on people who'd just lived through some kind of terrible emergency.

Call me a skeptic, but I think it's even *creepier* to see someone who's just suffered disaster and think, *Hey, great, they're vulnerable and I can screw 'em over,* than to actually *plan* the disaster. So I just don't see the point in trying to make some kind of case proving that the Bay Bridge was an inside job—it's ever so much more evil if it *wasn't* an inside job.

Thinking this stuff, talking it over with Ange, I started to feel like, somehow, the crowd's mood was changing. It was getting dark, and the temperature was dropping—it had started off as one of those San Francisco September days that are as hot as a July day anywhere else, but it was turning into one of those foggy San Francisco nights that makes you cold right to your marrow. The day's excitement was giving way to more anger and more fear, and it seemed to me that I was hearing a lot more crackling police radios, seeing a lot more helicopters and UAVs overhead.

We were stopped in a particularly dense spot near McAllister Street, so I got out my phone and watched Lemmy's copters' point of view for a while. There were a *lot* more cops, it was true. One of the copters was off at the fringe of the protest and as it swung around, I saw a line of police and military buses stretching out to infinity, seemingly all the way to the Embarcadero. Either those buses were there to bring about a zillion cops to the protest, or they were there to take a zillion protesters away in handcuffs. Or both.

"Lemmy," I said, showing him my screen. Ange pulled my hands lower so she could see, too—I was so freaked that I'd forgotten to take her height into account, which is pretty freaked, all right. Ange wasn't kind to people who were oblivious to the world of short people.

"Time to get out of Dodge," Lemmy said.

"Yeah," I said. "Let's go." We looked around, trying to figure out the shortest path out of the protest, starting to feel a little fear. As I scanned the crowd, I saw that I wasn't the only one getting wild-eyed. There were probably lots of other people who'd been tuned in to feeds from overhead and noticed the massing horde.

I looked back at my phone. "Something's weird."

Ange yanked my arm down, stared at my phone. "Can you be more specific?"

"No," I said. "I can't. But something's weird."

Lemmy peered intently at my screen.

"No police UAVs," he said.

We all looked up at the airspace over the protest. The density of UAVs—gliders and quadcopters—had definitely fallen off. "How do you know it's the police UAVs that are missing?" I said.

"They're the lowest flying," Lemmy said. "Better for getting face shots."

My mouth had gone dry. "Why would they ground all their UAVs?"

Lemmy looked at me with a crazy eye-roll. "Maybe they don't want to get any video of what's about to happen."

"Or maybe they're about to do something to the electronics," Ange said.

Lemmy and I both looked at her. She had a pit-bull look of determination on her face and she was digging through her bag. She pulled out two pairs of swim goggles and a stack of paper painter's masks. She pulled one pair of goggles over her eyes and passed the other to me, then used her free hand to produce a quart of milk of magnesia that she used to douse the painter's masks. She put one on, I put one on, and I handed one to Lemmy, but he wasn't paying attention. Instead, he'd crouched down and buried his face in his backpack and he was all but throwing its contents on the ground as he dug for something.

"Lemmy," I said, shaking the dripping mask under his nose. The liquid would neutralize some of the sting in any kind of pepper spray, and if they used some other chemical agent, the wet mask would trap more than a dry one. "Lemmy!"

He stood up so fast he caught me on the chin a little and would have sent me backwards on my ass if there'd been room for it. As it was, the people behind me caught me and steadied me, and I waved a quick thanks at them and turned back to see Lemmy holding a silver Ziploc bag.

"Phones," he said. "Quick!"

I recognized the bag: a Faraday pouch, the kind of thing you put your RFID-emitting ID, transit pass, toll road transponder, or passport into if you didn't want strangers to be able to read it.

But Faraday pouches weren't just good at keeping the stuff inside from communicating with the outside world: they were also good at keeping radio waves from the outside world from getting *inside* them. I yanked out my phone so fast I turned my jeans pocket inside out and scattered small change on the ground around our feet. Ange already had hers out. We dropped them in the bag and Lemmy shoved his in and sealed it and dropped it back in his backpack, then he took the mask from me and dug out his own goggles and pulled them on.

The people around us had seen this weird behavior and some of them were following us. Others were starting to push and panic, trying to get out, and I thought, *Oh God, there's going to be a stampede, we're going to die—*

And at that moment, there was a *crack* like the sky was a sheet of paper being torn in two by enormous, divine hands, and every electronic device in the vicinity sputtered and died.

They'd HERFed us.

HERF stands for High Energy Radio Frequency, and it basically means a big, nasty pulse of raw radio energy. You can build a HERF gun that will tune the power from a standard car battery, focusing it into a pencil-beam of ugly brute force by means of a mini satellite dish and use it to kill a laptop at twenty paces. The whole thing'll cost you under $200 if you're smart about parts.

Of course, if you're a big government or well-equipped police force, you don't need to homebrew anything like this. You can just go through a paramilitary mail-order catalog and buy some ginormous pulsed-energy appliances from off the shelf. From a law-enforcement perspective, they're like a friendly nuclear bomb, one that leaves all the people and buildings intact, but preserves that wicked electromagnetic pulse that turns anything more complicated than a 1975 diesel engine into a paperweight.

I figured that the police had HERFed the crowd, but that wasn't quite right. Later on, during the hearings on the September 24th Protest, police crowd-control specialists testified that they aimed the pulse weapon 100 feet over the crowd, instantly killing every UAV in the sky. These plummeted to the crowd below, and represented the first wave of casualties of the night. No fatalities, but one person was in a coma for six months, and another lost her left eye.

The specialists who testified swore that the mobile phones that they took out were unintentional, as were the firmware on all the cars that caught the edges of the burst. And the six people whose hearing aids died, and the twelve whose pacemakers stopped—entirely accidental and *most* unfortunate.

But they had to "preserve operational security," which is police-ese for "make sure no one could watch what they did next." And after all, they *had* given a "lawful order to disperse," though I can't say I heard it. Stuff happens, I suppose. All part of life in the big city.

I put my masked mouth right up to Lemmy's ear.

"Lemmy."

"Yeah?"

"You know that copter we landed on the roof, the one with low battery?"

"Yeah."

"You think it's still able to fly?"

"Dunno. Maybe. Why?"

"I think you should get it in the sky and start streaming video with infrared *right now*."

"Yeah."

He broke the seal on the Faraday pouch and spilled out the phones, handing me mine and Ange's, prodding his handset. The cellular towers had all been switched off at SFPD's request a moment before the HERF detonated, but Lemmy's phone included a 900Mhz direct radio link to his UAVs. 900Mhz was a good frequency, great for penetrating walls and other structures, but it was also a *busy* band, noisy with baby monitors and walkie-talkies and RC toys. Of course, all of *those* were pretty much toast at the moment, so Lemmy had the airwaves all to himself.

He grunted in satisfaction. "It's up," he said. "Maybe twenty-five minutes on the battery." A moment later: "It's got 4G, too. Must be picking up towers farther away from us—it's the altitude."

"Great," I said. "Get it over us."

"Yeah."

Ange, meanwhile, was hitting reload-reload-reload on her phone's WiFinder, waiting for the moment that the network the copter was retransmitting became available to her. "Got it," she said.

"Can you tweet out the URL for the livestream off the copter?"

"Derp. What do you think I'm doing?"

"Sorry."

I had my phone out, too, and signed on to the UAV's network, sent out my tweet.

"Can you shut down its network bridge?" I asked Lemmy. "There's going to be a zillion people trying to get online and none of the video'll make it out if they do."

"Yeah," Lemmy said. "Yeah, done."

"Okay," I said, and looked around for the first time since the pulse. "Holy mother of Zeus." It was as though all the light in the area had been sucked into the Earth, leaving us in a realm of shadows. All I could see, for as far as I could make out in every direction, were silhouettes, moving uneasily like stalks of wheat in a gathering storm. Here and there people had found flashlights or headlights, and these created pinpricks of illumination that stood out like searchlights.

Then, a wailing sound, a sound I hadn't heard since the day the Bay Bridge blew. It was the San Francisco air-raid siren, a sound like an effect from an old war movie. They used to test it every Tuesday afternoon, but after the trauma of its actual use following the attack on the bridge, they'd discontinued the tests. Too many people reacted to the sound with post-traumatic-stress freak-outs—crying jags, an uncontrollable urge to hide or get out of doors—or indoors—and various other low-grade psychotic reactions. There'd been a long debate and finally the city had settled on testing the alarm by playing three long beeps, three short beeps, and three long beeps—Morse code for SOS.

But now the siren blared, and it was louder than I remembered, though I couldn't see the nearest PA pole. It was so loud it felt like it was *inside* my head, so loud it made my teeth clench as it howled up and down its waveform, a sound that every cell in my body knew meant "Bad stuff is happening."

The silhouetted stalks of wheat began to waver more forcefully, colliding with one another as they tried to find some place away from that punishing sound.

Suddenly, the sound cut off, leaving behind a ringing silence that was almost as scary. Then, an echoing, giant voice broke out over the PA system. It was the voice of pure authority, like something engineered in a lab or coming off a text-to-speech library designed for maximum intimidation and terror.

"THIS IS AN UNLAWFUL GATHERING."

The words bounced around the precincts of the protests, blocks and blocks of it, like a tasteless parody of the People's Mic.

"YOU ARE SUBJECT TO SEARCH AND BACKGROUND CHECKS."

I thought of the copter zipping over our heads, streaming all this live to the Web. I wondered how many people were tuned in.

"THOSE WHO COOPERATE AND WHO HAVE NOT BRO-KEN LAWS WILL NOT BE ARRESTED."

There was pushing and shoving from nearby. I looked around

and saw that one of the pools of light belonged to a husky pro-
tester with a headlamp. He was taking off his baggy coat, revealing
a windbreaker emblazoned front and back with block-cap letters:
SFPD. I looked around from side to side and back and front and
saw that there were more SFPD windbreakers coming into view
as burly guys dotted around the crowd like raisins in rice pudding
revealed themselves.

But they weren't the only ones revealing their secret identities.
A dozen yards away, a trio of guys in all-tactical black, wearing
goggles and face masks, arranged in a flying wedge, forced their
way through the crowd, knocking people aside as they bulled in a
straight line. They snapped to a stop in front of a pair of young guys
with scared-pale faces and eyes wide enough to show the whites.
With no preamble or windup, two of the officers stuck them with
Tasers, and they fell to the ground like stunned oxen, twitching
and thrashing. One of them brushed a bystander with his hand
and she screamed and her head whipped back and hit the nose of
the man behind her, which began to gush blood.

The three guys in the flying wedge took no notice. They knelt
down and bound the two guys hand and foot with plastic cuffs,
cinching the bindings tight with savage yanks, looking like they
were trying to start balky gas mowers, then tossed the guys over
their shoulders like rolled-up rugs and bulled their way back out
of the crowd.

It was around then that the screams and the pushing started.

At first, it was a distant sound, sounding like it might be a block
away, and the pushing was just rippling waves back and forth
through the crowd, the person behind me taking a half step back
to absorb the shock of the person who'd just taken a half step into
her, banging into me, me taking a half step back and colliding with
Ange, who steadied me and took a half step back.

But the next wave was much stronger, not a half step push, but
a step and a half, and I got an elbow in the solar plexus that drove
the wind out of me and would have doubled me over if there were
room to double over. And the wave after that was like a mosh pit,
and the wave after that was like an earthquake, and the wave after

that was like—it was like being in a crowd of hundreds of thousands of people where panic had seized the night and was driving us insane.

Then someone had a brilliant idea.

"Mic check!"

I was irritated at first. Who the hell thought giving a speech at this juncture was going to improve things? But of course, it wasn't about giving a speech, it was about getting through the crowd's animal nature and to its human brain, the part that knew that pushing and shoving was a disaster waiting to happen.

"Mic check!" I called back, and others joined it.

"Mic check!"

"Mic check!"

The call rippled out in concentric circles through the human-swarm, and where it was heard, calmness came. A police snatch squad barreled past me, so close I could have stuck out a foot to trip them, but I did nothing, didn't even flinch. There was a calmness descending on me now, that calmness from the temple, the calmness I'd always sought in moments like this but found so rarely.

One of the husky SFPD guys was heading my way, various pieces of gear clipped to his belt, stuff that I found myself eyeing up curiously despite myself, wanting to know what all those gadgets were about. He stopped a few people away from me, facing a woman and a man who looked like they could have been my parents' friends, the sort they sometimes met for dinner and a show, back in the good days.

The policeman spoke to them authoritatively, and they both produced IDs. The policeman held up a PDA and snapped a photo of each, the ID briefly illuminated in a grid of red laser light, like a supermarket checkout. He stared at his display for a moment, then put it away. Next, they talked intensely for a few minutes, and then the couple handed over their phones, tapping out unlock codes first. They must have been in a radio-frequency shadow, shielded from the HERF blast, leaving their phones in working order. The officer stared at the cable jacks on the phone's underside for a minute before he pulled out a matching cable and inserted it. The cable ended with one of those intriguing boxes on his belt, and I thought I understood what was going on: the police were checking people, logging them, and *copying all the data off their phones* before letting them go.

I was agog. Somehow, this was worse than the snatch squads who'd taken people out of the crowd without so much as a word. Those phones would have so many intimate details of their owners' lives. Passwords. Address books of friends and family. GPS logs of all the locations they'd visited. Browser logs of all the websites they'd loaded. Their IMs, wall updates, tweets. I couldn't believe it.

When the officer was done, he took a pen out of a little arm-holster and scrawled something on the back of each of their hands. The couple were looking glazed-over and horrified. The officer smiled at them and explained something in detail, and they nodded in stunned silence.

The officer gave them a friendly slap on the shoulder and pointed, sending them off through the crowd. I moved to intercept them.

"Hey," I said. "Hey, wait!"

They stopped.

"What did he say to you? The cop, I mean."

The man—about sixty, with a friendly face and a neat little mustache and a soft Southern accent—said, "He said we could show this to anyone who stopped us and they'd let us through." He held up his hand, showed me the mark. It looked like a graffiti tagger's mark, a scribble. Maybe it was his initials. "Special ink," the man said.

"Did he make a copy of your phones?"

The woman nodded. She was about the same age, with a good haircut and chunky wooden jewelry around her neck and wrists, like an old hippie maybe. "Yeah. And he deleted our photos." She frowned. "I had some pictures of my grandchildren on there." They both spoke like they were in a dream or a nightmare.

"Thanks," I said.

"Yeah," they said, and moved off.

The officer had moved on to someone else. He scanned the ID, took the phone. This time, he searched the guy. The guy was black. Maybe that had something to do with it. The cop searched his bag, his pockets. By then, the guy's phone had locked up again and the cop made him unlock it. The guy looked like he wanted to cry—or hit the cop. The cop was clearly enjoying this. He scribbled on the guy's hand and sent him on his way.

Ange and Lemmy had been watching, too. We exchanged horrified looks. Another snatch squad sent a shock wave rippling through the crowd, and this time I did fall over, scraping my palms a little on the ground. The pain seemed to wake me up. I knew what I had to do.

"Mic check!" I called.

Ange gave me an alarmed look.

"Mic check!" I called again.

Ange repeated it. So did Lemmy. The call went around.

"The police are recording IDs.

"And copying the data off your phones.

"And erasing the photos.

"Without a warrant.

"Without charges.

"This is illegal.

"It's a crime.

"It's still a crime when the police do it.

"The police don't get to make up the law as they go."

The officer caught this and looked up at me. I resisted the temptation to speak faster. The People's Mic required slow, measured speech.

"Don't comply.

"Demand a lawyer.

"Refuse to allow them to break the law."

The cop was moving toward me now, plowing through the crowd, reaching for something on his belt. Pepper spray? A Taser? No—a long plastic handcuff strip.

"I think he's going to arrest me now.

"For telling you to uphold the law.

"Think about that."

The policeman was close enough to reach out and grab me when a guy stepped out of the crowd and interposed himself between me and him. I only saw his back—a green Army-surplus parka with a head of long hair protruding from it. He had three earrings in his left ear and two in his right. I saw it all in photographic clarity, limned with the light from the officer's flashlight.

The policeman tried to sidestep him, but two more people stepped in his way. Then more. I took a step back and people closed ranks around me. The officer shouted something. No one repeated it. He didn't have the People's Mic.

"You can go now."

I don't know what possessed me to say it. It just popped out.

"You can go now." The crowd repeated it, the sound rippling out.

"You can go now." It became a chant. "You can go now."

Four little words. Not "Screw you, pig!" or "This is what democracy looks like." Instead, it was a group of people asserting that they were capable of looking after themselves, and dismissing the "public servant" who'd come along to send them off to bed like naughty children.

"You can go now."

The cop stopped. His expression had changed from the confident, condescending friendliness with which he'd addressed the people he'd searched to something between rage and terror. His hand moved toward his belt, which was hung with all sorts of things that had pistol grips or aerosol buttons—"nonlethal" weapons he could use to shock us, gas us, immobilize us. More people joined the crowd between the cop and me, and I had to stand on tiptoes to see that behind him, the crowd had parted, leaving a clear walkway for him to turn around and leave.

"You can go now."

Hundreds of us were chanting it now. We weren't angry anymore. And we weren't laughing, either. There was no mockery in this. *We've got this. You're not needed. Go do something else.* That's what it meant.

"You can go now."

The cop turned on his heel and walked slowly away, his head held high, chin out, shoulders rigid. Even though he had been on the verge of gassing me a moment before, I felt a moment's pity for him. All he had was authority, and we'd taken that away from him. Now he was just a man in a kid's dress-up future-soldier costume, retreating from the "civilians" he was supposed to be guardian and master to.

A sound is just a shock wave, vibrating at a certain pitch and frequency. In thin air, there aren't many molecules for the shock wave to push ahead of itself, so the sound travels slowly and dies quickly. But in dense substances—steel and stone and water— sound travels fast and for a long, long way, because the shock wave has so much material to work with as it pushes forward and out.

We were packed in dense and thick, and our ideas traveled like sound vibrating along a steel beam. *You can go now* was rippling away from us like rings in a pond. The crowd lurched toward Market Street: one step, two steps. After a day of gathering—gathering our numbers and our strength—we were on the march. We were going to go somewhere.

Ange twined her fingers with mine, and I threw my arm around Lemmy's neck. We must have looked like Dorothy, the Tin Man, and the Scarecrow setting off down the Yellow Brick Road. Another step. *You can go now.* And so can we. Another step.

I had just a moment's warning—a general commotion, angry shouts, an elbow in the back as the person behind me was shoved forward—and then the snatch squad had me.

It was just a confusion of hands at first. Strong hands, all over my body. Then a meaty arm put me in a headlock, squeezing hard on my neck, choking so hard I couldn't get a sip of air down my throat. The hands on my arms yanked them behind my back, twisting them painfully in some kind of martial arts come-along hold that made me feel like they would be torn off at the shoulders.

The plastic handcuff bit cruelly into my left wrist and I'd have screamed if I'd had the breath for it. I thrashed instead, and there was a red-black haze creeping in around the edges of my vision. I registered screaming—Ange, other voices—and was lifted off my feet briefly and shoved this way and then that.

And then I was on the ground, gasping for breath, and the hands were gone. Ange was beside me, and she grabbed my goggles and pulled them over my eyes and pulled my mask up over my mouth, her fingers shaking with haste and desperation. I brought my hands up to help her and saw that the plastic cuff was still fastened to my left wrist—but not my right. I levered myself to my feet, feeling like I might retch at any minute. Lemmy was standing beside me, his jacket torn, seeping blood from an ugly, swelling bruise on his cheek. He pressed one hand to the wound and gave me a quick thumbs-up with the other.

"What happened?" I said.

"You were de-arrested," Ange said, matter-of-factly. I looked around. A guy with wild dreadlocks beside me was wearing what looked like a police-issue gas mask and carrying what was definitely a police-issue riot shield. Behind him, a short woman was wearing a police helmet. A few more police helmets bobbed around the crowd.

"What did they do to the cops?" I said.

Lemmy shrugged. "Not much. Took their stuff as they retreated. Don't worry, no one beat up a cop or anything."

We were still on the march. The crowd took another shuddering step toward Market Street. The mask over my face made it hard to breathe, and my goggles were fogging up. I was just about to clean them when the gas fell.

They were dropping it from nearly invisible, nearly silent black aerostats, little toy blimps that used whispering electric motors to keep themselves in place. I'd helped build some at Noisebridge once, a side project of the space-program team, who had also launched a lighter-than-air weather balloon with two cameras into the upper atmosphere, snapping pictures of the planet below it, curving away like the ball we knew it to be but could never see. The aerostats were as light and flimsy as a dry cleaner's plastic suit bag. The way they hovered in place was eerie—prod one with your finger and it would waft away like dandelion fluff, then return to the exact same location with tiny, precise bursts from its little fans. The ones I'd played with had reminded me of jellyfish, and not in a good way. They were like brainless, drifting aliens, and I'd instinctively feared them. Like they might have a sting waiting for the unwary.

The gas canisters slung under their bellies released their payloads with little near-synchronized *pops*, popcorn kernels detonating in a pan, and we all looked up at once, then—

—Panic.

The gas had been released from four or five yards over our heads, far enough up that it formed a drifting cloud that you could actually watch for a moment, which we did, and then as the reality of the falling chemical poison sank in, we all tried to simultaneously hit the ground *and* run away, anything to get away from the floating, descending toxin.

I was jostled this way and that, knocked to the ground, stamped on—one hard boot landed on my head, another got me in the kidney—dragged to my feet by anonymous hands, shoved, knocked down again, picked up again.

Then the choking started, and with it, choked screams. Then vomiting. Maybe there was something in the gas to make you puke, or maybe it was its victims' bodies trying desperately to expel the noxious foreign substance from every orifice. I was splashed with puke from all sides, and I slipped in it as I got to my hands and knees, then to my knees, then to my feet.

I'd caught some of the gas through my painter's mask, but not much. I was having a little trouble breathing, and my eyes were watering inside my goggles from the irritants that had climbed up my sinuses. I was half blind and it was dark, and there was only one thing I could think: *Ange.*

I scanned for her, but couldn't find her. A few other people had gotten to their feet, and I heard and then saw quadcopters and gliders start to crisscross the airspace over our heads again. I was sure they had their nightscopes on and were getting lots of footage. I supposed they'd be able to get nice, long, clear pictures of anyone who showed up with goggles and masks—"troublemakers" who'd come expecting that the police would deploy chemical agents against them for having an opinion.

I called Ange's name through my mask, and it came out muffled, and when I breathed deep to shout louder, I caught a mouthful of the chemicals clinging to the mask's outside, sucked through its pores and around its sides, and doubled over coughing, swallowing hard to keep from vomiting. I did *not* want to vomit into my mask, and I did *not* want to take my mask off and show my face.

I started grabbing the people on the ground around me and helping them to their feet. I had no idea where Ange was, but if she was one of those people thrashing in their own vomit on the ground, I hoped that someone was helping her up.

I reached for a big guy with a short, military brush cut who was holding his head and groaning, and something stopped me, rooted me to the spot with an irrational icicle of fear stabbing me right in the spine. I squinted at the man, and then it hit me—an ugly gnarl of scar tissue that ran from the crown of his head to his thick neck. I'd seen it before, in the back of an all-black luxury car whose back doors had no handles. It was Knothead, the Zyz goon.

He was only a few yards behind where I'd been. Close enough to keep a good eye on me, if that's what he'd been doing there. Far enough away that he couldn't have quite reached out and grabbed me, if that was his goal.

I took a step backwards, landing on someone's fingers, jerking my foot up, nearly skidding on a slick of used food and toxic chemicals. I caught my balance, took another step. Knothead hadn't spotted me yet. He wasn't wearing tactical black, but I saw that his blue jeans had a couple of bulging cargo pockets, and there were a few little bulges around his waistline.

I took another step and looked carefully around me. Would Knothead have been here alone? Would he have had Timmy with him? Zyz didn't strike me as the kind of organization that sent its goons out on their own. I looked all around me, finding new reservoirs of panic and fear, searching the crowd for guys who could be Timmy, wondering if he might be wearing a wig or some other disguise. I didn't see him, but I *did* spot Lemmy helping an older guy who was limping, his arm around Lemmy's shoulders. I started to move toward him, and then I felt a hand take mine. For a glorious moment, I thought Ange had crept up on me and grabbed my hand—somehow, I could feel that these were a woman's fingers.

Then the fingers grabbed hold of my thumb and did something awful and painful to it, something that made my head snap back in pain. I cried out, the sound muffled by my mask, and tried to squirm away from the terrible, wrenching pain. That only made it worse. I went up on my tiptoes, in agony, and managed to twist around and see who was the author of my suffering.

It was Carrie Johnstone, dressed like a sitcom housewife doing the grocery shopping in track pants, a loose SFSU sweatshirt, her hair tied back in a scrunchie. It was such a great disguise, so utterly unlike her efficient, ruthless persona, that I couldn't figure out where I knew that stern face from at first. When I did, I gasped harder. "Hello, Marcus," she said, and relaxed her grip on my thumb, just a little, so that I could catch my breath and focus for a moment. She watched my eyes carefully and when she was convinced that I was paying full attention, she brought her other hand out from beneath her sweatshirt. In it, she held a little two-pronged, pistol-gripped tactical black gizmo. A Taser.

"I'd prefer not to use this," she said. "Because then I'd have to carry you. That would be conspicuous. And I might have to drop you. You wouldn't like that. Am I being clear?" I nodded and swallowed a few times behind my mask. She made the Taser vanish. "Smart boy. Come along now. We've got to move."

It was full night now, and as the people around us regained their feet, there was chaos—shoving and pushing in the dark, crying and some screams and retching. Every now and again, I'd hear someone shout, "Mic check," and some weak echoes as people tried to establish order, but Carrie Johnstone always steered me away from those places, pushing me ahead of her like a battering ram, still gripping my thumb but hardly twisting it. Instead, she pulled it this way and that, steering me with it as if it were a joystick.

Somewhere behind us, I could hear the police bullhorns giving orders to sit down and put your hands on your head, and then I heard Johnstone curse, and she started pushing me faster.

The night blurred past, but something was nagging at me. Carrie Johnstone and Knothead had been at the protest, looking for me, I suppose, and they'd have been caught in the HERF burst. They were all about tactical this and tactical that, but would they have thought to put their clever devices inside Faraday pouches? Johnstone said the reason she hadn't Tased me was that she didn't want to carry me, but really, would it be that hard for her to drag me out of the crowd? Would it be that conspicuous? I was willing to bet that Johnstone could bench-press a water buffalo.

And the million-dollar question: Was there enough electronic circuitry in a dumb little Taser to make it vulnerable to a HERF blast?

I crashed into an old man whose face was streaked with dirt and tears, his face looming out of the night, eyes wide and surprised. He barely had time to register the fact that I was about to collide with him before we were going down in a tangle. As we fell, I felt Carrie Johnstone's grip tighten on my thumb, try to wrench it into that special configuration of torment, and slip.

I coiled my legs under me and sprang into the night like a jackrabbit, scrambling to get away, using hands and feet to get through the crowd, running blindly in the darkness. Behind me, I heard outraged cries and wondered if they were from the people I'd hurtled past, or from people who were being tossed aside by the vengeful hands of Carrie Johnstone. I ran so hard I lost my breath and couldn't catch it, couldn't get even a sip of air to pass my throat, but I forced myself to run on, even as my vision blackened around the edges, telescoping again.

I had been running west, and something about the buildings around me made me think I was getting away from the protest's center, out toward the edge. Soon I might escape to the real world, a place away from relentless pursuers and gas and crowds. Keeping that in my mind, I forced one foot in front of the other, gulping like a fish in my wet, claustrophobic mask.

It wasn't going to work. I wasn't going to make it. Any second now, I was going to fall to my knees and a second after that, Carrie Johnstone would have me. Even without the Taser, she was going to have to carry me—things inside me were wearing out, bursting, breaking, and once I stopped moving, I wouldn't be able to start again.

But there was the edge of the crowd, I could see it. See the place where the wall of people ended and the city began. Just a few more steps. The lights ahead glittered in my foggy, steamed-up goggles. I was so fixated on them, I didn't even see the police line that divided the protest from the real world, a line of helmeted men wearing bouquets of plastic handcuffs at their waists, hard-faced, hands encased in black gloves. I almost stopped myself then, but I didn't. Maybe I couldn't have. In any event, I was pretty sure that Carrie Johnstone couldn't kidnap me from jail.

One step, two steps, and then I was crashing into a policeman—I actually smelled his cologne and the hamburger on his breath as he absorbed the weak momentum of my last stumbling rush. He steadied me, took in my mask and goggles, spotted the plastic handcuff around one wrist, grabbed hold of the loose cuff, jerked my arm around, grabbed my other arm, and cuffed it. I was handled as impersonally as a sack of potatoes as another cop stepped forward out of the line and directed me to one of the waiting buses I'd spotted from the sky.

Before he put me inside, he patted me down, reaching for my phone, then stopping when his gloved hand encountered some of the vomit I'd been spattered with. He said, "That a cell phone?"

"Yeah," I said. "It's dead, though."

"Right," he said. "They'll take it from you when you get processed anyway."

There were already a couple dozen people in the darkness and quiet of the bus. Some were young, some were old, some were brown or Asian, some were white. It was laid out like a school bus, the kind of thing I'd ridden a thousand times on school trips, except for the steel mesh separating the driver's seat and back of the bus from the rest of the interior. Each seat held two people, and they were loading us from the back forward. I was halfway down the bus's length, and I had a seatmate, a guy in black jeans and sweatshirt. He was unconscious and breathing shallowly. The officer who led me to him didn't say anything as he guided me down into the seat, with an impersonal air that was neither hostile nor friendly. I jostled the guy and he made a whimpering noise, like a hurt animal.

"I think this guy needs medical help," I said, squirming in my seat to find a comfortable way of sitting with my arms lashed together behind me.

"He'll get it," the cop said. "Soon as he's processed."

There were murmured conversations around me, the voices tight and scared, like the voices of kids hiding from a killer in a slasher movie. I stared out the windows, looking for any sign of Carrie Johnstone or Knothead—or Ange or Lemmy, for that matter. At five-minute intervals, I remembered that I had forgotten to write a lawyer's phone number on my arm and thought about what an idiot I was. Against all odds, I actually drifted off to sleep for a while, leaning forward with my head against the back of the seat in front of mine. I guess my body had used up so much adrenaline that there just wasn't anything left to keep me awake. On top of everything else, I had the mother of all caffeine-withdrawal headaches. I would have happily eaten a pound of espresso beans and asked for seconds.

I woke up when someone was plunked down in the seat in front of mine. I looked up groggily and saw that it was a girl about my age. She was Middle Eastern–looking, with designer clothes and long hair that had mostly escaped from its ponytail. She had a look of utter, grim determination.

"Hey," I said to the cop. "Hey, are we going to get to go to the bathroom soon?"

"After you're processed," the cop said.

"When's that?"

"Later."

"Come on, we've been in here forever. Could you at least take my cuffs off?"

"No." The cop turned on his heel and left. The weird thing was how impersonal the whole thing had been. The guy could have been telling a panhandler that he didn't have any spare change.

"How long have you been in here?" the girl said.

"I don't know," I said. "I nodded off. A while. Do you know what time it is?"

She shrugged. "I think it must be after eleven."

"What's going on out there?"

"Oh," she said. "They're questioning everyone. If they don't like your answers, you go behind the fence."

"The fence?"

"You didn't see it? There's a big area, a block square. All fenced in with movable barriers. They don't like you, they put you there. Then they talk to you some more. If they still don't like you, they bring you here. You didn't go to the fence, huh?"

I thought about explaining that I'd been chased into a cop by a psychotic war-criminal merc. I said, "Nope. Just got grabbed and put here."

She shook her head. "Not me. They grabbed me, checked my ID, penned me in, checked my ID again, put me here. Bastards."

"Why do you think they grabbed you?"

She shrugged again. "I don't know. Racism? These days, having an Egyptian last name is like being called Jasmina Bin Terrorist Al Jihad. Or maybe it's because I belong to ECWR."

"What's that?"

"Women's group," she said. "The Egyptian Center for Women's Rights. Solidarity with women in the Middle East. The women came out for the revolutions, helped overthrow the dictators, spilled their blood. Then the new 'revolutionary' governments sent them back home, started running around talking about 'modesty' and 'a women's place.' So we talk about it here, have discussion groups, produce literature about what the Koran actually says about women. We call them out for their bullshit." She shrugged again. "So maybe that's it. I don't know. I tried to call my family when I was in the fenced area, but my phone didn't work. No one's did."

Huh. "Do you have a lawyer you could call?"

"No," she said. "But my mother would know someone—once she got over having a heart attack about me being arrested. What does it matter, though?"

I dropped my voice to a whisper. "I have a working phone."

The unconscious guy next to me stirred. He cracked one eyelid and said something indistinct.

"What?" I said, leaning in.

"415-285-1011," he said. "National Lawyers Guild number for San Francisco. If you've got a phone, I'd appreciate it if you'd call them for me."

There was a guard sitting at the front of the bus, on the other side of the heavy wire mesh that enclosed us. He wasn't paying much attention. Or maybe he had a hidden mic and was listening to every word through a headphone in the ear I couldn't see.

"Right," I said. "Do you think you could get your fingers in my pocket if I move around so you can reach?"

He shifted, made a hissing noise like a teakettle. "Don't think so. I expect my arm's busted."

582 | **cory doctorow**

I looked more closely. The arm closest to me was definitely at a funny angle. He must have been in agony. I turned back to the girl ahead of me. "Do you think you could get the phone out of my pocket?"

She craned around to look at me. "Maybe," she said, doubtfully. "How are we going to dial it?"

"Dunno," I said. "Let's burn that bridge when we come to it."

I twisted around to get my hip to stick out in the vicinity of the girl's bound hands. I jostled the guy with the broken arm in the process and he made another hissing sound, but didn't say anything when I said, "Sorry."

The next part was really hard. We had both moved so we were sitting on the seats with our legs in the aisle. My phone was in my front pocket, so to get it close to her, I had to turn around so I wasn't facing her anymore and scooch backwards to where her hands had been. Then she had to find my pocket with her bound hands, working blind, facing away from me.

"Ew," she said.

"It's not mine," I said. "Someone puked on me."

"That's so much more comforting, thanks."

She got her thumb and forefinger into my pocket, pushed in farther, gripped my phone, started to tug it out of my pocket. She got it most of the way out and lost her grip and I thought the phone was going to fall on the floor, but I kind of twisted my hip so that it ended up slipping back. She tried again and this time, she got it out.

"Give me a sec," she said. "These cuffs are so tight I can barely move my hands, and wriggling like that didn't help."

"Take your time," I said. "Can you get the phone into my hand?" I backed up until my fingers brushed hers and she pressed the phone into my hand.

While she flexed her fingers and wrists, trying to get the blood to circulate, I turned my phone around in my hands behind my back. I remembered the days when phones had actual buttons you could find by touch and dial without seeing them. I could feel the phone in my hand, in its familiar grip, my thumb over the power button. I turned it on and ran my finger over the screen, feeling the familiar haptic buzz—the little vibrations the phone emitted each time my finger brushed over a "hot" region on the screen to let me know that I was in a spot that could make the phone do something. Running my fingertip up the screen, I carefully counted out the four buzzes from bottom to top, and the three from left to right, trying to figure out where the number pad layout was drawn. This was the lock screen for my phone, which I'd configured to take a superstrong eight-digit password. Because, you know, I'm paranoid like that.

Gee, thanks, paranoid me. I was going to have to try to key in eight numbers correctly, blind, with half-numb hands. Without alerting the police.

"What are you doing?" the girl in front of me asked.

"I *think* my finger is on the number one. Is that right?"

"I don't know, you're holding the phone upside down."

Oh, this was going to be great. I rotated my wrists around so that the screen was facing her. Incidentally, this also made my fingers feel like I was trying to do the world's stupidest and hardest magic trick.

"Your fingers are on the one, the nine, the three, and the six."

Now I rearranged my hand again so that only one of my index fingers was on the glass. So now I had my hands in the stupid-magic-trick pose, *and* was gripping the phone only by its edges.

"Now your finger is on the one."

I moved it. "Three, right?"

"Right, but you got the two on the way."

I bit my tongue and started to count in my head. When I got to twenty, she said, "Okay, it's reset."

It took six tries. After the fifth try, the phone locked itself and we had to wait for ten tense minutes until it unlocked itself. Security is awesome.

"Okay, you've done it," she said. I could barely feel my hands.

"Who do we call first?"

"My mom," she said. "She knows a crapload of lawyers."

It took more fumbling to press the button that brought up the dialer and then an eternity to get her mom's number keyed in correctly. At least the dialer let me press the backspace button when I screwed up.

"You've done it!" she said, loud enough that people in the other seats shifted and looked around. I closed my hand around my phone, trying to hide it without inadvertently pressing any of the buttons. We waited until everyone had gone back to their solitary misery, and then I said, "Okay, how do we do this?"

"Do what?"

"I'm going to call your mom, right? How are you going to talk to her from up there, when the phone is down here?"

"Oh."

"Yeah."

"How high can you get your arms?"

I tried. It actually felt good to lift them some, working the kinks out of my shoulder blades, but I was left wishing I'd gone to more yoga classes with Ange. The woman—I still didn't know her name, isn't that funny?—shifted behind me, and I felt her prod the call button with her nose or tongue, and then my fingertips tingled with the sound of the phone ringing. From where I sat, I saw several of my fellow prisoners watching with expressions ranging from bemusement to delight to fear. I heard/felt someone answer, a kind of *buzz-buzz?* that my fingers translated as *Hello?* and then the girl whispered, "Mama," and started to talk in a low, urgent whisper, speaking a language I didn't know—Arabic, I guess? Is that what they speak in Egypt?

The bus was brightly lit, but we had been locked in it for ages—hours, it felt like—since the last prisoners were brought in. Surely the guard at the front was half asleep or bored stupid, or maybe he was stupid to begin with. Either way, I felt a welcome sense of superiority. They might be heavily armed, they might be able to arrest us and stick us in their plastic cuffs, they might be able to jail us and try us for crimes they'd invented just for the occasion, but they couldn't control us utterly and totally. Here we were, right in the belly of the beast, and we'd cooperated to establish a channel to the outside world. Between the gas and the violence and the sleep deprivation, I felt a strange madness creep over me, a sense that I was invulnerable and invincible, that I was destined to win, because I was able to do the things that the hero of a story would do, and don't heroes always win?

The first clue I had as to my total vincibility, my utter vulnerability, was when the eyes of the prisoners behind me on the bus widened in unison, turning to comical expressions of horror that made them all look like they were somehow related, cousins in a family of genetically frightened people.

The next clue was the terrified squeak from the girl behind me, and then the final clue a bare instant later: the phone knocked out of my hands, my wrists grabbed by a gloved hand and yanked so high and so fast that I barely had time to lever myself out of the seat, bending almost double, forehead impacting painfully with the floor as I sought to escape the wrenching, tearing agony in my shoulders.

Then there was a face beside mine, so close I heard the click of its teeth in my ear, so close I could smell the gum on its breath. It belonged to my tormentor, who said, "Kid, no one likes a smart-ass." My hands were released and I whimpered as my arms snapped back, my fists kind of bouncing off my butt, my face grinding into the dirty floor of the bus.

Before I could get my breath, the same hands had my ankles and the familiar, dread sound of plastic handcuffs being ratcheted along their closure mechanism ripped through the air as one ankle, then the other, were cinched tight enough to hurt. The hands kept moving. My wrists were jerked back as the plastic between them was caught and hauled back up, the man working over me grunting softly—a curiously tender sound—and another set of cuffs were attached to the plastic between them. Then my ankles were hauled up toward my wrists and my fogged-over brain realized that I was about to be hogtied.

I kicked and bucked and shouted something, I don't know what—maybe not even words. Just a kind of howl, a *NO* that ripped from my guts to my throat. I began to worm my way down the length of the bus, trying to get away from the tormentor and his hands. The other prisoners got their feet out of the way, giving me passage, and I heard them shout things at the guard who was pursuing me: "Shame!" in a dozen voices.

I reached the cage at the back of the bus and squirmed and wormed my way around on it, turning to face back up the aisle.

586 | **cory doctorow**

The police officer—a young white guy whose hat had been knocked off, a look on his face like a vengeful god—was trying to come after me, but the other prisoners on the bus had stretched their ankles back into the aisles, making a forest of legs that the cop had to bull past. He reached for the nightstick on his belt, had it halfway out of its ring, when he seemed to think better of it and shifted his grip to his can of Mace.

He lifted it up like bug spray, shifting the mask around his neck over his face as he did, settling the goggles around his eyes with gloved fingers. The prisoners who saw what he was doing retracted their legs, one by one, until the way between the guard and me was open.

He blinked twice at me.

"It's okay," I said. "I'll sit quietly. You don't have to tie me up—"

He took two steps toward me, holding the Mace in front of him like a vampire hunter holding up a crucifix. Like a vampire, I shrank away from it. My world telescoped down to the nozzle of the Mace bottle, the square aperture with the little round nozzle within. "Please," I said. His finger tightened on the trigger. The bottle was inches from my face, aimed right at a spot midway between my mouth and nose.

"Tom," a voice called from the front of the bus. "What the hell is going on here?"

The guard's finger froze. He slipped the bottle back into its pouch on his Batman belt, turned around on his heel, looked up the length of the bus at an older cop with a couple stripes on his shoulder, an inspector.

The guard walked the length of the bus to his boss and the two of them had a quiet, intense conversation. Every pair of eyes on the bus was glued to them, every ear cocked for them. Tom's back was to me, and I could see from where I stood that his shoulders were as tight as a tennis racket. It was clear to me that he was getting some kind of dressing-down. I confess that I felt a little smug to see this guy get told off, but mostly I was still crapping myself with residual fear.

Tom got off the bus, and the inspector marched down the bus without a word, grabbed me by the arm, and half dragged me back to my seat, while I tried to keep upright by shuffling my bound feet in a frantic penguin-gait. He pushed me impersonally into my seat and turned on his heel without a word.

"You should have called the lawyers first," the guy beside me said.

I didn't say anything. The lights in the bus went off and the engine roared to life and we were off.

The girl in front of me apologized over the bump and the growl of the bus as we rattled through the night. The irony was that her mom had been so freaked out that the girl hadn't managed to convey anything useful to her. On the plus side, the girl—whose name was Dalia—managed to retrieve my phone after Officer Friendly knocked it out of my hands. She'd managed to drop it into one of her boot cuffs, and promised to get it back to me as soon as she had the chance. I wasn't too optimistic about such a chance coming up, being bound hand and foot as I was, but I appreciated the thought. In the meantime, I gave her my name and told her that if she wouldn't mind googling me and getting my email address to get me the phone back when the time came, I'd appreciate it an awful lot.

The bus wasn't going very fast or very far. Out the window, it was all a confusion of traffic—lots of other police buses—and long delays. Several times we stopped for long periods—it felt like hours, and certainly my arms and shoulders told me it was an eternity—before moving on. I dozed several times, once flopping onto the guy with the broken arm, who made a weak whimper that was worse than a scream.

We got to where we were going just as the sun was coming up. It was a nondescript warehouse-type building, swarming with cops. They took us off the bus two at a time, spaced out by ten or twenty minutes. I guessed that this must be "processing." They left the people who couldn't walk until last. Two burly cops carried me off the bus like a sack of garbage, then went back for my seatmate. I shouted that he needed medical attention. They pretended they didn't hear.

No one asked me why I was bound at the ankles, and no one

moved to release me. I was hefted from one station to the next. First I was propped up in a chair in front of a trestle table where a couple of bleary cops with ruggedized laptops—about one millionth as cool and military-looking as the ones that Timmy and Knothead had—fingerprinted me, retina-scanned me, swabbed my cheek for DNA, and then took my name and address and Social Security number. I told them I declined to answer any further questions. I told them I wanted to see a lawyer. I told them I needed to pee. I asked them what I was under arrest for. (I'd drilled this routine a zillion times, but it was a lot harder to do in handcuffs than it was in front of the bedroom mirror when I was having what Mom called *collywobbles* about the thought of being arrested some day.)

They weren't impressed. Their responses, in order, were "Spell Yallow again?" "We don't have any further questions," "Later," "Later," and "Disorderly conduct and conspiracy to disturb the peace."

They called out to someone else and then I was picked up—the whole chair came with me this time—and taken to a fingerprinting station.

Then they took me indoors and led me to a cold, bright room that looked like it had once been a supervisor's office, or maybe a foreman's room, and strip-searched me. At least they cut loose my cuffs for this. I chafed at my wrists and ankles, doing my best not to whimper as the blood started to flow to them again. There were fifteen or twenty other guys in there, and we avoided one another's eyes as we stripped off our clothes and stood shivering and naked while more bored cops went from one person to the next, searching our clothes with hands clad in surgical gloves, like we were infected with some kind of vermin or virus. They looked in our armpits, under our testicles, up our butts. It was one of the most humiliating experiences of my life, partly because it was so bored and clinical. These guys had nothing personal against us. They could have been government health workers inspecting beef on the way to market.

It's surprising how philosophical being shivering, terrified, and naked in police custody can make you. If you'd have asked me how

I'd have felt about these guys beforehand, I would have told you that I hated them, thought they were gutless cowards and worse. They were traitors to humanity, people who made their living defending the interests of the wealthy and corrupt and powerful from everyone else. I'd seen them commit violence, seen them arrive at a peaceful protest dressed up like science fiction super-soldiers, seen them bristling with (supposedly) nonlethal weapons and treating people who were scared and upset about the world like vermin.

But there we were, two groups of human beings in a cold room, one group naked, one group wearing overblown Halloween costumes, and none of us wanted to be there. We had parts we'd been given by some weird, unimaginable authority, "the system," and now we had to act them out. I could see that the cops in the room would rather have been pretty much anywhere else, doing pretty much anything else. But there they were, looking up our buttholes and getting ready to throw us into cages.

There was a knife-edged moment where I felt like I could just pull on my underwear and walk up to the nearest cop and say, "Come on, dude, let's be reasonable about this," and we could have talked it over like real people who lived in the same city with the same problems. This guy might have kids who were going to get stuck paying off a quarter million bucks' worth of student debt or he'd lose his house; that guy was young enough that he might actually be living with his parents and trying to pay off that debt.

The moment stretched and broke. Our clothes were patted down and shaken out, then we were allowed to dress again. They cuffed us again, too. I silently begged the universe to keep me free from ankle cuffs and thought I'd made it, when the cop who was trussing me up seemed to remember that I'd been ankle-cuffed and reached for his belt again.

"It's okay," I said. "You don't have to do that."

He pretended he didn't hear me, but grabbed one of my ankles and started to cinch the zip tie around it.

"Come on, man," I said, wheedling and whining now, hating the sound of it in my voice. "It's really not necessary."

The guy made eye contact with me and grunted. "You did

something to earn those cuffs. Not my job to figure out whether it's time to get rid of 'em."

I squeezed my eyes shut. This guy had no idea why I'd been cuffed, but because I'd been cuffed, I obviously deserved to be cuffed. Tom was long gone, and so was the inspector who'd rescued me. I could imagine wearing leg cuffs all the way to the courthouse and the judge, and being denied bail because I was the kind of dangerous offender who got leg bindings.

I shuffled out of the foreman's office and into the main building. The cavernous space had been fitted with mesh cages, stretching in corridors as far as I could see. The cages were made of chain-link and steel poles, the poles bolted to the floor and ceiling at precise intervals, slicing the room into little pens. Each one had an electric lock fitted to its hasp, an open-air chemical toilet, and a collection of grim-looking prisoners. Men were on one side of the central aisle, women on the other.

One by one, the cops tossed us into different "cells," following instructions on their hardened, tactical handheld computers. I decided that "tactical" was the world's most boring fashion statement. Sometimes, they put guys into cells that were so full there was no room to sit, other guys went into cells where they were virtually on their own. Several cells sat empty. Whatever sorting and packing algorithm was being used to incarcerate us, it had a sense of humor.

I ended up in one of the nearly empty ones, and was glad that my hands had been cuffed in front of me, because I was finally able to take the piss that had been trying to batter its way to freedom for the past several hours, sitting down on the exposed toilet and hunching over for privacy, then fumbling my underwear and pants back up.

Within a few hours, the cell had gone from empty to full. Yes, I said hours. More hours went by. It felt like we'd been there for a day, though there was no daylight, and everyone had had their watches and phones confiscated. I got to know some of the guys in my cell, and someone tried a mic check and gave a little speech about how much it sucked that we were being held this way and asked the cops to uphold the law and give us our phone calls and food and water. He got cheers from the other protesters in the cells, and the cops pretended they didn't hear.

Hours oozed past.

People had come and gone for so long that I stopped paying attention. I was hungry and thirsty, and the toilet was overflowing and making revolting smells and starting to ooze a sickening chemical slick that reduced the space in the cell. Finally, I realized that the whole place was quieter and emptier than it had been before. More people were going than coming. They weren't coming back. So they were going *somewhere*, possibly to get their phone calls and their hearings.

Finally, officers came for me, two of them. They sliced the middle of the cuffs around my ankles so that I could walk, and I saw that nearly all the cells toward the front of the building were empty. A tingle of hope came into my belly, joining the hunger growls and the pasty, parched thirst.

We came out to the same foreman's room where I'd been searched. A woman police officer, older, black, took my fingerprints again, read notes off a screen, typed, didn't say anything. It's a good thing she didn't, because I kept forgetting that I wasn't going to say anything to *her* unless I had a lawyer present.

She nodded at the guys who'd brought me out and they gripped my arms and walked me to the door. I emerged to cold, gray daylight and a light drizzle. There were thousands of people standing across the street, holding signs and chanting. The officers brought me to the curb, then let go.

"You're done," one said.

"What?" I said.

"Go," the other one said. "You're done."

"What about the charges?"

"What charges? You want us to press charges?"

After all that, they were just going to let me go. Some part of me wanted to say, *Hell yeah, I want you to press charges. Otherwise, what the hell just happened here? A kidnapping?*

The people across the street with the signs and banners were angry. Now I understood why.

"What a load of bullshit," I said, with feeling.

The cops' faces slammed shut. I stood my ground. I was scared as hell, but I stood my ground. Let 'em grab me, chain me up, arrest me, put me in jail, waterboard me, try me, find me guilty, send me up for life. That *was* a load of bullshit, and I had every right to say it.

We stared at each other like dogs about to fight. I noticed that the people across the street had gotten quieter, then louder. I was peripherally aware of a lot of people with a lot of cameraphones maneuvering into position near me. I guess the cops were, too. One of them turned and walked back. Then the other one.

I was shaking, my fists clenched so hard my fingernails actually broke the skin on my palms in a couple of places.

The protesters patted me on the back. It seemed that they knew what I was freaking out about. There was a table laden with free food—someone had brought down a whole crapton of lentils and rice and PB&J sandwiches and hot pizzas—and five different people asked if I had any money to get home and whether I needed to talk to a doctor.

I sat down on the curb amid the shouting, jostling people and wolfed down about a hundred thousand calories' worth of food, eating mechanically, stopping only once I'd run out of food. Then I got up, dusted off my filthy clothes, and walked away, finding my way home, though I couldn't even tell you how I got there.

chapter 14

Mom and Dad were gray-faced when I knocked on the door. I tried to make a joke of it. "I'd have thought that you guys'd be used to this by now." My voice cracked a little on the last couple words, and they gave me enormous hugs. They'd figured out where I was, and confirmed it by calling my phone, which Dalia had answered, telling them all about what had happened on the bus. Mom and Dad had dipped into their line of credit to pay a lawyer to start shouting at the SFPD about me, but she was only one of hundreds of lawyers so employed and my parents had had no idea that I was released until I stumbled up the walk.

I wanted to shower for a hundred years. I wanted to sleep for a millennium. But before I did anything, I wanted to find Ange.

"She got home ten hours ago," Mom said. "But her mother said she went right back out to the chicken farm." That was what the press was calling the place we'd all been held, down in South San Francisco, the name coming from the cameraphone photos that had already appeared online, making the place look like some kind of nightmarish poultry factory.

No doubt Ange was waiting for me there and I'd missed her in the horde. How the hell did people live before phones?

"Can I borrow your phone?" I said.

Mom handed it to me, and I spent a couple moments unfogging my brain enough to get it to cough up Ange's phone number, which had been my first speed dial for years. "Have you heard from him?" she said as soon as she picked up.

"Kind of," I said.

"Where the hell *are* you?"

"Home," I said.

"What the hell are you doing *there*?"

"Preparing to estivate," I said. Estivate is a very handy verb: it's a kind of hibernation, "a prolonged state of torpor or dormancy." Just where I was heading.

"Not until I get there. How *dare* you get out of jail without my finding you?"

"I know," I said. "I'm a rotter. Sorry, darling."

"Have yourself bathed, waxed, perfumed, and put into bed. I'll be there in thirty-five minutes."

"Aye, aye, Cap'n."

The reunion, when it came, was just what I needed and then some. Both of us had been hurt. Ange had been gassed and trampled, arrested and freed, and while her story had some minor variations in its specifics, it came out to about the same thing as mine. She'd been with Lemmy through most of the process—they'd stayed together somehow, Lemmy bodily lifting Ange free of the crowd at one point when the crushing started, holding her over his head like a freaky circus act. She'd seen him again after they were released, and promised to call him as soon as she found me.

We talked about it for a few minutes, kissing each other in the places where we were bruised or hurt, holding each other, murmuring to each other, until sleep took us.

And the next day, I went to work.

Well, of course I did. It was Tuesday, and the election was coming up, and someone had to get Joseph Noss elected, and it was going to be me. A hundred times on the way to work, I reached for my phone—to make a reminder for myself, to send a text to Ange (who was still sleeping in my bed; her first class didn't start until after lunch), to check the weather for that night, to read what my tweeps had to say. Each time, I thought, *Crap, I've lost my phone.* Got to call it from my laptop and talk to Dalia and arrange to get it back from her. Then I thought, *Huh, I should really make a note about that, now, where's my phone?* And it began again. It was so funny I forgot to laugh.

I came through the door of the Joe for Senate office and stopped. Something was different. I couldn't put my finger on it at first, and then I realized what it was.

Everyone was staring at me.

Every single person in the office was watching me with owl-eyed intensity, giving off a mixture of awe and fear. I gave a little half wave and took off my jacket and headed for my desk, plunked down in my seat, pulled out Lurch, and plugged in my monitor and keyboard and mouse and started entering the passwords that got my disks mounted and my network connection going. There was near-total silence as I did this, and it was so unnerving that I fatfingered my password twice before getting it.

I sat down at my computer and started going through my start-of-day routine: downloading my email, checking the server log summaries to see if we were in danger of running out of bits, kicking off my own personal backups—stationkeeping stuff I could have done while half asleep.

I started off half asleep—or half distracted—and so it was only after a few minutes that I pounced on my mouse and started un-closing the browser tabs I'd just closed, hammering on crtl-F12 with a series of *whaps* so hard I actually felt the spring under the key start to lose its sprungedness. I clicked and clicked again.

Then I got up from my desk and looked into the sea of stares. "Can someone please explain to me what the hell's going on?"

As one, the whole office turned to look at Liam, who got up and came over to my desk.

"You wanna get a cup of coffee?" he said.

I realized that that was exactly what I wanted, more than pretty much anything in the entire goddamned universe. I let him steer me up to Dolores Park, stopping at the Turk's to get a cup to go and a thermosful for after that. We perched on a bench and Liam waited patiently while I drank my first cup and poured myself a second one. Then he raised his eyebrows at me, silently asking if it was time to hear what he had to say. I nodded.

"Joe came into the office on Monday breathing fire. He kept asking where you were, getting Flor to call your phone, getting me to send you email. He had something he really, *really* wanted to talk to you about, and he couldn't reach you, so finally, he came and got me. He said I got computers and the Internet and stuff and asked if I had access to our 'web thing.' Well, I knew where you kept the sealed envelope with the admin passwords, so the answer was technically yes.

"Then he told me about what you'd suggested at the protest, hosting all those darknet docs. He couldn't believe that there were all these people in the streets of San Francisco pissed off about the kind of thing that was in those docs, but that they'd gotten practically no mainstream media publication and no one had made a political issue of it. He said that the Dems and the Republicans didn't want to start everyone thinking about how corrupt the system was, how money bought policy, how scummy the whole Sacramento scene was at the state house. He'd been thinking about it all weekend and had decided that this was going to be the thing that made him different from the regular candidates. Flor tried to argue with him, but you know how he gets when he's sure about something. He was *sure*.

"So he tried to explain to me what you'd suggested, some kind of voting system or something? He couldn't really explain it. After a while, I said, 'Look, I can pull down all the darknet docs and put them up on our server in a couple hours, but I have *no* idea how to do all this other stuff, and if I tried, I'd probably leave the whole thing in such an insecure mess that someone'd take us down and replace the whole site with pictures of penises in about ten seconds flat.'"

I winced. "So what did he say?"

"He said that he'd rather beg forgiveness than ask permission, and told me to just put all the docs up, now, and he'd take care of the rest. The next thing I knew, he was calling in the press team and the next thing I knew after that, they were all checking to see if we could handle the capacity if, like, *millions* of people all came to download the docs at once. I was like, erm, yeah, I *think*. I mean, I knew we were on a cloud machine that could expand if we needed it. I tried calling the data center, but I didn't have your passphrase, so all they would tell me is that their servers could handle anything up to and including the entire state accessing us at once."

"Is that what happened?" The server logs showed that our traffic had hit over a million simultaneous connections overnight, and the rate was climbing.

"Oh no," he said. "Worse. I mean: 'more.' There was a *lot* of interest from out of state. At this rate, it's like the whole *world* wants to know about it. I mean, you've seen the news, right? It was the lead on every broadcast yesterday, and it's been trending on Twitter since about ten seconds after it went live. We've all been waiting for you to come in and get some decent analytics for it. I tried, but . . ." He shrugged. "Well, I'm just the T-shirt guy, right?"

I took a really, really deep breath. "I've been in jail."

"I figured," he said. "That was the leading theory. Joe was going to try to find your parents today if you didn't show up. What happened to your phone, by the way? I've been calling and calling."

"It's a long story," I said. I wondered why Dalia wasn't answering the phone anymore. Maybe she was answering calls where the return number showed up as "Mom," and ignoring the rest. Maybe the battery was dead. If that was the case, I wasn't going to be able to get my phone back until she got in touch with me. Great. "Where's Joe?"

"He's doing a press conference about this at Rootstrikers," he said. "They're an activist group that does something with getting the money out of politics. They're pretty excited about all this."

"Huh," I said, and reviewed what I'd just been told in my head. I mean, basically they'd taken my idea and *run* with it, and it had worked out *well*. So far, anyway. I wondered how long it could last, and decided that wasn't my job. My job was to keep the website online while Joe was off being Joe. The coffee was in my veins now, turning my thick, sluggish blood into quicksilver. It was time to go make some technology work. I was good at that.

Meantime, though: "What about the other thing, the vote-getting machine?"

"Yeah," Liam said. "That. He told me about it, but I couldn't really figure out what he was talking about. Something to mine your social-media contacts?"

"Basically," I said, and ran it down for him.

"Oh," he said. "That is awesome. And we could use the whole thing as a decision-making process, any time some big campaign issue comes up, or after he's in office, get the whole Joe for Senate machine to have instant runoff polls to see what we should do. That sounds *wicked*. Are we doing that, too?"

"That depends on whether we can find the time, now that the darknet docs are live." It's funny; even though the darknet docs had basically taken over my life, I was a lot more excited about this vote-getting machine, and half wished that I could just focus on that. I'd have to find some time to do it.

But first, I had to harden our infrastructure.

I figured the first thing to do was get us spanned out across a *lot* of cloud servers. My predecessor had gotten us hosted on Amazon's cloud, which was as robust as they came, an inconceivable network of humming racks in data centers all over the world, overseen by lab-coated priests who could diagnose and swap out a faulty component in two minutes flat, fed by twisted fiber-optic bundles as thick as my arm, and cooled by enormous chillers with carbon footprints the size of cities. Amazon was a great choice if you wanted to get hosted by someone who'd keep your servers online no matter how popular they got.

However, they were a *terrible* choice for hosting your data if you were worried about the police going bugnuts on you. You see, the police don't necessarily know how to seize just one customer's data from a global network of server racks. If you're doing something with your data that was going to *really* interest the cops, then you had to be prepared for someone powerful calling up Amazon's lawyers and saying, "We need to investigate one of your customers, and since we don't know how to take one customer's data off your servers, we're coming over with a couple of sixteen wheelers and taking it *all* away until we finish our investigations." Or, as the Godfather might have said, "Nice cloud; it'd be a shame if something were to happen to it."

Amazon had a lot, so they had a lot to lose, and while they'd been a good choice for our nice, boring campaign site, they sucked at providing infrastructure for ground zero in the new infowar. I'd heard a seminar about this from some of the Tor hackers at Noisebridge, and they'd mentioned a bunch of ballsy, free-speech-oriented cloud providers that could take us on. They were the projects of eccentric weirdos, free-speech nuts; bashed-together hackerspace side projects; sketchy-sketchy services with one foot in the porn industry and the other in organized crime. Most of them couldn't take a credit card payment because they'd been cut off by everyone from American Express to Visa to Mastercard to PayPal. Instead, they received payment through wire transfers, Western Union money orders, and other weird and cumbersome measures. I groaned and facepalmed and went and talked to Flor about this.

I'd been afraid to face Flor. I remembered her warning about dragging the campaign into anything "leet" and had a feeling that she was probably already furious with me. But I hadn't bargained on what it meant for the idea to come from Joe. Joe and Flor may have argued about this, but once Joe won the argument, Flor was behind him a hundred percent. Like most of us, she was ready to march into the sun for him, and as soon as I made it clear why I needed her to take the campaign credit card down the street to a liquor store and buy a Western Union order for a random dude—I didn't even know where he lived—she agreed.

"Just let me talk to him first," she said. I had a moment's impatience, because I felt like my parent wanted to look over my homework—finding bulletproof web hosting was my department. But then she got on the phone with the guy I'd chosen and exchanged some quick IMs with, and quickly negotiated better terms than I'd been able to get, including thirty-day billing for our future bandwidth bills and a 24/7 cellular number for support calls.

"Sounds like a good guy," she said, as she pulled on her jacket and picked up her purse and marched out into the Mission to find a Western Union office.

Joe got back in the late afternoon, just as I was finishing the switchover to our new host. I had set up two more backup clouds for us to move onto if we needed to, one in a country I'd never heard of in Central Asia. Flor had gone out for two more money orders and I'd written the scripts to keep us all in sync. I also made sure to register a bunch of variants on our domain, joenossforsenate.com, in other countries, snagging the .se (Sweden) and the .nz (New Zealand), figuring that it would be a lot harder to convince two countries on the other side of the planet with totally different legal systems to nuke our DNS than it would be to just get Verisign, who runs all the .com domains, to take down the U.S. version.

Joe listened to me report on all this and nodded his head soberly. "Marcus," he said, "I knew you'd be the right guy for this. Thanks for all the good thought and hard work you put into this. Now, Flor tells me you've been in jail. Were you at the chicken farm?"

I found that my voice had disappeared and tears had welled up behind my eyes. I nodded silently.

Normally, Joe looked, well, *statesmanlike* is probably the best word for it. Like someone who might be photographed at any instant and, if he was, would look as though he were carefully considering how to pilot the nation and its interests. But for an instant, something flashed to the surface that I'd never seen on his face before, a momentary glimpse of something like an Old Testament prophet who's about to lay down some smiting on a foolish tribe that had strayed from the path. The fact that he felt that way on *my* behalf made it all the more powerful—made me like him even more.

"Marcus," he said. "I have been around the block a few times. I've seen all manner of brutalities inflicted in the name of public order and keeping the peace. But the *premeditation* of what happened to you and the others, the sheer *militarization* of it—" He shook his head. "All I can say is, it's not to be tolerated. The fact that the SFPD had prepared for the future of protest by buying fleets of gas-spraying drones and turning a titanic building into an internment center—it can't stand. It won't. I'm sure you've heard about the class action suits pending against the city." I hadn't, but then I hadn't been doing *anything* except trying to get our infrastructure secured. "As someone who served in this city's government for many years, I wouldn't blame you if you joined them."

"Thank you," I said. The lump in my throat had gone down, and Joe had regained his normal "statesman" look. We were back to baseline.

"Now, about these documents. I'm sorry if I stepped on your

toes by having Liam work on this while you were away. He told
me that he couldn't do as good a job as you could, but perfection
wasn't as important as timeliness. There was a lot of interest in
those documents after the demonstrations, and I felt that we could
seize on that interest if we moved quickly."

"Uh," I said. He was apologizing to me? "Well, it's your campaign, right? I'm not going to chew you out for running it the way
you want to."

He smiled. "Yes, of course. But I hired you to do a job, and the
last thing I want to do is make it harder for you to do that job."

I waved him off. "I don't mind, really. But is it working?"

There was another flash, and I got a glimpse of Joe Noss, the
imp. The glee in his eyes was unmistakable. "Oh, it's working. I've
gotten more airtime in the past twenty-four hours than I have for
the whole campaign. Everyone seems to get the connection between the weekend's events and the documents we're publishing.
We can barely keep up with the requests to act as official campaign
volunteers, going through all that data and making sense of it. I
only check in a few times a day, but from what I hear, there's plenty
there for Sacramento—and the rest of the country—to chew on.
My advisory committee squawked and one of them quit. They're
worried, sensibly enough, that there's stuff in that archive that
could expose us to liability, and they're right to worry. I tried to
explain to Liam what you'd suggested about this but—" He spread
his hands and shrugged.

"I know," I said. "He told me." I'd been giving that some
thought. "I bet I can get it up now, though. I was going to try and
do the moderation system tonight, see if I couldn't bang something
together that would only show the public the checked documents.
Sounds like we could use the volunteers to go through what's left
pretty quickly, assuming you trust them. And then we're going to
get to work on this vote getting machine, somewhere for all that
positive energy to go."

"I trust them to do a better job than is being done now," he said.
"They're substantially better than nothing. But Marcus, you have
been in jail, you've been gassed, you've been beaten. I don't expect
you to work through the night, too."

I shrugged. "It's not that hard," I said. "I mean, no big deal. I've pulled plenty of all-nighters, and—"

He held his hands up and I fell silent. "Let me put this another way: as your employer, I don't want you to work on this until you've gotten a good night's sleep and had a chance to see your loved ones and start to recover from your trauma. It's not a request, Marcus, it's an order."

Part of me wanted to argue, but I told that part to shut up. "Yes, sir," I said.

"Good man," he said. "But if you should want to stay a little late tonight and possibly turn up a little early tomorrow, I wouldn't take it amiss."

"Yes, sir!" I said.

"Good man," he repeated.

Mom and Dad were surprisingly cool about everything. I tried about six Skype calls to my old phone, but Dalia wasn't answering. Finally, I gave up and dialed into it and picked up my voicemail (about a million messages from Mom, Dad, Ange, Liam, Flor, and Joe, preceded by a series of panicked calls from a woman speaking Arabic whom I took to be Dalia's mother, who must have had kittens when her conversation with her daughter was so rudely cut short and redialed my number). Then I found an old phone and brought its firmware up to date and stuck in a pay-as-you-go SIM I bought at the Walgreens down the hill and changed the outgoing voicemail on the old phone to a message telling people to use this number until I could get a new SIM from my phone carrier.

I *did* work a little on Joe's darknet moderation site before bed, despite what he'd said, because while Joe was a nice guy to insist, the darknet was *my* project, and just because I was working on it, it didn't mean I was working on it for *him*. I worked until the muscles that allowed my eyes to focus on my screen went on strike, and I blinked hard, brushed my teeth, stripped off, and fell face-first into bed, amid all the junk I'd dropped there, not even feeling the sharp corners that dug into me.

I was 99.9999 percent of the way to sleepyland when my eyes opened so fast I heard the *click* of my eyelids ungumming.

Lemmy's quadcopter.

We'd put it in the sky just before the gas attacks on the crowd, *after* the police thought that every camera had been killed. The tweet telling people where to look for its feed hadn't gone out, but that didn't mean it didn't create and store that feed. I pounced on my laptop and after a few minutes' dicking around, found the file I was looking for.

It was all in ghostly night-vision monochrome, with false-color splotches of orange and red where the people gathered. The SFPD stood out hotter than the rest, with bright red splotches on their hands and feet—I wondered if they were using boot- and glove-warmers? We didn't get the firing of the HERF gun on the camera, but we did get some *amazing* footage of the gas blimps setting sail, moving into position like sinister circus balloons, unleashing their chemical rain, a kind of gray static that fell on the screaming, ter-rified crowd below. The gassing went on and on and on, different blimps releasing at different times, filling the air with wave after wave of choking chemical droplets.

I'd lived through this on the ground, but I hadn't *seen* it, not the way I could see it now. Watching thousands and thousands and *thousands* of Americans of all stripes, choking and falling down—kids, moms, dads, old, young, writhing, crawling over one another, vomiting, screaming. I know that worse things have hap-pened. I know that bombs have fallen on cities, mustard gas sent over trenches, people machine-gunned wholesale.

But this was *here*. This was San Francisco. America. The twenty-first century. I had been in that crowd. It had just happened.

And yet life was continuing the way it had. The world didn't stop. No one declared that "everything was different now." No one was going to remember September 24th as "the day everything changed."

If some foreign power, some religious terrorist, had gassed hun-dreds of thousands of Americans in the streets of San Francisco, they'd be rearranging all the furniture in government to make way for the new agencies that would swoop in to make sure that "never again" would such a thing happen "on U.S. soil." Why did the fact that we'd all bought the gas with our tax dollars make the gas ac-ceptable?

I wanted to put this online, but I didn't have the energy to do it all over again, make *another* darknet site, try to get people interested in it. I was about to go back to bed when it hit me: I didn't *need* to do anything with the darknet this time. This video was *ours*, mine and Lemmy's. It wasn't a secret who recorded it or where it was recorded. I laughed. I could stick this on YouTube. I could tweet it from my own account! I'd gotten so used to operating in secret that I'd forgotten that I didn't have to.

I posted the video to the Internet Archive, YouTube, and popped a torrent on The Pirate Bay for good measure, wrote a paragraph explaining that I'd shot this at the demonstration after the HERF event, pasted it in, tweeted it, and crawled beneath the covers.

Ange woke me up at 6 A.M. by ringing my phone. When I'd set it up the night before, I'd forgotten to configure it to stay silent before 7 A.M., so the ringing drilled into my ears at oh-dark-hundred and dragged me back from the land of nod. "Morning, beautiful," I said.

"You could have told me you had video of the gassing," she said.

"I forgot," I said. I was still half asleep.

There was a long pause at the other end of the line. "You forgot?"

"I forgot I'd made the video."

Another silence. "Okay, under any other circumstances, that would be really lame, but I guess you've been pretty distracted lately. Fine. You get a walk. This time. Still—holy shit, dude, what the hell?"

"Are people talking about it?"

"It got a million YouTube views before it got taken down. The Archive version's still up and the torrent's being seeded by about a thousand people."

"Taken down, huh?" I tried to find some reservoir of naiveté in me that could be surprised to discover that the SFPD had ways of taking down files that embarrassed it.

"Temporary injunction," she said. "That's what the YouTube page says. I bet you're going to get a visit from a process server today."

"You think *they're* going to sue *me*?"

"Sure," she said. "No recording in a frozen zone, remember?" There'd been a bunch of news stories for years about police departments declaring certain areas to be "frozen zones" because a "major operation" was taking place, and no press had been allowed.

"Frozen zone my butt. The courts've said that the press can go into a frozen zone."

"Are you the press?"

"Well, a million people looked at my video. I'd say the answer is yes."

I could hear her smiling on the other end of the phone. "Well, *I* agree with you. But you'll have to explain it to a judge if you want to make it stick."

"Great," I said. "I'll get right on that. After I get Joe Noss elected, sue the SFPD for police brutality and unlawful detention, and rescue two people I don't like very much from the clutches of a band of ruthless international mercenaries."

"You make it sound so hard," she said. "Come on, dude, you're *M1k3y*!"

"And I've got to get my phone number transferred to this new SIM."

"Yeah, that sounds like a total bitch. Phone companies suck. Good thing you've got me."

"I do," I said. "Indeed I do."

So that was that day: getting the rest of the stuff built for Joe, getting a whole raft of emails from reporters—some of whom I knew from my M1k3y days—asking if they could license "my" video for their networks. I laughed and said, "License, schmicense, it's all over the net, duh." That was good enough for Al Jazeera and Russia Today and *The Guardian*, but all the big American networks wanted me to sign these release forms saying that if anyone sued them for posting the video, they could sue *me* for letting them post it. Invariably, these "contracts" came as noneditable PDFs so that I couldn't delete the offending clauses before signing them. The first three times this happened, I just opened the PDFs in a graphics-editing program and drew big black boxes over everything in the contract apart from the bit where I said they could use the video, pasted my signature into the bottom, and filled in the date and sent it back. After that, I stopped bothering. I noticed that most of the networks I gave this treatment to later ended up running the video, sometimes with "Courtesy of Marcus Yallow" underneath, but more often with their big fat logos superimposed over the picture and "All rights reserved" messages that made me hoot with indignant laughter.

My new phone rang at 2 A.M. Like an idiot, I'd forgotten *again* to apply the setting that turned off the ringer after bedtime. I swiped at the ANSWER button.

"Ange," I said. "It's the middle of the goddamned night. I love you and all—"

"We love you, too, M1k3y." It was another one of those text-to-speech voices. This one was female and had a crappy Australian accent.

"Good-bye," I said.

"You haven't done anything about Carrie Johnstone," a different voice said. This one was male and sounded like Yoda.

"You called me to tell me that? I already knew that."

"Masha and Zeb are depending on you." The female voice this time. I wondered if there were really two people on the call. It could have been one guy. Or one woman. Or a hundred people typing into a group-edited page and firing off the results to a text-to-speech engine.

"I've done everything I told Masha I would do and then some. If you want to save her, you should do it yourself."

"We sent you Johnstone's d0x," the male voice said.

"You did."

"Did you look at them?" This was a new voice, impossibly deep, like a cartoon bullfrog. It had a Texas accent.

"No," I lied.

"You should look at them. Johnstone's a very naughty girl. You could tell the world about it. You've got the platform. Especially now."

I sat up in bed. "Listen," I said. "I don't take advice from anonymous strangers. If you've got something to say to me, you can say it to my face. It's easy to sit there in your parents' basements telling me how I should be risking my life, but as far as I'm concerned, you're just another gang of creeps who get their kicks from spying on people."

"So much drama," the Australian voice said again. "We've handed you Johnstone on a platter. You've got the home addresses of everyone she loves, her Social Security number, her ex-husbands, her criminal record, the institution where her daddy is drying out from his latest Vicodin binge. You put all that online, you watch how fast she comes around to bargain."

"Why would she bargain with me *after* I put all her secrets online?"

"Oh," the Yoda voice said, "because she doesn't know what *else* you have. We told you, Ms. Johnstone's been a *very* naughty girl. You remember what we did to your computer? You'd be amazed at how many other peoples' computers we've pwned."

I groaned and pulled my knees up to my chest. "If you guys are all so leet and badass, why don't you do this? Why aren't *you* destroying Carrie Johnstone?"

"We are, Marcus. But you are our instrument in this mission. You are the perfect weapon to use to destroy one of the worst people on Earth. You should feel special."

I hung up.

Look, *you* try to get to sleep after a call like that. I'd spent several mesmerized hours staring at Carrie Johnstone's d0x already, but being gassed, beaten, shackled, nearly kidnapped, taken into custody, and then released to an insanely busy work situation had managed to drive the details out of my mind. And it wasn't as if I'd gotten through all of them. There were *thousands* of files in the Johnstone d0x. It was like a miniature ship-in-a-bottle version of the darknet docs, a mammoth library of sleaze and misery blended with a million irrelevant facts, cryptic files, and weird irrelevancies. I'd become a one-man version of the Department of Homeland Security, sitting on top of a haystack the size of the universe, trying to find the needles.

I dove back into the Johnstone d0x. The conversation with the

608 | **cory doctorow**

freaky, computer-voiced Anons had rattled me, but it had also intrigued me. I'd had nightmares about Johnstone, and there was something evilly attractive about giving her a nightmare for a change.

The conversation had equipped me with some search terms to use on the trove, and I saw that yup, her family was pretty screwed up, and that there were a bunch of phone numbers and addresses for relatives. Some of them were important people—there was an uncle who was a judge in Texas—and some were only noteworthy because they were in rehab or had some embarrassing criminal charge in their records. Once I started to search on *their* names, I saw that a lot of them had received "consulting" payments from Zyz, and while I didn't know enough about finance to know exactly what that meant, I assumed that it was either a way for Johnstone to rip off Zyz by sending a lot of money to her family, or some kind of slimy money-laundering. No reason it couldn't be both, either.

There were a few folders of photos. The most disturbing of these were clearly taken by the webcam on Johnstone's computer without her knowledge. In several, she wore pajamas or only a bra, and in one, she had a finger rammed up one nostril to the second knuckle. My first thought was how humiliating it would be to her if I released these pictures. My second thought was to feel sick at the number of pictures like this of me that there had to be floating around, and to wonder what all my robot-voiced "friends" might do with them if they decided I wasn't on their side.

A file called "searchterms.txt" turned out to be exactly what it sounded like: everything Carrie Johnstone had plugged into a search engine, harvested from her browser's cache of search queries. I started looking through it and quickly looked away. I hated Carrie Johnstone, but I didn't need to know what kind of breast cancer she was looking into, about her research into antidepressant drugs, or the names of the stars whose "nude photos" she was searching for.

I shook myself like a dog shaking off water, and retreated to the emotionally safer distance of all those payments from Zyz. Looking at several different files, I saw that everything that had to do with a payment used the string "IBAN," which stood for

International Bank Account Number, and had to be specified for wire transfers. From there, it only took a few seconds to produce a list of every file that had to do with payments and start looking through them. I quickly saw that Johnstone controlled and moved a *lot* of Zyz money, and that her payments went to a lot of political action committees. I wondered if maybe her family was channeling the PAC money as well.

A few seconds on the Web and I saw that Johnstone's favorite PACs were big donors to politicians who supported easy debt-collection laws, and it clicked. The darknet docs might tell the story of the pressure to wipe out the families of kids with student debt, but here was the smoking gun, the money paid from Zyz to fronts that went on to fatten up politicians who went along with the deal.

It was 3 A.M. I had work the next day. It was going to be a big day. There was a pretty good chance all our servers would be taken down by some scary lawyer-threat somewhere and I'd have to have a clear head to fix that. But who the hell could sleep under these circumstances? Who was I kidding? I was up for the count.

I took my laptop down into the kitchen and made myself cheese on toast—always my favorite midnight feast—and dithered in front of the coffee machine for ten minutes, trying to decide whether I should or shouldn't have a cup. If I drank coffee now, I really *would* be up for the rest of the night. But even if I didn't, I was pretty sure that I wasn't going back to bed, and a little of the old bean juice would sure help sharpen my wits.

Who was I kidding? I loaded up the AeroPress and made myself a double, and then made another to keep it company. I sat down at the kitchen table with the machine and kept on reading. I even went back to the pictures.

A chat request popped up on my screen. That didn't happen often. Ever since I'd gotten the job with Joe, I'd kept my main ID logged out, and the only handle I left logged in was one that almost no one knew about.

> hey jolu
> hey mr nite owl - good to see im not the only one awake at o-dark-hunnerd
> why are you up?

> fight with kylie
> oh

I paused.

> you mean you two are . . .
> kinda. its complicated

I had no idea that Jolu had any kind of romantic life, though it stood to reason. But Kylie? She was old! Oh, chronologically she was only a couple years older than us. But she was such a grown-up. She'd run that meeting like a boss.

> listen you want to get a slice of pie?

It was the first sensible suggestion anyone had made to me all night.

> hell yeah
> ill be there in 15

San Francisco isn't a bad place to get a slice of pie at three in the morning. I'm willing to believe that New York might be better, but it's not like we lacked for choice in any event. We ended up in the Tenderloin at one of those '50s-retro places that stayed open 24 hours and catered to a weird blend of jet-lagged tourists, hookers, off-duty cops, homeless people, and night-shifters. And us.

"I think you should do something really *lateral*," Jolu said, after I had him up to speed. "I mean, you've got these two groups of weird-ass crooks hoping to make you jump one way or the other, and they're both calculating your next move to see if they can get inside it, steer it. They're smart, nuts, and totally lacking in ethics. The only way you're going to get ahead of them is by doing something totally, absolutely whacked out. Move to Albania. Rappel off the Golden Gate Bridge. Become a Trappist monk."

"That's really helpful, thanks."

"Oh, come on, it's a major advance on 'When in trouble or in doubt . . .'"

"Again, this is less than helpful."

"It's four in the morning, cut me a break."

This wasn't the first time I'd found myself in an all-night diner with Jolu, and all the nights we'd passed in this kind of place had a certain sameness to them—I'd swear that some of the skeezy drunks and cracked-out weirdos holding down the booths around us were there the last time we'd been here. It's funny how comforting it was to inhabit the sheer weirdness of eating a slice of bad blueberry pie and good ice cream in the middle of the night sitting next to a guy with a face full of broken veins like a map of the California state highway system, a crooked nose, and a pink ballerina's tutu around his prodigious middle. Especially when that guy is trading unintelligible drunken remarks with a skinny one-armed guy with a heavily tattooed scalp, bare feet, and long fingernails painted with glitter polish.

"Marcus," Jolu said, "seriously. This is some bad stuff you've gotten involved with, and you're letting yourself be driven by what other people are doing, instead of choosing a path and making other people decide what to do about *you*. There's no reason for that. Look at it this way: all these people—the weirdos who rooted your computer, these mercenaries—have a lot of advantages over you. They're organized, they have money, they have technical expertise you lack."

"Gee, thanks, Jolu."

"Wait for it. They also all have to have meetings to decide what to do next. *You* can just decide on your own. That means that you can do something, force them to all sit down and figure out their next course of action, and while they're doing that, you can *change direction*, so that by the time they've worked out their response, it no longer applies. They have lots of advantages, but this is *your* advantage, and you've more or less surrendered it."

I thought about it. I couldn't think of anything wrong with his logic. And yet . . . "Okay, but there's only one problem: *I don't know what to do.*"

"The first step to solving the problem is framing the problem," Jolu said with a wise smile. "What if you put together a bunch of possible courses of action, all more or less independent of one another, and had them in your pocket, metaphorically, so that you could just jump and jive and zig and zag on a moment's notice?"

"Again," I said, "it's a nice theory, but it requires me to think up not just one, but *several* courses of action."

"That's not so hard," Jolu said. "You could publish everything on the Joe Noss for Senate website—explain what happened, put up Johnstone's d0x, and hit 'save.'"

I winced. "Jesus, Jolu, that'd be—"

"—Unexpected," he said. "And weird. And a little destructive, though I'd bet that Joe would forgive you. You could dump it all on Barbara Stratford. You could hit your Anon pals up for Carrie Johnstone's passwords and pastebin them, make her life busy as hell for a while, put her on the back foot. You could surrender yourself at the closest Zyz office, demand that they kidnap you, freak them right the hell out. Or call the FBI and report a kidnapping. Any and all of the above, and more."

Each one of these gave me a little shiver of excitement and fear. It was just the sort of thing Jolu excelled at—coming up with scary, smart, dumb ideas. I needed to change the subject before he got me too freaked out.

"So, you and Kylie, huh?"

He banged his forehead on the table. Twice. "I'm an idiot. First of all, I was dumb enough to date someone from work, and second of all, I was dumb enough to date someone a hundred times smarter than me. She's already figured out that there's only two ways this can go if we let it get any more serious: either we break up and one of us has to leave the company, or we stay together forever. And she wants to know which one it's going to be, *right now,* because she says it's stupid to pretend that this isn't the case, and to be forced into some big emotional scene that we can see coming from here."

I boggled. This was so totally different from what Ange and I were like. I mean, she was my *girlfriend,* but we lived at our parents' houses, she didn't have a job, much less a job working with me, and we were more worried about hacking justice forcibly into American politics than we were about what The Future of the Relationship might hold. Somehow, while I was off being a debt-stricken college dropout, Jolu had turned into an adult.

"Are you going to get *married*?"

I must have sounded pretty intense, because he laughed—and so did the weirdos at the next table. "Come on, Marcus, I'm nineteen years old. That's a little young, but it's not as if I'm a kid anymore. I don't know if I want to get married to Kylie right now, but the idea of getting married isn't the worst one I've ever heard. Lots of people do it, you know."

"I know," I said. "But—" I couldn't find the words. *But getting married is for old people.*

"My parents got engaged when they were eighteen. Like I said, I don't know for sure if Kylie is the person I want to spend the rest of my life with, but there's a good chance she is. I mean, how do you feel about Ange? Are you planning on breaking up with her?"

"No! I mean, of course not! We had a big fight last week and I was ready to stick my head in the oven. I get sick just thinking about it."

"There you go, then. You're planning on spending forever with her. You just haven't admitted it. And from what I know about her, she's in the same place. Kylie's twenty-five, she was in a long-term relationship before, and so she knows that there's a point where you've got to fish or cut bait."

"You make it sound so romantic."

"There's nothing romantic about pretending you're not heading toward a lifelong commitment. How long are you and Ange going to stay together? It's a question worth asking yourself—and Ange."

"How come no matter what, we always end up talking about my problems?"

He grinned. "Well, it's always easier to give advice than to take it, duh."

"So maybe I should give *you* advice."

"Marcus, you're one of my oldest friends. If you had advice for me, I'd listen closely."

"And once again, I've managed to put myself on the spot."

"Yeah. It's one of your most endearing traits."

"Argh. Okay, well, for whatever it's worth, I really like Kylie. I don't know her very well, but from what I've seen, she seems like really good people. And it sounds like she makes you happy. But Jolu—" I fussed with my pie and the spreading ice cream slick beside the cooling slice. "Well, buddy, I mean, I think most people today like to spend awhile making sure they know each other really well before they commit to forever. It sounds like Kylie thinks you can't afford to do that because if you decide you're not going to keep it up, you'll have to walk away from your job or she will. But what if you promised each other that no matter what, neither one of you will expect the other to quit? I mean, that may be a hard promise to keep, but is it any harder to keep than 'I promise to marry you and be with you forever until I die'?"

He chewed this over while I felt just a *little* bit smug. He was right: it was easier to give advice than to get it.

"Huh," he said. "You're not bad. Okay, that's worth a try. Now, what are *you* going to do?"

My mood fell. "I have no idea," I said. "Everything you've told me makes sense, but I don't know where to start."

"Start at the beginning," he said. "Move one step in the direction of your goal. Remember that you can change direction to maneuver around obstacles. You don't need a plan, you need a *vector.*"

I finished my ice cream and left the pie. The sun was starting to come up, and Ange would be waking up soon. We'd hardly seen each other that week, and all Jolu's talk about breaking up made me really want to see her. I figured I could go by the Korean walnut-cake place she loved and bring over a box and grab a shower and have breakfast with her family before work.

As it turned out, Ange's mom had an early appointment, and her sister was staying at a friend's place, so we had a rather indulgent time in her bed, replenishing our strength with walnut cakes as required. I had this gnawing feeling that I was going to be late for work, but every time I looked at the clock, it was still ungodly early, and we returned to our business. In the end, I rolled up to work ten minutes early, grinning like a dirty fool and feeling better than I had in weeks.

Jolu was right: I just needed to take a step in the direction I wanted to head and stay flexible enough to keep moving that way no matter what happened. And of all the problems I had, the biggest one was Carrie Johnstone. For so long as she was gunning for me, I couldn't be safe enough to do anything else. I would have to do something about her, and I was going to need Joe Noss's help to do it.

"Where's Joe?" I said. Early as I was, Flor was always earlier.

She gave me a searching look, as if trying to figure out what to tell me, then she seemed to come to a decision. "He's talking to the FBI," she said.

"The FBI? Like the FBI FBI? The guys with the sunglasses and the suits, those guys?"

"Those guys," she said.

"Oh. Um, is someone trying to kill him or something?"

Flor smiled a little. "Nothing like that. At least, not yet. If he goes all the way, the way I think he can, I'm sure that'll come.

"No, the FBI wants to talk to him about the documents we're hosting on our website."

"Oh." Of course they did. And once they started talking to him about this, it was only a matter of time until they came to talk to me. And then I'd either have to lie to a bunch of hardcore fed cops, or tell them what was going on. Neither of those were my ideal position. "Does he have a lawyer with him?"

Flor smiled again. "Yes, Marcus, he has the campaign's law-yer with him. Harry has known Joe since they were in college to-gether. I'm sure he'll do very well."

"Well, that's good." I swallowed. "The campaign has a lawyer?"

"Yes, since the beginning. He was one of the people who pushed Joe to run as an independent."

"Does that mean that if the FBI wants to talk to the rest of us that he'll come with?"

"Marcus," Flor said, "you work for this campaign, and so yes, the campaign's lawyer will represent you any time something you've done in connection with this campaign becomes an issue with law-enforcement. But don't worry too much. Joe talked to Harry before he had Liam post those documents. He understood the risks. He's gone to talk to the FBI to preempt them coming around here to talk to the rest of us. It's just part of the job."

"Okay," I said, "thanks."

"On the other hand," she said, and I glimpsed the *other* Flor, the one I'd seen the day I was hired, the slightly scary, stern one. "If you've done something that *isn't* part of this campaign, something that might make the FBI or some other law-enforcement agency want to take some action against you, something that might embroil this campaign in needless controversy, then you will find yourself answering to *me,* because we've discussed this already, and I believe we have an agreement on this. Am I right?"

"Right," I said. I felt sure my guilt was scrawled across my face, but I made myself stay calm and look just slightly to one side of her steady gaze.

I sat down at my computer to discover that I was actually a pretty smart guy. Amazon had terminated our hosting in the night, and the system had seamlessly switched us over to our first fallback cloud provider with such grace and speed that none of the uptime monitors had even noticed. That reminded me that I still needed to get my phone number back—if the uptime monitor had squawked, the messages would have gone to my phone, wherever it had disappeared to—and I dialed into the carrier's customer service line and started a timer going just to see how long it took the rocket scientists at the phone company to take my request. It had ticked past the thirty-five-minute mark when a shadow loomed over my shoulder, and I turned around to see Joe, looking like he'd been through the wringer.

I hung up the phone. "Hi, Joe," I said.

"Hello, Marcus."

"How're things?"

"Things are complicated," he said. "Perhaps you and I could sit down for a few minutes?"

I knew then that I was about to be fired. "Sure," I said. I locked my computer's screen and followed him into the boardroom and closed the door behind me.

"Let me tell you a few things, Marcus, before we get to chatting. If you don't mind?"

"No," I said, feeling that tight, bloodless feeling in my face and extremities. "Not at all."

"First: I believe that my opponents are behind this FBI business. They don't like the attention this has brought to the campaign, so they've put me in the soup with the law. Monroe, in particular, has had a longstanding relationship with Zyz and its subsidiaries through his career in Sacramento. I'm not in the least bit surprised to hear that he's hurting over this and wants to hit us back.

"Second: I value the work you've done here, and I credit you with coming up with this whole plan. I think you're a bright young man, and I hope you'll stay in touch with me no matter what happens.

"Third: That said, the FBI say that they're reasonably certain that you aren't just someone who happened to suggest posting these documents to our site. They seem to believe you had something to do with their initial publication.

"Fourth: I don't know if that's true or not, but in the course of our discussion, we covered several possibilities for what could happen with you and this campaign. In the end, they reluctantly but firmly agreed that if you were no longer formally associated with this office, they would not pursue any further investigations about your role in those documents to date. This was not an easy offer to come by, and in my view, it represents an internal conflict in their upper echelons, who are simultaneously outraged over these leaks and over the intelligence they contain. They don't want another WikiLeaks trial on their hands, especially since this one doesn't have the same national security dimensions of that entire affair. Very little of this material is technically classified or even secret, and Harry pointed out that the few documents that have surfaced with those labels would likely have been released if they were targeted by a Freedom of Information Act request.

"But still. They don't like the *look* of the thing. Here's this young man with a history of what they consider to be antisocial computer use, and he's implicated in both the release *and* the publication of these documents. They worry that if the story gets out, they'll look incompetent or worse."

"But if I get fired—"

"Marcus, I'm not going to fire you. Be clear on that. But we're talking about optics here, the appearance of the thing. You're right that if you were fired at this juncture, it would make you look more guilty and it would make me look more foolish. But if you were to, say, go off on your own to pursue private consulting work, then the campaign could pay you a decent retainer for your work to date, a sum more or less equal to what you'd have taken home in the event that you'd worked through to election day. You'll be paid your normal salary to the end of the pay period, in exchange for being available to Liam if he needs help getting up to speed on the really excellent systems you've built for us. And should I take office, well, there's always the possibility that you would find work in my office doing the very consulting you'd set out to do while you were on your own."

"I thought you said I wasn't being fired?" The anger bubbled in me, made me want to do something *stupid*. I literally bit the inside of my cheek to keep from saying anything more.

His expression didn't change. "You're not being fired, Marcus. You're not being thrown under the bus, either. That's what the FBI expected of me, you know. They wanted me to turn you over, denounce you as a criminal who'd used my office and its technology to commit your crimes. That was what my opponents were hoping for, too."

He dropped his voice. "The Bureau has some pure fools and vicious idiots in it, but it is not, at its core, rotten. What's more, even the most foolish, vicious Feeb at HQ has some self-respect and doesn't want to be used as a game token by scheming politicians who're hoping to score points with the electorate during the midterms. It wasn't easy to broker this deal, and Harry is still surprised we got it out of them. It's the best deal we're likely to get. It's a deal that keeps you from being investigated by the federal police, and one that lets you keep your pay. It does mean you can't keep coming here and you can't be a part of our team, and I promise you, Marcus, that however much you hate that idea, I hate it even more. I think that losing you is going to *cost us*, and if I get elected, it will be in spite of losing you."

I believed every word. When Joe Noss told you something, straight and even, looking you in the eye, you couldn't help but believe him. My anger drained away.

"I can't take the money," I said.

He shook his head once, minutely, but it was a gesture of total negation. "That's not optional. You were hired for this job, you were counting on that wage. The political machinations of unethical men and women shouldn't take money out of your pocket."

"That was money that you fund-raised for your campaign. Your donors didn't kick it in to pay me not to work for you."

"Marcus, that's very big of you, but I anticipate paying that sum out of my own savings. Flor will paper it over. I can afford it."

"I'll just donate it back to your campaign."

He sat back, looking suddenly exhausted and beaten. "I can't stop you from doing that, but I urge you to give it some thought before you rush into this."

"I will," I said. "I think I need to go now." The lack of sleep from the night before was catching up with me. Tears were welling up behind my eyes, which was always a sign that I wasn't in my right head. I decided that Joe was right about making up my mind about the money later. I started to wonder how much of a good guy Joe Noss could be when he was ready to fire people for "optics" and then quietly rehire them later. I think I said thank you or words to that effect, and stepped, wooden-faced, into the office. There were always ten or fifteen people in the office: volunteers staffing phones or collating literature, a cluster of desks where the campaign strategist and the speechwriter and the PR guy all sat, people whose jobs I didn't even know. I'd met them all, but I only knew half of them by name. Now they were all staring at me, and pretending not to, as I crossed to my desk. There was a cardboard banker's box on my chair, and as I drew up to it, I saw that the few things I'd brought into work had been gathered into the box. I looked at Flor, and she nodded at me and gave me a sympathetic look. I supposed she had packed the box for me, and I supposed that this was a kindness, since it let me leave faster. I got into my jacket, slid Lurch into my backpack, picked up my box, and left without saying another word.

Liam met me on the sidewalk just outside the office.

"Dude," he said. "This is *weak*." I hated the way Liam talked, but I decided to forgive him. I knew that if I lost my temper, it would be ugly. I wasn't in a good place.

"You've got my number, right?" is what I said. "In case you've got any tech problems? You know where the passwords are, too. I'll email you the full server details and customer service info for all the hosts and stuff when I get home."

He looked searchingly at my face. I looked back into his eyes. He blinked. "Is it true you were behind the darknet docs all the time?"

I didn't say anything. I was tired of lying, but I still reflexively felt that going public about this was a bad idea. I was pretty sure that Carrie Johnstone had been the one to tell Joe's opponents that he had someone working for him who was behind the darknet. She must have figured that isolating me was the first step to neutralizing me. She was probably right.

"Thanks for everything, Liam" is what I said.

He studied my face a moment longer. "I don't want the job," he said. "I'm going to quit."

"Don't do that," I said.

"Why the hell not?"

"Because the world will be a better place if Joe Noss is elected to the California Senate than it will be if one of those other two schmucks makes it into office."

He barked a laugh. "You're kidding, right? You really think it makes a difference who we vote for? After you've seen the darknet docs, seen how someone uses the system to get rich, then uses their riches to change the system to keep them that way? Jesus, Marcus, what is this, high school civics? Come on, bro, you of all people should know better than that."

"If you really believe that, why were you working for Joe in the first place?" It was weird sticking up for the guy who'd just fired me, especially since I was starting to get pretty pissed off about being fired. I mean, *optics*? What the hell kind of reason was *that* to fire someone? (The nagging voice in my head told me that it was a perfectly good reason if you were running for office, especially if the person generating the bad optics had lied to you—or at least failed to mention some very important information.)

"It's a job. Who gives a damn? Might as well be flipping burgers or walking dogs."

I started to say something about how you shouldn't do a job

you don't care about, but I remembered all those months I'd spent knocking on every door I could find, handing out résumés like chewing gum, and all the big, fat NOs that had got me. "Listen, Liam," I said. But there wasn't anything to say to Liam. The fact was, he was probably right. "Forget it," I said. "Call me if you need tech support, okay?"

"Yeah," he said. There was a second where we might have given each other a big, back-slapping dude-hug, but neither of us moved. Liam had looked up to me so much, and it had been nice, but it had also been *weird,* all that adulation. I had a feeling I wouldn't have to worry about it anymore.

Once upon a time, my government turned my city into a police state, kidnapped me, and tortured me. When I got free, I decided that the problem wasn't the system, but who was running it. Bad guys had gotten into places of high office. We needed good apples. I worked my butt off to get people to vote for good apples. We had elections. We installed the kind of apples everyone agreed would be the kind of apples we could be proud of. They said good things. A few real dirtbags like Carrie Johnstone lost their jobs.

And then, well, the good apples turned out to act pretty much *exactly* like the bad apples. Oh, they had *reasons.* There were emergencies. Circumstances. It was all really regrettable.

But there were always emergencies, weren't there? My whole nineteen years on this earth had been one long emergency, according to all the papers and the TV. When would the emergencies finally end? Would there be a day when unicorns pranced through the Mission and pronounced an end to hostilities around the world, a return to the promised normalcy, with jobs and freedom for all?

Hell no. If someone like Joe Noss could turn out to be just another politician, then so could anyone and everyone. Carrie Johnstone had been fired, but she ended up getting more money, more power, and more authority, with even fewer checks on her ruthlessness. Carrie Johnstone was always going to end up on top. I'd been an idiot to think that we could elect someone who'd make it all better. I once thought that Liam was an idealistic fool who lacked the sophistication to appreciate just how good it could all be if we just had the right people out there, passing good laws and making good government. Now I saw who the fool was. It was the idiot I saw in the mirror every morning, and I was getting pretty sick of his face.

Ange didn't answer emails or IMs, and didn't pick up her phone. Who cared? What I was about to do wasn't about her, it was about me.

Setting up the first darknet docs site had taken a fair bit of work. It was a lot easier the second time around, and now I had all of the Johnstone d0x in a nice, safe, untraceable place. I wrote a blog post explaining what these docs were, who they belonged to, and even how I'd come by them, gritting my teeth until they hurt and typing out the admission that I'd been rooted by a gang of anonymous trolls who'd done the same thing to my archnemesis.

Jolu was right. I'd spent far too long letting Johnstone drive me ahead of her like a terrified, bleating sheep. It was time I started leading the chase, instead of just running away in terror.

I didn't publish the post. I almost did. But I didn't.

Instead, what I did was email the post, along with the darknet link, to <pr@zyzglobal.com>, <carrie.johnstone@zyzglobal.com> and <press@zyzglobal.com.> I copied in <webmaster@zyzglobal. com> for good measure—practically no one read the webmaster@ account for their domains these days (the address was a spam magnet like no other), but it seemed like a good time to be thorough.

I had just hit SEND and begun to (metaphorically) crap my pants when Ange called.

"What's up? I had class."

"I got fired. Carrie Johnstone told Joe Noss's opponents that I'd been the one behind the darknet docs, and they called the FBI. Joe negotiated my freedom in exchange for shitcanning me. So I got home and emailed Carrie Johnstone a copy of her d0x. I've just sent a copy of the darknet address to your Tunisian Pirate Party email address. If I go missing, spread it around, okay?"

"Marcus?"

"Yes?"

"What did you just say?"

I repeated it.

"That's what I thought you said." There was a long silence.

"Hello?"

"I'm here."

"I'm not going to apologize," I said. "It's my life. I'm tired of running away. I'm tired of being a stupid idealist. It's time to take charge, time to *do* something. I'm sorry I didn't talk to you beforehand, but—"

"I wasn't going to ask you to apologize," she said. "You don't owe me an explanation. It's pretty clear you don't owe me anything. Don't worry, I'll get that darknet address and keep it safe and make sure everyone knows about it if you go missing." I had never heard the tone of voice she was using at that moment. I couldn't tell if she was angry or scared or maybe even . . . proud?

"Oh," I said. "Well."

"Well, I think I'd better go," she said, and the line cut off. Not proud, then.

My parents were both out for a change. Dad was doing some grocery shopping and Mom had a client meeting. The house felt more than empty—it felt hollow. Spooky. Every creak and bang was a squad of Zyz mercs about to break down my door and kidnap me.

And even though I knew that was the one thing they couldn't afford to do now that I had my finger over the button, I was sure I was about to get snatched. Or maybe they'd take my parents. Or Ange. What had been Jolu's other suggestions for actions I could take? Move to Albania. I didn't even have a valid passport—the one I'd used to go see Mom's relatives in the UK had expired two years before. I could dump it all on Barbara Stratford. Well, why not? She'd helped last time.

I got my bike out of the garage and set off for the *San Francisco Bay Guardian*'s offices. I was nearly there when my phone rang. The caller ID didn't know the return number. I answered.

"Yeah?"

"You're some kind of trouble-magnet, aren't you?"

It took me a minute to place the voice, mostly because I'd internally decided that I'd never hear it again.

"Masha?"

"You busy?"

"What?"

"From what I can see, you're somewhere by the Embarcadero. Judging from your rate of travel, you're either on a bus that's making a lot of stops, or a bicycle. And from what I can see, you're no longer listed as CTO of the Joe Noss for California Senate campaign on their website, so I'm thinking you might not be totally busy. So how about you turn off your phone altogether, remove the battery, and meet me where your idiot school-buddy tried to wrassle me. Do you know the place?"

The day Masha had disappeared—the first time—she'd tried to take me with her, and we'd been shadowed by Charles Walker, a drooling gorilla from Chavez High who would have dearly loved to narc me out to Homeland Security. Masha had kicked his ass, flashed her DHS ID, and threatened to arrest him. It had been on one of the alleys off Jackson, up on Nob Hill. I wasn't exactly sure which one, but I thought I'd recognize it again if I saw it.

"I know the place."

The line went dead. People kept hanging up on me. It wasn't a very pleasant experience. As I pedaled for downtown, I realized I didn't want pleasant experiences anymore. I was done with trying to optimize my life for what would make me happy. From now on, I was going to optimize my life for whatever worked at the moment. Happiness was overrated.

I was nearly convinced I had the wrong alley. I waited ten minutes, then fifteen, then I walked off. I got to the end of the block and I turned around and walked back. I looked down the alleyway. It wasn't much of an alleyway—just a narrow space between two buildings, wide enough for the fire exits and trash cans. The fifteen minutes I'd spent standing in the alley had been enough time for me to memorize every single feature of the place, from the ancient, mossy urine streaks on the wall to the dents in the trash cans. And now I could see that something was different. Hadn't *that* trash can been over *there*? It had been. I took a cautious step into the alleyway and my palms slicked with sweat, because I could tell, somehow, that there was someone in there with me. I took another step.

"Back here," a voice said from behind the trash cans. I tried to peek over them, but couldn't quite see, so I went deeper in and came around them.

Masha was sitting with her back against the wall. She looked like she was on her way to the gym, in track pants and a loose T-shirt, her hair in a pink scrunchie, a gym bag beside her. Her hair was mousy no-color brown, and she was wearing big fake designer shades. She could have been rich or poor, teenaged or in her late twenties. I wouldn't have given her a second look if I'd sat next to her on BART. I wasn't sure it *was* her, until she lowered her shades on her nose and skewered me on her glare.

"Have a seat," she said, and gestured at the space next to her behind the trash cans. She'd put down a piece of new cardboard there, which was a nice touch and made me think this wasn't the first time she'd done this. I lowered myself into a cross-legged position.

"Nice to see you," I said. "A bit unexpected."

"Yeah," she said. "Zeb and I walked out of there a few days ago, but it's been busy."

"Walked out of there."

"Those Zyz people, they're mostly meatheads that couldn't cut it in the DHS, so they went private sector, tripled their pay, and set out on their own. They have a *lot* of faith in their systems. Like, say, if a vendor says a CCTV is secure, they believe it. Same with electronic door locks, tracking ankle cuffs, and perimeter sensors."

"Oh," I said. I'd always known that Masha was a million times more badass than I was, but in all this business about saving her, I'd somehow come to think of her as a damsel in distress. "Did you have to come far?"

"Are you asking where I was held?"

I shrugged.

"Are you sure you want to know that?"

I shrugged again. "Probably not. All this spy shit, I pretty much totally hate it, to tell you the truth. Is Zeb okay?"

"Zeb's as good as he has any right to expect. Better. He's doing some stuff on his own for a while."

I mentally translated this as *We had a big fight and split up.* "Oh."

"So I wanted to say thanks," she said. "You've done some stuff that needed doing, but you did it for me and Zeb and that was damned good of you. Even if 'spy shit' isn't your thing."

"Yeah," I said. "Well, glad to be of service, even if you didn't need me in the end."

"Oh, I needed you. Zyz's been in an absolute *panic* pretty much since the moment they grabbed us. I figured out pretty quick that you were behind it. They were awfully anxious to know what had gotten out, what else might come out, and how they could stop it. They had a lot of really *sincere* questions for me. But it was an excellent distraction, and from what I can tell, all the people who supplied me with that material are happy with how it's gotten out. There was a *lot* more material waiting for me when I got back on-line. Enough to keep me busy for a really long time." She was being super macha, but I was starting to see that there was something wrong with her. She rooted in her gym bag for a water bottle and took a slug of it. I saw big, ugly bruises—no, *welts*—on her wrists and at her throat. I swallowed.

"Well, glad to be of service. Wish I'd known, since I happened upon some more 'material' of my own recently." I told her about Carrie Johnstone's d0x and the source of them.

"I see," she said, in sober tones. "And where are these files now?"

"I emailed them to Zyz corporate headquarters," I said.

I have to admit, I was a little proud of the silence that followed. She might have been James Bond–meets–Spider-Man, but I'd managed to do something so heroically crazy-stupid-brave that I'd rendered her speechless. But the silence went on, and on, and on. I peered at her shades, trying to see if she'd fallen asleep behind them.

"Um?"

"Shush," she said. "I'm figuring angles."

"Oh."

She lowered her head for a moment, and I heard her muttering to herself. There was a raw ligature mark around the back of her neck, which disappeared beneath her chin.

"So if I have this straight, you've sent all this in to Zyz and to Johnstone personally. You've implied that you're ready to publish it at the drop of a hat, but as far as they know, you haven't actually done anything about getting it published, right?"

"Pretty much. I've locked down the server my blog is on six ways to midnight, because I figured they'd be after it with everything they had. I'm half convinced they're going to come after me personally again, but that was always a certainty. They've tried to snatch me twice now. There's nothing I could do that would stop them from coming a third time."

She nodded along with me and held up her hand as I came to the end. "What if I could stop them?"

"What do you mean?"

"What if I could negotiate something with them, so that they made a meaningful promise to leave you alone, and you agreed to leave the Johnstone d0x alone?"

"Just so I'm clear on this: you've just escaped from a secret prison run by these goons, and now you're proposing to negotiate with them for *my* safety? As we say on the Internets: double-you-tee-eff."

"Oh," she said. "Marcus, come on. I'm not doing this to negotiate for *your* safety. I'm negotiating for *mine*."

Derp. "Right," I said. "Right. And Zeb's."

"Zeb, you, me, your little girlie, all of them. Zyz is stupid and evil, but it's a *business*. Money talks and bullshit walks. What you're about to dump, it will cost them plenty. If we give them a chance to cut their losses, they're going to do that."

"What about Johnstone? Won't she come after me after she's fired?"

"They won't fire her," she said. "Whatever reasons they have to fire her, you can be sure she has amassed a fat dossier of reasons why they *shouldn't* fire her. That woman's got the survival instincts of a cockroach. She only goes when she's ready to go. The U.S. Army only fired her once she was ready to be fired, once she'd set up the Zyz deal to step into. She *let them* fire her."

"You sound almost like you admire her," I said.

"The only day I wouldn't piss on Carrie Johnstone is the day she caught fire," Masha said, without the slightest hesitation or expression. "But if you're not prepared to learn from the teachers that life gives you, you'll always be ignorant. I've paid for every lesson that Carrie Johnstone has taught me, and I'm going to get my money's worth."

Sitting with Masha was like sitting on a razor's edge. On one side was my old life: safe little Marcus with his safe little life, in the system, applying for jobs, building his little electronics projects. On the other side was the life that I'd have if I followed Masha: violence, secrecy, poverty—but also power, strength, and adventure. I could disappear from the world, become a ghost and a legend, a fugitive who only gave the system what I deemed it deserved, not what it demanded.

After all, wasn't the *system* the problem? No matter who we voted for, the government always seemed to win. What was the point of living out my little fantasy of democratic change and justice when the real action was being fought out in secrecy, with anonymous envelopes of cash, encrypted whispers, secret bunkers, and secret deals?

Masha got to her feet and I was alarmed to see how slowly and painfully she moved. I was even more alarmed by how heavily she leaned against the wall. "Gimme a little help here," she said.

I hastened to stand beside her and let her put her arm around my shoulders, putting a lot of weight on me. Her hair tickled my cheek. It still smelled of her hair dye, a smell I remembered from being a kid who tried a different hair color every week. Back when I felt like I could express who I was and what I felt with my *hair*.

"Come on," she said. "Let's go use your network connection to do some negotiating before they scramble the black helicopters and nuke your ass."

"I haven't agreed to the deal," I said. I was practically holding her upright at this point, and I was amazed by how light she was, how little there was to her under her exercise clothes.

"Yeah," she said. "And what else are you going to do, dipshit?"

"Yeah," I said. "All right. Let me go get my bike."

"Screw that. If it's locked up, you can get it later. If it's not, someone else will get it and you won't have to worry about it. Get us a cab. I've got money."

Mom and Dad had left me a note saying they'd gone to a meeting with their accountant and telling me they'd be home for dinner. I raided the fridge for Masha while she used the shower and settled in in my room. I sat down on the end of my bed and watched her gnaw at a hunk of cheese and a tray of cookies while her fingers flew over her keyboard. She stopped typing after a while and spun around on my chair, her wet hair whipping around her shoulder, leaving watermarks on her T-shirt. "Okay," she said. "Now we wait. I gave them an hour, so let's assume they'll get back to us within two hours."

"I don't like the idea of Carrie Johnstone just getting away with this," I said.

She looked at me like I was a simpleton. I hated that look. "People like Carrie Johnstone always *get away* with stuff, until someone shoots them or they retire to some distant dictatorship where no one can get at them. She's not going to court. She'll never go to court. No one will ever arrest her. No one can afford to arrest her. You need to get past this romantic idea of justice and realize that some stuff just *is*."

"I hate that," I said. "It's like there's no human beings in the chain of responsibility, just things-that-happen. It's the ultimate cop-out. The system did it. The company did it. The government did it. What about the person who pulls the trigger?"

"Yeah," she said. "Well, that's a nice fairy tale. Have you got any juice or soda, something with sugar? I'm crashing here. Maybe some coffee."

I made her an *epic* cup of coffee. I may not be a ninja secret agent, but that's one thing I could most certainly do. She drank it with something approaching the proper reverence, sent me for another, drank that, and said, "Okay, this'll do." But the way she said it, I could tell that it was Masha-ese for HOLY CRAP THAT IS *AWESOME* COFFEE.

Then she typed some more. Then she typed some more. Then she made a face like she smelled something bad and her fingers bounced over the keys like a troupe of ten meth-addled acrobats on eighty-nine little trampolines. Then some more typing, her teeth bared like an animal. I tried to peek over her shoulder—I used a polarized laptop shield that made it impossible to see the screen unless you were looking at it straight on—and she batted me aside without even seeing me. More typing.

"Yeah, that'll do it," she said, and pulled out the plug and the battery in two smooth motions, thoroughly nuking the virtual machine she'd been working inside of and erasing all the passwords and keys she might have entered. I didn't even bother to object. I wasn't even particularly offended.

"That'll do it, huh?"

"You just nuke any copies you have of those files, starting with the darknet site you gave them details on, and you can forget about Zyz and Carrie Johnstone forever. I've taken the precaution of emailing myself a full set of docs, so that's that. They want to know if you want your old phone back."

"Huh?"

"They burgled some Egyptian girl's house after grabbing your old handset's location from the carrier's network."

"Jesus. Did they hurt anyone?"

"They didn't mention, so I'm assuming no. They're capable of *some* subtlety. Sounds like it bought you some time, in any event. You want it back? They've probably filled it with every bug and trojan known to the human race, of course."

"Forget it," I said.

"Smart guy," she said.

"Yeah," I said. "Well, thanks, I guess." It felt like something simultaneously monumental and *boring* had just happened. Once again, someone else had solved my problems for me. People thought M1k3y was some kind of action hero, but I was just a player in someone else's plot.

She climbed painfully to her feet, faced me. "You did pretty great, Marcus. I gave you a lot of shit, but you did great. I relied on you, and I got you into trouble. I'm glad I was able to clean up my mess. And I saved my own ass, too, I think." She wobbled a little on her legs, then put her arm out to steady herself and caught hold of my shoulder in a death grip that I barely noticed, because she was staring at me with huge, liquid brown eyes.

It was one of those moments, those girl-boy moments, where there's breath passing between you, gazes locked, a kind of falling feeling from every nerve ending, inside and out. I let the moment move me and her together, and let the kiss that had been waiting inside us come out. It went on for a long, long time and she squeezed me like I was the only thing holding her up. We came up for breath and she went on holding me, turning her face into my chest. I could feel the dampness from her hair, but I could also tell by the little shaking movements of her back and chest that she was crying. Hey, so was I.

She snuffled up her snot and wiped her cheeks on my T-shirt and let go of me. "Well," she said, with a sad smile, "nice to see you again, Marcus. I'll look you up the next time I'm in the neighborhood."

"Yeah," I said. "Sounds good."

The door opened downstairs and my parents' voices came up through the vents, talking about money worries and what to have for dinner. We stood, eyes locked, until they moved into the kitchen, then we descended the stairs in silence. I opened the front door and Masha slipped out into the street, limping down Potrero Hill with her gym bag over her shoulder. I watched her until she turned onto 24th Street, but she never looked back at me.

Then I went inside and told my parents I'd lost my job.

Ange could tell something was up from the minute I called her, I could hear it in her voice, and she met me at a burrito joint around the corner from Noisebridge, coming straight to the table and sitting down opposite me without a hug or a kiss or any of the other normal pleasantries.

"I saw Masha," I said. "And she spoke to Johnstone's people, and they say it's over."

"Over," she said, flatly.

"As in, we don't have anything to do with them, they don't have anything to do with us. Over."

"Oh," she said. She bit her lip, the way she did when she was thinking hard. "Over. You believe her."

"Yeah," I said. "I do."

"Oh."

I'd thought about this next part a thousand times, rehearsed every way it could go, hated all of them, decided I needed to do it anyway.

"Ange," I said.

She started crying before I said anything else, so I guess my voice must have conveyed some secret message to her in the cipher known only to our bodies and subconscious minds.

"What comes after this?" I said, trying to keep my voice even. Other people in the restaurant were staring at us, even though I'd deliberately staked out a place in the back corner.

"What do you mean?" she said, taking napkins out of the dispenser on the table and wiping at her eyes.

"I mean, do we just keep dating forever? Do we get married?"

"You . . ." She blinked. "You want to get married?"

"No," I said. "Do you?"

"No," she said.

"Ever?"

"Well, I don't know. Maybe."

"But not to me."

"I didn't say that, Marcus. Jesus, you're being such a freak. Are you breaking up with me?"

I willed myself not to flinch away from her angry gaze. "I just feel like there comes a point where you have to ask yourself: Is this going to go on forever, or isn't it? Are we doing this for the long haul, or is this just something we're doing for now?"

"That is the stupidest thing I've ever heard," she said. "This isn't binary. We can be boyfriend and girlfriend without being husband and wife. We're young. What the hell is this all about?"

I thought about the weird silences with Van, the kiss with Masha, the times I'd woken up next to Ange and just watched her breathe, in love with every curve and angle of her face. "I—" I thought about being a person who did things, instead of someone that the world did stuff to. I thought about the system and how broken it all was. "Look, it's been intense lately. I don't know what I'm feeling anymore. I'm just not sure about anything anymore."

"That's it? You're not *sure*? Since when was anything *sure*? Listen, you lunk, you say that you're not sure about anything. Are you sure that you're happier when you're with me than when I'm not there? Not all the time, but on balance, most of the time?"

It was such a weird, Ange way of framing the question. But I gave it thought. "Yeah," I said. "Yeah, I am sure about that. But, Ange—"

She wadded up the napkin and dropped it on the table. "That's something I'm sure of, too. But you're clearly going through some crazy mental crap, and if you need to work it out, you need to work it out. Give me a call when you've sorted it out. Maybe I'll still be around."

It took everything I had not to chase after her as she left the burrito place, but I stayed in my seat, facing away from the door, staring at the burrito cooling in front of me. I gave her a decent interval to get a ways down Mission Street, then I left the place myself, leaving the food untouched.

I hung around across the street from the Joe Noss for State Senate campaign office, wearing track pants and a hooded sweatshirt and carrying a gym bag, figuring that what worked for Masha would probably work for me. Autumn was upon us, and the sun had set early, making me just one more anonymous, slightly menacing guy with his hands in his pockets on a street in the upper Mission. But I wasn't clutching a vial of rock. I was holding onto a USB stick.

I hadn't been able to talk this over with anyone. Talking to Darryl meant talking to Van, and that meant being a theoretically single man talking to his theoretical best friend's girlfriend who had some kind of theoretical crush on him that might or might not be theoretically mutual. Jolu was busy with Kylie, because what had failed so miserably for me had worked really well for him. And of course, there was no way to talk to Ange about anything now, and maybe never again.

Liam left the building. Then the speechwriter and the researchers whose names I forgot. Then some volunteers, with Flor behind them. I was sure I'd seen Joe go in there, but Flor locked the door behind her, so maybe I'd missed Joe somehow. But I'd seen a few lights on inside the office as she shut the door, and so I hung tight. Joe came out twenty minutes later, wearing his Joe uniform, his cardigan buttoned high against the chill night.

I crossed the street and matched his stride. He looked at me, did a double take.

"Hello, Marcus," he said, his voice gentle and unconcerned. Statesmanlike.

I held out my closed fist, hand down. "Here," I said.

He held his hand out, let me transfer the USB stick to him. He felt it, put it in his pocket.

"Do I want to know what this is?"

"No," I said. "But your friend in the FBI might."

"Aha," he said, and patted his pocket. "Well, I'll take that under advisement."

We walked on for a few steps.

"Is this going to get me into trouble, Marcus?"

"No," I said.

"Is it going to get *you* into trouble?"

"Don't know," I said. "Are you going to win the election?"

"It seems likely," he said. "That vote machine idea of yours—Woah. Though nothing's certain in politics."

"I know," I said. "I'm a member of the network. I recruited sixteen people from my contact list. Maybe I'll get a pizza-and-beer party invite."

He stifled a small, sad laugh. "You're always welcome to pizza on me, Marcus."

"Well, that's good," I said. "Keep them honest, okay?"

"I'll certainly try."

"And keep yourself honest."

"Yes, that much you can be sure of," he said.

I walked away.

As I walked into the night, back toward home, I felt a huge weight lift from my shoulders. It's funny, because I assumed that after I had started the chain of events that would lead to Carrie Johnstone's d0x ending up in an FBI agent's possession, I would be clobbered by worry. Would Carrie Johnstone come back for me? Would Zyz come after me? They'd have no reason to assume I turned over the d0x to the FBI, but no reason not to, either. Hell, maybe the FBI wouldn't do anything—what had Joe said? *Even the most foolish, vicious Feeb at HQ has some self-respect and doesn't want to be used as a game token by scheming politicians who're hoping to score points with the electorate during the midterms.* Maybe they'd just drop it in a shredder.

But somehow, that little voice I knew to be my own, the little voice that told me all the time about the ways I'd screwed up, the way I'd let other people do the driving, the way I let life push me around—that little voice shut up the instant I did something. And not just something: the exact thing I knew to be right. Because if the system was broken, if Carrie Johnstone wasn't going to ever pay consequences for her actions, it wasn't because "the system" failed to get her. It was because people like me chose not to act when we could. The system was people, and I was part of it, part of its problems, and I was going to be part of the solution from now on.

I'd had eight months to debug Secret Project X-1. I even made a special midsummer trip to the Mojave, where the gypsum dust was nearly identical to the stuff you got out on the playa. I'd watched with glee and pride as X-1 sucked up the sun's rays, turned them into a laser beam, and used that to sinter fine white powder into 3D shapes. First a little skull ring. Then a toy car. Then some chainmail, the links already formed and joined, one of the coolest tricks 3D printing had to offer. I gave a presentation on my progress one night at Noisebridge, and resulting praise had given me a glow you could have seen with a spy drone.

But *now, here,* on the *actual* playa, the goddamned machine *wouldn't work.* Lemmy sat in his lounger nearby, sipping electrolyte drink from a CamelBak and making helpful suggestions, as well as several unhelpful ones. Burners passing by stopped and asked what I was doing, and I let Lemmy explain it to them so that I could concentrate on the infernal and stubborn machine.

I only stopped when I found that even the light from my headlamp wasn't sufficient for seeing what I was doing, and then I stretched all the aches and pains out of my body, swilled a pint of cold brew, and proceeded to dance my skinny ass off for forty-five minutes straight, chasing after a giant art car blasting ferocious dubstep as it crawled across the open playa. I stopped as a thunderstrike of inspiration struck me, and I *ran* straight back to camp, unlocked Lemmy's car, and used its dome light to confirm that yes, I had in fact inserted a critical part of the power assembly backwards. I turned it around, slotted it in, and heard the familiar boot sequence kick in as the stored power from the solar panels kicked the 3D printer to life.

I wasn't a total moron after all.

It didn't matter how much dancing I'd done the night before, I was for goddamned sure getting up at first light to crank up X-1. I had a lot of printing to do. I puttered around it as the blue arc of laser light shone out of its guts, making it glow like a lantern in the pink dawn.

People stopped and asked me what it was doing. I gave them trinkets: bone-white skull rings; renderings of perfect knots and other mathematical solids; strange, ghostly figurines. I had a whole library of 3D shapes I'd plundered from Thingiverse when I realized that I was going to have a real, functional 3D printer on the playa this year. Word got around, and by the time Lemmy got out of bed, a huge crowd had gathered around our camp: dancers who'd been up all night, their pupils the size of saucers; early risers with yoga mats; college kids who'd somehow found themselves at the burn; and a familiar jawa with crossed bandoliers over her chest, emphasizing her breasts.

"Hi, Ange," I said, leaving Lemmy to run the machine while I grabbed us a jar of cold brew and walked off a ways with her. She pulled down her mask. The sun had toasted a smattering of freckles around her nose and cheeks. I gave her first slurp at the coffee, then I had one. Then we hugged. It was awkward.

It was wonderful.

"Hey, Marcus. Congratulations on getting it working."

"Yeah," I said. All I wanted to do was hug her again.

"So," I said.

"So," she said.

"I'm an idiot," I said.

"Yeah," she said.

"I've missed you."

"Yeah," she said again. "I missed you, too. Like fire. Like part of me had been cut away."

I dropped my voice. "I gave Johnstone's d0x to the FBI."

She blinked twice. "When?"

"Back in October."

"And you're still here, huh?"

"Yeah," I said. "I guess that means they didn't do anything with it."

"Or maybe it means they *did* do something with it."

I found my mouth was hanging open. "You know," I said. "That possibility never occurred to me."

"Yeah," she said. "You have a tendency to see the bad side of things."

"I guess I do."

We didn't say anything for a while, just drank our coffee.

"Have you seen anything great yet?"

"No," I said. "I've been working on that goddamned machine since the moment we arrived."

"I haven't been to the temple yet," she said.

I took the hint. "I bet Lemmy'll be okay with the printer for a while."

"You think?"

"Yeah. Let's go."

"You spending much time at the protests?" she said.

"Every day," I said. "Trying to figure out how to do more with the kind of technology we build at Noisebridge to help make them harder to bust up. Better antikettling stuff, HERF shielding, effective treatments for gas poisoning and those dazzler lasers and sound cannons they're using now. Been arrested a few times, but I keep going back."

"I think that's great," she said. "Seriously great. I'm proud of you."

"Thank you," I said. "That means a lot." It really did. I didn't hold her hand, but oh, how I wanted to. "What about you?"

"College," she said. "College, college, college. Doing a double courseload to get out as fast as I can. My student debt, God, it's like the national debt of some drowning island nation."

"There's still time to drop out," I said.

"Yeah, yeah. We can't all be professional revolutionaries."

Not if you're drowning in student debt, is what I didn't say, because I didn't want to fight with Ange. More than anything, I didn't want to fight with Ange.

The temple came into sight. It was even more amazing than last year's, and it was surrounded by art bikes and milling crowds of people dropping off their memorials or reading them or making them. By some unspoken agreement, we walked to them in silence.

By the same unspoken agreement, we took each other's hands.

When we sat down in the central atrium and the first deep *Omm* moved through us, tears began to flow. Ange was crying, and so was I. Our fingers were interlocked, and squeezed so hard that my knuckles creaked. But the sound kept coming, and with it, a kind of peace. Peace wasn't something I'd had much of in the last year, and I barely recognized it—and then I sank into it.

My eyes closed, I sensed someone settle to the floor next to me. I opened my eyes. I knew before they opened who it would be.

Masha's hair was pink again, and she looked better than she had the last time I'd seen her, but she also looked older. There were deep worry lines around her mouth and eyes. They looked good on her somehow. Her eyes were the same, and just as I'd remembered them.

She and I looked into each other's eyes for a long time. I squeezed Ange's fingers and sensed her looking at Masha, too. The three of us stared at one another, three pairs of eyes, three brains, three sets of hands, three *people* inside the crowd, inside the temple, inside Black Rock City, on the skin of the planet.

Then Masha stood up, blew us both a kiss, and smiled in a way that made her look ten years old and made me feel like I'd been blessed by a holy woman. I gathered Ange into a hug that started off stiff and awkward and then turned into the most familiar feeling in the world.

afterword

by Aaron Swartz, Demand Progress
(cofounder, Reddit.com)

Hi there, I'm Aaron. I've been given this little space here at the end of the book because I'm a flesh-and-blood human and, as such, I can tell you something you wouldn't believe if it came out of the mouth of any of those fictional characters:

This stuff is real.

Sure, there isn't anyone actually named Marcus or Ange, at least not that I know, but I do know real people just like them. If you want, you can go to San Francisco and meet them. And while you're there, you can play D&D with John Gilmore or build a rocket ship at Noisebridge or work with some hippies on an art project for Burning Man.

And if some of the more conspiracy-minded stuff in the book seems too wild to be true, well, just google Blackwater, Xe, or Blue Coat. (I myself have an FOIA request in to learn more about "persona management software," but the Feds say it'll take three more *years* to redact all the relevant documents.)

Now I hope you had fun staying up all night reading about these things, but this next part is important, so pay attention: what's going on now isn't some reality TV show you can just sit at home and watch. This is your life, this is your country—and if you want to keep it safe, you need to get involved.

I know it's easy to feel like you're powerless, like there's nothing you can do to slow down or stop "the system." Like all the calls are made by shadowy and powerful forces far outside your control. I feel that way, too, sometimes. But it just isn't true.

A little over a year ago, a friend called to tell me about an obscure bill he'd heard of called the Combating Online Infringement and Counterfeits Act, or COICA. As I read the bill, I started to get more and more worried: under its provisions, the government would be allowed to censor websites it didn't like without so much as a trial. It would be the first time the U.S. government was given the power to censor its citizens' access to the net.

The bill had just been introduced a day or two ago, but it already had a couple dozen senators cosponsoring it. And, despite there never being any debate, it was already scheduled for a vote in just a couple days. Nobody had ever reported on it, and that was just the point: they wanted to rush this thing through before anyone noticed.

Luckily, my friend noticed. We stayed up all weekend and launched a website explaining what the bill did, with a petition you could sign opposing it that would look up the phone numbers for your representatives. We told a few friends about it and they told a few friends and within a couple days we had over 200,000 people on our petition. It was incredible.

Well, the people pushing this bill didn't stop. They spent literally tens of millions of dollars lobbying for it. The head of every major media company flew out to Washington, DC, and met with the president's chief of staff to politely remind him of the millions of dollars they'd donated to the president's campaign and explain how what they wanted—the only thing they wanted—was for this bill to pass.

But the public pressure kept building. To try to throw people off the trail, they kept changing the name of the bill—calling it PIPA and SOPA and even the E-PARASITES Act—but no matter what they called it, more and more people kept telling their friends about it and getting more and more people opposed. Soon, the signers on our petition stretched into the millions.

We managed to stall them for over a year through various tactics, but they realized if they waited much longer they might never get their chance to pass this bill. So they scheduled it for a vote first thing after they got back from winter break.

But while members of Congress were off on winter break, holding town halls and public meetings back home, people started visiting them. Across the country, members started getting asked by their constituents why they were supporting that nasty Internet censorship bill. And members started getting scared—some going so far as to respond by attacking *me*.

But it wasn't about me anymore—it was never about me. From the beginning, it was about citizens taking things into their own hands: making YouTube videos and writing songs opposing the bill, making graphs showing how much money the bill's cosponsors had received from the industries pushing it, and organizing boycotts putting pressure on the companies who'd endorsed the bill.

And it worked—it took the bill from a political nonissue that was poised to pass unanimously to a toxic football no one wanted to touch. Even the bill's cosponsors started rushing to issue statements opposing it! Boy, were those media moguls pissed. . . .

This is not how the system is supposed to work. A ragtag bunch of kids doesn't stop one of the most powerful forces in Washington just by typing on their laptops!

But it did happen. And you can make it happen again.

The system is changing. Thanks to the Internet, everyday people can learn about and organize around an issue even if the system is determined to ignore it. Now, maybe we won't win every time—this is real life, after all—but we finally have a chance.

But it only works if you take part. And now that you've read this book and learned how to do it, you're perfectly suited to make it happen again. That's right: now it's up to you to change the system.

Aaron Swartz

acknowledgments

Many thanks to the people who helped with suggestions and technical details to make this book work: Jacob Appelbaum, Aaron Swartz, Quinn Norton, Tiffiniy Cheng, Nicholas Reville, Holmes Wilson, Joe Trippi, Danny O'Brien, Tim Hardy, Nat Torkington, Thomas Gideon, Roger Dingledine, Barry Warsaw, Gord Doctorow, James Gleick, Lee Maguire.

Thanks to my campmates at Liminal Labs for introducing me to Burning Man and making me so welcome there.

Thanks to John Perry Barlow, John Gilmore, Mitch Kapor, and Wil Wheaton for letting me give them a cameo (and thanks again to Gilmore for his plotting suggestions!).

Thanks to my agents, Russ Galen, Danny Baror, Heather Baror, and Justin Manask, for the awesome work in bringing *Little Brother* and *Homeland* to the world.

Thanks to all the fans and readers, the librarians and teachers, and hackers and remixers and *especially* the booksellers who put my books into peoples' hands.

Thanks to my editors, especially Patrick Nielsen Hayden, who has always improved my books.

bibliography

When I was a kid, facts were hard to come by. If you wanted to know how to hack a pay phone, you'd have to find someone else who knew how to do it, and get them to teach you. Or you'd have to find operating manuals for pay phones and pore over them until you came up with your own method. There's nothing wrong with either of these solutions, except that they're slow and can be tedious.

Today, facts are cheap. As I type this in early 2012, a Google search for "How to hack a pay phone" gives back a full screen of detailed YouTube videos full of fascinating and often practical advice on getting pay phones to dance to your will. So if you know or suspect that a thing is possible, it's easy to discover whether someone has managed it, and how they did it. Just bear in mind Arthur C. Clarke's first law: "When a distinguished but elderly scientist states that something is possible, he is almost certainly right. When he states that something is impossible, he is very probably wrong." If you're trying to do something that everyone on the net swears is impossible, it may still be worth a go on your own in case you think of something they've never imagined.

With *Homeland*—and in *Little Brother*—I've tried to give you some scenarios and keywords that might expand your impression of what is and isn't possible, to give you the search terms you'll need to educate yourself and get yourself doing cool stuff. So, for example, if you google "hackerspaces" you'll find that places like Noisebridge are very real and have spread all over the world (Noisebridge is also real!). You can join your local hackerspace. If it doesn't exist yet, you can *start* it. Just google "how do I start a hackerspace?" And while you're searching, try "drone" and "tor project" and "lawful intercept." You'll be amazed, scared, energized, and empowered by what you find there.

Wikipedia is an *amazing* place to do research, but you have to know how to use it. Your teachers have probably told you that Wikipedia has no place in your education, and I'm sorry to say that I think that this is a lazy and dumb approach. There are two secrets to doing amazing research on Wikipedia:

1. Check the sources, not the article.

In an ideal world, all the factual assertions in a Wikipedia article will have a citation to a source at the bottom of the article. Wikipedia hasn't achieved this ideal state (yet—that's what all those [citation needed] marks in the articles are about) but a surprising number of the facts in a Wikipedia article will have a corresponding source at the bottom. *That*'s where your research should take you when you're reading an article. Wikipedia is where your research should start, not where it should end.

2. Check the "Talk" link.

Every Wikipedia article has a "Talk" link that goes to a page where everyone who cares about the article discusses its state. If someone has a weird idea about a subject and finds a source somewhere on the net to support it, they might just stick it into the Wikipedia article. But chances are that this will spark a heated debate on the Talk page about whether the source is "reputable" and whether its facts belong in an encyclopedia.

Armed with the original sources *and* the informed discussion about whether those sources are good ones, you can use Wikipedia to get an amazing education.

Beyond Wikipedia, there are some other sites you should really have a look at if you want to learn more about the material in this book. First Codecademy (www.codecademy.com), which contains step-by-step lessons to learn how to program, starting from no knowledge. You can even get them by email, one page at a time. While you're chewing on that, check out the Tor Project (www.tor project.org) and find out how to run your own darknet projects. If you're looking to use an operating system that lets you control your whole computer, down to the bare metal, then you want GNU/Linux. I like the Ubuntu flavor best (www.ubuntu.com). It runs on any and every computer, and is really easy to get started with. And if you have an Android phone, get jailbreaking! The CyanogenMod project (www.cyanogenmod.com) is a free/open version of the Android operating system, with all kinds of excellent features, including several that will help you protect your privacy.

Now, all this stuff is well and good, but only if the Internet stays free and open. If your country acquires the same awful censorship and surveillance used in China and Middle Eastern dictatorships, you won't be able to get at this stuff and learn to use it. There are lots of threats to this freedom, and every country has groups devoted to stopping them. In the United States and Canada (and worldwide!) there's the Electronic Frontier Foundation (www .eff.org), where I used to work. In the UK, there's the Open Rights Group (www.openrightsgroup.org), which I helped to found. In Australia, there's Electronic Frontiers Australia (www.efa.org.au). In New Zealand, there's Creative Freedom (www.creativefreedom .org.nz). There are also global groups like Creative Commons (www.creativecommons.org) and groups with lots of local affiliates like The Pirate Party (www.pp-international.net).

There are lots of thinkers on this stuff whom I have a lot of respect for. If you want to know about teens, privacy, and networked communications, read danah boyd's blog (www.zephoria.org/ thoughts). For more on Anonymous, 4chan and /b/, read Gabriella Coleman's blog and papers (http://gabriellacoleman.org/blog/). For the future of news and newspapers, read Dan Gillmor (www.dang illmor.com), especially his excellent recent book, *Mediactive* (www .mediactive.com). For the relationship of leaks to the news, follow Heather Brooke (www.heatherbrooke.org) and read her history of WikiLeaks, *The Revolution Will Be Digitised*. To understand how the net is changing the world, read Clay Shirky (www.shirky.com), and his latest book, the kick-ass *Here Comes Everybody*. If you want to fight for free and fair elections in America without undue influence from power and money, read Lawrence Lessig (www.twitter .com/lessig) and join Rootstrikers (www.rootstrikers.org), where activists are making it happen.

Finally, if you want to understand randomness, information theory, and the strange world at the center of mathematics, run, don't walk, and get a copy of James Gleick's 2011 book *The Information*. It's where I got all the good stuff about Gödel and Chaitin from.

There's plenty more—more than would ever fit between the covers of a book, so much that you need the whole net for it. I write on a daily website called Boing Boing (www.boingboing .net), where I keep up to date on the latest stuff. I hope to see you there.

Turn the page for a sneak peek at Cory Doctorow's

attack
surface

Available October 2020

That was why I loved technology: if you use it right, it gives you power—and takes away other peoples' privacy. I was on my sixteenth straight hour at the main telcoms data-center for Bltz, the capital of Slovstakia. Those are both aliases, obviously. Unlike certain persons I could name, I keep my secrets.

Sixteen hours, for what my boss had assured the client—the Slovstakian Interior Ministry—would be a three-hour job. You don't get as high as she did in the Stasi without knowing how to be a tactical asshole when the situation demands it.

I just wish she'd let me recon the data-center before she handed down the work estimate. The thing is, the communications infrastructure of Slovstakia was built long before the Berlin Wall fell, and it consisted of copper wires wrapped in newspaper and dipped in gutta-percha. After the Wall came down, responsibility for the telcoms had been transferred to the loving hands of Anton Tkachi, who had once been a top spook in Soviet Slovstakia. There are a lot of decades in which it would suck to have your telcoms run by an incompetent, greedy kleptocrat, but the 1990s represented a particularly poorly chosen decade to have sat out the normal cycle of telcoms upgrades. Because internet.

After Tkachi was purged—imprisoned 2005, hospitalized with "mental illness" in 2006, dead in 2007—the Slovstakian Ministry of Communications cycled through a succession of contract operators—Swisscom, T-Mob, Vodaphone, Orange (God help us all)—each of which billed the country for some of the jankiest telcoms gear you've ever seen, the thrice-brewed teabags of the telecommunications world, stuff that had been in *was zones,* leaving each layer of gear half-configured, half-secured, and half-documented.

The internet in Slovstakia sucked monkey shit.

Anyway, my boss, Ilsa, She-Wolf of the SS, promised the Interior Ministry that I would only need three hours, and the Interior Ministry had called up the telcoms ministry and given them orders to be nice to the Americanski lady who was coming over to do top-secret work for them, and give her everything she needed. I can tell that they laid it on thick, because when I first arrived at the country's main data-center, a big old brutalist pile that I had to stop and take a picture of for my collection of Soviet Brutalist Buildings That They Used to Shoot You for Taking Pictures Of— hashtags are for losers who voluntarily submit to 280-character straitjackets (and sentences can too a preposition end with)—the guy on the desk sent me straight to the director of telcoms security.

His name was Litvinchuk and he was *tightly wound*. You could tell because he had his own force of telcoms cops dressed like RoboCop standing guard outside his door with guns longer than their legs, reeking of garlic sausage and the sweat of a thousand layers of Kevlar. Litvinchuk welcomed me cordially, gave me a long-ass speech about how excited he was to have some fresh foreign contractors in his data-center (again) and especially ones from a company as expensive as Xoth Intelligence.

"Wait, that's not right word," he said, in a broad Yakov Smirnoff accent (he had a master's from the London School of Economics and I'd watched him do a TEDx talk where he sounded like a BBC World Service newsreader). "Exclusive? Illustrious?" He looked to me—specifically, to my tits, which was where every Slovstakian official I'd met addressed his remarks. I didn't cross my arms.

"Infamous," I said.

He smirked. "I'm sure. Miss Maximow"—he pronounced the w as a v, as they always did as soon as I got east of France—"we are all very excited to have you at our premises. However, I'm sure you understand that we must be careful to keep records of which contractors work on our sensitive systems." He slid a paperclipped form across his desk to me. I counted to seven—more efficient and just as effective as ten—and picked it up. Nine pages, smudgily photocopied, full of questions like "List all NGOs and charitable organizations to which you have contributed, directly or indirectly."

"No," I said.

He gave me his best fish-face, which I'm sure was super-effective against the farm boys cosplaying Judge Dredd in the hallway. But I'd been glared at by Ilsa, She-Wolf of the etc., etc., and had been inured to even the hairiest of eyeballs.

"I must insist," he said.

"I don't fill in this kind of form," I said. "Company policy. Xoth has negotiated blanket permission to access your premises from the Interior Ministry for all its personnel." This was true. I hated paperwork, and this kind of paperwork the most—the kind that asked you questions you could never fully or honestly answer, so that there'd always be an official crime to pin on you if you stepped on the wrong toes. Lucky for me, Xoth had a no-exceptions policy that techs were not allowed to fill in any official documentation at client sites. I'd take notes on my own work, but they'd go up the chain to my boss—Ilsa, She-Wolf etc.—who'd sanitize them and pass them back to the Interior Ministry for their own logs, omitting key details so that we would be able to bill them for any future maintenance.

I did my best to look bored—not hard, I was so bored my eyeballs ached—and stared at this post-Soviet phone commissar.

"I will fill it out for you," he said.

I shrugged.

He worked quickly, pen dancing over the paper. Not his first paper-pushing rodeo. He passed it back to me. "Sign." He smiled. It wasn't a nice smile.

I looked down. It was all in Cyrillic.

"Nope," I said.

He switched off the smile. "Madam." He made it sound like *missy*. I could tell we weren't going to get along. "You will not get into my data-center until we have gathered basic information. That is our protocol."

He stared at me, fish-face plus plus, clearly waiting for me to lose my cool. Long before Ilsa began her regime of hard-core stoicism training, I had mastered situations like this. You don't get far in the DHS if you don't know how to bureaucracy. I turned boredom up by a notch. I tried to project the sense that I had more time to burn than he did.

He held out his hand. I'd assumed he'd be a short-fingered vulgarian, but he had pianist's fingers, and a hell of a manicure, the kind of thing that made me feel self-conscious about my lack of girly cred. "ID."

Xoth gives us fancy ID cards to wear on client sites, with RFIDs and sapphire-coated smart chips and holograms, props for impressing rubes. I could knock one up in an afternoon. I unclipped mine from my lanyard and handed it over.

The pen danced again at the bottom of the form, and he turned the paper to show me. He'd added "signed, per, Masha Maximow" to the signature line. *Good for you, Boris. You made a funny.* What an asshole.

"We done?"

He carefully made a xerox on a desktop printer/scanner/copier—one that I knew five different exploits for, and could use to take over his whole network, if I wanted to—and handed it to me. "For your records."

I folded it into quarters and stuck it in my back pocket. "Which way?"

He said something in Russki and one of the Stormtroopers struggled in under the weight of his body armor and escorted me to the data-center. I took one look at the racks and racks of hardware, zipped up my fleece against the icy wind of the chillers, and got to work. It was going to be a long three hours.

By the time I finally finished, I was freezing and swearing. My hoodie was totally inadequate and I suspected that my long-fingered vulgarian had ordered one of his Armored Borises to turn the thermostat down to sub-Arctic.

But it was done, and the test-cases ran, and so I got up off the folding chair I'd been hauling around the data-center's corridors as I moved from one rack to another, tracing wires, untangling the hairball of grifty IT contractor shortcuts and fat-fingering.

Surveying my work, I had a deep feeling of . . . Well, to be honest, a deep feeling of pointlessness. I'd labored for sixteen hours—fifteen if you subtract meals and pee breaks—getting the Xoth Sectec network appliance installed, and all I had to show for my trouble was an inconspicuous black one-unit-high server box, mounted on the bottom shelf of the furthest rack (this was Xoth policy—put our gear in the most out-of-way place, just in case barbarian hordes topple our dictator clients and storm the gates, looking for mediagenic evidence of collaboration with evil surveillance contractors) (that would be me).

But now I got to celebrate. I looked over my shoulder and made sure I was alone—the RoboCops had made a point of standing behind me, watching my ass, as I dragged my chair around— bent down and touched my toes, feeling the awesome stretch in my hamstrings and the unkinking of my neck and shoulders as my hair brushed the ground. Then I stood, cracked my knuckles, plugged my laptop into my phone, and tunneled out to a network box I'd left in my hotel room that morning, making sure it was all charged up and successfully connected to the hotel's wifi, which (see above) sucked monkey shit. I fired up a virtual machine on my laptop, choosing a container with a fully patched version of the latest freebie version of Windows, and used its browser to connect to Facebook.

The Slovstakian uprising hadn't figured out that the only real use for Facebook in a revolution was as a place to teach people how to use something *more secure than Facebook*. All their communications was in a couple of groups that they accessed over Facebook's Tor Hidden Service, good old https://facebookcorewwwi.onion, which was pretty good operational security (if I did say so myself).

Their problem was that they were way, way outgunned—as of now, they were facing down the best Xoth had to offer (at least, the best Xoth had to offer in its middle-upper pricing tier). Things were about to get very, very bad for the plucky demonstrators of Slovstakia.

The virtual Windows box in my virtual machine connected through the hotel's network to Tor—The Onion Router, a system that bounced network connections all over the world, separately encrypting each hop, making it much harder to trace, intercept, or modify its users' packets—and to Facebook's hidden service, a darknet site based in a much nicer data-center than this one, in an out-of-the-way corner of Oregon with remarkably low year-round temperatures (ambient chilling is the number one money-saver when it comes to running a building full of superheated computers).

I alt-tabbed into my monitor for the Sectec box beside me, using an untunneled interface on my phone's native network connection. That Sectec box could handle ten million simultaneous connections, combing through all their packet-streams using machine-learning models originally developed to recognize cancer cells on a microscope slide (fun fact!). Sure enough, it registered the existence of a stock Windows laptop in the Sofitel Bltz, communicating over Tor. It profiled the machine by fingerprinting its packets, did a quick lookup in Xoth's customer-facing API to find a viable exploit against that configuration, and injected a redirect to the virtual machine on my laptop. I pinned the monitor window to the top of my desktop and flipped back to the VM, watching as the browser's location bar flickered to an innocuous-seeming error message, and by flipping to a diagnostic view of the VM, I could see the payload strike home.

It used a zero-day for Tor Browser—always based on a slightly out-of-date version of Firefox and thus conveniently vulnerable to yesterday's exploits—to bust out of the browser's sandbox and into the OS. Then it deployed a higher-value exploit, one that attacked Windows, and inserted some persistent code that could bypass the bootloader's integrity check, hooking into a module that loaded later in the process. In less than five seconds, it was done: the virtual machine was fully compromised, and it was already trying to hook into my webcam and mic; scouring my hard drive for interesting files; snaffling up saved password files from my browser, and loading its keylogger. Since all that was happening in a virtual machine—not an actual computer, just a piece of software pretending to be a computer—none of that stuff really happened, thankfully.

Now it was time to really test it. Sectec has a mode where it can scour all the traffic in and out of the network for specific email addresses and usernames, to locate specific people. I gave it Litvinchuk's email address, and waited for his computer to make itself known. Took less than a minute—he was polling the ministry's mail server every sixty seconds. Two minutes later, I controlled his computer and I was cataloguing his porn habits and downloading his search history. I have a useful script for this; it locates anything in my targets' computers that make mention of *me*, because I am a nosy bitch and they should know better, really.

Litvinchuk was into some predictably gross porn—why is it *always* being peed on?!—and had googled the shit out of me. He also had a covert agent who'd searched my room; they had put a location logger on my phone using a crufty network appliance I'd already discovered in my epic debugging session in the data-center. I could have fed that logger false data, but I turned it off because fuck him sideways. I downloaded half a gig of videos of Litvinchuk in full-bore German heavy latex, gleaming with piss, then stood, stretched again, and shut my lid.

I'd started my adventure at 4 p.m. the day before. Now it was 8 a.m. and that meant that the demonstrations in the main square would be down to skeleton crews. Anyone interesting only came out after suppertime and worked the barricades in the dark, when the bad stuff always kicked off. That's when the provocateurs and neofascists came out—often the same people—and the hard-core protesters had to work extra hard.

I called the Sofitel on the way back and ordered room service. All they had was breakfast and I wanted dinner, so I ordered triple, and gave up on explaining that I only needed one set of cutlery.

I arrived at the room's door at the same time as the confused waiter. I waved at him and carded the door open, then followed him and his cart in. He was one of those order guys you saw around the hotel, someone who'd once had a job in Soviet brute-force heavy industry but ended up pushing room service trolleys when it all went to China. Those guys never spoke English, not like their strapping sons, who spoke gamer-international, the language of Let's Play videos and image boards. "Dobre," I said, "Pajalsta," and took the folio from him and added a ten-euro tip—everything at the Sofitel was denominated in euros, ever since the local currency had collapsed. I hadn't even bothered to change any cash on this trip, but I had bought a 10,000,000,000-dinar note from an enterprising street seller who'd been targeting the tourist trade. I liked the engraving of the opera house on the back, but the Boris on the front was a unibrowed thick-fingered vulgarian straight out of central casting. I kept forgetting to google him, but I was pretty sure he was being celebrated for something suitably terrible, purging Armenians or collaborating with Stalin.

My alarm went off four hours later. I found my bathing suit and underwater MP3 player and the hotel robe, made sure all my devices were powered down with their USB ports covered, and headed for the pool.

Swimming—even with loud tunes—always churns my subconscious, boredom forcing it to look inward at its neglected corners. So somewhere around the fiftieth lap (it was a small pool), I remembered what was happening that day. I did the time zone calculation in my head and realized there was still time to do something about it. *Fucketty shitbuckets.* I hauled myself out of the pool and toward a towel.

I perched, dripping, on the room's desk chair and powered up my phone for a quick peek at the pictures of the screw-heads on my laptop. I had covered all the screws with glitter nail polish and shot clear pics of each one, with a little label beside it, so that I could easily verify whether someone had unscrewed my laptop lid and done something sneaky, like inserting a hardware keylogger or, you know, some Semtex and packing nails. I used an open-source astronomy package designed to match pictures with known constellations to verify two of the seven screws. The glitter patterns had become old friends by this point, since I checked them every time I'd been out of sight of my computer before powering it up again.

I booted it, pulled the towel over my head (to defeat hidden cameras), and keyed in my passphrase while going "AAAAH" medium-loud, just to defeat anyone trying to guess my passphrase from the sounds of my fingers on the keys. Xoth had an airgap room for really sensitive stuff, walls shielded with Faraday cage, full of computers that undercover Xoth techs bought by walking into consumer electronics stores and buying computers off the shelf without ever letting them out of their sight. After being flashed with a Xoth version of TAILS, a paranoid Linux distro, wifi cards and Bluetooth radios ripped out with pliers. Their USB ports were covered with 3-D printed snaps that couldn't be removed without shattering them. You brought your encrypted data in on a thumb drive, requisitioned a machine, broke the seal, plugged in your USB stick and read the data, then handed the machine back to a tech to be flashed and resealed. Compared to that shit, I wasn't all that paranoid.

Litvinchuk had been a busy Boris: my computer downloaded and sorted his own wiretap orders as he took the Sectec out for a spin. I looked through the list, and yup, I already knew a lot of those names. They were the people I was planning to meet for drinks in a few hours. I made a few quick revisions to my Cryptoparty slides.

It was getting to be time for lunch-ish or dinner-esque, whatever you call a 3 p.m. meal. I was about to phone down for room service when my phone alarmed me, which isn't something it does often, because I've turned off every notifier.

When that chirp goes off it is a pure sphincter-tightener.

"Wedding of Marcus Yallow and Ange Carvelli" and a shortened URL. Because livestreaming. Because Marcus. Because exhibitionist attention-whore. Because shithead.

God, he drove me crazy. I fired up the livestream. They'd made everyone they loved fly to Boston for the wedding, because of the girl's grad school schedule, and they'd filled the hall with robots they borrowed from the MIT Media Lab to give it some nerd cred. Of course she didn't wear white. Her dress was ribbed with EL wire that pulsed in time with the music, and Marcus's suit—Beatles black, with a narrow tie and drainpipe pants that made his legs look even scrawnier than usual—was also wired up, but it only pulsed when they touched, moving bands of light across its surface from the point of contact.

Okay, that *was* pretty cool.

The officiant was a prominent Cambridge hacker, one of the ones they'd hauled in when they were after Chelsea Manning. She'd been a kid then, but now she looked older, her wife holding their kids on her lap off to one side. She wore a colander on her head, because she was ordained in the Church of the Flying Spaghetti Monster, which was frankly too much.

Marcus and his girlie exchanged vows. Marcus promised to make her coffee, rub her feet (ugh), review her code, and say sorry and mean it; she promised to back down when she was wrong, forgive him when he apologized, and love him "until the wheels come off" (double ugh). They kissed and received their applause. I gave it three minutes, making sure that the ceremony was well and truly done and the reception about to start. I'm not a monster.

Here's the thing about Cambridge: they have drone delivery there. For a little extra, you can time the delivery to the minute. I checked the time in the corner of the screen. There was a big window right behind the officiant with a view of the Charles River and the snow and the tracks of students' boots. I checked the time again.

The drone came right up to the window and rapped on it politely. It had four big rotors and a sensor package that fed me all kinds of telemetry on the activity in the room, from Bluetooth device IDs to lidar outlines of all the humans in the space. The wedding livestream showed it tapping on the window from the bride and groom's POV (the stream ran off about a dozen cameras and was smart enough to switch between them based on which one was capturing the most action); the stream from the drone showed me the opposite view, Marcus and his girl and all their nice nerdly friends and family gaping at the fisheye camera.

Marcus broke the tableau by opening the window, and the drone daintily coasted into the room and deployed its box into his hands. He pulled the ripstrip on the plasticky wrapping and revealed the gift-wrapped box within. She took the card out of the envelope and read it. I admit it gave me a shiver to hear her say my name.

When Marcus heard it, his face did a funny. *That* gave me a shiver too—a different kind. He and I have a complicated history. I rubbed my fingers, the ones he'd broken when I was only sixteen. He did it in order to steal my phone, because I had a video that exonerated him of being a terrorist. Complicated. Those fingers hurt whenever I thought of him.

He looked at the drone's sensor package. "Thank you, Masha," he said. "Wherever you are." The usual was for this to be a recording that you could watch later, but if you were a creepy stalker chick (ahem), you could watch it in real time. I emojied the drone and it bobbled a curtsey and gave me five seconds to commit another \$50 to hold on to it for five more minutes, because it had other packages to deliver. I released it and its feed died.

On the livestream, I watched them unwrap my gift. I'd almost sent them a bag of kopi luwak, which is a kind of coffee bean that's fed raw to a civet cat, then harvested from its poop and roasted, but then I'd read an animal welfare article about the treatment of civet cats. So I'd given them a Raspi Altair 8080: that is, a 1974 "personal computer" that you controlled with a row of faceplate switches and read using peanut-bulb blinkenlights, which had been painstakingly restored with a Raspberry Pi open-source CPU inside it, giving it approximately eight bazillion times the computing power. Most of the interior was left empty by the refit, and the craftswoman who'd sold it to me had filled the empty space with a bunch of carved wooden automata that cranked a set of irregular gears around in whirring circles while the computer was operating, which you could see if you swapped in the optional transparent case.

Marcus knew exactly what it was (because I'd found it through his Twitter feed) and how much it cost (because he'd moaned about never being able to afford it, not in a million years), and he had a look of profoundly satisfying shock on his face. He told his girlie all about it in that spittle-flecked hyperactive mode he slipped into when he was really, really excited. The expression that crossed her face was even more satisfying: a mix of jealousy and appreciation that I reveled in like the petty, terrible person I am.

I felt like the fairy who curses Sleeping Beauty out of spite when she thinks she hasn't been invited to her christening, except that this was a wedding and not a christening. Oh, and they invited me, of course.

But I had work to do. Hey, I'd sent a thoughtful gift, even if I totally upstaged their stupid nerd chic wedding. Shoulda had a more nerdy wedding, if they didn't want to get upstaged.

I was still hungry and now it was getting to be time to head out to the square. Room service at the Sofitel sucked anyway. I'd get a doner kebab. Hell, I'd get a sack of them and bring them along.

The vegan café where my pet revolutionary cell met was called the Danube Bar Resto, and they could always be found there before the night's action, because fuck opsec, why not just make it easy for the secret police to round you all up somewhere far from a crowd? I despair.

Kriztina was already there, chowing down on something that had never had the chance to breathe and live and run and play. I cracked open the crumpled top on my sack of kebab and let her smell the meaty perfume. "Save room," I said.

She laugh-choked and gave me a mouth-full thumbs-up as I sat down next to her. There were eight of them in Kriztina's little cell, a couple of graphic designers, two webmonkeys, a poet (seriously), and the rest didn't even pretend to be employed. Few under-thirties in Slovstakia were, after all.

"You want drink?" Oksana always had spending money. I'd pegged her as a snitch when I first met her, but it turned out she just made good money working for a law firm that did a lot of western business and didn't mind having a trans girl for a paralegal. Once I'd satisfied myself that she didn't appear anywhere in Litvin-chuk's master lists of turncoats, I'd come to like her. She reminded me of some of the women I'd known in the Middle East, brave fuckers who'd managed to look like a million bucks even as their cities were being pounded to gravel around their pretty shoulders, fearless beneath their hijabs and glamorous even when they were covered in dust and blood.

"Sure." It would be something with wheatgrass and live microbes and probably twigs, but mostly orange juice and mango pulp. The guy who ran the place liked to talk about how the chlorophyll "oxygenated" your blood—of course chlorophyll only makes oxygen in the presence of sunlight, and if you've got sunlight in your colon, you've got big problems. Even if you could get grass to fill your back passage with oxygen, it's not like your asshole has any way to absorb it. I get my oxygen the old-fashioned way: I breathe.

"Tonight—" Kriztina started. I held up a hand.

"Batteries or bags," I said. Everyone looked embarrassed. Those of us whose phones had removable batteries removed them. The rest of them put their phones into the Faraday bags I'd handed out when I first started hanging out with these amateurs.

"Before we talk about tonight, I want to walk you through some new precautions." They groaned. I was such a buzzkill. "First: running Paranoid Android is no longer optional. You have to get the nightly build, every night, and you have to check the signatures, every single time." The groans were louder. "I'm not fucking around, people. The Interior Ministry now has a network appliance that gets a fresh load of exploits three times a day. If you're not fresh, you're meat.

"Second, make sure your IMSI-catcher countermeasures are up to date. They just bought an update package for their fake cell towers and they'll be capturing the unique IDs of every phone that answers a ping from them. The app your phone used last week to tell a fake tower from a real one? Useless now. Update, update, update. Check every signature, too.

"Third, make sure your smart-meters aren't sneaking back online. After Minsk, the Interior Ministry's really looking for a chance to pull the same trick, turn off heat in the middle of February for anyone they suspect of demonstrations.

"Finally, everyone has to wear dazzle, no exceptions." Again with the groans, but I got the tubes out of my bag and passed them around. The dazzle was super-reflective in visible light and infrared and anyone who tried to take a picture of someone wearing it would just get a lens flare and jitter from their camera's overloaded sensors. It had been developed for paparazzi-haunted celebs, but the smell of the stuff and the greasy feel it left on your skin—not to mention persistent rumors that it was a powerful carcinogen—had doomed it to an existence as a novelty item used only by teenagers on class picture day and surveillance-haunted weirdos.

I slurped the green juice Oksana had just handed me and was

pleasantly surprised to discover that it tanged unmistakably of tequila. She winked at me. Oh, Oksana, you are a hero.

"Get to it," I said. "Update before we leave. Remember, opsec is a team sport. Your mistake exposes all your friends."

They got to it. Kriztina and Oksana and I checked everyone else's work, and then each other's. Friends don't let friends leak data. We also smeared each other with dazzle, and they made jokes in Boris about the smell, which I could almost follow, though my Boris was a lot worse than everyone else's English.

"Nazis tonight," Kriztina said, looking at her phone. She knew people who knew people, because Slovstakia was so small that everyone was someone's cousin. That meant that when someone's idiot skinhead cousin and his friends started boozing and heil-ing and getting all suited and booted, which meant telescoping steel rods (the must-have neo-Nazi fashion accessory of the season) and brass knucks. The neo-Nazis were someone's useful idiots; they'd come out to the demonstrations and shout about bringing down the government, and then they'd start giving those one-armed salutes and charging the police lines.

It wasn't that they lacked sincerity—they really did hate immigrants, especially refugees, especially brown ones; as well as Russians, Jews, Muslims, queers, vegans, the European parliament, and every single member of the national congress, personally. They may have even come by those views organically, by dint of their own intolerant knuckleheaded generalized resentment. But these characters also had money, a clubhouse, a source for those nifty telescoping batons, and someone had given them workshops on how to make a really effective Molotov, without which they would surely have removed themselves from the gene pool already.

I'd been inside Litvinchuk's network for a month, ever since I landed in-country to backstop the sales team that was working him, feeding them URLs of pastebins where hackers dumped sensitive data they'd pulled out of his data-centers, data we also trickled to his political rivals, making him look worse and worse and making the case to give us a shitpile of reserve-currency dollars better and better.

So I knew what his theory was on the skinheads: he blamed the Kremlin. He blamed the Kremlin for *everything*. It wasn't a bad strategy—Moscow certainly did like to meddle in the affairs of its former satellite states. But I had figured out which personal accounts his own senior staff were using, and done some digging there, and I thought that maybe the skinheads were actually unwitting skirmishers in the civil service empire-building that Borises excelled at. Which didn't necessarily mean the Kremlin had clean hands; maybe they were backing one of Litvinchuk's lieutenants in the hopes of destabilizing things and replacing their canny adversary with someone dumber and more biddable.

"What do we do about it?"

Kriztina and her cell exchanged looks, then muttered phrases in Boris that I couldn't follow. This turned into an argument that got quieter—not louder—as it intensified, dropping to hisses and whispers that were every bit as attention-grabbing as any shouting match. It was lucky for them that the Danube Bar Resto's other customers weren't snitches (I was pretty sure, anyway).

"Pawel says we should back out when they show up. Oksana says we should go to the other side of the square, and move if they go where we are."

"What do you think?"

Kriztina made a face. "I hear that they're going to go in hard tonight. Maybe the big one. It's bad. If we're in the background when they go over the barricades—"

I nodded. "You don't want everyone in the world to associate you with a bunch of thugs who crack heads with the cops."

"Yes, but also, we don't want to sit by and let cops bust our heads to prove we're not with them."

"That's sensible."

Oksana shook her head. "We must protect ourselves," she said. "Helmets, masks."

"Masks don't stop bullets," Pawel said.

"I agree. Masks don't stop bullets. If they start shooting, you'll have to shelter or run. Nothing's going to change that."

He made a sour face.

The tension was palpable. Kriztina's pretty face looked sad. Her little cell had been good friends before they'd been "dangerous radicals." I didn't have that problem because I didn't have friends.

"It's true that you can't survive bullets and it's true that the pinheads are going to try to provoke something terrible if they can. It's true that the cops on the other side are scared shitless and haven't been paid in a month. There are some factors you can control, and some you can't. Wishing things were different won't make them different. It's okay to call it a night and try again later. Maybe the cops and the Nazis will cancel each other out."

All of them shook their heads in unison and started talking. Even the bystander vegans couldn't ignore the racket. Kriztina flushed and waved her hands like a conductor and they quieted down. The staring vegans pretended to stop staring.

"Maybe we can win them over," Kriztina said, quietly. Everyone groaned. This was Kriztina's go-to fantasy. None of us had even been alive in 1993 when the tanks rolled in Moscow to put down Yeltsin's ragtag band of radicals, but of course they all knew the story of how his young, idealistic supporters had spoken to the soldiers about the justice of their cause and then the tank drivers had refused to roll over the revolutionaries. Then there had been borscht and vodka for all the Borises, and the big Boris, Boris Yeltsin, had led the USSR to a peaceful transition.

Pawel broke the tension. "You first." We all laughed.

I knew what to say next. "It's been an honor to serve for you. We will drink together tomorrow, here or in Valhalla." Wrong mythos, but there isn't a Boris alive who can resist a good Viking benediction.

We paid the bill and I chugged down my wheatgrass margarita, and Oksana linked arms with me as we left the Bar Resto, while Kriztina expertly relieved me of the bag of doners and handed them around. We ate as we walked. I pulled out my phone at a red light, one last slot-machine pull at my social-media feeds, and saw Marcus and his girlie, smiling radiantly as they got on a tandem recumbent bike to ride off to their honeymoon, looking so sweetly in love I nearly tossed my kebab.

Kriztina saw something in my face, and let her hand touch mine. She gave me one of her pretty, youthful sisterly smiles and I smiled back. Once, I'd had female friends who'd been there when some stupid boy did some stupid thing, and even though I didn't have that anymore, Kriztina let me pretend I did, sometimes.

As we got closer to the main square, we ran into other groups heading the same way. A month ago, the nightly demonstrations had been the exclusive purview of hard-core street fighters in his-'n'-hers Black Bloc/Pussy Riot masks. But after an initial rush of head-beating that rose, briefly, to the notice of people outside of this corner of the world, the police had fallen back and the numbers of babushkas and families with kids went up. There were even theme nights, like the potluck night where everyone had brought a covered dish and shared it with the other protesters and some of the cops and soldiers.

Then the neo-Nazis started crashing the police lines and the cops stopped accepting free chow from the likes of us. Now, nightly skirmishes were standard issue and the families were staying home in growing numbers. But the night was a relatively warm one—warm enough to walk without gloves, at least for a few hundred meters—and there were more kids than I'd seen in at least a week. The older ones bounced alongside their parents, the younger ones were in their arms, dozing or watching videos on phones. Of course the idents of those phones were being sucked out of them by the fake cell towers cutting right through their defenseless devices' perimeters.

The square buzzed with good energy. There was a line of grannies who had brought out pots and wooden spoons and were whanging away at them, chanting something in Boris that made everyone understand. Kriztina tried to translate but it was all tangled up with some Baba Yaga story that every Slovstakian learned with their mother's borscht recipe.

We stopped by a barrel fire and distributed the last couple kebabs to the people there. A girl I'd seen around emerged from the crowd and stole Kriztina away to hold a muttered conference that I followed by watching the body language out of the corner of my eye. I decided some of Kriztina's contacts had someone on the inside of the neo-Nazi camp, and judging from her reaction, the news was very bad.

"What?" I asked. She shook her head. "*What?*"

"Ten p.m.," she said, "they charge. Supposedly some of the cops will go over to their side. There's been money changing hands."

That was one of the problems with putting your cops on half pay: someone might pay the other half. The Slovstakian police had developed a keen instinct for staying one jump ahead of purges and turnovers—the ones that didn't develop that instinct ended up in their own cells, or dead at their own colleagues' hands.

"How many?"

Borises are world-class shruggers, even adorable pixies like Kriztina. If the English have two hundred words for "passive-aggressive" and the Inuit have two hundred words for "snow," then Borises can convey two hundred gradations of emotions with their shoulders. I read this one as "Some, enough, too many—we're fucked."

"No martyrs, Kriztina. If it's that bad, we can come back another night."

"If it's that bad, there may not be another night."

That fatalism.

"Fine," I said. "Then we do something about it."

"Like what?"

"Like you get me a place to sit and keep everyone else away from me for an hour."

The crash barricades around the square had been long colonized by tarps and turned into shelters where protesters could get away from the lines when they needed a break. Kriztina returned after a few minutes to lead me to an empty corner of the warren. It smelled of BO and cabbage farts, but was in the lee of the wind and private enough. Doubling my long coat's tails under my butt for insulation, I sat down cross-legged and tethered my laptop. A few minutes later, I was staring at Litvinchuk's email spool. I had remote desktop on his computer and could have used his own webmail interface, but it was faster to just slither into his mail server itself. Thankfully, one of his first edicts on taking over the ministry had been to migrate everyone off Gmail—which was secured by 24/7 ninja hackers who'd eat me for breakfast—and onto a hosted mail server in the same data-center I'd spent sixteen hours in, which was secured by wishful thinking, bubblegum, and spit. That meant that if the US State Department wanted to pwn the Slovstakian government, it would have to engage in a trivial hack against that machine, rather than facing Google's notoriously vicious lawyers.

The guiding light of Boris politics was "trust no one." Which meant that they had to do it all for themselves.

Litvinchuk's cell-site simulators all fed into a big analytics system that mapped social graphs and compiled dossiers. He'd demanded that the chiefs of the police and military gather the identifiers of all their personnel so that they could be white-listed in the system—it wouldn't do to have every riot cop placed under suspicion because they were present at every riot. The file was in his saved email.

I tabbed over to a different interface, tunneled into the Xoth appliance. It quickly digested the file and spat out all the SMS messages sent to or from any cop since I'd switched it on. I called Kriztina over. She hunkered down next to me, passed me a thermos of coffee she'd acquired somewhere. It was terrible, and reminded me of Marcus. Marcus and his precious coffee—he wouldn't last ten hours in a real radical uprising, because he wouldn't be able to find artisanal coffee roasters in the melee.

"Kriztina, help me search these for texts about letting the Nazis get past the lines."

She looked at my screen, the long scrolling list of texts from cops' phones.

"What is that?"

"It's what it looks like. Every message sent from or to a cop's phone in the past ten hours or so. I can't read it, though, which is why I need your help."

She boggled, all cheekbones and tilted eyes and sensuous lips. Then she started mousing the scroll up and down to read through them. "Holy shit," she said in Slovstakian, which was one of the few phrases I knew. Then, to her credit, she seemed to get past her surprise and dug into the messages themselves. "How do I search?"

"Here." I opened up a search dialogue. "Let me know if you need help with wildcards."

672 | cory doctorow

Kriztina wasn't a hacker, but I'd taught her a little regular expressions-fu to help her with an earlier project. Regexps are one of the secret weapons of hackerdom: compact search strings that parse through huge files for incredibly specific patterns. If you didn't fuck them up, which most people did.

She tried a few tentative searches. "Am I looking for names? Passwords?"

"Something that would freak out the Interior Ministry. We're going to forward a bunch of these to them."

She stopped and stared at me, all eyelashes. "It's a joke?"

"It won't look like it came from us. It'll look like it came from a source inside the ministry."

She stared some more, the hamsters running around on their wheels behind her eyes. "Masha, how do you do this?"

"We had a deal. I'd help you and you wouldn't ask me questions." I'd struck that deal with her after our first night on the barricades together, when I'd showed her how to flash her phone with Paranoid Android and we'd watched the Stingrays bounce off it as she moved around the square. She "knew" I did something for an American security contractor and had googled my connection with "M1k3y," whom she worshipped (naturally). I'd read the messages she'd sent to her cell's chat channel sticking up for me as a trustworthy sidekick to their Americanski Hero. A couple of the others had wisely (and almost correctly) assumed I was a police informant. It looked like maybe she was regretting not listening to them.

I waited. Talking first would surrender the initiative, make me look weak.

"If we can't trust you, we're already dead," she said, finally.

"That's true. Luckily, you can trust me. Search."

We worked through some queries together, and I showed her how to use wildcards to expand her searches without having them spill over the whole mountain of short messages. It would have gone faster if I could read the Cyrillic characters, but I had to rely on Kriztina for that.

When we had a good representative sample—a round hundred, enough to be convincing, not so many that Litvinchuk wouldn't be able to digest them—I composed an email to him in English. This wasn't as weird as it might seem: he had recruited senior staff from all over Europe and a couple of South African merc types, and they used a kind of pidgin English among themselves, with generous pastings from Google Translate, because opsec, right?

Fractured English was a lot easier to fake than native speech. Even so, I wasn't going to leave this to chance. I grabbed a couple thousand emails from the mid-level bureaucrat I was planning on impersonating and threw them into a cloud machine where I kept a fork of Anonymouth, a plagiarism detector that used "stylometry" to profile the grammar, syntax, and vocabulary from a training set, then evaluated new texts to see if they seemed to be by the same author. I'd trained my Anonymouth on several thousand individual profiles from journalists and bloggers to every one of my bosses, which was sometimes handy in figuring out when someone was using a ghostwriter or had delegated to a subordinate. Mainly, I used it for my own impersonations.

I'm sure that other people have thought about using stylometry to fine-tune impersonations, but no one's talking about it that I can find. It didn't take much work for me to tweak Anonymouth to give me a ranked-order list of suggestions to make my own forgery *less detectable to Anonymouth*—shorten this sentence, find a synonym for that word, add a couple of commas. After a few passes through, my forgeries could fool humans *and* robots, every time.

I had a guy in mind for my whistleblower—one of the South Africans, Nicholas Van Dijk. I'd seen him in action in a bunch of flamewars with his Slovstakian counterparts, friction that would make him a believable rat. I played it up, giving Nicholas some thinly veiled grievances about how much dough his enemies were raking in for their treachery, and fishing for a little finder's fee for his being such a straight arrow. Verisimilitude. Litvinchuk would go predictably apeshit when he learned that his corps was riddled with traitors, but even he'd notice something was off if a dijkhead like Van Dijk were to narc out his teammates without trying to get something for himself in the deal.

A couple passes through Anonymouth and I had a candidate text, along with a URL for a pastebin that I'd put all the SMSes into.

No one at the Interior Ministry used PGP for email, because no normal human does, and so it was simplicity itself to manufacture an email in Litvinchuk's inbox that was indistinguishable from the real thing. I even forged the headers, for the same reason that a dollhouse builder paints tiny titles on the spines of the books in the living room—even though no one will ever see them, there's professional pride in getting the details right.

Also, I had a script that did it for me.

"Now what?" Kriztina looked adorably worried, like I might grow fangs and tear her throat out.

"Now we give Litvinchuk fifteen minutes to check his email. If he hasn't by then, we text him from Van Dijk's phone. Which reminds me." Alt-tab, alt-tab, paste in the number, three clicks, and I'd disconnected Van Dijk's actual phone from the network, making sure that Litvinchuk couldn't reach him.

It was very dark now, and cold, and my ungloved fingers burned. Typing done for now, I tugged on my gloves, turning on the built-in warmers. I'd charged them all day, and they should be good for a full night on the barricades. Kriztina's gloves had cigarette burns on the fingers that must have let the cold in. Filthy habit. Served her right.

The square was more crowded now. Barrel fires burned, and in their flickering light and the last purple of the sunset, I saw a lot of flimsy homemade armor.

"You guys are in so much trouble."

"Why?"

I pointed at a young dude who was handing out painter's masks. "Because those masks won't do shit against tear gas or pepper spray."

"I know." She did fatalistic really well.

"Well?"

She shrugged in Boris. "It makes them feel like they're doing something."

"Feeling isn't enough," I said. "Maybe in the past, in the Vaclav Havel days or whatever. Back then you had these basket-case Borises who ran their secret police on vodka and purges and relied on their own engineering talent to make listening devices the size of refrigerators that needed hourly repairs and oil changes. Now, spooks like Litvinchuk can fly to DC every couple years for the Snooper's Ball trade show, where the best-capitalized surveillance companies in the world lay out their wares for anyone to buy. Sure, they're all backdoored by the Russians, the Chinese, or the Americans, but they're still about a million times better than anything Slovstakia is going to produce on its own, and they will peel you and your friends like oranges.

"Not just surveillance, either—you should see the brochures from the less-lethals industry these days. Melt-your-face pain rays, pepper spray and nerve gas aerostats, sound weapons to make you shit your pants—"

"I know, I know. You tell me this all the time. What do you want me to do? I try to be smarter, try to make my friends smarter, but what can I do about all these people—"

I could feel the heat rising through my body. "The fact that you don't have a solution doesn't mean that you don't need to find one and it doesn't mean that one can't be found. You and your seven friends aren't going to change shit, you need all these people, and you know something they don't know, and until they know it, they are going to get creamed." My hands shook. I stuffed them in my pockets. I shook my head, cleared out the screams ringing in my ears, screams from another place and another time. "You need to be better because this is serious and if you're not better, you'll die. You understand that? You can run from these jokers, hide with Paranoid Android and Faraday pouches, but you will make mistakes and the computers they run will catch those mistakes, and when they do—"

There was doner kebab coming up my gullet, and I couldn't talk anymore without puking, or maybe sobbing, and I couldn't tell you which would be worse. I'm not an idiot: I was talking to myself more than I was talking to her. Having a day job where you help repressive regimes spy on their dissidents and a hobby where you help those dissidents evade detection is self-destructive.

I get that.

But tell me that *you* don't do anything self-contradictory. Tell me that you don't find yourself dissociating, doing something you know you'll regret later, something you know is wrong, and doing it anyway, like you're watching yourself do it.

I just have a more dramatic version is all.

Kriztina must have seen something in my face, which I hated. It wasn't her business what was going on in my heart or my head.

But she took me in a big hug, which Borises also specialize in. It was a good hug. I snuffled the snot back in, willed my tears away, and hugged her back. She was tiny underneath all those layers.

"It's okay," she said. "We know you're only trying to keep us safe. We will do our best."

Your best won't be good enough, I didn't say. I took her hand. "Let's stroll."

The protest crowd was big now, throngs, really, and some of them were singing folk songs in rounds, deep voices and then the high, sweet ones.

Kriztina sang along under her breath. The song floated across the square and it changed the rhythm of the night, made people stamp their feet in time with it, made them lift their heads to the police lines. Some of those cops nodded along with the singers. I wondered if they were the same guys who'd agreed to let the neo-Nazis get through their lines and smash the parliament.

"What do the words mean?"

Kriztina's eyes were warm when she turned to me. "Most of it is nonsense, you know, 'Slovstakia, our mother, on your bosom we were fed,' but the good parts are very good, I think, 'all of us together, different though we are, will work together always, strong through understanding, invincible unless we forget who we are and attack our brothers—'"

"No way."

"Seriously. The words were written by a poet in the seventeenth century after a terrible civil war. I modernized it a little in the translation, but—" She shrugged. "It's our old problem, this kind of infighting. Always someone who wants to build himself a little empire, have ten cars and five mansions, and always the rest of us in the square, fighting about it. Spending blood. But from what you say, maybe this time we lose, no matter how much blood."

I looked at the police lines, the milling crowds. It was full dark now and there were huge steam clouds sweeping the square, pouring off the barrel fires, lit by the huge LED banks that shone out from behind the cops, putting them in shadow and the protesters in full, photographable glare. Their support poles glittered with unblinking CCTV eyes. The police vans ringing the square sported small forests of weird antennas, ingesting all the invisible communications flying around the square, raiding phones for virtual identity papers at the speed of thought.

"You guys are pretty much fucked," I said.

Kriztina grinned. "You sound like a Slovstakian."

"Ha ha. The truth is that it's a lot harder to defend than it is to attack. If you make one mistake, Litvinchuk and his goons will have you. You have to be perfect. They need to find one imperfection."

"You make it sound like we should be attacking."

I stopped walking. Yeah, of course that was what we should be doing. Not just playing around at the edges, pitting one adversary against another with false-flag emails—we should be doing a full-court disruption to their whole network, shutting down their comms when they needed it the most, infecting their phones and servers with malware, making a copy of everything they said and did and siphoning it off to a leaks site on the darknet that we'd unveil at the worst possible moment.

I checked my phone. Nearly fifteen minutes had gone by.

"I think you should," I said. "But once you do, the game will change. Once they know that you're completely inside their network, they'll have two choices: turn and run or crush you like bugs. I think they'll go for option two."

"Masha." My name sounded weird and natural at the same time when she said it. It was a Russian name, once upon a time, and there were Borises in my ancestry stretching back to the Ashkenaz diaspora. Not just Jews, either: in the old photos, my grandmother looked like a Cossack in drag. Cheekbones like snowplows, eyes tilted like a Tolkien elf. I turned to stare at her. "Masha, we are not inside their network. *You* are."

Oh.

"Oh." It was true, of course. I'd taught them a little ("teach a woman to phish . . .") but if I packed up and left, as I was scheduled to do in two weeks, they'd be sitting ducks.

"I could provide remote support," I said. "We'll encrypt emails, I'll send you the best stuff."

She shook her head. "You can't be our savior, Masha. We need to save ourselves. Look at them," she said, and pointed.

It was the painters, the Colorful Revolutionaries, who took their inspiration from those nuts in Macedonia who'd gone around splashing all the public monuments and government buildings with brightly colored paint. Long after the "revolutionaries" had been chased away or arrested, the paint remained. It had built up a lot of hope (and made a ton of money for Chinese power-washer manufacturers). In Macedonia, "vandalism" was a misdemeanor and the worst they could do to you is give you a ticket for it. Slovstakia's parliament hadn't hesitated to make vandalism a felony, of course. They'd watched Macedonia just as closely as their citizens had.

Slovstakia's painters had perfected the color wars, loading their slings with cheap latex balloons filled with different colors of long-lasting paint, swollen eggs they whirled in a blur over their heads before releasing them in flight, arcing toward their targets. It was like Jackson Pollock versus Goliath.

Like all the radical cells, they did their own thing, separate from Kriztina and her group. No one was sure where they'd show up or what they'd do when they got there. Litvinchuk had a fat file on known and suspected members, and I'd toyed with joining them when I got to Slovstakia, before deciding that they were too low-tech for me to work with. You couldn't deny that they were effective: they'd been working their way along the top row of windows, egging each other on with feats of breathtaking long-distance accuracy, bull's-eyeing each window in succession from left to right. The cops below them on the line, behind their shields and faceplates, flinched every time one of those bright balloons arced over their heads. The floodlights caught the colored mist that spread out from each bursting bladder, and I imagined that it was powder-coating the cops underneath in a rainbow of paint and glitter. Glitter was the pubic lice of the Colorful Revolutionaries, spreading inexorably through even the slightest glancing contact, impossible to be rid of.

The cops. I checked the time on my phone again. It had been sixteen minutes since I'd sent that email to Litvinchuk and there was no sign of the chaos that was supposed to ensue. Shit.

"I think we've got to find a place to sit down and plug in my laptop again," I said, tilting my head at the cops.

"Shit."

"Yeah."

We looked around for a place to sit. There'd been benches in the square, two administrations ago. Then the first wave of protests hit, mild ones by day, that involved thousands of people sitting politely in the square on every single bench, eating ice cream. There was no law against eating ice cream, and you're not loitering if you're sitting in a designated sitting zone. The last act of the old prime minister—long since deposed after a no-confidence vote and a midnight flight in the presidential jet loaded with bales of paper euros, so much of it that they burned out six bill-counting machines before giving up and weighing it by the ton to estimate its value—had been to remove all the benches and replace them with waist-high "leaning benches" that tilted at a seventy-degree angle. That'll teach those ice-cream-eating motherfuckers!

But there wasn't anywhere to sit, so that naughty old Boris had the last laugh, I guess.

"Here," Kriztina said, taking off her coat, leaving her in nothing but an oversized sweater that made her look even tinier and younger and more vulnerable. She folded the coat and set it down on a clean-ish patch of asphalt.

"You're such a martyr." I settled down onto it and dug in my bag for my phone. "And thank you." Before I had my lid up, there was a commotion from the police line. A flying squad in Vader-chic riot gear had emerged from the parliament building with guns at the ready, and they now stood behind the line of rank-and-file cops, barking orders. "Holy shit." I put my laptop away and Kriztina pulled me and her coat from the ground. Everyone in the crowd was holding up a phone to capture the commotion; the clever ones had the phones mounted backward on long, telescoping selfie sticks that towered over the crowd.

"I guess Litvinchuk got the email, huh?"

People were streaming past in all directions now, jostling us. The guns the new goons were pointing at their police colleagues were also pointed into the crowd. Any shots that missed (or pierced, I suppose) those cops would be headed straight at us. The crowd was sorting itself into a giant V shape with a clear space behind the police line, protesters crammed in on the side, selfie sticks and phones going like crazy.

We were also crammed in with the crowd, because Kriztina had all but lifted me off my feet and dragged me out of the potential line of fire.

It was a tense standoff. The cops were shouting at the goons, the goons were shouting at the cops, gun muzzles were out. One of the Colorful Revolutionaries stepped out into the empty V of space, a girl barely five feet tall, with that telling coltishness of early adolescence, and fitted a paint balloon to the pocket of her sling. She began to spin. The crowd held its breath, then someone shouted something that I semi-translated as "Don't do it, you idiot," in a voice that was half-hysterical twitter. The girl's eyes were narrowed in concentration and the sling whirled around her head, its whistle cutting through the crowd noise, and she bared her teeth and grunted like a shot-putter as she let it fly, and it flew true, the crowd turning as one to watch it arc through the cold air and the harsh LED light to spatter, perfect dead center, on the ass of one of the riot cops. She pumped her fist and dove for the safety of the crowd as the cop spun with a yelp and instinctively reached for his besplattered ass—then brought his hands unbelieving to his eyes, the banana-yellow glitter paint sparkling on his Kevlar gloves. The goons behind him had, as one, aimed their guns at him and I swear I could see their fingers tightening on the triggers— but miraculously, none of them shot this dumb Boris fuck in the back and sent his lungs sailing over the square. When the paint-spattered cop went for *his* gun, his comrade had the presence of mind to slap it out of his hand, and it skated across the icy square toward the crowd, skittering and then gliding, revolving slowly.

There followed one of those don't-know-whether-to-shit-or-go-blind silences as everyone—protesters, cops, elite goons, and let's not forget the neo-Nazi skinheads—contemplated their next course of action.

The leader of Litvinchuk's goons was faster than the rest of us. He barked an order and his boys all settled their muzzles back into an even distribution across the police lines, and the cops re-formed themselves back into an uneasy line, facing them. The chief goon barked out names—the names we'd provided—and pulled officers out of their line, one at a time, cuffed them, and led them away.

When the first one went, the crowd's curiosity, already close to peak, blew through all its limits. But then as more and more were led away, that curiosity and the insistent buzz of people narrating the action into their phones reached a feverish intensity.

By the time it was done, half the cops on the line were gone. A few of the goons moved to fill in the empty spaces, standing shoulder to shoulder with the cops they'd just been pointing their guns at. The remaining cops were more freaked out than the crowd. I looked around for the neo-Nazis, easy enough to spot—skinhead uniforms, always clumped together, always glaring at anyone who glanced their way, always with cans of beer—and couldn't spot them at first. Ah, there they were, way at the back, talking urgently among themselves, waving their hands, even shoving each other. They must have been in a fury: ready to rush the lines, keyed up for serious out-of-control violence, now trying to master all that psycho energy. Some were doubtless considering the short numbers on the police line and wondering if they could break through even without turncoats ready to help them with it; the others likely remembering the savage reputation of Litvinchuk's private enforcers, the country's most fearsome torturers and disappearers of political enemies, the only force whose pay was never delayed, let alone cut.

Alcohol is a hell of a drug. The pinhead who broke free of his friends was so drunk he was practically horizontal, not so much running as failing to completely fall, but his Klaxon was working and he opened his big dumb mouth wide enough to let out all the drunksound that was begging to be free. His war-yodel drew the attention of everyone in the square, and he had that nice, big open V-shaped empty space to charge through, holding his piece of rebar up in one hand like a villager with a pitchfork, heading straight for the gun that had gone skittering away.

The leader of the goon squad shouted an instruction at him, just once, loud enough to be heard over the drunkspeak. Then, goon-prime tipped a finger at one of his men, who raised his rifle, aimed, and blew the Nazi's head off with an expanding round that sent bone fragments and chunks of brain out in a fan behind him.

One thousand camera-phone eyes captured the scene from every angle.

The first scream—a dude, somewhere behind me—was quickly joined by more. Someone jostled me, then again, harder, and then hard enough that I went down on one knee, Kriztina hauling me back up to my feet with her tiny, strong hands. "Thanks," I managed, before we were swept up by more running bodies, having to run and push ourselves just to keep from being trampled.

Then we couldn't hear the screaming anymore, not over the sound-weapons that the cops had switched on. These sonic cannons combined very loud sound with very low sounds with gut-twisting efficacy, literally making you feel like you were about to shit yourself even as your ears shut down. The crowd was virtually immobilized as people froze and twisted and covered their ears. After a pitiless interval, the cannons finally switched off, leaving a post-concert whine ringing behind them, the death throes of our inner ear hairs.

I couldn't see the cops anymore—too many bodies, the neat V erased by a tangle of people, many weeping or holding their torsos or heads. A loud pronouncement, too distorted to make out.

"What did he say?" I said to Kriztina, making sure she could see my face, read my lips.

"He wants us to go." Her voice sounded like it was coming from the bottom of a well.

"I want to go," I said.

She nodded. We looked around for the rest of our group, but it was hopeless. People were milling about, hopeless and aimless, crying or searching for their friends. I pulled out my phone. No signal. In situations like this, the cops are always trying to strike a delicate balance between keeping the internet service turned on (and spying on everyone) and turning it off (and preventing everyone from coordinating). I guessed that they'd decided they had all the data they needed on the protesters to find them later, so now it was time to get rid of them. There were some who weren't going to be moving under their own power—people who had been hurt in the stampede and were lying on the frozen cobblestones, either alone or, if they were lucky, in the arms of someone. I remembered all those families I'd seen, all those kids.

Some people get overwhelmed by situations like that. I've seen it happen and I understand it. I'm not one of those people, though. My limbic system—the fight-or-flight response—and I are on speaking terms, but we've got an arrangement: it doesn't bother me and I won't bother it. So what I felt was urgency to get gone, but not fear. I felt for the people lying on the ground, but a foreigner who couldn't speak their language was going to be less than useless compared to someone who knew where the hospital was and how to talk to the paramedics, and that someone would reach them soon enough.

Kriztina, though, was in rough shape. Her face was so bloodless it was almost green, and her teeth were chattering. Probably a little shock, plus the temperature had dropped another ten degrees. "Come on." I pulled her toward the ring road around the square, toward a road I recognized as leading toward my hotel. It would be safe.

Kriztina let me lead her along for a few minutes, at first with a big group of crying and scared (former) protesters, then in a thinner and thinner crowd as we moved toward the business district and the Sofitel.

Look: I'm a compartmentalizer. It's my superpower. Part of me had just watched a guy get killed, sorta-kinda because of me, and had been in a stampede. Part of me knew that I'd done something insanely risky that night, something that could cost me my job and worse. Part of me, though, was thinking about the fact that I was responsible for this little sidekick-slash-sister of mine, a hobby that had metastasized into a moral duty, and that she was as keyed up and adrenalized as I was. Neither of our phones was working, and if Litvinchuk held true to form, they'd stay dead for hours, meaning that no one could get through to us or vice versa for the foreseeable, which meant I'd have to keep her out of trouble. I had a hotel room of my own and the turndown service would have left us chocolates to replenish our blood sugar after that intense experience, which was good first-aid protocol, so it was practically medical advice that said we would have to go into my hotel room and get the fuck away from all that danger that she doubtless wanted to drag me back into.

I took her hand in mine as we turned into the Sofitel's road, and I felt her trembling. I hoped that was cold, or excitement, because trauma was going to be a pain in the ass. The Sofitel had two big Borises out front with semiautos and body armor. They glared at us as we approached. I glared back. Glaring isn't personal with Borises: they see smiling as a sign of insincerity.

I held out my room key. One of them took it from me without a word and touched it to an NFC reader on his belt. It lit up green. He nodded. "Welcome."

I began to lead Kriztina through the door, but Boris #2 put a hand on her shoulder and held a hand out, presumably for a key, though I'm guessing a bribe would have worked just as well. "She's with me," I said. Boris 2 pretended he didn't understand. I took the liberty of moving his hand—I'm no black belt, but I've always found jujitsu more relaxing than yoga—and yanking Kriztina into the hotel. I wasn't in the mood for this. The guard shouted at us and followed us in, slinging his gun and reaching for me. I was *not* in the mood for this. I sent him sprawling on his ass, and by this time, the check-in clerk had come out from behind her desk. She and I had already crossed swords when I'd checked in and they hadn't wanted to bill the room to the corporate booker, demanding a credit card from me. I don't do reimbursement, and so I'd just flipped down the seat attachment on my suitcase and opened my laptop and started answering email, studiously ignoring her until such time as her boss's boss had spoken to my boss and sorted things out. Sitting on the suitcase's cool little seat instead of one of the lobby sofas weirded out everyone who came in or out of the lobby, as intended, and kept things moving along.

She recognized me right away and, I'm sure, realized that I would be the world's biggest pain in the ass if she got in my way.

"My friend is coming with me."

"She must be on the register."

"No," I said, and dragged Kriztina past her to the elevators.

She dogged our heels. "I'm sorry, madam, but all guests have to be on the register, it is a regulation."

"I'll add her to the register later, when I check out."

She followed us into the elevator. "Madam—"

"Does the regulation say when guests have to be added to the register?"

"Madam, it's our policy—"

"Good, we can discuss the policy in the morning. Good night."

I felt her eyes burning into my back from the closing elevator doors as I dragged Kriztina toward my room door. She wasn't going to evict me in the middle of the night, not with all the cops busy somewhere else. I was willing to bet that if I were a dude coming back to the Sofitel late at night with a couple of underage hookers, no one would bat an eye, state of emergency or no state of emergency. But let a lady try and show some sisterly solidarity, and suddenly it was ENFORCE ALL THE POLICIES. Fuck that.